# College life 402;

## *Undergrad Completion*

J.B. Vample

Book Eight

The College Life Series

COLLEGE LIFE 402-Undergrad Completion

Copyright © 2019 by Jessyca B. Vample

Printed in the United States of America

First Printing, 2020

ISBN-13: 978-1-7323178-5-7 (eBook edition)
ISBN-13: 978-1-7323178-4-0 (Paperback edition)

For information contact; email: JBVample@yahoo.com

Website: www.jbvample.com

Book cover design by: Najla Qamber Designs

In loving memory of my grandmother, Marlene. Thank you for passing your love of writing to me. I promise to continue to make you proud. I'll miss you and love you forever.

# Chapter 1

"This is our last semester dawg!" Mark Johnson bellowed through the door of the girls' Winfield home.

Startled, Alexandra Chisolm pulled her head out of the refrigerator; she nearly dropped a carton of juice in the process. "Boy!" she barked, slamming the carton on the counter. "You still haven't heard of knocking?" Her hand was on her chest as she tried to steady her breathing. "And why do you always have to be so damn *loud*?"

"'Cause it's our last semester dawg!" Mark repeated, voice still on high. "So stop girlin' and get excited."

Alex fixed a blank stare on her tall, dark-skinned friend for several seconds, before a smile appeared on her face. Mark might have been obnoxious, but he was right; the final semester of college was now upon them. It made returning to Paradise Valley University bittersweet.

"Whatever, just give me a hug, crazy," Alex chortled, walking over and wrapping her arms around him. "It's good to see you."

"You wanna get your greasy hands off my man?" Malajia Simmons jeered, heading downstairs.

Alex and Mark parted as Alex shot Malajia a glare. "Malajia, don't start your crap," she ground out. "And my hands aren't even—"

"Don't care anymore," Malajia rudely cut in, waving a manicured hand in Alex's direction. She jumped down the last step and practically ran into Mark's open arms. "Baby!" she shrieked.

"Ugh," Alex grimaced. She watched in disgust as Mark and Malajia began kissing heavily in front of her. "*Seriously,* right in my face?"

"Take your lonely ass upstairs then," Mark joked.

"This is *my* damn house," Alex flashed back, annoyed as she went to retrieve her juice from the counter. "And on that note, *you* can leave."

"You ain't gotta go a damn step babe," Malajia cut in, plopping down on the couch. "Her and them run-down snow boots she brought back in this house don't run shit up in here."

"God, shut up will you?" Alex huffed.

Malajia ignored her as she examined her burgundy nails. "Where is everybody else?" she wondered.

"David and Josh are back," Mark informed them, sitting on an accent chair.

"I would *hope* so, since they rode with *you*," Malajia sneered, earning a side-glance from Mark.

"Don't let your smart mouth talk you out of me taking you to dinner later," he grunted.

A look of confusion fell upon Malajia's face. "So going to the *caf* is taking me to dinner now?" she sneered. "You cheap bastard."

Alex shook her head at the banter as she poured herself some juice. "Before I put this back, anybody want some?" she offered of the orange juice. When Malajia accepted, Alex poured a glass and brought it to her.

Malajia took the glass and turned her face up. "This ain't no real orange juice," she scoffed.

Alex fixed an angry gaze upon Malajia. "You know what, forget it," she griped, snatching the glass back. "You're so damn ungrateful."

"How you mad at *me* because *you* bought cheap ass juice?" Malajia returned, fighting to keep her laughter in. "It ain't even juice, it's *drink*," she mocked. "How much was that gallon jug, fifty cents?"

"Shut *up*," Alex barked from the kitchen.

Malajia dissolved into laughter, relishing Alex's annoyance. Being able to do that every day was one of the things that she looked forward to every semester.

The door opened, and Malajia jumped up upon seeing who walked in. "Booski!" she screamed, darting for Chasity, nearly knocking her down as she hugged her.

"Girl!" Chasity Parker barked, dropping a bag to the floor.

"You didn't react like that when *I* walked in here earlier," Alex fussed, folding her arms.

Malajia released Chasity from her embrace. "'Cause I wasn't excited to see *you*," she sneered. "I'm just kidding," Malajia chuckled, seeing the hurt look on Alex's pretty, dark brown face. "Come hug me."

"No, screw you," Alex scoffed, holding her hand up to halt Malajia's approach.

Mark glanced up at Chasity, who was approaching the stairs. "Satan," he jeered. "Where's Jason?"

"Jackass, walking in *now*," Chasity threw back, heading up the stairs.

Mark's mouth fell open as his head snapped towards Malajia. "Babe, you gonna let your girl call me names?"

"You called her Satan *first*," Malajia pointed out, shrugging.

Mark flagged Malajia with his hand.

"Chaz, you've got to learn to pare down babe," Jason Adams called out as he set foot in the house, dragging two large suitcases behind him.

"No matter how many times you say that, it's never gonna happen," Chasity hurled down the steps.

Jason rolled his eyes as he adjusted the bags in his hands.

"Bro," Mark smiled, holding his hand out for Jason to shake.

Jason paused short of heading up the stairs. "You *do* see that my hands are full, don't you?" he ground out.

Mark pointed to Jason as he gave a nod. "Misguided

frustration 'cause you gotta drag them heavy ass bags upstairs," he acknowledged. "I get it and I forgive you."

Jason let out a huff. "That woman has *way* too much stuff."

"So does *this* one," Mark chuckled, pointing to Malajia.

"Oh shut up, Mark. You act like *you* carried my shit in here," Malajia threw back, running her hand through her long, wavy dark brown locks.

Mark gave Malajia a blank stare. "That's it, you walking to the caf by your goddamn self," he spat, shaking his hand in her direction.

Malajia flagged Mark with her hand.

Jason shook his head. "You two make me tired," he grunted, heading up the steps with Chasity's bags.

Malajia glanced over and caught Mark staring at her with disgust. "*What* boy?" she hissed.

"You stay showing off," Mark spat.

Malajia tossed her hands in the air in frustration. "On second thought, Alex bring that watery ass drink back so I can splash it in Mark's face," she bit out, earning an exaggerated gasp from Mark.

Alex rolled her eyes and sipped her juice.


Emily Harris unzipped one of her suitcases and removed some clothes. As she began to place the items in a drawer, the door swung open, startling her. She let out a scream.

"Emily you got company," Malajia announced, strolling in. She frowned in confusion when she noticed that Emily had her hand over her chest, trying to catch her breath. "What's wrong with *you*?" she asked.

Emily looked at Malajia like the girl had lost her mind. "Malajia, you just scared me half to death!" she exclaimed.

Malajia waved her hand dismissively. "Stop being dramatic," she scoffed. "Will is downstairs."

Emily quickly tossed the clothes in her hands in the drawer and darted over to the full-length mirror on her roommate's closet door.

Malajia smiled as she folded her arms. "You hype as shit you about to see your boyfriend," she teased.

Emily smoothed her hand down her pink turtleneck sweater. "He's not my boyfriend," she denied. Even though she and Will Palmer had been talking since last semester, the pair elected not to date seriously, but to keep their friendship platonic.

"Uh huh," Malajia mocked, eyeing the shirts in Emily's open drawers. "Hurry up and go see him before he leaves."

Emily flung her sandy brown, relaxed, shoulder length hair over her shoulder as she headed for the door. She stopped and flashed a skeptical glance Malajia's way; the girl was thumbing through the tops Emily had just put away. "Mel?"

"Huh?" Malajia asked, not bothering to stop.

"What are you doing?"

Malajia jerked her head up and regarded Emily with an attitude. "Checking out your shirts, damn can I *look*?" she barked.

Emily laughed. "Why are you *mad*?"

"'Cause I'm sick of everybody thinking I'mma steal their shit," Malajia fussed, shaking her hand in Emily's direction.

Emily's mouth dropped open. "*I* don't think that!"

"Well, you *should* 'cause it's true," Malajia quickly threw out, snatching a red t-shirt from Emily's drawer.

"No!" Emily shrieked, trying to grab it from Malajia.

"Red looks better on *me*, it's too dark for your bright ass," Malajia barked, referencing Emily's light complexion in contrast to her own brown skin tone.

"That doesn't make any *sense*," Emily flashed back. "*Chasity* is as light as *I* am and she wears *black all the time*."

A silly look fell upon Malajia's face.

Emily rubbed her face with her hand. "Please just give me my shirt back, I haven't worn it yet," she demanded.

"I need something to wear for laundry day, just let me

have it!" Malajia snapped the shirt at Emily several times until the fabric hit her in the face.

"Malajia my eye!" Emily shrieked as Malajia ran out of the room.

Will glanced up at the staircase as Malajia came flying down the steps with Emily following close behind.

"Will, Emily's tryna steal my clothes," Malajia lied, running around the couch.

Emily chased her around as she rubbed her eye with her hand. "Malajia stop playing," she panted.

"Ahhhh, you out of breath and shit," Malajia teased, still dodging Emily.

Will shook his head in amusement. "The fun is starting already, huh?" he joked at the scene.

Emily stopped running and folded her arms in a huff. "No," she grunted.

Malajia stopped running and started hopping from side to side, twirling the shirt around. "I'mma wear it while I eat hot wings and use it as a napkin," she taunted.

Emily just stared at her, eyes narrowed. She glanced up at the staircase as Chasity walked down.

"Hey Will," Chasity said, nonchalant as she walked over to Malajia.

"Hi," Will smiled.

Malajia held the shirt up at Chasity. "Chaz guess—" before Malajia could finish, Chasity snatched the shirt from her. "Bitch what the hell are you doing?" Malajia snapped.

Chasity held the shirt out of Malajia's reach. "Stop stealing people's shit," Chasity scolded. Having been in her room, with her door cracked, she had heard everything.

"I didn't—"

"Shut up, yes you did, I heard your loud ass," Chasity barked, interrupting Malajia's protest yet again.

Emily smiled as Chasity tossed her shirt back. "Thank you, Chaz," she beamed.

"Shut up, Emily," Malajia huffed, folding her arms. "You know what Chaz? For your interference with my new shirt, just know I'm gonna be *all* up in *your* closet later."

Chasity slowly folded her arms as she stared at Malajia.

"You got all the expensive shit, *anyway*," Malajia added. "Emily's shirt feels like Alex fabric."

Chasity narrowed her hazel eyes as Emily made a face at Malajia. "Don't get killed before you graduate," Chasity warned.

Malajia rolled her eyes. "Whatever," she bit back, playing with her hair. "Anyway, Alex is at the bookstore and her room door is open, you wanna go put sticky notes all over her stuff?"

Chasity flung some of her long curled, black hair over her shoulder, before amusement set in on her pretty face. "Yeah," she agreed, before both girls took off running up the steps, laughing.

Emily gasped. "Aww, come on you two, don't be mean," she called up the steps after them.

"Shut up," Chasity hurled back, the same time that Malajia spat, "You mind your goddamn business, Emily," from upstairs.

Emily shook her head. She tossed the t-shirt on the couch, before sitting down. Will took a seat next to her. He smiled at her before giving her a hug. "Hi," he said.

Emily returned his smile and his hug. She'd forgotten, with all of Malajia's nonsense, to properly greet him when she came downstairs. "Hi," she replied as they parted.

"How was your trip in?" Will asked, adjusting his position.

"It was good, my dad dropped me off," Emily answered. "How has everything been?" she asked, curious. "I know we haven't talked in a few weeks... Sorry about—"

"No, don't apologize," he cut in, touching her shoulder. "You were traveling with your father, I understand. But things have been good, I've picked up another job."

"Really?" Emily asked. "Where?"

"At a restaurant in the same mall as the movie theater," he answered, running a hand over his freshly cut dark hair.

"I'll be bartending there."

Concern fell upon Emily's face. "You sure you're not taking on too much?" she wondered. "I mean, you're already a manager at the theater all day, then you'll be going straight there to bartend?"

Will chuckled. "Well, bartending is only a few nights," he pointed out. "I appreciate your concern, but I can handle it, and the best part is that I'm *finally* going to be able to move out of my parents' basement."

Emily smiled bright. "That's great," she beamed.

"Yeah, I found a two-bedroom apartment not too far from work," he informed, excited. "Just enough space for me and Anthony."

Emily was overjoyed. She knew how much Will, who had been staying with his parents along with his two-year-old son Anthony, couldn't wait to get his own place. "I'm happy for you," she said.

"Thanks," he smiled back. "It'll be a few more weeks before I can move in, but once I do, I'd love for you to come see it. I still owe you a home cooked dinner."

"It's a date," Emily's eyes widened. "No, I mean—I just—"

Will laughed a little. *She's so damn cute when she's being all nervous.* "No, I know what you meant," he cut in.

"Okay," she breathed, nervously pushing her hair behind her ear as she glanced away from his gaze. Emily hadn't realized how much she'd missed talking to Will, until he was sitting in front of her. She'd almost forgotten how handsome he was.

The door opening snapped Emily out of her thoughts.

"Hey guys," Alex smiled, walking in, carrying a bag in her hand.

"Hey," both Emily and Will returned.

"Is the bookstore crowded?" Emily asked. "I have to get over there myself."

"Oh, I wish you would've said something, we could've gone together," Alex said, setting her bag on a nearby chair.

"But no, it's not crowded. At least not *now*—" Her words were interrupted when Chasity and Malajia bolted down the steps.

Alex watched in confusion as the girls ran for the door in a hurry. "Where are you two going so fast?" Alex asked, confused.

"No time to explain," Malajia quickly stated, running out behind Chasity.

As the door slammed shut, Alex glanced at an equally confused Emily. "What's with *them*?"

Emily felt laughter bubbling up. "I have no idea," she lied.

Not wanting to dwell, Alex shrugged and headed up the steps.

Once Alex was out of sight, Will turned to Emily, amused. "Wait, didn't they—"

Emily put her hand up, to silence him. "Three, two, one," she laughed.

As if on cue, they heard Alex yell, "What the hell?! Why are there sticky notes all over my freakin' room?!"

# Chapter 2

"Thanks for coming over to help me bring my things in Josh," Sidra Howard said, grateful as she sat on her bed and unzipped one of her suitcases.

"It's no problem," Josh Hampton grunted, setting the heavy bag on the floor. He wiped his face with his shirt. "Did you *always* have this much stuff?" he wondered, looking around at the luggage and bins scattered on her side of the room.

Sidra glanced at the horde. "I *think* so," she chuckled.

Josh shook his head. "That's not even including the stuff you left in here over break," he reminded her.

Sidra pushed some of her straight long brown hair over her shoulder. "Well, I'll just have to make sure that Daddy brings help when he comes to get my stuff before graduation."

Josh shrugged, then pointed to a bottle of spring water sitting on Sidra's dresser. "You mind if I get some of that?" he asked.

"Of *course* not," Sidra returned, gesturing for him to take it. As Josh retrieved the bottle and began to drink from it, Sidra found herself staring at him—something that she found herself doing a lot lately. She focused on his handsome face, brown skin and toned body. *I wonder if he's been lifting weights. He looks like he's been lifting weights*, she thought. Sidra shook the thoughts from her head as Josh headed for the door.

"I'm gonna finish unpacking my own crap, I'll be back

later," he announced, walking out.

"Okay," Sidra returned, tone somber. "Oh hey," she called after him.

Josh turned around and poked his head back into the room. "What's up?"

"Umm, you maybe want to go grab some lunch when you're finished?" she asked, hopeful.

Josh winced. "Sorry, I ate already," he declined.

"Oh…" Sidra tried her best to hide her disappointment. She waved a delicate hand. "Okay that's fine, not surprised. It *is* after two."

"I'll just see you and the others later for dinner," he added. "Looks like you'll be awhile anyway," he chuckled, gesturing to her belongings.

Sidra feigned a smile. "Yes, I suppose you're right," she agreed. "See you later."

"Later."

She craned her neck to watch him walk down the steps, before letting out a long sigh. She was disappointed about not being able to have lunch with Josh. Which was odd; it was only lunch in the cafeteria after all. *Sidra, stop being weird,* she told herself.

Pushing her hair behind her ear, Sidra grabbed a stack of folded items from a suitcase and made her way over to her drawer. As she proceeded to put the items away, she heard her phone ringing. She walked over to her bed and glanced at it. James' number flashed across the screen; she stared at it until the ringing stopped.

"I'll call him back," she muttered to herself. Normally, she'd snatch the phone up in a hurry when he called. But Sidra just wanted to put her things away as quickly as possible, and once she started talking on the phone, she knew she would be distracted… At least, that's what Sidra told herself.

Chasity walked to the door and knocked.

Sidra looked over at her and giggled. "Why are you knocking when the door is already open?" she wondered as

Chasity walked in.

"Don't know exactly," Chasity shrugged, glancing around the room. "Damn, I think you actually have more shit than *I* do."

"I doubt it," Sidra chuckled, extending her arms for a hug. "This is going to be our last return to school hug."

Chasity eyed Sidra skeptically as she slowly moved in for an embrace. "Sidra, don't start that weird sentimental shit," she jeered.

"Too late," Sidra chortled, wrapping her arms around Chasity. "Where are you coming from? Jason's?" she asked, parting.

Chasity pushed her hair over her shoulder. "Nah, me and Malajia were at the mall."

"You get anything good?" Sidra asked, going back to putting her things away.

"*I* did," Chasity said, laughter in her voice.

"Mel get you to buy *her* something?" Sidra joked.

Chasity examined her manicured nails. "She *tried*."

Sidra had a thought. "Oh, I saw Alex a little earlier, and she said that if I saw you before *she* did for me to let her know," she said.

Chasity's eyes widened. "Alex is here *now*?"

Sidra shot a skeptical glance Chasity's way. "Yeah, she's in her room," she slowly put out. "Should I *not* tell her that you're here?"

"I'm sure she just heard me." Chasity closed her eyes when she heard Alex's room door open. "Shit," she muttered.

Concern masked Sidra's face. "What's wrong?"

Before Chasity could answer or react, Alex, rolled up magazine in hand, ran over to Chasity and swatted her on the behind with it.

"Ow!" Chasity shrieked, spinning around to face her. "What the hell, Alex?!"

"Did you just pop her on the butt like she's a child?" Sidra laughed.

"*Yes* Sidra," Alex fussed, grabbing hold of Chasity's

arm. "Because *this* heffa and her simple ass friend put sticky notes all over my damn bedroom," she continued, swatting Chasity again.

Sidra's mouth fell open. "Are you serious?" she asked.

"Where did you get this hard ass magazine from?!" Chasity wailed, trying to shield her behind with her hand.

"Move your hand or I'm gonna hit it," Alex ordered.

Chasity busted out laughing before Alex swatted her again. "Stop beating on me, Alex."

Alex swatted her again, earning a backhand to her arm from a now agitated Chasity.

"That *hurts*, goddamn it!" Chasity snarled.

"It's what you deserve," Alex fussed, pointing the magazine in Chasity's face.

Chasity smacked it out of her face. "You have no proof that I had anything to do with that," she argued.

"I *know* it was you," Alex hurled back. "*Emily* told me." Alex stormed towards the steps. "Where the hell is that damn Malajia?"

Chasity leaned over the stair banister as Alex ran down. "Malajia, Emily snitched on us! Alex is coming down to beat you with a magazine that she got off her parents' coffee table," she hollered before heading down the steps, with Sidra close behind.

"You damn right I am," Alex confirmed, reaching the bottom of the staircase.

Malajia, who was in the kitchen, dropped to the floor upon seeing Alex. "I'm innocent!" she yelled, trying to stuff her tall, slender body into the cabinet under the sink.

"Girl!" Alex barked, grabbing Malajia's leg, and dragging her out. "Take this spanking like a woman," she ordered, giving Malajia several swats to her behind and legs with the magazine.

Malajia began screaming at the top of her lungs as she flopped around on the hard floor, kicking her legs wildly in the air.

Sidra covered her ears. "Malajia come *on*," she

complained. "You know it doesn't even hurt that badly."

"Ouch!" Malajia bellowed, trying to slap Alex's hand as she took another hit to her thigh. "You know you didn't hit *Chasity* that damn hard."

"She *did*, actually," Chasity chuckled.

Alex smacked Malajia's hand out of the way as she hit her again. "I'm sick of you messing with me," she hissed through clenched teeth. Alex delivered one last swat to Malajia's behind.

"Ow! You hit me with the fuckin' corner," Malajia fumed, frantically rubbing her butt.

Alex mugged Malajia on the side of her head, before tossing the magazine on the counter. "Serves your ass right," she sneered, walking away. "It was probably *your* idea."

"It *was*," Malajia confirmed, disheveled and standing from the floor. "And it was *worth* it."

Alex shook her head as she flopped down on the couch, catching her breath. "And why was there a picture of a *penis* on the one stuck to my pillow?" she ranted, still upset.

Malajia snickered as she looked at Chasity, who was fighting to keep her laughter in. "We thought you could use one," Chasity joked, before snickering at the anger on Alex's face. Malajia busted out laughing. "*She* drew it," Chasity told, pointing to Malajia.

"And it was a good penis if I do say so myself," Malajia boasted.

Sidra shook her head and folded her arms. "You two are dangerous together, you know that?" she said.

"Only when we're bored," Malajia reasoned, smoothing her hair down.

"Y'all *both* make me sick," Alex scoffed.


Josh, hearing a knock on his room door, tossed the school supplies on his unmade bed. "Since when do you guys *knock*?" he chuckled, pulling the door open. "Oh shit," he sputtered, seeing who was standing there. "December."

December Harley, Josh's ex-girlfriend, had a mask of anger frozen on her dark brown face, and a plastic bag in her hand. "Here's your shit," she spat out, shoving the bag into his hands. The last thing that December wanted to come back to school to was any reminder of Josh in her room.

Josh opened the bag and peered inside. "You didn't have to go through the trouble of coming over to bring this to me," he said, sincere. "It's just a t-shirt and a hat..." he looked into the bag again. "And the stuffed bear that I gave you," he added, somber. "I would've come and grabbed it."

"I don't want you in my damn house," December hissed, turning to walk away. "You can burn that bear for all I care."

Josh reached out and gently grabbed her arm, stopping her. "Can you just hold on a second so we can talk?" he begged.

December snatched away from him as she spun around. "We have *nothing* to talk about," she barked.

Josh looked at the floor.

"What could you *possibly* have to say to me?" December mocked. "What? That you're sorry for cheating on me."

Josh looked up at her, frowning. "I never *cheated* on you," he denied.

"Maybe not *physically*," she argued. "But *mentally* and *emotionally*, you cheated, and with your best friend."

Josh took a deep breath as he stood there, taking the verbal lashing from December. Josh wished more than anything that he could find something to say to make up for what he'd done. Last semester, he had started a relationship with December, after promising her that he didn't have feelings for Sidra. However, December soon learned the truth—that Josh was deeply in love with his best friend. She'd overheard Sidra talking to her brother after a football game.

Josh wasn't surprised when December immediately broke up with him. He knew that she was angry; he just wished that she didn't hate him.

"I know that I messed up," he said, tone sincere. "But

you *have* to know that I never meant for any of this to happen."

December rolled her big brown eyes. "Yeah I know, you never meant to get *caught*."

"No, that's not it..." Josh sighed. "I promise you, I tried to put the feelings that I had for Sidra out of my head... I know that I shouldn't have started a relationship with you until they *were*...but you *gotta* know that I care about you."

December folded her arms as she held her piercing gaze. "You care about *me*, but you're in *love* with *her*," she spat.

Josh fought to keep his eyes on her as the truth was hurled at him. "I'm sorry," was all that he could say.

December sucked her teeth. "Save it, and while you're *at* it, why don't you save the *next* girl from this nonsense."

"There is no *next* girl," Josh assured her.

"You're not gonna have *any* girl if you don't get over her!" December erupted, stomping her foot on the floor. "I don't *get* it! Sidra doesn't *want* you Joshua! She has a boyfriend."

"I *know* that!" Josh yelled back.

"Then *why* does she get all of your damn feelings?!" December hurled. "*I* wanted to be with you, *I* cared about you, and—" She paused when she felt tears prick her eyes. "*I* couldn't get all of you because *she* has it... That's not fair."

Josh wanted to reach out. To grab hold of December and hug her. But he knew that she would only push him away. "No, it's *not* fair to you," he admitted.

December wiped her eyes. "You know what the worst part is for me?" she asked; he just stared at her. "That I *still* have feelings for you. And now *I* have to wait until they're gone before I can allow myself to date anyone else... Thanks, thanks for ruining me for the next guy."

Josh rubbed his face with his hand. He felt like the worst person on the face of the earth. Not only had he hurt December, but he had delayed any chance of her moving on. "I'm sorry," he repeated.

"Yeah, that you *are*, you asshole," she hissed, storming

out of the room and slamming the door.

Furious, Josh tossed the bag to the floor and gave it a kick.


"Yo, what's the plan for tonight?" Mark asked, opening a bottle of soda.

Malajia pulled open a bag of chips. "*Whatever* it is, it better be fun," she griped.

In the girls' house later that afternoon, most of the group were lounging in the living room, trying to decide what to do for their first night back on campus. As it was tradition for them to do *something* entertaining.

Alex retrieved her mug of tea from the microwave and carefully walked into the living room. "You know the school is doing another game night in the SDC," she informed, taking a careful sip.

"We did that shit like *two times* already," Chasity scoffed, leaning back against Jason as she sat on his lap. "And the last one was wack."

Alex paused mid-sip and fixed a stern gaze upon Chasity. "Why do you have to be rude all your life?" she hissed. "I was just passing on information. I don't see *you* offering a suggest—"

"Oh my God, just shut up," Chasity spat, earning a snicker from Jason.

"Salty," Malajia commented of Alex's interruption.

Alex took another sip of her tea. "Make me pop you again, Chasity," she warned.

"Could've *sworn* I just said shut up," Chasity huffed, tired of hearing Alex's voice.

Jason chuckled. "Oh yeah, Chaz told me how you spanked her earlier Alex," he mentioned.

Chasity rolled her eyes. "Never said spank," she jeered.

"Yeah well, that's *my* job anyway," he joked in return.

Chasity turned and fixed a stern gaze on Jason, who stared back at her, amusement on his handsome face.

"Seriously?" she chided.

Jason put his hands up in surrender. "I'm sorry, I couldn't resist," he laughed.

Mark leaned over and held up his hand for Jason to high five it. "I hear that, brother," he approved.

"Jason, don't high five his dumbass," Malajia ordered.

"Oh, I *wasn't*," Jason assured, wrapping his arms around Chasity's slender waist.

Mark shot Malajia a glare. "Why I gotta be a dumbass?" he barked.

"It doesn't even matter," Malajia dismissed, eating chips.

"Anyway," Alex cut in. "Does anybody *else* have any ideas? Since mine was shot down."

Mark snapped his fingers after a few moments of silence. "I got it," he announced, excited. "Let's play strip spades." His suggestion was met with groans and frowns.

Malajia, both embarrassed and annoyed, smacked her hand against her forehead. "See *this* is why I called you a dumbass," she groaned and looked at Chasity. "Chasity, trade me boyfriends. I'm sick of him."

Jason frowned in confusion. "The hell?"

"*Fuck* no," Chasity spat out, disgusted.

"*Please*?!" Malajia begged, slapping the arm of the chair with her hand repeatedly. "He's fuckin' irkin'."

Mark snapped his head towards Malajia and pointed at her. "Hey, hey!" he barked, earning a glare from her. "You're stuck with me, so *deal* with it."

Malajia flagged him with her hand as she played in her hair.

Emily put her hand up. "*I* may have an idea of what we can do," she put in, grabbing everyone's attention.

"This better not be nothing corny Emily," Malajia sneered, shaking her hand in Emily's direction.

"It just may *be*," Emily chuckled, adjusting herself in her seat. "Why don't we have a puzzle contest?" She tried not to laugh at the confused looks on her friends' faces.

"A *what*?" Sidra asked, pushing hair over her shoulder.

"Well, we can go buy some cheap puzzles from the store, pick teams and put them together." Emily glanced at the group as the room fell silent. "Well...what do you think?"

"That has got to be the *dumbest* fuckin' thing that I've ever heard," Chasity slowly put out, earning a playful nudge to her back, from Jason.

Emily busted out laughing. "Is it *that* bad?"

"We're like thirty years old, don't nobody wanna put together no damn puzzles," Malajia sneered.

"Naw, baby girl is on to something," Mark cut in, rubbing his chin.

Emily smiled brightly. "See?" she gestured to him. "At least *somebody* likes it."

"Yeah, this is good. Drunk puzzle party," Mark declared, excited.

Emily's smile faded. "Um, *that's* not what—"

"Naw listen, we can time it for like every ten minutes and shit, and whatever team has the least amount of pieces put together in those ten minutes, gotta take a shot." Mark was bubbling with excitement at the idea.

Alex scrunched her face up as she took another sip of her tea. "Why does everything either have to be freaky or drunk related, with you?" she hurled at Mark.

"Why *you* touching cups and shit when you been playing with yourself all day, lonely ass?" Mark returned.

Sidra put her hand over her mouth in shock. "Whoa!" she gasped as laughter bubbled up.

"Yooo chill, Mark," Jason laughed.

Chasity couldn't say a word because she was practically screaming with laughter. Mark's comeback, paired with the angry look on Alex's face, was almost too much for her to take.

"Yes baby!" Malajia bellowed, slapping Mark a high five. "You're back on my good side for that comeback. You sexy, chocolate, big dicked daddy."

Mark busted out laughing.

"Eww! Why would you say that shit out loud?" Chasity snapped, all traces of amusement gone.

"What the hell?!" Jason exclaimed, disgusted. "Malajia, you trippin'."

"Oh come the hell *on*," Sidra griped of Malajia's explicit words. "God. If it's not him, it's *you*."

"Malajia, you're banned from drinking tonight, you're already on ten," Alex sneered, heading back into the kitchen.

Amused, Malajia just shrugged.

Sidra shook her head, then glanced over at Emily, who had a pillow over her face shaking with laughter. "Em, were you laughing this whole time?"

Emily pulled the pillow down, tears were streaming down her face. "What is *wrong* with you people?" she managed to get out between laughs.


David Summers adjusted the collar on his blue coat before knocking on the door. He smiled at the person who answered.

"Hi David," the short, curvy woman smiled.

"Hey Nicole," David gushed. Aside from the excitement over this being his last semester of college, David couldn't wait to return to campus to see Nicole Elliot, the brown skinned beauty that he had gone out with last semester.

"Come in, silly," Nicole giggled, gesturing for him to come inside. She shut the door behind him as he turned to face her, and she pulled him into a hug.

David, standing at six feet tall, almost wanted to pick Nicole's five-foot five frame off the floor. "How was your break?" he asked as they parted.

"Good, just spent time with the family mostly," Nicole answered, grabbing for the handle of a large plastic bin.

David grabbed it for her. "I got it," he smiled, dragging it to her bed.

"Thank you," she returned, sitting on her bed as she pushed some of her hair twists over her shoulder. "Do you have anything planned for your first night back?"

David watched as she removed items from the bin. "Don't know," he replied. "I'm pretty sure my friends will come up with something."

"Oh," Nicole shrugged. She placed some toiletry items on her bed before glancing up at David. "Um…I wanted to tell you something," she began, much to his anticipation.

"Um, okay," he hesitantly put out.

"It's not a big deal, but since we've been talking like every day over break and have been out… I think you should know."

This time David looked worried. "Do I *really* want to know?"

"You *should*," she urged. Nicole took a deep breath. "I used to mess with—*talk* to someone here on campus," she revealed.

"Anybody *I* know?" David questioned, folding his arms.

"I don't think so, but *Mark* knows him," Nicole answered. "They play basketball a lot."

David looked confused.

"His name is Quincy," she revealed.

David shook his head. "Doesn't ring a bell, really," he muttered. "He was your boyfriend?" he asked.

Nicole hesitated. "Not *necessarily*," she alluded. "We were—*are* just friends." She fiddled with her hands. "But we used to mess around from time to time."

David lowered his head momentarily. *Great, just great. Her ex fling is an athletic jock and I'm just some corny nerd.* "So, you were friends with benefits? That's what you're telling me?"

Nicole nodded. "Yeah. But I promise that that has long been over, and we really *are just* friends."

"Why are you telling me this?" David asked.

"I just didn't want you to be blindsided by that," she explained. "People talk."

David gave a small nod. "That, they do," he agreed. He ran a hand over his cut hair. "Do you um…do you think that he wants you back by any chance?"

Nicole made a face. "I don't *think* so," she answered honestly. "I mean, the way he goes through the dance team on this campus, I highly doubt it," she chuckled.

David found nothing funny about the situation. All that he could focus on was that the woman that he liked, was still friends with someone who she used to have sex with. He didn't know if he could be okay with that.

Nicole smiled. "Look David, I just wanted to be honest," she said, sensing his hesitation. "You have nothing to worry about when it comes to him. I like *you*."

David let out a deep sigh, still uneasy. "I like you too." Hearing his cell phone ring, he grabbed it from his jeans pocket. "Yeah Mark?" he answered, tone dry.

"Whatchu doin'?" Mark asked.

"I'm at Nicole's," David answered, scratching his head. "Why, what's up?"

"We about to play a game, so hurry up and bring your glasses home."

David rolled his eyes; he was in no mood for Mark's nonsense. "I'm in the middle of a conversation man, what game—"

"Don't be asking me no questions dawg just hurry up, we got drinks," Mark barked, then hung up.

David stared at the phone. "He just hung up on me," he said in disbelief.

"You guys are about to play a game?" Nicole asked, refolding one of her towels.

David looked confused. "How did—"

"Mark is *really* loud," she giggled.

David nodded in agreement. "Yeah." He wasn't surprised that Mark and his surround sound voice could be heard through the phone. "I'm gonna go and let you finish unpacking."

Nicole watched as David walked to the door. "David, are you okay with what I told you?" she asked.

David turned and looked at her as he reached for the doorknob. "Sure, I'm good," he answered before walking out the door.

# Chapter 3

"Who bought this cheap ass liquor?" Malajia fumed, pointing to a large bottle of dark liquor on the dining room table. "And the shit is *brown*."

Mark pointed to Chasity. "Yo, *she*—"

"Boy you better point that ashy ass finger somewhere else," Chasity barked, opening a box of pizza.

Mark quickly glanced at his finger. "It's not even ashy," he argued.

"Ashy, dirty, I don't give a fuck," Chasity threw back.

Mark sucked his teeth as he snatched a piece of paper towel from a roll on the table. "Whatever yo, I *asked* you if I should get it, and you said—"

"I said get that cheap ass bottle of bullshit out my face," Chasity recalled, cutting Mark off.

"*Exactly*, and I asked you what kind I should get *instead*, and you told me to fuck off," Mark shot back.

"*So?*" Chasity frowned.

"*So* since you didn't give me any advice, I went with the cheap shit, and we drinkin' it," Mark spat out, grabbing a slice of pizza.

Chasity rolled her eyes and looked over at Jason, who was opening a bottle of soda. "I told your ass not to leave me in the store with him," she griped.

"Baby, I had to go pick up the pizza," Jason laughed back.

Mark flagged Chasity with his hand. "I don't give a shit *what* y'all say," he griped. "Y'all drinking this whole damn bottle. You not gonna waste *my* seven dollars."

"*Seven* dollars?" Malajia sneered. "This big ass gallon was *seven* dollars?" Mark fixed an angry gaze. "You tryna kill us?"

"Will you shut your dramatic ass up?" Mark hurled back. "Always whining, you don't even know what it tastes like."

"She doesn't *have* to, it smells like lighter fluid," Sidra scoffed, taking a whiff from the open bottle. "I'm not drinking that."

"Y'all think I'm playing, this *will* get drank," Mark promised, unfazed by the complaints going on around him.

Alex trotted downstairs. "Who picked out the puzzles?" she asked, glancing into a toy store shopping bag.

"Emily," Sidra replied, grabbing a slice of pizza.

Alex looked over and put her hands on her hips. "I thought you guys were *tired* of pizza," she said, noticing the unfamiliar name on the boxes.

"No, we're tired of that raggedy ass *Pizza Shack* that you and Josh keep tryna feed people," Malajia sniped. Sidra almost spat her food out as she tried not to laugh. "That shit be dry."

"I thought you said it was *greasy*," Alex grunted.

"Same difference," Malajia spat.

Alex looked bewildered. "It's the total *opposite*—"

"Bottom line, we don't like it and don't you bring that shit in here when you go back to work this semester," Malajia snapped, smacking her hand on the arm of her chair.

Alex rolled her eyes. "Whatever Malajia, I don't even know why I argue with you anymore," she ground out.

David walked through the door and removed his coat. "Hey guys," he greeted, tone dry.

"You okay?" Sidra asked, picking up on his tone.

David flopped down on the couch and sighed. "Yeah, I'm fine," he muttered. "It's nothing."

"That sounds like a lie," Chasity observed, putting a slice of pizza on her plate. She noticed that Malajia was reaching for her slice and smacked her hand away. "What the hell are you doing?"

"I'm getting a slice," Malajia explained, reaching again.

"Get your own damn slice out the box, you moron," Chasity fussed, moving her plate out the way.

"The cheese is all uneven on those!" Malajia exclaimed, pointing in the box.

David shook his head at the banter. "Mark, how well do you know Quincy?" he asked.

"Who?" Mark questioned.

"The guy you play basketball with?" David clarified

"Oh Q-dub?" Mark answered, taking a bite out of his pizza.

David frowned. "*Who*?"

Mark snickered as he swallowed his food. "That's his nickname," he said. "I mean we cool and all. Why? He got beef?"

"Nah," David shook his head. "But, apparently Nicole used to date him."

Mark looked up from his food. "I *told* you that was her boyfriend!" he wailed.

David looked confused. "*That's* who you were talking about?" he asked. David recalled the time when Mark told him that he played basketball with Nicole's boyfriend, when it was revealed that David had a crush on her. But after Nicole denied having one, David brushed the information off. "So you *weren't* lying, huh?"

"Naw, I *wasn't* and I think you owe me an apology for accusing me of it," Mark sniped, folding his arms.

"Boy ain't nobody apologizing to you because you didn't lie *one* time," Malajia spat out, as David went to speak. Mark made a face at her.

"How did you find out that they used to date?" Sidra asked.

"She *told* me," David revealed. "Well, she didn't say that he was her boyfriend exactly. She said that they were just…messing around."

"So they were fuckin'," Chasity concluded, eating her food.

"There you go," Malajia agreed, pointing a finger at Chasity.

David smacked his face in embarrassment.

"Classy Chasity, just classy," Sidra scoffed, flinging her hair over her shoulder.

Chasity flashed a frown Sidra's way. "What? Is that not what they were doing?" she argued.

"You could be a little less crass about it," Sidra fussed.

Chasity set her pizza back on her plate and clasped her hands together. "Sorry, I forgot that I was in the presence of someone who doesn't use adult words," she jeered.

Sidra narrowed her eyes at her.

"I meant to say that..." Chasity sucked her teeth. "I can't think of anything. They were fuckin'."

Jason put his hand over his face as he laughed.

Sidra glanced at him. "Jason, tame her please," she hissed.

"Nah, I love her how she is," Jason crooned, flashing a smile Chasity's way.

Chasity eyed him seductively. "You *better*."

Sidra flagged Chasity with her hand. "Anyway David," she said, focusing her attention on him. "How do you feel about that?"

David shrugged. "I don't know," he admitted. "I mean, I'm not naïve to think that she doesn't have a past... I just didn't think that I'd have to see it on *campus*."

"I don't get what the big deal is, as long as she ain't tryna mess with him *again*," Mark put in. "Chicks that *I* used to mess with are still on campus, and Malajia doesn't have any problem seeing 'em. She knows that I'm all hers." He glanced at Malajia, who had a stern gaze fixed on him. "Ain't that right sugar face?"

Malajia's stern gaze turned into a glare as she grabbed a saltshaker from the table. "Bring up your old, ugly hoes again and I'm gonna shove this thing down your throat while you're sleeping," she threatened.

Mark's smile faded. "Probably a time when I should've kept my mouth shut, huh?" he muttered.

"One of a fuckin' million," Malajia ground out, slamming the shaker back on the table.

"David, don't start feeling insecure," Sidra advised, ignoring the brewing argument. "She was honest when she didn't have to be. I say you trust her." She examined her nails. "But just know that if she ever hurts you, we're beating her."

"Beating the *bullshit* outta her," Chasity stressed.

"Then I'mma spit on her," Malajia promised.

David managed a laugh. "Not necessary, but I appreciate it."

Three puzzle boxes, the bottle of rum, and plastic shot glasses sat in the middle of the girls' living room floor a half hour later.

"So, we have our teams picked," Alex said, rubbing her hands together.

"And *once again* you got the dry team," Malajia joked, pointing to Sidra and Josh.

"Whatever, and just like Halloween, *this* team is gonna win," Josh boasted, taking a sip of juice. He'd spent hours sulking in his room after his unexpected visit from December; it left Josh desperate to have a little fun to take his mind off of how terrible he felt.

"Hey, don't y'all losers still owe us a dinner?" Alex jumped in.

"And here goes the big one bringing up food again," Malajia jeered, adjusting her position on the floor. Alex leaned over and backhanded her on the arm, making Malajia snicker.

"How the hell did we get Emily on *our* team?" Chasity asked, adjusting her position on the carpeted floor.

"Stop it, Chaz," Jason chortled, grabbing some chips

from a nearby bowl. "You promised to be nicer this semester."

"No, I *didn't*," Chasity contradicted, face scrunched up.

"Hey, I spent a lot of nights alone in my room growing up, so I put a lot of puzzles together...you need me," Emily replied, reaching for one of the boxes.

Chasity looked confused. "That don't mean *shit*," she fussed. "You didn't put *this* one together before."

"Hey, hey, I'm still good at solving puzzles," Emily laughed, pointing at Chasity.

Mark looked at David, who was cleaning his glasses lenses with the bottom of his sweatshirt. "*You* better be good at solving puzzles or you *and* those glasses are going right over there with the corny trio," he said, gesturing to Alex, Josh and Sidra.

"Shut up and open the damn box," David ordered, pointing to their puzzle.

A person from each team grabbed a box, opened it, and dumped the pieces in a pile. "Okay, so every ten minutes, we stop and see how far we got. The team with the least amount done gotta take a shot of this cheap ass rum," Mark explained.

"Somebody is gonna die tonight," Jason joked, cracking his knuckles.

Mark set the timer on his phone and put it in the middle of the floor. "Y'all ready?" he asked, eager to get started.

"Just come on," Alex urged, reaching for a puzzle piece.

"Aaaaaand go!" Mark sounded off.

"You yelled *right* in my damn ear," Malajia fussed, nudging Mark.

As the teams frantically began trying to put the five hundred-piece puzzles together, the infighting began.

"Why the fuck would you put that there?" Chasity snapped, moving the piece that Emily had just placed.

"It *goes* there!" Emily exclaimed,

"It's not even the same damn *color*," Chasity returned.

"Chaz, look at the box, it *goes* there," Jason assured,

showing Chasity the picture on the lid.

"I don't give a damn about that box," Chasity fussed, slapping it from Jason's hand.

"Emily why did you pick puzzles with all these goddamn pieces?" Malajia griped, sorting through the massive pile in front of her.

"Yo, Mel, stop fuckin' complaining and *help* with this shit," Mark demanded, connecting some pieces.

"Mark, those pieces aren't connecting," David observed, pointing to Mark's work. When Mark tried to force the pieces together, David sucked his teeth and reached for them. "The pieces don't fit together."

Mark smacked his hand away. "Fuck outta my space dawg," he spat. "Worry about your *own* pieces."

"They all have to be put together *eventually*. We're on the same damn team," David argued.

Malajia let out a groan as she searched for pieces to put together. Giving up, she glanced over at Alex's team, who were working quietly together. Malajia leaned over to examine their work. "How far y'all got?" she asked.

"Girl move," Alex demanded, giving Malajia a nudge.

"Yeah, turn those big ass eyes back to your *own* team," Sidra spat out.

Malajia threw her head back and groaned loudly. "That was so corny."

"Malajia! I swear to God, if we lose because of your non-helping ass, you're taking my shot," Mark fussed.

"I ain't taking *shit*," Malajia threw back, unfazed.

When the buzzer on Mark's phone finally went off, the groups immediately stopped working. "Alright, let's see what we have," Alex said, glancing at the three piles. Eyeing one group, she laughed. "You guys lose."

"How so?" Jason charged, pointing to another pile. "We *clearly* have more put together."

"No, y'all clearly *don't*," Mark laughed. "Ahhh, y'all gotta take a shot."

Chasity pulled her hands down her face. "I told you we

should've started with the colorful part first," she barked, pointing to the box. "We could've gotten more done."

"Hey, if you spent *less* time yelling at us, and more time putting the damn pieces together, we wouldn't *be* in this position," Jason threw back.

Chasity's eyes widened. "So this is *my* fault?"

Jason took the shot that Mark had poured and pushed it in Chasity's face, "Just take your shot," he ordered.

Chasity rolled her eyes and snatched the small cup from him. "Yeah, whatever," she muttered.

Both Jason and Chasity held their cups to their lips. "It *smells* like it's about to make my chest hurt," Chasity complained.

Jason shook his head as he and Chasity both downed their shots. Chasity nearly spat hers out as the taste got caught in the back of her throat.

"Shit," Jason coughed, feeling the heat in his chest. "That shit is the worst."

Chasity tossed her cup on the floor in anger and pinched the bridge of her nose. She felt like she wanted to throw up.

"How does it taste?" Malajia teased.

"Like fuckin' acid," Chasity grunted, patting her chest.

Malajia laughed, then looked at Emily who was holding her shot in her hand. "Naw chick, you better down that shot," she ordered.

Emily stared at the brown liquid, her face scrunched up. "I can't drink this," she declined.

"Emily, stop tryna use your sophomore year alcoholism to get out of taking that shot," Malajia threw back.

Emily rolled her eyes. "That's *not* what I'm doing," she promised. "I just can't do shots... Can I at least mix it?"

"No, ain't no mixies, that's not the rules," Malajia hissed, shaking her hand in Emily's direction. "And Alex, you *better* not say nothing," she directed at Alex.

"I didn't even open my mouth!" Alex exclaimed.

Had it been last year, last *semester* even, Alex would have tried to intervene on Emily's behalf. But after having a major blow up with Emily last semester due to overstepping her boundaries, Alex was learning to back off.

"Malajia, I'm not taking this shot by itself," Emily refused.

"God, just come the fuck *on* before I quit," Chasity spat, fanning herself with her hand. She was still feeling the burn of the cheap rum in her chest.

Before either Emily or Malajia said another word, Jason took Emily's shot from her and quickly downed it.

"Goddamn it!" he wailed, slamming his hand on the floor. The bitter taste and high proof was almost unbearable.

"That's what you get for trying to be the hero," Chasity spat at him.

"Not now, Chasity," Jason grunted, pinching the bridge of his nose with two fingers. "My damn eyes are watering."

"He cryin' and shit," Mark laughed.

Jason flipped him off in retaliation.

Emily leaned over and patted Jason's arm. "Thanks Jase," she smiled.

"Cheatin' ass," Malajia mumbled. "Next round, your loser ass is *taking* that shot, Emily."


Malajia's prediction didn't come true; it was *her* team who lost next round.

"This is some straight up bullshit!" Mark boomed. "We ain't lose."

Sidra stared at him in disbelief. "You only have two more pieces than you did *last* round," she observed.

"But they make the puzzle *bigger*," Mark argued.

"Shut up, you sound stupid," Malajia spat at Mark. "I told you to stop concentrating on that dickhead ass rainbow in the corner."

Mark narrowed his eyes at her. "I'm sick of your shit, you sleepin' on the floor tonight," Mark threw back, putting his finger in Malajia's face. "In your *own* room."

Malajia put her hand in his face. "Boy, if you don't—"

"Shut up all that damn noise and take your damn shot," Jason ordered, pouring three shots.

"I'm not drinking that shit," Malajia refused, flinging her hand at the shot.

"Hold on, you just criticized Emily for not wanting to drink, and now *you* go and do the same *thing*?" Alex chided, folding her arms.

"*I* ain't Emily," Malajia sneered.

As David quickly took his shot with not so much as a scrunched face, Mark grabbed both his and Malajia's cups. "Mel, nobody has time for your shit, just take it."

"Get that out my face," Malajia spat out.

"Take it or I'm holdin' out for two weeks," Mark warned.

Malajia's eyes widened. "Why you always gotta show off?" she sneered, snatching the cup from him. She sucked her teeth and took the shot. Angry at the taste, Malajia threw the small plastic cup across the room. "I swear to God, Mark, you're going to hell for buying that shit," she complained, rubbing her chest.

After another round of losing, Malajia was at her wits end. "No, no! I'm not doing another shot of that," Malajia refused.

Mark held the shot that he'd just poured for her, in her face. "Come on and just drink it so we can start the next round," he huffed.

Malajia flopped around on the floor. "That shit is *nasty*," she fumed, pointing to the bottle.

"It's actually not that bad," David shrugged, taking his shot.

"That's 'cause your damn taste buds are damaged from that nasty ass food that your dad used to make," Mark joked.

David thought for a moment. "Yeah, you may be right," he agreed, amused.

Mark faced Malajia again. "Malajia, stop whining. You know the rules," Mark said, pushing the cup in her direction.

"I swear to God, I'm about to cry," Malajia whined,

fanning her eyes with her hand. "I can't do it."

Sidra rolled her eyes, "Stop being so damn dramatic," she huffed. "You're holding up the game."

"Fuck this game!" Malajia erupted.

Chasity put her hand on her forehead. "Either that shot or Malajia's damn mouth gave me a headache," she complained in an aside to Jason.

"Shut up Chasity," Malajia barked, then turned to Sidra. "How come *y'all* haven't lost a round yet?" she sniped.

"Because instead of arguing with one another, we're working *together* to get the puzzle done," Alex threw back. "Shut your damn mouth, and maybe *your* team can stop losing."

Malajia stared at Alex for several seconds. "You know what, fuck you *and* this puzzle," she muttered, breaking apart their half-finished puzzle.

"Are you kidding me?!" Alex wailed, watching Malajia spread their pieces around.

Angry, Sidra slapped Malajia's hand away. "You're such an asshole!" she fumed.

Malajia tossed a few puzzle pieces across the floor. "You mad your puzzle messed up," she teased, putting her finger in Sidra's face. "Now you gotta drink that pissy ass liquor."

Sidra gritted her teeth, reached over, and started breaking apart Malajia's teams puzzle. "Now *your* puzzle is messed up."

Mark shook his head as his girlfriend and childhood friend began tossing puzzle pieces at each other. "See what you done started Malajia?" he griped.

"Shut up," Malajia hissed, then grabbed for Chasity's teams puzzle. "*Your* shit is fucked up too."

"I don't give a shit about this stupid ass puzzle," Chasity dismissed, running a hand through her hair.

Malajia tossed a few pieces at Chasity. "I bet you do *now*," she taunted.

Angry, Chasity picked up a handful of pieces and threw

them at Malajia's face. "Leave me the fuck alone," she hissed.

Malajia let out a scream. "Damn bitch, my eyes!" she wailed, rubbing her eye. She then grabbed another handful of pieces and tossed them at Emily, who let out a shriek as she shielded her face.

"I didn't even *do* anything!" Emily wailed.

"This was *your* dumbass idea," Malajia returned, gathering up more pieces.

"Malajia, will you chill the hell out?" Alex cut in, fed up with Malajia's antics. "You're mixing all the puzzles up." Alex put her hands over her face as puzzle pieces came flying at her. "Let one of those things hit me in the eye Malajia, and it's *on*."

"Fuck you *and* your eye," Malajia spat. Feeling puzzle pieces hit her on her arm, her eyes widened as she faced Mark. "Oh for real Mark, is that what we're doing now, turning on each other?" she spat, throwing pieces at him.

Mark flinched. "Ow! You didn't have to throw them that damn hard," he barked. He then grabbed for more pieces as Malajia reached for more.

Without warning, everyone except for Alex, grabbed puzzle pieces and darted away from each other.

Alex shook her head as puzzle pieces went flying throughout the room and her friends began running around the living room, chasing each other.

"Y'all are childish, I quit," Alex huffed, standing up from the floor. As she turned to walk away, she felt puzzle pieces hit her back. "Who did that?" she snapped, spinning around.

"Chasity," Sidra ratted, ducking under the dining room table.

"Was that necessary?" Alex fussed, eyes fixed on Chasity with an angry gaze.

"I didn't like the way the back of your head looked just now," Chasity threw back, running behind the couch.

Alex let out a loud huff. "That does it," she fumed,

grabbing pieces off the floor.

Mark, after hurling pieces at Josh, rushed over and kicked the pieces that Alex was reaching for, out of the way. "You don't get none," he laughed.

"I hate you!" Alex screamed, slapping him on his arm.

Mark didn't get a chance to register the sting from the slap because he'd been hit in the chest with a hoard of puzzle pieces. He looked up at his friends wide-eyed. "Really, all y'all against a brotha now?"

"You shouldn't have brought that nasty ass liquor," Jason ground out.

Mark pulled his hands down his face. "Y'all got it," he nodded, before quickly scooping up a handful. "It's on now." Taking off running, Mark hurled his pieces at David, hitting him in the face.

"Come on man," David complained, as his glasses fell off.

"Get him, he can't see," Mark laughed.

David quickly retrieved his glasses from the floor and shielded his face as he took off running up the steps, with most of the group chasing him, throwing puzzle pieces in the process.

Alex, upon hearing David scream, stomped her foot on the floor. "You guys are making too much noise!" she yelled up the steps, "And making a damn mess!"

"She's right, everybody in Alex's room!" Malajia yelled.

Hearing running footsteps heading to the back room, Alex shrieked. "No!" as she ran up the steps. "Y'all play too much!"

# Chapter 4

"My schedule this semester is some bullshit," Mark complained, tossing the printout into his book bag.

Sidra chuckled. "What's wrong with it?" she wondered, adjusting her book bag on her shoulder as she, Malajia, Mark, and Alex walked through the campus quad to their respective destinations.

"They *all* hard as shit," Mark complained, exasperated. "Principles of Managerial Accounting…I fuckin' *hate* Accounting. English Lit 4, Advanced Econ, Financial Management, and Advanced Marketing… I'mma fail like shit."

"You better *not*," Sidra scoffed. "I'll slap you silly if you don't graduate on time."

"He's *already* silly," Alex teased, smoothing some wavy tendrils back up into her ponytail.

Mark rolled his eyes at Alex's comment. "Whatever yo," he sneered.

"Don't tease my man," Malajia jeered, cutting her eye at Alex.

Alex was unfazed. "Girl please," she dismissed, with a wave of her hand.

Malajia turned her attention to Mark. "Babe, I don't understand *why* you choose Accounting as your major if you hate it so much," she asked, confused. "Every semester you bitchin' about those classes."

"'Cause it's gonna make me money when I get out of here," Mark answered honestly.

Upon graduating high school, Mark had no idea what he wanted to do as far as a career was concerned. His father was a successful accountant, so Mark picked that as his major, in hopes of making a living. "And how you talkin' about *me* Mel, when you complain about *Spanish* all the time?"

"Spanish ain't my major," Malajia threw back.

Mark let out a little laugh. "Good point," he admitted.

"Look, it doesn't matter *what* classes you have, just make sure you do what you need to do so that we all walk across that stage together in May," Alex said, glancing at her watch. "I gotta get to this bookstore. See you guys."

"Later sis," Sidra said as Alex headed off to her destination. Hearing a notification on her phone, she glanced at it.

"Ahhh, she gotta go stand in that long ass line because her cheap ass bought the wrong book, thinkin' she was getting a bargain and shit," Malajia teased, pushing her hair over her shoulder.

Mark let out a laugh. "A damn shame."

Hearing Sidra suck her teeth, Malajia glanced over. "What's wrong Sid?"

Sidra let out a groan and tossed her phone into her purse as the three continued ambling through the campus grounds. "My mom keeps texting me about ideas for this stupid wedding," she griped, adjusting the collar of her coat.

Mark chuckled. "Marcus is *actually* going through with marrying India, huh?"

"Ugh, can you not say that name in my presence? I'd like to keep my pancakes down," Sidra scoffed. It was no secret that Sidra was less than pleased with her brother's choice in his on-again / off-again girlfriend of the last five years. But her displeasure hit the roof when Marcus revealed to Sidra last semester that he would be marrying the woman.

Malajia winced. "I feel for you Sid," she sympathized. "I couldn't imagine having someone I can't stand as an in-law."

Sidra looked at her. "I thought you couldn't stand your sister Tanya's husband," she said.

Malajia quickly shook her head. "No, I can't stand *Tanya*," she jeered of her eldest sister. "There's a difference."

Sidra rolled her eyes at Malajia. "Anyway," she grunted, adjusting the glove on her hand. "I have to talk some sense into my brother. He can*not* go through with this."

"When is this wedding supposed to happen anyway?" Mark asked.

Sidra let out a long sigh. "I don't even *know*," she answered, tone not hiding her disdain. "They can't even make a damn decision on the *date*. But they swear it's gonna be sometime this year."

"Bet money he ends up calling it off," Malajia predicted.

"It would take something more drastic than India cutting up his clothes and breaking his game system," Sidra huffed.

Mark's head snapped in Sidra's direction. "Damn, homegirl broke the system?" he asked, astonished. "Oh she's *definitely* batshit crazy."

Sidra rolled her eyes; she'd had enough 'India' talk. "I have to go guys," she sulked, heading off in another direction.

Mark let out a little laugh as Malajia shook her head. "My prediction, Sid is gonna complain all the way up until they say 'I do'," he chortled, putting his arm around Malajia's shoulder.

"God, can she move into y'all house for the semester?" Malajia pleaded.

This time Mark laughed fully. "Naw, but *you* can," he returned.

"Naw, I'm good," Malajia returned, amusement in her voice. "I'm used to living with women. I wouldn't know what to do in a house full of men."

Mark shrugged as they continued to walk.


Chasity busted through the doors of the Science building and approached Jason; he was leaned up against the iron banister, looking at his cell phone, waiting for her to emerge.

Jason smiled at the sight of her. "You're in a good mood, I see," he mused, noticing the broad smile on her face and pep in her step.

"Hell yeah," she confirmed, placing her printed class schedule in her purse. "I only have computer related classes this semester," she revealed, pushing her hair behind her ear.

"Oh yeah?" Jason smiled. "No more math?"

"Nope," she beamed. It was no secret that Chasity hated any class that was related to math.

"No more late-night tutor sessions, I guess," Jason concluded.

Chasity smiled. "We can still have late-night sessions, just no *math* will be involved."

Knowing what that meant, Jason took a step closer to her. "Damn a late night, let's go have a session *now*," he proposed, a lustful look on his face.

"Calm your horny ass down boy, it hasn't even been three hours," Chasity sneered.

Jason laughed. "Funny."

Chasity adjusted her purse on her shoulder. "I don't think I've ever been this happy with a class schedule before. I don't even care that it's freakin' brick out here," she mused of the frigid weather. Feeling a cold breeze chill her entire body, she shivered. "Yeah, I lied, I care."

Jason placed his arm around her and pulled her close. "You wanna go get something to eat?"

"Sure," she said as they began walking down the path.

As they ambled along the crowded walkway, Jason let out a sigh. "Guess who called me while you were getting your schedule," he said.

Chasity stopped walking. "It better not be who the fuck I *think* it is," she hissed.

Jason stopped and looked at her. "Who?" he wondered, confused.

Chasity shot him a knowing look.

Jason's eyes widened as he came to a realization. "Who? *Paris?*" he scoffed of his ex-girlfriend.

"Jason, if I get my hands around her neck again, I *won't* let go," Chasity fumed.

Just the mention of Jason's ex's name sent Chasity into a fit of rage. Having been introduced to his ex-girlfriend Paris by Jason's mother at a football game last semester, Chasity had to deal with her insecurities when it came to Jason and his feelings for his ex. After a confrontation with Paris, and on the verge of breaking things off with Jason for her own sanity, Chasity hoped to never have to hear the girl's name ever again. Jason, who blew up at Paris over the situation, was eager to keep her name out of his mouth and his mind.

"I promise, it wasn't," Jason assured. "She won't be calling me anymore."

"Oh? Did she die?" Chasity asked, feigning concern.

Jason smirked and shook his head in amusement. "You're so beautiful when you're spiteful," he chortled. Chasity shrugged. "But no, she didn't die, she—"

"Baby, as long as she wasn't the one on your phone, I don't *care* what happened to her," Chasity cut in.

Jason nodded. "Noted," he said. "...It was my mother."

Chasity tilted her head. Jason's somber demeanor at the mention of his mother wasn't missed by her. "You still not speaking to her?" she asked.

Jason shook his head. After giving his mother a verbal lashing over trying to destroy his relationship with Chasity, Jason wasn't too eager to exchange words with her. But it didn't mean that it didn't affect him.

"I guess you staying with me most of the break, didn't give her the hint that you're still mad at her," Chasity commented.

"Apparently *not*," Jason muttered. He let out a deep sigh. "She left a message saying that she wishes me a good semester, that she loves me and hopes that I start talking to her again before graduation, blah, blah, fuckin' blah."

Chasity shook her head. "Look Jase, as much as I appreciate you sticking up for me, I know how close you are to your mom, so if you want—"

"I *don't*," he cut in, stern. "I meant what I said to her. If she can't respect *you*, she and *I* have nothing to talk about. It is what it is."

"Okay," Chasity said after a moment. "Well look on the bright side."

Jason raised an inquisitive eyebrow. "What bright side?"

"At least she's trying to contact you," Chasity pointed out. "So maybe all hope isn't lost with her."

"Yeah, that doesn't matter," Jason grunted.

"It *should*," Chasity returned, even toned. "At least she cares."

Jason held a sympathetic gaze on Chasity; he had a feeling as to what she was alluding to. "Your father still hasn't contacted you, has he?"

She shook her head. "Since I texted him back last semester? No."

Jason ran a hand over his head and let out an agitated sigh. He was tired of Chasity's father neglecting her. "Next time I see him, can I punch him?"

Chasity couldn't help but chuckle. "He's not worth the energy."

"Oh it *will* be worth it," Jason disagreed. He watched as Chasity went to say something, but hesitated as she held her hand out in front of her. "What's wrong?" he asked, concerned.

"I can't feel my fingers," she ground out. They were so deep in conversation that Chasity had forgotten that they were still outside in the bitter cold. That was, until she felt a tingling sensation on her hands.

Jason grabbed one of her hands and gave it a kiss, enclosing it in his. "Come on, let's get out of this cold," he said, leading her down the path.


"I can't believe I bought the wrong book," Alex griped to herself as she stood in the long line at the campus bookstore. Having been in the crowded bookstore for twenty minutes, Alex was berating herself for her mistake.

Glancing at her watch for the third time, she let out a heavy sigh. "God, why is it taking so long for this damn line to move?" she wondered aloud. "What? Are they *making* the damn money they're using to pay?"

"I think it's just one cashier today," a man behind her commented.

Alex immediately spun around, a stunned look on her face. "Uh hey," she stammered to the familiar face.

"Hey," Eric Wendell returned, adjusting the stack of books in his hand.

Alex smiled as she stared at him. She hadn't spoken to her former friend and casual sex partner since she'd gone to his room to apologize for her harsh treatment of him. Though he had yet to forgive her, he at least was speaking.

"Social Psychology, huh?" Alex commented finally, gesturing to one of the books in his hand.

Eric glanced down at said book, then gave a nod. "Yeah."

"I took that class, my sophomore year," Alex replied, moving some hair from her face. "You'll like it."

"I hope so," Eric commented.

Alex nodded as she moved up in line, with Eric close behind. His presence was overpowering in a good way; she'd missed it. After a few seconds of silence, Alex spun around to face him once again. "So um…how was your break?"

"It was okay," Eric answered.

"You do anything interesting?" she pressed, hoping to engage him more.

Eric shook his head slightly. "Not really."

Alex glanced down at the book in her hand. *You're trying too hard, Alex*, she thought. "Oh…okay," she muttered.

Eric suddenly sucked his teeth loudly.

Alex was confused. *Shit, what did I do? What did I say?*

"Damn it, I forgot something," he grunted. "Now I have to get out of line."

"Oh," Alex replied, relieved that it wasn't her presence that had garnered the reaction from him. "Do you want me to hold your spot in line?" she offered.

"Nah, I'll be fine," he said, stepping aside. "See you around, Alex."

"See you, Eric," she replied as he walked off. Alex went to turn around, but had a thought. *Screw it.* "Eric," she called.

He turned around. "What's up?"

She hesitated for a moment, then took a deep breath. "Okay so I was thinking that maybe sometime this week before things get crazy with classes that…maybe we can go get some coffee or something?" she asked, hopeful.

Eric stared at her, not uttering a word.

Alex started to panic on the inside, though she didn't let it show. "I heard that they opened a new donut place in the SDC and I *also* heard the coffee is really good there…better than that instant stuff at least." *You're rambling!*

Eric let out a sigh. "Uh yeah, I'm sorry Alex, but I don't think that's a good idea."

His words smacked her in the face. As much as Alex didn't want the regret to show, it did. "O-kay."

"Sorry, but I'm just not in a place where I can hang out with you."

Alex rolled her eyes. "It's just coffee Eric," she said.

"It's just *you*, Alex," Eric amended. Alex looked down at the floor. "I can't right now, I hope you understand."

Alex shrugged slightly. "I guess I have no choice, *but* to," she sulked.

"I'm sorry…enjoy your coffee," he said, before walking off, leaving Alex standing there hurt.

"Yeah, thanks," she muttered to herself.


Will looked up from his basket of French fries and stared at Emily. A blank expression was on her face as she stared at the table. "Are you okay?" he asked.

Emily glanced up at him. "Uh…I don't know," she

answered slowly.

"What do you mean?"

Emily sighed as she pushed her hair behind her ear. "I had a meeting with the Education department earlier," she revealed.

Will sat there as she paused. "Well?" he pressed, when she still didn't answer. "What happened?"

She picked up her half-eaten burger. "My student teaching assignment at Paradise Valley Elementary starts in two weeks," she sighed. After getting her classes situated and attending her meeting, Emily decided to take a trip off campus and meet Will at the mall food court to have lunch with him during his break.

"Why do you seem upset about it?" he wondered. "I thought you were looking forward to this, at least that's what you told me last semester."

"I know, I guess now that it's finally *here*, I'm just nervous." She let out another sigh.

Although Emily was looking forward to getting some real experience in her Early Childhood Education major, she had to admit that the thought of being in charge of a room full of students, even if they were children, had her on edge.

"What if they don't listen to me? What if they don't like my assignments? What if the real teacher who I'll be shadowing tells my professor that I'm not cut out to be a teacher?" Emily stressed.

"Em, you're going to give yourself a panic attack and you haven't even stepped foot inside the classroom yet," Will pointed out, reaching for his soda.

Emily set her food back down and put her face in her hands. "God," she groaned.

"You really gotta relax," Will pressed.

"No, no it's not that," Emily muttered, face still in her hands. "There was ketchup on my hand and now it's on my face."

Will tried not to laugh, but was unsuccessful. He grabbed a napkin and held it close to her face. "Here you go."

Emily removed her hands from her face. She did in fact have ketchup on her cheek.

Will laughed some more.

"I'm glad that this is funny to you," she sneered, taking the tissue from him.

"Would it make you feel better if I put ketchup on *my* face?" he asked.

Emily wiped her face. "No silly."

Will dipped his finger in the leftover ketchup in his fry basket. "Too late," he blurted out as he ran his finger across his cheek.

Emily couldn't help but laugh. She appreciated his effort at making her feel less embarrassed. She picked up a clean napkin, leaned over, and wiped the condiment from his smiling face. "Thanks."

"Anytime," he said, taking a sip of his drink. "Look, I get that you're nervous about your assignment, but I don't want you to put yourself down before even giving yourself a chance."

Emily sat back in her seat as she folded her arms. "I can't help it, my confidence when it comes to *anything* has always been low," she said, honest.

"Well, it's time to change that part of yourself," Will advised.

Emily shrugged. "Easier said than done," she sulked.

Will leaned forward. "Well, you can always get some practice in beforehand," he suggested.

Emily looked at her nails. "Yeah? How will I do that?" she wondered, unenthused.

"By hanging out with Anthony."

Emily looked up at him. "*Now?*"

Will laughed. "No, not *now*, but I'm hoping *soon*," he replied. "I would like for my son to get to know my friend."

Emily nervously bit her bottom lip.

"Don't worry, he won't bite you," Will joked. "Unless you take his favorite toy away from him."

Emily let out a chuckle. She had to admit that she was

still apprehensive about meeting Will's son, but she didn't know exactly why; he was just a child after all. "Okay tell you what, before I start my assignment, I'll let you introduce us," she promised.

Will's smile could have lit the entire mall food court. "Great," he beamed. "I'll bring cookies."


"Stop holding on to it!" Malajia yelled at Mark as she held her hands out.

"You can't tell me how long to hold it," Mark returned, holding a round plastic toy. "I can hold—" he jumped when the top of the toy opened and out popped rubber snakes. "Shit!" he bellowed.

"That's what the hell you get, cheatin' ass," Malajia sneered, pointing to the floor. "Now pick up them snakes."

"Shut up," Mark returned, bending to retrieve the colorful items from the floor. Having gotten through a day of running around, Mark and Malajia returned to the girls' house for some R&R. To them, that meant playing a makeshift game of hot potato, using a wind-up ball, filled with rubber snakes.

"Y'all still playing that dumbass game?" Chasity asked as she and Jason walked down the stairs.

"It's fun, you should play," Malajia suggested, adjusting the bracelet on her wrist.

Jason stared at Mark as he continued to pick up the snakes. "Bruh, it's like five snakes, why is it taking you so long?" he teased.

"Shut up, my damn back hurts," Mark griped.

"Stop girlin' and stuff the damn things back in the ball," Malajia mocked, waving her hand at him dismissively.

Mark stood upright and angrily stuffed the contents back into the ball, mumbling something under his breath.

"Start the timer," Malajia urged. "Mr. and Mrs. Adams, come play with us."

"Not interested," Chasity muttered, folding her arms.

"Yes you *are*, get over here and catch these balls... I mean this ball," Malajia joked, much to the amusement of the guys.

Chasity rolled her eyes. "Shut up," she hissed.

Mark winded up the toy. "Mel, stop asking, just *make* them," he cut in. "Whoever has it when the snakes pop out gotta clean the bathroom in both the houses." He then immediately tossed the ball to Jason.

"Hell no," Jason refused, tossing the ball to Chasity, who caught it, then immediately threw it to Malajia.

"Y'all got me chopped if you think I'm cleaning y'all guys' nasty ass bathroom," Malajia scoffed, tossing the ball to Mark.

"I'm sure our bathroom is *pristine* compared to *y'all* pad filled bathroom," Mark mocked, tossing it to Jason.

"So, you think we just throw fuckin' pads all around the bathroom?" Chasity asked, annoyed.

"Chaz, he's stupid, don't pay him no mind," Malajia dismissed as the ball came flying at her. She let out a little scream as she threw it back to Jason. She was determined not to lose.

As soon as Jason caught it, he threw it to Mark, who glanced at the front door as it opened.

"Hey guys," Alex sighed, walking in and closing the door behind her.

"Catch thickums," Mark said, tossing the ball to her.

Alex caught it with both hands, a confused look on her face. "What in the world—" she screamed and jumped back as the snakes popped out of the top of the ball. "What is this?!" she wailed as her friends erupted with laughter.

"You gotta clean the house bathrooms," Mark teased, pointing. "In *both* houses."

Alex stared at the group as if they had lost their minds. "Y'all are crazy and that's *not* happening," she refused, tossing the ball on the accent chair, along with her book bag.

"Fine," Mark sighed, heading for the door. "Let me go make sure I have all my shit together for class tomorrow before we go to dinner."

"You're actually preparing for class *ahead* of time?" Jason asked, amused as he followed suit.

"Hell yeah. Shit, I'd hate to be like Alex's silly ass and have the wrong book and shit," Mark laughed.

"Not funny, get out," Alex ground out.

"Was already leaving," Mark threw back, walking out the door with Jason.

As the door closed, Alex removed her coat, walked over to the couch, and slung it over the back of it, before flopping face down on the cushions. This caught both Chasity and Malajia's attention. They walked over and stared down at her.

"You never had to flop down that hard," Malajia teased, earning a snicker from Chasity.

"Malajia, go away please," Alex warned, tone low, muffled by the cushions.

"Nah, I think I'll stay and annoy you some more," Malajia mocked.

Alex, face still smashed on the cushions, let out a groan.

"You sure you wanna lay your face on those cushions?" Chasity asked, when Alex didn't move.

"Sure, why not?" Alex replied, tone even.

"I fucked on them last night," Chasity jeered.

Alex immediately bolted up as Malajia busted out laughing. "Oh come on," Alex complained. "House rules, sex in your own damn rooms."

"I'm joking," Chasity promised, amusement in her voice.

"Funny," Alex scoffed, leaning back against the couch. She sighed as the girls took seats on both sides of her.

"What's wrong Mama Bear?" Malajia asked, noticing Alex's sullen demeanor.

Alex glanced at Malajia and smiled. "Aww, that's so cute, you called me 'Mama Bear'."

"See, never mind," Malajia scoffed of Alex's mushiness. "You always gotta ruin shit. Why you look all salty in the face, fat ass?"

Alex narrowed her eyes at Malajia, then turned her attention to Chasity, who was laughing. "She's not funny, and you *know* it," she griped.

"I'm hilarious and *you* know it," Malajia threw back.

"Anyway," Alex dismissed, with a wave of her hand. "Guess who I ran into today?"

"Not a *comb*," Malajia muttered of Alex's wild hair. The response made Chasity, who was already doubling over with laughter, scream louder.

Alex moved to get up from the couch. "Forget it," she fussed.

Malajia laughed as she grabbed hold of Alex's arm. "I'm just kidding," she assured, amused at Alex's annoyance. "Who did you run into?"

Alex ran her hand over her forehead. "Eric," she revealed. "He was in the bookstore."

"How was *that*?" Chasity wondered, laughter now subsided.

"Awkward as hell," Alex admitted, adjusting her back against the couch cushions.

"Yeah I can imagine," Malajia added. "You haven't spoken to him in a minute."

"I know," Alex agreed. "I apologized to him before we left school—"

"Did he forgive you?" Chasity asked.

Alex shook her head. "No...at least he didn't *say* that he did." She let out another sigh. "But he's *speaking* to me at least...or at least he *was*." She looked down at her hands. "I'm pretty sure my overly eager ass went and messed that up."

"What did you do?" Malajia asked, adjusting her position on the couch.

"I asked him out for coffee," Alex revealed, glancing at Malajia. "I knew it was too soon but I did it anyway... I couldn't help it, being near him again brought back all of these feelings..."

Chasity and Malajia were silent as Alex continued to reflect.

"I really miss him, and I thought that maybe if we started to hang out again, even if it was just for coffee that we could maybe get back to where things were before—"

"You started acting like an ass?" Malajia cut in.

Alex rolled her eyes. "Yeah," she admitted. "Anyway, I wasted my breath because he shot me down."

"Oooooohhhh," Malajia commented, putting her hand over her mouth. She could only imagine how terrible Alex felt.

"Yeah," Alex sulked. "I had egg *all* over my face and I swear to God Malajia, if you make a smart assed comment about me talking about food, I'm gonna smack you."

Malajia's mouth fell open. "Give me some damn credit, I *can* be sensitive you ass."

Chasity shook her head at Malajia's comeback, then focused her attention on Alex. "Can I ask you something?"

Alex looked at her. "Sure," she sulked.

"Why did you ask him out?" Chasity asked.

Alex looked confused. "I just *said* why."

"I can hear," Chasity sneered. "But I'm confused. Eric already said that he doesn't want to be just friends with you. And you *know* this, yet you tried to ask him out knowing that *you* still don't want what *he* wants… You're playing again."

Alex's eyes widened. "No, I'm *not*," she argued. "I'm not trying to sleep with him again; I just want us to be friends."

"He doesn't *want* that," Chasity reiterated through clenched teeth and poked Alex in the forehead.

"Ouch!" Alex shrieked, putting her hand over the spot where she was poked. "You didn't have to use your nail."

"I'm surprised her finger didn't *break* on it, as hardheaded as you are, Alex." Malajia chimed in.

Alex sucked her teeth as she gave the spot a rub. "Are you two done beating up on me? Can I go sulk in my room now?" she ground out.

"You may," Malajia granted, gesturing towards the staircase.

Alex stood up, then headed for the stairs. "This still stings Chasity," she grunted, walking up.

"Well maybe it'll mask the sting of your pride," Chasity threw back, earning a loud snicker from Malajia.

Chasity snapped her head in Malajia's direction. "You just fuckin' spit on me," she snapped, smacking the laughing Malajia with a pillow.

# Chapter 5

"Yo, somebody go in that kitchen and tell the cooks to stop making this nasty ass fuckin' lasagna," Mark complained, shoving his plate away from him.

"Every time they have lasagna, you get it and then complain about it," David laughed.

"'Cause I be hopin' that they actually get it *right* one time," Mark explained, folding his arms on the tabletop. Having gotten through their first day of classes, some of the group migrated to the cafeteria for dinner.

"God boy, *here*," Malajia ground out, breaking a piece of her hoagie and giving it to Mark. "*Please* stop getting the fuckin' lasagna. I'm sick of hearing you whine about it."

Mark mumbled something under his breath as he took a bite of the Italian hoagie.

"How was everyone's first day of classes?" David asked, taking a sip of juice.

"Dawg, nobody tryna talk about no classes right now," Mark sneered.

David picked up his turkey and cheese hoagie. "Don't get mad at *me* because your accounting professor gave you homework on two chapters," he threw back.

Mark pounded his fist on the table. "He ain't even go *over* them shits," he fussed, still upset over his assignment. "How you gonna give us homework for shit we didn't even *talk* about? What kind of shit is that?"

"It's called *college*," Alex pointed out, tone sarcastic. She had grown tired of Mark's complaining. "I'm sure you've heard of it; you've only been *in* it for four years."

Mark flashed a scowl Alex's way. "How's Eric Alex?" he threw back. Malajia nearly choked on her soda.

Alex's eyes widened. "*Really*, asshole?" she fumed as Malajia began coughing.

"Mark!" Malajia barked in between coughs. "Damn it!"

"Babe, she started with me," Mark defended, pointing at Alex.

"So *what*," Malajia fumed, nudging him on the arm. "I told you no teasing…at least not yet."

"So, you told him my business, *again*?" Alex hurled at Malajia.

"Oh stop acting all shocked, you already knew I was," Malajia drawled, waving a dismissive hand, much to Alex's annoyance. Malajia turned to Mark. "You're on time out," she hissed.

Mark sucked his teeth.

David ate some chips. "Mark, I swear, you stay getting in trouble," he teased.

"David, there go Nicole with Quincy," Mark immediately spat out, pointing behind David.

David quickly jerked his head around. "What?" he panicked, nearly knocking his basket of chips on the floor.

Malajia sucked her teeth as she backhanded Mark on the arm. "Chill the hell out," she snapped.

Realizing that he had been duped, David frowned and faced Mark, who was doubled over with laughter. "You're an asshole, you know that?" David fumed.

"Stop messin' with me then," Mark threw back, laughter subsiding.

Annoyed and shaken, David grabbed his coat, his remaining food, and stood up. "I'm outta here," he muttered.

"Tell Nicole I said 'hi'," Mark called after him.

Malajia, totally over her boyfriend's antics, leaned her elbow on the table and placed her head in her hands.

Mark leaned close to her. "What's wro—"

"Just shut up!" she barked.


David adjusted the knit hat on his head as he approached the steps to his house. Reaching for the doorknob, he paused. *I wonder what Nicole is doing*, he thought. Mark's little prank made him realize that he hadn't spoken to her all day. Shoving his hands in his coat pockets, he turned around and headed back out the gates.

Ignoring the harsh, cold wind, David made his way to the entrance of Paradise Terrace. Greeting dorm mates in passing, he walked to Nicole's room. As he went to knock, the door opened, startling him. It wasn't the fact that the door opened before he could knock that had David's eyes nearly popping out of his head; it was the fact that a tall, muscular, dark skinned man, walked out.

"Thanks again Nicky," the man called back into the room.

"No problem," Nicole replied.

David held his stunned gaze as the guy smiled. "What's up man?" the guy greeted as he walked away.

David followed the man's progress until he turned the corner, before turning back to the door, which was cracked. After a moment of hesitation, David gave the door a tap.

"Come in," Nicole called, glancing up from her textbook. She smiled when she saw David. "Hey you."

Closing the door behind him, David forced a smile "Hey."

"I wasn't expecting to see you today," she said, voice cheerful.

David fixed his eyes on her disheveled bed. *Yeah, I bet*, he thought. "Uh, why would you say that?" he asked, removing his hat.

Nicole shrugged as she retrieved another textbook from the floor. "I figured with it being the first day of classes that you would be swamped with homework," she reasoned. "Just like *I* am."

David nodded "Oh," he muttered. "Is that what you were doing with that guy that I saw leaving just now?"

Nicole looked up at him. "You saw Quincy leave just now?"

David's eyes widened. "*That* was Quincy?" he asked. Nicole nodded.

David ran a hand over his head as he took a deep breath. "Um, o-kay," he grumbled. *What the hell was he doing in here?* As much as he tried to keep his imagination at bay, it was unsuccessful. All sorts of scenarios were playing in his head.

"David, he was here to get some notes from me for History," she placated, seeing the panic on David's face. "That's all. I told you, you have nothing to worry about."

David still looked like he was about to throw up as he unzipped his coat.

"Summers, come sit down, you look like you're about to fall out," she giggled.

David sighed as he walked over to her bed.

"Take off your coat crazy, it's blazing in here," she ordered.

David did as he was told, then sat on the bed next to Nicole.

Nicole took her hand and ran it over David's hair. "Do you want me to introduce you two so you can see for yourself that he has no interest in me, other than just being a friend?"

"No, it's fine," David pouted.

When David didn't make eye contact with her, she tapped his shoulder, causing him to turn around. "How was your day...before *this*, I mean?"

David shrugged. "It was fine," he replied. "I think I'm really gonna enjoy my Advanced Physics—I don't understand why he needs notes after only the first day. What, he wasn't in class?"

Nicole put her hand over her face and laughed at David's instant subject switch. "He was late and got locked out the class, if you *must* know," she revealed.

David rolled his eyes. "How stupid," he muttered, staring down at his hands.

She shook her head. "You look like you could use some hot chocolate, you want me to make you some?" she offered, at an attempt to change the subject.

David sat in silence, staring out in front of him. He hadn't even heard her question due to his racing mind.

"Do you wanna kiss me?" Nicole blurted out.

David immediately snapped out of his daze. "Huh?" he sputtered, eyes wide.

"I *thought* that would get your attention," she chuckled. David gave a nervous laugh. "You want some hot chocolate?" she offered once again.

David nodded. "Yeah, thanks." David watched as Nicole stood up and walked over to her microwave to retrieve the box of instant hot chocolate from atop of it.

Realizing that he was still feeling on edge, he stood up. "On second thought, I'm gonna head out," he said.

Nicole looked at him as she grabbed a mug. "Oh, okay then." Her voice didn't hide her disappointment.

David grabbed his coat from the floor and walked over to her. "Sorry, I just remembered that I have another assignment to finish up."

Nicole reached up and gave him a hug. "I understand," she assured. "Call me before you go to sleep?" she put out, voice hopeful.

"Okay," he agreed. As Nicole went to give him a kiss, he turned his head and her lips landed on his cheek. "Night," he said, walking out the door.

Nicole sighed as the door closed. "Night," she said to the empty room.


Malajia unlocked the door and pushed it open. Cradling a small box in her hand, she walked over to the couch. "I haven't been here a whole *week* yet and my parents already sent me a package," she gushed, setting the box on the coffee table. "They love me and shit."

Chasity shook her head as she removed her coat. "I've had to be subjected to this damn care package conversation since we left the post office, do I really have to hear it now that we're home?" she ground out.

Malajia looked at her. "Yes, yes you do," she mocked.

Chasity rolled her eyes as she sat on the accent chair.

Malajia took a seat on the couch. "Don't be bitter because your mom didn't send you anything," she teased, amusement in her voice.

Chasity shot Malajia a glare. "You get *one* care package in four years—"

"Shut up, nobody asked you all that," Malajia cut in, waving her hand in Chasity's direction.

"Yeah, that's what I thought," Chasity sneered, examining her nails. "Besides, I got *my* care package in the mail *yesterday*."

Malajia sucked her teeth. "Was it from your dad?" she hissed.

"No, it was from *yours*," Chasity threw back.

Malajia's mouth dropped open at the immediate come back. "Bitch," she spat. "Good one though, I'm proud of you."

Chasity smirked.

Malajia sat up in her seat and reached for her package. "There better be blank checks in here," she said. She eyed the address on the box, or lack thereof. "They were so fast to get this out that they forgot to put the return address on it?" She shrugged, then ripped the box open.

Malajia was excited as she removed a card from the box. "'Malajia, have a good semester. Love you'," she read aloud.

"You do *not* have to be cheesin' that hard," Chasity teased.

"Keep talking and you won't get any— Ooh candy," she beamed, pulling three boxes of her favorite candy out. Setting the contents on the table, Malajia reached back in and retrieved small boxes of crackers, cookies, and popcorn, along with a small pack of tea, and a white mug with a red heart on it.

"Um…this heart ass mug is weird, but they're on point with the snacks," Malajia mused.

Chasity held her hand out. "Give me those cookies," she ordered.

"Bitch no," Malajia scoffed, moving the box out of reach. She grabbed the tea pack. "Here, you can have this nasty ass tea," she offered, handing it to her.

"I can't *eat* tea," Chasity barked, smacking Malajia's hand away.

"Well your ungrateful ass don't get nothin' then," Malajia ground out, putting the items back in the box.

Chasity sucked her teeth and stood up from the chair.

"Where are you going?" Malajia asked, as Chasity grabbed her coat from the chair.

"To that donut place," Chasity replied.

Malajia jumped up. "Ooh, I want donuts. I'm coming too," she said, grabbing her coat.

"No, you eat those dry ass cookies."

"Fuck those cookies," Malajia scoffed, following Chasity out of the door.


"Stop walking so damn close to me," Chasity griped as she and Malajia made their way to the SDC.

"Girl shut up, I walk where I want," Malajia threw back, bundling her coat to her neck. "Besides, your hell flames are keeping me warm."

Chasity rolled her eyes, but decided it wasn't worth the energy to respond.

As the girls entered the small donut shop within the SDC, Malajia rubbed her hands together. "Yessss, it smells like all kinds of sugary heaven in here."

Chasity shook her head as she eyed the selections on the glass-covered trays behind the counter.

Malajia leaned in close. "Two glazed and a powdered donut on you?" she hinted.

Chasity let out a loud groan as she tried to keep from backhanding Malajia across her face.

Malajia frowned as she looked at Chasity. "I don't appreciate the attitude," she hissed.

Fed up with Malajia's lack of respect for her personal space and her voice, Chasity jerked around and faced Malajia, pointing her finger in her face. "Malajia, I swear to God—"

"What kind of donut can I get for you?" a female voice behind the counter said, interrupting the impending argument.

Both girls turned around and stared at the cashier in shock. "What…the…fuck?" Chasity hissed.

"You've *got* to be kidding me," Malajia added, annoyed.

Jackie Stevens smiled. "Nice seeing you again Chasity and Malajia," she said.

"Bitch please," Chasity spat out. "The fuck are you doing here?"

"I work here," Jackie shrugged.

"*Why?*" Malajia fussed. The last person that she wanted handling her donuts was her enemy.

"Well, like I told you when I saw you a few weeks ago, I'm back at school part-time," Jackie replied, adjusting the uniform hat on her head. "I'm doing work study, so, here I am."

"There *is* no work study for part-time students you fuckin' liar," Chasity snarled.

Malajia busted out laughing.

Jackie rolled her eyes and let out a huff. "Well, I'm *working* and *studying* so technically—"

"*Technically,* we don't care," Malajia interrupted, flinging her hair over her shoulders. "You could've stayed in whatever gutter you pulled yourself out of."

"That's nice Malajia, real nice," Jackie spat, voice

dripping with sarcasm.

Chasity fixed an angry gaze. The more Jackie spoke, the more she wanted to lunge across that counter and smash her face into the donuts.

Malajia on the other hand had questions; she wanted to know exactly the mess that they were about to have to deal with now that Jackie was back. "So what, are the *rest* of the ratchet, rat crew back too?" she hissed to Jackie. "All of y'all raggedy asses dropped out at the same time."

Jackie shook her head. "Shawna got a record after getting caught stealing from the Mega Mart, Trina got pregnant and Dawn...who knows," Jackie informed them.

"Not surprised," Malajia spat out. "I'm sure Trina and her hoe ass is a *stellar* mother," she grunted, sarcastic.

Jackie tilted her head as she fixed a long gaze on Malajia. "She wouldn't know because she got an abortion."

Malajia frowned slightly, then looked away. If coming face-to-face with Jackie for the second time in weeks, wasn't bad enough. The girl completely ruined her mood by mentioning Trina's abortion. Although Malajia knew that Jackie had no idea how the mere mention of the word, brought back the memories of her *own* abortion, Malajia still wanted to slap her for it.

"I've had enough bullshit for one day," Chasity huffed, unaware of the anxiety that suddenly came over Malajia. "Fuck her, I'm leaving," she announced to Malajia.

Malajia watched as Chasity headed out of the shop and turned to follow.

"Malajia," Jackie called.

Malajia stopped and looked at her, frowning. "What?"

"You don't want your donuts?" she asked, giving her hat another adjustment.

"No, I don't want *anything* that your scaly hands touch," Malajia threw back.

"Well, *that's* good to know," Jackie replied, much to Malajia's confusion.

"Whatever bitch," Malajia scoffed. "Stay away from us."

"Gladly," Jackie bit out as Malajia walked out of the shop.


Sidra rubbed her forehead as she stared at the images on her laptop. "I should have never opened this email, I swear," she muttered. Just as she reached for her cup of tea, her cell phone rang. Without looking at the caller ID, she grabbed the phone.

"Yes Mama, why are you sending this stuff to me?" Sidra spat into the phone.

A deep chuckle came through the line. "I prefer *Daddy*," the man joked.

Sidra's eyes widened as she recognized the voice. "Ooh, sorry James," she said. "Hi."

"Hi," James Grant returned, amusement in his voice. "Expecting your mother, I take it?"

"Yeah," Sidra sighed. "But to be honest, I'm glad it *wasn't* her."

"Oh?"

Sidra rose from her seat at her desk and made her way over to the bed. "Yeah, she agreed to help my brother plan his stupid wedding that shouldn't even be happening in the *first* place," she vented, flopping down on the bed. "And now she's trying to drag me into the planning by sending me— swatches and décor ideas." She sucked her teeth. "Every time I think of this damn disaster of a wedding and of the *bride*, it gives me a headache."

"Okay sweetheart," James cut in. He sensed that Sidra's tempter was simmering and nearing its boiling point. "How about a subject change?"

"Yes please," Sidra sighed.

"I'll be in Virginia in two weeks, I'd love to spend some time with you," James said, tone hopeful.

"Sounds good," she replied, tone dry.

James chuckled. "I was hoping for a little more enthusiasm."

Sidra rolled her eyes, though she didn't mean to.

"Especially since we haven't been talking that often," he added. "You don't answer my calls as much."

Sidra rubbed her face with her hand. James had a point; out of the many times that he had called Sidra over the past week, she had only answered half the time. She didn't know why, but she just wasn't that pressed to spend hours on the phone with him like she used to. "I'm sorry, I've just been really busy with classes," she explained. "This is my last semester after all. You know that they want to make us suffer as much as possible."

"I suppose you have a point," James agreed.

Sidra glanced at her watch. "Speaking of classes, I have to go," she told him. "I almost forgot about my debate assignment."

"Oh okay." James didn't even try to hide his disappointment. "Well, I guess I'll call you later tonight."

"Sounds good, bye." Sidra ended her call and tossed her phone on the bed, letting out a long sigh. As she headed for her laptop again, she heard voices from downstairs. Curious, she walked out of the room.

Walking downstairs, she looked bewildered as she saw Mark holding the door to their refrigerator open, peering inside. "*What* are you doing here?" she blurted out, startling him.

Mark let out a yelp, as he spun around. "Damn Sid, announce yourself next time," he barked.

Sidra scrunched her face up as she was getting ready to fire off a retort but hearing the front door open, she spun around. Seeing Josh walk in, she immediately forgot about Mark.

"Hey Sid," Josh greeted.

Sidra offered a small wave and slight smile to go along with it. "Hi Josh."

"I don't mean to barge in here, but that fool in your fridge is taking too long," Josh explained. "We're supposed to be going to the gym."

Sidra stared at Josh as he spoke. *Yeah, you do look like you've been lifting some weights,* she thought, eyeing his physique.

Shaking her head to snap herself out of her daze, Sidra looked back at Mark, who was now doing a dance in front of the refrigerator. "Mark," she sighed. "*Why* are you in our fridge?"

Mark opened the freezer. "Malajia said that I could have the leftover spaghetti from yesterday," Mark explained, grabbing a half gallon of ice cream from the freezer.

"You know that's *ice cream*, right?" she pointed out.

Mark opened the container. "Is it?" he mocked.

Sucking her teeth, Sidra headed into the kitchen. She took the ice cream from Mark and placed it back in the freezer, then reached into the refrigerator and pulled out the container that he was looking for. "Here, now go, I have work to do," she said, nudging him away.

"Can I get a fork?" Mark asked. "I'm tryna finish this while I'm walking to the gym."

As Sidra went to grab a fork, Josh stared at Mark, shaking his head at him. "That is some greedy shit," he commented.

"Don't mind my business Joshua," Mark spat as Sidra handed him the utensil.

Sidra watched as both men headed for the door. "Josh," she called.

Josh spun around, looking at her.

"Have fun at the gym," she said.

Mark looked confused; Josh just chuckled. "Thanks...I guess."

"Sidra, that was weird," Mark jeered as he walked out the door.

"Shut up and eat your damn spaghetti." Josh spat at him, following him out of the house.

Once the door closed, Sidra smacked her forehead. "'Have fun at the gym'? What is wrong with you?"

The door opened once again. Seeing the girls walk in,

Sidra folded her arms. "Malajia, your man just left here with a container of food," she announced.

Malajia cradled a grocery bag as she walked to the kitchen. "I know, I just saw his greedy ass chewing and shit," she replied, setting the bag on the counter. She, along with Alex, Chasity and Emily, had just returned from the grocery store.

Alex walked over to Malajia and peered into her bag. "Do you have the shredded cheese in your bag?" she asked.

"Alex, I told you about letting that itchy ass shirt fabric touch me!" Malajia snapped in dramatic fashion.

"Girl!" Alex barked. "That's the second time today you made a loud outburst for no damn reason."

Malajia flagged Alex with her hand.

Alex reached into Malajia's bag and yanked the pack of shredded cheddar cheese from it. "Just give me the damn cheese," she fumed, teeth clenched. "Sick of you."

"My outbursts were justified," Malajia threw back.

Sidra looked confused. "*What* happened?" she wondered, curious.

Emily busted out laughing as she leaned against the counter. "Alex was trying to decide on which pack of ground beef to buy for tonight's chili dinner, and out of nowhere, Malajia throws her head back and shouts 'Alex, stop staring at the damn meat like you wanna give it a'... Wait what did you call it Malajia?"

"A twirly," Malajia answered.

Chasity busted out laughing.

"Oh yeah," Emily laughed. "Everybody who was within ear shot, looked at Alex. *Including* an old lady."

Sidra turned to Malajia, who was snickering. "What is *wrong* with you girl?" she hurled.

"Sidra, she spent like twenty minutes examining the fuckin' packs," Malajia explained, reliving the incident. "Like, pick one, and come the hell on."

"Not *only* did I have to endure people staring at me, I had to listen to Chasity's cackling ass laugh the whole damn ride back here," Alex fussed, folding her arms. "I had to drive her car because she couldn't stop laughing."

"You should've seen her face," Chasity said, laughter subsiding. "Her eyes got big as shit."

"Whatever," Alex grunted.

Sidra scanned the grocery items on the counter. Zoning in on something, she reached for it. "You got those dry donuts from the grocery store?" she scoffed.

"Yeah," Malajia grunted.

"Why?" Sidra wondered. "I heard that the donuts at the shop here on campus are *ten* times better."

"Don't nobody want donuts that Jackie been breathing on," Malajia grimaced, opening a bottle of soda.

Sidra's mouth fell open. "Wait, Jackie is actually back on campus?"

"Yup and she's shedding her scales on the donuts," Malajia scoffed.

Sidra sucked her teeth. "Damn it, why couldn't she just wait until we graduated?" Sidra recalled Malajia telling her that Jackie planned to return to Paradise Valley University over the winter. She never thought that Jackie would make good on it.

"'Cause she's just that damn spiteful," Malajia grumbled.

Sidra looked over at Chasity. "I'm surprised you didn't punch her on sight," she said.

Chasity pushed her hair over her shoulder as she began putting the groceries in the cabinets. "I don't have time to be worrying about that bitch," she scoffed.

Alex chuckled. "Not that I'm not happy that you haven't resorted to violence, but if this was *last year,* her face would have been in your hand by now," she said.

"Look I'm trying to *graduate*," Chasity threw back. Alex nodded in agreement. "I'm not gonna jeopardize that by cracking her damn face."

"If we do it off campus, we won't get kicked out," Malajia mumbled. "I'm just saying," she shrugged when the other girls looked at her with confusion.

"Yeah?" Alex questioned, folding her arms. "Do the words 'jail' and 'President Bennett's office' kick that stupid logic out of your head?"

Malajia made a face at Alex as she reached for a glass in the cabinet above her.

# Chapter 6

Clutching her cell phone to her ear, Emily darted out of her house, closing the door behind her. "God, I'm gonna be late," she complained.

"You sound like you're in a hurry," Dru Harris said through the line.

Emily walked at a quick pace out of the complex gates. "I am," she admitted, though she wasn't too busy to take a call from her eldest brother. "I have a meeting with the department head to go over some last-minute details about my teaching assignment, then I have to go straight to class."

"Oh yeah, you start teaching tomorrow, right?" Dru asked.

Emily smiled. She didn't know why she thought Dru wouldn't remember their conversation about her assignment from days ago, but she was happy that he did. "Yeah," she answered.

"Are you excited?" he asked.

"I'm *nervous*," Emily confessed, adjusting the book bag on her shoulder. "I guess I'm excited *too*, but the nervousness outweighs that."

A chuckle came through the line. "You'll be fine," he assured.

Emily shook her head. "Everybody keeps telling me that, but I still don't believe it," she sighed.

There was a pause on the line. "Will tells you that too, huh?" Dru assumed.

Emily once again shook her head. "Dru, don't start," she

warned. This wasn't the first time that her brother has brought up Will while talking with her.

"Em, I've said this before, I need to meet this man that has been occupying all of my sister's time," he demanded.

Emily rolled her eyes to the sky. "It's not even *all* of it," she pointed out.

"*Enough* of it," Dru amended.

"He's not even my *boyfriend*," Emily insisted.

"Not the point," Dru teased. "I can hear the smile in your voice every time you mention him."

"I think you're just imagining things," Emily muttered.

"Nah, I know what I'm talking about," Dru insisted. "He may not be your *boyfriend*, but it's clear that you like this dude."

Emily took the path towards the English building. "Fine Dru, if it'll make you feel better, I'll introduce you to him when you come down for graduation," she offered.

Dru gasped. "You're making me wait that long?"

"Yes," Emily chuckled.

"Fine," Dru muttered. "But look, I gotta get back to work but before I go, I need you to tell me what you want for your birthday."

Emily squinted her eyes in confusion. "My birthday?" she questioned.

"Yes, your birthday."

*For my mother to apologize to me*, Emily thought. "Umm, I don't know right now, can I think about it?" she asked, sullen.

"Of course, talk to you later."

"Bye." Emily hung up, then stuffed the phone into her book bag. Pausing short of walking up the building steps, she let out a deep sigh. Yet another birthday was approaching, and she was still estranged from her mother. Trying to push the somber thoughts aside, Emily headed inside.

Malajia walked into her class hall and sat in the back

row. Mark, whom she sat next to, looked over at her.

"Hey sugar foot," he smiled.

Malajia, not impressed with the new pet name, flashed a scowl his way. "Call me that again and I swear I'll dump you," she grunted.

Mark laughed as he pulled his notebook out of his book bag.

Malajia sighed as she glanced at her watch. "I'm like ten minutes late and the damn professor isn't even *here*," she complained, craning her neck to scan the front of the hall. "I already didn't feel like taking that long ass hike from the house to this building, so he *better* show up."

Mark tapped his pencil on his desk. "Shiiit, he can stay his ass *wherever* he's at," he replied. "I'm not in the mood for no marketing bullshit today."

Malajia shot him a knowing look. "You didn't finish your assignment from last class, *did* you?"

"Nope," Mark threw back.

Malajia shook her head. "Mark if you fail, I'm leaving you," she ground out.

Mark sucked his teeth. "Yeah, yeah," he replied dismissively. After a few moments of comfortable silence, Mark looked at Malajia. "So, Queen Evil doesn't want to do anything for her birthday this year," he announced. "You wanna take advantage of a free Valentine's Day and do something together? It'll be our first one as a couple."

"*First* of all, I told you about calling my bestie names," Malajia spat out of Chasity. A smile then broke across her face. "But yeah, I *do*."

"Good...now I actually have to think of something," Mark said, putting his hand on his chin.

"Babe we don't have to do anything fancy," Malajia assured. "As long as I'm with you, it'll be a great Valentine's Day."

"So that means we can just spend the whole day butt ass naked in bed?" Mark wondered, eyes lighting up at the possibility.

*"Hell* no, you cheap ass freak," Malajia snapped.

Mark busted out laughing. "I *knew* you were lying your ass off."

"You damn right. As much as you get on my damn nerves, you *better* do something fancy," she fussed, folding her arms.

Mark put his hand over his face and shook his head. "Noted," he said finally.

Malajia fixed an angry gaze on him. "I'm not fuckin' around with you Mark," she fumed.

Mark chuckled as he put his hand on her arm. "I got you," he promised.

"Fine," she grunted, rolling her eyes.

Seeing some of his classmates stand from their seats, Mark looked at his watch. "Whelp-ah, looks like Professor Collins ain't showing up," he said, ecstatic. "Let's bounce baby."

Malajia grabbed her belongings. As they both rose from their seats, the door opened, sending several disappointed, groaning students back to their chairs.

"Please excuse my tardiness," Professor Collins apologized as he made his way to the front of the room.

Mark sucked his teeth and flopped down in his seat. "Come on *man*," he complained.

"We salty," Malajia chortled, sitting back down.


Sidra let out a loud groan as she bundled her scarf up to her neck. "It does *not* have to be this cold out," she complained to Josh as she exited the post office.

"Sid, it's February, what do you expect?" he teased, pulling his gloves on.

"Funny," she grumbled, inciting a slight laugh from Josh.

Making their way through the hordes of students, Sidra needed anything to take her mind off of the bitter cold wind whipping around her. "Do you have anything planned for

Valentine's Day?" she asked, adjusting the purse strap on her shoulder.

"Um...no, not really," Josh sulked.

Sidra, having realized her insensitivity, winced. "Oh I'm sorry Josh, I didn't—"

"It's okay," Josh assured.

"No, what I meant was—" she ran her hand over her hair. "Instead of celebrating Chaz's birthday like we *normally* do, I think everybody is doing their own thing for Valentine's Day."

"I figured," Josh replied. "Chaz really doesn't want to do anything this year, huh?"

Sidra shook her head, hoping that Josh wouldn't hold her question against her. "No," she replied. "We asked her what she wanted to do, and she said, and I quote; 'not a damn muthafreakin' thing."

Josh shot her a quizzical look. "Chaz said 'freakin'?"

Sidra laughed. "No, I cleaned it up of course," she admitted.

"Of course," Josh chuckled, nodding his head. After a few moments of silence, Josh was about to say something, when he saw someone that he recognized.

"Hey Laurie," he smiled to the young woman.

"Hey yourself, my favorite project partner," the pretty, brown-skinned woman smiled back as she approached. "I went to the library earlier and checked out that book that we needed."

"Oh good," Josh breathed. "I was planning on going myself later."

"See, I got you boo," Laurie crooned.

Sidra stared as the two kept talking; Josh hadn't bothered to introduce them. If that didn't bother Sidra, the fact that the girl called Josh 'boo' sure did. *Who calls a man, who isn't their boyfriend, boo?*

"Cool, you know I appreciate you." Josh smiled, adjusting his book bag on his shoulder. "I have to get to class, I'll call you later."

"We're still on for Friday, right?" Laurie called after Josh as he and Sidra continued on their way.

"Yeah," Josh replied.

Sidra was silent for a few moments as they walked. "So…she seemed nice," she said finally.

"Yeah, she's cool," Josh replied nonchalantly. "We're working on a class project together."

"Oh okay." Sidra adjusted her purse strap once more. "You're going to be working on the project on a Friday?" she pressed. "That's some serious dedication."

Josh scratched his head, almost as if he didn't want to answer. "Uh…no." Sidra glanced at him. "She asked me to dinner."

"Oh?" Sidra gasped. As far as she knew, Josh was putting his dating life on hold. "You mean on a *date*?"

Josh shook his head. "No, not really, just dinner," he replied.

Sidra felt a flutter in the pit of her stomach. The idea of another woman asking Josh out, made her feel sick. "Well that was *bold*," she stated.

"Maybe," he agreed. "Anyway, like I said it's just dinner. She knows that I'm not looking for a relationship."

Sidra frowned. "I take it she doesn't care since she wants to go out with you *anyway*."

Josh adjusted his book bag. "She's not *looking* for a relationship *either*," he revealed.

"Oh *really*?" Sidra sneered.

Josh looked at her. "What are you trying to say?" he ground out.

Sidra put her hand up. "Look, she might not want a relationship, which by the way, I think is bullshit," she argued.

Josh raised an eyebrow as Sidra ranted on.

"And even if she *was* being honest about that, I'm pretty sure, that girl wants something *else*," Sidra concluded.

Josh stopped walking and stared at Sidra, who in turned halted her own progress. "So?" he replied.

Sidra's eyes widened. "And you're *okay* with that?"

Josh shrugged. "Maybe."

Sidra ran her hand over her hair. Josh never struck her as the casual sex type. "Josh…" she paused for a moment to calm herself down. If the thought of Josh going on a date made her feel sick, the thought of him having sex made her feel worse. "You're not that type of guy."

"Never said I *was*," Josh threw back. "However, I'm single and allowed to do what I *want*."

"And that includes screwing someone you don't *know*?"

Josh held a stern gaze on Sidra. "Don't judge me," he spat.

Sidra was taken aback, and it showed on her face. "I'm *not* judging you," she threw back, annoyed.

"Seems like you *are*," Josh argued. "But you have no *right* to."

Sidra's eyes widened yet again. "What does *that* mean?"

"It *means* that unless you're still a virgin, which I'm pretty sure you're *not*, you can't judge *anybody* for having sex, no matter *who* it's with," he argued.

Sidra's mouth fell open as she came to a realization. *Josh thinks that I had sex with James.* She wondered if she should tell him that she was still a virgin; she *wanted* to. Then it dawned on her: *why should it matter? Why should I make it his business? And why am I making his sex life, mine?*

Sidra let out a sigh as she checked her attitude. "You're right, I'm sorry."

"It's fine," he said, voice dripping with disdain.

"No really, what you do is your business," Sidra added.

"No need to dwell on it, let's just go," Josh spat.

Sidra held her gaze on Josh as he walked off. *He's really pissed at me,* she thought as she slowly headed off in an attempt to catch up to him. She felt horrible. She'd upset him, and she hadn't meant to. She wanted to call after him, but he was several strides in front of her. *Keep your mouth shut*

*Sidra, you've said enough.*

Emily jotted some notes down, only to quickly erase them. "Come on, think," she coaxed herself, leaning back in her seat. Trying to finalize her mock lesson for her assignment the next day was stressing her out, among other things. The sound of Malajia yelling from downstairs, didn't help.

"Emilyyy! Will just pulled up in front of the hooouuuse!" Malajia screamed.

"Oh my God, will you shut the fuck *up!*" Chasity hollered from her room.

"Really Malajia?!" Alex followed up. "You were right by my damn ear with all that noise."

Emily shook her head and stood from her desk. "Wow, just wow," she muttered. She gave herself a once over in the mirror. "Come on Emily," she reassured herself. "This shouldn't stress you this much."

She opened the door, then headed out into the hall just as Chasity emerged from her room. Emily giggled at the annoyed look on Chasity's face.

"She's fuckin' irkin', yo," Chasity bit out of Malajia as both she and Emily walked down the stairs.

Malajia glanced up from the couch; she laughed at the disgust on Chasity's face. "Did I disturb your studying boo?" she teased.

Chasity narrowed her eyes at Malajia. "I should've gotten my own apartment," she grunted, heading for the kitchen.

"I hear you Chaz, and I share your sentiment trust me," Sidra commented from the dining room table. "That damn girl almost gave me a heart attack."

"Malajia, you never can use your inside voice," Emily commented, smoothing her sweatshirt down.

"Isn't she ridiculous?" Alex fumed, rubbing her ear. "I swear, I hear a ringing in my ear."

"Look, I was *trying* to be a good housemate and let Emily know that her company was here," Malajia explained, pointing to herself.

"You could've walked up the *damn steps* and told her," Sidra hissed. "Instead of busting out people's damn eardrums."

"Oh shut up," Malajia dismissed, waving her hand.

Emily scratched her head. "Malajia, you said Will was here?"

"His car is out there," Sidra informed, pointing to the window.

Emily headed over to the bay window in the living room and glanced out of it. She watched Will close his car door and walk up to the house. He was carrying a book bag and holding what appeared to be a large blanket.

Spinning around, Emily faced the girls. "Okay so, I think I should probably mention that—" she paused when she saw a mug of tea on the coffee table. "You may want to move that tea from the table," she advised, pointing to it.

"Why? I'm about to drink it," Malajia replied, confused.

Emily walked over and carefully grabbed the hot cup off the table. "Just trust me," she urged, taking it to the kitchen.

Before anybody could comment on Emily's weird request, Will knocked on the door. Emily darted over, opening it. She smiled at Will and stepped aside to let him in.

"It's freezing out there," Will commented as Emily quickly shut the door behind him.

"So, you decided to wear your blanket outside?" Chasity mocked, eyeing the brightly colored throw covering the upper half of Will's body.

Will chuckled. "I needed the extra covering." Noticing the confusion on the girls' faces, Will glanced at Emily. "You didn't tell them?" he assumed.

Emily winced. "Was getting ready to but—"

"Tell us *what*?" Alex pressed, curious.

Will removed the cover from his body, revealing a snowsuit-covered, sleeping child. He set the blanket on the chair in front of him, then carefully turned the child around for the girls to see. "Ladies, meet Anthony," he beamed.

"Oh my God, he's so cute!" Sidra shrieked. The loud squeal not only startled the adults in the room, but Anthony as well, who jerked awake. An ear-piercing cry followed.

"Damn it Sidra!" Malajia barked, as Sidra placed her hands over her mouth. "And you talk about *me* busting eardrums."

"I'm so sorry," Sidra apologized sincerely.

Will chuckled as he tried to calm the little boy down. "It's okay Tony, the crazy lady didn't mean to scare you," he teased.

Sidra lowered her head in embarrassment as her friends laughed at her.

As Will sat on the couch and removed the heavy snowsuit from his son, who was finally calming down, Emily went into the kitchen and searched the cabinets. Not finding what she was looking for, she closed the cabinet door and frowned. "What happened to that pack of butter cookies that was in here?" she asked.

Malajia looked at her. "You mean the purple pack?"

Emily eyed Malajia skeptically. "Yes."

"I ate those," Malajia admitted.

Emily's eyes widened. "The *whole* pack?!" she exclaimed. Malajia shrugged. "By your*self*?"

"Look, in my defense—they were some good ass cookies," Malajia returned at a sad attempt to defend her greedy actions.

"Seriously?" Emily was annoyed. She'd bought those cookies after giving Will the okay to introduce her to Anthony that day. She had planned on giving them to the little boy.

"Emily it's okay, I have some in my bag for him," Will cut in.

Emily shook her head at Malajia as she walked back into the living room.

Malajia turned around to see Alex staring at her.

"What?" she snapped.

"You don't have to eat *every* damn snack in the house," Alex spat out. "There are other people living here."

"Shut the hell up, you just mad 'cause *your* fat ass ain't get to 'em first," Malajia threw back, flicking her hair over her shoulder.

Alex made a face in retaliation.


Emily took a bite of her cookie and watched as Anthony made his way around the room, throwing his soft toy ball around. In the forty-five minutes that he'd been at the house, the toddler went from fussy, to apprehensive, to playful.

"He has so much energy," Emily mused, watching the boy roam.

"Yeah, I know," Will chuckled, keeping a close eye on his son. "And he'll keep that energy all damn night because of that nap he took earlier."

Emily giggled. "Maybe I should've just gone over your place so you wouldn't have had to bring him out."

Will shrugged. "Nah, I was cool with coming to you," he assured; he touched her arm with his hand. "Thanks for agreeing to meet him," he said, grateful. "I know you were apprehensive."

Emily offered a warm smile. "You're welcome." She adjusted her position on the couch. "And the apprehension was never because of *him*," she assured. "It was *me*. I was afraid that he wouldn't take to me."

"I already told you he *would*," Will stated. "*Especially* since you were the one who gave him that cookie that's still in his hand."

Emily nodded. "Yeah, you did." She ran a hand through her hair. "Also…I think I was just a little confused on why you wanted me to meet him in the first place," she admitted.

A look of confusion fell upon Will's face. "What do you mean?"

"Well…I guess I just figured that you would want to

introduce your child to someone who's actually your girlfriend and not just a friend," she explained, though Emily was not sure how well she was doing it. "Friends come and go you know."

"So do *girlfriends*," Will pointed out.

Emily winced. "Point made."

"Title doesn't mean anything to me, regarding who I bring around my son," he said. It's the *person* and you're a good—no *great* person, who I'm honored to know and who I want my son to know."

Emily blushed and looked down at her hands.

"I mean, I know that we've only known each other a few months but…you've become important to me," Will admitted.

"Really?" Emily questioned. Though she felt that Will was telling the truth about how he felt about her, she just wasn't used to a man having those feelings for *her*, so she still felt the need to question.

Will nodded. "Absolutely," he confirmed.

Emily stared at him, taking in his face and the intensity in his eyes as he held his gaze on her. *God, he's so handsome. I wonder what*—she refused to finish her thought. *Nope, nope, don't even go there.* She cleared her throat and glanced away; *time for a subject change.* "Um, so how do you like the new apartment? Did you—" Anthony's loud squeal of delight interrupted Emily's question.

Both she and Will glanced over and saw him standing by the staircase. He was watching Chasity as she walked down the steps.

Chasity looked down at the boy and smiled. "What's all that noise for?" she cooed, kneeling in front of him.

"Hi," Anthony made out.

"Hi cutie," Chasity smiled, holding her hand out for him to shake. Anthony eagerly placed his hand in Chasity's outstretched one. Feeling something squishy, Chasity made a face and looked down to see a smashed tan substance. "Tell me this is a chewed-up cookie and not something else," she directed to Will, who immediately jumped up with a tissue.

"It's a cookie, sorry about that," he winced, handing the tissue to Chasity. "I swore he ate it."

Chasity stood up as she wiped her hand clean. "It's fine," she assured, heading for the kitchen with Anthony running behind her in close pursuit. "Why are you running up on me little one?" she teased as she washed her hands in the sink. Anthony just stared up at her, smiling.

Emily let out a giggle. "You have a pint-sized admirer, Chasity," she mused.

Will ran a hand on top of his head. "Yeah, when you went upstairs earlier, he tried to go after you," he chuckled.

"Well, you better get him, because I'm about to go out," Chasity announced.

"Chasity!" Alex yelled from upstairs.

Chasity ignored her as she headed for the door.

Emily looked at Chasity. "You didn't hear her?" she wondered.

"I did," Chasity confirmed, putting on her coat.

"Chasity?" Alex belted out again as she stepped out of her room. From downstairs, they heard Alex knock on a door. "Chaz?"

Emily covered her mouth to conceal her laugher while Chasity stood by the couch, examining her nails. "She's down here Alex," Emily announced after a moment.

Alex made her way down, to see Chasity standing there staring at her. "You *know* you heard me," Alex put out, annoyed.

Chasity shrugged as if she didn't care. "What do you want?"

Alex stood there in stunned silence. "Really? You—" she put her hand up in an effort to calm herself; she wanted to curse Chasity out for being outright ignorant. "Are you heading out?"

Agitated, Chasity gestured to the coat that she was wearing. "What do you *want*?" she barked.

"Calm down," Alex bit back. "Can you stop by the mall

and pick up that—*thing*?" she asked, eyes shifting.

Chasity rolled her eyes. "You mean your vibrator? Sure, I'll pick it up for you," she mocked, walking out the door, leaving Alex standing there with her mouth open in shock.

Alex turned to Emily and Will, who both stared back at her. "Yeah, like she would *actually* pick up a vibrator for me," Alex ground out, heading for the steps. "She's such an asshole."

"Alex, there's a child here," Emily reminded, pointing to Anthony.

Alex winced. "Sorry," she apologized, trotting up the steps.

Emily just shook her head as Will laughed.


"You fix your damn faces," Malajia barked at Chasity and Jason as she removed her coat and slid into the booth.

"I know, right?" Mark agreed, sliding in next to her. "We've had to put up with y'all damn attitudes through the entire movie."

Jason and Chasity, who were seated across from them at the diner, both looked at their friends as if they had lost their minds. "You crashed our damn date night," Jason reminded, exasperated.

Mark flagged Jason with his hand dismissively.

"And ran your fuckin' mouths through the *whole* damn movie," Chasity added. "And you question our damn *attitude*?"

Malajia pointed her finger at Chasity. "*First* of all, *you always* have a damn attitude," she sneered. Chasity flipped Malajia the finger. "*Second*, that movie was dry as shit and *third,* you invited us on a double date with you."

Chasity looked like she wanted to smash Malajia's face on the table. "No the fuck we *didn't*!" she exclaimed, slamming her hand on it instead.

"Where did you get *that* from?" Jason asked, confused.

Malajia looked to Mark for backup, but all she received

was a shaken head from him.

"Naw babe, that didn't happen," Mark confirmed.

Malajia frowned. "It didn't?"

"No," Mark assured, amused. "We saw them walking to the car and asked them if we could go with them. They told us to go to hell, and we jumped in the car when Chaz unlocked the door."

Malajia snickered; she remembered the incident clearly. She turned back to face Jason and Chasity, and flagged them with her hand. "So what, y'all already knew we wasn't gonna let y'all go out without us," she said, flinging her hair over her shoulders.

Chasity rubbed her temples as the waiter brought them menus. Earlier, she'd headed to the mall to pick something up, then went back to campus to wait for Jason to get out of the library so they could go on their date. The last thing she had wanted, was for their alone time to be crashed by Malajia and Mark. "I swear to God, I can't wait to graduate so I don't have to see this idiot every day."

"You aren't gonna get rid of me *that* easily sister," Malajia teased, relishing Chasity's annoyance. "Keep talking, I'll move right in your neighborhood."

"Who says that I'm staying in West Chester?" Chasity sneered.

"It doesn't matter, I'm following you *anywhere*," Malajia barked, clapping her hands with each word. The dramatic response made Jason and Mark laugh. Chasity just shook her head in disgust.

"Anyway, what are you guys planning for Valentine's Day?" Mark asked.

"You mean my *birthday*?" Chasity bit out.

Mark shook his hand in Chasity's direction. "You had three years of this, it ain't about you no more," he joked.

Chasity couldn't help but laugh. "I hate you," she said, reaching for her menu. "My parents forever screwed me with this 'born on a holiday' shit."

"Naw, they screwed *each other*, *you* just happened to

pop your happy ass *out* on the holiday," Malajia teased.

"Fuck you Buttons," Chasity replied as the waiter approached.

"Fuck you *too*, Pebbles," Malajia threw back.

Once orders were placed and the waiter returned with their drink order, Mark folded his arms on the table. "So anyway, y'all got any plans?"

"Yeah, *we* do," Jason said, gesturing to Chasity.

Mark sucked his teeth. "Ain't nobody tryna crash y'all Valen-Birthday shit," he ground out. "I was just asking."

"Don't get all swole up in the chest at *me*, after the shit you pulled today," Jason threw back, reaching for his glass of water.

"Whatever," Mark grunted, reaching for his glass of iced tea. "What I have planned for me and Mel, don't include y'all *anyway*."

"Ooh, you planned something already?" Malajia beamed, glancing over at Mark. "You gonna spill some details?" she asked, clasping her hands together.

"Nope," Mark returned, taking a sip of his tea. Malajia sucked her teeth as Mark pulled the glass from his lips, frowning in disgust. "Come on with this bland ass tea and shit," he complained.

"You didn't hear the waiter say that the tea was unsweetened?" Jason asked, bewildered.

Mark stared at him for several seconds. "Maybe I didn't," he admitted, reaching for the sugar packets. "Shut up Jason," he grunted when Jason snickered.

Malajia placed a straw in her glass of soda and prepared to take a sip, but a notification from her phone stopped her. "This better not be Alex about that damn thing you picked up earlier," she griped, reaching into her purse. "Chasity, answer your damn phone so she can stop bugging *me*."

"Nope," Chasity refused, sipping her fruit punch.

"What thing are y'all talking about?" Mark asked, curious.

Malajia looked at her phone. "Something for Emily," she

answered, scrolling. "The hell?" she blurted out as she eyed a message.

Mark glanced at her. "What's wrong?"

"Somebody just texted me a blurry ass picture," Malajia frowned. "No message or nothing, just a blur."

"Who is it from?" Mark wondered, glancing at Malajia's phone.

"I don't know, I have no idea whose number this is," Malajia fussed. "It just says 'unknown.'"

"Is it that same number that you kept getting texts from a few months ago?" Chasity asked, recalling Malajia's complaints of this happening before.

Malajia shook her head. "No, I blocked that number a long time ago," she assured. "I must have a recycled phone number or something."

"Malajia, your number hasn't changed since freshman year," Chasity pointed out. "And you didn't start getting those weird messages until last semester."

"Yeah well..." Malajia spat, unable to think of a good explanation. "Whatever, this number is about to get this block too... After I figure out what this is a picture of," she added, bringing the phone close to her face in an effort to make out the image. "It looks like a blurred penis."

Mark quickly reached for the phone. "Who's sending you dick pics?" he barked. "I'll choke slam the shit outta 'unknown'."

Malajia busted out laughing as she handed him the phone. "I'm kidding," she teased. "It looks like a close-up of a hand or something."

"Yeah it better be *just* a damn hand," Mark grunted, handing Malajia her phone back. "And it *better* not be on no damn dick."

Malajia laughed again.

# Chapter 7

Emily walked down the steps, book bag in hand. "Morning," she greeted to Alex and Sidra in the kitchen.

Sidra smiled at her. "Morning," she returned, scooping freshly made oatmeal from a small pot into a bowl. "Do you want some breakfast?" she offered.

Emily smoothed her hand down her pink cardigan, sighing in the process. "No, I'm fine thanks."

Alex chuckled. "We know you're not fond of oatmeal," she said. "I made cheese eggs and bacon. Help yourself."

Emily sat on the arm of the couch. "No, it's not that. I actually *like* the way Sidra makes oatmeal," she said.

Sidra playfully tapped Alex's arm. "See, I told you I make the best oatmeal," she grinned.

Alex just shook her head in amusement.

"I just don't have much of an appetite," Emily admitted.

Alex grabbed her plate of food and walked to the dining room table. "Nervous, huh?"

Emily nodded.

"Don't be, you'll be fine," Alex assured her, sitting at the table.

Here it was, the first day of Emily's teaching assignment, and Emily's nerves hadn't gotten any better. She was exhausted, a result of not getting any sleep the night before. She let out another long sigh. "You know I just—"

"Hey Miss teacher," Malajia beamed, trotting down the steps. She was holding something behind her back.

Emily managed a smile. "*Student* teacher," she

corrected, looking at Malajia.

"Same difference," Malajia shrugged.

Sidra joined Alex at the table with her food. "You know you saying 'same difference' is an oxymoron, right?" she scoffed.

"Don't call me a moron, dress slacks," Malajia threw back.

Sidra stared at Malajia, dumbfounded. "Wow," she muttered after a moment.

Malajia moved over towards the couch, then when Emily wasn't looking, gestured to Alex.

Alex quickly took a bite of bacon, then signaled for Emily. "Em, I know you're not hungry sweetie, but you really should put *something* in your stomach," she advised.

"Yeah, at least have one bite," Sidra added.

Emily stood from her seat. "Yeah, you're right," she admitted, making her way towards the kitchen.

With Emily's focus elsewhere, Malajia quickly pulled the small box that she was holding from behind her back, and proceeded to unzip Emily's book bag. Just as she was about to stuff the box into her bag, Emily nearly turned around.

"Make sure you get a glass of juice out the fridge," Sidra quickly blurted out, halting Emily's progress out of the kitchen.

Emily grabbed the juice from the refrigerator. "Are there any to-go cups in here?" she asked.

Malajia quickly stuffed the box in the bag and zipped it back up. She then walked to the kitchen and grabbed the carton of juice from Emily. "Thanks girl, I'm thirsty," she said, drinking the rest of the juice, straight from the carton.

Emily tossed her hands in the air in frustration. "I have to go," she muttered, grabbing a piece of bacon from a plate on the counter. She took a bite of it as she grabbed her book bag. "See you."

"Good luck sweetie," Alex called after her as Emily headed out the door.

Malajia walked over to the table and set the empty juice

carton down. "She looks so studious with her little sweater on," she mused. She glanced around and saw Sidra and Alex frowning at her. "What?"

"You're replacing that damn juice," Alex sneered.

Malajia scoffed. "That little ass swig? Y'all got me chopped," she refused, walking away.

"At least put the damn thing in the trash!" Sidra yelled after her.

"Nope, you got it," Malajia flashed back, walking back upstairs.

Sidra sucked her teeth as she went back to her food.

"Stop shaking," Emily coaxed herself as she slowly walked up the steps to Paradise Valley Elementary school. She had hoped that the scenic ten-minute bus ride would calm her a little bit, but it hadn't. Reaching the school entrance, Emily pulled the door open. She scanned the hallway, taking in the atmosphere. It was bright and colorful, what she'd expected from an elementary school. Classroom doors were decorated using different themes; she smiled at the sight. Arts and crafts was something that she was fond of and hoped to incorporate in one of her lessons.

Stopping by a chair, Emily grabbed a piece of paper from a pocket of her book bag. Checking the class information, she made her way to her assigned room, stopping in front of it.

"Here goes nothing," she said to herself, before opening the door. A smiling young woman immediately acknowledged her.

"Hi, you must be Emily Harris from Paradise Valley University," the bubbly dark-skinned woman greeted, crossing the room, hand outstretched.

"Yes," Emily smiled, shaking the woman's hand.

"I'm Ms. Olivia to the children, but *you* can call me Livy."

"Nice to meet you Livy," Emily smiled, glancing around

the colorfully decorated classroom. "I know that I'm super early—"

"No, you're fine," Olivia assured, walking back to her desk. "We can get to know each other a bit." Seeing that Emily hadn't moved from her spot in front of the door, Olivia giggled. "You can put your things in that closet over there," she stated, pointing to the door. "And you have a desk near the window."

Emily nodded as she walked over to the closet. She removed her coat and hung it on a hanger.

Olivia watched as Emily made her way over to her assigned desk and plopped her book bag down next to it.

"You don't talk much do you?" Olivia joked, sitting down.

Emily felt the urge to look down at the floor in embarrassment. *Stop that—you're grown. Look people in the eye.* Listening to the voice in her head, Emily pushed some of her hair behind her ear as she smiled again. "Sorry if I seem standoffish, I'm just nervous."

Olivia waved her hand. "Oh its fine, I understand," she said. "*I* was nervous my first day too, but I quickly learned that these little ones are harmless. They're just little people who are eager to learn…and play."

"Yeah, I love children," Emily mused, sitting down.

"Are you looking to teach kindergarten when you graduate?" Olivia asked.

"I'm not sure yet," Emily replied, feeling some of the nervousness ease. "I know that I want to teach children, but I'm still trying to figure out what grade."

"Well I'll tell you that kindergarten students take a lot of energy, but they are the most fun to teach," Olivia replied, twirling an apple on her desk. "Plus, I love art and I have an excuse to play with finger paints and crafts."

"I love art too," Emily beamed. "I had to do a few mock assignments for my education classes and I found myself coming up with a lot of art projects."

"I'd love to take a look at them," Olivia offered. "I was

told by the office that you'll be here two days a week for the duration of your assignment." Emily nodded. "For the first few weeks, I'll let you shadow me and after that I'm going to let you actually run the class."

Emily's eyes widened as she gulped. "By myself?"

Olivia giggled at the horrified look on Emily's face. "I'll be in here with you," she promised. "But it'll be good practice for you. You'll do just fine; I can see it already."

"I hope you're right," Emily muttered. The sound of the school bell startled her.

Olivia glanced at the door, then turned back to Emily. "It's almost show time," she said, standing from her desk as loud chatter and running could be heard through the hall.

Emily simply nodded, waiting in anticipation. Reaching into her book bag for her notebook, she frowned when she felt something weird. Pulling a small brown box from the bag, she eyed it with suspicion. *What the heck? I didn't put this in here.* Opening it, her confusion gave way to a bright smile. Tears pricked the back of her eyes as she pulled a glass apple from inside the box, accompanied with a note written on a pink index card.

*Happy first day of teaching, baby sis. You've got this.*
*Xoxo,*
*Alex, Chasity, Malajia and Sidra*

Emily wiped the forming tears from her eyes and set the apple on her desk. Knowing that she had support from her friends meant the world to her; it helped her confidence. *Yeah, you've got this.*

She rose from her seat as the door opened.


Alex closed her textbook and placed the cap on her highlighter. "I'm so over words right now," she griped, gathering her belongings from the library table.

"Tell me about it," Sidra complained. "I'm about to buy a damn gavel just so I can beat this Prosecution Process textbook with it."

Alex chuckled. Having been in the library drafting two papers for over three hours, Alex was desperate to put some distance between herself and the building; she was certain Sidra was as well. "Do you regret choosing your major?"

"No," Sidra shook her head and rubbed the back of her neck. "I mean it's a lot of work and I get frustrated sometimes, but I still want to be a lawyer."

"Yeah, I feel the same about becoming an editor," Alex said, pulling her hair into a wild ponytail. "Don't get me wrong, I'm sick of synonyms, adverbs, and damn revisions, but I know that once I get into my field, I'll love it."

Sidra packed her textbooks and notes away in her book bag. "You can feel free to revise any of my papers, anytime," she said.

Alex waved her hand at Sidra dismissively. "Honey you don't need revisions. Your papers are always on point."

"I will take that lie and run with it," Sidra joked, slinging the book bag over her shoulder. "This homework has me in cranky mode."

Alex placed her arm around Sidra's shoulder. "Come on Princess, let's go grab something to eat," she suggested. "Food always seems to calm your crankiness."

"Yeah, if it's covered in chocolate…and caffeine," Sidra grunted.

"Hot chocolate with whipped cream on top, it is," Alex smiled as both girls headed through the stacks.

Upon reaching the exit, Alex glanced at something and came to a halt. "Shit," she hissed.

Sidra frowned in concern. "What's wrong?"

"Um…Eric is over there," Alex whispered, pointing.

"Eric?" Sidra repeated, voice loud.

"Shhhhh!" Alex panicked, as she saw Eric look behind him from his place by the information desk. "Don't make him look over here, baby Malajia."

Sidra put her hands on her hips and regarded Alex sternly. "First of all, *never* could I be as loud as Malajia," she spat out. "Second, what's with the nervousness? You guys are cordial now."

Alex shrugged. "I honestly don't know," she admitted, staring at him.

Sidra gave Alex a sympathetic look as she came to a realization. "Oooh, you're still embarrassed that you asked him out and he declined, huh?"

Alex rolled her eyes. "No, but thanks for that reminder," she ground out.

"Sorry," Sidra said, fixing her bag on her shoulder. *I can't seem to say anything right lately.* First her mini argument with Josh days ago, and now she was making Alex feel bad.

"I just…I honestly think that he's seeing someone now," Alex admitted.

"Did he *say* that he was seeing someone?" Sidra asked.

Alex sighed. "No," she answered.

"Then what would make you think that?" Sidra pressed.

Alex shrugged. "Because he's a great guy, so I'm sure *someone* has caught his interest by now," she sulked.

Sidra shifted her weight from one foot to the other. "Well if it makes you feel better, *I* haven't seen him around campus with a girl," she placated.

Alex just looked at her.

"I mean, not with one girl in *particular*," Sidra corrected. "I've seen him walking in groups that consists of a few girls, but if he was in a relationship then maybe he'd be hanging with just one."

Confusion was written on Alex's face. "Sidra, that doesn't mean *anything*," she argued.

"On *this* campus, it does," Sidra shot back. "Everybody knows who everybody is dating, and at some point, the couples are seen together."

"Anybody seen you around here with *James*?" Alex questioned, tone smart.

Sidra made a face. "James doesn't *go* here," she pointed out.

"Well, maybe Eric's *girlfriend* doesn't go here *either*,"

Alex shot back. She put her hand on her head. "See? Now I have images of him and this unknown chick in my head. Thanks a lot."

Sidra threw her hands up as Alex walked off. "I'm sorry, I was only trying to help," she called after her. When Alex didn't stop walking, Sidra let out a sigh. "I'll treat for the hot chocolate."

"Yes, yes you *will*," Alex agreed, walking out of the building.

"You think that she'll like these flowers?" David asked Mark, as he held a bouquet of red roses in his hand.

"Dawg, you asked me that like eight times already," Mark barked, pulling a burgundy sweater over his head. "They all dried out now and shit."

David glanced at the flowers as he pushed his glasses up on his nose. "Shut up, they are *not*," he grunted. "Always lyin'."

Mark sucked his teeth. "David, Valentine's Day ain't until tomorrow," he teased, grabbing his watch off his nightstand. "Why did you buy those things *today*?"

"I guess I wanted to make sure that the guy in the store didn't run out before I had a chance to get them," David shrugged. It was his first Valentine's Day with Nicole; David wanted to make sure he had the necessities.

"First of all," Mark began, placing his watch on his wrist. "There's no way that weird ass guy is gonna run out of those roses... They raggedy as shit bro."

David flagged him with his hand in retaliation.

"Second...relax. You're being extra," Mark added.

"What do you mean?" David wondered.

"You running around here like a fool, asking people about candy and flowers, like you never had a Valentine before."

"You mean the one I had in the fifth grade?" David sneered. "I didn't have to do much to impress the girl then, besides let her put my glasses on."

Mark busted out laughing. "Oh yeah I remember. That's when she ran off with them and you ran into the door trying to run after her."

David held an angry gaze on Mark as he laughed at David's past trauma. "Real funny," he spat out. "If I remember correctly, didn't she pull *your* pants down in front of the whole class?"

"Hey, hey, this ain't about me," Mark immediately cut in, making David smirk. "Anyway, Nicole is a country girl who don't want much," Mark pointed out. "I mean that in a *good* way," he amended when he caught a quizzical look from David. "Just spend some time with her. Grab some movies, pick up dinner and go chill."

David sighed. "Yeah well, that's about all I can afford to do *anyway* since I had to buy a new laptop," he sulked.

"Damn, that dinosaur you had with no auto save finally bit it, huh?" Mark joked.

"Yep, the other day," David confirmed before letting out a quick sigh. "But you're right. I'll just do something simple... It's not like we've made anything official anyway, we're just dating."

"Yeah well, I don't see her dating anybody else *but* you, so y'all official," Mark pointed out.

"Thanks bro," David said, grateful. As he went to walk out of Mark's room, he was stopped by the sound of Mark clearing his throat, loudly. "You need some water or something?" David laughed, turning back around.

Mark held his hand out. "Give me the flowers," he demanded.

David's eyes widened. "But—"

"Give me the goddamn flowers DJ!" Mark snapped, making David flinch.

David sucked his teeth and reluctantly handed over the bouquet of wilted roses. "Did you have to use both my first and middle initial?" he sneered.

"Would you have preferred me to say the *full* names,

David Joseph?" Mark threw back, before breaking the stems in half. "Dawg, I'm doing you a favor," Mark barked, when David began to protest. "These things are shriveled as shit." He tossed the crumbled flowers in the trash.

David let out a loud groan and stormed out of the room.

"Don't you go buying no more from that damn man!" Mark yelled after him. "If you gonna get flowers go to the damn flower shop."

"Damn it!" David complained, shutting his bedroom door.

# Chapter 8

Malajia sat on the couch in her living room, twirling a few strands of her curled hair around her finger and spinning a single red rose in her other hand.

She had awakened that morning with anticipation, but as the day went on, her excitement waned. It was now early evening, and she hadn't seen Mark all day. The only communication that she had from her boyfriend was when he called her and told her to be ready in an hour. That was almost an hour and twenty minutes ago.

"He better come the hell on," Malajia griped, glancing at her watch.

As if on cue, Mark walked through the door. "You ready?" he asked, a smile on his face.

Malajia shot him a glare. "I've *been* ready," she sniped. "All damn day."

Mark closed the door behind him, then closed the distance between them. Leaning in for a kiss, he was stunned when Malajia backed away from him. "What's wrong?"

Malajia stared daggers at him. *Is he fuckin' serious?* "Sooo, you just gonna act like you ain't have me waiting all damn day to see you?" she hissed. "It's like seven o'clock."

Mark stood up straight and rubbed the back of his head with his hand. "Babe, I'm sorry. I had some things to take care of," he explained.

Malajia wasn't trying to hear any of what Mark was saying. She just stared at him for several seconds. "On Valentine's Day?!" she exploded. "On *all* days to do your pointless bullshit, it had to be on *this* day?"

Mark just stood there as Malajia continued to rant.

"What, did you take your ass to the gym? To play ball with Quincy's bald ass?"

Mark successfully concealed a snicker as he continued to stand there, taking the lashing.

"Or, no—I know what you did, you were playing that bum ass video game all day. Is that what you did?" Malajia tossed the rose on the table. "This isn't even my goddamn rose," she hissed. "I found this on the table when I came downstairs this morning. At least *somebody's* boyfriend was nice to them today... I shoulda' made Chaz do something with the group for her birthday. At least I would be having *fun* right now."

Mark folded his arms. "Are you done?" he asked after a few seconds.

Malajia stood up from the couch and pointed in Mark's face. "No, you know what—"

"Let me rephrase that," Mark interrupted, putting his hand on top of hers and lowering it from his face. "You're done. Shut your mouth for five seconds, grab your coat and bring your fine ass out to this car."

Malajia looked at Mark like he was crazy. She had every intention of unloading her vocabulary of profanity at him, but decided against it. "Whatever," she muttered, grabbing her coat from the arm of the couch.

Mark watched her pass him in route to the door. "You look pretty," he said.

"Whatever," Malajia reiterated, yanking the door open.

Mark shook his head in amusement and followed suit.


The car ride off campus was silent as Malajia spent the time staring out of the window, seething quietly. She was disappointed. Disappointed that Mark hadn't put any effort into their first Valentine's Day together. Disappointed that she had gotten her hopes up only to be let down.

Disappointed that as the hours passed by, she watched Emily trot out the door with her small teddy bear for her movie with Will. She saw the several gifts sent to Chasity by Jason, before Chasity was picked up for a romantic evening, and she watched the delivery man deliver two dozen roses, necklace, and fruit arrangement to Sidra from James.

*I should've hung out with Alex, at least we would be bored together*, she thought. The car stopping in front of a small restaurant on the corner of a block snapped her out of her thoughts.

"Come on cranky," Mark teased, stepping out of the car.

Malajia rolled her eyes as Mark walked around to her side and opened the door for her. "I'm not even in the mood for no damn dinner," she grunted.

"Yeah okay," Mark dismissed, taking her hand and gently pulling her from the car. "We both know how your mood changes after you eat."

Malajia stared at the side of Mark's head as they navigated the sidewalk. He was taking this whole thing as a joke. "You think this is funny?" she hissed.

"Yes," Mark chuckled.

Malajia sucked her teeth and pulled her hand from his. "Just know that you're about to be on the *longest* couple time out ever," she spat out. "You gets *no* part of me for a month."

"If you say so," Mark nonchalantly replied.

Malajia rolled her eyes and cursed under her breath as they began to pass the restaurant. She stopped as Mark kept going. "Where the hell are you going?"

"Down this alley way," Mark informed.

"Boy!—"

"Malajia, chill," Mark calmly urged, reaching his hand out. "Come on. Trust me."

Malajia reluctantly took hold of Mark's hand. She was silent as Mark led her down a well-lit alleyway. The narrow path gave way to what looked like the back of the restaurant. As they kept walking, Malajia's eyes lit up as she laid eyes on a small skating rink, with white lights and red flowers draping on the perimeter. The center of the ice was illuminated by a large heart monogram. Her mouth fell open when she looked off to the side; there was a small dining area enclosed in glass, overlooking the ice-skating rink.

"Finally, I got you to be quiet," Mark joked, leading Malajia along the candlelit path, through the glass doors.

Malajia looked around the dimly lit intimate space. The round table set for two with its candelabra centerpiece, and china place settings, was placed right near the window. As she suspected from the outside glance, it overlooked the rink perfectly. She even had a perfect view of the clear, star-filled sky.

Feeling overwhelmed, Malajia spun around to face Mark, who was smiling brightly at her. "You...you did all this?" she asked in disbelief.

"I told you, I got you," he replied, grabbing a dozen red roses from the table. "Happy Valentine's Day, my pain in the ass," he joked, handing them to her.

Malajia let out a laugh as happy tears filled her eyes. "Happy Valentine's Day," she returned, then wrapped her arms around his strong body and squeezed tight. She leaned in for a kiss, but Mark pulled away, shocking her.

"Naw bee, if you kiss me now, we're not gonna make it through dinner," Mark teased. "I'll clear this damn table in a minute."

"You're always so damn horny," Malajia chided, giving him a light tap on the arm. As Mark pulled her chair out, allowing her to sit, she eyed a long box set in front of her plate. "Oooh, ooh, can I open it?" she squealed.

"Yes," he replied, pushing his seat up to the table.

Malajia ripped the red wrapping paper from the present with haste, then opened the black box. Her eyes sparkled when she laid eyes on the silver bracelet consisting of five charms. "Oh my God... It's beautiful," she breathed.

Mark leaned over and took it from her, placing it on her wrist. "So, I wanted to start a charm bracelet for you. I'll add to it over time," he explained. "I tried to find something that had meaning…which by the way was a pain in the ass to find."

Malajia laughed as she examined the bracelet resting on her slender wrist. "Tell me what they mean," she smiled, pointing to the silver charms.

Mark pointed to one. "Okay, so the schoolhouse represents the middle school where we first met."

"You mean where I threw dirt in your face when you tried to give me a wedgie?" Malajia recalled, amused.

Mark narrowed his eyes at her. "Focus Mel," he ground out, earning a giggle from her. "The apple represents food, 'cause your ass is always hungry."

"True, as are *you*," Malajia mused.

"Yeah, we have that in common," Mark chuckled, pointing to the third charm. "The card represents games, 'cause we always have fun together…no matter *how* stupid the game is."

Malajia stared at Mark with adoration and longing as he continued talking.

"The smiley face represents laughter because you make me laugh, even when I feel like I can't." He paused for a moment as a wave of emotion hit him and grabbed hold of the last charm. "And the heart, well…" Mark looked into Malajia's brown eyes. "You're my heart…and I love you," he said sincerely, touching her face. Malajia put her hand over his. "So…those are your charms."

A tear spilled down Malajia's cheek as she stared at the man before her. A man who had shown her that not all men are just after one thing from her. That not all men would hurt her. A man who went out of his way to make her feel special. A man that she had deep feelings for— deeper than anything she'd ever felt before. "Did…did you just say that you love me?" she asked.

Mark nodded as he held her face. "Yeah…was that corny?" he asked.

Malajia shook her head. "No," she sniffled. "It was perfect…I love you too."

Mark smiled. "Yeah?"

She nodded. "Yeah," she confirmed. She leaned in and was elated that he had finally allowed her to plant a kiss on his lips. "Can we go in the bathroom and have a quickie?" she asked once they parted.

Mark shook his hand in her direction as he signaled for the waitress who was standing by. "Chill babe," he said.

"Please?" Malajia returned. At that point, her hormones were in overdrive.

Mark laughed at her eagerness. For once, the roles were reversed. "I promise I'll handle all that, later on."

"You *better*," Malajia threw back.

After enjoying their romantic candlelit meal, the pair took advantage of the private rink.

"How did you pull this off?" Malajia asked, flinging her hair over her shoulder as she skated a circle around Mark with ease.

"It wasn't as hard as you might think," Mark replied, skating around her. "You'd never believe whose place this is."

"Whose?"

"Praz's," Mark revealed.

"What?!" she exclaimed, intrigued. "*Drink making* Praz?"

Mark nodded.

"*Six-year student* Praz?" Malajia added. "*Used to have a crush on me,* Praz?"

"Hey, chill, he ain't have no crush on you," Mark denied.

Malajia giggled. "Whatever gets you through the day babe."

"Anyway, I ran into him while I was in town a week ago and we started catching up," Mark said. "He said he was taking his girl on a trip after Valentine's Day, since she had to work, and I told him that I was trying to find a nice spot to take you. That's when he mentioned that he had this restaurant. He said that nobody used the back room yet, and I asked if I could use it... He closed the rink off for me for tonight, set up the lights and everything."

"Wow," Malajia breathed.

"Yeah, and get this, his name ain't even *Praz*," Mark added. Malajia looked intrigued. "His name is Preston Randle Zuric."

"The hell?!" Malajia belted out, then laughed. "Now *that's* how you shorten a damn name."

"I know, right?" Mark agreed, laughter in his voice.

Malajia skated up to Mark. "Tell him I said 'thank you'. Tonight was perfect." She wrapped her arms around his neck. "And I'm sorry for giving you attitude earlier. If I had known—"

"It's okay, that was the whole point," Mark cut in. "I wanted to surprise you. I knew you didn't expect much from me, but I wanted to prove you wrong."

"You *did*," Malajia confirmed. "Now if you can just be like this *every* day," she joked.

"Nah, too much energy," Mark jeered.

Malajia shook her head, amused, before they kissed.

"Hey, no getting busy on the ice," a familiar voice said, halting the couple's make out session.

"Who would do it on some cold ass ice?" Mark muttered, seeing Praz walk out of the dining area.

"Hey Preston," Malajia teased, wrapping her arms around Mark's waist.

"Funny," Praz chortled.

"You have a great place here," she smiled.

"Thank you, I'm glad that you enjoyed it," Praz smiled back. "Just came out to see if you guys needed anything else."

"Nope, we're good," Mark nodded. "Thanks again for the hook up."

"Anything to help you make the day special for my former crush."

"See, I *told* you," Malajia laughed as she tapped Mark on the arm.

"Don't get drop-kicked *Preston*," Mark spat out.

Praz laughed as he put his hands up. "I'm just joking around, nothing but respect," he assured. "Mel has always been like a sister to me. Anyway, I gotta go get ready for this trip tomorrow, my staff will take care of anything else. Night."

"Bye," Malajia said as Praz disappeared through the doors. She then glanced up at Mark, a knowing look in her eyes. "You wanna head home?" she crooned.

"Absolutely," Mark returned, catching her gaze.


David adjusted the throw blanket around his and Nicole's shoulders as they snuggled on her bed. The room was illuminated by the light of her flat screen television and a nearby lamp.

"You want me to turn the heat up?" Nicole asked, leaning her head against his chest, before letting out a small cough.

"Nope, it's fine," David replied, wrapping his arms around Nicole. "Are *you* cold?"

"A little, but it's just chills, this blanket and your arms are keeping me warm," Nicole smiled, rubbing his hand with her own.

David was grateful that Nicole wasn't facing him; otherwise, she would have seen him blush. "It was nice of your roommate to leave us alone for a few hours."

Taking Mark's advice and keeping it simple, David arrived at Nicole's room, small gift bag, DVD's and take-out in hand. Finding that Nicole was battling a cold, he was glad that he decided to do just that.

"Oh please, that heffa is somewhere being a ho," Nicole joked. "She's out of this room damn near every night."

David chuckled. "Well, at least you get the room to yourself often."

"True," she giggled, then coughed. The coughing spell caused her to sit up; it gave David access to her back in order to pat it for her. "Thanks. I hope I don't get you sick," she grimaced, once the coughing subsided.

"It's okay," David assured. "I'll just go cough in Mark's face; it'll pay him back for destroying the flowers that I was going to give to you."

Nicole shook her head in amusement as she reached for her gift bag. "Well, I happen to like this candy apple that you bought me better, anyway," she smiled, removing the caramel and chocolate covered apple, with red and pink chocolate chips. "I love apples."

"I'm glad that you like it," David smiled in return. "I hope the card wasn't too cheesy."

"Summers, your gift *and* card are perfect," Nicole assured, returning to her resting spot on David's chest. "I like this better than fancy dinners and stuff. I prefer things sweet and simple."

"Well, one of these days I'll take you to someplace fancy *anyway*," David chuckled.

"I'm fine with that too," Nicole returned, patting his leg. She grabbed the remote and flicked on the DVD player. "Oh, can you please pass me my juice over on my nightstand?"

"Sure," David said. As he pulled the juice away from the stand, he accidentally knocked something over. "Crap, sorry," he muttered, handing Nicole her juice. He leaned over to grab the fallen objects from the floor. One of which was a small alarm clock, the other a Valentine's Day card. However, it wasn't the one that *he* had given to her.

David frowned slightly and put the alarm clock back. Then he glanced at Nicole, who was drinking her juice while clicking buttons on the remote. Curiosity getting the best of him, David opened the card. His eyes fixed in an angry stare as he read the written words.

*'Happy Valentine's Day to the best friend a guy could ask for,*
*-Q'*

*Son of a bitch*, David thought as he resisted the urge to rip the card into pieces.

"You okay Summers?" Nicole asked, unaware of what David had seen, or what he was feeling. "Did the stuff fall behind the stand or something?"

"No," David grumbled, putting the card down beside the clock and leaning back against the pillow. As Nicole adjusted herself against him once more, David let out a quick sigh. *Why is he giving her Valentine's Day cards? And why is she accepting them?*

Despite the thoughts running through David's mind, he remained quiet as the movie began to play.

"I've seen this movie about a hundred times, it's one of my favorites," she mused after a few moments of silence.

*Is that how many times you've seen it with Quincy?* He thought. Realizing that the sniping thoughts in his head would not cease until he said something, David rubbed the back of his neck and took a deep breath.

"Quincy gave you a Valentine's Day card?" he asked, already knowing the answer.

Nicole sat up and turned around to face him. "Huh?" she questioned.

David stared at her, annoyed. *I hope you're not about to try and play stupid with me.* David grabbed the card from the nightstand and opened it, showing the writing to her. "*This* card?" he pressed.

Nicole rolled her eyes as she tried to take the card from him, but frowned when David quickly moved it out of her reach. "David, it's nothing. It's just a friendship card."

"Friends don't give friends Valentine's Day cards," David spat.

"Me and *my* friends do," Nicole threw back, placing her hand on her hip. "And like I told you *before*, Quincy *is* my friend."

"Oh, so you gave *him* one too?" David sneered, slamming the card closed. Feeling his eyes sting, he removed his glasses and pinched the bridge of his nose.

Nicole sighed. "Look, it's just something that we do as friends. It's no big deal."

"You didn't give *me* one," David pointed out.

"I *did* buy you one, but I coughed on it by accident and spit got on it so I didn't want to give it to you," Nicole spat back. "It's over there in the trash if you want proof. I wrote you a note and *everything*."

The confession made David crack a smile.

"It's not funny," she pouted. "I wanted to cook dinner for you and everything, but I started feeling worse."

"It's fine," David assured her.

"No, I really wanted to do something special," Nicole insisted. "Because I don't just think of *you* as my *friend*. I was hoping... I'm hoping that I can call you my *boyfriend*."

David stared at her, surprise written on his face. "Really?" he asked.

Nicole didn't initially respond; she was fixated on his eyes, which were light brown. "You have nice eyes, never really noticed them with your glasses on."

"Yeah? Well I can't see for shit right now," he jeered, gesturing to the glasses held in his hand.

"Stop it," she chuckled, giving his arm a poke. "But seriously, I really like you and I want to see where our relationship goes." David just stared at her with a calm expression, even though on the inside, he was doing cartwheels. This had been what he wished for ever since he had first laid eyes on her. "That stupid card doesn't mean anything, you can tear it—" Not waiting for her to even finish, David ripped the card in half, inciting a giggle from Nicole. "Feel better?"

"A little," David replied.

Nicole grabbed his hand and held it. "So? What do you say? Do you wanna be my boyfriend?"

"This is not how I saw this conversation going," David chortled.

Nicole raised an arched eyebrow. "Oh what, you wanted to be the one to ask *me*?"

"Well, yeah."

Nicole rolled her eyes to the ceiling. "Get out of the gender role thing Summers, I'm perfectly okay with being the one to initiate this relationship," she stated. "But if it makes you feel better, *you* were the one who asked me out first."

"That is true," David mused, then let out a sigh. "I don't mean to accuse you of anything, I'm just…" *I'm freakin' insecure!* "I don't know, forget it," he said, despite what was screaming in his head. "You say I don't have anything to worry about, then I believe you."

"You sure?"

"Yeah," David assured. "So, it's safe to actually call you my girlfriend?" he concluded.

"Absolutely," Nicole beamed.

Happy about the turn of events, and proud to call the woman that he admired his actual girlfriend, David smiled the brightest smile. Ignoring the fact that Nicole was battling a cold and risking his own health, David leaned in and planted a kiss on Nicole's cheek. When Nicole tried to move her lips to his, he pulled her back.

"I'm sorry, I know you don't want to get sick," Nicole apologized, embarrassed.

David just nodded, even though that wasn't the truth. *Getting sick isn't my concern. Not wanting to get all hot and bothered is.*

As Nicole settled back against David, he placed his glasses back on his face. Wrapping his arms around Nicole, David stared at the screen as she began to rewind the movie. *Stupid!* he chided himself.

# Chapter 9

"I can't wait until this damn case is over," James vented as he unbuttoned his suit jacket.

Sidra rested her head against the headrest of the luxury car she was riding in with James. "Yeah, I can imagine," she sympathized. "You've been working a lot of late hours. More than usual."

"Tell me about it," James sighed. "It's been going for weeks. I'm still mad that I couldn't get here for Valentine's Day to see you."

Sidra grabbed James' hand and held it. "I keep telling you, it's no big deal," she insisted. "I understand that you had to work." Sidra awoke that day to a visit from James, whom she hadn't seen since her winter break. Feeling guilty for missing Valentine's Day nearly three weeks ago, James showed up with a luxury car, complete with a driver, to whisk her away for the day.

"It *is* a big deal," James uttered. "I love my career, but this working hours on end, especially for someone *else's* firm, is starting to get to me."

"Well, have you thought about starting your *own* firm?" Sidra asked.

James sighed, "Of course I've *thought* about it," he replied. "The question is, should I actually *do* it."

Sidra adjusted her position in her seat and faced him. "Maybe you *should*," she pressed. "You're an amazing lawyer. You can build your clientele like that," she smiled, snapping her fingers.

James smiled back at her, focusing on her beautiful face and listening to her encouraging words. "If I did, would you come and work for me?"

"Uh, no," she chortled.

James let out a gasp. "Why not?"

"I couldn't see myself working with my boyfriend," she explained, "Especially an experienced boyfriend. I'd be working under you and I'd feel inadequate. Not to mention I'd probably hate you as a boss."

James chuckled. "Noted," he replied, staring at her intently. "Well, I can think of something *else* that I'm experienced in."

Sidra stared at him.

"You would work under me, and you wouldn't hate me," he crooned.

Sidra felt a wave of heat fall over her. "James," she breathed. "Please stop."

"I know, I'm sorry, I couldn't resist," he replied, squeezing her hand and giving it a kiss.

Sidra just turned away and glanced out the window. Even after all this time, she still wasn't ready for sex. But she was starting to wonder if James was still okay with waiting.

"Enough about me and my whining. Have you looked into what law school that you want to go to after you graduate?" he asked, snapping Sidra out of her thoughts.

Sidra pondered his question. "I have, actually," she said. James stared at her in anticipation. "Logan School of Law here in Virginia, Reed Law in California and Ruby West Law in Pennsylvania."

James nodded in approval. "All three are great schools," he replied, adjusting his necktie. "California, huh?" he said, after a moment.

Sidra shrugged. "It's just an option."

"Well, if you recall me telling you, *I* went to Reed Law," James reminded. "I know a few people on the board… Maybe I can put in a good word for you."

"I appreciate you wanting to help," she returned,

grateful. "But I'd rather get in on my own. I don't want to start off my law career with any handouts."

"Fair enough," James approved, leaning back in his seat.

Sidra glanced out the window once again as they rode in silence. Normally, whenever they were in each other's presence, they could hardly stop talking. Now, Sidra was fine with the silence.

"I was thinking," James began.

Sidra fought the urge to roll her eyes. She was enjoying the quiet. "What were you thinking?" she asked, feigning enthusiasm.

"After dinner, we can go check out this art show that they're having near the hotel that I'm staying in."

Sidra winced; the idea of spending part of the evening standing around in some stuffy art gallery wasn't high on her list of fun things to do. "Um…honestly, I'm not really a big fan of art shows," she replied, looking at him.

James was bewildered. "You're kidding," he assumed.

Sidra shook her head. "Never could get into them," she explained. "I guess I'm just not the artsy type."

James' expression hadn't changed. "Huh," he muttered, rubbing his chin. "I thought that would have come up in one of our conversations."

"Well, it *wouldn't* because it doesn't interest me," she returned, trying to remain polite, even though she was becoming annoyed with his persistence. She touched his arm. "Can we maybe go bowling or something?"

"Bowling?" James chortled. "I don't take you for the bowling type."

"What does *that* mean?" Sidra frowned.

"That you don't seem like the type who would prefer bowling over *art*." James was a little taken aback by her attitude. "It's fine, I didn't mean to upset you Sidra. I was just making an observation."

Sidra looked away briefly. *What is your attitude for girl? He didn't say anything wrong.*

"I'll just give the tickets to my coworker who will be

traveling up here soon," James muttered. "Bowling is fine, whatever you want."

Sidra sighed. *Damn, you made him feel bad you idiot. What is wrong with you?* "I'm sorry, I didn't mean to sound ungrateful," she pacified. "Since you spent your money, we can go."

"It's fine," he reiterated, voice tired. Mood dampened, James just stared out the window, continuing their ride in silence.

"Did you know that Paradise Valley University is hosting a college tour this spring?" Alex asked, full of enthusiasm. "I read it on a flyer earlier."

"Nobody cares," Chasity spat, removing a box of cake mix from the store shelf and examining it.

Alex rolled her eyes. "Well...*I* care," she muttered. "And I think that we should volunteer to be tour guides."

Chasity shot Alex a challenging look. "Who's *we*? You speak French now?"

"No I *don't*, heffa," Alex hissed, earning a smirk from Chasity as she placed the box of mix and a container of icing in the shopping cart. With classes done for the day, Chasity was taking advantage of her free time and doing a little shopping at the Mega Mart. Alex, who had time before heading to work, decided to tag along.

"Anyway," Alex sneered. "I think it'll be fun to be tour guides for the potential freshman class. We can make it fun." She was brimming with excitement at the opportunity. "I know *my* tour guide was pretty boring when I came." She picked up a jar of sprinkles. "How was *your* tour experience?"

"I wouldn't know, I didn't have a tour guide," Chasity replied, eyeing items on the shelves.

Alex shot Chasity a glance. "What do you mean?" she charged. "What, you didn't come for the tour?"

"I didn't say that," Chasity clarified, fixing her gaze on

the red sprinkles that Alex was placing in the cart. "I walked the campus by myself. You know I don't like people and what the hell are you getting those sprinkles for?"

"Aren't you making a cake later?" Alex questioned, tone not hiding her aggravation. "I figured we could put them on top."

Chasity snatched the sprinkles from Alex and shoved them back on the shelf. "Not a goddamn soul asked you for a suggestion," she snarled.

Alex sucked her teeth.

"You weren't getting any of this cake *anyway*," Chasity added.

Alex waved her hand dismissively at Chasity. "Girl, you must have cramps today because you're being extra for no reason."

"No, I *always* have a reason," Chasity threw back, tone even as she pushed her cart down the aisle, Alex walking alongside her.

"Whatever, like I said, I think it'll be fun to be tour guides. *We* can make it fun," Alex insisted, going back to the original topic of discussion. "I'm gonna sign us up."

"Alex, don't put my name on that goddamn list," Chasity warned.

"Not paying you any mind, I'm signing you up," Alex mocked, earning a groan from Chasity. Alex giggled. "So who's the cake *for* anyway?"

Chasity frowned in confusion. "Not *you*," she huffed, rolling her eyes.

"My God girl, just answer the question," Alex bit back, tossing a hand up in frustration.

Chasity shook her head. "It's for Sidra," she answered. "She asked me to pick up some mix and food coloring. I think she's gonna try to experiment on it or something."

"Yeah, that sounds like her. The bougie baker," Alex joked. "*Speaking* of cake, Emily's birthday is coming up."

"Yes, I know," Chasity replied, grabbing a few more items from a shelf.

"And it's a big one, her twenty-first," Alex pointed out.

"I *know*," Chasity spat out. "She's *my* friend too, Alex. I am privy to that type of information."

"I'm trying to think of something fun for us to do," Alex continued, ignoring Chasity's smart reply. "But I'm coming up blank... Or should I say, what I'm coming up with would be fun for '*freshman*' Emily, not 'senior, grown ass woman, cussing my ass out', Emily."

"And cussed your ass out *good*," Chasity teased recalling the verbal showdown between Emily and Alex the previous semester—over Alex's nosiness and blatant disrespect of Emily and Will's relationship.

Alex stopped walking and stared daggers at Chasity, who found Alex's annoyance amusing. "Do *you* have any damn ideas?"

"No, just *ask* her what she wants to do." Chasity watched with agitation when Alex turned around and started back down the bakery aisle. "What are you doing?" she hissed.

"Just bring the cart and hush," Alex demanded.

Chasity let out a loud sigh, but complied. She stood there, arms folded and annoyed as Alex stood in front of the cake mixes.

"Knowing Em, she'll say 'nothing' because she thinks that we won't do anything for her," Alex stressed, grabbing a box of cake mix.

"Ask her *anyway*," Chasity insisted. She thought for a moment. "Never mind, no matter *what* she says, this damn group will plan what they *want* to plan."

"That's not necessarily true," Alex contradicted.

"No?" Chasity challenged. "How many times have I told y'all that I didn't want to do anything for my birthday and y'all drag me out and get me drunk *anyway*?"

"That's because we know that *you're* just being difficult," Alex answered, matter-of-factly. "You know you enjoyed every single birthday celebration that we had for you."

"Not the hangovers," Chasity muttered, making a face.

"Learn to handle your liquor, light weight," Alex goaded, grabbing another bottle of sprinkles. Chasity narrowed her eyes at Alex. "You know what, *I'm* gonna make us a cake tonight and I'll decorate it with—"

"I said nobody wants those!" Chasity snapped, smacking Alex's hand, which held the offensive cake sprinkles.

Startled, Alex lost her grip and dropped the small glass bottle to the floor. It shattered. "Chasity!" she exclaimed, eyeing the multicolored sprinkles scattered across the floor.

"Oh shit," Chasity laughed. Pushing her cart in front of Alex, Chasity blocked Alex's path as she made her getaway out of the aisle.

Angry, and unable to make a hasty departure without moving the cart, Alex smacked the handle. "You play too damn much!" she yelled after her. Eyeing the sprinkles once more, she sucked her teeth and stomped her foot on the floor. "Clean up on aisle three," she announced.


Malajia opened her mailbox and removed the envelopes inside. Closing the box and locking it, she began to flip through the contents. Not being in a rush, and relishing the heat inside the small space, Malajia leaned against a wall located near a cluster of mailboxes and began opening them.

"Boring, nobody wants to see the pictures from your baby shower, cousin," she muttered to herself. She opened another envelope and pulled a letter out. "No Grandma, I'm not coming to your church when I come home; stop asking me." She pulled a ten-dollar bill from the envelope. "But I *will* use this money for a wing and fry platter."

Her eyes fixed on a red envelope with no return address. "Who the hell is *this* from?" She opened it and removed the card. Confusion set in as Malajia eyed the picture of a teddy bear holding a heart on the front. She opened the card and read the handwritten note. "*To Malajia, a special card for a special person. I love you.*" she read aloud. Perplexity still masked her face before realization cut in; she sucked her teeth.

"Geri, I'mma kick your corny ass," Malajia mused to herself. It'd been weeks since Malajia had checked her mail. With she and Geri's relationship being closer than ever, she assumed that the card was just a sweet gesture from her. "You couldn't at least sign your damn name? And why does your handwriting look like a fourth grader wrote it?"

Having had enough of the post office, Malajia clutched her mail in her hand. As she proceeded to make her way out of the small office, she collided with someone on their way to their mailbox. The impact knocked the mail from Malajia's hand.

"Shit! Jackie, move!" Malajia barked.

Jackie put her hands up. "It *clearly* was an accident," she threw back.

"You see how small this space is, you should've waited until I got out," Malajia fussed.

Jackie rolled her eyes, as Malajia quickly bent to retrieve her items from the floor. "Whatever," Jackie huffed.

"Yeah, whatever," Malajia bit back, moving around Jackie to get to the exit.

Spinning around, Jackie frowned at Malajia's departing figure. Glancing down, she spotted another piece of Malajia's mail still lying on the floor. Jackie quickly retrieved it; her eyes glanced over the words written in the card.

"Malajia," Jackie called, voice dripping with disdain.

Malajia, spun around. "What?" she asked, exasperated. When Jackie didn't respond right away, Malajia sucked her teeth and walked back up to her. "What?!" she barked, making Jackie flinch.

"Um—you left this," Jackie stammered.

Malajia looked down at the card and snatched it.

"How's Mark, Malajia?" Jackie spat out as Malajia went to walk away once again.

"*Excuse* me, bitch?" Malajia challenged, turning back around. "The fuck are you asking about my man for?"

"Oh, so he *is* still your man?" Jackie sneered, folding her arms.

"What do you mean *still*?" Malajia questioned, confused. "He's been that for a *year*, not that it's any of *your* damn business."

"I'm just curious why you're getting Valentine's Day cards mailed to you when your man is here on campus," Jackie hurled, visibly upset.

Malajia was reaching her boiling point with Jackie's prodding and blatant disrespect. She took a step towards her. "*First* of all, keep Mark's name out of your nasty, random, dirty dick-sucking mouth," she said, tone nasty. "Yeah, the whole school knew," she spat, seeing Jackie make a face. "*Second*, not that I owe you an explanation, but this card is from my sister."

"Oh *really*?" Jackie challenged.

Malajia looked confused. "Why am I even—bitch bye," she threw back, before sauntering away, leaving Jackie standing there seething.

# Chapter 10

Sidra reached for the hot cup of tea on her nightstand and took a careful sip while reading the contents of a law school brochure. "Why am I even looking at this California school? There's no way I'm moving across country," she muttered to herself. Hearing her phone ring, she quickly reached for it, hoping that it would be James. Seeing her brother's name flash through her video call, she sighed.

"Hey Marcus," she answered, tone dry.

"Damn sis," Marcus chuckled. "You sound as dry as you *look*."

Sidra made a face. "Don't make me block you from my video call list," she warned.

"Were you expecting someone *else* to call?" Marcus assumed.

Sidra sighed, taking another sip of her tea. "Yeah, James," she sulked. "I think he's mad at me."

"What did you do?" Marcus asked point blank.

"When he was here a few days ago, I got snippy with him," Sidra admitted.

"Why?" Marcus asked.

"It doesn't even matter," Sidra grumbled. "I don't know what's going on with me lately, I just keep saying the wrong things to people. First Josh, and now James."

"Is that why you keep talking shit about India?"

Sidra scoffed. "No, I just don't like her."

"Yeah, it was worth a shot," Marcus joked.

Sidra rolled her eyes. "Is there a reason you called? And

don't let it be about this damn wedding."

"Okay, you're about to be pissed, 'cause that's why I'm calling," Marcus confirmed. "You know I can see you right?" he asked when Sidra rolled her eyes. He then took a short pause. "So, we settled on a date..."

Sidra tilted her head when he hesitated. "And that *is*?" she ground out.

"April 25th," he answered hesitantly.

Sidra rubbed her eyes as she sighed; she regretted answering Marcus's call. "Great, so I have a whole year to come up with an excuse not to show," she spat.

"*This* year sis," he clarified.

Sidra bolted up, spilling some of her tea on her thigh. "Ouch! Shit!" she screamed.

"What happened?" Marcus asked, concerned.

Sidra set the cup back on her nightstand. She wiped her leg off with her cover and pulled the pant leg up to check for red marks or welts. "I just spilled tea on my damn leg," she fumed.

"Are you okay?"

"No Marcus, I'm *not* okay!" she wailed, holding a hand on her leg. "That's two months away, are you out of your damn mind?!"

Marcus paused for a moment. "I was talking about your leg," he clarified.

Sidra gritted her teeth. "Marcus, I can't deal with you right now," she fussed. Feeling the sting from the burn, she winced.

"Sidra, I know it's a short time, but we have our reasons for pushing it up," he vaguely explained. "It'll be small and simple, don't worry. We might even just go to the courthouse and have a reception afterwards."

"Yeah, I'm sure Mama would *love* a shotgun wedding for her son," Sidra scoffed, sarcastic. "Look I have to go. Thanks to you, I need to ice my leg."

"Nobody told you to be dramatic," Marcus teased.

Not saying another word, Sidra held up her middle

finger. She pulled the phone close to give her brother maximum view of the vulgar gesture, before abruptly ending the phone call. "I can't believe we both came from the same parents," she said to herself.

Sidra painstakingly made her way downstairs. Heading in the kitchen, she grabbed a small towel from a drawer then opened the freezer. Grabbing two ice trays, she let out a loud groan then slammed them on the counter. "Who keeps putting these damn trays back in here empty?!" she yelled to an empty house. "I know it was that simple ass Malajia," she fumed. In pain and needing to ice her burn, Sidra headed out the door.

Sidra banged on the guys' door once she arrived. She stared wide-eyed as the door opened; Josh stared back at her.

"Hey Sidra," he said.

Sidra swallowed hard. "Um, hey Josh," she stammered. "Can I come in?"

Josh stepped aside. "Sure," he said as she walked in. "What's the matter?" he asked, noticing her limp and panicked voice.

Sidra spun around to face him, rubbing her leg. "Um, I know you're probably still mad at me, but—"

"I'm not mad at you," he cut in.

Sidra stared at him. "Oh...well, that's good to hear," she replied, pushing her hair behind her ears. Clearly Sidra had been stressed for nothing; Josh seemed to have forgotten about their conversation regarding his project partner. "Silly question, do you guys have ice?"

Josh chuckled. "Ice?" he repeated.

Sidra nodded. "Yeah. The trays in my house are empty and I'm in desperate need," she answered. As Josh walked into the kitchen, Sidra rubbed her leg. "Ouch," she muttered.

"You want it in a bowl or you want to just take the tray?" Josh asked, removing a tray from the freezer.

"Um, can you put it in a towel? I need it for my leg," she

explained. "I burned myself."

Josh looked up from the tray. "How did you burn yourself?" he asked, grabbing a clean dishtowel from the drawer.

"Tea, if you can believe that," she informed, trying to mask the pain in her voice. "I was on the phone with Marcus and he said something that made me mad, so I jumped up and spilled it on myself."

Josh placed several ice cubes in the towel and closed it. "Damn, that sucks," he sympathized.

"Tell me about it," she grumbled. "I think I might need to go to the hospital... This thing really hurts."

Josh held the towel in his hand. "Let me take a look at it," he offered.

Sidra stared at him wide-eyed. "Huh?"

"Your burn, let me see it," Josh reiterated.

"Um, you wanna look at my leg?" she stammered.

Josh shot her a knowing look. "Sidra, you wear skirts every day that it's not cold outside, I've seen your leg before," he pointed out, amused.

"Yeah...right," Sidra agreed. *God, stop acting like he just asked to see your panties,* she thought. Sidra gingerly rolled up her blue yoga pants to just above where the burn was. "Gross," she winced, eyeing her discolored skin.

Josh set the ice-filled towel on the coffee table next to where Sidra stood, and kneeled in front of her. She stared down at him as he gently touched her leg. The soft touch sent tingles through Sidra's body. Tingles that she wasn't expecting.

"It doesn't look too bad, probably just hurts more than anything," Josh observed, maneuvering her leg a bit in order to get a better look.

Sidra saw Josh's lips move but didn't hear him speak; she was in a daze as she continued to stare down at him. She didn't know when it happened, but she had stopped focusing on the pain and only on his touch. Closing her eyes, she let her mind drift. It wasn't until she heard his loud voice that she snapped out of it.

"Huh? What?" she sputtered.

"You're choking me with my own shirt," Josh told. He was grabbing her hand, which unbeknownst to Sidra, was tightly clutching part of his shirt.

"Oh God, I'm so sorry," she apologized, embarrassed. She immediately let go and Josh rose to his feet. "I guess it was just...the pain."

"It's fine," he assured, grabbing the ice from the table and handing it to her. "Just ice it for a while, and then let it get some air. You'll be fine."

"Okay, thanks," Sidra said.

"If you want, you can chill here for a bit to start the process," Josh offered. "I'm about to head out, but—"

"Oh? Where are you going?"

"Um...*out*," Josh replied.

Sidra took the answer and his hesitation, as basically telling her that it was none of her business. "Got it," she mumbled. "Thanks for the offer, but I'm gonna just go home."

Josh stared at her. She seemed weird, nervous even. "You okay?" he wondered, "*Besides* the burn I mean."

"Um hmm, yep," Sidra immediately threw back. Truth was, she wasn't okay, Josh was standing too close to her. They had been close together in the past, but this was making her feel *different*. And uncomfortable. "See you."

As Josh moved aside to let her pass, Sidra, in her haste, bumped into the coffee table, hitting her leg on the corner. "Shit!" she shrieked, grabbing her leg in pain.

"Ooh, you alright?" Josh panicked, reaching down.

Sidra jerked her leg away. "No don't touch it!" she barked.

Josh quickly retreated. "Sorry," he said, putting his hands up.

Sidra felt bad for her outburst; she knew that he was only trying to help. It wasn't *his* fault that she was being clumsy. "No, I didn't mean to yell, it just—"

"Hurts, I know," Josh finished. "I'm just gonna go grab a bag of ice from the store for you."

"You don't have to do that," she muttered, hobbling on one foot.

Josh walked over to her. "Stop it," he said, reaching for her hand. "Just so you're not alarmed, I'm gonna pick you up and carry you to your house. Are you okay with that?"

*I don't think it's a good idea for you to touch me right now,* she thought, afraid of how her body would react in Josh's arms. She immediately shook the thought from her head. "Yes, I'm fine with that."

Without another word, Josh opened the door, before sweeping Sidra up in his arms with one swift motion.

*God, he's so strong—Stop that!* Sidra wrapped her arms around his neck as he carried her out the door.

Emily walked into the house and shut the door behind her. Noticing Sidra sitting on the couch, leg propped on a pillow, she frowned. "What's wrong with your leg?" she asked, dropping her book bag near the steps.

Sidra glanced at Emily and shook her head. "I'm a klutz," she replied. "I burned *and* hit my leg on a table."

"Burned it with *what*?" Emily asked, curious.

"Tea," Sidra answered, adjusting her position on the couch.

Emily winced. "Aww," she sympathized, sitting on the couch next to her.

"Thanks," Sidra sighed, turning the TV down with the remote. "If this day wasn't bad enough, I learned that my brother finally decided when to have that raggedy wedding of his."

Emily leaned her elbow on the back of the couch. "When?"

Sidra looked at her. "April," she grunted.

Emily stared at her for a moment. "Wait, April of *this* year?" she asked. Emily was well aware of how much Sidra was dreading this wedding; the fact that it was now so close, she could only imagine how angry Sidra was.

"Yes, can you believe that mess?" Sidra vented. "Talking about he has a reason why they're moving it up and they might just go to the courthouse." Emily placed a sympathetic hand on Sidra's arm as she continued to vent. "Ole' poor ass, shotgun wedding. That is *not* how my family does things."

"I'm sorry Sid," Emily pacified.

Sidra took a deep breath and waved a dismissive hand. "I don't mean to bother you with this nonsense," she said. "How was your day sweetie? How's your teaching assignment going?" It had been a while since Emily shared her progress.

Emily let out a sigh as she clutched a throw pillow to her chest. "It's good," she answered, tone dry. "I ran my first class solo today."

Sidra's eyes widened in excitement. "That's great Em," she beamed. "How was it? Were you nervous?"

"Yeah, I was nervous but I think I did okay," Emily replied, tone not changing.

Sidra squinted, picking up on Emily's somber attitude. "Why do I get the feeling that you're not excited about your accomplishment?"

Emily sighed again. "It's not that," she assured. "I'm really enjoying the assignment."

"Then why do you look *and* sound like you feel otherwise?" Sidra asked.

Emily hesitated. "My brother Dru sent me a text when I was on my way back from the school," she informed, grabbing the phone from her book bag.

"What's so wrong about *that*?" Sidra wondered. She knew that Emily was in a good place with both of her brothers. Why would a text from one of them affect Emily in such a bad way?

"You'll see," Emily replied, scrolling through her messages.

Confused, but curious, Sidra stared at Emily intently as she began to read the message in her phone.

Emily cleared her throat. "This part is from Dru. '*Emily, Mom sent me this*'"

Sidra frowned.

"*This* is from my mother," Emily spat, reading. "'*Dru, thanks for calling me and telling me about Emily's student teaching assignment a few weeks ago. She is a chip off the old teacher block. I appreciate you giving me updates on how she is doing. Tell her to reach out when she finds time.*'"

"Wait, what?" Sidra reacted as Emily put the phone down. "So she texts your brother to offer well wishes about you, but she doesn't text *you*?" Sidra was annoyed for Emily.

"Yeah, she has this habit of talking to everyone about me, *but* me," Emily vented.

"Are you okay?" Sidra asked, holding a sympathetic gaze.

"No, no I'm not," Emily admitted, frustrated. She looked at Sidra. "You know what's sad?"

Sidra shook her head.

"I originally wanted to become a teacher *because* of my mother," Emily revealed. "I used to look forward to when she would come home from work and tell me about how the day with her students was... It was like those students gave her purpose and I wanted that same feeling."

Sidra tilted her head as she continued to listen.

Emily glanced down at her hands. "Even though, over time, my reasons for wanting to become a teacher had nothing to do with her, it still would've been nice to talk to her about my assignment... To share with her how I was feeling, to tell her about how my first day went—to hear her say that she was proud of me, *if* that's even possible."

Sidra reached over and rubbed Emily's shoulder. "Even though she's acting a fool, she can't *not* be proud of you," she consoled.

Emily shook her head. "Two years Sidra... It's been two years," she sulked.

"I know, sweetie," Sidra soothed.

Emily felt tears forming in her eyes; she quickly wiped them away. "I still can't believe she's doing this to me, and has the *nerve* to say 'tell her to reach out when she finds time'? Is she serious?" she fussed, wiping her eyes again. "I told Dru not to give me anymore messages from her. If she can't contact me directly, then I don't need to hear what she has to say."

"And you're absolutely right," Sidra agreed. "I hate that you're going through this."

Emily shrugged. "It's probably for the best that we're not talking," she said, somber. "If she was still in my life, she'd still be trying to control me."

"If it means anything, I don't think at this point in your life, she *can* control you," Sidra stated. "You're not that person anymore."

"Yeah," Emily sulked, looking down at her hands again.

Sidra gently patted her leg. "You want me to make you brownies?" she smiled. "That's the one thing that seems to make *all* of us feel better."

Emily managed a small laugh. "Yes, thank you."

# Chapter 11

"Yo," Mark began as he grabbed a slice of pizza from the tray. "We talk a lot of shit about this Shack pizza but admit it, you're gonna miss it when we graduate."

"Hell no I'm *not*," Malajia scoffed. "I've eaten enough of this pizza to last me a lifetime."

Alex and Josh shot each other glances. They'd almost regretted asking the group to meet them for lunch that Saturday before ending their shift.

"For somebody who talks about the food all the time, you sure don't have a problem stuffing your damn *face* with it," Alex ground out.

"It's free, you damn *right* I'mma eat it," Malajia threw back, taking a bite of her slice of pepperoni pizza.

Alex shook her head, then glanced up when she saw David walk in. "Hey stranger," she teased as David removed his knit hat and coat.

"Hey guys, sorry I'm late," David apologized, taking a seat at the table.

"Yeah, we *know* why you're late," Mark teased. "Been mixing your city with her country, huh?" Once the comment left Mark's lips, he immediately put his head down and sipped his drink.

Silence fell over the table as the group stared at Mark, who was desperately trying not to laugh.

"That had to be the *corniest* innuendo ever," Chasity sneered, causing laughter to erupt.

"I know, that's why I didn't say nothin' else," Mark

admitted, laughing. "I hoped y'all would forget."

"Anyway, I wasn't mixing *anything*," David clarified, reaching for a slice of pizza. "I missed the bus, so I decided to walk."

"Pay him no mind," Sidra said of Mark with a wave of her hand.

"Yeah, it's just that we haven't seen much of you since you and Nicole became an official couple," Alex grinned, letting her hair down from her wild ponytail. She then began to fluff her hair out with her hands.

"Come on with all that, you getting them naps all on the pizza," Malajia jeered, flinging her hand in Alex's direction.

Alex stared blankly at Malajia, then looked at Mark. "If she keeps messing with me, I'm cutting off your free pizza supply," she warned.

Malajia sucked her teeth. "You ain't—"

"Mel chill," Mark ordered, laughter in his voice. "You fuckin' up the free shit."

"David," Sidra cut in, reaching for her cup of soda. "You should tell Nicole to come hang out with us girls sometime."

David nodded in agreement. "I think she'd enjoy that," he mused. "She's always asking about you girls. And Chasity—she said that you don't talk to her now that you two no longer have class together."

Chasity looked up from her plate of salad, bewildered. "Was I *supposed* to?" she asked smartly.

Snickers resonated around the table.

David narrowed his eyes at Chasity. "Really?" he jeered.

Malajia laughed as Chasity shot David a challenging look. "You're really surprised? You *know* she's rude," Malajia commented, gesturing to Chasity.

"We'd *love* to have Nicole hang with us," Alex chimed in, excited.

"Speak for yourself," Chasity muttered, eating her food.

Jason playfully nudged her. "Stop it," he chortled.

"Cool, I'll extend the invite," David agreed. He folded his arms on the table. "How is your leg by the way, Sid?" he asked. His question incited groans from the group.

"God, *please* don't ask the drama queen about that damn leg," Chasity griped.

"What's wrong?" David laughed as Sidra rolled her eyes.

"Nothing," Sidra spat. "They're just being assholes, as *usual*."

Chasity looked at Sidra as if she had lost her mind. "Really?" she hurled at Sidra. "Have you or have you *not* been milking that damn bruised leg for three days now?"

"It still *hurts*!" Sidra exclaimed. "You've *seen* me limping and you've *seen* the burn on my leg. I had to go to the emergency room and *everything*."

"Girl, you went a day later and they gave your ass ointment and sent you home," Malajia recalled.

Sidra sucked her teeth.

"Little ass burn and shit," Mark teased. "You can put a bandage on that and be done with it."

Malajia laughed. "Right, talking about 'can y'all please fill up the ice trays, I need the ice for my leg' and shit."

Sidra flashed a scowl Malajia's way. "No, I said fill the ice trays up in *general*," she clarified. "Who the hell wants to open the freezer for ice and see empty trays? Like, the sink is right there, *Malajia*."

Malajia flagged Sidra with her hand. "Keep the damn juice in the fridge and you wouldn't *need* ice," she argued.

"That makes no sense! Just fill the fuckin' trays back up, we've *all* been telling you that shit," Chasity snapped, directing her glare at Malajia.

"This is true," Alex cosigned.

Malajia narrowed her eyes. "Y'all some nagging ass heffas, I swear to God," she spat, picking pepperoni off of her pizza.

Sidra sipped her drink. "Look, back to my leg, I don't appreciate the insensitivity," she bit out. She pointed to Chasity. "Chaz, I took care of *you* when you were sick freshman year. You can't extend the same courtesy? Selfish."

Chasity was confused. "Bitch, I had the *flu and* a *stomach virus*," she reminded.

"Still," Sidra maintained.

"I could barely *move* but you want me to help *your* fully functioning ass down the steps at seven in the morning so you can get coffee? You lost your mind," Chasity argued.

Sidra held a scowl on her face as her friends laughed at her expense. "All of you can take the nearest train straight to hell," she spat out.

Alex laughed. "Okay let's leave Sid alone, she *did* really injure herself and we *should* be more sensitive," she pacified, looking at her watch.

"Thank you, Alex," Sidra approved, folding her arms.

"I guess we know who'll be rubbing ointment on that damn leg later," Malajia mocked, pointing her pizza crust Alex's way.

Sidra made a face at Malajia.

Alex just shook her head. "Let me clean these tables off and clock out so we can get out of here," she added, rising from her seat.

"Right behind you," Josh announced, standing up.


"I want something sweet," Emily declared as the group walked through campus. "I should've grabbed some of those cookies."

Having left the Pizza Shack over twenty minutes ago, the group was now back on campus. The cold air kept most of the students inside, so the group was taking advantage of the vacant paths.

"Why don't we go grab some hot chocolates from the donut shop?" David suggested. "I keep hearing about how good they are."

"I say we do it," Alex agreed, adjusting her scarf. "*Especially* since I hear that Jackie's not working there anymore. Apparently, the slacker quit."

"Can we not talk about that troll?" Malajia requested,

voice not hiding her disdain. "I just ate." Just the mention of Jackie's name killed her mood. Malajia still couldn't get over how Jackie tried to come at her over a card that she wrongly assumed was from a man other than Mark.

"You should've slapped her ass for what she said," Chasity spat out. She remembered Malajia barging through her door after the encounter, ranting about it.

"Trust me, I *wanted* to," Malajia assured. "But like you, I'm trying to graduate."

"Y'all already know how Jackie is," Jason put in. "Ignore her ass and let her be miserable."

"I agree with Jase," Alex added.

*Easier said than done*, Malajia thought, but elected not to respond.

As the group made their way past the sports field in route to the donut shop, something caught Mark's eye. "Who put that volleyball court up?" he wondered. "It ain't even spring yet."

"Maybe they wanted to get it up early," Josh shrugged. "Spring is technically about two weeks away."

"You sure can't tell by this arctic weather out here today," Alex chortled of the frigid air.

"Yo Josh, remember when we used to play volleyball in high school?" Mark reminisced.

"Yeah, you used to get so mad when you'd lose," Josh recalled, laughter in his voice.

Mark stopped walking and frowned at Josh. "When have I *ever* lost at volleyball?" he questioned, bite in his voice.

Josh looked confused as he too stopped walking. "Dude, you lost like a hundred times!"

The rest of the group halted their paces as the quarrel ensued.

"To the actual *volleyball team*, maybe, not to *your* non-spiking ass," Mark threw back.

Josh stared at Mark for several seconds. "*I* was *on* the volleyball team, you idiot."

Mark flagged Josh with his hand. "Whatever yo, you

didn't beat me."

"Oh, I *did*," Josh maintained, confident.

Mark looked at David for validation. "David—"

"He *did*, Mark," David laughed. "Every single game you played against him, you lost."

"Thank you!" Josh exclaimed, tossing his arms in the air. "I'm glad I had witnesses."

Malajia looked at Sidra. "Is that true?" she asked.

"Absolutely," Sidra confirmed. "Then after Mark would lose, he'd get mad and throw the ball behind the bleachers."

Malajia laughed. "Sounds about right."

Mark, annoyed, pointed at Josh. "You always bringing up old victories and shit," he griped.

"*You're* the one who brought up volleyball to *me*," Josh returned. Mark's irritation was amusing to him. "You're just mad because *you* have no victories to relive. With *your* non-spiking ass."

Mark quickly removed his gloves. "Bet money you can't beat me *now*," he challenged.

"Are you serious?" Josh frowned.

"You damn skippy, let's go, right now," Mark demanded.

Josh pondered the challenge for a moment, then nodded in agreement. "You're on," he accepted, unbuttoning his coat.

The girls complained as Mark and Josh removed their coats.

"Here we go," Sidra sighed.

"Mark, put your damn coat back on, it's freezing out here," Malajia demanded.

Mark turned and faced Malajia, "Nah babe. Josh out here chuckling at me and shit, tryna play me," he fussed, slamming his coat on the ground. "I'm about to shut his ass the hell up."

Mark and Josh walked towards the volleyball net.

"So much for hot chocolate," Alex muttered as the rest of the group reluctantly followed.

Mark looked around, then spotted a red ball laying off to the side. "Bet. This'll work," he mused of the lightweight ball. "You ready?" Mark asked, holding the ball in position as he stood in front of the net.

Not saying a word, Josh prompted him to throw the ball.

Mark tossed the ball up and smacked it over the net. Josh, reacting quickly, jumped up and spiked the ball, hitting Mark square in his face with it. "Shit!" Mark barked, rubbing his face as Josh busted out laughing. Lucky for him, the beach ball was low on air, otherwise the impact would have been much worse. "Fuck this, I'm not taking this ass woopin' by myself. Jase!"

Laughing, Jason removed his coat and gloves. "I knew this was coming," he mused, walking over to the net.

"I got you Josh," David said, removing his outerwear.

"He ain't even ask you to play," Mark griped at David as he headed over to the net.

As the guys taunted each other, Alex looked at the girls. "Soooo, we're really gonna stand here and watch them run around with no coats on in below twenty-degree weather?"

"Yep," Chasity replied nonchalantly at the same time that Malajia said, "Uh huh."

"Not like anybody can stop them really," Emily chortled, folding her arms across her chest.

Alex shook her head, sighed, and settled in to watch the show.

"Y'all ready to get this beat down?" Josh taunted, tossing the ball in the air.

"Man, the only thing you're gonna beat is your meat later, lonely ass," Mark threw back.

Caught off guard by the crude remark, Josh dropped the ball and regarded him with shock. "Really?!" Josh barked, embarrassed.

"Oh come on!" Alex wailed as Emily covered her face in embarrassment.

"Bro," Jason laughed at Mark. "You could've kept that comment to yourself."

Mark just shrugged.

"Do you *always* have to be so damn rude?" Sidra hurled to Mark. She then turned to Malajia, who was doubled over with laughter. "It's not funny," she chided. She sucked her teeth when Malajia kept laughing.


Alex glanced at her watch, squinting in the process. After standing outside witnessing the guys play an intense game of volleyball for over a half hour, she had grown tired. "Guys, come on, when is this game gonna be over?" she complained.

"Yeah exactly, it's like nine to two," Chasity fussed. "It's cold as shit out here. If I get sick, I'm coughing in all y'all damn faces."

Josh shook his head as he held the ball in his hands. "I keep *telling* Mark to give it up, he won't listen," he laughed.

"Look the game ain't over," Mark ground out. "The game goes to ten, last time I checked, y'all asses had *nine*."

Josh tossed the ball over the net; Mark jumped up and hit it back over. "Yeah!" he boasted.

David dove for the ball, hitting it up far enough to where Josh was able to jump up and spike it over the net. "Fuck!" Mark yelled, as the ball flew past him. Jason tried to dive for it, but missed and fell on the ground.

"Yes, great teamwork," Josh commended of David, giving him a high five.

Mark stomped his foot as Jason picked himself up from the cold ground. "Come the fuck on Jason, how you keep missing hits and shit!" he yelled.

Jason brushed the dirt from his black, long sleeved shirt. "Yo, who the fuck are you yelling at?!" he yelled back.

"You keep missing those easy ass points," Mark argued. "How the hell they beat us by eight points?"

Jason looked shocked. "*First* of all, I'm the reason we have *any* points in the *first* place," he threw back, pointing to himself. "You haven't done *shit* to help us win."

"Bullshit," Mark disagreed.

"No?" Jason challenged. "Name *one* time during this game where a ball that *you* hit flew past them or hit the ground," Jason folded his arms. "Exactly," he said when Mark didn't respond. "*I'm* the one who got dirt all over my clothes, tearing my damn self up on this hard ass ground trying to make points. *You* don't do *shit* but stand by the damn net with your scared ass."

"Man shut up," Mark spat out. "You should be ashamed of yourself, how you play football, but suck at volleyball?"

Jason looked like he wanted to drag Mark through the dirt by his face. "Football and volleyball are two totally different sports you jackass!"

"It's still a *sport*, asshole."

"Don't *you* play *basketball* you fuckin' moron?" Jason countered.

"Not all the *time* though," Mark returned.

Jason put his hands on his face and pulled down. "I swear to God," he seethed.

Chasity and Malajia shook their heads at their boyfriends. "They stay arguing," Malajia commented. "Over *dumb* shit too."

Sidra, Alex, and Emily exchanged glances. "Sound familiar?" Alex mocked.

"Shut up," Chasity spat back.

Sidra shivered. "Seriously guys, is the game over, can we go now?" she pleaded, folding her arms across her chest. "My leg is really bothering me."

Chasity rolled her eyes. "Sidra, I cannot continue to stand next to you if you're gonna be dramatic," she said.

Sidra sucked her teeth. "It *does*," she whined.

"Nah, fuck this. The game is going to twenty," Mark demanded.

"Oh no the hell it's *not*," Malajia refused. "No damn that, get your coat Johnson. Like right now or you're on time out."

"You can't put me on time out for tryna win," Mark

frowned.

"You already *lost!*" Malajia erupted, holding her arms out. "Get over it, let's fuckin' *go.*"

"Fine, how about twelve?" Mark amended.

"Dude, you're at two points and we have *ten,*" Josh pointed out, annoyed. "There is *no* way you're gonna come up."

"Just throw the goddamn ball," Mark demanded, holding his hands out.

Frustrated with Mark's antics, Josh tossed the ball up and hit it with force, sending the ball flying over the net and striking Mark in his chest.

"Ow!" Mark barked, then turned to Jason with his arms up. "Jase, where were *you!*"

"I swear to God!" Jason snapped. He was over Mark's nonsense, the cold, and the game in general.

"How you snappin' at *him* when the ball was right in *your* face?" Chasity barked at Mark as Jason retrieved his coat and gloves from the ground.

"Chaz don't even bother, he's too damn stupid," Jason sniped, heading over to her. "I'm done, let's go."

Mark looked at Malajia as the rest of the group began filing away. "How you gonna stand there and let them talk shit about me like that?"

Malajia causally examined her gloves. "I would've defended you, but they had a point," she mocked.

Mark flagged her with his hand. "You on time out," he spat, walking away.

"*For what*?!" she yelled after him.

# Chapter 12

Sidra walked down the steps with Emily in tow. "I'm going to the store to pick up something to make for dinner, so what do you want to eat?" she asked, putting her coat on.

Malajia turned her attention away from the movie that was playing on the screen. "Ooh, can you fry some fish?" Malajia asked, hopeful.

Sidra rolled her eyes. "Malajia, you know I don't fry food," she scoffed. "I'll *bake* some—"

"Nah, we don't want that. Chaz if Sidra gets the fish, can you fry it? We like yours," Malajia quickly cut in, looking at Chasity.

Chasity couldn't help but laugh. "Yeah," she agreed.

Sidra stood there with her mouth open as Alex and Emily laughed. "Do you have a problem with my baked fish?" she asked, insulted.

"Sidra the only way to eat fish is to fry it, nobody wants no healthy ass baked fish," Malajia threw back, flicking her hand in Sidra's direction. "We don't know *why* you keep making that shit."

Sidra narrowed her eyes as she slowly looked at Emily, who was still laughing. "You're gonna laugh yourself out of this ride to Will's job," she warned.

Emily adjusted the knit hat on her head. "I don't mind the bus," she shrugged, amused.

"Ooooh she told your ass," Malajia taunted, clapping. "Fuck that ride and fuck that fish she was tryna make."

Sidra flagged Malajia with her hand. "Whatever, come on Em," she hissed, opening the door. "I'll make sure that I'll get enough fish for everybody *but her* rude behind."

Malajia shrugged. "I'll just eat yours," she stated, unfazed.

Sidra rolled her eyes. She had a thought as she was about to walk out the door. "Oh, Marcus is supposed to be coming down here to see me in a few days, so just giving you a heads up that he'll be over," she informed.

"Oh really? Any special occasion?" Alex wondered, pushing hair off of her neck.

Sidra shrugged as she adjusted a bracelet on her wrist. "He said he wanted to talk to me in person," she answered, dry. "He knows I'm pissed at him, so he probably wants to bribe me so I can be happy about this bullshit that's about to take place."

"Would a bribe actually *work?*" Alex chuckled.

"Nope," Sidra snapped as she walked out the door.

"See you ladies later," Emily waved, closing the door behind her.

Going back to watching the movie, Malajia let out a sigh as she focused on the images on the screen. "This movie is ass, who picked it?"

"*You* did," Alex threw back, grabbing a handful of popcorn from the bowl in front of her.

Malajia shook her head. "Y'all gotta stop letting me do that," she muttered. Her phone rang and she retrieved it from the cushion next to her. She glanced at the caller ID and threw her head back, letting out a loud, agitated groan.

"Him *again?*" Chasity assumed, amused.

"Yes, like come *on*, I haven't been in for fifteen minutes," Malajia ground out, putting the phone to her ear. "*Yes* Mark…What? …I *just* made you soup *and* tea! …Well what the fuck did you do with it?! …I swear to God—No, I'm not coming back over there… That's not my problem… I *said* no!"

Alex laughed as Malajia abruptly ended the phone call. "What is it *this* time?" she wondered.

"His sick ass talking about he spilled the soup on his way to the bathroom," Malajia hissed. "Talking about now he's laying in it."

Alex laughed. "Chaz, didn't Jason call you not too long ago with something like that?"

Chasity rolled her eyes. "Yeah, talking about, can I make him some minestrone soup," she spat out. "I don't even know what the fuck that *is*." She ran a hand through her hair. "Men are such freakin' babies when they're sick."

Alex amused, nodded in agreement. No one was surprised when the guys started falling victim to severe colds, days after their volleyball game. The combination of the frigid air and them sweating, did them in.

"*Three days* of this shit," Malajia griped. "This is ridiculous, it's a damn *cold*."

"Come on ladies, don't be like that," Alex chided. "They take care of *you* when you're not feeling well."

"Yeah, yeah," Chasity reluctantly agreed, examining her nails.

"Please," Malajia scoffed. "Mark don't do *shit* but get on my nerves when I'm sick."

Alex shook her head. "Girl, stop whining and go take care of your sick, soggy man," she teased, reaching for more popcorn.

Malajia looked at her. "Can *you* go?" she asked. "You can have him for the day, I don't even care."

Alex made a face. "No thank you," she scoffed, giving Malajia a nudge with her hand. "Go be a girlfriend."

Chasity sighed. "Let me go check on this boy," she said, standing up. "You coming?" she asked Malajia on her way to the door.

"I guess," Malajia relented, standing up. "You gonna make that minestrone?" she teased.

"Fuck no...I'll buy that shit," Chasity replied, walking

out the door.


David sneezed and sniffled before putting the phone back to his ear. "Sorry about that," he mumbled, flopping down on his bed.

"Poor baby," Nicole sympathized. "Has it gotten worse?"

"I don't think so," David replied, pulling the cover up over his body. "It's still the same hell it's been for the past three days."

"Aww, I understand how you feel," she placated. "I have some homemade vapor rub that my grandma sent me that last time that *I* got sick. I can bring it to you. I'll even make you some soup and tea," she offered.

David coughed briefly before closing his eyes. "I appreciate it, but I don't want you to get sick again," he declined. "I'll be okay."

"Oh," Nicole replied, not hiding the disappointment in her voice. "I mean, you came over and kept me company when *I* was sick...brought me tea and stuff. I just wanted to return the favor, that's all." She frowned when she didn't get a response. "David?" she called.

David didn't hear her; he had unintentionally fallen asleep. As he turned over in bed, the phone fell to the floor.


"How did your tall ass knock the soup over?" Malajia fussed, placing a handful of soup soiled paper towels in the trash.

"I already told you," Mark hissed in between coughs. "I knocked it over on my way to the bathroom."

Malajia placed her hands on her hips. "Mark, the soup was on your nightstand, which is on the *side* of your bed, not in front of it, so unless you were being extra, there was *no* way you could've knocked it over."

Mark stared at her for a moment. "Okay, *maybe* it wasn't on my way to the bathroom," he admitted.

Malajia's eyes widened once she came to a realization. "You knocked it over on purpose, *didn't* you?" she barked. "You did that so I would come the hell back over here."

"Why are you yelling?" Mark griped, placing his hands on his head.

Malajia walked over and smacked his hands down.

"Ow!" Mark bellowed.

"Cut that shit out. That didn't hurt and I'm not even yelling," she pointed out, tone angry. "That was some stupid shit...and you *purposely* laid in it. You had noodles all on your damn face, were you eating it from the damn floor, nasty? Who *does* that?"

Mark jerked the covers over his body. "Look, I just wanted you to come back over, sue me for missing you," he grunted.

Malajia rolled her eyes. "You are so damn dramatic," she hissed.

Mark, tired of feeling like death and of the verbal lashing, slammed his hand on the bed. "Look here damn it," he snapped. Malajia shot him a challenging look. "You need to kill all that attitude. Don't I take care of *you* when you on your period, with those cramps, bleeding all over the place and shit? And I don't complain."

"*First* of all, don't nobody be bleeding all over the damn place," she threw back. "That is such a *man* thing to say."

"Yeah whatever," Mark mumbled.

"Yeah, *whatever* is right," she agreed, angry. "You're such an asshole. What happened to the Mark from Valentine's Day? I want *him* back."

"He's down the toilet with the *rest* of my waste," Mark threw back.

"*And* you're gross," Malajia scoffed. "Look fool, I don't *mind* taking care of you when you're sick, but you over here doing extra *dumb* shit, like kicking the covers off, then talking about you cold."

Mark fought to contain his chuckle, but was unsuccessful.

"Or, purposely putting a damn pillow over your face, talking about you can't breathe," Malajia continued to rant.

"I only put the pillow over my face to drown out all that damn yelling you was doing," Mark defended. "Now can you please go check on my tea?"

Malajia glared daggers at Mark and stormed out of the room, slamming the door behind her. Mark flinched at the loud smack, then laughed to himself. "Never gets old," he mused before having a coughing spell.

Malajia folded her arms as she walked over to Chasity, who was standing in the hall. She rolled her eyes and Chasity shook her head at the loud, exaggerated coughing coming from Mark's room.

"Oh come on!" Malajia yelled back at the door. "You know you don't have to cough that hard." She then looked at Chasity, who was examining her nails.

"Mark being a dramatic asshole?" Chasity asked, already knowing the answer.

Malajia shot Chasity a knowing look. "Chasity, he danced on my last nerve like a half hour ago, I'm ready to let him choke on his own mucus."

"Gross," Chasity stated flatly.

Malajia let out a sigh as she moved her neck from side to side. "Anyway, what are you doing out here?"

"Waiting on the water to boil for Jason's tea," Chasity replied.

"Oh," Malajia muttered. "I didn't hear yelling coming from Jason's room, so I'm assuming that he wasn't working your nerves like that fool in *there*." She gestured her head towards Mark's room.

Chasity chuckled. "No, he's not so bad," she replied. "Maybe because he's been half asleep since I got here."

"Lucky *you*," Malajia griped, pointing to the door. "I wish *this* ass would go to sleep."

Before Chasity could open her mouth to respond, she

heard Jason call her name from his room. Chasity stood in silence.

"He just called you," Malajia pointed out.

"Shhhh," Chasity hissed, waving her hand. "If he thinks I'm downstairs he'll shut up."

Malajia's eyes widened in shock, "I thought you said he wasn't bad."

"Bitch I lied, he's been whining the whole damn time," Chasity whispered, angry. "This tall ass man takes tackles during football and shakes it off, but gets a cold and all of a sudden he can't do *shit* for himself," she fussed, pointing back towards Jason's room.

Malajia put her hand over her mouth as she tried to conceal her laughter.

"Chaz," Jason's cracking voice called through the closed door.

Chasity stomped her foot on the floor and let out a whine. "Yes?" she answered.

"Can you come hand me the remote?"

Chasity frowned in confusion. "Jason, the remote is right on the floor beside the bed."

"I know, but I don't wanna move from under the covers or my chills are gonna start again."

Chasity stared at the closed door for several seething seconds. "This muthafucka don't have no damn chills," she whispered in anger as she repeatedly flicked her hand in the direction of the door.

Malajia busted out laughing.

"I swear to God, they *can't* be serious," Chasity barked. "They're doing this shit on purpose, I swear I hear laughter in his damn voice."

"I wouldn't be surprised," Malajia ground out. "At least *yours* didn't spill soup on purpose and lay in it to get your attention."

"Chaaaaz!"

"I'm coming!" Chasity yelled back, stomping towards the door.

The sound of Mark's loud voice interrupted Malajia's laughter. "Mel, is my tea done yet?"

"Shut up! Just shut the hell up!" Malajia screamed at the door.


Nicole sat at her desk, flipping through the pages of her textbook, while simultaneously jotting down notes. Having a thought, she grabbed her phone from her desk and dialed David's number. She let out a sigh when his voicemail picked up. "Hey, it's Nicole...just calling to check on you. Call me later."

Setting the phone back down, she began writing again; a task that lasted only mere seconds. She pushed her seat back and stood up. Moving quickly, she tossed a few items into a small bag, grabbed her coat and left the room.

Nicole's brisk walk took her straight to the front door of the guys' house. She adjusted the bag in her hand before giving the door a knock.

"It's open!" a voice called from the other side.

Nicole opened the door and walked in. "Hey Josh," she smiled.

Josh, wrapped up in a comforter, looked up from his plate of spaghetti and smiled. "Hey—"

Before he or Nicole could say another word, they were startled by Chasity and Malajia, who ran down the stairs and flew towards the door.

"Hi girls," Nicole greeted, offering an enthused wave.

"What's up Nicole?" Chasity hurriedly threw out, opening the door.

"Hi Nicole. Josh, they're *your* problem now," Malajia added, running out the house behind Chasity, slamming the door behind her.

Nicole, perplexed, turned to Josh. "Um...what was *that* all about?" she asked, amused.

Josh scooped some spaghetti onto his fork. "Their boyfriends are running them crazy," he answered.

"Oh," was all that Nicole could say before she saw Mark and Jason walk down the stairs, stopping in the middle of the staircase.

"Yo Josh, how fast did they run outta here?" Jason laughed.

"If Nicole was in the way, she would've gotten knocked over," Josh replied, taking another bite. "What did y'all ask them to do *this* time?"

"I asked Mel to wipe my ass for me," Mark answered.

Josh nearly choked on his mouthful of food. He started coughing as he reached for his glass of water. "The hell?" he spat in between coughs.

"I told Chaz that I pissed in the bed because I was too weak to make it to the bathroom," Jason added.

Mark looked back at Jason. "Yo, you ain't really piss in the bed, did you?"

Jason shot Mark a frown. "*No* I didn't do that shit," he barked, nudging him in the back of the head. "Stop asking me stupid questions."

Mark rubbed the back of his head as he looked back at Josh. "Anyway, next thing we knew, they ran outta our rooms and we heard them running down the stairs."

"Y'all are wrong for playing up your sickness," Josh chided.

"Man, we ain't playing *shit*, these damn colds are in the way," Mark threw back, rubbing the back of his neck. "But what better way to get through it than to annoy the women in our lives?"

Nicole's mouth fell open. "That's terrible," she commented, laughter in her voice.

"As much as they put *us* through with those damn mouths of theirs, it's *justified*," Mark returned.

Jason laughed. "Don't worry, I'm sure we'll pay for it later," he assured.

"Shit, I'm *already* on time out," Mark joked, then pointed to Josh. "How *you* talking about somebody playing up a cold and you down here wrapped in a damn tent?" he sniped. "It ain't even cold in here."

"*I'm* cold," Josh hissed through clenched teeth.

Jason shook his head and began heading back up the stairs.

"Bro, can you make me some tea?" Mark asked jokingly, following Jason up the steps.

"Fuck no," Jason barked.

Nicole giggled. "Never a dull moment with you guys," she commented, hearing the room doors close.

"Nope, never," Josh admitted. "David's in his room, I think he just woke up. I heard movement."

"Thanks." Nicole trotted up the steps and headed straight for David's door. She gave the door a light tap.

"It's open," David said through the door.

Nicole opened the door and walked in. "How are you feeling Summers?" she asked.

David sat up in his bed. He hadn't expected her, but he was happy to see her. "I'm okay."

"Somehow I don't believe you," Nicole replied, removing her coat and slinging it over the back of his chair.

David rubbed his eyes with his hand. "I thought you were supposed to be working on your project for Marketing?"

Nicole shrugged. "I was, but I didn't like the way you sounded on the phone earlier," she explained, sitting next to him. "You know, when you fell asleep on me."

"Sorry about that," David muttered.

"Not your fault, I understand," Nicole assured. "I just wanted to come over and check on you. I even brought the rub that I mentioned earlier."

David sat and watched as Nicole began removing items from her bag. "Thanks, I appreciate it."

"No need to thank me," Nicole grinned, opening the small container of vapor rub.

"Whoa," David commented of the strong smell, fanning his nose. "That opened my chest up and it's not even *on* me yet."

Nicole glanced at the substance. "Yeah, it *is* a bit strong, but it works," she admitted, scooping some in her hand. "Here, let me put some on your chest, you'll be feeling better in no time."

David began to get nervous when Nicole lifted his t-shirt and gently rubbed the substance on his bare chest. So much so that he took hold of her hand and removed it. "I can do it," he sputtered, adjusting his position on his bed. "I appreciate you, but I got it."

Nicole frowned in confusion. She didn't understand why he was so jumpy when she touched him. "Um, what's wrong—"

"Nothing, I just don't want to get you sick," he immediately cut in, holding his hand out. "Let me see it please?"

Nicole let out a sigh as she handed the container to him. "Sure," she muttered.


Sidra smoothed her hand against the linen napkin on the table in front of her. Picking up her glass of virgin strawberry daiquiri, she took a long sip through the straw and set the glass back on the table. Glancing at her watch, she took a deep breath.

After a long week, which included three tests, Sidra wasn't in the best of moods. But when her brother called her to let her know that he was coming in town that Friday afternoon and to meet him at the restaurant that they had dinner at the last time he visited, she tried to push her bad mood aside.

Glancing at her watch again, she let out a groan. She grabbed her phone from the table and dialed a number. Placing it to her ear, she tapped her long, manicured nails on the table. "Marcus, where are you? I'm starving," she hissed into the phone once the line picked up.

"I'm about to walk in now," Marcus said after a moment of hesitation. "Umm...so you didn't eat anything all day?"

Sidra frowned. "I ate earlier, but it's been hours," she replied. "I'm waiting on *you*, so hurry up."

"Uh…soooo you're at that angry place you get to when you haven't eaten in a while, huh?"

Sidra was becoming annoyed. "What are you—Marcus can you just come on please?" she begged.

Marcus sounded like he was talking to someone in the background. "Okay I—okay I'm walking in now. See you in a minute."

Sidra held a confused look on her face as the call ended. Marcus was acting funny, but she was too hungry to figure out why. She took another long sip of her drink then glanced at the door. Seeing him walk in, she couldn't help but smile. Marcus may have been working her nerves, but she was always happy to see him.

She stood up and held her arms out for a hug as he walked over to her. "About time," Sidra commented, hugging him.

Marcus hugged her back. "Sorry about the hold up," he apologized, gesturing for Sidra to sit. He took his seat after. "You look good," he smiled.

She flagged him with her hand. "I know, boy."

Marcus let out a laugh. "And *this* is why your nickname is Princess," he said.

Sidra giggled as she picked up her menu.

Marcus stared at Sidra as she studied the items on the menu. "So how was your week?" he asked.

"Long," she answered, not bothering to look up. "Too many tests, not enough sleep."

Marcus nodded. "I hear you."

Sidra finally glanced up. "I think I'm just gonna get the pasta primavera that I had last time I was—"

"Sidra, I brought India here to have dinner with us," Marcus blurted out. He put his hands over his face to block out the enraged look on Sidra's face. "She's waiting in the entryway for me to give her the signal to come in."

Sidra scratched her head. "I'm sorry, I thought that I

heard you say that you brought India...*India*, the girl who I *don't* like, here to where I go to school, to have *dinner* with us," she fumed.

Marcus put his hands up cautiously. "Listen Sidra—"

"Are you out of your—Are you *kidding* me?!" she snapped, slamming her menu on the table.

Marcus rubbed his face as Sidra made a move to get up. She refused to sit and break bread with her soon to be sister-in-law. Especially on her turf.

"You ambushed me and I don't appreciate it," Sidra snarled, grabbing her purse.

"Wait, don't go, *please*," her brother begged, stopping Sidra in her tracks. "Look, I'm sorry that I pulled this on you, but I was desperate. I need you to at least *try* to get along with her."

"Marcus—"

"*Please?*" he pleaded.

Sidra had every intention of walking out of that restaurant, but the desperation in her brother's eyes made her relent. She tossed her hands up, went to her seat, and flopped down. Folding her arms, she looked down at the table. "I will sit here, but I'm not speaking," she grunted.

"Fair enough," Marcus said, looking over towards the entry. He signaled to the young woman standing there. She walked over. Marcus looked back at Sidra, who was staring at her nails. "I will make this up to you."

"Yes, yes you *will*. And it'll take more than a stupid dinner," Sidra sniped.

"About time," India Pratt ground out, rolling her eyes at Marcus as she approached the table. She removed her coat and slung it on the back of a chair.

"Look, she had no idea you were coming, so cut me some slack," Marcus threw back as India sat down.

India flagged her hand at Marcus. "Whatever," she huffed.

Sidra sat there, seething at the bickering taking place in front of her. *If she hits or throws anything at my brother, I'm dragging this bitch.*

India looked at Sidra. "Hello Sidra," she spoke.

Sidra looked at her, no traces of warmth on her face. She just didn't understand what kept her brother running back to this girl. Sure, she was attractive, with her caramel skin, voluptuous frame and stylish short hair. But all Sidra could see when she looked at India was how much drama the woman created for Marcus. "India," she spat.

March pinched the bridge of his nose. *God help me*, he thought, sighing.

Sidra kept her promise; she sat through dinner but barely said two words. It had been an hour and to say that she was over this entire dinner was an understatement.

"So, I'm sure you've heard that we're getting married in April," India mentioned, sipping her water.

"I *heard*," Sidra ground out.

"Yeah, I told her we might go to the justice of the peace—"

India snapped her head in Marcus's direction. "Uh, no we're *not*," she scoffed. "No, I said I wanted a *small wedding*, not to get married at some courthouse."

Marcus looked confused. "What wedding do you think we can plan and *pay for* in two months?" he argued.

"Figure it out," India spat, putting her hand up at him.

Sidra put a hand up; she wasn't just going to sit there and let India talk down to Marcus. "You can't tell him to just *figure it out*. He's *right*," she spat.

India looked at Sidra, raising an eyebrow. "*You* would be okay with a justice of the peace wedding?" she challenged. "I highly doubt it, Princess."

Sidra frowned. "What did you call me?" she bit out.

"Sidra," Marcus warned.

"I called you Princess," India replied, unfazed.

"Are you my parents?" Sidra asked, tone angry.

India looked confused. "No."

"My brothers, my boyfriend, my *friend?*"

India folded her arms. "Apparently *not*," she hissed.

"Then don't *ever* call me Princess," Sidra fussed. "That nickname is a term of endearment from people who actually *matter* to me."

"What is your damn problem Sidra?" India snapped.

"I don't like you," Sidra threw back.

"You don't even *know* me like that!"

"I know enough about you *not to like you*," Sidra countered, pointing at her. "Oh you're shocked?" she mocked when India rolled her eyes. "Just *last week* you poured bleach on my brother's clothes, and now you expect me to sit here and play *nice* with you?"

"Your brother has a bad habit of running to his family every time we have a disagreement," India spat, and side-eyed Marcus.

"Don't do that," Marcus warned, eyeing her back.

"No, his *bad habit* is *you*," Sidra spat. "And he needs to drop you."

India put her hand on her stomach and smirked. "Well, even if he *wanted* to, he *can't.*"

Sidra narrowed her eyes. "Whatever, I'm done here," she scoffed, grabbing her purse.

"Sidra, India is pregnant," Marcus revealed. He couldn't take the bickering anymore, nor could he hold their secret.

Sidra's eyes widened as she tried to process the words that had come out of her brother's mouth. "Wait—*what?*" she barked finally.

"It's true," Marcus confirmed as India nodded.

"A few weeks," India added, clutching her stomach.

Sidra put her hand over her face. *He is so damn stupid! How can they bring a baby into this wreck of a relationship?!*

"Look, it wasn't planned but it's happening," Marcus added, picking up on Sidra's feelings. "*That's* why we're moving the wedding up."

"Excuse me for a minute," India said, standing up. "Full bladder."

"Ugh," Sidra scoffed as India headed for the bathroom.

With India gone, Sidra fixed her gaze on her brother. "Marcus...are you serious?"

Marcus nodded. "India is pretty excited."

"I don't care about *her*. How do *you* feel about this?" Sidra pressed, leaning forward.

Marcus thought for a moment. "I'm pretty excited about becoming a father," he admitted, smiling. "It's unexpected but I'm looking forward to meeting my child."

Sidra sighed as she sat back in her seat. Hearing Marcus speak about his future child made her lower her defenses a bit. After all, despite how she felt about the mother, that child would be her niece or nephew.

Marcus put his hand on the table. "Look, I know you have your reservations, but whether you like it or not, you're going to be an aunt."

"Yeah, I know," Sidra sighed. "You know I'll love that baby."

"I know you will," Marcus smiled at her. "And I don't expect for you to like India, I'm just asking that for the sake of the baby can you try to be civil?"

Sidra rolled her eyes. "I can be civil, but my feelings won't change," she maintained. "I don't like what she does to you."

"I'm fine, don't worry so much," he said.

*Easier said than done.* Sidra ran a hand through her hair. "Well...congratulations."

"Thank you."

# Chapter 13

"I'm so glad spring is finally here," Alex rejoiced, plopping down on the bench along the campus commons area.

"Alex, you act like we ain't out here feeling the sun *with* you," Malajia griped.

Alex narrowed her eyes at Malajia as she adjusted the zipper on her sweat jacket, but refrained from responding.

After weeks of dealing with the harsh frigid winter weather, Virginia was finally starting to see a change in the seasons. The warm sun and light breeze brought most of the campus outside, milling about and relaxing in between classes on the building steps and benches. This included Alex, Sidra, Malajia, and Mark.

"Can you believe it's almost the end of March?" Sidra commented, adjusting the purse on her lap.

"*Again*, we *all* have calendars, we know what month it is," Malajia sneered, flinging her hair over her shoulder. "God, where is Chasity? You two are irkin'."

Mark snickered at her response.

Sidra flagged Malajia dismissively. "I was saying that to say that we don't have much longer to go before we graduate," she mused, excited. "*Graduate*. That's insane."

"No what's *insane* is that Marcus is about to be a dad," Mark laughed, earning a side-glance from Sidra.

After coming back from her dreaded dinner with Marcus and India three weeks ago, the first thing Sidra did was run in the house and spill the news to the girls. After much reservation, plenty of conversations with her mother and lots of thinking, Sidra had come to terms with the situation and was actually beginning to get excited about her niece or nephew.

"You keep your jokes about my brother's parental abilities to yourself, you hear me?" Sidra scolded.

"Not a chance in hell," Mark refused. "As many times as he clowned *me* over the years? Oh I'm due payback."

Sidra rolled her eyes. "Go ahead, it's all fun and games until *you* have a baby, and people start questioning your abilities," she threw back. "That's if Malajia even *wants* one."

Mark's smile faded as he shot a sideway glance at Malajia. *Shit*, he thought. Even though Sidra had no idea, Mark suspected her words might have struck a nerve with Malajia—especially after the termination of Malajia's pregnancy last year.

Malajia, who was staring off into space, caught Mark's glance. "What?" she questioned, confused. When Mark gestured towards Sidra, Malajia sucked her teeth. "Oh, ain't nobody thinking about Sidra's stupid remark." She stood from her seat. "I gotta go."

"Where are you going?" Alex asked as Malajia gathered her jacket from the bench. "I wanted to ask your opinion on my idea for Emily's birthday."

Malajia let out a loud sigh. "Alex, we've been sitting here for like a half hour and *now* you wanna bring that up right when I'm about to leave?" she sneered.

Alex made a face in retaliation as Sidra snickered. "Just tell me what you think so I can finalize the damn plans," Alex fussed. "All that extra talking you're always doing is unnecessary."

Malajia tossed her arm up in frustration. "*You* just said like eighty-five extra words your-damn-self," she jeered.

Sidra put a hand on Alex's shoulder to stop her from jumping up at Malajia. She chuckled. "Alex, we like the idea, go ahead with the plans," she placated.

"Thank you, *Sidra*," Alex ground out, eyeing Malajia with disdain.

"Look, just make sure you have some drinks on deck," Malajia said, unfazed by Alex's attitude.

Alex rolled her eyes. "Emily doesn't *drink*," she spat.

"But the *rest* of us *do*, stop acting new," Malajia countered. She tapped Mark's shoulder. "Come on Mark, we got class."

"Ughhh," Mark groaned, hopping up from his seat. "Time to go fail this quiz."

Alex just rolled her eyes as he and Malajia walked off. She looked at Sidra, who was trying to suppress a laugh. "She's on my nerves," Alex griped of Malajia.

"You act like this is something *new*," Sidra laughed.


Alex cradled the cordless phone between her shoulder and her ear as she jotted down notes on a piece of paper. "Okay, so we have to be there by eight?" she said into the phone. "You said it's BYOB right? ...And we pick the one that we want to do right? ...Perfect." Alex smiled as she jotted down more notes. "Okay, see you Saturday."

"Your plans all finished?" Leroy, manager of the Pizza Shack commented in passing, as Alex hung up the phone.

"Yep, all set," she confirmed, placing the top back on her ink pen. "Thanks again for giving me Saturday off so I can celebrate my friend's birthday," she added, grateful. When Alex began to feel bad because she was scheduled to work on Emily's upcoming birthday, her boss immediately switched the day with another waitress.

"Not a problem. Anything for my favorite waitress," Leroy mused, adjusting several stacks of plastic cups.

"Oh, so you mean to tell me that I'm just your favorite waitress and not your favorite employee *over all*?" Alex teased, feigning hurt, placing her hands on her hips.

"Well, when you can get pizzas out in record time like *Josh*, you can have his spot," Leroy returned, earning a giggle from Alex. She had to admit, even though she wouldn't necessarily miss working as a waitress upon graduating college, she sure would miss working with her boss.

Leroy glanced over at the front counter when he heard the door open. He smiled when he saw a patron walk in. "Alex, your pretty little friend is here," he announced.

"Which one?" Alex asked, adjusting the straps of her apron.

"The *mean* one," he returned, still smiling. "I like 'em mean."

Alex laughed and grabbed a small dishtowel from behind the counter. As Leroy walked off, Alex turned around and sure enough, Chasity was standing there. "Hey 'mean one'," she joked.

Chasity looked confused. "What?"

Alex shook her head. "Nothing," she dismissed. "I think my boss has a crush on you."

Chasity frowned in disgust. "Eww," she scoffed.

Alex playfully swatted her arm with the towel. "Don't be rude," she chortled.

"That towel better not had been dirty," Chasity warned.

"Oh hush your mouth," Alex returned, waving her hand at her. "Did you order the cake?"

"No," Chasity replied nonchalantly.

Alex stood there, waiting on an explanation as to why Chasity did not complete the task that she left earlier to do. When she gave none, Alex became frustrated. "Why *not*?" she barked.

Chasity frowned. "Calm down," she warned.

Alex sucked her teeth.

"And to answer your *question*, Sidra said that *she* was making Emily's cake," Chasity informed. "She's been hype about doing it for weeks."

"She's really gonna attempt to make that cake with all of those layers in the different shades of pink?" Alex questioned.

"Yep," Chasity confirmed. "Bet money that shit comes out all one color."

Alex shook her head as she began wiping the counter. "Well, I can't knock her for trying," she shrugged. "But we should just pick up an extra one just in case."

"Alright," Chasity agreed, adjusting her purse on her shoulder. "I *did* however, pick out her present."

"*Did* you?" Alex asked, intrigued. "What did you get? Can I see it?" she pressed, peering over the counter, looking for a bag.

"No," Chasity bluntly stated.

Alex's mouth fell open in shock. "Why *not*?"

"Just concentrate on what *you're* supposed to set up, alright," Chasity sneered.

"It better not be anything *remotely* smart assed," Alex warned.

"Worry about what *you're* doing," Chasity reiterated, this time slowly and through clenched teeth.

"Fine," Alex relented. "I really think she's going to like what we're planning. It's so *her*."

"For *once*, I agree with you," Chasity jeered.

Alex made a face in retaliation. "Funny," she ground out. "Anyway, I gotta get back to work. You hungry?"

"Not for *this* food," Chasity scoffed, walking towards the door.

"Forget you then, heffa," Alex hurled at her back. Chasity smirked then walked out of the restaurant. Alex shook her head and went back to wiping the counter top.


"Okay guys, just one more problem and we're finished for the day," Emily said, standing in front of the blackboard. "You ready?" she asked the fifteen eager faces in front of her.

"Yes!" the kindergarteners bellowed.

Olivia giggled as Emily playfully covered her ears.

Emily grabbed a large card; it had a word with a picture

next to it. "Okay guys, what is this word?" she asked, pointing to it.

"Cloud," the class wailed in unison.

"Very good," Emily beamed. "And how many letters does the word 'cloud' have?" When the class hesitated, she began pointing to each letter. "Come on, count with me," she urged, then smiled as the class began slowly counting with her.

"One, two, three, four, five!"

"Very good," Emily replied. "There are five letters in the word 'cloud'... And can you tell me a word that rhymes with 'cloud'?"

"Loud!" several students bellowed, along with several other words.

Emily laughed. The children always brightened her day. She set the card down and began clapping. "Good job class, give yourself a clap." She pushed some of her hair behind her ear as she moved around the desk. "Well that's it for the day," she said, hearing the bell ring. "You little ones have a—"

"Hold on, before we all leave for the weekend, we have something that we want to give Miss Emily, right class?" Olivia asked, standing from her seat at Emily's desk.

"Yeeesss," the classroom erupted.

Emily looked skeptical. "They do?" she asked.

Olivia nodded. "Yes and they're really excited about it," she beamed, opening the closet and pulling something out of it. "Okay everybody, just like we practiced," she urged.

Emily faced the front of the class as the children rose from their desks and eagerly approached the desk.

"On three," Olivia prompted, then started counting.

"Happy birthday Miss. Emily!" the boys and girls wailed.

Emily put her hand over her chest and smiled the brightest smile. She glanced over at Olivia, who was walking over to her, holding a cake, a large birthday card, and small gift bag with a pink balloon attached. "Awww, you guys are so sweet," she gushed. "Thank you."

Olivia set the items on the desk in front of Emily. "They couldn't wait to say happy birthday to you," she giggled. "All week, they kept asking, 'is it time yet'?"

Emily laughed.

"Do you like your cake?" A little girl asked.

Emily bent down in front of her. "I *love* my cake," she cooed.

"Miss Olivia let us sign the card," a little boy added.

Emily opened the large card and began reading all of the scribbled names. She felt herself getting choked up. After the morning that she'd had, she was pleasantly surprised and grateful that the class did that for her.

"Miss Emily, are you crying?" another student asked.

"No," Emily lied, laughter in her voice. "Thank you guys."

"Okay, go get your things together," Olivia ordered. "Your parents are waiting for you."

"Can we have some cake?"

"You have to ask Miss Emily," Olivia said. "It's her cake."

"Of *course* you can have some cake. *Everybody* can," Emily said, setting her card down. She grabbed the plastic knife off and began cutting as the children rejoiced.

As Emily and Olivia worked swiftly to cut up and wrap the small pieces into pieces of paper towels for the children, Emily looked over at Olivia.

"Thanks for this Livy," she said.

"Oh you're welcome hon," Olivia smiled. "You are doing such a great job. The children love you."

"Awww, I love them too," Emily returned. "Their little faces make my day."

As the last child filtered out of the classroom, Olivia began straightening up. "You have any plans for your *actual* birthday tomorrow?"

Emily sighed. "No," she sulked.

"What about your friends?" Olivia asked. "Are *they*

planning anything for you?"

"I have no idea," Emily shrugged. "Which is just as well, I'm not really in the mood to do anything anyway."

Olivia shot her a sympathetic look. "No?" Emily shook her head. "It's your twenty-first birthday, you're supposed to go out and have a crazy time. And take twenty-one shots."

Emily shook her head as she winced. "Yeah, I don't think so," she chuckled. "Shots are *not* my thing, let alone *twenty-one* of them. I'd die."

Olivia giggled. "Well, I hope that you end up having fun anyway. You deserve it."

"Thanks."

"You go ahead and head out, I'll clean up," Olivia declared. "Go," she chuckled when Emily went to protest. "Enjoy your birthday weekend."

"Thanks." Emily headed to the closet to grab her jacket.


"So the plan is, we're gonna wake her up at midnight by throwing ice water in her face," Malajia suggested to Sidra, Chasity, and Alex as they sat around the dining room table, eating snacks.

"Why would we throw water on her face?" Sidra asked, annoyed.

"So she can wake up," Malajia explained.

"As opposed to *what*? Just *waking* her up?" Chasity sniped. She put her hand up when Malajia went to speak. "Just shut up," she barked.

Alex laughed at the silly look on Malajia's face. "Oh Sidra, how did your cake turn out?" she asked, excited.

"I think it turned out pretty good if I *do* say so myself," Sidra boasted, folding her arms on the tabletop.

"Don't nobody believe that shit," Malajia threw out, shaking her hand in Sidra's direction. "You might as well bring that cake out and let me cut into it."

"You're not cutting into a *damn* thing," Sidra refused, reaching for a corn chip from a bag. "I worked too hard on it for your greedy butt to mess with it."

"Fine, fuck that cake," Malajia spat. "I'll just cut the backup cake. Chaz where is it?" Chasity quickly shot Malajia a wide-eyed glance, as Alex quickly shook her head.

"Backup cake? *What* backup cake?" Sidra asked, looking back and forth between the girls.

Malajia winced. "Oops, my bad," she uttered.

Alex tossed her head back and let out a groan as Chasity put her face in her hand and shook her head.

"Never, she can *never* just keep her fuckin' mouth shut," Chasity bit out.

"I *said* my bad, shit," Malajia barked, tossing her arms in the air.

Sidra looked hurt. "You really bought a backup cake?" she asked, upset. "What? You don't trust that I did a good job?"

Chasity looked at her. "Well honestly—"

"Hey Emily!" Alex exclaimed as the door opened. She was glad for the interruption; she just knew that Chasity was about to say something mean and Sidra was feeling offended enough.

Emily walked in and closed the door behind her. "Hey," she greeted, walking towards the table, items in hand.

"Whatcha got there?" Malajia asked, pointing to the box and bag in Emily's hand.

Emily glanced down at the box. "Oh, the students got me a cake and a gift for my birthday," she smiled. "Do you want so—"

"Yep!" Malajia jumped up and grabbed the box of cake from Emily and sat back down.

Alex leaned over the table to try to peer inside the white box. "Ooh, is that butter cream—"

"Alex, you ain't gettin' none!" Malajia erupted, pulling the box closer to her.

Seeing the angry look on Alex's face, Emily couldn't help but laugh. "Wow," she commented.

"That was nice of them to do that for you Em," Sidra

commented, ignoring the side bickering.

"Yeah," Emily sighed. "They made me this little clay sculpture too," she said, removing the small colorful egg-shaped sculpture from a bag.

"What *is* it?" Chasity chortled.

Emily tilted her head. "I think it's supposed to be an Easter egg."

"It ain't even *Easter* though," Malajia teased.

"Malajia, I will *pay* you to be quiet for *ten* minutes!" Alex barked, putting her hands on her head. She'd been over Malajia's nonsense for the past hour.

Cutting a piece of cake with the plastic knife that was inside the box, Malajia smirked. "Ain't shit I can do with that poor ass dollar," she mocked, earning a snicker from Chasity.

Ignoring the banter, Emily set her gift bag on the couch and flopped down on the accent chair next to it. A long sigh soon followed.

"What's wrong sweetie?" Sidra asked. "Aren't you excited about your birthday tomorrow?"

Emily ran her hand through her hair. "Yeah, I guess," she muttered.

"You *guess*?" Sidra pressed.

"I don't know; I guess I'm just feeling a little let down," Emily admitted. "I was hoping that my brothers would be able to come down and see me this weekend, but they can't."

"Oooh, I'm sorry Em," Alex sympathized.

"Thanks," Emily sulked. "I mean, Dru said that he was *sending* me something, but it's not the same, you know?"

"Yeah I know," Alex placated.

"And my dad is traveling, so *he* can't be here," Emily added. "And...that's it." She knew mentioning her mother or sister not being around was pointless; Emily never expected them to show up for her anyway.

"Well...do you have anything *else* planned?" Alex asked, eyes shifting. Chasity, Malajia, and Sidra shot her side-glances.

*Nope, nothing, nada, and I guess nobody else does*

*either,* she thought. Emily had to admit that not only was she feeling let down by her family, but the same also applied to her friends. She secretly hoped that at least *they* would make a big deal out of her twenty-first birthday, like they did for *each other's.* But showing her disappointment wouldn't change a thing. She rose from her seat. "I'll probably just catch up on some much-needed sleep."

Sidra followed Emily's progress as she headed for the stairs. "Cheer up, Em," she said.

"I will," Emily replied, disappearing up the steps.

Once they heard the door close, Chasity tossed a balled-up napkin at Alex. "You can't lie for *shit*," she sniped.

"What do you mean?!" Alex exclaimed, laughter in her voice.

"That obvious inflection on the word 'else' for one," Sidra teased.

"And those shifty ass eyes," Malajia added. "About to give up the plans and shit."

Alex rolled her eyes. "Whatever," she threw back.


Emily pulled her comforter up to her neck as she rolled over in bed. After being up for half the night with a heavy mind, she was happy to finally be able to drift off to sleep. Just as the swirls of dreamland began to take hold, loud voices startled her awake.

"Happy birthdaaaayyy!" They bellowed at the top of their lungs. Letting out a scream, Emily jerked so hard that she rolled out of bed.

"Oh shit," Chasity laughed as Alex bent down to help Emily up.

"What?—wait—" Emily was trying to catch her breath and focus her eyes.

Sidra turned on the lamp. It was then that Emily was able to see the girls standing there. "Did we scare you?" Sidra giggled.

Emily put her hand on her chest as she sat on her bed.

"Yes," she admitted once she calmed down. "You nearly gave me a heart attack, but thank you."

"Yeah well, this was the most dramatic way that we could think of to wake you up," Alex chuckled, running her hand over her bonnet-covered head.

"No, *I* suggested that we throw water on her," Malajia grunted.

"Girl, we already told you that we weren't doing that to her," Sidra hissed, glaring at her.

Malajia folded her arms in a huff as she mumbled something incoherently.

Sidra sat down on Emily's bed next to her. "So, how do you feel?" she quipped, putting her arm around her.

Emily ran her hand over her disheveled hair. "No different, really," she said.

"You *will* once you take these shots," Malajia beamed, pulling a shot glass and a small bottle from the pockets of her robe. She handed Emily the shot glass. "It's drinkin' time."

"Seriously?" Alex fussed, watching Malajia open the bottle of rum.

"Malajia, I'm not doing this," Emily tiredly said, holding the shot glass away from her.

"And she *knows* that. She doesn't *listen*," Alex fumed, shooting Malajia a death stare. "What is *wrong* with you?"

Malajia stared at the bonnet sitting on top of Alex's puffy hair. "Don't talk shit to *me* when *you're* standing there looking like a fat ass mushroom with that thing sitting on top of your head like that," she bit back.

Sidra put her hand over her face and shook her head; Emily covered her mouth and snickered.

Alex looked at Chasity, who was laughing.

"Don't look over here, I told you the other *day* to stop coming out the room with that bullshit on," Chasity jeered. "You look crazy."

"*She* don't listen," Malajia chimed in, swirling the liquor around in the bottle.

"Shut up, both of you," Alex barked. "And leave my

bonnet alone. You don't have to look at it."

"How can we *not*, as big as your fuckin' head is," Chasity muttered.

Sidra desperately tried to keep her laughter in. "Okay, we didn't wake Em up for all that," she cut in, putting her hand up. "Malajia, she's not drinking your shots, you wasted your money." She leaned down and grabbed a small bottle from the floor, then showed it to Emily. "I brought up a wine cooler, do you want *that*?"

Emily smiled as she took it. "Yeah, that'll work."

"That's so wack yo," Malajia commented. "You're supposed to get drunk, not sip some watered-down cooler."

"Malajia do me a favor?" Chasity asked, tone calm, polite even.

"What's that sis?" Malajia replied.

"Shut up," Chasity threw back in the same polite tone.

Malajia couldn't help but laugh.

Alex shook her head. "We're going to let you get back to sleep Em, but we wanted to be the first ones to wish you a happy birthday," she said. "We want to take you to breakfast and then we all have something planned later tonight."

Emily was grinning from ear to ear as she grabbed her phone from the floor by her bed. They had thought of her after all. "That sounds wonderful, thanks girls," she gushed. Her day was looking up already. "And um...you weren't the first ones to wish me happy birthday," she slowly revealed, glancing at her cell phone. "*Will* was...he texted me at twelve exactly." She giggled at the salty looks on her friends' faces.

"He hype as shit, tryna get first dibs," Malajia mocked; Emily shook her head in amusement. Malajia snapped her head towards Alex. "This is *your* fault," she hurled.

"What did *I* do?" Alex wailed.

"If you would've taken that stupid bonnet off, we would've come out the rooms *sooner*," Malajia threw back. "You always fuckin' shit up."

Alex glanced at Sidra. "Sidra, hand me that magazine on

your desk please," she prompted.

"Shit!" Malajia hissed, running out of the room.

Alex, not waiting for Sidra to move, snatched the magazine off the desk and rolled it as she chased Malajia out of the room.

# Chapter 14

"Daddy, stop apologizing. I know that you would be here if you *could*," Emily said, slowly pacing her bedroom.

"I can't help but feel bad," Mr. Harris said. "It's your twenty-first birthday and I can't even take you to dinner."

Emily smiled. She knew that her father felt bad when he missed major moments in his children's lives. He always did, even when they were little. But she knew that it wasn't for lack of trying.

"It's okay, my friends have things planned for me today, so I'm happy," Emily stated. "Don't stress yourself."

"Thank you for being so understanding," Mr. Harris said. "I have to get to this meeting, but enjoy your day and make sure you call me later."

"I will," Emily promised. "Bye."

Once Emily ended her call, she walked over to the floor-length mirror and glanced at it. Smiling to herself, she remembered how she looked when she first came to school at the age of seventeen. The ponytails, the frumpy clothes, the crippling shyness. Emily couldn't believe how much she had changed, not only as a person, but even in the way she looked. Her brown hair was curled and pinned to one side. Form fitting skinny jeans, paired with a pale pink off the shoulder top and nude ankle boots, not only made her look her age, but accentuated her slim figure. Her modest silver jewelry and subtle makeup brought out her features.

"You look cute," Emily smiled to herself, grabbing her nude purse from her desk. She trotted out of the room and down the steps.

"Hey there pretty birthday girl," Sidra smiled as Emily reached the bottom of the stairs.

"Thanks," Emily beamed, placing the strap of her purse on her shoulder. "Thanks again for taking me to breakfast—"

"Emily, don't get all fussy bus on us and start thanking us every five minutes," Malajia jeered, shaking her hand in Emily's direction.

Alex playfully backhanded Malajia on the arm as she looked at Emily. "Ignore her," she said. "But no need to thank us."

"Alright ladies, let's get going," Sidra ordered, looking at her watch. "Those pancakes are calling my name."

"How a pancake call you without any lips?" Malajia mocked. Sidra shot Malajia a confused look as Emily snickered loudly.

Chasity pinched the bridge of her nose. "I swear to God, don't let her sit next to me," she griped. "You sound just like Mark's stupid ass."

"They can try to stop me from sitting by you if they *want* to, I'll sit right on your damn face," Malajia threw back, examining her nails.

Chasity looked utterly disgusted. "Eww! You wanna rephrase that shit?"

"Nope," Malajia returned, unfazed.

Alex shook her head. "Look you two, don't—" A knock at the door interrupted her warning.

"That better not be who I *think* it is," Sidra said as Emily headed for the door.

Chasity looked at Malajia as she retrieved her car keys from her purse. "Malajia, tell your fuckin' greedy ass boyfriend that he's not coming with us," she barked.

"Why it gotta be *my* man?!" Malajia exclaimed, pointing to herself.

"Did he or did he *not* come over earlier, talking about 'y'all ready'?" Chasity reminded.

Unable to justify the accusation, Malajia lowered her

head and shook it. "Yeah I know," she chuckled.

Emily opened the door. Her bright smile gave way to pure shock as she laid eyes on the person standing on their front step. "What the hell?" she blurted out instantaneously. "Mommy?!"

"*Mommy?*" the girls repeated in unison, as they all turned around to see Ms. Harris standing outside.

"Hello Emily," Ms. Harris said, a stern look on her face, arms folded. Emily just stood there, frozen in silence, the shock not leaving her face. "Can I come in?"

Emily snapped out of her haze and hesitantly moved aside to allow her mother—a woman who she had not seen or spoken to in what seemed like forever—to step foot inside her home.

Ms. Harris glanced around and laid eyes on the four girls standing near the dining room table. The astonishment hadn't left their faces. Emily's mother was the last person *anyone* expected to visit.

Neither one got the chance to say anything, because Emily stepped right in. "Mom, what are you doing here?" she asked, the shock wearing off, giving way to frustration.

Ms. Harris fixed her gaze on Emily. Her daughter looked so different; she sounded different. Gone was that low-pitched voice. "Well, I figured it had been a while, so I decided to come see you," she answered.

Emily was truly confused, and it showed all over her face. "*Huh?*"

"Yes," Ms. Harris nodded.

Emily shook her head in disbelief. *What the hell?! Is she insane?!* "So…instead of *calling* me after all this time to establish a *dialogue*, you decide to do one of your *pop-up visits*?" she hissed.

"Ooh," Sidra gasped, then immediately covered her mouth. "Sorry," she muttered in embarrassment as the other girls hissed at her to be quiet. They began to quietly gesture to each other. The strained exchange between mother and daughter was uncomfortable for them, especially since no one had ever seen Emily be snide with her mother before.

"Um, Emily, we're gonna just leave you two alone to let you catch up," Alex quickly put out as they began making their way to the door.

"Wait a second, I thought we were going to breakfast," Emily frowned.

"You two can just go without us," Sidra quickly put in as they paused.

"I think that is a good idea," Ms. Harris put in, looking at Emily.

"Uh *no*, the girls have plans for me and it's not fair to them *or* me to change them," Emily replied.

"No, Em its fine, we weren't gonna go *out*, out until later tonight anyway," Alex assured, tone nervous. "Your mom isn't ruining anything."

Emily shot Alex a wide-eyed glance. *Shut up Alex! You're not helping!*

"Um, yeah, we gotta go," Malajia quickly put out as the girls tried once again to run for the door. They couldn't get out of the house fast enough.

"Just a second," Ms. Harris called to them, halting their progress once again.

"Goddamn it," Chasity huffed under her breath as they spun around to face Ms. Harris once again. Alex lightly backhanded her.

"I apologize for coming into your house and not speaking," Ms. Harris said. That not only shocked the girls, but Emily herself. Her mother had never liked Emily's friends and the woman never had a problem ignoring or being rude to them; Emily surely wasn't expecting any sort of cordial encounter.

"It's fine," Malajia once again put out with haste. "We really have to—"

"It was nice seeing you girls again," Ms. Harris said, ignoring the girls' impatience as they stood there. "Let me see if I can remember your names." She tapped her chin with her finger as she tried to remember. "Oh, I got it. Alice,

Sierra, Cassidy and Maria," she slowly put out as she pointed to each girl.

Emily put her hand over her face and shook her head. *God, please don't let one of them go off,* she thought.

The girls stood there for a moment, shooting each other glances.

"Alice?" Alex mouthed to them, face turned up. It was clear that she hated that name more than *Alexandra.* Chasity rolled her eyes and shook her head.

"Am I right?" Ms. Harris pressed, when they didn't respond.

"Yep, those are our names, we gotta go," Chasity quickly blurted out. At that point, she didn't care that Ms. Harris butchered her name. She just wanted to get out of the house.

As the girls hurried out of the door, Malajia turned to Alex. "Ahh, she called you 'Alice'," she teased.

"Shut up '*Maria*'," Alex threw back as she closed the door behind her.

Emily faced her mother once again. "Mom—"

"Emily," Ms. Harris began, putting her hand up, cutting Emily's words short. "I know that I shouldn't have popped up on you unannounced. But… It's your birthday and I wanted to see you."

Emily sighed as she turned away. Just like always, her mood dampened when her mother inserted herself into Emily's plans without considering her daughter's feelings. Although she missed her mother, Emily wasn't over how her mother had treated her, and she certainly didn't want to dredge up bad feelings on a day that she was supposed to be carefree and having the time of her life, with her second family.

Sensing Emily's hesitation and agitation, Ms. Harris decided not to start up the inevitable conversation right then and there. "Will you come to breakfast with me?" she asked, hope in her voice.

Emily just stared at her. At that point, she felt that she

had no choice *but* to go. She might have been upset, but Emily didn't have the heart to turn her mother down, especially when the woman sounded and looked hopeful. "Sure," Emily muttered, tone unenthused.

"Yo, her mom really showed up and crashed y'all damn plans?" Mark laughed, cutting his pancakes with his fork.

"I wouldn't say *that*," Sidra replied, pouring sugar into her cup of tea. "Em would have come with us, but we knew that she really needed to talk to her mother."

Upon leaving the house, the girls decided to cancel their diner plans, and opted instead to just hit the cafeteria for breakfast. In route, they met up with Mark and Jason, who were already on their way there.

"That's crazy. It's really been that damn long since her mother spoke to her?" Jason asked, pouring syrup on his waffles.

"Yup," Chasity confirmed, picking up a piece of her French toast with her fork.

Jason shook his head in disbelief. "And this is all because Emily *moved out*."

"I never thought I'd say this, but Emily's mom is even pettier than *Brenda*," Chasity jeered. "And that's nearly impossible to accomplish."

"Stop it," Alex chided, pointing her fork in Chasity's direction. "You shouldn't speak ill of the dead."

Chasity rolled her eyes. "Oh chill the hell out *Alice*," she mocked, reaching for her cup of juice.

Malajia nearly spat the chewed-up bacon out of her mouth as she tried to contain a laugh. Alex rolled her eyes and let out a loud sigh. "Yo, that was hilarious," Malajia recalled, wiping her mouth with a napkin.

"You act like she didn't butcher *all* of our names," Alex spat.

"*I* actually *like* the name 'Sierra'," Sidra chuckled.

"Alex, just mad 'cause her name sound old as shit,"

Malajia teased. "*Just because* you hate it so much, we're gonna start calling you that *all* the time."

"You better *not*," Alex warned.

"You don't scare nobody, Alice," Malajia mocked, earning a laugh from Mark.

"I hate you," Alex ground out.

"We know you don't mean that, Alice," Mark teased.

"Cut it out!" Alex fumed, slamming her hand on the table.

"You seem upset, Alice," Jason chimed in.

Alex sucked her teeth. "Really Jason?" she sneered.

Sidra put her hands up in mid-laugh. "Come on guys, leave her alone," she cut in.

"Thank you, Sidra," Alex replied, grateful. "It's nice to know that I have at least *one* friend at this table."

Sidra snickered. "You know that Alice doesn't like her name."

Alex tossed her hands up in the air in frustration as laughter broke out around the table.

"Yeeesssss Princess!" Malajia rejoiced, giving the laughing Sidra a high five. "I was hoping you would join the team."

Sidra looked at Alex. "I'm sorry, I *had* to," she explained.

"I swear, all of you make me sick," Alex fussed, folding her arms. "Always gotta tag team *one* damn person."

"Shut up Alice," Mark taunted, earning more snickers from the table.

Emily sat across from her mother at the small diner minutes from campus. While her mother was ravenous, eating her order of pancakes, eggs and grits, Emily barely touched her Belgian waffle. She still had a hard time wrapping her head around the fact that her mother was actually in town, sitting in front of her, after all of the time that had passed.

Ms. Harris looked up from her plate of half eaten food and met eyes with Emily, who was staring at her. "You're not going to eat?" she asked.

"Mommy," Emily replied, tone unenthused. "What are you doing here?" She wasn't in the mood for small talk; she wanted to get to the point of her mother's impromptu visit.

"Like I said back at the house, I came to see you," Ms. Harris reiterated. "It's your birthday after all."

Emily squinted as she tried to remain calm. "Why show up for *this* birthday when you didn't show up for the *last* one?"

Ms. Harris reached for her glass of juice and took a sip, not bothering to answer.

"I mean, who talked you into coming here?" Emily pressed. "Was it Daddy? Well, it *couldn't* be him because you don't talk to him that much. It wasn't Jazmine, because, well…she couldn't care less about anything that has to do with me— Was it Brad? Dru?"

"It was Dru," Ms. Harris confirmed.

Emily shook her head. *So that's what he meant when he said that he was sending me something for my birthday,* she thought. "So, it took *Dru* to tell you about yourself, for you to actually come and see me?" That was more of a statement, than a question. "That's nice."

Ms. Harris fixed a stern gaze upon Emily. Although her daughter's voice was calm, her tone was snarky. This wasn't an Emily that she was used to; she didn't like it. "You may be upset with me Emily, but that doesn't give you the right to get smart with me," she chastised.

"I'm not getting smart," Emily countered, folding her arms.

"You don't think so?" Ms. Harris challenged, folding her arms in retaliation. "Because it sure sounds like it to *me*."

Emily rolled her eyes. As far as she was concerned, her mother was lucky that a smart tone was the only thing that she received, and not a slammed door in her face earlier. "Mom, with all due respect—"

"Oh, *now* you want to acknowledge respect?" Ms. Harris hissed.

"As much of it as I can *possibly* give to you at this very moment," Emily threw back.

Her mother shot her a challenging look, a look that if it were a few years ago, would have shut Emily right up.

"You can't show up here after *all* this time and expect everything to be normal," Emily fussed. "*Especially* when you haven't even said that you're sorry."

Ms. Harris let out a huff. "Look, I might have overreacted—"

"*Might* have?" Emily interrupted, shocked. "Might— Mom, you practically *disowned* me," she reminded. "You didn't answer any of my phone calls and the only reason why you spoke to me last year was because I was at Grandma's funeral. If she hadn't passed, you probably wouldn't have spoken to me at *all*!"

"That's not true," Ms. Harris denied.

Emily rolled her eyes and placed her hands on both sides of her head in exasperation. Her mother wasn't taking responsibility for her own actions once again, and Emily was over it. "Yes Mom, that *is* true," she argued. "All because I moved out."

Ms. Harris slammed her napkin on the table. "You just up and *told* me that you were leaving!" she snapped. The bass in her voice startled Emily. Even though her mother tried to play up the polite act, it was quite clear to Emily, and some of the nearby patrons, that she was outraged. "You didn't discuss it with me, you didn't ask me how I *felt*... After *everything* that I have done for you, you acted like you just didn't care."

"You know what, at that point I *didn't*," Emily barked back. "Talking to you about it wouldn't have made you feel any differently. It was like you never wanted me to leave."

"You're my baby—"

"I'm *not* a baby," Emily cut in, angry. "And you have *three* other children. Why were you clinging to only *me*?"

"*You* needed the most attention," Ms. Harris explained. "You needed the most hand-holding—"

"See, *that's* why I left, Mom. I was *nineteen* and you were treating me like I was *five*," Emily fumed. "It was like you were holding my neck, trying to keep me close to you. I couldn't *breathe* Mom. I was failing my—"

"Oh so now we're back to you blaming me for failing your classes your sophomore year, huh?" Ms. Harris sneered.

"I failed because I was *stressed*. I was *stressed* because of *you*," Emily argued. "I go to school in Virginia, and you were controlling me from freakin' *New Jersey*." She stared at her mother with pleading eyes, hoping that she would understand where Emily was coming from. Hoping that she would understand why her daughter had to do what she did. "...I started drinking my sophomore year," she revealed, much to Ms. Harris's shock.

Ms. Harris's eyes widened in anger. "You *what*?" she barked.

Emily had debated whether to reveal to her mother the struggles that she went through her sophomore year. But she knew that her mother wasn't taking what she was saying seriously, and had hoped that revealing the extent of the damage that she had done to Emily by controlling her, would help her understand.

Emily looked nervous, but it only lasted a second as she gathered her nerve to keep talking. "I was so stressed out, that...I started drinking as a way to deal with it," she explained.

Ms. Harris shook her head with vigor. "No, that wasn't because of me," she refused to believe. "It was because you were hanging around those girls."

Emily's eyes widened. "Are you *serious*, right now?" she ground out.

"Absolutely," Ms. Harris maintained. "You allowed those heathens to influence you, *that's* why you started drinking."

"So in *your* mind, I was weak enough to let someone

talk me into doing something that I knew was wrong?" Emily sniped.

"*Clearly* that was the case." Ms. Harris hissed.

"Yeah well, it wouldn't be the first time," Emily threw back.

Ms. Harris frowned. "What is *that* supposed to mean?" she challenged.

"Never mind," Emily dismissed. Her mother wasn't accepting one of her secrets; there was no way that she would accept the other.

"I knew I was right in wanting you to come back home," Ms. Harris grunted. "I *knew* you couldn't handle being on your own."

Emily just stared at her mother, shaking her head.

"Not *only* were you failing, but you were being a drunk. I didn't raise you like that," her mother stated. "If you would've staying in New Jersey you would've—"

"Still been living at home being controlled by *you*," Emily put in.

"Stop being dramatic," Ms. Harris spat. Emily let out a sigh. "You're throwing a temper tantrum and it's getting on my nerves," her mother continued. She watched as a fed-up Emily gathered her belongings. "Little girl, where are you going?"

Emily rose from her seat. "I'm a *woman* Mom," she threw back. "And *clearly* this issue between us isn't going to be resolved, because you refuse to believe that you did anything wrong."

"I raised you. I did what a mother was *supposed* to do," Ms. Harris snapped.

"Yeah, you raised me," Emily agreed. "You *raised* me to feel like I needed to depend on you for everything. You *raised* me to be afraid of being on my own. You *raised* me to believe that I didn't need anybody else but *you*." Emily slung her purse over her shoulder. "You favored me over your other children and that caused them to hate me. But you probably loved that, because it gave me nobody else to turn to but *you*."

Ms. Harris's mouth fell open as she listened to the words that Emily was spewing.

"You made me weak," Emily added. "And it's clear that that weak girl was the same girl that you were expecting to see when you popped up today…am I right?" she shook her head when her mother didn't answer. "Well, I'm not that girl anymore and if you want to have a *real* conversation, then you know where to find me."

Ms. Harris watched in stunned silence as Emily walked out of the restaurant.

# Chapter 15

The bus ride back to campus didn't help in calming Emily down. In fact, the quiet ride only intensified her burdening thoughts, because she had time to dwell on them. Once the bus arrived at her stop, she got off and walked in seething silence through campus to her house. Opening the door, Emily removed her jacket and slammed it on the couch, along with her purse, before flopping down on it. She was too upset to even speak to the girls, who were all in the living room.

"You okay sweetie?" Sidra asked.

"Nope," Emily muttered.

Alex frowned in concern. "How was breakfast with your mom?" she asked.

"I don't want to talk about it," Emily grunted, folding her arms.

"Fair enough," Alex replied.

Malajia glanced over at Alex in shock. "What Alex?" she teased. "You mean you're not gonna sit in her face and press her to talk about it?"

Alex narrowed her eyes at Malajia. "What? I'm trying to *change*, okay," she hissed.

Malajia just chuckled.

"You not wanting to talk about it is understandable," Sidra added, ignoring the side conversation.

Emily bolted up in her seat. "No, you know what, I *do* want to talk about it," she fumed. "My mother is *unbelievable.* Unbelievably *crazy.*"

"You're *just now* figuring that out?" Chasity sneered. Her smart comment earned her a backhand to the arm from Sidra, who was standing next to her.

"Right?" Malajia agreed, amusement in her voice.

"I guess I always knew," Emily reiterated. "I mean, she *still* hasn't apologized to me. She thinks that she has done nothing wrong."

"That's ridiculous," Malajia griped.

"Yeah, I know," Emily agreed, furious. "You wanna know what's even *more* ridiculous? She blames *you* girls for me drinking sophomore year."

"She *what*?!" Sidra exclaimed as Alex looked confused.

"What, did we force the bottles of that strong ass, red drink to your lips?" Malajia added, annoyed. "We didn't even *know* that you were drinking at first."

"Truth be told Emily, I'm not surprised by that," Chasity declared, running her hand through her hair. "What *does* surprise me is that you told her in the *first* place."

"Shit, I thought that you would have taken that to your grave, when it came to her smothering ass," Malajia commented.

Emily sighed. "I guess I just thought that maybe hearing what I went through would make her realize—" Emily quickly shook her head. "Never mind, *obviously* it didn't work."

Alex walked over and sat down beside Emily. "Em, this may be a silly question but—"

"If you *know* it's gonna be silly, why are you even about to ask it?" Malajia cut in, annoyed.

Alex shot her a glance, before pointing to Sidra. "Smack her for me, will you Sid?"

"She ain't gonna—Ouch!" Malajia bellowed as Sidra backhanded her on the arm.

Alex turned back to Emily, whose face was glum. "Do you think you'll ever tell your mom about you losing your virginity?" she asked.

Emily looked at Alex as if she was crazy. "You're joking right?"

Alex shook her head. "Maybe having an adult conversation like that will make her realize that you're not a kid anymore."

"Doubt it," Emily grunted. She looked around the room. "Just curious, when you girls lost your virginity…how did *your* moms take it when you told them?"

Sidra raised her hand. "Well, I'm still a virgin so this doesn't apply to me," she chuckled. "But I *will* say that my mom has always been open with me about sex…sometimes *too* open."

"You only saying that 'cause she uses the actual words for sex organs and not those childish ass words that *you* use like nunu's and hoho's," Malajia mocked, running a hand over her hair.

"Not *once* have I used nunu's and hoho's," Sidra sneered, clapping her hands in agitation.

Malajia busted out laughing.

"Snacks and goodies don't sound any better," Chasity teased, laughter in her voice. Alex snickered. "What word do you use to say dick? Pecker? Peter?"

"Naw, she say 'noodle' and shit," Malajia teased.

Sidra put her hand over her face. "No, I call it a…pee pee." She shook her head in embarrassment as her friends laughed at her.

"Pee Pee?!" Malajia wailed. "What *are* you, *three*?"

"Look, I've just always called it that," Sidra explained. "I can say the *actual* word if I want to."

Chasity couldn't stop laughing. "You are such a *child*," she mocked. "Come on Sidra, say it, say penis."

Malajia got in her face. "Penis, peeeennniiiisss," she taunted as Sidra covered her face in embarrassment.

"Y'all are terrible," Alex chortled. "Leave that girl and her rated PG words alone."

"Nah, she can say it if she wants to, right Sidra?" Chasity pressed, pointing at her. "Go ahead and say it."

Malajia removed Sidra's hands from her face and held them. "You red as shit," she teased.

Sidra sucked her teeth. "I am *not*," she grunted. "I can say it." She cleared her throat. "P—pe—ugh!"

"She can't say it!" Malajia blurted out at Sidra's stammering. This was beyond hilarious to her.

"Leave me alone," Sidra whined, jerking her hands out of Malajia's grasp.

"Aww, it's okay, you fuckin' baby," Chasity mocked, patting Sidra on the arm.

"Shut up, we can't *all* be vulgar," Sidra argued.

"Saying the normal, medical terms for body parts isn't vulgar sweetie," Alex cut in, amused.

"Whatever," Sidra hissed. "Can we get back to Emily's question please? Since none of you answered her."

"Do you even say *vagina*?" Malajia wondered, still not ready to let Sidra off the hook. "I mean you do *have* one."

"Shut up!" Sidra barked, stomping her foot on the floor.

"Okay, okay," Alex put in, putting her hands up. "To answer your question Em, my mom didn't freak out when I told her," Alex said. "Even though I was sixteen, she knew that I was thinking of doing it because we had the sex talk beforehand... I had a boyfriend after all."

Emily just sat in silence as she listened.

"I think that Trisha wanted to freak out a little bit when I told her," Chasity chuckled, recalling how wide her mother's eyes had gotten after she'd told her that she was no longer a virgin. "I mean, they know it's gonna happen eventually, but who *really* wants to hear that their daughter is doing the grownup." Chasity looked at Sidra. "Do you like that, instead of saying 'sex'?" he teased.

Sidra made a face at her. "Ha ha," she sneered, much to Chasity's amusement.

"Did *Brenda* ever talk to you about sex?" Alex asked Chasity, curious. "You were living with her before you got here after all."

"If by talking to me, you mean throwing a half empty

liquor bottle at my head, accusing me of being a whore because I missed my curfew *one* time, then *yeah* she talked to me," Chasity sniped.

Alex was regretful of her question. "I'm so—"

"You always gotta be the one to bring up old, traumatic memories and shit," Malajia fussed, cutting Alex off, flinging her hand in Alex's direction.

"It's fine," Chasity assured. "Trisha had the 'talk' with me way before I left... Y'all remember, I told you she bought me a box of condoms when I turned sixteen."

"Shit *my* mom had the talk with us as soon as we started our damn periods," Malajia recalled, fingering the curls on her head. "It went something like this: 'You don't want all these damn kids like *I* got? Use a damn condom and get your ass on birth control'."

Emily giggled as snickers rang out around the room.

"Y'all think I'm playing," Malajia declared. "When Melissa was born, and she would cry one of her high-pitched, screamin' ass cries, Mom would hold her right in my damn face and say 'You want this? Huh? No? Well then make whoever it is, strap the hell up'."

"Well as non-conventional as that talk *was*," Alex giggled. "At least you listened. You might be having sex, but you haven't had any unplanned pregnancies."

Malajia just glanced at the floor as she pushed some of her hair behind her ears. *I wish.* "Yeah," was all that she could mutter.

Emily sighed as she looked down at her hands. "I just feel like...maybe if Mom would have talked to me about sex instead of avoiding the topic or trying to shield me from it, then maybe..." She ran a hand down her arm as she paused. "Nothing."

"You think that you might not have done it, if you would've been more educated about it...about guys in *general*?" Alex asked, tone caring.

Emily shrugged as she glanced at her. "I don't know," she replied, voice somber. Hearing a notification on her phone, she retrieved it from her purse and looked at it. Shaking her head, she let out a sigh. *"Emily, it's clear that coming was a mistake,"* she read aloud. *"We both need time to cool down, so I'm going back home. Enjoy your birthday. Mommy."*

The girls stared at her sympathetically. "Sorry sis," Alex said, patting Emily on her leg.

"Yeah, sorry Em," Sidra added.

"It's whatever. I don't want to talk about my mother anymore." Emily stood up from the couch. The day was too dim for her; she needed a pick me up.

"I think I know what will cheer you up," Malajia alluded.

Emily stared at her nails. "What's that?" she asked dryly.

"Some shots!" Malajia exclaimed, then dissolved into laughter. "I'm joking," she assured when all eyes laid on her. "Chaz, let's give Em her gift."

Emily instantly perked up. "Gift, you got me a gift?" She smiled as Chasity headed up the steps.

"I still don't understand *why* I couldn't go with you two to help pick out her gift," Sidra grunted at Malajia.

"'Cause your input wasn't needed," Malajia shot back, unfazed by Sidra's annoyance. "Chaz and I are perfectly capable of picking out a damn birthday present."

"*Chaz* maybe, but *your* cheap behind, not hardly," Sidra countered, folding her arms smugly.

Malajia shot Sidra a glare before getting close to her face. "Vagina," she barked.

"Eww! *Come* on," Sidra sneered, covering her ears. The reaction caused laughter to erupt from Emily and Alex.

Chasity walked downstairs carrying a small gift bag. "Mel, why are you down here yelling out private parts?" she wondered.

"'Cause Sidra is tryna play me," Malajia explained.

Sidra flagged Malajia with her hand. She felt no need to continue the back and forth.

Chasity handed Emily the bag. Not hesitating even for a

moment, Emily removed the pink tissue paper and retrieved the black felt box. Smiling brightly, she opened it and laid eyes on the silver bangle bracelet. Her name was engraved in cursive with a small butterfly on either side.

"It's beautiful," Emily squealed, placing the delicate bracelet on her small wrist.

"The butterflies are a symbol," Chasity explained. "Kind of like your transformation."

Emily stared at the engraving in awe as she ran her finger across it.

"Yeah, see you were a sluggish worm when you first came here, and now you've turned into a butterfly," Malajia added, folding her arms in confidence. The room went silent. Malajia just stood there; Sidra pinched the bridge of her nose. Emily tried not to laugh, while Alex looked confused.

Chasity took a deep breath as she stared out in front of her. "Caterpillar," she corrected, tone even.

Malajia looked at her. "What?"

"It's a fuckin' *caterpillar*," Chasity repeated, trying not to show her agitation over Malajia's sheer stupidity.

Malajia sucked her teeth. "Do they *not* slide their asses on the ground like worms?" she threw back defensively.

Chasity shook her head. "Never mind yo," she hissed.

"I'm just saying, you correcting me and shit, but it's the same damn thing," Malajia fussed.

"It's *not*, but okay," Chasity contradicted.

"Malajia..." Alex let out a deep sigh.

"*What?*" Malajia hissed, snapping her head in Alex's direction. "I *know* that a caterpillar turns into a butterfly and not a damn worm. I'm not stupid. I just didn't feel like saying that long ass word."

Sidra lost it. "But in you *not* saying the right word, you caused this extra side conversation and ended up saying it *anyway!*"

"Sidra, just don't even bother," Chasity advised. She was learning more and more that engaging her best friend in her own stupidity only prolonged the irritation. "You're gonna give yourself a headache."

"She's so damn simple," Sidra ranted, folding her arms. "And for no *reason*."

"I know," Chasity agreed. Malajia sucked her teeth.

Alex shook her head emphatically—an effort to shake the last five minutes from her memories. She looked over at Emily. "I'm glad that you love your gift, and the day isn't over," she smiled. "We have something else special planned for you a little later."

"Thank you girls," Emily gushed, on the verge of tears. "You're really turning this day around for me."

"We're glad that we're able to," Sidra smiled. "We love you."

"Fussy bus," Malajia coughed, earning a glare from Sidra.

"I hate you," Sidra seethed, inciting a laugh and a shrug from Malajia.


Emily stepped out of Chasity's car later that evening brimming with excitement. After spending the early part of the afternoon relaxing with the girls, Emily was intrigued when they told her to get into the car, but without telling her their destination.

Emily glanced up at the sign on the building. *Valley Paint Studio,* she silently read.

Alex looked at Emily, excited. "So Em, we spent a long time trying to think of something to do for your birthday," she began. "We wanted to do something that we knew you'd enjoy and we know that you—"

"God, will you *come on*?" Chasity rudely interrupted. She'd barely gotten any sleep since waking Emily up early that morning to wish her a happy birthday, and she was practically exhausted.

"I know, all tryna make pointless ass speeches and shit," Malajia added.

Alex ignored them. "Come on Em," she pressed,

gesturing towards the entrance.

Emily made her way into the building with the girls close behind. Stepping through the doors, Emily was directed down a small hallway. The walls were covered in paintings. Turning the corner, she entered a room and spotted two rows of tables, with small painting easels. Each chair was decorated with pink and white balloons, and streamers. Off in the corner was a table covered with pans of ingredients used for building burger sliders, salad fixings, French fries, sodas and wine coolers. On a small table beside it, was a round cake covered in white icing with decorative plates, cups, and cutlery laying on the table next to it.

Emily smiled ear to ear. "Oh my God—" Before she could finish her emotional response, a door opened and the guys, with Will included, popped out.

"Surprise!" they yelled.

Emily giggled at the dumb looks on their faces.

"Y'all late as *shit!*" Malajia snapped, snatching her jacket off.

"You were supposed to be in here when she walked through the *door*," Sidra added, agitated.

"What was the point of even hiding in there?" Chasity sniped.

"You guys can't follow instructions to save your life," Alex berated.

"Hey, kill all this back talkin' bullshit," Mark barked, rubbing the back of his neck. "Hiding was *Will's* idea," he quickly shot out.

Will looked stunned. "Huh?" he replied, confused.

"How about a 'thank you' for setting everything up," Jason threw out.

Malajia sucked her teeth. "Y'all ain't set up *shit*, the damn *workers* did," she sneered, heading over to the table. "Always lying."

"Well, we *supervised*, so hush your face," Jason threw back. "*You* weren't here to do it."

Malajia looked at Mark with her mouth open. "You gonna let him talk to me like that?" she fussed, pointing to Jason.

"Yup," Mark returned, unfazed.

While the side conversations were happening, Emily walked over to Will. "Thanks for being a part of this," she smiled.

"Where *else* would I be?" he cooed, putting his arm around her. Emily blushed as she looked at the floor.

"Who keeps buying these nasty ass, orange wine coolers?!" Malajia bellowed, holding one up.

All the guys simultaneously pointed to a stunned Will. "Wait, *what?*" he stammered.

"Okay, so the purpose of paint 'n sips is to express yourself through painting, while enjoying food and drinks," a bubbling young woman explained, standing in front of the room.

"Yeah, no shit," Chasity mumbled, earning herself a nudge to her leg from Jason.

"Stop it," he whispered, amused.

"So if you look here, I have a painting that I've already done," the woman said, pointing to her colorful painting of a moonlit path, with figures of people standing in the middle. "But I have a blank canvas and we're going to paint it together."

Malajia leaned over to Chasity as she munched on her burger. "That painting looks hard as shit," she muttered. "*Don't* it Chaz?"

"Malajia, move," Chasity barked, nudging her. "You're getting ketchup all on my damn side."

"That's not ketchup, that's paint," Malajia explained, wiping her hand with a napkin.

"Where on *any* of these plates, do you fuckin' see red paint?" Chasity threw back, flashing a glare her way.

Malajia glanced at her plate, which consisted of yellow, white, blue, black and green paint. Malajia went to open her mouth to speak, but was immediately cut off by Chasity.

"Shut up," Chasity spat out.

"Shhh," Alex hissed from the other side of the table.

"Is Alice telling us to shush?" Malajia mocked. "I can't see with these easels in the damn way."

Alex moved her head and glanced at Malajia through the space between her and David's easel. "Make me come over there, hear?" she warned.

"Guys, pay attention," Sidra demanded, swirling one of her brushes in water.

"*You* pay attention," Malajia shot back. "She didn't tell us to dip our damn brush in the water yet."

Sidra ignored Malajia; she signaled for the woman to continue.

"So I'll start to recreate this portrait and you'll paint along with me," she instructed. "There is no right or wrong way to do this; everyone paints differently. No two paintings will look the same. Just relax and have fun."

The group began prepping their brushes as the woman started drawing the first lines.

"I'm not gonna have fun with these sweet ass coolers," Malajia grunted, downing the last bit in her bottle. "Where's the liquor?"

"I got some back in my room," Mark crooned, dipping his brush in water. "I'll pour it on you and lick it off later."

"Yeeesss," Malajia rejoiced, doing a dance in her seat.

"Can you two *not* act like freaks for *five* minutes?" Sidra hissed as laughter rang through the room. "You're embarrassing."

"Nope," Malajia answered, running her paint-dipped brush along her canvas. "Shit, I used too much paint!"

"A little paint goes a long way," the woman smiled at Malajia's outburst. "So you don't need to use that much."

"She won't listen, *trust* me," Chasity griped, pointing to

Malajia, who was busy scooping more paint onto her brush.

Sidra tilted her head as she gazed at her painting. "It's coming together pretty nicely, if I do say so myself," she said. Nearly thirty minutes into the painting session and the group was beginning to see their work come to life.

Josh glanced at her work. "Yeah, looks a hell of a lot better than that bowl you painted at the orchard," he teased.

Sidra giggled and gave Josh a playful nudge. "Very funny Joshua," she threw back. "*Yours* was no better."

"True," he agreed, dipping his brush into some paint.

"I don't know what the hell this *is* but it ain't no damn moonlit path," Mark griped, pointing to his picture.

Jason glanced over at it. "Did you bother following any directions at *all*?" he laughed at the distorted images on Mark's easel.

"Nope," Mark admitted, taking a sip of his drink.

Malajia let out a loud groan as she slammed her paintbrush down. "I need more white paint," she announced. Looking over at Chasity, she tried to reach over and dip her brush onto Chasity's plate.

"Get out my face!" Chasity snapped, nudging her away.

"I need some of your paint," Malajia threw back. "My moon ain't colored in all the way."

"Bitch no," Chasity spat out. "Nobod*y* told you to make your fuckin' moon that damn big and *nobody* told you to put those stupid ass white dots all over your picture."

"They're fireflies," Malajia explained. "She said we can make it our own."

Chasity rolled her eyes. "*Why* do y'all keep letting her sit next to me?" she huffed at the group.

"Yeah, like we have a *choice* in the matter," Alex muttered, swirling her paintbrush in a nearby cup. "God forbid anybody *else* sits next to her bestie."

Malajia made a face at Alex through the space between

the easels. "You just mad 'cause nobody wants to sit next to *you*," she threw back. "That's why your painting sucks ass… Let me get some of your paint."

"*Hell* no," Alex immediately threw back, wiping the brush on a napkin. "And you haven't even *seen* my painting."

Malajia sucked her teeth as she looked over at Mark. "Babe, let me get some paint."

"No. You already used my blue paint, creating imaginary lakes and shit," Mark returned. "And you *betta* not say I'm on time out," he added when Malajia opened her mouth to speak. "I should put *you* on time out for that."

Malajia waved her hand at him, then stood up and grabbed her painting. Walking around the other side of the table, she took her brush and tried to dip it in Emily's paint.

"No!" Emily shrieked, blocking the plate with her arm. "You already took some of mine earlier. I don't have any more to spare."

Malajia stomped her foot on the floor. "Come *on*. The lady won't give me no more," she whined.

"That's because you went up there like *three times* for more," Alex put in, dipping her brush, yet again.

David put his brush down and glanced over at his cup of soda. Noticing that the once clear soda was darkened, accompanied by the paint on his cup, he frowned. "Alex, you've been cleaning your brush in my soda!" he exclaimed.

Alex's head snapped in his direction. Her eyes widened as she realized what she had done. "I am *so* sorry, sweetie," she apologized. "I didn't realize how close our cups were."

David put his hand over his throat. "I think I drank some of it a few minutes ago," he gagged.

"I'm sorry!" Alex was mortified as she patted his back.

"Ahhh, David got paint in his throat and shit," Mark laughed.

Alex rolled her eyes at Mark, before turning her attention back to David. "It's non-toxic paint so you should be fine," she placated.

"Nicole gonna kick your ass if David dies and shit,"

Mark teased.

"Shut up, will you?" Alex barked.

Malajia reached over Sidra's shoulder. "Let me get some paint," she softly said. In the process of reaching over, Malajia accidentally bumped Sidra's arm, causing Sidra to smear paint where she didn't want it.

"Damn it Malajia!" Sidra hollered.

"Why you so *hype*?" Malajia hurled back. "It *clearly* was an accident."

"I don't care if it *was*, you have been getting on people's nerves about paint the *whole* time," Sidra fumed. "And now you made me put blue paint on my moon."

Malajia stared at Sidra for a moment, before sticking her brush out and smearing the drop of blue paint across Sidra's canvas. "It can be fixed."

Sidra smacked her hand. "What are you doing?!"

"I'm making the moon, blue," Malajia explained. "Have you never heard of one? Duh."

"Blue moons aren't *actually* blue, you idiot," Sidra fumed.

"*Yours* is," Malajia laughed.

Furious, Sidra dipped her paintbrush in black paint and drew a quick line across Malajia's moon.

"You petty ass bitch!" Malajia erupted.

"Now, fix *that*," Sidra taunted, slamming her paintbrush on the table.

Malajia stormed around to her station, sat down, and began to furiously paint an image on her easel.

"Um, do any of you need any help?" the instructor asked.

"No, I think you'd do better to leave us be," Josh chuckled. "You don't want to get in this crossfire."

After a few moments, Malajia finished and held her picture up. "Sidra, this is for you," she grunted.

Sidra stood up and frowned as she eyed Malajia's painting. "What the hell *is* that?" she asked, confused.

Alex glanced up. "Really Malajia?" she scoffed at the

image.

"Is that a picture of a behind in the moon?" Sidra ground out.

"No, it's not a *behind*," Malajia mocked. "It's an *ass*. And it symbolizes *me* mooning *your* stuck-up ass."

Sidra rolled her eyes. "You're childish."

"And *you're* gonna get a glimpse of this big black ass *every* damn night, 'cause I'm hanging this picture right above your bed," Malajia countered.

Jason put his paintbrush down. "I think it's safe to say that this session is over," he chortled.

"Yeah," Alex agreed. "Let's cut the cake."

"I want everybody to show their pictures first," Emily smiled. Everyone glanced around at each other's work once they turned their easels around.

"Jason, why is your path going up to the sky?" Malajia laughed.

"Hey, I'm not artistic okay, back off," Jason returned.

Chasity sucked her teeth. "Leave his picture alone," she ground out. "*You're* one to talk with that drunk ass picture *you* got."

"*My* picture expresses how I feel and I *feel* like showing Sidra my ass right now," Malajia spat out, shooting Sidra a glance. "I *should* paint some lips on it."

"Bite me," Sidra threw back.

"So Mark, you were really over there drawing statues?" David quipped, trying to deflect the group's attention from the bickering. "Why?"

"'Cause I messed up in the beginning," Mark answered. "And they're not statues...they're liquor bottles." He sucked his teeth. "Look, she said make it our own."

"That meant *adding* things, not completely ignoring the instructions," Alex fussed.

"Hey, you interpreted one thing and I interpreted another," Mark ground out. "You shouldn't talk with your decrepit ass moon and shit. It ain't even *round*."

"Shut up, it is *so*," Alex threw back. She looked around

as the group shook their heads, contradicting what she said. "No?"

"It looks more like an egg," Will observed.

"Will stop tryna be nice. That shit look like a spattered hot ass mess," Mark cut in.

"Can I cut my cake now, please?" Emily pleaded, noticing the angered look on Alex's face. She wanted to keep the mood as light as it could be.

Sidra clasped her hands together. "Em, I can't *wait* for you to cut it," she beamed. "I made you the perfect cake."

"You made it?" Emily asked as everyone approached the cake table. Sidra nodded enthusiastically. "Thank you."

"There are five shades of pink," Sidra added, proud.

"Are there *even* five shades of pink?" Malajia spat.

"Yes," the group answered in unison.

"I knew that," Malajia muttered, folding her arms.

Sidra smiled brightly as she handed Emily the cake knife. She watched with glee as Emily cut the cake and placed a piece on a plate. Seeing the slice, Sidra stomped her foot on the floor.

"Noooo!" she whined. "What happened?"

Chasity held her hand out in front of Alex's face. "You owe me ten dollars."

Alex let out a quick sigh. "I'll give it to you when I get paid," she stated, resolved.

Malajia busted out laughing at the dark-pink-colored sponge cake. "Ahhhh, it came out one color and shit," she mocked. "You thought you was doing something special. Ole' one shade ass cake and shit."

"It's okay Sidra, I still love it," Emily promised, cutting another piece.

"I'm sure it still tastes good," Josh cut in.

"It's gonna taste like food coloring and Sidra's tears," Malajia laughed. "Betchu' wish you didn't make us leave that back-up cake home now *do* you?"

Sidra was seething as she stared at Malajia.

# Chapter 16

"You sure you don't need for me to go over more notes with you before your study group?" David asked Nicole as they ambled along the path to the library.

Nicole giggled. "No, I'm fine," she assured, looping her hand through his arm. "I appreciate all of the notes that you've already given to me. Besides, I'm going to a study group, so if I need anything else, I'm sure my group members will have it...at least I *hope* so."

"True," David replied, running a hand over his head.

"Thanks for walking me to the library though," Nicole smiled.

"No problem," David returned, adjusting his book bag with his free hand. "I have time to kill before my next class anyway."

Reaching the library steps, Nicole stood on the second step so that she was eye level with David. She smiled at him as he adjusted his glasses. "Do you want to come over later?" she asked, tone seductive.

"Um, sure...we can study for these midterms together."

Nicole grabbed his hand and held it. "Well, I'll be studying *here* for most of the day, so I don't think I'll want to study *later on*," she returned.

"Oh." David scratched his head. "Well, that's fine, I'm free either way. What do you want to do later, then?" he asked, oblivious. "Watch a movie?"

Nicole fought the urge to roll her eyes. *God boy, take the hint.* "Um…we can put on a movie if you want," she said. "Won't be interested in *watching* it though."

David looked confused as he scratched his head yet again. "Well, why—" He glanced up and met Nicole's piercing gaze. His eyes widened. "Ooooh," he muttered. *You know what she wants, say something dummy!* But his mouth refused to speak.

"So…what do you say? You wanna come over?" Nicole smiled.

David swallowed hard. "Uh…I uh—I can't," he hesitantly put out. "I have somewhere to be."

Nicole frowned. "But, you *just* said—"

"I know, but I just remembered that I already have plans later." David gave Nicole a quick pat on her arm as he backed away from her.

"David—"

"I'll call you later," he interrupted, before scurrying off.

Nicole stood there bewildered as she watched him hurry down the path. *What is his deal?* She thought as someone touched her shoulder. She spun around. "What's up Quincy?"

"What do you look all mad in the face for?" Quincy asked, amused.

"Nothing, you ready for this study group?" she deflected. When Quincy nodded, Nicole made her way up the steps with him following close behind.


David practically ran all the way back to his house, berating himself in the process. Kicking the door open, he slammed his book bag to the floor. "Stupid," he hissed to himself. He flopped down on the couch and threw his head back against the couch cushions. "Idiot!"

"Yo, why you down here talking to yourself, crazy?" Mark teased, heading down the steps.

*'Cause I'm a complete idiot,* he thought. "Just got a bad test grade, that's all," David lied.

"Bullshit. *You?*" Mark questioned in disbelief. "What did

you *get*?"

"A 'B'," David replied, tone even.

Mark stared blankly for several seconds. "I should come over there and punch your glasses off," he griped.

David couldn't help but snicker. "It's fine," he sighed, rubbing his forehead. He needed to talk about something and he wasn't sure how it would be taken. "Uh, bro, what are you about to do?"

"Go play ball with Josh," Mark answered, looking at his watch.

"Don't you have class?" David asked.

"Fuck that class," Mark ground out. When David rolled his eyes, Mark laughed. "Nah, the professor canceled it for the day. Why what's up?"

David thought for a moment. *Don't even bring it up, he'll just tease you.* "You mind if I play basketball with y'all?"

"Did you *have* to say the whole word?" Mark jeered. "Just say 'ball' we all know what it means."

David stood up from the couch. "Whatever, can I play or not?"

"Fine, just know it'll be two on one," Mark chortled.

"Are you gonna be my partner?" David asked, hopeful.

"*Fuck* no!" Mark barked, earning a frown from David.


"I can't believe you actually signed their names up for that, Alex," Jason chuckled, scanning over the notes in his notebook.

"Look, I already told them that I was doing it," Alex said, trotting down the steps of the English building.

Jason shot Alex a knowing look. "And what did they say?" he asked, already knowing the answer.

Alex moved some hair from her face. "They told me that if I signed them up, they'd perm my hair while I'm asleep."

Jason busted out laughing.

"And then cut it off afterwards...then make a doll out of

it and stick pins in it." Alex added. She joined him in laughter. "Look, they may hate me *now*, but I know that it'll be good for all of us to do this."

"Giving campus tours to potential freshman is *not* some of the girls' idea of a 'good' thing," Jason advised. "You already *know* who I'm talking about." Jason had already advised Alex not to place that girl's name on the volunteer list when they had passed by the signup sheet on their way out of the English building. But in typical Alex fashion, she didn't listen.

"Oh I know. *She* was the one who said she would cut my hair off and make a doll out of it," Alex jeered. "Your girlfriend is evil."

Jason shook his head in amusement. Hearing his cell phone ring, Jason retrieved it from his jeans pocket. Rolling his eyes at the caller ID, he let out a groan then answered the phone. "Yes Mom," he answered, some bite in his voice. "Okay... Yes, that would make sense... No, you don't have to open them, I'll get them when I come home for break in a few weeks... Yes, I am... I appreciate you letting me know, but I really need to go... Bye."

Alex looked on as Jason mumbled a curse word, shoving his phone back into his pocket. "Should I even ask?"

"Nope," Jason answered.

"Fair enough," Alex shrugged as they turned the corner, heading for the campus quad. "So, with spring break coming up in a few weeks, do you have anything planned?"

Jason let out a sigh; he was dreading going back home for break. He knew that he would be forced to interact with his mother, something that he wasn't fully ready to do. "No, nothing that I know of," he answered honestly.

"Yeah, same here," Alex replied, adjusting the gold hoop earring in her ear. She glanced up and locked eyes with Eric as he approached along the same path. She always felt awkward when she saw him, but it didn't help that he was walking with a young woman. "Shit," she whispered in a quiet aside to Jason.

Jason didn't get to react or respond, because they had stopped right in front of the pair.

"Hey Jason, how's it going?" Eric greeted, shaking Jason's hand.

"Pretty good, man," Jason replied.

"Cool," Eric replied, then looked at Alex. "Hey."

"Hey," Alex put out, trying not to focus on the girl standing next to him.

Feeling the tension, Jason glanced at his watch. "So um, I'm gonna head—"

Alex quickly grabbed his arm and held onto it as Jason went to walk away. The gesture stopped him. She was waiting for Eric to say something, or at least leave. When he didn't, Alex extended her hand in front of the woman. "I'm Alex."

"I'm—"

"Sorry, this is Chelsea," Eric introduced.

The tall, shapely caramel skinned woman smiled. "I love your hair," she complimented, shaking Alex's hand.

"Thank you," Alex blushed.

Chelsea ran a hand over her ponytail. "I would kill for natural waves like that."

"Thank you," Alex repeated. *God, she seems nice. I can't hate her.*

"You know, I've heard a lot about you," Chelsea said, wagging her finger harmlessly in Alex's direction.

Alex was perplexed. "*Have* you?"

"Yeah," she confirmed, pointing to Eric. "I swear, *this* guy here—"

"Chelsea, we should get going to the restaurant so we can get a table," Eric abruptly cut in, nervous.

Chelsea shot him a skeptical look. "*What* restaurant?" she asked. "Last time I checked, we were going to the cafeteria."

Eric gently grabbed Chelsea's arm. "Let's just go," he ordered through clenched teeth.

Chelsea shrugged as she allowed herself to be led away.

"Whatever you say, E."

Alex stood there in silence, not even bothering to turn around to watch Eric and Chelsea walk off.

Jason tried to find the right words to say. Knowing their history, he figured Alex was probably feeling terrible.

"Should I even ask?" he asked finally.

"Nope," Alex immediately replied, staring at the ground.

"Fair enough," Jason replied.

Alex went to take a step forward, then immediately stopped and turned to Jason. "Do you think I'm stupid?" she asked.

The question took him by surprise. "Ummm, no," Jason replied.

"No, seriously," Alex pressed.

"I *am* being serious," Jason insisted, confused. "What are you getting at?"

Alex ran her hand over her hair. "I just feel—" she let out a quick sigh. "I don't know. I just—I still have hope that somewhere down the line we can be together."

"I thought you didn't *want* that," Jason pointed out.

"I mean I *didn't*," Alex replied. "But now I'm starting to realize that maybe I *do*. It's crazy, even though I *saw* him with that girl, I *still* have hope."

Jason folded his arms. "Is that so?"

Alex nodded. "Yeah," she admitted, embarrassed. "That's why I asked you if you thought I was stupid. Because I *feel* like I'm being stupid for thinking that way… I mean I would *never* go after him while he's dating someone, but…should they break up—" Alex shook her head in an effort to shake the thoughts brewing in her head. "Never mind, that's wrong of me to even think. If he's happy, then I want that for him."

Jason rubbed his chin as he pondered Alex's revelation. "You want my opinion?"

Alex nodded. "I *need* a man's opinion."

"I don't think he's dating that girl we just saw," Jason stated.

Alex's eyes widened. "You *don't?*"

Jason shook his head. "It was something off about her interaction when it came to you," he stated. "She was all too excited to tell you about how much he talked about you."

Alex thought back. "I guess," she slowly put out. "But why would he put on a front?"

Jason shot Alex a knowing look. "You're *really* asking me that?"

Alex giggled. "Point taken."

Jason patted Alex on the shoulder. "Look, I don't know what Eric's situation is regarding if he's dating anybody on campus or not. Honestly, I don't pay attention to other people's business," he said. "But, if it turns out that he's *not* with anybody, and you feel like you really want to try something *real* this time—"

Alex looked away, a guilty look on her face.

"Then put that pride aside and go for it… But you better be ready this time," Jason advised, voice stern. "No man is gonna let you play him twice."

"Ouch," Alex grimaced. Having the reality of how she had treated Eric thrown in her face, was what she both needed and dreaded. *Why am I going through all of this? Am I even really ready to start a new relationship?* "You're right, thank you."

"Anytime," Jason smiled. "Can I go now? My study group is probably cussing me out right now."

Alex laughed. "Yeah, sorry," she apologized. "I need to get my butt to the library to study for these midterms myself."

"Later," Jason said, before heading off towards his destination.

Standing alone, Alex's smile faded as she let another sigh come out. She knew Eric was long gone, but she glanced back anyway. *Alex, fix your shit.*


"This simple bitch just told my class that she's moving

the midterm up from Friday to Monday," Chasity fumed of her professor, sauntering down the halls of the Science building alongside Malajia. "Talking about she gotta leave to go home on Tuesday."

Malajia pushed some of her hair behind her ear. "Can she *do* that?" she asked dryly.

"Apparently *so*," Chasity fussed, glancing at her watch. "Apparently *all* of these overpaid professors on this damn campus can do what the hell they *wanna* do."

"Yeah well, they love to torture us," Malajia commented, tone not changing. She glanced over at Chasity as they continued their pace out of the building. "My Spanish midterm is on Monday too; can you go over some stuff with me?"

Chasity shot her a glance. Malajia seemed off to her; her tone was dry and she hadn't made a single attempt at one joke. "Yeah," Chasity replied, tone even.

"Thanks," Malajia muttered, reaching the bottom of the steps. Looking out ahead of her, Malajia rolled her eyes. The person she least wanted to see was approaching. "God, will this maggot die already?" she mumbled to Chasity.

Jackie stopped right in front of them. "Hello Chasity," she greeted, clutching her books to her chest.

"Ugh," Chasity scoffed, rolling her eyes.

Jackie let out a quick sigh. "Chasity, do you *ever* think we could get to a place where we can at least be *civil*?"

Chasity looked at Jackie as if she was crazy. "No," she stated bluntly. "And for *what*?"

"Just trying to be a *mature adult*, that's all," Jackie huffed.

"Of all the words that I can think of to describe you, 'mature' and 'adult' aren't *any* of them," Chasity sniped.

Jackie shook her head at Chasity, then shot a glare Malajia's way. "Malajia," she spat.

"Ashy," Malajia hissed back.

Jackie looked Malajia up and down. "I'm surprised you're not in the post office receiving more late

Valentine's Day cards," she ground out.

"What I *receive*, is none of your business, you dirty dick magnet," Malajia threw back. "How's that itch you got, nasty ass?"

Jackie rolled her eyes. "Whatever," she sneered. "I'll have you know, that despite what my past reputation was, my *magnet* only attracts *one* dick these days."

"Whether it's one dirty dick or ten, it's still gross and so are you," Malajia sneered, disgusted.

Jackie fixed her gaze on Malajia. "Go ahead and make your little jokes," she bit out. "But I *will* say that it's amazing the number of good men out here that ungrateful women throw away." She smirked. "And they're just waiting for the *right* woman to make them whole again."

"Bitch ain't *nothin'* right about *you*," Malajia spat back.

"Jackie walk the fuck away," Chasity jumped in. She was tired of the girl taking up her airspace.

Jackie shrugged. "Enjoy your day ladies," she returned, unfazed, before moving around them to head up the steps.

"Why the *fuck* does she keep talking to me?" Chasity complained to Malajia.

"I have no idea," Malajia admitted dryly. "You would think that her stupid ass would get the hint that you will never like her."

Chasity ran a hand through her hair as she started walking again, with Malajia in tow. "Is it just me, or does it seem like she moved her hatred from me, to *you*?"

"It's not just you," Malajia admitted. "She's been pissing me off every chance she gets. Like she got a grudge against me or something."

"Have any idea why she seems to have a hard-on for you?" Chasity jeered.

Malajia chuckled a bit. "I don't have anything that her ass would want, so who knows," she replied. She let out a heavy sigh. "Anyway, I gotta get to this raggedy class. I'll see you later."

"Okay," Chasity said. She stared at Malajia as she went

to walk away. "Malajia, are you alright?"

Malajia turned around. "What? You mean about Jackie?"

"No, fuck her," Chasity clarified. "I mean in *general*. You seem...not like yourself."

Malajia held a steady look on her face. *No, I'm not. I feel like straight shit.* "Yeah, I'm good," she lied. "Just trying to get through these midterms alive."

Chasity held a skeptical gaze. "If you say so."

"Let me find out you love me and shit," Malajia smiled, attempting a joke.

"See, never mind," Chasity scoffed, walking off, leaving Malajia to laugh. Once Chasity was out of sight, Malajia's smile gave way to a somber look, accompanied by a deep sigh. Glancing at her watch, she headed off to her destination.

Sidra pulled her car into a parking space as she spoke into her earpiece. "Mama, I swear, I'm becoming obsessed with baby stuff," she gushed.

"Sidra, don't you—"

"Calm down Mama," Sidra giggled. "That doesn't mean that *I* want babies now."

A deep sigh of relief came through the line. "Thank God," Mrs. Howard whispered. "Princess, don't play with my heart like that. You better finish college and law school. I'm not playing with you."

"Trust me, *I'm* not playing with me," Sidra laughed. "But, seriously. Every little pacifier, bottle, onesie; I just *have* to buy it. I can't wait until Marcus's baby gets here."

"Yeah, I'm getting used to the idea of being a grandmother myself," Mrs. Howard said, smile prominent in her voice. "I talked to Marcus and India the other—"

"Ugh," Sidra scoffed.

"Sidra—"

"I know, I know," Sidra groaned. "Be civil. I'm *trying*."

She let out a sigh. "What did they say?"

"Well, they both said that they were going to go to pre-martial counseling," her mother finished.

"Oh *really*?" Sidra replied, unenthused.

"Yeah," Mrs. Howard confirmed. "I guess they figured that their issues were getting out of hand, so they wanted to get a handle on them before the baby is born."

Sidra rolled her eyes. "Nothing but a pure break up between those two is going to fix that train wreck of a relationship. But we *both* know how desperate she is to get married so she's not gonna be the one to do it."

"What happened to you trying?" her mother asked.

"That doesn't mean that I can't vent to you," Sidra pointed out. She glanced at her watch. "Mama, I gotta go. This homework is calling my name and I'm trying not to ignore it."

Mrs. Howard laughed. "Alright, I'll talk to you later. Love you."

"Love you too." Sidra ended the call, then stepped out of the car.

Seeing Nicole across the path, leaving the guys' house, Sidra waved. "Hi Nicole," she called.

Nicole spun around, smiled, then waved back. She stood as Sidra trotted up to her.

"Nobody's home?" Sidra asked.

"Apparently *not*," Nicole muttered. "I've been trying to get ahold of David since the other day."

Sidra frowned. "You haven't spoken to him?"

Nicole shook her head.

*That's weird*, Sidra thought, but neglected to speak those words out loud. "Well, I'm sure he has a reason. Midterms are next week and I'm sure you know by now how David gets with his studies," she placated.

Nicole looked at the concrete ground. "I guess," she sulked, kicking a pebble with her sneaker.

"And of course, he's a *senior* now, so…" Sidra rubbed the back of her neck, hoping that Nicole's mind would ease.

She didn't get to find out either way, because both girls saw David heading through the gates. *Speak of the devil.*

"David," Nicole said.

The look of panic set on David's face as he stopped in front of them. "He—hey Nicole," he stammered.

Nicole tilted her head. "Why do you look funny?" she asked.

"Yeah, why do you look funny?" Sidra wondered as well.

David shot Sidra a stern look, in return Sidra winced. "Didn't mean to ask that out loud," she stated, looking away. "I'm gonna go—"

"Hold up a sec, Sid," David interrupted.

Sidra looked confused for a moment, but shrugged. "Okay."

"I've been trying to reach you," Nicole began.

"I'm sorry, I've been studying," David apologized. "I know it's no excuse for not returning your phone calls though."

"I guess I get it," Nicole said, tone calm. "Do you have class right now?"

"No," David said.

"You want company?" Nicole asked. David's eyes widened.

"Uh, I can't have company at the moment because Sidra and I are about to go to the store," David sputtered.

"We *are*?" Sidra asked. *What the hell, David?*

David shot Sidra a pleading glance. *Please go along with it.*

Sidra was beyond bewildered and it showed on her face. She didn't know what was going on with David, but seeing the desperation on his face, she decided to play along. She lightly tapped herself on the head. "That's right, we are...duh," she said. "I nearly forgot about that."

David smiled at Sidra, then turned back to Nicole, who didn't hide her disappointment.

"Oh...okay," Nicole said. "I guess I'll talk to you later

then."

David nodded. "I'll call you when I get back, okay," he promised as Nicole walked off.

"Sure," Nicole replied, tone sullen, continuing her walk towards the gate.

David followed Nicole's progress, until Sidra smacked him on the arm, snapping him out of his trance. "Ow!" he bellowed, rubbing his arm.

"What was that about?" Sidra hissed. "Look, whatever reason you have for not hanging with your girlfriend, is your business, but don't drag *me* into it."

"It's not what you think," David promised, sensing Sidra's anger with him. "I promise I'm not doing anything shady. I just...can't hang out right now and didn't want to hurt her feelings...that's all."

Sidra stared at him, skeptical. She wasn't sure if he was telling the truth, but then she remembered, this was David after all. "Fine David," she relented.

David patted Sidra on the arm. "Thanks for covering," he smiled, then went to walk away.

"Hold up, Summers," Sidra called, halting his progress.

"Yeah?" he asked, spinning around.

"You might as well get in the car, because you're coming to the store with me," Sidra demanded.

David's mouth fell open. "Huh?" he said. "But I—"

"I don't like being part of a lie, so we might as well make it true," Sidra maintained, adjusting the purse on her shoulder. "Besides, I *do* need to go anyway."

David stared at Sidra, who pointed in the direction of her car.

"Get to walking, brother," she ordered. Resolved, David lowered his head as he headed towards the car.

# Chapter 17

"Going anywhere fun for spring break?" Will asked Emily as he handed her a glass of juice.

Emily sighed. "Nope," and took a sip. "Well…I can't say that. I'm actually going to Jersey." Needing a break from her studies, Emily decided that the best way to unwind was to spend some time with Will and Anthony in his new apartment, ten minutes from campus. Other than the couch and small end table in the living room, the furniture was scarce in the two-bedroom apartment, but that didn't bother her in the least. She was just happy that Will was finally settled.

Will glanced at her, a shocked look on his face. "*Really?*" He figured since Emily's mother and sister lived in Jersey, that she would stay as far away as possible.

Emily nodded. "Yeah, Dru asked me to come."

"I thought you were still upset with him," Will frowned.

"I'm *not upset*," Emily assured. "I mean, I wish that he would have given me a heads up that Mom was coming down on my birthday, but I know he meant well."

Will nodded as he kept his eye on Anthony, who was busy running around the living room. "Well, that's good," he commented.

"Yeah, I miss my brothers, so it'll be good to see them," Emily said. "And it's not like they live on the same block as my mom, so I'll be fine."

"Have you spoken to her since your birthday?" Will asked.

"Nope," Emily ground out, examining her nails.

"How does that make you feel?" Will pressed, noticing that Emily wasn't making eye contact with him.

Emily let out another sigh. "Like she hasn't changed," she sulked. "Like she expected me to just let everything go and 'respect' her, but she can't respect *me* and admit that she did wrong by me."

Will just held a sympathetic look on his face as Emily kept talking. He wanted to reach across the couch and hug her.

"It's sad because…I do miss her, but—"

"You can't deal with things being the same," Will finished.

"Yeah," Emily replied, somber.

"Well, if it's worth anything, I hope that you have a good time when you go back," Will said. *I'll miss you*, he thought, but decided against saying it out loud.

"Thanks." Emily folded her arms. "I'm okay, really," she promised. Her sullen demeanor gave way to a bright smile once Anthony stood in front of her, holding something.

"Emmy," the toddler cooed.

Will put his hand over his face and shook his head in embarrassment as Emily giggled. "Dude, her name is Em-i-ly," he chortled.

"Aww, he can call me Emmy," Emily smiled at the little boy. "Whatchu' got there?"

Anthony handed her a soggy piece of fruit. "Apple."

"Uh—oh," Emily sputtered as Anthony dropped the soggy apple into Emily's outstretched hand.

Will quickly retrieved it from Emily's hand and set it on the nearby end table. "Sorry about that," he said, shaking his head. "Bruh, go find your truck."

Emily giggled as she wiped her hand on a napkin. She let out a laugh when Anthony completely ignored his father's command and climbed on the couch, squeezing in between them.

Will stared at him. "So you're just not gonna listen,

son?" he said.

Anthony didn't verbally respond, but the boy leaning his head on Emily's shoulder gave Will the answer that he sought. "*And* you're trying to steal my friend?"

Emily tapped Will on his arm. "Leave him alone," she teased.

Will shrugged as he adjusted the cushion behind him. "Well, at least he has good taste in women."

Emily blushed as she glanced away from Will.

Will, noticing, craned his neck to get a better view of Emily's face. "Are you blushing?" he teased.

"No," Emily lied, amusement in her voice.


"I can't believe they ran out of my favorite ice cream," Sidra complained as she walked out of the frozen aisle of the Mega Mart with a quiet David following behind. "They can never keep things stocked in this damn store."

"Yeah," David muttered.

Sidra glanced behind at him. "You still mad that I dragged you here?" she wondered. David had been quiet ever since he got in her car.

David shook his head. "No, I needed stuff too," he replied.

"Oh okay," Sidra said. A few moments later, as they approached yet another aisle, Sidra flung her hair over her shoulder. "Are you ready for midterms?" she asked, attempting to make conversation.

"As ready as I'm *gonna* be," he returned. "I think I crammed enough."

"Yeah, I told Nicole that's why she hadn't heard from you," Sidra replied.

David felt a chill go down his spine at the mention of Nicole's name.

"I told her how you get with your studies," Sidra continued, unaware of what David was feeling.

"Yeah," David muttered. As Sidra began placing items

into her cart, David let out a sigh. Something was plaguing him, and he couldn't hold it in any longer. At that moment, he figured that Sidra was the best person that he could confide in. "Um Sid, can I ask you a personal question?"

Sidra was focused on the label on the box of hot chocolate in her hand. "Sure sweetie," she said.

David took a deep breath. "Okay so…" he hesitated. *Just ask!* "So okay…are you still a virgin?" he asked.

She snapped her head towards him.

David's eyes widened. "Sorry, I didn't mean to—"

"Yes, I still am. I'm not mad, I'm just confused as to why you asked," she said. "That question came out of nowhere."

"I know," David admitted. "So…how does James feel about that?"

Sidra was still confused about David's line of questioning; it was strange. Nevertheless, she had no problem answering him. "James is perfectly fine with it," she replied. "I mean he doesn't have much of a *choice*… I'm just not ready—wait, did he say something to you?"

Anger flashed in Sidra's grey eyes and David immediately put his hands up. "Oh no, no, nothing like *that*," he assured.

Sidra relaxed her frown. "Oh," she said, then started walking with David in tow. "But yeah, like I said, he's fine with it. We talked about it when we first became a couple, so he was well aware of what he was getting into…or *not* getting into." Sidra shook her head at her sad attempt at a joke. "Ignore that last part."

"Noted," David said. He scratched his head. "So he already knew that you were a virgin and he was able to make the decision on if he wanted to continue being with you, knowing that you were inexperienced," he said. It was more to himself, than to Sidra.

Sidra raised an eyebrow. "Uh…yeah," she returned, skeptical. "Where is this—"

"Can I ask you something else?" David cut in.

Sidra hesitated. "Sure," she answered, finally.

"What if it were the other way around?" he began.

"Meaning?" Sidra asked.

"What if *James* was the virgin and *you weren't?*" David finished.

Sidra stopped walking and faced him. "Where is this coming from?" she wondered.

"I'm just curious," David explained. "If James was a virgin and you weren't...how would you feel about that?"

Sidra thought for a moment. "I mean, I guess I wouldn't think anything of it," she put out. "I would figure that he was saving himself for the right woman, maybe...I guess...I don't know."

"You wouldn't think it was weird that a grown man in his twenties, was still a virgin?"

Sidra shrugged. "Not really," she said. "David, what's with all the virgin talk?" she asked. David pinched the bridge of his nose. "Is Nicole a virgin?"

David hesitated, then shook his head. "No...*she's* not the virgin," he vaguely replied.

Sidra stared at David for a few moments, before realization set in. Her eyes widened. "David, are *you* a virgin?!" she exclaimed.

David quickly put his finger up to his mouth as he looked around in a panic, "Shhhhhh!" he hissed.

"Sorry," Sidra winced. "But seriously, *you're* a virgin?" she repeated, this time at a volume only the two of them could hear.

David took a deep breath. "Yeah."

Sidra was in total shock. She could have sworn that all of her guy friends had given up their V-card a long time ago. "Really?"

"Yes," David stated.

"Oh," Sidra breathed. "And Nicole isn't?"

"No."

"Oh," Sidra repeated. That seemed to be her go-to response. "Well sweetie, I find that admirable."

David rolled his eyes. "Come on Sid, don't patronize me," he ground out, turning away.

"I'm *not*," Sidra assured, grabbing his arm. "I'm telling the truth."

"Then why did you react how you did?" he asked point-blank.

"You mean with shock?" Sidra frowned; David nodded.

"Because I *was*, I had no idea that you never had sex."

"*Who* would I have had it with?" David sneered. "The nerd never had a girlfriend until now."

Sidra tilted her head at him. "You're not a nerd," she placated, tapping his arm. "You never told the guys?"

"Why? So Mark can make jokes about it every chance he gets?" David scoffed. "No, I get enough jokes about my glasses... They'll just think I'm pathetic."

"David, jokes aside, you know that your brothers won't judge you," she said. David just shrugged. "And Mark has gotten a *lot* better."

"Yeah, I know," David admitted, tone sullen.

"Well, how does *Nicole* feel about that?" she wondered. David just looked at her, not saying a word, but his silence spoke volumes, "You didn't tell her?"

"No," David admitted shamefully.

"David," Sidra's tone was chastising.

"I know," David agreed, rubbing his face. "And she's trying to get closer to me and I...I'm avoiding her."

Sidra frowned. "You *know* that's messed up right?" David hung his head. "David, she's gonna think that you're losing interest in her."

"I'm *not* though," David assured.

"But she's going to *feel* that way," Sidra insisted. "You have to tell her."

"I know...but I—she's gonna think I'm pathetic," David put out.

"I doubt that," Sidra contradicted. "She seems to really like you... You can't keep that from her. *Especially* if it's making you act weird towards her."

David sighed. "You're right," he admitted. "I'll do it...just don't know when yet."

Sidra gave David another pat on the arm. "And you know what, if she *does* start acting funny after you tell her, then she isn't the girl for you...and I'll be happy to smack her for you."

David managed a chuckle as he shook his head. "Thank you." He reached out and gave Sidra a big hug. "I appreciate you."

"You *better*," Sidra joked, rubbing his back. "You're welcome."


Malajia sat at her dining room table, concentrating on the words in her textbook. Of all the things on her mind at that moment, midterms were the last thing that she actually cared about. However, knowing that her grades depended on her concentration, she tried her best to focus.

Her cell phone ringing made her lose her place. Letting out a sigh, she reached for her phone as she rubbed the back of her neck. Not bothering to glance at the caller ID, she answered.

"Hello?" she frowned when no one answered. "Hello?... I know someone is there, I hear your stupid ass breathing." She pulled the phone from her ear. Glancing at the caller ID, she realized that the number wasn't one that she recognized. Rolling her eyes, she placed her phone back to her ear. "Wrong number, weirdo," she hissed into the phone then immediately hung up. "Idiot," she mumbled to herself.

A few seconds later, just as Malajia picked up her pencil to begin jotting down notes, her phone rang again. She snatched it from the table and put it to her ear. "What?!" she barked.

"Damn babe, it's me, you cool?" Mark answered, stunned by Malajia's reaction.

Feeling both bad and relieved, Malajia let out a sigh. "Sorry," she said, rubbing her eyes. "Somebody called a few minutes ago, breathing all in the phone, not saying nothin' and shit."

"Oh," Mark replied. "Whose number was it?"

"I have no idea," Malajia answered honestly. "What's up?"

"I called to see what you were doing," Mark said.

"Just studying." Malajia's tone was somber, something that wasn't missed by Mark. As a matter of fact, it'd been something that he had noticed over the past few days.

"You okay?" he asked, point-blank.

"You're the second person who asked me that," Malajia huffed. "I'm fine."

"If people are asking, then maybe it's clear to us that you're *not* fine," Mark returned, tone stern. Malajia was silent. "Okay, if you say you're fine, you're fine."

"Okay," Malajia mumbled, staring at her book.

"You wanna go grab something to eat after you finish studying?" Mark asked. "I don't know about *you*, but I'm in the mood for some hoagies."

"Sounds good," Malajia responded, tone dry. "Give me like an hour."

"You got it," Mark said. "See you."

"Bye." Malajia ended the call and placed the phone back on the table. Letting out another deep sigh, she closed her textbook. "I don't feel like this bullshit anymore," she grunted to herself. As she began gathering her study items from the table, the front door opened.

"Malajia, you missed a huge sale at the mall today," Sidra gushed, walking in holding several bags.

"Girl, you know I don't have no damn money," Malajia muttered, capping her highlighter.

"Since *when* has that ever stopped you from going?" Sidra chuckled.

Malajia just shrugged.

"Anyway, you've got to see what I bought for the baby," Sidra squealed, tossing the bags on the couch. With her niece or nephew constantly on her mind, Sidra could not resist it any longer; she had to shop. Luckily for David, she didn't drag him to the mall while they were out the day before. "Baby?" Malajia frowned. "*What* baby?" "Marcus's baby," Sidra clarified. Malajia shot her a confused look. "Damn Auntie, isn't that girl only like two months pregnant?" Sidra put a hand on her hip. "Look, it's never too early to shop okay?" she threw back, tossing her purse on the couch.

"No, I guess *not*," Malajia agreed, rubbing the back of her neck. "I hope you got gender neutral stuff, 'cause you're not gonna know for some time what they're having."

"Yeah I know," Sidra replied, sitting on the chair across from Malajia. "I swear, every time I talk to Marcus, he just seems so excited, you know?"

"Yeah, I'm sure," Malajia said.

"He's even more excited about this, than that wedding," Sidra said. "Now that I think about it, he hasn't mentioned it recently and it's supposed to be the end of this month."

Malajia shook her head. "Damn that came up fast."

"Tell me about it," Sidra grunted. "But they're in counseling now, so maybe they'll postpone it until they're finished with the sessions."

"Maybe he'll call it off all together," Malajia jeered, glancing at her phone.

Sidra stared at Malajia. "Don't get my hopes up like that," she said, inciting a slight chuckle from Malajia. Sidra waved her hand in a dismissive gesture. "Anyway, my parents are pretty excited too…about the *baby* I mean," she continued.

Malajia chuckled again. "I'm sure that baby will be just as spoiled as *you* are," she joked.

"Funny," Sidra grunted. "This whole thing is making me think about being a mother one day," she continued after a few seconds of silence. She looked at Malajia. "Have you thought about having kids?"

Malajia felt a chill go down her spine. "Uh huh," she

answered, not lifting her head.

"*Really?*" Sidra questioned, eyeing Malajia in disbelief. That made Malajia look at Sidra. "Why did you say it like that?" she ground out.

"I'm just shocked, that's all," Sidra returned, brushing some hair from her face. "I mean, I never took you for the 'having a baby' type. I figured you'd be too concerned with your figure. Or not having enough time to party."

Malajia frowned. "Why do you keep making smart ass comments implying that I don't want kids?" she snapped.

The humor left Sidra's face. "Mel, I was only *joking*," Sidra assured. "If I offended you, I'm sorry."

Malajia felt bad for snapping; she knew that Sidra didn't mean any harm. Her mood had been off lately and she knew exactly why. As much as she tried to push it out of her mind, her thoughts plagued her.

"Its fine, don't worry about it," Malajia said with a wave of her hand.

"I know you'll make a great mom one day," Sidra placated.

"Thanks," Malajia muttered, running her hand over her hair, "Sorry I snapped, just…these um, midterms." Malajia gestured her head to Sidra's bags. "Show me what you got."

Sidra happily jumped up and grabbed the bags. "You've *got* to see these pacifiers, they're so cute," she gushed, reaching inside the bag as she headed back over to Malajia.

As Sidra dug through the contents, something caught Malajia's eye, sending her hand into the bag. "Girl!" she exclaimed, retrieving a small item. "I thought you got gender neutral things."

Sidra rolled her eyes. "It *is*," she argued

Malajia held up the item as she eyed Sidra skeptically. "Crazy, does this bright pink, porcelain bunny bank *look* gender neutral to you?" she questioned.

"Pink *is* gender neutral," Sidra laughed. "You forget that *my* favorite color is blue."

"Yeah okay," Malajia rolled her eyes. "And I suppose

those pink dresses in that bag are neutral too huh?"

"Okay, okay," Sidra relented, knowing that the jig was up. "I'm hoping that they're having a little girl," she admitted. "A little princess, like me."

"Nobody wants another *you*," Malajia teased, carefully placing the bank on the table. Sidra made a face in retaliation.


Alex wiped the last of the tables off with a cloth. After barely making it out of midterm number two of the week, Alex was almost too drained to work her shift. "Josh, the next time that I agree to work during midterms, smack me," she joked, heading over to the counter.

Josh, who was busy tying the strings on his apron, let out a small laugh. "One, I won't smack you," he said. "*Two*, there won't be a next time. We'll be graduating."

Alex smacked her forehead with her palm. "Oh yeah, that's right."

Josh chuckled.

Alex chuckled herself. "I'm so tired, I'm surprised that I even *remembered* that I had to work today."

"It was like that for me the other day," Josh said, washing his hands in the sink.

"How many midterms have you taken so far this week?" Alex asked, adjusting some pencils in a cup.

"Three," Josh answered. "The last two are tomorrow."

"Lucky *you*, *my* last one is on Friday," Alex shook her head. "I don't understand why we couldn't take it on Wednesday, why is he waiting to torture us on *Friday*?"

"Who knows?" Josh replied, glancing up. His eyes widened at the sight of a patron who just walked in. "Um Alex don't look now but Eric—"

Josh didn't get to finish before Alex spun around to face the entryway.

"I said *don't* look," Josh muttered.

Ignoring Josh, Alex walked up to the ordering counter

and smiled. "Hey Eric," she said. "Taking a meal break from midterms huh?"

Eric ran his hand over his head. "Yeah, I guess you could say that," he murmured.

"You eating in or out—" Alex paused when she realized her innuendo.

Josh, having heard, snickered hard. Alex turned around and shot him a death stare. Catching the look, Josh put his hands up in surrender and went back to prepping his station.

Embarrassed, Alex faced Eric once more. "Um, I mean—"

"I *know* what you mean," Eric chortled. "Carry out. Large pizza, half cheese, half supreme."

Alex jotted down the order on her note pad. "Josh—"

"I heard. On it," Josh returned from his station.

"How are your tests going?" Alex asked Eric, who stood before her, trying not to make eye contact.

"They were okay," he replied. "I took my last one earlier today."

Alex tossed her hands up in the air. "God, everybody is getting done early but *me*," she huffed.

"Ah, I see where that would annoy you, especially when *you're* used to finishing first," Eric joked.

Alex didn't get a chance to blush at the innuendo because Josh had cut in with his own remark. "Ha! Good one, man," Josh bellowed from the back.

Alex rolled her eyes and shook her head at Josh. He was being way too silly today. "Funny," she mocked. "At least I don't feel so bad for *my* vulgar slip."

Eric smiled. "I figured I'd ease your embarrassment."

Alex tilted her head. *He's being nice…and chatty, and is he flirting?* "I appreciate it," she returned, grateful.

Hearing his phone ring, Eric grabbed it from his jacket pocket and glanced at it. "I'm gonna take this outside," he announced, pointing to it.

Alex nodded. "Your pizza will be done in a few minutes," she said.

Eric nodded in return and put the phone to his ear as he walked out of the restaurant.

Alex glanced back at Josh. "Did he seem like he was flirting to you?" she asked, when she was sure that the door closed.

Josh poked his head out from behind the pizza oven. "Huh?" he asked.

Alex twisted her lip. "Oh *now* you don't hear anything, huh?" she ground out.

Josh could do nothing but laugh.

# Chapter 18

"You gonna eat that?" Mark asked, pointing to the half-eaten hoagie on Malajia's plate.

Malajia turned from the window that she was glancing out of. "Huh?" she frowned.

"Your sandwich," Mark amended. "You barely touched it."

"Oh," Malajia replied, gesturing to the sandwich. "Go ahead greedy."

Rubbing his hands together, Mark reached out and grabbed the hoagie from Malajia's basket as she went back to gazing out of the window of the small sandwich place. As promised, Mark picked her up and took her off campus to lunch. He even took Malajia to a movie first, hoping that it would relax her mind enough to let him know what was really going on with her. But her silence throughout the car ride, movie, and now lunch, made him think twice.

"Mel, what's going on with you?" Mark asked point-blank.

"Huh?" she repeated, facing him once more.

"What is going on with you?" Mark repeated, enunciating each word.

"I'm fine, like I told you *earlier*," Malajia grunted.

"See I don't believe you," Mark pressed.

Malajia frowned. "Why *not*?"

"You've been acting really funny lately," he pointed out.

"*How*?" she snapped.

Mark shot her a knowing look. "Come on Malajia," he

said. Malajia folded her arms and shot him a challenging look. "First off, you've been *really* quiet and that is sooooo not like you."

She shot him a glare. "You being smart?" she hissed.

"Just stating the obvious," he returned. "You wanna tell me what's going on?"

Malajia just stared at Mark in silence for a few moments. She had every intention of giving an excuse or making a joke to deflect, but she couldn't, not anymore. She took a deep breath. "Okay so...it's been a year," she vaguely put out.

"A year of *what?*" Mark asked, confused.

Malajia nervously rubbed her arm. "A year since...um...since I had my abortion," she slowly put out.

Mark set his food down, his face masked with sympathy. He felt horrible; he had completely forgotten. "Oooooh," he sputtered. "I'm sorry—"

"Don't be sorry, I don't want your sympathy or pity," Malajia cut in, putting a hand up.

"I'm not pitying you," Mark frowned.

Malajia sighed. She hadn't meant for her words to come out so harsh. "No, I didn't mean it like that," she clarified. "I meant that...I don't want you to feel sorry for me."

Mark looked confused. "That don't sound no *better*," he pointed out. He took a deep breath as Malajia stared at him. "Look Mel—"

"Mark...can you just let me deal with this please?" she interrupted. "I mean... I just...I'll be over it in a few days," she assured. Malajia had no idea that the anniversary of the most difficult decision that she ever had to make in her young life would affect her the way that it did. But when she woke up nearly a week before, feeling a cloud of sadness fall over her, Malajia realized that she couldn't run from it.

Mark wasn't convinced and it showed on his face. "Malajia, I doubt that you will be *over* this in a *few days*," he contradicted. "I mean, it's been a *year* and you're *still* not."

She rolled her eyes at him.

"You don't talk about it," he said. "Don't you think you

*should?*"

"No, no I *don't*," Malajia ground out.

"You know what holding stuff in, does," Mark threw back, unfazed by Malajia's attitude. "Our relationship almost ended *because* of it."

"You really wanna throw that in my face right now?" Malajia spat, shooting him a death stare.

"I'm just making a point, Malajia," Mark insisted, voice calm. "I'm not trying to piss you off."

Malajia's face relaxed from its frown. "Yeah, I know," she admitted. "I just...there is nothing to talk about. I did it and I can't take it back. Don't even know if I would *want* to, even if it *was* a possibility."

"The point isn't in you regretting your decision or not, the point is that in order for you not to go crazy...you should *talk* about it," Mark pressed. "If you don't want to talk to *me* about it...talk to your mom, your counselor back home, or your best friend."

Malajia frowned. "Hell *no* I'm not telling my mom," she barked. "She had seven kids, you really think she would be understanding of one of her daughters having an abortion?" She ran her hand through her hair. "The counselor, therapist lady...she was good with helping me deal with the whole 'blaming myself for being beat up' thing, but...I don't know. It's just not something that I want to talk to her about. She'd probably tell my parents." Malajia let out another sigh. "And...I *can't* tell Chasity... After what she went through, she'd probably hate me for what I did."

"I think you're just telling yourself those things to avoid doing what you *should* do," Mark pointed out.

"No, I'm telling myself these things because they *will happen*," Malajia grumbled.

Mark shook his head as he reached for the rest of Malajia's sandwich. "Whatever you say," he relented.

Malajia stared at him while he took a bite. "Thanks for trying to cheer me up though," she said sincerely, reaching out and touching his arm. "You irk my life but I appreciate you."

Mark chuckled. "Likewise."


Josh took a bite of his hamburger and set it back on his plate. "I don't know what they put in this burger, but it's really good," he mused.

Sidra giggled as she picked up her turkey wrap. "I guess they learned the power of seasoning," she joked.

"You may be right," Josh returned, wiping the ketchup from his mouth with a napkin. "How's things going by the way?"

Sidra looked up from her plate. "Huh?"

"I feel like we haven't really sat down one on one in a while," Josh pointed out.

*Trust me, I'm aware*, she thought. She hated that she wasn't spending as much time with Josh as she used to. She wasn't sure if it was him avoiding her, or the other way around. "Well. We've both been busy with classes, tests and um...*relationships*." She looked off to the side, wondering if Josh picked up on her not so subtle hint.

"You must be talking about yours with James, because unless you know something that *I* don't know about my love life, last time I checked I was still single," Josh returned, reaching for some French fries on his plate.

Sidra looked skeptical. "Oh?" she put out. "Not dating at *all*?"

"Define *dating*?" Josh threw back.

Sidra took a deep breath. *That means he's having causal sex*. Just the thought of that bothered her. "Never mind," she muttered.

"How's things with James?" Josh deflected.

Sidra was still focused on her inner thoughts. "Um, things are fine," she answered.

"*Just* fine?" Josh pressed, raising an eyebrow.

Sidra shrugged. "No, things are good... Just—"

"Just *what*?" Josh interrupted, a frown of concern

masked his brown face. "He's still treating you right, right?" Josh might be coming to terms with the fact that he would never be with Sidra romantically, but that didn't mean that he wouldn't hesitate to go toe to toe with James over her. She was still his friend after all.

"Of *course* he's still treating me right," Sidra assured. "It's just that..." *I'm starting to feel differently about him, and I don't know why.* She paused for a moment; that was the first time that she admitted to herself that something was different when it came to how she felt for James. She didn't know why that was the case, but what she did know was that she didn't want to talk about it with Josh. "Let's talk about something else."

Before Josh could utter another word, Sidra's phone beeped.

"Sorry, hold on a second," she said, reaching for it. Glancing at the message on the screen her eyes nearly popped out of her head. *'The wedding is off.'* Sidra bolted from her seat. "Josh, sweetie, I have to make a phone call," she announced, darting away from the table and out of the cafeteria.

Standing on the front steps, she hit the call button. "Marcus, tell me that my eyes weren't deceiving me just now," she barked into the phone when her brother answered.

Marcus let out a sigh. "No, it's true," he clarified, tone sullen. "The wedding was called off."

Sidra was grateful that she wasn't video chatting, because he would have seen the look of pure delight on her face. "Well...what happened?" she asked, feigning concern. *Not that it matters.*

"Mom told you that we were going to pre-marital counseling, right?" Marcus began.

"Yeah."

"Well, while we were in the sessions, I realized that we put each other through too much shit... Our relationship is toxic right now and if we're going to even *try* to make it work, we need a hell of a lot more than a few therapy sessions," her brother explained, then sighed. "Getting married is the *last* thing that we should be doing right now, so...I called it off."

Sidra closed her eyes and tilted her head to the sky. Her prayers were answered. "So um...how did she take it?" she wondered. "Not that it *matters*."

"Sidra," Marcus warned.

"Sorry," she returned. Sure, Sidra was excited, but she had to remember that her brother was hurting.

"I mean, of *course* she's not happy about it," Marcus said. "She's pissed, to say the least. She said if we aren't getting married, then there is no need for us to be together. So, I'm moving out."

"She's not going to make it difficult for you to be a part of that baby's life now that you're not together anymore, *is* she?" Sidra ground out. "I mean, I know that she's petty, but I hope she has an *ounce* of maturity in her."

"Honestly Sidra, I don't know," Marcus admitted. "But I'll tell you one thing, I don't care *how* she feels, she's not gonna keep me from my child."

Sidra smiled proudly. Not only had her brother seen the light finally, but he was determined to be a good father, despite having a troublesome woman as the mother of his child.

"But look, I gotta go," Marcus said. "Mom wants me to come over."

"She knows?" Sidra asked.

"Yeah," he sulked.

"Well, at least you have all the support you need," Sidra tried to console. "Love you."

"Love you too."

Sidra looked at the phone once her brother hung up. She was smiling from ear to ear. A tap to her shoulder, brought her out of her blissful moment. Spinning around, she saw Josh standing there holding her jacket and purse.

"I have to get to class and I didn't want to leave your stuff sitting in there," he announced, handing the items to her. He was shocked when Sidra wrapped her arms around him and gave him a big hug. "This is a pretty exaggerated 'thank you' for bringing your things out," he joked.

Sidra parted from him. "I am in *the* best mood right now," she gurgled. "I think I want to celebrate with a big, calorie filled ice cream sundae from the ice cream shop. You wanna go after you get out of class?" she proposed. "My treat."

Josh thought for a moment. "Let me make sure I don't have a ton of homework before I give you an answer."

Sidra put her hands up. "Fair enough," she replied. "See you later."

"See you," Josh said, giving her a nod before walking off, leaving Sidra to stare at his departing back.


"Mom, when I get home next week, can we go to a spa or something? Just you and me?" Malajia asked her mother over her phone.

"Sure sweetie, I'll make sure to carve out some time," Mrs. Simmons said. "Any particular one that you want to go to?"

Malajia shook her head, even though her mother couldn't see her. "No. It doesn't matter, any one is fine."

"Okay, I'll get on that." Still feeling guilty over brushing Malajia off over the years and making her feel that she wasn't as important as her other daughters, Mrs. Simmons had made a promise to herself that whenever Malajia asked to spend time with her, she would make sure to do it. "How were midterms?"

Malajia sat down at the dining room table. "They were fine," she answered, tone sullen. "Glad that they're over."

"You don't *sound* thrilled that they're over," Mrs. Simmons observed. "You sound sad even, are you okay?"

Malajia rolled her eyes. *If one more person asks me if I'm okay.* "I'm fine, just tired."

Mrs. Simmons hesitated for a moment. "Well…okay

baby, get some re—Girl!" she barked.

Malajia frowned. "Huh? What did I do?"

"No, not *you*," Mrs. Simmons clarified. "Your damn sister got her little sneaky ass into my new perfume— Melissa! I swear to God!"

Malajia couldn't help but smirk. Her youngest sister, now nearly six years old, was getting herself into trouble more and more. "Mom, go handle your child," she teased.

"I'mma *handle* her little butt alright," Mrs. Simmons hissed. "I'll call you later."

"Okay." Malajia hung up the phone and set it on the table in front of her. Hearing a sound from upstairs, she frowned as she concentrated on it. Recognizing the noise as a ringtone, she looked confused. "Is that Sidra's phone?" she muttered to herself. Shrugging once the ringing stopped, she glanced at the door as it opened.

"Hey, boo thang," Malajia smiled, seeing Chasity walk through the door.

Chasity turned her lip up. "Ugh," she scoffed. Malajia chuckled as Chasity walked over and sat at the table.

Malajia opened her mouth to speak, but was interrupted by the ringing of Sidra's phone once again. "What the hell, man?" she complained.

"Is that Sidra's phone?" Chasity asked, pointing to the steps.

"*Sounds* like that wack ass ringtone of hers," Malajia jeered. "I'm surprised Princess perfect left it."

Chasity shrugged as she fiddled with the bracelets on her wrist.

"You doing anything spoiled and expensive for spring break?" Malajia joked.

Chasity smirked. "Nah, I think I'm just gonna chill at home."

"In your big expensive house with your spoiled ass," Malajia chortled.

"Still hating after all these years, huh?"

"Absolutely." Both girls groaned when they heard

Sidra's phone ring again. "I can't take that ringtone!" Malajia covered her ears. "It's worse than that damn beep tone that Alex got."

Chasity didn't get a chance to respond; the door opened and Alex ran in with Emily trailing behind.

"Alex, you cheated!" Emily wailed, closing the door behind her. "You tripped me."

Alex spun around and faced Emily, stunned. "I did *not*!" she exclaimed. "You tripped over your own foot as soon as you stepped off the bus."

"You wanna explain why you're sweatin' all over the damn rug?" Chasity scoffed at a glistening Alex, who in turn stuck her tongue out at her.

"Shut up Chasity," Alex hissed, tossing her purse on the couch. "Anyway, me and Emily made a bet that whoever makes it back to the house from the bus stop first, has to cook dinner for the house tonight."

Malajia and Chasity stared at them.

"Why are you two looking at us like we're crazy?" Alex slowly asked.

"You went through all that when we all said that we were gonna eat at the caf tonight," Malajia bit out.

Emily tossed her hands in the air. "Dang it Alex," she fussed, heading for the kitchen in search of a cold bottle of water

Alex busted out laughing. "Damn, that *was* my idea, huh?" She glanced at the ceiling when she heard a noise. "What's that noise?"

"Sidra's fuckin' phone is ringing again," Malajia griped.

As if on cue, Sidra barged through the door. "Hey—"

"Sidra, *please* go answer your phone, it rang like eighty times," Malajia charged.

"Hello to you *too*," Sidra sneered. She adjusted the strap of her purse on her shoulder. "And I'm sure it wasn't *eighty* times, oh dramatic one."

Sidra jogged up the steps and into her room.

She closed the door behind her and grabbed her phone

from her desk. Glancing at the call log, she frowned. "Mama, why did you call me so many times?" she wondered aloud.

She immediately hit the redial button and put the phone to her ear. She ran her hand over her hair as she waited for her mother to answer. "Mama hey—huh? ...I left my phone in my room by accident...what's wrong? Why do you sound like that?" The confusion left Sidra's face and gave way to pure shock. "Wait, what... She *what*?!"

The conversation between the four girls downstairs was interrupted by the sound of screams coming from Sidra's room.

"What the hell?!" Alex exclaimed.

The girls immediately jumped up from their seats, and were already in mid-charge to the staircase when they heard the door open.

"Sidra! Are you okay?" Emily called up the steps as a hysterical Sidra darted down. Sidra was panicked; she was wringing her hands and beginning to hyperventilate.

"Sidra, what happened?" Chasity demanded.

Emily tried to grab Sidra's hand, but Sidra jerked it away as tears formed in her eyes. "You're scaring us, what's wrong?" Emily panicked.

"Sis, calm down, what happened?" Malajia pressed.

"She—she got rid of it," Sidra stammered, tears spilling down her cheeks as she ran her trembling hands over her face.

"What?" Alex frowned. "What are you talking about sweetie?"

"She—she got rid of—"

"Sidra!" Chasity clapped her hands in Sidra's face once, in an effort to get her to focus enough to form a complete sentence.

"She got rid of my brother's baby!" Sidra screamed.

"Sweetie, you have to elaborate," Alex said, calm. "We're trying to understand."

"India!" Sidra hollered. "That fuckin' bitch!" Sidra began pacing the floor in front of her stunned friends. "She got an abortion!"

Emily's eyes widened. "She *what*?!" she exclaimed. Malajia's eyes shifted as she listened to Sidra continue her rampage.

"Apparently she was so angry at the fact that Marcus called the wedding off, that she went and got rid of the baby," Sidra revealed, furious. "Talking about since he didn't want to marry her, then there was no need for her to keep the baby." Sidra stopped pacing and put her hand over her face once again. "My brother—" She broke down crying. "He's so hurt—" Sidra removed her hand from her face and balled up her fist. "How could she do something like that?! How could she be so fuckin' selfish? She killed a baby! She killed my brother's baby."

"I'm so sorry Sid," Alex consoled as she moved in for a hug. Sidra was too distraught to let anyone touch her. She moved away and taking the hint, Alex backed up.

"How could she—that bitch!" Sidra fumed, wiping tears from her face. "She needs to go to jail for that! *Anybody* who does that—it's wrong! It's so wrong."

Malajia was still silent.

Sidra was furious; her family was hurting, *she* was hurting. "How can anyone take an innocent life like that? What the hell is *wrong* with people?"

Malajia took a deep breath. She understood why Sidra was angry; she was angry *for* Sidra. But she couldn't just let her friend say something like that, judging all women who decided to make the choice that *she* did, out of rage.

"Sidra…you don't really mean that do you?" Malajia softly put in. "That anybody who gets an abortion…is wrong."

"Yes, the hell I *do* mean that shit," Sidra maintained, angry. "Every damn word of it."

Malajia scratched her head as she wondered if she should even continue with the conversation. But she started it; Malajia felt she had no choice *but* to. "Sidra...while India was wrong for getting an abortion out of spite for your brother..." she paused.

Sidra snapped her head in Malajia's direction. "I know *damn* well you're not gonna stand here in my face after I just *told* you that she got rid of my brother's *baby*. A *life*, and justify abortions to me."

"All I'm saying is that you can't judge every situation based on *hers*. You can't make a blanket statement like that, it's not okay," Malajia said, tone as calm as she could get it in that moment. "You don't know how difficult a decision like that *is*," she continued when Sidra just stared daggers at her. "You don't know what goes through the mind of a woman who goes through that."

Alex touched Malajia's arm. "Mel, maybe this isn't the time," she softly said. Malajia looked at her. Alex, seeing her glare, backed off.

"I can judge whoever the hell I *want*. It's *my* niece or nephew that won't get a chance to be born," Sidra raged, pointing to herself. "How dare you!"

Malajia put her hands up in surrender. "I'm sorry okay," she said. "Look, I understand—"

"You don't understand *shit*!" Sidra yelled, pointing her finger in Malajia's face.

"I do *so*," Malajia threw back, angry.

"Okay you two, seriously this is not the time to argue with each other," Alex cut in. She didn't care how passionate the girls were about their stances; she wasn't going to stand by and watch them fight.

"No, Malajia's shallow ass thinks she understands what I'm feeling, I'm trying to figure out exactly *what* she understands," Sidra mocked.

Malajia scoffed as she shook her head. "I understand more than you *think*," she sneered.

Sidra folded her arms. "Is that so?"

"Yes," Malajia assured. "*You're* the one who doesn't understand. Having an abortion done is probably one of the most *difficult* things that a woman can go through," she argued. "It's bad enough that she has to constantly live with that decision, day in and day out. But the *last* thing she needs is to be judged for it."

Sidra stared at Malajia in disbelief. "Are you kidding me?" she ranted. "Are you standing in my face as *my friend* defending that girl?"

"I'm not even *talking* about what India did. *That* shit was fucked up." Malajia threw back. "I'm—I'm talking about in *general*, Sid."

"And what makes you the fuckin' expert on that bullshit?!" Sidra yelled.

"Yo, y'all gotta chill," Chasity urged.

Malajia put her hand up at Sidra. She was desperately trying to keep herself calm; the last thing that she wanted to do was say something that she regretted. "Sidra—"

Sidra stepped closer to Malajia's face. "No! You need to tell me to my face why you're defending it," she yelled.

Malajia went to walk away. "I'll talk to you when you calm down," she said.

Sidra grabbed Malajia's arm to stop her. "*Tell* me goddamn it!"

Malajia spun around, snatching her arm from Sidra's grasp. "Because *I had* one!" she yelled. Just as soon as the words left her mouth, Malajia wished that she could take them back. But she couldn't. Malajia looked around as her friends stared at her, in stunned silence.

"Malajia," Emily sputtered. "You—"

Alex was dumbfounded. "What? *When?*—I mean—"

"Last year," Malajia revealed, regretful. The only ones who hadn't said a word were Chasity and Sidra. "It was Tyrone's," she added after a moment. "The last time I was with him before he attacked me for the last time, I—" she shook her head. "Anyway, two months later I found out I was pregnant."

Chasity just shook her head as she looked off to the side. Sidra, on the other hand, was staring Malajia dead in her face with a mask of indifference.

Malajia ran her hand through her hair. "I couldn't—after *everything* he did to me, I just *couldn't* have it," she sighed, feeling tears well up in her eyes. "So I got an abortion... I didn't tell anybody, I just went by myself and did it."

"I'm sure that was hard for you to do," Alex commented after a moment. She was still in shock, as she was sure the other girls were.

Malajia nodded, wiping her eyes.

"I'm sorry that you had to go through that," Emily sympathized, rubbing Malajia's shoulder.

"Thank you," Malajia muttered.

Sidra's eyes narrowed as she stared at Malajia, a woman whom she had known since she was a child. "You killed your baby?" she snarled.

Those venomous words hit Malajia like a ton of bricks and it showed on her face.

"I *knew* you were selfish, I just didn't realize *how* much, until now," Sidra fumed. Emily put her hand over her mouth in shock.

Malajia's eyes filled with tears once again. "What?" she gasped.

"Sidra, don't do that," Alex urged. "Don't say something that you'll regret."

"The *only* thing that I regret is knowing this *baby killer* in front of me," Sidra raged, flinging her hand in Malajia's direction.

Chasity snapped out of her stunned silence. "Sidra! Don't be a bitch," she barked.

"No! *Malajia* is the bitch," Sidra threw back. She stared at Malajia, who looked like she wanted to pass out. "So your irresponsible ass makes a bad decision, and you made your child pay the price for it. Instead of owning up to your responsibility, you took the cowards way out. I hope you're happy, you fuckin' monster."

Malajia put her hand over her chest as she tried to steady her breathing. Everything that Sidra was hurling at her was the same way that she felt about herself, even though she tried to tell herself otherwise. All of Malajia's fears were brought to light—that she could possibly lose the respect of her friends over her decision. She felt herself nearing a break down as the tears spilled down her cheeks.

Sidra just shook her head and looked at Malajia with pure hatred. "You disgust me, and I'm sorry that I even know you," she spat before turning away and storming towards the door.

"Sidra," Malajia called out, voice almost pleading.

Ignoring her, Sidra snatched open the door.

"Sidra," Malajia repeated as she tried to take a step forward.

Chasity grabbed Malajia's arm to steady her, before her best friend collapsed.

"Sidra don't leave!" Emily exclaimed, then flinched when the door slammed shut behind her.

Malajia broke down crying. "What did I do?" she sobbed. She jerked her arm out of Chasity's grip and bolted up the steps.

Hearing the door slam, Alex put her hand over her head. "Oh my God," she gasped.

Chasity headed for the steps. "One of y'all go talk some sense into Sidra's ignorant ass," she demanded, angry, before jogging up the steps.

Alex and Emily looked at each other, neither one knowing what to say. "Em—"

"Alex, I can't," Emily immediately cut in, nervous. "Did you see how angry she was?"

"Yes, we *all* did," Alex replied. She took a deep breath. "We'll *both* go," she proposed.

Emily stood for a moment, uncertainty on her face, before giving a slight nod.

# Chapter 19

Chasity banged on Malajia's door. "Malajia, open the door," she ordered. She couldn't even focus on what she had just learned, and the conversation that she knew she would have to have with Malajia. The only thing that was on her mind was trying to make sure that Malajia was okay. And judging by Malajia's hysterical cries that came through her locked bedroom door, she knew that she wasn't.

Chasity banged again. "Mel, *please* open the door."

Raising her hand to bang once more, she changed her mind and put it down. "Shit," she whispered to herself. Letting out a sigh, she grabbed her phone from her jeans pocket and dialed a number. Stepping away from the door, she waited for an answer. "Hey, where are you? ...Well, you need to get over here like now... It's Malajia... No, she's not alright. Just get here."

Ending the call, Chasity glanced back at the closed door before shaking her head and heading back down the steps.


Mark hurried into the house to find Chasity sitting on the couch alone.

"I got here as fast as I could," he said, closing the door. "I was off campus when you called."

Chasity just nodded as she stared at him with her arms folded. With Alex and Emily having gone after Sidra, Chasity, not wanting to leave Malajia in the house alone, elected to stay and wait for Mark to arrive. "She's locked in her room."

Mark sighed, glanced up the steps, and proceeded to head up. Pausing, he turned around and faced Chasity once again. "Chaz, what happened?" he asked.

Chasity rubbed her face with her hand before taking a deep breath. "Um...Sidra found out that Marcus's...*whatever* she is, aborted his baby because he called off the wedding," she answered, tone low.

Mark frowned. "Wait, *what?*" Sidra had told him two days ago about the wedding being called off. He expected India to be angry, but never in a million years did he think that she would do something like that.

"Yeah," Chasity confirmed, slowly standing up from the couch. "Sidra was angry, and she went off...the rant turned from India, to her opinion on abortion in general."

Mark closed his eyes and pinched the bridge of his nose. "Mel was here for that?"

Chasity slowly nodded. "And Malajia... Well, she tried to reason with Sidra, and long story short...she ended up telling more than I think she wanted to."

Mark stared at Chasity. "*What* did she tell exactly?" he wondered, careful. He had no idea if Malajia actually told them about her abortion; she had been so adamant about keeping that to herself.

Chasity paused and shot him a knowing look. "Judging by your lack of confusion or shock...I think you already know."

*Yep, she told them.* Mark could do nothing but nod in confirmation.

Chasity let out a sigh. The events of the evening had mentally drained her. She had to get out of the house. "Good luck," she said, heading for the door.

Mark spun around to face her departing back. He couldn't help but wonder if Chasity was upset with Malajia over her decision. It was something that Malajia had feared. "Chaz," he called.

She turned around and looked at him, not saying a word.

Mark realized however that his only concern was

checking on Malajia. Whatever issues, if any, between her and Chasity should be handled between the two of them. "Thanks for calling me," he said.

"You're welcome," Chasity returned, walking out the door and shutting it behind her.

Mark headed up the steps and walked to Malajia's closed door. He gave the knob a twist; it was locked. He then gave the door a light tap.

"Mel," he called. He heard no response. "Baby…can you open the door? Chaz told me what happened… I came to check on you." Still, he heard no answer. He let out another sigh as he ran his hand over the back of his neck. This was killing him. "Tell you what, I'll just sit out here until you're ready to open the door, okay?" He put his hand on the door. "Okay," he muttered, taking a seat on the floor. He placed his back against the door and leaned his head against it. Not more than a minute later, he heard movement, followed by the sound of the lock turning. Mark quickly stood up and turned around, just in time to see the door open.

With caring eyes, he saw Malajia standing before him, eyes red and tears staining her face. She looked fragile, broken.

"Malajia—"

"I'm not okay," she admitted as she broke down crying once again.

Mark just reached out and wrapped his arms around her, holding her as she buried her face in his chest and wept.

Sidra, still fuming, paced the grass in front of the duck pond behind the houses. After storming out of her house, she'd sat on the bench near the pond, before she felt the tears build back up in her eyes. Ignoring the calls from her mother, calls from Alex and Emily, and not having the mental strength to talk to her brother, she called James. When he didn't pick up after the third time that she called, she stood and began her pacing.

"Pick up the damn phone James," she hissed at the phone in her hand. She had every intention of tossing her phone in the pond in anger, yet decided against it. She needed to talk; she needed to vent. She needed to cry and at that moment, there was only one person that Sidra felt that she could do that with.

Sidra walked around to the guys' house and knocked before twisting the doorknob. Finding the living room empty, she headed up the steps. Standing in front of Josh's door, she knocked.

Josh opened the door and was met with the tear stained face of Sidra. A look of concern was held on his face. "What's wrong?"

Sidra sniffled. "Josh, I need—" she glanced past him and laid eyes on a young woman, sitting at his desk. Sidra's eyes widened. "Oh my God, I—I'm sorry, I didn't mean to bother you."

Sidra turned to walk away, but Josh gently caught her by the arm. "No, no it's okay," he assured.

Josh looked at the woman. "Do you mind if we finish this later?" he asked.

"Yeah, that's fine," she said, gathering her book bag.

Sidra wiped her face with her hand as the girl stood from her seat and headed to the door. "See you Josh."

"I'll call you tomorrow," he called after her as she walked down the steps.

Josh pulled Sidra into the room and shut the door behind him. Sidra spun around to face him. "Josh, you didn't have to make your company leave."

"It's cool," he assured. "I was helping her with an assignment from our class, don't worry about it."

Sidra glanced at the floor as more tears began to flow. "What's the matter?" Josh pressed. "What happened?"

Unable to speak, Sidra just broke down crying. She walked over to him and buried her face into his chest.

Josh put his arms around her and hugged her. As much as he wanted to know what had Sidra so distraught, he felt it would be better to just let her cry.

Until he heard a knock on his door.

"Who is it?" he called, without looking up.

"It's Alex and Emily," the voice called from the other side.

Sidra quickly lifted her head.

Josh looked at Sidra, raising his eyebrow in skepticism when she shook her head 'no.' "What's up ladies?" he called through the door.

"Um, is Sidra there by any chance?"

This time Sidra shook her head emphatically. The last thing that she wanted to do was talk to any of the girls. "Please don't tell them I'm here," she whispered to Josh.

Josh put his hand up at her, telling her to keep quiet. He then pointed to a corner. Taking the hint, Sidra headed over and stood out of sight of the doorway. Josh opened the door a crack.

"I'm sorry, what did you say?" he asked, coming face to face with the girls.

"Is Sidra here?" Alex repeated.

Josh shook his head. "No, she's not here."

Alex threw her head back. "Damn it," she hissed to Emily.

"Everything okay?" he asked, already having an idea that it wasn't.

"No, not really," Emily stated, shaking her head. "If you see her, can you please tell her to come home?"

Josh's curiosity was at an all-time high. "Yeah, I'll tell her," he assured. "No problem."

"Thanks," Alex muttered, before she and Emily headed down the stairs. Josh followed their progress until he heard the door shut. Turning to see Sidra come away from her corner, he stared at her.

"You want to tell me what happened?" he asked.

Sidra shook her head. "Can I just sit in here with you for a while?" she sniffled.

Josh nodded as he walked over to his bed and sat down.

"Sure," he said, moving a pillow aside. Sidra sat next to him, then leaned her head on his shoulder, prompting him to put his arm around her. Hearing her phone ring, she glanced at the caller ID. *Now you call back*, she thought seeing James's name flash. Shaking her head, Sidra turned her phone off and tossed it on the floor.

"Am I a selfish person?" Malajia asked Mark as he opened a can of soda for her.

"No, you're *not*," Mark answered, handing her the can. Malajia took a sip and placed the can on the nightstand next to her.

"Babe, don't let what Sidra said make you question yourself," Mark added. "She might have been upset over what happened, but what she said was fucked up."

Malajia sighed. After having had a good cry in Mark's arms, for what seemed like forever, she was finally able to pull herself together enough to tell him exactly what happened. Understandably, Mark was upset with Sidra.

"She's entitled to her opinion," Malajia sulked.

"*Not* when her opinion is that you are selfish and a coward," Mark fumed. "I swear, I love Sidra to death, but she's always looked down her damn nose at people."

"Everything she accused me of…I swear to God, I've been thinking the same thing about myself," Malajia revealed. Mark just looked at her. "I mean…did I really do the right thing? Should I have—" she felt tears fill her eyes again. "What if I messed something up by doing that? What if I can't have any more kids?"

"Malajia—"

"What if I can't give *you* kids?" she panicked, interrupting Mark.

Mark put his hand out. "Stop that," he ordered. She let out a groan in frustration as she wiped the tears from her eyes. "If we're meant to have children, we *will*. Stop beating yourself up." His tone was stern. "You were in a fucked-up position and you did what you felt was best. I've told you that before. Stop. Beating. Your. Self. Up."

"I can't help it," she sniffled. "Mark...I'm scared that I'll never get over it."

Mark sighed as he reached out and gently touched her face. He knew that no matter what he said, as long as Malajia questioned her decision, she would never get to a point where she could put it past her. "I wish I could make everything that you're feeling, go away," he said.

"I know," she said.

"I wish that I would have known—I wish that I could have been there for you," Mark put out.

Malajia looked at him. "I know," she assured. "Can you just hold me?" she asked, feeling herself getting ready to cry again.

Mark nodded. "Of course. Anything you need."


"Alex, are you riding home with me or no?" Chasity asked Alex, tossing some items into a suitcase.

"It would be nice," Alex chortled, standing in the doorway of Chasity's bedroom. "But if not, it's cool. I can take the bus."

Chasity glanced up at Alex and narrowed her eyes. "Don't feed me that bullshit," she hissed. "Just be ready tomorrow by twelve."

Alex clasped her hands together. "You know I love you, right?"

"Yeah, yeah," Chasity grumbled, zipping her bag.

Spring break was upon the campus once more. With tensions still high within the house, the group couldn't wait to put some distance between themselves and the campus.

The humor left Alex's face as she watched Chasity maneuver around her room, putting items in their place. "Have you talked to Sidra at all?"

"Nope," Chasity put out instantaneously. "You?"

"I have... I mean, I can tell she's still upset," Alex said.

It had been days since the blow up and Alex had wished the tension would be resolved before leaving for break. But sadly, it wasn't. "Why haven't *you* spoken to her?"

"Because if I talk to Sidra right now, I might slap the shit outta her," Chasity admitted. "Her whole fuckin' attitude is disgusting."

"I know, I know," Alex placated. "She won't even *look* at Malajia."

"Can we not talk about this anymore?" Chasity hissed, shooting Alex a glare. Just thinking about how Sidra had hurt Malajia's feelings didn't sit well with Chasity. Especially since she hadn't even gotten the chance to talk to Malajia herself about how she was feeling; Malajia seemed to be avoiding her. "Don't you have packing to do?"

"Yeah, I'll get on it," Alex sighed. "Remind me to give you gas money too."

"Alex, you still owe me gas money from the *last* break," Chasity sneered, putting her hands on her hips.

Alex snickered. "I pick up my check today."

Chasity narrowed her eyes. "Whatever, keep that shit. Just get out."

"Yes ma'am," Alex chortled, walking out of Chasity's room.


Sidra placed her bag into the trunk of her car and slammed it shut. She, unlike everyone else in her house who was leaving tomorrow, decided to leave that day. She needed to put some distance between herself and campus.

"Leaving now?" Josh asked, heading over, a jacket in hand.

Sidra managed a smile at the sight of him. "Yeah, I gotta get out of here," she said. "I just wanna go home and hug my brother."

"I get it," Josh sympathized. "Have you talked to him?"

Sidra shook her head. "He's not answering my calls," she sighed. "But my mom got him to at least text *her* so at least he's communicating with *someone*."

Josh nodded. "Here, you left this," he said, handing her the dark blue jean jacket.

Sidra retrieved it from his grasp. "Thanks," she said. "And thanks for letting me spend the night the other day... I just couldn't be in this house."

"You're welcome," Josh returned.

"Thanks for listening to me...and for not expressing your opinion on any of this."

"I'll save it for another time," Josh said. Upon hearing what happened between Sidra and Malajia, both from Sidra and in talking to Alex while at work, Josh had his own opinions. But instead of giving her attitude like Mark did, Josh elected to remain neutral, knowing that what Sidra needed was comfort.

She pushed her hair behind her ears. "Oh and tell Mark I said thanks for giving me the cold shoulder," she spat.

Josh shook his head. "Malajia is the woman that he loves, Sidra," he pointed out. "He can't remain neutral...you can't *expect* him to."

"Yeah well, whatever," Sidra grumbled. "I gotta get going. When you get home, we should go hang out or something."

"I'll actually be staying with Mom in Jersey for spring break," Josh announced.

"Oh," Sidra put out.

"Yeah, she wants me and Sarah to go to the shore with her so...I'm going," Josh explained.

Sidra forced a smile. "I hope you have fun. You deserve it."

"Thanks. Just call me if you need to," he said, before giving her a quick hug.

"I will." Sidra watched as Josh walked away, sighing in the process. As she opened her car door to step in, she glanced up and saw Malajia heading into the house. The two women locked eyes, staring at each other.

Although Malajia was still hurt, she didn't hate Sidra.

For that, she couldn't just let Sidra leave without saying something to her. They hadn't spoken in days. "Be safe," Malajia said.

Sidra looked like she wanted to say something in return, but decided against it. Rolling her eyes, she just stepped into her car. Malajia didn't wait for the car to pull off; she sucked her teeth and headed in the house.

As Malajia shut the door, she saw Chasity walk down the steps. They stopped in front of each other and Malajia's eyes widened at the stern look on Chasity's face. *Shit, she wants to talk,* Malajia panicked. She had been intentionally avoiding a conversation with Chasity. Suddenly, Malajia retrieved the phone from her pocket and put it to her ear.

"Yeah? ...No I already said—"

"Malajia," Chasity stared at her for a moment as she folded her arms. "You know there's nobody on that phone."

"Chaz, you're being rude. I'm talking," Malajia spat, pointing to the phone.

Chasity took a deep breath and pinched the bridge of her nose. She was trying her best to remain calm. "It didn't even *ring.*"

Malajia put her finger up to silence her as she continued talking.

Fed up, Chasity sucked her teeth. "Fine," she huffed, storming out of the house, slamming the door in the process.

Malajia removed the phone from her ear and sighed as she flopped down on the chair. "Great...just great," she muttered to herself, defeated.

# Chapter 20

"You're leaving tonight?" David asked, standing in Nicole's doorway.

"Yeah," she nodded. "My bus leaves in an hour actually."

David glanced at the floor. "Oh," he said, rubbing the back of his neck. He had hoped that he could go to a movie with Nicole that night, thinking that they both wouldn't be leaving until the next day. That hope was gone once Nicole called him and told him that she would in fact be leaving that afternoon. "I hope you have a safe trip."

"Thanks," she muttered, placing some items in the top of her closet.

"You need a ride to the bus stop?" he asked. "I can see if Mark will let me hold his car for a few...I can even wait with you."

Nicole flung her twists over her shoulder. "No need, I have a ride already," she said, tone sharp. "My friend is going to take me."

David, noticing her tone and stiff demeanor, looked concerned. "Is something wrong?"

"You mean besides the fact that you've been avoiding me?" Nicole blurted out.

David closed his eyes. *I knew this was coming.* "I'm sorry, I was busy studying," he explained, hoping that Nicole would believe him.

"David, I see you hanging with your friends around campus, so you're *not* studying every single minute of every single day," she argued. David looked guilty. "So obviously there is something wrong here. Even though you're pretending it's *not.*"

David could've kicked himself. Nicole was feeling insecure and angry with him, and he could solve that by simply telling her the truth: that he was a virgin and that he was embarrassed by it. "Nicole, look—" He took a deep breath, trying to find the right words to say. "I'm sorry," was all that he could get out.

Nicole sucked her teeth as she went back to gathering items.

"Look," he said, putting his hand up. "There's nothing wrong here, okay," David lied. "I promise I'll make more time for you."

Nicole stared at him. She couldn't help but soften her frown. *He's so cute when he's nervous.* "You promise?"

David nodded enthusiastically. "Absolutely."

"And you'll stop acting weird when I try to touch you?" she asked.

That question took David by surprise, even though he knew exactly what she meant. "Um, what do you mean?"

She shot him a knowing look. "David—"

David crossed the room and wrapped his arms around Nicole in a tight, secure hug. *Please drop this subject.* Nicole, seemingly happy for his touch, wrapped her arms around him in return, relishing the hug.

"I'm gonna miss you," she crooned against his chest, feeling better.

"I'll miss you too," David smiled as they parted.

Hearing a knock at the door, Nicole spun around. "It's open."

"Yo, you ready to get to this bus stop?" Quincy asked, entering the room.

David's eyes widened slightly. *The hell? Him again!*

"My bad, what's good man?" Quincy nodded to David.

*Well...Nothing now!* "You're taking Nicole to the bus stop?" he asked, trying to keep as calm as he possibly could.

"David, he has to ride by there on his way to work, so he offered to take me," Nicole cut in, grabbing her bag.

David just stared at her.

"Is that an issue?" she asked.

*Your ex-friend with benefits giving you a ride, yes, it's an issue.* "Um—"

"Man, no disrespect, I was just looking out for a friend," Quincy cut in.

David wanted to throw something right at his face. But the last thing he needed was for Quincy to see him rattled. "No it's—" he cleared his throat. "It's cool."

Nicole stared at David. "You sure?"

*No.* "Sure, I'd take you myself but I have no car—" *Damn it! Shut up David, you already look pathetic.* "I mean, have a safe trip Nicole."

Nicole walked over and gave David a kiss on the cheek. "I'll call you when I get home, okay?"

David feigned a smile. "Okay."


"You riding home with Chaz, or are your peoples coming to pick you up?" Mark asked Jason, watching him fix a sandwich in their kitchen.

"I'm riding with Chaz," Jason answered, scooping mustard out of a small jar. "Heading out tomorrow."

"Yeah, me too," Mark said. "Leaving in the morning that is."

Jason nodded as he put the finishing touches on his turkey and cheese sandwich.

"Yo, can you make me one?" Mark asked.

"No," Jason said, placing the top back on the mustard and mayonnaise.

"Come on bro, look out for the cookout," Mark pleaded, holding his arms up.

Jason raised an eyebrow. "*What* cookout?" he sneered, earning a chuckle from Mark. "And no, make your own." He moved the sandwich items in Mark's direction.

Mark rolled his eyes. "Fine," he muttered, grabbing a plate. As he began to prepare his sandwich, he let out a sigh. Pausing, Mark glanced up at the cabinet as Jason opened a bag of chips. "Bro, can I ask you a serious question?"

"Sure," Jason answered.

"How do you stay out of issues between Chasity and the other girls?" Mark asked, tone serious.

Jason paused, mid-bite of a chip. "Meaning?"

Mark faced him, folding his arms. "I mean...when Chaz gets into it with the other girls...how do you stay out of it? Like, how do you not let it affect *your* relationship with them?"

Jason set his food down. "This about Malajia and Sidra?" He knew exactly what had happened; Chasity had told him when she left her house that night after Mark came to tend to Malajia. He also knew how *she* felt about the situation.

"Yeah," Mark admitted. "I mean, I love Sidra like a sister, you know that." Jason nodded. "But yo, she said some foul shit to my lady and I don't appreciate that shit."

"I hear you," Jason sympathized.

"So, how do you *deal* with that? 'Cause I want to check Sidra's ass," Mark vented. "I mean I'm not gonna come at her disrespectful. But she's dead wrong and needs to be told about her damn self."

Jason sighed. He knew exactly how Mark was feeling. Being with Chasity, he'd witnessed her get into it with pretty much everyone. "Look, I won't lie. It's hard," Jason admitted. "When Chaz got into it with the girls, with *Malajia* especially, she was hurt and I *hate* to see her hurt."

"It's rough bro," Mark sighed, running a hand over his head. "Seeing Mel cry, makes me want to tear this whole fuckin' *campus* down."

"Yep," Jason agreed. "Brick by brick."

"You damn right," Mark followed up.

"But we *both* know that eventually, they're going to work it out. They always *do*," Jason pointed out. "As much as we *want* to step in, we *can't*."

"Have you ever given any of them the cold shoulder over a fight?" Mark asked.

"Probably," Jason chuckled. "Some things I can't help."

Mark gave a nod. "I'll just throw my cold shoulder heavy at Sidra until she apologizes," he said. "She *better* apologize to my baby."

Jason patted Mark on his shoulder. "They'll be fine," he assured.

Mark nodded in appreciation, then went back to making his sandwich. As Jason grabbed his food and proceeded to head out of the kitchen, Mark had another thought. "One more thing Jase."

Jason turned and faced him, not saying a word.

"Is Chasity mad at Malajia?" Mark put out.

Jason looked confused.

"Over what she did?" Mark clarified.

Jason shook his head. "She's not mad, she's...*bothered*."

"Damn...that's what she was afraid of," Mark sulked.

"It's not what you think," Jason assured. "They'll talk about it. Don't worry."

Mark managed a smile. "Thanks man," he said as Jason headed up the steps. Mark stood still for several moments, thoughts wandering, before going back to his sandwich.


"How are you getting back to Jersey?" Alex asked Emily as both girls carried their bags down the steps.

"Brad is coming to pick me up," Emily answered, plunking her bag down on the floor.

"Well, that's cool," Alex beamed. "But I would've thought that you would ride with *us*."

Emily giggled. "I doubt that Chaz would have driven me to Jersey."

"I'm sure she would've—" Alex insisted.

"No, she *wouldn't* have," Chasity cut in, walking from the kitchen.

Emily laughed as Alex shook her head. "*See?* Told you," Emily said.

Alex waved her hand dismissively as Chasity headed up the steps.

Malajia poked her head out of her room as Chasity walked into her room and shut her door. Relieved that the door was shut, Malajia grabbed her bag and proceeded to head for the steps. Right before she was able to make it downstairs, Chasity's room door opened.

"Malajia, come here," Chasity demanded.

*Shit!* "Chaz, my parents are on their way," Malajia informed, glancing at her watch.

"They're not here *now*, so come here," Chasity urged, signaling Malajia with her finger.

Malajia rolled her eyes. "What do you want?"

"What do you *think*?" Chasity returned.

"You want to talk *now*?" Malajia ground out. "We're about to leave for break."

"No shit," Chasity sneered. "Now if you want to make this difficult, we *can*."

Malajia, drained and in no mood to argue, dropped her bag on the floor and walked, arms folded, past Chasity and into her room. Chasity followed and shut the door. Malajia flopped down on Chasity's bed as Chasity stood with her back against the door, folding her arms.

"You didn't have to threaten me," Malajia began, annoyed.

"You're in here, aren't you?" Chasity returned, unfazed my Malajia's anger.

"Whatever," Malajia mumbled. "You wanna talk? Talk."

"Why are you avoiding me?" Chasity charged.

Malajia frowned. "I'm not—"

"Don't lie to me, Malajia," Chasity fumed. "You *are*. And I want to know *why*?"

Malajia let out a groan. She wasn't planning on having this conversation, but it was clear that Chasity wasn't letting up, so she figured she might as well get it out. "Why do you *think?*"

"*You* tell *me*," Chasity insisted.

"Because I didn't want to *have this* damn conversation," Malajia fussed. "You think I want to hear why you're pissed at me? You think I want to argue with you? *Especially* now?"

"You think I'm mad at you?" Chasity was curious as to where Malajia was going with her accusation.

"Yes! Yes, I think you're mad at me," Malajia erupted, bolting from the bed. "I know that you *hate* the fact that I got an abortion... There, I said it."

Chasity frowned. "I don't hate the fact that you got an abortion," she said, much to Malajia's surprise. "What? You think I mirror Sidra's feelings about it? Huh?"

Malajia turned away, not bothering to answer.

"Well, I *don't*," Chasity spat out. "Contrary to what you think about me, I don't judge people on shit like that. It's not my place."

"I don't think that about you," Malajia said, facing her.

"Yeah, you *do*," Chasity argued. "But I'm telling you to your face that I don't hate *or* judge you for what you did."

Malajia took a deep breath. "You don't?"

Chasity shook her head, no. "I *am* however, irritated with you," she added.

Malajia stared at her. "Why?"

Chasity took a step forward. "Malajia, why did you feel that you had to go by yourself?" she asked.

Malajia looked at the floor. "I had nobody to go with me," she muttered.

"No?" Chasity pressed, angry. "Nobody? Not *one* person could have been there for you while you went through that?"

Malajia closed her eyes and let out a sigh. She knew what Chasity was hinting at. "Chaz—"

"*Nobody*?!" Chasity yelled.

"I couldn't tell you okay!" Malajia yelled back. "I just— I *couldn't* tell you."

"Why *not*?" Chasity demanded.

"How could I look you in the face after you lost *your*

baby and tell you that I was getting rid of *mine*?!" Malajia belted out.

Chasity's eyes widened at Malajia's revelation. Malajia felt herself tear up. "I couldn't tell you." Her voice cracked slightly.

Chasity stared at Malajia as she tried to process what she'd just heard. "So...the reason why you went by yourself...is because of *me*."

Malajia wiped a tear from her eye. "That's not what I'm—" Flustered, she let out a loud sigh. "I couldn't tell Mark, I couldn't tell my parents, the other girls—" she shook her head. "The only person I *would* have, was you."

"But because I had a miscarriage, you *didn't*," Chasity finished. She shook her head when Malajia looked at the floor. "Mel...I don't want you to *ever* feel like you can't tell me something. That I wouldn't be there for you," she said, voice stern.

"Chaz—"

"Listen to me," Chasity interrupted. "I appreciate that you cared about my feelings, but I'm irritated with you because, you put *mine* before yours."

Malajia didn't say anything, she just listened.

"If you didn't *want* to tell me, fine, but the fact that you felt you *couldn't*..." Chasity didn't know when it had happened, but she felt herself getting emotional. "It sucks because—I would've been there for you, like you were there for *me*... You didn't have to go through that by yourself."

Malajia glanced up at Chasity. To see tears in her friend's eyes, just made Malajia appreciate their friendship even more, and made her realize that she was worried over nothing.

"I'm sorry," Chasity said.

Malajia tilted her head. "Why are you apologizing?"

"For making you feel like I wouldn't support you."

Malajia reached out and hugged Chasity, who in turn wrapped her arms around her. "I don't think that," she assured. "It was my own stupid conscious. I know that you care about me. I know that you would've been there."

The women parted from their embrace and Chasity wiped the tears from her eyes. "If you know that, then stop being stupid," Chasity jeered, giving Malajia a soft tap to the side of her head. A gesture that made Malajia crack a smile. "I'm serious. I don't care *what* it is. If you need somebody, I'm here. I may not agree with everything, but…I'm *here*."

"I hear you and I know that… Thank you," Malajia replied, grateful.

"At least until we graduate, then you're on your own," Chasity joked.

Malajia laughed. "You always gotta ruin a sentimental moment, you jackass," she chortled. "I've already told you, you're stuck with me."

"Yeah, yeah, I know." Chasity pushed her hair over her shoulder. "You okay?"

"Getting there," Malajia answered honestly.

"I usually don't speak for other people, but…Alex and Emily don't feel any differently about you… They're worried about you though, you should talk to them."

"I will. I know that they've been walking on eggshells around me," Malajia said, running a hand over her hair. "I hate it."

"Yeah," Chasity agreed. "You want me to cuss Sidra out for you?"

Malajia chuckled. "No…she's entitled to her opinion."

"Sidra is judgmental and I hate that shit," she fussed. "I thought *Alex's* ass was bad."

"I know but…it's *her* opinion."

Chasity nodded. "Fine…I won't say anything," she promised. "At *all*."

Malajia gave Chasity a knowing look. "Chaz, don't ice her out."

"Too late," Chasity put out.

Malajia put her hand over her face and shook her head.

# Chapter 21

Jason flipped through his piles of mail as he sat at his family's dining room table. Being home on spring break for two days now, he was finally able to sit down and go through it. "So many damn graduate schools," he griped, eyeing the many envelopes.

Taking a sip of his juice, he turned around when he heard footsteps approach. "Hey Mom," Jason put out, tone dry as his mother walked up to him.

"Hey," Mrs. Adams said, taking a seat at the table with him.

*Great, there goes my peace,* he thought, taking another sip of his juice.

His mother could feel the tension already. "Have you decided on what school you want to apply to?" She asked, at an attempt to make conversation.

"No," Jason answered, opening a letter.

"Oh," she replied. "So, you *have* made the decision to attend grad school?"

Jason read over a letter. "Yes."

"Oh." Mrs. Adams fiddled with her hands. "So…do you have anything planned during your time here?"

Jason pinched the bridge of his nose. *Pleeeaaase just leave me alone.* "Not really," he answered, unenthused.

"You're not going to spend a few days over Chasity's house?" Mrs. Adams pressed.

Jason shot her a glance. "Do you *want* me to spend a few days over Chasity's house?" he asked, some bite in his voice.

"No, of *course* not." His mother let out a quick sigh when he raised an eyebrow at her. "That's not what I meant," she amended. "I meant that... I'm happy that you decided to stay *here.*"

"Yeah well, this is my home, so I have to be here at *some* point," Jason grumbled, gathering his items and rising from the table. He wished more than anything that he would have gone to the store with his father and brother. It would have prevented this very conversation. "I'm gonna go sit out back."

"Jason, wait a minute," Mrs. Adams called at his departing back. Jason stopped and turned around. "I hate this," she said, standing from her seat. "I hate the strain between us."

"*You* caused this, Mom," Jason stated, voice stern. "I'm gonna respect you but I'm *not* gonna pretend like I'm not still upset with you."

"I know," she said. "You're a good son, always *have* been and I hate that I hurt you."

Jason resisted the urge to roll his eyes.

She took a step towards him. "I want to make things right and I have an idea about how to start."

"And that *is*?" Jason asked, curious.

"I think that we should have lunch," his mother suggested, much to Jason's confusion.

"Lunch?" he questioned, frowning. "*That's* how you're going to fix this...by going out to *eat*?"

Mrs. Adams nodded. "Yes," she confirmed. "You, me...Chasity...and her mother."

Jason's eyes nearly popped out of his head at the suggestion. "Wait a minute." He put his hand up. "Mom, I already told you—"

"I know what you said," she cut in. "That if I'm not sincere in my attempt to make things work with Chasity, that you're not going to let me talk to her...I heard you."

"So, what are you *doing*?" Jason asked.

"I sincerely want to have a sit down and talk to her. To

get to know her," she proposed. "And since I know that you probably won't allow a sit down between us *alone*, I figured you can come and as a mother, I'm sure *her* mother wouldn't mind meeting either."

"*Her* mother knows me," Jason spat.

"I'm sure she does," Mrs. Adams returned. "But she doesn't know *me* and I'm curious to meet her, just as I'm sure, she would be curious to meet *me*."

*Yeah, she's curious alright*, Jason thought. He had a pretty good idea of how Trisha felt about his mother, having heard things from Chasity. He just remained silent as his mother continued to talk.

"Besides, if you two are going to be together, I think it will be a good idea for *all* of us to talk, you know."

"Um..." Jason slowly put out, still skeptical.

"So do you think that you can convince them both to come?" his mother asked, hopeful.

Jason rubbed his chin with his hand as he pondered the suggestion. As much as he wanted to tell his mother no, Jason couldn't overlook the fact that she seemed to be making an effort. Something that he had begged her to do in the past. Though he was still cautious, he decided that it was worth a shot.

"I'll talk to Chasity to see how she feels," he promised.

Mrs. Adams flashed a smile, the first one since Jason had been home. "Thank you, sweetie," she gushed, walking over and giving him a hug. "As soon as you get confirmation, I'll make the reservation," she stated, parting from their brief embrace.

"Okay," Jason replied, watching her walk out of the dining room. Once the room was clear, he let out a sigh. He already knew that this wasn't going to be an easy conversation between him and Chasity.

Chasity sat across a small bistro table, staring at Jason with disbelief. "She *what*?" she ground out.

Jason sighed as he reached for his sandwich. "Yep. Lunch, with you and Ms. Trisha." Jason knew that he had to tell Chasity about his mother's proposal, however he didn't want to do it over the phone. Instead, he opted to take her to lunch to break the news. In a public place, Jason figured that Chasity would be less inclined to throw something.

Chasity put her elbows on the table and leaned her face on her fingertips. "Jason...I don't know," she hesitated. Chasity wanted Jason to get back to a good place with his mother, but she wished it didn't require her having to actually talk to Mrs. Adams.

"I understand your apprehension. I'm a little apprehensive *myself*," Jason admitted. "But I want to believe that she's making an effort for my sake. I at least want to give her that chance."

Chasity rolled her eyes.

"I'll be there with you," he promised.

"I know that, and I know that you'll do your best to not let her say or do anything slick," Chasity replied, meeting his gaze. "But after the shit she pulled last semester, I don't know if I can sit and be civil."

Jason sighed yet again. "I completely understand."

"And you *know* my *mother* won't be able to either," Chasity pointed out. "Trisha has been *begging* me to let her get at your mom for a while now."

"Yeah, I know," Jason said, rubbing his face.

"Only because of the fact that she's your mother, did I tell her to back off," Chasity added. "If she sits at that table with your mom, there is no telling what she might say or *do*."

Jason leaned back in his seat. "This is a whole goddamn mess," he commented.

"Yep," Chasity agreed.

Jason shook his head. "I'm sorry that it's *my* mom who is causing this nonsense," he began. "I can handle the tension, but I don't *like* it. I want us to have peace. I want our families to get along."

"I know," Chasity sighed, poking at her sandwich.

"I just…if this sit down can start the process of us achieving that then I would like for us to give it a shot." Jason held a pleading gaze on Chasity. "I promise, if I feel like anything crazy is going to happen, I'll get you out of there and I'll never ask you to do it again."

Chasity hesitated for a moment as she pondered the invitation. "Fine, I'll go," she reluctantly agreed. "I'll get Mom to come too."

Jason smiled gratefully. "Thank you so much." He raised an eyebrow. "You think you can control her temper?" he joked.

Chasity shot him a knowing look. "I can't even control my *own* temper, you think I can control *hers*?" she mocked.

Jason couldn't help but let out a little laugh.

"But I'll handle it," she assured.

Jason reached over, grabbed her hand and kissed it. "You know I appreciate you."

"You damn well *better*," Chasity hissed through clenched teeth, giving Jason's hand a slight twist.

"Ouch," he winced. "That was petty."

"Why do you think I did it?" Chasity replied, unfazed.

Jason just shook his head at her. "Smart ass."


"You sure you're gonna be okay here, by yourself?" Dru asked, gathering his briefcase and coffee mug from his kitchen table.

Emily closed the refrigerator door, a carton of milk in hand; she chuckled. "I'm twenty-one years old, I *think* I can handle being in an apartment by myself."

"Funny," Dru returned, rubbing his chin with his hand. "I've moved since you were last in Jersey, so was just making sure you were cool in this new area."

"I'll be fine. If I get lost, I'll just find a nice policeman to get me back to my parents," Emily mocked.

Dru laughed. "Okay fine," he relented, heading for the door. "Oh, if Brad drops by, *please* don't let him in the fridge. I swear he's been stealing food."

Emily giggled. "You went from sharing an apartment, to moving into the same building," she said, pouring some milk into a bowl of cereal. "You two never *could* be separated."

"He *follows* me, I can't shake him." Dru shook his head, opening the door. "Later."

Emily waved to him as she placed the now empty milk carton in the trash. Grabbing her bowl, she made her way to the living room and flopped down on the couch. She flipped on the TV and scooped a spoonful of cereal out of the bowl. As soon as she put the spoon into her mouth, she heard her cell phone ring. Luckily for her, she'd left it on the coffee table after she'd spoken to her father earlier.

Smiling, she reached for the phone. "I hope this is you, Will," she said to herself. Not taking her eyes off the flat screen television in front of her, she answered the phone. "Hello?"

There was a brief pause. "Emily...its Mommy."

Emily choked on the cereal in her mouth. *What the hell?!* That was the last person that she was expecting. Setting her bowl down, Emily patted her chest and began coughing. Once she gathered herself, she placed the phone back to her ear. "Um...yes?" she answered, after clearing her throat.

"Are you okay?" Ms. Harris asked, voice not hiding her concern. "You sounded like you were choking."

"Just a little," Emily replied, tensing in her seat. "I'm okay though."

"How is your break so far?" Ms. Harris asked.

Emily pulled the phone away from her ear and stared at it. Her mother was acting way too nice. After their last encounter, she was expecting hostility. "It's fine, I'm staying with Dru," Emily finally answered.

"I know, Dru told me."

"Of *course* he did," Emily mumbled. *The snitch strikes again.*

"Listen, I wanted to ask you something," Ms. Harris

began.

Emily let out a sigh. "Yes?"

"Can you come over to the house sometime before you leave to go back to school?" her mother inquired.

That question took Emily by surprise. "Huh?"

"I would like to see you," Ms. Harris reiterated.

The last thing that Emily wanted to do on her break was have another argument with her mother. "Mom I—"

"Emily, please can you just stop over?" she insisted. "I'll make some lunch and we can talk."

*No! She just wants to yell at you some more!* Emily wanted more than anything to listen to the voice in her head. But once again she relented. She stomped her foot on the floor and let out a sigh. *You'll never learn.* "Okay," Emily answered finally, in her best "sweet" voice. "When I decide which day, I'll let you know."

"Sounds good," Ms. Harris gushed, smile practically beaming through the line. "Do you want me to make you anything in particular?"

"No, whatever you want to make is fine." Emily had a thought. "Mom…Jaz isn't going to be there is she?" Seeing her mother was one thing, but she refused to lay eyes on her big sister. That was negative energy that she could not handle.

Ms. Harris sighed. "No, she won't."

"Then I'll see you soon," Emily said.

"Good. Can't wait."

Emily shook her head. *That makes one of us.* "Bye Mom."

Upon ending the phone call, Emily glanced at the bowl of cereal. "There goes my appetite," she grunted.


Malajia adjusted the fluffy white robe as she leaned back against a cushy sofa. "That mani-pedi was *everything*, Mom," she mused, examining her freshly manicured nails.

"I'm liking this color, too. Never thought to try this iridescent shade."

Mrs. Simmons glanced over at Malajia's outstretched hand. "Yeah, I like that," she agreed of the shiny purplish color. Making good on her promise to Malajia about spending time at a spa together, Mrs. Simmons took her daughter to a day spa. They enjoyed facials, body scrubs, manicures, pedicures, and were now relaxing in a private room, while they awaited their massages.

Mrs. Simmons leaned back against the cushions. "I swear, I can live here," she cooed, relishing the sound of the fountain and the flicker of the tea light candles around the room.

"Now you know Dad and those critters you call children, won't let you go," Malajia teased.

"*Who?*" Mrs. Simmons joked, earning a laugh from Malajia. "No, my family is my life, y'all know that."

Malajia nodded. "Yeah," she agreed. She adjusted herself on the couch so that she would be facing her mother. "Mom, thanks again for bringing me here."

Mrs. Simmons glanced over at her. "No problem," she smiled. "I promised you that I would... Besides, you seem like you needed some relaxation."

*Tell me about it*, Malajia thought as her mother continued.

"We *both* did," Mrs. Simmons added, adjusting the belt of her robe. "It's nice to spend some time together, just the two of us."

Malajia nodded. "Yeah," she admitted. "I know that a lot of times, especially before last year, I made it seem like I never wanted to hang with you...or that you embarrassed me... I mean you *did*—"

"That *one* time," Mrs. Simmons cut in, laughing.

Malajia shot her mother a knowing look. "Mom, between you leaving the house in a raggedy scarf, cussing me out in public, and you trying to hit me with that shoe every five minutes... You were embarrassing."

"Well, if you didn't show your *ass*, maybe you wouldn't have *gotten* the shoe," she threw back.

Malajia shook her head as her laughter subsided. "No but it *is* nice to spend time together." She leaned her elbow on the back of the couch. "I guess the older I get, the more I realize how important it is to have a close relationship with you guys."

"I know that I didn't always make it easy for you to come talk to me," Mrs. Simmons said, tone somber.

Malajia glanced down. "Mom, that's not what I meant—"

"I know, but as a mother I should have made more time for you," she insisted. "And made sure that I acknowledged you *all* the time, not only when you did something wrong."

Malajia learned after her youngest sister was born, that she only seemed to gain attention from her parents when she got on their nerves. Subconsciously, she acted out, exaggerated stories and purposely irritated them. Not because she enjoyed getting yelled at, but because Malajia was crying for their attention. It was a relief that her mother finally saw that. "Not gonna lie, it's funny seeing you guys get all red in the face when you're mad," Malajia said at an attempt at a joke.

Mrs. Simmons held a gaze on her daughter. "Don't make jokes," she said, stern. "You make jokes to avoid getting into deep conversations. You're an adult now; it's time to stop that."

"Okay," Malajia mouthed, focusing her attention on a nearby candle.

"So," Mrs. Simmons began, giving Malajia a pat on her knee. "How are things? I mean outside of classes. How are you?"

Malajia forced a smile. "I'm fine," she said.

"How's Mark?" her mother asked. "Everything good with you two?"

Malajia let a genuine smile come through at the mention of Mark. "Yeah, things are good with us," she said, pushing her hair behind her ears. "He really *is* a good man."

Mrs. Simmons smiled. "I *know* he is," she agreed. "Despite what your crazy father thinks, *I* always liked Mark."

"You lie like a rug," Malajia laughed.

"No, I'm serious," Mrs. Simmons insisted, amused. "I mean, he's always been silly and a bit over the top but then again, so are *you*. So…I like him. You two fit."

"True," Malajia agreed. "Thanks." Malajia was truly enjoying the conversation with her mother. She felt comfortable, like she could tell her anything…like she *wanted* to tell her *everything.*

"How are the girls?" Mrs. Simmons asked, unaware of Malajia's burdening thoughts.

She glanced away. "Um…they're fine," she muttered. "Chasity…Alex…Emily…they're fine."

Mrs. Simmons frowned. "And *Sidra?*"

"I don't know," Malajia answered vaguely. "Can't say that I really *care* right now."

"You two have a fight or something?" her mother asked.

"You could say that," Malajia replied.

"Oh… Well, that's a shame," Mrs. Simmons commented, eyeing one of the spa workers open the door to their room. "Nobody wants to fight with their friends, but you'll make up. You always *do.*"

Malajia stared at her nails. "Maybe."

"You want to tell me what happened? Maybe I can offer some advice on how to fix whatever the problem is," Mrs. Simmons signaled for the worker to approach. "I *am* the mother of seven girls after all. All you girls *do* is fight."

"Um…" Malajia hesitated. In order to tell her mother about what happened with Sidra, Malajia would have to divulge *all* the information, and that was something that she was trying to get the courage to do. "I *do*, but—"

"Sorry to interrupt but would you ladies care for some sparkling wine?" the woman asked, holding a tray with two glasses and a bottle of sparkling wine sitting on top of it.

"Yes please," Malajia immediately cut in before her

mother had a chance to respond. She was going to need some liquid courage.

Smiling, the woman filled both glasses with the bubbly beverage and set them on the table in front of them. Malajia reached for her glass as the woman walked away, taking the bottle with her.

"Can you leave the bottle?" Malajia blurted out. Mrs. Simmons raised an eyebrow at Malajia as the woman complied. Once she was out of the room, Mrs. Simmons turned to Malajia, who had begun downing her drink.

"You plan on getting drunk before we go eat lunch?" Mrs. Simmons quipped.

Malajia didn't answer as she drank the rest of her beverage. She then poured herself another glass and prepared to drink it, but decided against it. Setting the glass down, Malajia sighed, running her hand over her face. "Mom, I have to tell you something," Malajia began. "But...you have to promise not to hate me afterwards."

Mrs. Simmons frowned. "Why would you say that? I could never hate you."

*Don't be so sure.* "Can you promise me?" Malajia pressed, staring long at her mother.

Mrs. Simmons began to get worried, based off Malajia's tone and nervous look. "I promise...what's up?"

"Um...I have something to tell you."

"You *said* that," Mrs. Simmons's tone was comforting. "So what is it?" she gestured to Malajia's glass. "Judging by the way you downed that wine, I'm pretty sure you're not pregnant." She waited for Malajia to respond. When she didn't, opting instead to glance at her hands, Mrs. Simmons gently grabbed Malajia's chin and guided her gaze towards her. "*Are* you?"

Malajia shook her head. "No, I'm not pregnant," she assured. Seemingly relieved, her mother removed her hand from her chin and let out a sigh. "I um...I *was* though," Malajia revealed.

Mrs. Simmons fixed a stern gaze. "You were *what?*"

Malajia felt like she wanted to get up and run out of the spa, but she had already started her confession; she might as well finish it. "I was...pregnant." Malajia wished that she could block out the horrified look on her mother's face.

"Malajia," her mother breathed. "Honey, I—"

"You always told me to use protection, I know," Malajia cut in. "I heard you... I just didn't *listen*."

Mrs. Simmons put her hand over her face as she took several deep breaths in an effort to calm herself. She knew that Malajia was grown, so an angry reaction wasn't something that she wanted to give. "Okay, okay," she repeated, as if she was giving herself a pep talk. She then put her hand up. "Wait, you said *was*," she recalled. "When?"

Malajia bit her bottom lip. "Um...a little over a year ago..." she fiddled with the fabric on her robe. "It was...Tyrone's."

"That fuckin' abuser?!" Mrs. Simmons erupted. "I *hate* the fact that he *ever* touched you."

"You and me *both*," Malajia agreed.

Mrs. Simmons took a deep breath, calming herself. "So what happened to the baby?" she asked. "Did you miscarry?"

Malajia shook her head as she hesitated to speak. If she thought telling her friends was hard, this was even worse. "I um—when I found out, I just—" Malajia felt like she couldn't breathe, like she was going to explode.

"Malajia, just tell me, sweetie," Mrs. Simmons pressed, calm.

"Mommy, I had an abortion," Malajia blurted out. She sat there, staring at her mother, hoping that she would say something. It was out, and Malajia couldn't take it back. She just wanted a reaction, any reaction. But what she got was a stunned look from her mother.

"Can you say something please?" Malajia begged. Tears filled her eyes when she still got no response. Unable to stand the silence anymore, Malajia went to stand up, but was stopped by her mother's hand grabbing her wrist.

"Sit down," Mrs. Simmons ordered, tone calm, caring.

Before Malajia knew it, her mother had pulled her into a warm hug. Something that Malajia needed. "I'm sorry that you had to go through that," she breathed against Malajia's hair.

Malajia didn't speak; she just held on to her mom as her tears flowed.

"I don't hate you... I'm hurt for you," Mrs. Simmons consoled, rubbing Malajia's back. "No parent wants their children to suffer. We do our best to shield you from things and unfortunately no matter how hard we try, we *can't*."

Malajia moved from her mother's embrace and sniffled as her mother wiped the tears from her face. She found it hard to speak. Telling her mother was a load off, but in releasing that information, her emotions were overwhelming her.

"Does he know?"

Malajia shook her head. "I haven't seen or spoken to that bastard since the last time he put his hands on me."

Mrs. Simmons nodded. "Good," she fumed. If he was standing in that room, she would have killed him herself. "Do you regret it?" she wondered.

"Sometimes," Malajia admitted, through her sniffles. "Um...I know I did what I felt was best at the time, but I can't help but wonder if..." She shook her head as she wiped some tears from her cheeks. "My thoughts are all over the damn place and I don't know how to deal with them. I thought I was okay, and then one year hit and I just started feeling depressed."

"I'm going to take you to the family doctor just to get you checked out," Mrs. Simmons stated. "I know that you've probably already been to one down in Virginia, but for my own sanity, *I'm* taking you, okay?"

Malajia nodded.

Mrs. Simmons stared at Malajia. "I know how you feel," she said after a moment. Malajia looked confused. "I know, because...*I* had one myself."

Malajia's eyes widened. "You *what*?"

"Yeah," Mrs. Simmons admitted. "I was young, and this was before I had any of you girls…before I met your father even. I had unprotected sex with my boyfriend at the time, and it happened," she recalled. "I told my mother and she told me that it was on me and that she wasn't going to help me…not that I blamed her. But I wasn't ready to be a mother and he wasn't ready to be a father…so I made the decision."

Malajia had no idea about any of this. "Does Dad know about this?"

Mrs. Simmons nodded. "Yes. I told him not long after we started getting serious," she answered.

Malajia took a few deep breaths. She felt some relief, that someone knew how she was feeling. "Does it get better?"

"Like anything else, with time things heal… You don't forget, but you eventually find peace with it," Mrs. Simmons placated. "I still think about it from time to time. But I'm at peace. One day *you* will be too."

Malajia used the sleeve of her robe to wipe her face. "I swear to God, I could never do this again."

"I hope that you wouldn't *have* to."

"Yeah," Malajia agreed, wiping her face once more.

"Does Mark know?"

Malajia nodded. "Yeah and he's been supportive," she said.

Mrs. Simmons gave Malajia's arm a rub. "Good," she approved.

"Mom, can you please not tell anybody about this?" Malajia pleaded.

"Of *course* I won't," Mrs. Simmons promised.

Malajia looked down at her hands. "Dad either," she muttered.

Mrs. Simmons sighed. "I don't make it a practice to keep things from your father. *Especially* when it comes to our children," she stated. Malajia sighed. "But, I won't say anything… You'll need to tell him eventually."

Malajia was full of dread. "He'll kill me, Mom."

"No, he won't," Mrs. Simmons assured. "You're his daughter, the most *like* him actually. Will he be upset? Yes. He'll hurt for you but he won't hate you."

Malajia just glanced off to the side.

"You don't need to do it now," Mrs. Simmons assured. "But when you're ready, you *should*."

"Okay." Malajia had no idea when she would be ready to tell her father, she just knew that it wouldn't be any time soon.

"You feeling a little better?" Mrs. Simmons asked, pushing some of Malajia's hair behind her shoulder. Malajia nodded. "I love you, Malajia."

"Love you too."

"You want some more wine?" her mother asked.

"No, I think I'm good," Malajia said, putting her hand up. "I just realized that stuff is nasty."

Her mother giggled.

# Chapter 22

Sidra poked at the food on the plate in front of her. The shrimp pasta with pesto that she had ordered certainly smelled good, but she just couldn't bring herself to eat it. She had been sitting at the small table in a corner of an Italian restaurant for the past half hour, just staring at it.

Sighing, she reached for her glass of seltzer with lemon and took a sip as she grabbed the cell phone from her purse. Scrolling through her phone, she noticed a few text messages from James. Rolling her eyes, she scrolled by them. *I'm not in the mood for him right now*, she thought.

Dialing a number, she put the phone to her ear. "Chasity pick up, you know you see me calling," she grunted as the phone kept ringing. When it went to voicemail, she sucked her teeth. "Bitch," she hissed to herself. That had been the fifth time that she'd called Chasity within the past few days with no answer.

Seeing another message pop up from James, Sidra let out a huff. "Fine," she grunted, dialing his number.

"Are you ignoring me?" James charged, picking up after the first ring.

Sidra pinched the bridge of her nose. She hadn't spoken to James since before she left school for spring break. That was nearly four days ago and even then, the conversation was brief. She stuck to telling him what happened with the baby but that was the extent of it. "No, I'm not," she lied. "I'm having lunch, so I had my phone on silent."

"Oh…are you at home?" he wondered.

Sidra took another sip of her drink. "No, I'm at a restaurant."

"Out with friends?"

"Nope, by myself." Sidra's tone was unenthused, a bit sharp even. "Left the hairdresser earlier and decided to stop in."

"I thought you hated eating out alone," James commented.

"Yeah, well nobody is here to eat with me, so I have no choice."

The sniping wasn't missed by James. "Sidra...what's the problem?"

"I don't have a problem," Sidra returned, defiantly.

"I beg to differ," James insisted, tone stern. "You have an attitude. And while I understand that you're still upset over what happened, you don't have to take it out on *me*."

Sidra looked at her phone in disbelief before putting it back to her ear. "Who are you talking to?"

"Excuse me?"

"You heard me," she fussed. "Don't tell me how to feel. What? You like it better when I just smile and pretend everything is okay? You like when I do that?"

There was a pause on the line. "Sidra, calm down."

"Don't tell—" Sidra paused and glanced around the half-empty restaurant. She realized, by a few glances, that she had just yelled. Letting out a sigh, she leaned her elbow on the table. "James...I'm not in the mood for this conversation right now."

"Doesn't matter, I haven't spoken to you in days and *clearly* you're upset."

"If you tell me that I should get over it—"

"Stop," James cut in, halting Sidra's rant. "I'm not referring to your brother. I'm *referring* to the other thing and we need to talk about it," he pressed.

"Talk...about...what?" Sidra was on the verge of throwing her phone on the floor.

"You're still pissed at me because I didn't answer when you called that night."

"James—"

"I already *told* you that I was in court," James cut in. "I *couldn't* answer my phone."

Sidra's free hand balled up the napkin on her lap. "You weren't even arguing your case that night."

"So *what*?" James argued. "I had to listen, take notes. Sidra, you're a future lawyer, you should be *somewhat* aware of the rules by now."

Sidra sucked her teeth.

"And I called you back as soon as I was *able* to, but you didn't answer," he reminded.

"Yes, I know that," Sidra spat out.

"Then what is the attitude for?"

Sidra rolled her eyes. She knew that she was acting a bit unreasonable. Yet Sidra still felt that if James had only noticed that she'd called several times and sent several messages within a few minutes, that he could've sent a text or something, acknowledging her. Then again, it wasn't his fault that any of this happened, so giving James a hard time about it all was unnecessary. "I'm fine now, forget it," she said after a moment.

"Are you sure?"

"Yeah," she muttered.

James let out a sigh. "Look Sidra, I don't want you to *not* express yourself," he began. "But, there is a better way of doing it," he chided. "If you were upset with me in the beginning, fine. But ignoring me and being short was not the way to handle it."

Sidra frowned. *Is he chastising me? Like a fuckin' child?* She rubbed her forehead. *I need to calm myself before I cuss him a new ass.* "James, I gotta go."

James sighed again. "Fine Sidra, I'll call you later."

"Uh huh," Sidra said in a phony 'nice' voice before ending the call. Resolved to not eating, Sidra signaled to the waiter for the check.


The drive from the restaurant to her home was a short one. Sidra didn't care about the highway that day; she wished that she could have driven longer. Emerging from her car, she slowly approached the door of her house. Upon entering, she acknowledged her mother, who was sitting in the living room, on the couch, talking on the phone. Sidra tossed her purse on the stand near the door and proceeded to the kitchen, doggie bag in hand.

"I'll call you later," Mrs. Howard whispered into the phone. Hanging the phone up, she looked at Sidra's departing figure. "Sidra can you come here, please?" she called.

Sidra turned around and headed back into the living room. "Yeah Mama?" her voice, like her eyes, were tired.

Mrs. Howard patted the cushion next to her on the couch. "Come sit down."

Sidra stood there. "Can whatever this is, wait?" she pleaded. She was in no mood for any conversation or even company at that point. "I just want to put this food away and go take a nap."

"Set your food on the stand and come here, please," Mrs. Howard ordered, tone calm.

Sidra let out a loud sigh as she set her bag down. "Fine," she huffed under her breath.

"You say something?" Mrs. Howard asked as Sidra approached the couch.

"No," Sidra lied, flopping down next to her mother. She folded her arms like a child and stared at the wall in front of her.

Mrs. Howard gave her a once over. "Your hair looks nice," she said of Sidra's flowing curls, which hung to her chest.

Sidra gave her mother a side-glance. *I know damn well this isn't what you wanted to talk to me about.* "Thank you. I had the ends trimmed a bit," she said. "Is it noticeable?"

Mrs. Howard smoothed some of Sidra's hair. "No, not really," she answered.

Sidra took a deep breath. "Mama…you didn't want me to sit here to talk hair, did you?" she asked, trying to keep her temper in check. She might have been irritated, but one person she knew not to snap out on, was her mother. Vanessa Howard may have been prim and proper, but she did not play.

"No, that's not what I want to talk to you about," Mrs. Howard assured. "I talked to Marcus," she revealed after a moment.

Sidra perked up, turning in her seat. "How is he? I still haven't spoken to him," she pressed. "He won't answer the phone."

"He's fine," she answered. "Better, actually."

Sidra frowned. "Better?" she hissed. "How can he be *better* after what happened? I mean, that was his *baby* after all."

Mrs. Howard rubbed one of her hands with the other. "Sidra, India is pregnant."

Sidra's frown grew deeper on her brow. "*Again?*" she fussed.

Mrs. Howard shook her head. "Not again, *still*."

Sidra was utterly confused, and it showed. "I don't—"

"She never got an abortion. She just told *Marcus* that she did."

Sidra's mouth dropped open. "Wait, she *what*?!" she erupted. She was furious. "What kind of—What the hell is *wrong* with her? Why would she put him *through* that? The *family* through that?"

"Because the girl is an idiot," Mrs. Howard stated matter-of-factly. "Marcus left and India was angry, so she told him that she got the abortion to get back at him. Then days ago, she called him and told him that she lied and that she wanted him back." She took a deep breath. "Marcus didn't believe her so he made her go to the doctor with him and they confirmed that the baby is still there. And doing well actually."

Sidra was seething; she shook her head emphatically.

"Mama, I swear if he goes back to her—"

"He assured your father and I that he isn't," Mrs. Howard cut in. "He's gonna support her through the pregnancy then when the baby is born, he's going for custody…well joint. I told him to go for full custody because *clearly* the girl is unstable, but…we know Marcus."

Sidra let out a sigh. "Well I'm glad that the baby is okay." She rubbed the back of her neck. "It's a relief that she didn't actually *do* that horrible thing."

Mrs. Howard stared at her. "Which brings me to the *other* thing that I wanted to talk to you about."

Sidra looked curious, but didn't say anything.

"I spoke to Evelyn today."

Sidra looked unfazed. It wasn't rare for her mother to converse with Malajia's mother. She didn't understand why it was news. "Um…okay."

"And…she told me that she had spoken to Malajia the other day."

Sidra squinted. "*About?*"

"I think you know," Mrs. Howard alluded.

Sidra stared at her mother momentarily, until realization set in. "I don't want to talk about this," she fussed, rising to her feet.

"Sit," Mrs. Howard commanded. Sidra immediately complied. "I can't help but be a little disappointed in you Princess." Mrs. Howard couldn't believe her ears when Malajia's mother informed her of the argument that had happened between Sidra and Malajia. Normally the mothers stayed out of the girls' disagreements, especially now that they were grown women. However, this was something that Mrs. Howard could not let slide without having a conversation with her daughter.

"Mama, can you stay out of this please?"

"No, honey I *can't*," Mrs. Howard insisted. "At least not until I talk to you."

Sidra rolled her eyes. At this point, she was too annoyed and bothered to care about how she came off to her mother. "I don't want to hear it."

"Well you're going to listen *anyway*," Mrs. Howard demanded.

Sidra held her focus on the lamp beside her. She was afraid that if she looked her mother in the eye that she would start to cry. That was the extent of her frustration.

"Did you mean what you said to Malajia?" she asked.

"Yep," Sidra answered immediately, eyes not leaving the object.

Mrs. Howard slowly shook her head. "I don't believe that."

Sidra tossed her hands up in frustration. "What do you want me to say?" she fussed. "You expect me to change my views and my opinion because India lied about the abortion?" she turned in her seat to face her mother.

"So, you're okay with verbally attacking your friend the way that you did?" Mrs. Howard snapped back. "You've known that girl since you two were children, and you're going to sit here in my face and tell me that you are *okay* with tearing her down the way that you did? Over her decision to do something that you should *pray* that you *never* have to do?"

"What exactly did you hear that I said, Mama?" Sidra ground out.

Mrs. Howard frowned. "That you called Malajia selfish, a coward and a *monster* for having her abortion."

Sidra smirked. "Well, for once 'exaggerating Malajia', told the *truth*."

"This is not *funny*, Sidra." Her mother's tone and look were scolding.

"I'm not *laughing*," Sidra countered. "So what? Malajia told *her* mom to tell *my* mom? How elementary school."

"No, actually Malajia asked her not to say anything, but Evelyn told her that she was going to tell me *anyway* because she felt that you needed a talking to," she informed. "We both know how Evelyn is about her girls. The same way that *I* am with you and your brothers. You have been friends *too* long for this."

Sidra shrugged. "Friend or no friend, I still believe what I believe," she maintained. "*That's* not changing."

Mrs. Howard pinched the bridge of her nose. "I understand that. I'm not telling you to change how you feel. I'm just saying that there is a better way that you go about things. Your friend stood there and revealed something to you that I'm sure was hard for her to do and instead of offering your support as her friend, you verbally attack her for it... Does that seem right to you?"

Sidra turned away from her mother once more.

"Judging by your lack of response, I think you know that you were wrong," her mother confirmed.

"I'm wrong about having an opinion?" Sidra felt tears well up.

"No, for how you *reacted*." Mrs. Howard moved some of Sidra's hair over her shoulder. "I know you have compassion, and judging by your tears, you feel it."

Sidra wiped her eyes with the back of her hand.

"I know you don't like to admit that you're wrong...you never *did*," Mrs. Howard said. She grabbed Sidra's hand and held it. "I share your opinion... I don't like the idea of abortions, especially when women use it carelessly. But in *Malajia's* case..." she sighed. "She had a hard decision to make Sidra, and she *made* it. I'm sure she's beating herself up enough... She doesn't need the people she loves to do that to her as well."

Sidra let out a sigh as she shook her head. She was mentally exhausted. She was happy that her niece or nephew was still well, but on the other hand she was feeling the blow up with Malajia.

Mrs. Howard figured that she had said enough. She patted Sidra on her leg. "I'll leave you alone now," she said, then stood from the couch. "Be the woman that I know you are. The woman that I *raised* you to be…go talk to your friend Princess."

"Not right now," Sidra muttered.

"When you're ready."

Sidra watched her mother walk away and head up the steps. Letting out another sigh, she kicked the leg of the coffee table and leaned her head back against the couch cushions. Burdening thoughts swirled in her head.

# Chapter 23

Jason glanced at his watch, then ran his hands down his black button-down shirt. He took a sip of his water and checked the time once again.

"Jason," Mrs. Adams called, reaching for her glass of sangria.

He looked up, eyes wide. "Huh?"

"That's the fourth time that you've looked at your watch," she observed, taking a quick sip of her drink. "We're early."

"I know," Jason returned. He tried to put on a brave front, but he was nervous, *more* than nervous. Days had passed and now he was sitting in a restaurant with his mother, waiting for Chasity and *her* mother to arrive for their planned lunch date.

Mrs. Adams shook her head. "Son. Relax," she urged. "Everything will be fine. I told you, I'm here to play nice."

"What do you mean *play*?" Jason frowned. The last thing he needed after promising Chasity that things would be fine, was his mother playing any games. "Mom seriously, I'm not—"

"I didn't mean it like that," Mrs. Adams insisted, touching his arm. She then grabbed the pitcher of sangria in front of her and filled his glass halfway. "You need to loosen up, Jase. Here, have some of this."

"No no, I think I need something a bit stronger," he said, glancing around for the waiter.

Mrs. Adams shook her head as she sat the pitcher back

in its place. "Suit yourself."

"Mom remember you promised that you were gonna be on your best behavior," Chasity said to Trisha as the two women walked down the busy sidewalk towards the restaurant.

"I didn't promise a *goddamn* thing," Trisha hissed, adjusting the large designer sunglasses on her face.

Chasity rolled her eyes. When she went to Trisha with the news of Nancy Adams's invitation, she wasn't surprised when Trisha jumped at the chance to meet the woman who had been shunning her daughter, face-to-face. Chasity only hoped that Trisha wouldn't do or say anything to make matters worse.

"Mom foreal, I need you to act like you have some sense, okay," Chasity urged, voice stern.

Trisha shot Chasity a side-glance. "Excuse *you*," she ground out.

Chasity narrowed her eyes at Trisha. "Don't do that. Don't act shocked that I'm saying that to you," Chasity returned, unfazed by Trisha's attitude. "I know how you feel about her, I *get* it. But I promised Jason that I would come here and—" she paused when Trisha focused her attention on the sparkling diamond watch on her own wrist. Chasity put her hand over the over-the-top piece of jewelry to grab her mother's attention. "Bring *you* here with good intentions," she finished through clenched teeth.

"My intentions are *fine*," Trisha assured. "She don't start nothin' it won't *be* nothin."

Chasity put her hand over her face and shook her head. She was so much like her mother, it was scary. "I swear to God, I will never understand why I couldn't put the fact that I was your kid together, *years* ago," she mocked.

"Hush," Trisha ordered.

Chasity shot her a glance. "Why do you have on that extra ass watch and that big ass diamond ring I hate?" she wondered, annoyed. "You don't need all those damn diamonds on."

"Look, I bust my ass for my damn diamonds *and yours*, smart ass," Trisha threw back. Chasity made a face. "Besides, little housewife Nancy likes to look down her nose at people, I just figured that I'd give her something sparkly to look at."

"Oh yeah, *that's* not petty and a blatant display of flaunting your wealth," Chasity sniped, rolling her eyes.

Trisha pursed her lips as she stared daggers at Chasity.

"Trisha, chill okay," Chasity ordered. "And the single lady who hasn't had a *date* since I stopped sticking pebbles in my damn diapers, should *not* make snide remarks about someone being a housewife," she mocked.

Annoyed, Trisha gave Chasity's arm a pinch.

"Ouch!" Chasity shrieked, grabbing her arm.

"Keep it up, hear?" Trisha chided. "I've told you about your damn mouth."

"Okay fine," Chasity huffed, giving her arm a rub. Approaching the restaurant, the two walked in.


Jason took a sip of his drink and nearly choked when he saw Chasity and Trisha walk through the doors. As the hostess walked them over, Jason stood from his seat. He greeted Chasity with a kiss to her cheek and a hug, then greeted Trisha with a hug.

"Good to see you again, Jason," Trisha beamed, removing her sunglasses.

"You too, Ms. Trisha," Jason smiled in return.

"Nice to see you again, Chasity," Mrs. Adams smiled, extending her hand.

Chasity stared at it for a moment, then shook her hand. "Likewise," she returned, hoping that her voice sounded pleasant. There were times when Chasity had no idea how her tone would come off.

It must have been polite enough, because Mrs. Adams

just nodded in return.

As everyone sat down, Jason took a deep breath, then looked at his mother. "Mom, this is Chasity's mother Patrisha Duvall... Ms. Trisha this is my mother, Nancy Adams," he introduced. He took a sip of his drink as he and Chasity locked eyes, hoping that neither woman would say anything smart.

Mrs. Adams flashed her smile once again. "Nice to finally meet you," she beamed.

"*Is* it?" Trisha sneered, phony nice voice on one hundred.

Chasity lowered her head as she played with the cloth napkin in front of her. "Jesus," she whispered to herself. *She's already starting.* "Didn't hear a word I said, *did* you?" she said in an aside to Trisha through clenched teeth.

"I heard you just fine," Trisha assured, smile still on her face.

Mrs. Adams, catching the snide response, did her best to not let it bother her. She just signaled for the waiter to come over.

Jason, also feeling the tension, looked at Chasity. "Chaz," he called.

She looked up at him. "Huh?"

"You need a drink?"

"Yes," she answered immediately.

"You want some of this sangria?" he asked, pointing to the pitcher.

"No, no, I need something stronger," she quickly put out. "What do you have in *your* glass?"

"Rum and cola," he answered, pointing to his glass.

"Yeah, I need that."

"I'll order you—"

"No, just give me yours," she insisted, holding her hand out. "Like *right* now."

*Yeah, she's stressed*, Jason observed. *Just like I am.* Without hesitation, he passed his glass to Chasity, who took it and immediately downed the rest of it. She put her hand over her face. "What, did they put a *drop* of soda in there?" she complained, pinching the bridge of her nose.

"Probably," Jason chuckled. The amusement immediately left his face when he noticed that both mothers were just staring at each other, not uttering a word. He let out a sigh, *this is gonna be a long lunch.*

The next hour was spent mostly in silence. Jason and Chasity exchanged awkward glances, accompanied by gestures for one of them to say something. Their mothers spent the time concentrated on eating their food.

Unable to take the silence anymore, Jason looked at Chasity. "Boy am I looking forward to graduation," he blurted out.

Chasity stared at him, fighting to hold her laugher in. "Really? *That's* what you come up with?" she jeered.

Jason couldn't help but laugh. "Well, I *am.*"

Mrs. Adams glanced at Jason, smiling. "You and I *both,* son," she gushed. "We're so proud of you. Have you decided on a graduate school yet?"

"I've filled out a few applications so far," he answered. "Trying to make sure that whichever one I choose has a good computer program."

Mrs. Adams took another sip of her sangria. "Makes sense," she agreed. She looked at Chasity. "So Chasity, are *you* going to graduate school?"

"Probably not," Chasity replied. "Four years has been enough."

"I guess I can understand that," Mrs. Adams nodded. "But I just wonder if you would want to take your education as far as—"

"She *said* she doesn't want to go, so she doesn't *have* to go," Trisha cut in, trying to keep her tempter in check. "Not everybody needs to go to graduate school."

Chasity glanced at Jason as his eyes widened. *And, it starts*, Jason thought.

Mrs. Adams put her hands up. "Wasn't saying that at all," she declared, tone calm, polite even. "Didn't mean anything by it." She reached for her fork and cut another piece of her food. "Chasity, do you still plan on pursuing a job in your chosen field?"

Chasity stared at Mrs. Adams as she continued.

Trisha, meanwhile, was seething. *If this bitch don't stop questioning my damn child.*

"What was it again? Web design?" Mrs. Adams pressed.

*You mean the field that you stated just consisted of me drawing pictures and letting someone smart do the work?* Chasity thought, recalling a snide comment that Mrs. Adams had made in the past. Despite her bitterness, she didn't let it show. "Um, yeah that's the plan," Chasity answered, playing with the straw in her empty water glass. "Might freelance for a while."

Mrs. Adams nodded. "Good," she commented, then turned her attention to Trisha. "So Patrisha, Jason tells me that you own a lucrative real estate company."

Trisha stared at her, eyes narrowing slightly.

"What's it called?" Mrs. Adams prodded.

"PMD Real Estates," Jason answered.

Mrs. Adams snapped her fingers. "That's right," she gasped. "I've heard of them...well *you*."

Trisha folded her arms and sat back in her seat. "I'm sure you *have*," she ground out. "My company brings in well over six figures every year."

"I can imagine," Mrs. Adams returned. "If you don't mind me asking, what does PMD stand for?"

"Patrisha Marie Duvall," Chasity answered, sensing her mother's agitation with the twenty questions.

"Oh..." Mrs. Adams took another sip of her drink. "I noticed Chasity, that *your* last name is different from your mother's."

Chasity and Trisha both looked confused, and so did Jason, who shot his mother a scolding look. "Mom, really?" Jason hissed.

Mrs. Adams looked shocked. "What? I'm just making an observation," she defended. "Trying to get to know them, that's all."

Trisha's temper was reaching the boiling point. She already had ill feelings for the woman before even laying eyes on her. Then to have to endure snide questions and snotty looks, it surely wasn't helping her opinion of Jason's mother.

Trisha smirked. "Yeah, our last names are different," she said, feigning amusement. "I guess that's what happens when you fuck your child's father in a one-night stand but don't marry him."

"Whoa!" Jason blurted out in shock. Chasity nearly choked on the piece of bread that was in her mouth.

As Chasity coughed and patted her chest, Trisha stared down Nancy Adams, who just feigned a smile.

"How nice," Mrs. Adams hissed.

"*Is* it now?" Trisha countered. "Does that answer your question? Do you have any *more* questions about my personal business?"

Mrs. Adams stared daggers at Trisha. "Look Trisha—"

"It's *Pa*trisha," Trisha corrected. "Trisha is a shortened name that I am called by people I *care* about, and *you* certainly aren't *one* of them."

Mrs. Adams gritted her teeth as Jason put his hand over his face and shook his head. He knew this wasn't going to end well.

Chasity pushed her seat back. The tension was too much for her. "Um, that dessert tray looks good, I'm gonna go get a closer look," she quickly said, standing from her seat.

"Sit down, Chasity," Trisha commanded. Chasity immediately complied, then leaned her elbow on the table and put her head in her hand.

"Look *Patrisha*," Mrs. Adams sneered, all traces of forced politeness gone. "This is the first time that I am meeting you, and I can honestly say that I have been nothing but cordial to you." She folded her arms. "So do you think that your damn attitude is really necessary?"

Jason pushed his seat back. "Chaz you were right, that dessert tray *does* look good. You wanna check it out?"

"Uh huh," Chasity made a move to get up once again.

"Jason sit down," Mrs. Adams commanded. Jason flopped back down in his seat, letting out a groan in the process.

"I said sit," Trisha hissed at Chasity.

Chasity rolled her eyes and pushed herself back up to the table. There was no escaping this situation, for her or Jason.

Trisha leaned forward, shooting a challenging look. "My attitude became *necessary* when I found out how you were treating my daughter," she spat. Mrs. Adams rolled her eyes. "As a matter of fact, you're lucky that my attitude is *all* you're getting. And not my expensive ass stiletto up your *ass.*"

Chasity tossed her hands in the air as Jason put his hand up. "Ladies can you *please*—"

"Jason, be quiet," his mother commanded.

Jason sucked his teeth as he signaled for the waiter. "Another drink. *Please* hurry," he called out.

Mrs. Adams frowned. "Was the threat *also* necessary?" she barked. "You're a grown woman."

"Ask me one more time if something is necessary," Trisha warned. "True, I may be grown, but don't let this money and this designer fool you honey. I will revert back into that dangerous teenager in a minute."

"*Please* don't," Chasity muttered.

"Shut up," Trisha hissed at her.

Chasity folded her arms in a huff, yet remained silent.

Mrs. Adams let out a sigh. "Threats aside Patrisha, I understand how you feel."

"No, you *don't*," Trisha countered. "See, I don't treat *your* son like shit. I don't talk down to him. I don't make him feel like he's not good enough for my daughter."

Chasity sat there and listened to her mother defend her, and in that moment, her embarrassment of Trisha's abrasive behavior was gone. Her mother had a right to be angry.

"I don't dig Chasity's ex-boyfriends out of the damn trash and flaunt them in Jason's face in order to not only intimidate him, make him feel insecure, but to try to ruin their relationship," Trisha continued to fume.

Mrs. Adams just sat there and listened, and so did Jason. This was nothing he hadn't said to his mother before.

"Let's set aside the fact that you didn't care about *my* child's feelings," Trisha ranted. "You completely disregarded the feelings of your own *son*. What kind of parent *purposely* tries to hurt their child?"

"I did not *purposely* try to hurt my child," Mrs. Adams snapped, slamming her hand on the table in frustration. "I—I thought that I was looking out for him."

"Mom, I told you that you didn't need to do that," Jason cut in. "That my relationship is *my* business."

"I know," Mrs. Adams admitted. "But—" She focused her attention on the visibly angry Trisha. "Listen, mother to mother, I apologize for hurting your daughter. I wouldn't want you to do that to Jason and I appreciate the fact that you care about him... He's told me."

Trisha just held her gaze, folding her arms in a huff.

Mrs. Adams then turned to Chasity. "Chasity, I apologize for going about things the way that I did. Not *only* that, but *what* I did...how I treated you. It was wrong, I know that, but—" She took a deep breath. "Grown woman to grown woman, I want you to try to understand where I was coming from—"

"She don't need to hear—"

Chasity put her hand up to silence Trisha and held her gaze on Mrs. Adams. "It's okay Mom," she assured. "Go ahead Ms. Nancy."

"No Chaz, your mom is right—"

"Jason, it's okay," Chasity insisted, cutting him off. She felt that this was something that she needed to hear.

Upon receiving the go ahead, Mrs. Adams leaned forward. "I'll admit that when Jason was with Paris, I never seen him affected the way that he was with *you*—that he *is* with you… There were times *especially* during his sophomore and junior year, that he was just so upset. I mean he looked broken and hurt and as his mother, it was hard to see him that way and I knew that it had to do with you."

Chasity held her gaze as she listened. She remembered those times too.

"And no matter *how* better things appeared, or what Jason said, I just held on to that because I want the best for my son and him being that hurt, was not the best thing for him." Mrs. Adams took another deep breath. "But I also have to realize that Jason is a grown man and knows what's best. He knew it was best for him to get rid of that cheating *ex* of his, and that being with *you* is what's best for him. So, who am I to question that?"

Chasity pondered Mrs. Adams's words, and knew that she needed to respond. She hesitated as she tried to gather her thoughts. "Ms. Nancy, look…to be honest I know those times that you were talking about," she began.

Jason shook his head. He had a feeling what Chasity was about to say, and he didn't feel that she owed anybody any explanation. "Baby—"

Chasity looked at him. "Stop," she stated. He closed his mouth and sat back in his seat.

She looked back to Jason's mother. "I'll admit that I wasn't that nice to Jason when I first met him," she admitted. "I did say things and acted in a way that would make anybody else run. *He didn't* and I didn't know how to handle that. That feeling, on top of never having to consider anybody else's feelings but my own for so long…" She paused as she tried to keep herself composed. "I'll admit that the way that I handled *certain* things that happened between Jason and I, wasn't the best way," she continued. "But I'm not that same person. At least I'm trying *not* to be. I honestly love your son and as angry as you make me, seeing the way he's affected when he's not in a good space with you, doesn't sit well with me."

Mrs. Adams just stared at Chasity, a trace of admiration lit in her eyes.

"I'm tired of this back and forth between us and I know *he* is too," Chasity said, gesturing to Jason. "So, I appreciate your apology and I accept it… I'm willing to try to get along if *you* are. Not for me, but for *him*."

A smile was bubbling within Jason. He couldn't believe that his mother and the woman that he loved were finally having a civilized conversation. He also felt his adoration for Chasity heighten; she was putting aside her own feelings in an attempt to resolve an issue that was clearly taking its toll on him. He hoped that his relief wasn't going to be short-lived; Jason had no idea how his mother would react.

Before Jason could give it another thought, Mrs. Adams rose from her seat and rounded the small table towards Chasity. Chasity didn't know what to expect, so she immediately frowned and scooted her seat close to her mother, who held an 'I dare you' expression on her face.

Mrs. Adams let out a little laugh. "I just want to give you a hug," she assured.

"Oh," Chasity said. She stood up, granting Mrs. Adams the opportunity to embrace her.

"Thank you," Mrs. Adams breathed before releasing Chasity. She then held on to Chasity's arms and smiled at her. "I appreciate your honesty and I can tell that you love Jason and God *knows* he loves *you*," she gushed. "I know things aren't always easy in a relationship, I've been married a long time, so I get it. And I'm not always that easy to deal with either, just ask my husband," she chuckled.

"Who you tellin'?" Jason muttered.

"Bottom line, as long as Jason is happy, *I'm* happy," Mrs. Adams smiled. "I won't be a problem for you anymore and I truly *am* ready to move forward and establish a relationship with you, Chasity."

Chasity nodded. "Okay," she agreed.

"About time," Jason broke in at an attempt to lighten the mood. "You women stress me out."

Mrs. Adams flagged Jason with her hand in amusement as she made her way over to Trisha. "I know you're irritated with me, but I want to hug *you too*," she offered, arms out. "They're obviously stuck with each other so, so are *we*," she grinned.

Trisha narrowed her eyes.

"What do you say? Give me a chance to make things right?" Mrs. Adams pressed.

Trisha stared at her for a moment, then removed the napkin from her lap. "For *her*," she began, gesturing to Chasity. "I can try," Trisha promised, standing and allowing an embrace.

"I admire how you stood up for your child," Mrs. Adams chortled. "A woman after my own heart."

"Uh huh, I'll drag *anybody*," Trisha chuckled in return.

"I know that's right," Mrs. Adams mused as they parted. "Come on girl, let's go to the bar and get us a *real* drink."

"Alright, drinks on *you*," Trisha agreed. Mrs. Adams clasped her hands in delight as she trotted in the direction of the restaurant bar. As Trisha went to grab her purse, Chasity tapped her on the shoulder, prompting Trisha to face her.

"Thank you," Chasity said, appreciative.

Trisha smiled. "You never have to thank me," she returned, then gave Chasity a kiss on the cheek. "You want me to cuss your father out too? I can do that right now, I'm on one."

Chasity chuckled a bit. "No, no you've done enough," she said. "Go have your drink."

"I'm about to get lit," Trisha beamed.

"Please, please don't ever say that again," Chasity begged, mortified as Jason busted out laughing. Shrugging, Trisha trotted off.

Chasity and Jason locked eyes with one another as Chasity flopped down in her seat. The two of them let out long sighs of relief. Without saying a word, Jason held his hand up and Chasity returned a high five. He grabbed her other hand as well and held on to it. Both smiling, both relieved, and relishing the turn of events that had just taken place.

"Thank you," Jason smiled at her. Chasity just gave a nod.

"You know they're probably gonna drink up that entire bar, right?" Chasity commented after a moment. "And Trisha is about to get really loud."

Jason laughed. "I don't even care, as long as they're not arguing."

# Chapter 24

Emily stood outside the home that she had lived in for nineteen years of her life and stared at the doorbell. She'd been standing there for what seemed like forever, but it only turned out to be five minutes.

*Just ring the damn bell*, she told herself. Letting out a long sigh, pushing some of her beveled hair behind her ear, Emily finally pressed the doorbell. She practically held her breath when she heard movement on the other side of the door. When it opened, she came face to face with her smiling mother.

"You made it," Ms. Harris beamed, signaling for Emily to enter.

Emily walked in and the familiar scent of lavender and vanilla hit her nose. Her mother always bought that same air freshener. "Yeah," she answered, removing her light jacket.

"Chilly out there?" Ms. Harris asked, returning to the pitcher of iced tea that she was making in the kitchen.

"A little, but nothing out of the ordinary for April," Emily answered, laying the jacket on the arm of an accent chair. She walked into the kitchen as her mother added more slices of lemon to the tea. Plates of food were laid out on the table.

"I made a grilled chicken salad, if that's okay," Ms. Harris announced. "And I made some lemon squares for a little dessert."

"Okay, that's fine," Emily said, rubbing her arm. If she was honest, she didn't have much of an appetite; her nerves were all wound up.

Pouring some tea into two ice-filled glasses, Ms. Harris gestured to the back door. "You want to sit out in the sunroom back there?"

Emily craned her neck to see. "You added a sunroom?"

"Yeah, I figured with the house empty, why not add it finally," Ms. Harris said. "I mean, I've been talking about getting one for years."

Emily couldn't help but focus on the fact that her mother had stated that her house was empty. As far as Emily knew, Jazmine was still living there. "Makes sense," Emily muttered.

Grabbing their plates, both women headed out to the new sunroom and sat on the cushioned furniture. Emily looked around. The sunroom was wall to wall windows, which allowed the view of the backyard, without having to bear the elements. "It's nice out here, Mom," she commented, taking a sip of her tea.

"Thanks," Ms. Harris returned, taking a sip of hers. "I spend a lot of time out here... I'm gonna start planting a garden within the next few weeks."

Emily nodded. "Oh, okay." As much as she was enjoying not being yelled at or criticized, Emily was pretty sure that sunrooms and gardens were not the reason why her mother invited her over.

"So...how's your break so far?" Ms. Harris asked, breaking through Emily's thoughts.

Emily set her glass down on the table in front of her. "It's been fine," she answered. "But uh, if I'm being honest, the last few days have brought on a little anxiety."

Ms. Harris glanced at Emily. "In anticipation of *this*, huh?" she wondered.

Emily held a gaze on her mother as she slowly nodded. "So...what's up Mom?" she asked point-blank. "I mean, the last time that we saw each other, we didn't exactly leave off on good terms."

"If you recall, *you're* the one who actually left," Ms. Harris recalled.

Emily held her gaze, not blinking. "Are we gonna do this again?" she challenged.

Ms. Harris sighed. She knew that comment was completely unnecessary and irrelevant. She wanted her daughter to come to the house so that she could have a conversation with her, not to upset her. "No," she said finally. "I um... I don't like how things have been between us Emily...how they *are* and I want us to try and fix that."

Emily looked away. "How do you expect that we do that?" she asked. "I'm not trying to go back to how things *were*. I'm not that person anymore, and that is what I was trying to get you to understand when we last talked."

"I get that, and I listened to what you said."

Emily looked back at her mother. "Listening is one thing, *hearing* it is another," she said, tone calm. "And I just don't think that you've done that."

Ms. Harris took a deep breath. "I'll admit that after our argument I was irritated. But after I had time to dwell on it— and it has been *all* that I have been thinking about..." she took another breath. "Emily—" she turned in her seat to face her daughter. "I understand that I handled you with kid gloves, I know that I overprotected you and I sheltered you *way* too much... But, I was doing that for your own good. At least *I* thought so."

Emily held her gaze. "Why *me* though?" she questioned, pushing more of her hair behind her ears. "Out of the four of us why only *me*, did you treat that way? Was it only because I was the youngest?"

Ms. Harris paused for a moment as she gathered her words. Feeling a bit emotional, she reached for a napkin and dabbed the corner of her eyes, much to Emily's confusion. She balled the napkin up in her hand and faced Emily once more. "I never told you this, but when you were just a baby you almost died."

Emily's eyes widened. "What?"

Ms. Harris nodded. "You were born premature," she revealed. Emily just sat with her mouth open. She had no idea. "After Jaz started getting older, I started getting sick and the doctors said—" she paused for a moment. "Long story short, they told me that I would eventually need to have a hysterectomy," her mother revealed, somber. "I knew that I wanted one more child before I lost my ability to bare children anymore."

Emily glanced down as she listened to her mother reveal her story.

"I prayed day and night for that chance… When I found out I was pregnant with you I was so happy and grateful," she reminisced, smiling. "Like when I was pregnant with your siblings, I felt like I did everything right. I took every precaution, followed my doctors' orders to a tee." Her smile faded. "And none of it was enough to prevent you from coming into this world two months early." She let out a sigh. "I couldn't even *hold* you after you were born because doctors were surrounding you, and *I* was rushed to surgery after… I woke up without my reproductive organs and was given the news that you probably weren't going to make it."

The knowledge that Emily almost didn't live hit her like a ton of bricks.

"I prayed every hour on the hour, and your father and I sat in that room and stared at you through that incubator," Ms. Harris continued. "I felt guilty, like something that I did or *didn't* do caused that to happen. I felt that I didn't do enough to protect you when it counted and I promised myself that if you pulled through, that I would never fail at that again…and by God's grace, you survived." She held her gaze on Emily. "Emily—I know that nobody understood, but me holding on to you so tight was because I wanted to keep you safe."

Emily took a deep breath as she processed everything that she had just heard. "Mom," she began, adjusting her position. "I understand that it must've been hard seeing me go through that. I, probably more than *anybody* appreciate you praying over me and being there every day while I got stronger…but…and I mean no disrespect, you really thought that it was okay to keep me under your thumb the way that you did?"

"I did, yes," Ms. Harris maintained. "In my mind as long as I kept you close, bad things wouldn't happen to you. As long as I kept you sheltered, you wouldn't have to deal with things that could hurt you."

Emily rolled her eyes. "Mom, I *understand* that a parent's job is to protect their children, but you can't *possibly* protect them from everything...from *life*," she argued. "That's unrealistic."

"I think I did a pretty good job of it," Ms. Harris countered. "You left for college unscathed and untouched."

"Mom, I think we need to table this for now," Emily uttered, she was beginning to get angry.

"No, don't get upset Emily, let's *talk* about it," her mother insisted. "Face it, my methods may have been questionable, but you were the perfect child growing up. Never doing anything wrong, never lying, never getting into trouble—"

"I needed guidance," Emily cut in, annoyed.

"I *gave* you guidance."

"No, you *babied* me," Emily insisted. "You refused to talk to me about *anything* that had to do with real life."

Ms. Harris shook her head. "That's not true."

"Yes, it *is*," Emily insisted. "When I tried to talk to you about boys, and had questions about things that I was feeling, you just basically told me not to worry about it... 'don't worry about that Emily', 'I'll tell you when you're older, Emily', 'you wanna go to the store with me, Emily?'" she mocked, recalling some of the dismissive things that her mother would say. "Well I *needed* to worry about those things because *those things* were a part of growing up. Something that you didn't *want* me to do."

"*Of course* I wanted you to grow up Emily, don't be silly," Ms. Harris dismissed. "I just felt that if you weren't exposed to certain things that you could avoid—"

The more and more Ms. Harris tried to explain her

actions, the more and more Emily felt herself losing control. "I couldn't avoid as much as you *thought* I could, because I lost my virginity at fifteen years old!" she blurted out.

Emily not only shocked her mother—who sat there with her eyes practically bulging, looking like the color had drained from her face—she shocked herself. She never intended on spilling that secret to her mother, at least not now.

Ms. Harris was horrified, one hand over her chest as she tried to control her breathing. "You—you *what?*" she barked. Emily looked like she wanted to get up and run away as fast as she could. "You…you lost—who?—fifteen? *Fifteen?*"

Emily pinched the bridge of her nose as she let out a long sigh. This was draining, but there was no turning back. "Yeah Mom…fifteen," she confirmed, voice calm, tired.

Ms. Harris was still in shock; she couldn't stop her stammering. "But—who? When?—*who?*"

"You remember that boy that I told you that I liked back in high school?" Emily asked. "The one who I asked you if I could go to the movies with?" Her mother just sat there, staring at her as she tried to remember. Emily gave a slight wave of her hand. "Doesn't matter," she dismissed. "Anyway, when I asked you and you said no, he called me and asked me to sneak out after you went to work and I did…and I—" she let out a frustrated sigh. "It happened in his basement and after that night he never spoke to me again."

Ms. Harris looked like she wanted to cry. "Did—did he—"

"No Mom, he didn't rape me," Emily assured, knowing what her mother was trying to say. "I consented to it…*shouldn't* have. I definitely regretted it but, I consented."

Ms. Harris grabbed Emily's hand and held it as Emily continued to speak.

"I was confused, hurt and angry," Emily vented. "I felt used and I wanted to talk to you about it but, I figured…what was the point?"

Ms. Harris let a few tears fall. She had missed an opportunity to be there for her daughter when Emily needed her most. It hit her hard. "Emily, I'm sorry," she sniffled. "I wish that you never had to go through that."

"I know, but I *did*," Emily pointed out.

Ms. Harris clutched Emily's hand. "Maybe if...if I would have talked to you about sex and boys and just things that a teenage girl with questions and hormones should have *known*...maybe you wouldn't have ended up in the situation that you were in."

Emily shrugged. "Maybe, maybe *not*...who knows," she said. "I said all that to say that no matter how hard you try, you can't protect me from life. You just *can't*."

Ms. Harris wiped her eyes.

"I had to leave here so that I could start *living* my life," Emily added. "If I hadn't, I would probably still be drinking."

Ms. Harris rubbed her face with her hands. "God," she sighed. "I didn't realize that I put you through so much... That I *stressed* you that much." She held a sorrowful gaze on her youngest child. "I just never thought that you'd get to a place where you didn't need me anymore and I guess I didn't know how to handle it."

"I never said that I didn't need you," Emily pointed out. "You're my mom, I will *always* need you. And I want to have a normal mother/daughter relationship *with* you," she stressed. "When I hear my friends talking about the relationships that they have with their mothers and the fact that they can talk to them about *anything*—I want that."

Ms. Harris nodded as she patted Emily's hand with her free hand. She was amazed. Emily had truly grown into a confident woman who had the ability to express herself. "I want that too," she said. "And I promise that I'll try."

"You sure?" Emily questioned, hopeful.

"Of course," Ms. Harris smiled, squeezing Emily's hand.

Emily let a slight smile come through. She was relieved and proud of herself for not backing down. While she was sure that her mother had good intentions, Emily knew that having an open relationship would take time. But if her mother was willing to work at it, so was she.

Ms. Harris let out a deep sigh. The entire conversation was intense, but she knew that it was something that needed to happen. She was finally getting her daughter back. She took a sip of tea as some thoughts swirled in her head. "Emily," she began.

Emily, reaching for her food, paused and looked at her.

"So um…have you—were there any other times after that—"

Emily couldn't help but giggle at her mother as the woman struggled to ask her a personal, adult question. *Yeah, this is definitely not gonna be an overnight thing.* "It was just the one time," she answered.

Ms. Harris breathed a sigh of relief. "Thank God." Emily shook her head. "Not that I don't expect it to happen again in the future," she immediately added, putting her hand up. "I'm just glad that you're *waiting*. When the right person comes along, you won't have to question their intentions."

Emily smiled and nodded. "Thanks Mommy."

Ms. Harris put her hand over her heart and tilted her head. "You called me 'Mommy', again," she beamed.

"I know," Emily smiled.

"Princess, you sure you don't wanna come in here and pick out something?" Mr. Howard asked, poking his head out of a small dessert café.

Sidra glanced up from her seat on the outside bench. She forced a smile. "No Daddy, I'm fine," she assured.

"You sure?" he pressed, a bright look in his eyes. "They have a ton of chocolate stuff in here."

Sidra held her smile; her family knew how much Sidra enjoyed a chocolate treat. In fact, when her family arrived down at Baltimore's harbor earlier that afternoon for a much-needed family outing, they made it a point to stop at every shop that they could find in order to find the perfect treat. Sidra, who would normally be the first in line, just didn't have the appetite.

"I'm sure," she said. "You can pick something for me if you want."

Mr. Howard smiled. "Really?"

Sidra nodded. "Yeah, I trust you." Sidra watched as her father eagerly headed back inside the café. He was always so excited about the smallest things, which Sidra always admired.

Letting out a sigh after a moment, Sidra reached for her phone. Scrolling through numbers, she settled on one in particular. Sidra stared at Malajia's name on the screen as she held her finger over the dial button. *Just dial it!*

"Calling James?" a voice asked, breaking Sidra's thoughts and startling her.

She immediately cleared her screen and put her phone back into her purse. "No," she muttered, looking up. "Did Dad send you out here to make absolutely sure that I wanted him to pick something for me?"

Marcus chuckled. "Nah, but that *would* be a thing that he would do," he joked, sitting down next to Sidra on the bench.

Sidra nodded in agreement. "Yeah," she sighed.

Marcus looked at her. She looked sad, a look that hadn't changed since he'd arrived at his parents' house earlier that day to come along for the day trip. "You okay?"

Sidra forced another smile as she looked at him. "Yeah, I'm okay," she lied. "Are *you*?"

Marcus nodded. "Now that I know that my baby is okay, yes, I'm good," he assured.

"Do you think that she'll *actually* do that the next time she gets mad at you?" Sidra asked. It had been on her mind heavy.

Marcus slowly shook his head. "No," he answered. "She's crazy but I *do* know that she wants the baby as much as I do. She's been apologizing to her damn stomach ever since we left the doctor." He took a deep breath. "Together or not, I'm going to be there for my child."

Sidra gave a nod. "You're gonna make a great dad."

Marcus smiled bright. "I damn sure *hope* so."

Sidra gave his leg a pat. "You *will*," she assured.

"Yeah." He rubbed the back of his neck. "This somber thing you got going on—you're still going to be an aunt. The wedding is off, *I'm* okay so, what's it about?"

"I don't know what you're talking about," Sidra denied. Marcus shot her a knowing look. "Sidra don't do that 'pretending' thing that you do," he scolded. She rolled her eyes. "Come on sis, what's up? Did you fight with James? One of the girls?"

She let out a sigh as she leaned forward and placed her head in her hands. "Yes, and yes."

Marcus patted Sidra on the back. "Figured," he said. "How is it gonna get resolved?"

"I don't know," she muttered, even though she knew exactly how to resolve *one* of the issues.

"Look, I'm sure anything that was said, can be fixed... Sometimes, *you* have to be the fixer," Marcus pointed out.

Marcus didn't say anything that Sidra wasn't already thinking. In fact, one reason why she wasn't enjoying her trip was because she was in a city where one of her best friends resided, and the only thing that she could think about was her.

She looked over at Marcus. "Do you plan on staying down here for a while?"

Marcus shrugged. "I *guess*. I followed you guys down here in my own car, in case my job called me in and I needed to leave, but it seems like that won't happen. So yeah, I'll be here until you guys leave." He looked at her skeptically. "Why?"

Sidra stared at him. "I need to borrow your car."


"Why must you chew your food so damn close to the camera?" Malajia fussed, staring at Mark with disgust through the video on her phone. As much as she missed seeing his face, she could have done without seeing him inhale his food while trying to have a phone conversation.

"Shut up," Mark threw back, swallowing the bite of food in his mouth. "You don't say nothin' when *you're* eating like a damn animal."

Malajia busted out laughing as she leaned over the counter island in her kitchen, holding her phone with both hands. "Whatever."

"Yeah, that's what I thought," Mark joked in return.

"I miss you," she said, laughter subsiding. With spring break being up in just two days, Malajia was happy that she would get to go back to seeing Mark every day.

"Miss you too," he returned. "You good?"

She nodded. "Yeah." She ran her hand over her hair. "Talking to Mom about everything helped me feel a lot better."

"That's good...still haven't told your dad yet?"

"Fuck no," she immediately returned, earning a chuckle from Mark.

"It's just as well, he'll just find a way to make it *my* fault."

Malajia giggled. "Sad, but true."

Mark paused for a moment. "Have you gotten a call from Sidra?"

"Nope."

Mark sucked his teeth. "I swear, I'mma twist the top off her salt shaker when we get back to campus."

Malajia frowned. "Hey, *I* use that damn shaker too."

"Well get ready to have some salty ass food," Mark returned, Malajia let out a little laugh. "Don't worry about it *or* her. Worry about yourself."

"Easier said than done," Malajia muttered, then took a sip of juice from a nearby glass.

"I know," Mark sympathized. He paused for a moment. "What color drawls you got on?"

Malajia spat out some of her juice. Once she gathered

her composure, she stared at the phone. "Red," she answered, wiping the counter with a paper towel.

"Ooh, my favorite color," Mark crooned. "Let me see 'em."

Malajia shook her head. "Sure, and while I'm at it, why don't I show you this big ass maxi pad I got *in* them," she mocked, making a face in the camera.

"I'm a grown ass man dawg, your period don't phase me."

"Yeah? Coming from the idiot that made a comment about me *bleeding* all over the place," Malajia reminded.

Mark was quiet for a moment. "*Still* bringing up old shit, I see," he jeered.

Malajia laughed. "Boy get off my phone so I can go take a damn nap."

"Fine," Mark sighed. "Talk to you later."

"Bye." Malajia hung up the phone, grabbed the rest of her juice and headed for the living room. For once, the house was empty; she intended to take advantage and get some rest. She knew it was only a matter of time before someone returned home.

Before she could even sit down on the couch, she heard a knock at the door. "Please God, don't be Aunt Joyce dropping Melissa's bad ass off," she pleaded as she headed for the door.

Opening it, Malajia was both startled and confused by the visitor. "Sidra," the response came out as a statement rather than a question.

Sidra fiddled with her fingers as she held her gaze on Malajia. She didn't know what to expect when she borrowed her brother's car and made the drive from the harbor to Malajia's house unannounced. Judging by the look on Malajia's face, Sidra wondered if she had made the right decision.

"Um… Hi, Malajia," Sidra uttered.

Malajia relaxed her face as she held her hand on the door. "Hi."

"Can I come in?" Sidra wondered when Malajia didn't move.

Malajia nodded as she moved aside to allow Sidra to enter. Sidra spun around to face Malajia as she closed the door.

"What's up Sidra?" Malajia asked. She was unsure of Sidra's reason for popping up. Especially since they hadn't spoken since their blow up, and that was over a week ago.

Sidra took a deep breath as she smoothed her shirt with her hands. "Um…" she gestured to the couch with her hand. "You mind if I sit?"

Malajia twisted her lip up. "No, no you *can't*," she ground out. When Sidra glanced at the floor, Malajia let out a huff. "Girl, sit down," she ordered. "Like I'm gonna keep you off of couches that I didn't pay for."

"Thanks," Sidra muttered as she walked to the couch and sat down with Malajia following suit. Sidra took a deep breath and looked around. "Did your mom redecorate?"

Malajia stared at her. "If by redecorate you mean, did she buy this *one* new throw pillow that my dad can't seem to stop sleeping on, then *yeah*, she did," she replied, unenthused, pointing to said colorful pillow.

Sidra wished she was in the mood to crack a smile at Malajia's response. Unfortunately, she wasn't. "Oh," was all that she could say.

Malajia ran her hand along the back of her neck and let out a sigh. She was tired and Sidra's pointless casual mentions weren't going over well with her. "Sidra come on…what's up? Why are you here?"

Sidra took another deep breath as she shifted in her seat. It was time to stop delaying the inevitable. "Okay. I was at the harbor earlier today, with my family…"

Malajia sat there, wondering where Sidra was going with the topic. "Uh huh," she muttered.

"Anyway, it was *supposed* to be a fun, family day trip. Just something to help us unwind after everything that has been going on and… I couldn't have any fun because all I could think about, was *you*."

Malajia tilted her head as Sidra continued to speak. "So I borrowed Marcus's car and left my family to come here and see you...to *talk* to you."

"You couldn't just *call* me?"

Sidra shook her head. "One, I was pretty sure that you wouldn't have answered, and two...what I have to say to you needs to be said in person."

Malajia let out a sigh as she adjusted her position. "I would've answered the phone, had you called," she assured. "Like I would have spoken to you, had you *allowed* me to after our fight."

Sidra wished she could have dissolved under Malajia's piercing gaze. "Right," she muttered.

"So, what do you want to talk to me about?" Malajia asked, point-blank.

Sidra squinted. "I think...you already know."

Malajia rubbed her face with her hand. "I can't do this right now," she huffed.

Sidra put her hand up. "Malajia just listen please," she pleaded.

Malajia stared at her, arms folded.

Sidra took a deep breath. "Look, I feel how I feel about abortions and I don't see that changing for me, at least no time *soon*," she began. "But despite my views, I shouldn't have come at you the way that I did," she admitted. "I was angry over what happened...over what I *thought* had happened and I took everything that I was feeling out on you and I *shouldn't* have."

"No, you *shouldn't* have," Malajia agreed, even toned. "Look Sidra, I respect the fact that you have your opinion. And I didn't mean to come at you like I was trying to change your mind set about abortions. I just wanted you to have a little compassion for those who have made that decision because it's not easy." Malajia shook her head. "It might have been bad timing on my part, because the situation wasn't about *me* and I *know* that, but..." she paused for a moment as she tried to keep herself calm. "Sidra, the way that you made me feel wasn't cool," she admitted, hurt. "You talked to me like you didn't know me, like you didn't give a shit about me, like I was just some...*baby killer*. I mean...it's *me*. We're like sisters; I love you like one and—that just wasn't cool."

Sidra lowered her head. She was already feeling bad enough, but seeing the hurt in Malajia's eyes and hearing it in her voice, made Sidra feel even worse. "I'm sorry, Malajia," she said, as tears filled her eyes. "I know I hurt your feelings... We can have a difference of opinion, but I should consider your feelings and I didn't do that... I'm sorry."

Malajia's demeanor softened a bit though on the inside, her feelings were still hurt. While she appreciated the fact that Sidra came to her and apologized, it didn't take away from how Malajia felt. She wasn't lying; Sidra had hurt her. And while it wasn't a physical pain, the words that Sidra spewed in her fit of rage hurt her worse than any punch did. Yet, she hated fighting with her friends; she just wanted this one to be over. "It's okay, I accept your apology," Malajia said after a moment.

Sidra wiped her eyes as she sniffled. "Can I have a hug?" she asked, holding her arms out.

Malajia gave a slight nod as she and Sidra hugged.

Sidra wiped her eyes again as they parted. "I swear, I'm starting to feel like a bad person," she admitted. "I'm saying all the wrong things, I'm arguing and getting angry for no good reason—I don't know what's going on with me."

Malajia grabbed a tissue from a holder on a side table and handed it to Sidra. "You're not a bad person," she said, even toned. "We all have our moments, it's okay."

Sidra wiped her eyes with the tissue. "I appreciate you saying that," she said. Malajia once again nodded. "I mean it Malajia, I'm *really* sorry."

"It's fine." Malajia tilted her head. "My mom made cake, you want some?" she offered.

Sidra nodded. "Yes, please."

# Chapter 25

"Emily, what is with all those bags?" Alex chuckled, seeing Emily place several grocery bags full of food and other items on the kitchen floor.

Emily stood up straight and stretched her back. "All this stuff is from my mom," Emily explained. Before leaving her brother's house to return to school, Emily was surprised by her mother. Ms. Harris had showed up at the apartment with several bags of groceries and toiletry items for Emily to take back to school with her.

"I could've helped you with those bags, you know," Alex chuckled.

Emily waved her hand dismissively. "Ahh, it's fine," she assured. "I swear, now that we're talking again, it's like she's making up for lost 'shopping' times."

Alex began to help Emily unpack the bags. "Well, at least we won't have to go grocery shopping for a while." Alex was excited as she placed several frozen meat packages, boxes of cereal, snacks, and canned goods on the counter.

Emily opened her mouth to speak, but was interrupted by the door opening. She and Alex glanced over to see Dru standing there, cradling two large packs of toilet paper.

"Emily, your mother has gone overboard," he griped, setting them at the bottom of the staircase.

Emily giggled, putting items away alongside Alex. "Are you really surprised?"

Dru shook his head in amusement. "No, not really," he

agreed. "I haven't seen her *this* shop happy since she redid you and Jaz's room after she put her out."

Emily bolted up right and stared at her brother with shock. "Wait, she put Jaz out?"

Dru raised an eyebrow. "Uh yeah, like a month ago," he confirmed. "You didn't know?"

"*No,* I didn't know," Emily declared. "She mentioned having the house to herself when I went over there, but I didn't think anything of that." She ran her hand through her hair. "Wow, never thought that Mommy would put *any* of her kids out."

"Yeah well, Mom was over her," Dru grunted, rubbing the back of his neck. "She's lazy, she can't keep a job… Hell, *I* even broke and recommended her for a position in another department in my company and she lost that one too."

Emily shook her head.

"But I think her last straw was when Jazmine bad-mouthed you after your birthday," her brother revealed.

Emily raised an eyebrow. "What did she *say?*"

"I think Mom said that she called you a…" he put his finger on his chin as he tried to recall the conversation between his mother and himself. "Yeah, it was after she told Jaz about the conversation that you and her had when she came to visit on your birthday. Apparently Jaz had called you a weak, alcoholic bitch."

*Wow!* Alex thought, shaking her head. Alex remained silent as she continued to put items away. She had no intention of making a comment, but she sure kept her ears perked.

"How nice," Emily spat, sarcastic.

"Yeah, Mom snapped on her and kicked her to the curb."

Emily shook her head. "Can't say that she didn't deserve it," she dismissed.

"Agreed," Dru said. "Anyway, I'm gonna get going," he announced, heading for the door.

"Bye," Emily waved. "Thanks for putting me up for the

week."

"Anytime," he smiled, turning around. "Oh, and don't think I forgot."

Emily tilted her head. "Forgot about *what?*"

"I'm supposed to meet your little friend," Dru ground out. "He's lucky I'm tired and need to get back...otherwise, it would be grillin' time."

Emily giggled, "I said graduation Dru." She waved to him. "Bye, drive safe."

Alex looked over at Emily once Dru walked out of the house. "You alright?" Alex asked.

Emily was confused. "Yeah, why?" she returned. "You mean what my sister said about me?"

Alex nodded. She couldn't help it; what Jazmine said was harsh and she just wanted to make sure that Emily was okay. Had it been her, Alex wouldn't have been.

"Yeah, I'm fine," Emily replied, putting items away. "Nothing Jazmine says about me shocks me anymore."

"You sure?" Alex pressed.

"Alex, I'm no longer weak, I'm not an alcoholic and I'm not a—b-word, so...yes. I'm sure. I'm fine," Emily insisted.

Alex held a sympathetic gaze.

"Let's just finish putting this stuff up," Emily suggested.

"Okay," Alex agreed, grabbing some items and getting to work.

Mark grunted as he fumbled with a small DVD player. "Mel, I love you to death, but if *one* more thing you own breaks, I'mma snap," he griped, much to Malajia's amusement.

"You act like shit breaking is *my* fault," she threw back, flipping through a stack of DVDs.

Mark held the player up as he snapped his head toward her. He'd come over to watch movies with her, but that plan was derailed once he tried to eject the old movie from the device, only to find it stuck.

"It *is* your fault, stop buying cheap shit," he countered.

She rolled her eyes. "Why would I pay a hundred dollars for a DVD player when the *twenty* dollar one does the same thing?" She pointed to her head. "Duh."

"'Cause the *cheap* ones do shit like hold a fuckin' DVD hostage...*duh.*"

Malajia made a face and flipped him the finger in retaliation. Mark rolled his eyes as he slammed the player on the TV stand. The disk popped out.

"See? It's still good," Malajia boasted, grabbing her can of soda from the floor and taking a sip.

"Yeah, yeah," Mark mumbled, picking the disk up from the floor. He looked at the title and frowned. "'Do me long dick daddy'?" he read aloud.

Malajia spat out her drink as she tried to hold in her laugh.

"Whatchu' doin' watching pornos when you got *me*?" Mark hurled, to the now laughing Malajia.

"I completely forgot that was in there," she laughed. "What? You're not here all the damn time, what do you want from me?" she sniped when Mark shook his head.

Mark had a thought, a sly smile forming on his face. "You wanna show me what you do when I'm not here?"

Malajia narrowed her eyes at him as his smile became wider. "You're so nasty," she jeered.

Mark nodded enthusiastically. As he scooted closer to Malajia, there was a knock at the door.

"Come in," Malajia called.

"No, no don't come in! I was about to see Malajia play with herself," Mark barked to the closed door.

Malajia threw a pillow at him. "Cut it out you freak," she chided as he laughed.

"Umm, is it safe to come in?" the muffled female voice on the other side asked.

"Yeah, come on," Malajia assured.

The door opened and Mark immediately rolled his eyes at the intruder. Malajia caught the gesture and shook her head, then glanced up. "What's up Sidra?"

Sidra stood in the doorway. "Hey, do you have any aspirin?" she asked, tone low.

Malajia shook her head. "Naw, try Chaz, she usually has some."

"She's not in her room," Sidra groaned, placing a hand on her head.

"What's wrong with you, somebody punch you in the head?" Malajia joked.

"No, I have a major headache," Sidra moaned, tilting her head. "Had it all day."

Mark sucked his teeth. "That's what the hell you get," he mumbled, examining the DVD player.

Malajia shot Mark a side-glance while Sidra frowned at him.

"Did you say something Mark?" Sidra challenged.

"Sure did," Mark spat out.

"Mark, cut it out," Malajia urged, running her hand over her forehead.

Mark stood from the floor. "Nah, I *won't*," he hissed.

Malajia sighed as he made his way to the door. Even though Sidra had apologized to Malajia, Mark had yet to let it go.

Sidra followed his progress as he moved around her. "What is your attitude about?" she barked.

"You foul," Mark hurled to a shocked Sidra. He turned to Malajia. "Let me know when she leaves."

Malajia just shook her head at him as he walked out of the room, leaving Sidra stunned.

"Well damn," Sidra commented, leaning against the TV stand.

"Sorry about that," Malajia muttered. "I guess he's still not over what you said."

"I don't get it, if *we're* good," Sidra began, gesturing her hand back and forth between herself and Malajia, "what is *he* still mad for?"

Malajia frowned slightly. "He's just being protective of

me," she pointed out. "*You* have a man, you should understand."

Sidra looked at her. "I *do* understand the need to be protective, however—"

"You should probably run to the store before they close to see if they have any aspirin." Malajia abruptly cut in.

Sidra was in too much pain to harp on being interrupted, a pet peeve of hers. "You're right," she agreed.

"Hope you feel better," Malajia offered.

"Thanks." Sidra replied, heading out of the room.

"Sure," Malajia muttered as the door closed.


Chasity cradled the phone between her ear and shoulder as she tried to eat the spaghetti on her plate. "Yeah... I know right... Exactly," she muttered into the line. Although her tone was bubbly, her face told a different story.

Jason, who sat quietly beside her on the living room couch, watched in amusement as Chasity entertained a phone conversation with his mother.

"I'm sure my mom wouldn't mind going for a drink with you..." Chasity said into the phone. "Um...you wanna do what? ...Girls spa day?" Chasity made a face and flopped back against the couch cushion as Mrs. Adams' ramblings continued.

Jason snickered loudly, earning a backhand to the arm from Chasity. She was far from amused.

"Um, Ms. Nancy, why don't I just give you my mom's number so you can call her about that... No, no, that's her office number, let me give you her personal number...like now." Chasity gave Mrs. Adams the phone number, something that seemed to satisfy her, because soon after, she ended their phone call.

Relieved, Chasity tossed her phone on the coffee table in front of her. "An hour Jason," she complained; her boyfriend laughed. "She kept me on the phone for an *hour*."

"Yep, Mom can certainly run up phone time," Jason

joked. "I swear, she can talk for hours."

Chasity pushed the spaghetti around on her plate. "God," she muttered.

Jason laughed. "She *likes* you now, so get used to it."

Chasity rolled her eyes. "Yeah well, I think I liked it better when she hated me."

Jason poked her on the leg as she went to stand up. "Hush," he chortled.

"Damn food is all cold now," she complained, going for the kitchen. Before she stepped foot inside, her phone rang. She let out a groan. "Jason, if that's your mom again, I'mma break up with you."

Jason raised an eyebrow at her. "Yeah a'ight," he challenged.

She set her plate down on the table, grabbed her phone, and winced. "Shit, it's Mom."

"What's wrong with *that*?" Jason wondered.

"She's probably gonna cuss me out about giving your mom her number," Chasity chuckled. "She hates people calling her personal line." Chasity put the phone to her ear. "Yes?" she answered.

There was a pause. "Why are you answering like I'm about to yell at you?" Trisha asked.

"*Aren't* you?" Chasity shot back.

"Um no...should I?"

"No," Chasity answered. "What's up?"

"Are you busy? Because I just heard some shit and I need to tell you about it."

Chasity frowned. "O-kay," she cautiously put out. "What's going on?"

"So, you know in my business I get a lot of information on properties," Trisha began.

Chasity looked confused as she sat back down on the couch. "Yeah, so?"

"*So*, I heard that one of the vacant buildings in Paradise Valley, not too far from their airport, was bought by a hotel chain," she informed. "A new hotel is going to be built there."

"Again, *so*?" Chasity was impatiently wondering where this conversation was going. She just wanted to eat her food. There was a pause on the line. "Chasity, the chain that bought it, is the one that your father works for," she revealed. "In fact, he will be closely overseeing that project, which means that he'll be spending a *lot* of time there in Virginia, not too far from *you*."

Chasity rolled her eyes. "Mom it doesn't matter if he was *five minutes* from me, we both know it won't make a difference," she dismissed. "He's not going to text me, call me, or come see me, so as much as I appreciate the heads up, it wasn't worth your time."

Trisha sighed; she felt bad for Chasity. Besides, she was still angry at Derrick for how his actions or lack thereof was affecting her daughter. "Okay sweetie, I just didn't want you to be blindsided—"

"By silence?" Chasity sniped. "Don't think that's possible."

"Okay, I'll drop it," Trisha promised. "I have to go, I'll call you later."

"Okay."

"Love—hold on," Trisha said. "Hmm, Nancy is calling my personal line."

Chasity's eyes widened. "Bye Mom," she quickly put out before hanging up.

Jason looked at her. "Everything okay?"

"Sure," Chasity replied. Although she played it off well, she couldn't help but feel upset at the news. Her dad was going to be physically closer to her, and still had yet to reach out to her.

Jason reached over and gave her arm a rub. He sensed that she wasn't being honest; her demeanor had changed in those brief moments while talking to her mother. But he wouldn't press her to talk about it.

Chasity went to grab her plate, but her phone rang yet again. "What the fuck?" glancing at the caller ID, she quickly tossed the phone to Jason. "It's your mom again, not it," she spat, getting up from the couch. "Damn it Chasity," Jason called after her as she went to the kitchen. Letting out a sigh, he answered her phone. "Hey Mom," he answered, running his hand down his face. As much as he was glad to have things back to normal between him and his mother, he wasn't in the mood for a long conversation. "Um, Chaz is doing something right now. You wanna call b—" his question was interrupted as his mother began talking. Jason rolled his eyes and leaned back against the cushions. "Uh huh," he muttered.

David stared at Nicole as she speared a large amount of salad with her fork. "Hungry huh?" he teased as she placed the forkful into her mouth.

She covered her mouth in an effort not to spit out her food, while she tried to contain her laugh. "This Caesar salad is really good," she replied once she swallowed her food.

"Yeah, I'm sure it tastes better than this pot pie I have," David joked, pointing to the half-eaten pie on his plate.

David returned to campus the day before with anticipation; he couldn't wait to see Nicole. Especially after the conversation that they had before they left for break. He wanted to make sure that she didn't feel neglected. When she arrived a day later and invited him to have lunch in the cafeteria with her, he jumped at the opportunity.

"How was it going to your mom's grave?" Nicole asked.

David sighed, folding his arms on the tabletop. He had spoken to Nicole the morning that he decided to go visit the cemetery.

"It was okay, I guess," he shrugged. "It was my first time going to the site since her funeral." David had made it a point to stay clear of his mother's gravesite; he wanted to remember her as she was before her sickness overtook her. Keeping the last picture that he took of her when she was healthy was a pleasant reminder. However, at the request of his father, he decided to go.

Nicole reached for her cup of soda. "Wow, eight years is a long time," she said.

David ran a hand over the top of his head. "She's not there," he said. "I mean, her *remains* are, but...*she's* not," he clarified.

Nicole nodded. "I can understand that," she empathized. "When I go home, I visit my parents' sites. I like to talk to them there."

"I'm not knocking that," David assured, spinning his fork around on the table. "It's just not for *me*." He halted his fork spinning and sat back in his seat. "Let's talk about something else," he suggested. The mood got too dim for him.

"Okay," Nicole agreed. "I think my grandparents are gonna get me a car before the start of next semester."

"Oh?" David smiled. "How do you know?"

"Because they said that they're gonna get me a car before the start of next semester," she chortled.

David laughed a bit. "Oh... Well that's good. Now you don't have to rely on buses anymore...or rides to and from them." *From one person in particular,* he thought.

"True," she shrugged. Hearing her name being called, Nicole glanced up the same time that David did.

*What in the entire hell?!* David fumed, seeing Quincy walk over. It was like he could sniff out when David was with Nicole.

"Hey big head, here's the money I owe you," Quincy said to Nicole, giving her arm a playful tap. "I was gonna drop it by your room, but saw you over here." He glanced at David, who was staring at him. "What's up Dave?"

"*David*," David corrected, jaw clenched.

"My bad," Quincy returned, apologetic. "Hope you had a good break."

*I wish you would have been hit by a car over break,* David thought, then immediately regretted it. *Okay, that was a bit callous.* He didn't get to respond because Nicole cut in.

"Thanks for bringing it," she said, taking the money from his hand. "You better get to class."

"Going," Quincy assured, then waved and walked off. David looked at Nicole as she put her money into her jeans pocket. "Um…you gave him money?"

Nicole looked up at him. "I wouldn't say that I gave him money, I let him borrow it for a burger while he waited with me at the bus stop."

David fought the urge to frown. "What's the difference between what you said and what I asked you?"

"You asked me if I gave him money and I *didn't*," she argued. "I let him *borrow* it."

David just stared at her. He was studying her face to see if she was joking or not; he couldn't tell.

Nicole touched his hand. "David, look—"

"It's fine, it's fine," he immediately cut in. Although David was tired of Quincy hanging around Nicole, and vice versa, he didn't want to seem like an insecure, jealous boyfriend. He wasn't sure if he was overreacting or not.

"David, you know nothing is go—"

"I said it's fine," David cut in yet again, gathering his books from the chair next to him. "I gotta get to class."

Nicole watched him stand up. "Are you mad?" she asked, tone sullen.

"Nope," he lied.

"If you're not mad, can I have a kiss?" Nicole smiled.

David leaned in and Nicole closed her eyes and tilted her chin up, allowing him direct access to her glossed lips. To her annoyance, David turned his head and kissed her on the cheek instead. "See you later," he said.

Nicole opened her eyes and sucked her teeth as David walked away. "Still giving me these damn adolescent kisses, I see," she muttered.

David, having heard what she said, stiffened and turned around. "What did you say?"

"Nothing David." This time Nicole was noticeably upset. "Have a good class."

Shaking his head, David walked out of the cafeteria.

# Chapter 26

Jason glanced at his watch as he made his way through the glass doors of the athletic department. He nodded at his football coach as the man walked out of the office.

"Jason, how's classes going?" the dark skinned, older man beamed, giving Jason a pat on his arm.

"Pretty good," Jason replied, adjusting the gym bag on his shoulder. "Just looking forward to graduating."

"Well, this school will certainly miss you. *Especially* the football field."

"Yeah well, playing football here has been a good experience," Jason mused. "But I'm sure the new team will be just as good."

Coach Robinson adjusted the baseball cap on his head as he made a face. "Not from what I've seen on the field for spring training," he jeered. "You should come to a few training sessions and show 'em a thing or two."

Jason laughed. "I'll be sure to do that," he promised. He pointed to a closed door in front of him. "Mr. Henderson wanted to see me about something?"

Coach Robinson nodded. "Yeah, he just wanted to talk to you about something that the department wants to do during commencement."

Jason looked confused. "Ummm, and he wants to see *me* about that?" He was on edge. He had no idea what the head of the athletic department wanted from him; the man hardly ever spoke to Jason unless it was after a winning game. Now knowing what the meeting was about, Jason was even more confused.

"Yep. So quit standing around and go into the office, Adams."

Jason shook his head. Coach Robinson usually called him by his last name when he was pushing him to the brink during practice. "Right," Jason replied, moving around him. "See you later."

Coach Robinson spun around and faced Jason's departing back. "You know that the pro league has their eye on you," he said.

Jason halted his progress and turned around.

"A lot of teams want you to play for them," Coach continued.

"That's not what I want to do, Coach," Jason ground out. "You knew when you *recruited* me that I only wanted to play for the scholarship, not to go pro."

"I know that, but think of the money," he pressed. "You're too gifted of an athlete not to see how far it can take you."

Jason began to feel frustrated. "Coach—"

"Not trying to pressure you," he immediately cut in, putting his hands up. "Just letting you know."

Jason took a deep breath in an effort to calm himself down. "Thanks," he said. "Later." Not allowing his coach the opportunity to get another word in, Jason headed over to the door and knocked. Receiving the okay to enter, Jason opened the door and walked over to the large wooden desk, hand outstretched.

Mr. Henderson stood from his seat and shook Jason's hand. "Thanks for coming in, Jason," he smiled.

"Sure." Jason set his bag on the floor near the seat across from Mr. Henderson and sat down. "Can't help but wonder what this is about though."

Mr. Henderson took his seat and folded his hands on the desk. "Well Jason, first of all, I wanted to congratulate you on an amazing four seasons here at this school. Paradise Valley University was honored to recruit you."

Jason blushed as he glanced down at his hands. He'd always been humble about his abilities; constant praise embarrassed him a little. "I appreciate that," he said. "Thank you for my scholarship by the way, it came in handy." Mr. Henderson nodded. "Yeah, you certainly are making the most of it. You've managed to maintain your B average," he commended.

"Thanks," Jason replied. "Not going to lie, it's been rough managing both football and my grades, but my education is important to me."

"Commendable," Mr. Henderson beamed. "Anyway, on to why I wanted to talk to you. This university has an award that we give to outstanding students who play for one of our teams. We only give one away per year and with your performance as both an athlete *and* student, we want to award it to *you*."

Jason's smile could have lit up the entire room. He still had almost two months left of school, and he was already being promised awards. "Oh…wow, that's awesome. Thank you." He stood up and shook the man's hand again. Grateful.

"You're welcome," Mr. Henderson returned, proud. "You will receive a plaque during the graduation ceremony. Your name and jersey number will be placed on our hall of fame wall along with the team trophies," he smiled. "You'll also receive a little something extra, but the final details of that have not been worked out just yet."

"Hey, I appreciate anything that I'm given," Jason beamed, grabbing his bag. "Thanks again."

"No problem, well-earned Jason, well-earned," Mr. Henderson boasted as Jason headed out the door.


Jason was still brimming with pride and excitement as he walked into the basketball court at the gym. Heading through the door, he set his gym bag on the floor by the bleachers.

Mark stopped dribbling and looked over at Jason. "About time bee. We were waiting for like forty-five minutes," he barked.

Jason frowned as he removed his water bottle from his bag.

Josh shook his head. "We've only been here for about five minutes," he contradicted, wiping the sweat from his face.

Mark shot him a glare. "Nobody asked you for the truth," he hissed, earning a snicker from Jason, who removed his sweat jacket.

Josh shook his head as he wiped more sweat from his face with his hand.

"Yo, why you sweatin' so damn much?" Mark mocked.

"It's hot as shit in here," Josh ground out, tossing his hands up.

"Take off that hot ass sweatshirt, then," Mark threw back, dribbling the ball. "You stupid as shit, cuz."

Josh flagged him with his hand. "Whatever," he spat, then turned to Jason. "You seem to be in a good mood bro, what's up?"

Mark scrunched his face up. "Why you all in the man's face and shit?"

"Will you shut up?!" Josh yelled. The outburst caused Mark to bust out laughing.

Jason shook his head in amusement. "Always messin' with people," he commented, holding his hand out for the basketball. "Anyway, I just came from the Athletic department."

"For what? Football season is over," Mark wondered. "You graduatin' dawg, you don't owe them no more practices."

Jason chuckled. "I know, but apparently they were so impressed with me as a player, that they want to give me an award during graduation," he beamed.

Josh and Mark clapped for him. "That's great, congratulations," Josh said.

"Thanks," Jason smiled. "I guess that last game I lost last season didn't tarnish my record *after* all."

"Man fuck that last game," Mark dismissed. "As many games as you won for this damn school?" Mark shook his hand in Jason's direction. "I heard this team *sucked* before you got here freshman year. You damn *right* they givin' you an award and they better give you some money to go along *with* it."

Jason scratched his head. "Yeah, I don't think that's gonna happen," he chortled.

"Five dollars or *something*," Mark pressed. "Cheap ass school and shit... Still not tryna go pro, huh?"

Jason shook his head. "If *one* more person asks me that," he warned.

"Shit you better than *me*," Mark said, ignoring Jason's attitude. "If I had to choose between going to grad school, where I'd have to suffer through more raggedy ass classes for another two years, or go make a ton of money *now*, doing shit I already know *how* to do? ...Man I'd be up on that field in a heartbeat."

"Yeah well, I'm glad to know that you finally acknowledge that I'm better than you," Jason teased. Mark flipped him off.

Josh opened his mouth to speak, but was interrupted by the sound of the door opening. "Sorry I'm late fellas," David apologized. "Got held up."

"At Nicole's?" Mark quickly assumed. He then pointed at David before David had a chance to respond. "My bro, gettin' it in before a game."

David stared at him. "Uh...*no*," he denied, removing his jacket. "I was at the library."

Mark looked angry. "*That's* not a good reason to be late," he barked. "*Sex* is a good reason to be late, not no damn dry ass library."

"Mark, chill out," Josh hurled. "Not *everybody* is interested in bangin' every five minutes."

David breathed a sigh of relief. *Thank you, Josh.* The last thing that he needed, on top of keeping his virginity a secret from both his friends *and* his girlfriend, was Mark goading him about his nonexistent sexual encounters.

"Who said anything about every five minutes?" Mark threw back, unfazed by Josh's annoyance. "You just mad 'cause you ain't gettin' none for *no* minutes."

"You don't know *what* I'm getting," Josh argued.

"Sure I do. *None*," Mark laughed. Josh narrowed his eyes at him. "Matter of fact, I don't want you touching my basketball. You been spending too much time in your room, jerk hands."

"Shut up," Josh hissed, holding his hands out. "Just pass the damn ball."

Mark passed Josh the ball; Josh began to dribble.

"Mark, lay off," Jason urged, stretching. "Josh has plenty of women coming over the house for him."

Mark sucked his teeth, "That's only 'cause they need help with those hard ass business classes he got with 'em," he goaded. "Data Management dates and shit."

Josh couldn't help but laugh. "Whatever, idiot," he threw back, tossing the ball back to Mark. "I'm just hanging out, nothing serious right now."

"There's nothing wrong with that," Jason approved.

"He lyin' like shit,'" Mark mocked, tossing the ball at Josh. He smacked it back at Mark, hitting him in the leg with the ball. "Goddamn it Josh!" he roared, grabbing his leg in dramatic fashion.

"Oh *come* on, it didn't even hit you that hard!" Josh exclaimed as David laughed, and Jason shook his head in disgust.


"How's your day going?" James crooned into the phone.

Sidra slowly steeped a cup of tea as she sat at the dining room table. "It's fine." Her tone was less than enthusiastic.

"You don't sound too convincing," James observed.

"Sorry," she sighed. "Honestly, I'm not feeling well." She rested her hand on her forehead.

"What's wrong?" he asked, concerned.

"Headache." It was the half-truth. While she did have a headache, something else was bothering her. She'd called James the night before and he didn't answer; he'd just called her back ten minutes ago.

"Sorry to hear that, sweetheart," James sympathized.

"Wish I was there to make it better."

Sidra rolled her eyes. *Yeah but we both know that's not happening anytime soon.* "I'll be fine," she grumbled. "So um, are you getting any time off *any*time soon?"

James noticed the bite in Sidra's voice. "Sidra...you know the answer to that," he answered calmly. "This case is really big and it's taking up a lot of my time. Hell, to even *call* you is losing me money," he joked.

"Is that why you didn't answer my phone call last night?" she spat.

"Hold on, I texted you and told you that I couldn't answer," James explained. "When I got a few minutes, I was planning on calling, but figured you'd be sleep."

Sidra rolled her eyes. "Late night had never stopped you from calling me back *before*," she harped, angry.

There was a pause on the line. "Sidra, don't start this nonsense okay, not today," he spat.

"What?" Sidra barked.

"I swear, it's like *every time* I talk to you, I get attitude," James pointed out, frustrated. "I don't know what's going on with you lately, but it seems like I can't do anything right."

Sidra rolled her eyes. "Whatever James, just go make your money."

"See?" James threw back. "That was unnecessary. I said that as a joke and you're taking it personal."

"No, what's unnecessary is the fact that I'm dealing with some stuff that I want to talk to you about because I'm supposed to be able to vent to you and you're always busy," Sidra sniped.

"You act like I haven't *always* been busy," James argued. "I make time for you, you know that."

"I don't know anything but the fact that my headache

just got worse," Sidra sneered, yanking her tea bag out of her mug.

"Yeah? Well thanks to you, *I* have one now," James spat back. "Call me when you cool off."

Sidra opened her mouth to respond, but James had hung up on her. "Asshole," she fumed through clenched teeth as she slammed her phone down on the table.

Sighing, she took a sip of her tea and immediately made a face. "Forgot the damn sugar," she griped of the bland taste. She tapped her fingernails on the tabletop as she stared at her phone. Debating with herself for a moment, she snatched it up. She pinched the bridge of her nose with two fingers as she waited for the person to answer. "Hey Josh... No, I'm not okay right now, I need to get out of this house...really? Are you sure? ...Okay, I'll be over in a few minutes."

This time, when she set the phone down, Sidra felt her mood lighten a bit. Josh seemed to have that effect on her lately. Hearing the door open, she looked over.

"Hey," she said to Malajia and Chasity as they walked in.

"Hey," Malajia returned, setting her purse on the chair.

Chasity sucked her teeth as she looked at her phone. "Who is this Virginia number calling me?" she questioned. "Yeah, it's getting blocked."

"What's wrong with you?" Malajia chuckled. "That old man from the gas station calling again?"

Chasity looked at Malajia, narrowing her eyes. "Why would he be calling my phone?" she slowly asked. "Why would he have my number?"

Malajia held up a finger. "*Obviously*, it was a joke," she threw back.

"*Obviously*, shut up," Chasity hissed.

Sidra snickered at the byplay. "Malajia, you know your jokes make no sense," she commented.

Malajia rolled her eyes, then shot Sidra a side-glance. "You say something, Sidra?"

Sidra, catching the bite in Malajia's tone, stood up from the table. "Wasn't important," she dismissed, pouring her cup of tea in the sink; she no longer had the desire to drink it. "I'll see you two later."

"Yeah," Malajia said as she and Chasity watched Sidra walk out the door without another word.

Chasity looked at Malajia, who was fiddling with the earring in her ear. Malajia glanced up and caught Chasity's stare. "What?"

"You shot a whole dagger at Sidra's face just now," Chasity joked.

Malajia frowned slightly. "No, I didn't."

"Yeah, you *did*," Chasity insisted.

Malajia sighed. "You're right. That wasn't cool," she admitted. "She was joking, I'm just…shit is just rubbing me the wrong way lately."

Chasity tilted her head as she folded her arms. "You're still mad at her," she observed. "I don't blame you," she added when Malajia didn't answer.

"*Should* I be still? I mean, she *did* apologize," Malajia wondered. As much as she felt justified in her feelings towards Sidra because of their argument, Malajia was starting to wonder if she was taking her grudge too far.

Chasity frowned in confusion. "So?" she scoffed. "Who says that's supposed to make shit better? She shouldn't have said it in the *first* place."

"*You've* said worse," Malajia jeered, rolling her eyes.

Chasity stared at her. "No, I *haven't*."

Malajia let out a deep sigh as Chasity walked up the steps. "No, no you haven't," she muttered to herself.


Sidra stirred her soup around in her bowl as she sat quietly across from Josh. Sighing, she sat the spoon down in the bowl and slid it away from her.

"What's wrong? Don't like it?" Josh asked, scooping up a spoonful of his soup. "I know it's my first time making it and all."

Sidra managed a smile. "No, I like it, I just—" she rested her elbows on the table. "Don't have much of an appetite."

Josh took a bite of his homemade chicken noodle soup and winced. "Damn, I think I overdid it with the salt," he grimaced.

Sidra chuckled slightly. "Josh, the soup is good," she assured.

Josh wiped his mouth with a napkin. "To *you*," he muttered, taking a long sip of his water.

Sidra played with the charm bracelet on her wrist. It had been the third night in a row that she had dinner with Josh. With Josh confining himself to the house when he wasn't in class in order to hammer out major homework assignments for the week, Sidra had an excuse to spend some one on one time with him, which she was enjoying.

"So, what's up with you?" Josh asked after finishing his water.

Sidra looked up. "Huh?"

"You've been hiding out here for the past few days pretty much," he said. "That's not like you."

"I'm not *hiding*," Sidra denied, frowning. "I just like your company."

Josh shot her a knowing look. "Sidra," he pressed.

"I'm serious, things are fine," Sidra insisted. That was a total lie. Between the argument that she had with James the other day and everything else that was on her mind, she felt like she was on the verge of a breakdown. The only bright spot was her time with Josh.

Josh studied her. "You know you can't lie to me, right?" he said.

Sidra sat up right in her seat. *Damn, I keep forgetting how well he knows me.* She sighed. "You don't really wanna hear it," she assured.

Josh opened his mouth to speak, but was interrupted by the door opening. Both he and Sidra looked over and saw Mark walk in. "What's up man?" Josh greeted, noticing the annoyed look on Mark's face.

Mark let out a loud sigh. "Fucking accounting homework is about to have me looking stupid all night," he grunted, heading for the kitchen.

Sidra, noticing that Mark hadn't even made eye contact with her, resisted the urge to say something smart. "Hi Mark," she ground out.

"Sidra," Mark spat, opening the refrigerator.

Sidra rolled her eyes. "Still not speaking to me?" she hissed.

"I *did* speak," Mark returned, slinging his book bag over his shoulder with one hand and shaking a bottle of orange juice with the other. "That's more than you deserve."

Sidra frowned as Josh looked at him. "Dude, come on," Josh stepped in.

Mark put his hand up. "I'm cool," he promised. "I'm gonna get to this homework."

Sidra rubbed one eye as Mark disappeared upstairs. "I can't believe he still has an attitude with me," she complained to Josh, who just looked at her. "He's never been this mad at me before."

Josh folded his arms on the table. "Well, I don't think he had a reason to be, until *now*," he stated bluntly.

Sidra looked shocked. "Wait, you're siding with him?" she bit out.

Josh had no intention of upsetting Sidra; the words just came out. Josh put his hands up. "Forget I said that," he said.

Sidra shook her head as she flung some of her hair over her shoulder. "I don't like this feeling," she vented.

"*What* feeling?" Josh probed.

"The feeling that people are upset with me," she clarified. "I mean even Malajia—"

Josh folded his arms on the tabletop again. "Mel is still upset?" he cut in.

"I honestly don't know," Sidra shrugged. "We talked and everything and she accepted my apology. But—"

Josh held his gaze on her. "But *what*?"

"I feel like things are still a little weird," Sidra confessed. "I don't get it. If she forgave me, why the attitude?"

Josh nodded slowly as he listened. He had things to say, but wondered if it was the right time to say them; Sidra seemed stressed enough. However, Sidra was his friend. It was his duty to be honest with her. "Sidra..." he rubbed his arm as he thought of where to begin. She just looked at him in anticipation. "I think you really need to—"

"You think I need to what?" Sidra asked, fixing an intense stare on him.

"Uh—I think you need to drink some more water if you're gonna finish that soup," he deflected.

Sidra managed a giggle as she stirred her soup once more. "How about I just make us something else," she proposed.

"Sure," Josh nodded as Sidra stood from the table and headed for the kitchen. *Yeah, it's not the time*, he thought, rubbing his face with his hand.

# Chapter 27

Standing in the Student Activities office, Alex retrieved a piece of paper from a folder. "So, *how* many high school students are expected to show up for the tour?" she asked the director.

Pushing her glasses up on her nose, the director picked up a piece of paper and closely examined it. "Several hundred," she replied. "We have about five high schools touring."

Alex nodded. With the campus tour coming up soon, Alex was anxious to get the details for her and the other girls. She wanted to be as prepared as possible. "Will my group be split up?"

"No, since we have a big turnout for tour guides this year, you and your friends can guide together."

"Can I pick who's in my tour group?" Alex pressed.

The woman thought for a moment, "Um...I don't think—"

"My little sister will be here touring, so I just wanted to be her guide, if possible," Alex requested. "I know she'd want that too."

"Her name?"

"Sahara Chisolm," Alex answered, scratching her head.

The woman nodded. "Okay, that shouldn't be a problem. Whatever group she's in, I'll put your group as the guide."

Alex smiled gratefully. "Thank you." Upon being dismissed, Alex trotted out of the office.

Cradling her books to her chest, she saw a familiar face

and smiled. "Stacey," she beamed, giving her friend a hug with one arm.

Stacey Addison gave Alex a hug in return. "Sorry, I didn't return your call the other day," she apologized, flinging her long box braids over her shoulder. "These professors are ridiculous with these tests. My face has been in books every damn minute."

Alex chuckled. "Tell me about it," she agreed. Alex smiled as she gestured to Stacey's hair. "I see you're trying pastels now," she teased of Stacey's brown braids, mixed with lavender, pale blue and pink synthetic hair.

Stacey giggled as she grabbed a few of her braids with her hand and looked at them. "Yeah, I drew a picture of a unicorn the other day and got inspired."

Alex shook her head; she knew that whatever Stacey was going to do upon leaving college, it was sure to be artistic. "Well, it looks cute," she complimented. "Oh, Sahara will be down here for the school tour."

Stacey beamed. "Aww, I love it," she said, clasping her hands together, "I can't wait to see her." Someone caught Stacey's eye and she signaled for them to come over. "Alex, I want you to meet somebody."

Alex stood in anticipation. Seeing a tall, dark skinned young man walk up to Stacey, she smiled. *Okay Stacey* she thought in approval of the handsome man.

"Alex, this is my boyfriend Greg. Greg, this is my sister from another mister, Alex," Stacey eagerly introduced.

Alex chuckled as she offered an outstretched hand. "Nice to meet you Greg," she smiled, as Greg shook her hand. "You're on the basketball team, right?"

Greg nodded. "Yeah," he smiled in return. "Oh and nice to meet you too."

Stacey looked at him. "Can you wait for me by class? I'll just be a minute," she said.

"Sure." He took off, leaving both women to follow his progress.

"I see where *your* time has *really* been," Alex teased,

giving Stacey a pat on her arm.

Stacey rolled her eyes. "No, I've really been *studying*," she assured. "*Most* of the time, anyway. I've been here three years, I had to snag *one* of these fine men eventually."

Alex laughed. "I hear that." She pointed at her. "Use protection."

"Always," Stacey returned, clutching her books to her chest. She peered at a classroom across from her as the door opened and students filtered out. "*Speaking* of fine men...what's up with you and Eric?"

Alex's smile faded as she glanced down at her sneakers. "A whole bunch of *nothing*," she sulked. She let out a quick sigh as she returned her gaze to Stacey. "He's moved on, can't say that I blame him."

Stacey frowned. "Moved on with *who*?"

"*Some* girl," Alex grimaced.

"You mean the girl that was with him a few weeks ago?" Stacey pressed.

Alex looked skeptical. "I believe so," she slowly put out. "Why?"

"Girl, that's not his girlfriend," Stacey dismissed with a wave of her hand.

Alex let out a huff. "Okay, so maybe she's just his *friend*. It doesn't matter—"

"No Alex, she's nothing to him but a *family member*," Stacey cut in. Alex's eyes widened. "She's his *cousin*."

"Wait...*what*?!" Alex exclaimed. She put her hands up. "Hold on, how do *you* know that?"

Stacey fiddled with the large purple hoop earring in her ear. "She *said* it," she revealed. "We were standing in line at the donut shop. She complimented me on my braids, and we started talking about *something*, then Eric walked in and she said 'hey cousin'."

Alex stared at her, blinking slowly. "Um..."

"And before you try to think of an excuse, think of *one* couple that calls each other *cousin*," Stacey interrupted, putting a finger up. "That would be creepy."

"Point taken," Alex muttered. She scratched her head in confusion. "Wow...that would explain the flirting that he did with me... But why would he make it seem like he was seeing her and he wasn't?"

Stacey tilted her head. "You really need an answer to that?" she chuckled. "Point is, he's still *single*. Girl, you better go grovel, *something*."

Alex flagged Stacey with her hand. "Alex doesn't grovel," she boasted.

"Yeah well *Alex* messed up pretty badly so she just had *better*," Stacey teased. Alex made a face. "I gotta go," Stacey said, heading in the same direction as her boyfriend. "See you later."

"Call me," Alex called after Stacey as she walked off. Turning to head for the exit, Alex couldn't help but let a slight smile come through.


Chasity was typing vigorously on her laptop. Reaching for her glass of iced tea, she let out a groan as something flashed across her screen. "I swear to God, work! Damn it!" she yelled at the data.

"Chasity, who are you yelling at?!" Alex shouted through her closed door.

Chasity rolled her eyes as she let out a heavy sigh. "My laptop!" she yelled back.

There was a pause. "Carry on," Alex said.

"Thanks," Chasity muttered, grabbing a nacho from the plate on her desk. She'd been glued to her desk in her room for what felt like hours, working on a coding assignment that had her stumped. But Chasity couldn't figure out if it was due to just her lack of knowledge on what it took to make her program work, or if her distractions had something to do with a voice message that she'd received earlier.

Taking a deep breath, Chasity put her fingers back to the keys and typed a few more lines. Hitting enter, the data flashed across the screen.

*Fuck! Fuck! Fuck!* Furious, Chasity gripped the sides of her desk, and took several deep breaths. Picking up her phone, she hit the video call button.

"Hey Chaz," Jason answered as his face appeared on her screen.

"What are you doing right now?" Chasity's tone did not hide her frustration.

"On my way to the library to finish this research paper," Jason answered.

Chasity pinched the bridge of her nose. "Shit," she mumbled. "That's right, you *did* say you had that going on today."

"Something wrong?"

"Yeah, I can't get this stupid ass program for Dr. Porter's class to work," Chasity vented. "I swear, I don't know what the hell I'm doing wrong. I wanted to see if you could help me."

"Never thought you'd actually come to me for help with computer codes," he chortled. "I'm usually the one asking *you* for help."

Chasity stared at the phone. Her eyes narrowed. "I'm lost, was that supposed to be funny?" she hissed.

Jason rubbed his face with his hand. "Alright, just relax," he placated. "Step away from the laptop before you throw it and I'll come over after I get out of here and see what I can do to help."

Chasity sighed. "Okay, see you later."

"See you."

Chasity ended the call. Just as she put the phone down on her desk, she heard a knock at the door. "Go *away* Malajia," she barked at it.

"It's not even *me* though," the muffled voice came through the door.

Chasity stared at the door, annoyed, for several seconds. "What the fuck?" she muttered to herself. Shaking her head, she stood from her seat and went for the door. Opening it, she found Malajia standing there eyes wide, alongside Emily, who had her hand over her face laughing.

"What?" Malajia asked, noticing the death stare that Chasity was giving.

"You make my face hurt, you know that right?" Chasity spat.

Malajia chuckled as Emily wiped a tear from her eye.

"That was sooo *stupid,*" Emily laughed. "She really just said, 'it's not even me though'."

Chasity shook her head as Malajia busted out laughing. "Don't laugh at her Emily, it only encourages her bullshit," Chasity ground out, moving aside to let them both in. "What do you want?" she asked, sitting back at her desk.

"Talent show, we wanna go so come on," Malajia explained, shaking a small bag of popcorn around in her hand.

Chasity stared, blinking slowly. "And you thought I'd rather see a bunch of no talent having idiots embarrass themselves on stage, than sit here and work on my homework?" she sneered.

"Do we *really* need to answer that?" Malajia countered.

"Point taken," Chasity muttered, leaning back in her seat.

Emily looked over at the food on Chasity's plate. "Ooh nachos," she beamed, reaching across the desk and grabbing a nacho from Chasity's plate.

"Girl, keep your thin ass fingers off my plate," Chasity griped, looking at her phone.

"Ahhh, you got your nacho taken," Malajia teased.

Emily stuffed the chip into her mouth, then glanced in Malajia's open bag of popcorn before digging her hand in and taking some, much to Malajia's displeasure.

"Emily you know how I feel about my food!" Malajia wailed, flicking her hand repeatedly in Emily's face.

Emily laughed as she stuffed the popcorn into her mouth.

Chasity rubbed her temples with her fingertips. "Malajia, can you take your surround sound outburst elsewhere?" she griped.

"What's wrong with *you*?" Malajia asked, taking some popcorn from her bag. "You pissed at that raggedy ass homework?"

"Yep," Chasity grunted. "Among other bullshit."

"*What* other bullshit?" Malajia probed.

Chasity examined her nails. "My ever-absentee sperm donor called me today," she revealed, voice dripping with disdain.

"Oh...well, that's great," Emily hesitantly replied. "*Isn't* it?" she wondered when Chasity scowled at her.

"No, no it's *not*," Chasity grunted.

"Did you actually talk to him?" Malajia asked.

"*Fuck* no," Chasity spat. "You don't play me after I open the door to you and expect me to talk. Fuck him. I let it go to voicemail."

Malajia sat on Chasity's bed. "Well, sweetie, what did the message say?" she pressed. She knew that Chasity's father was a sensitive subject for her; clearly whatever the man said had upset her.

Chasity shook her head. "A whole bunch of bullshit," she vented. "Talking about he's gonna come to campus and visit me soon."

Emily fiddled with her bracelet. "You don't think he's telling the truth?" she asked.

Malajia put her hand up at Emily. "Em, sweetie, just shhh," she advised, when Chasity looked at Emily like she had lost her mind.

"Derrick is a liar," Chasity reiterated. "I'm starting to realize that he's gonna reach out every few *months* or so just to ease his own conscious. Just like the *last* time he promised to start trying, this time will be no different." She glanced back at her laptop screen. "I just wish he'd leave me alone all together. Like...just stay gone."

Malajia poked her lip out. "Come on booski, don't get all sad on me," she said.

Chasity rolled her eyes. "Stop it."

"No, I'm serious," Malajia insisted. "I hate when people make you sad, it makes me wanna smack whoever did it and as cute as your father *is*, I'd gladly give him a two-piece to the face."

Chasity eyed Malajia in disgust. "Eww."

Malajia snickered.

"I know that I might be the minority in thinking this, but maybe your father will come around," Emily chimed in. "I mean, you never know. My mother finally got her mess together, so your dad could do the same."

Chasity looked at her. "Happy for you and your mother Emily, but my situation won't turn out the same," she rebuked, even toned.

Malajia stood from the bed. "That's it, you need a cheer up session," she said. "To the talent show we go."

"I'm really not trying to go to that bullshit," Chasity complained.

"Oh bitch, you *goin'*," Malajia demanded. "You not leaving me with Emily by myself." She then turned to Emily. "You know I love you, but you be dry."

"Yeah, yeah, I know," Emily chuckled, waving her hand at Malajia dismissively. "Oh, we should call Sidra and invite her."

"Ummm, no I think we should leave Sidra where she is," Malajia hesitantly put out. She wanted to enjoy herself and she felt that if Sidra was there, that her mood would change.

"Well, her feelings might be hurt if we don't at least *ask* her," Emily pressed. "We asked *Alex*, even though she doesn't want to go."

"I really don't care about Sidra's feelings at this moment," Malajia mumbled.

Emily looked at Malajia, skeptical. She noticed the difference in Malajia when it came to Sidra. "Are you two okay?"

"Who me and Chasity?" Malajia questioned, feigning confusion.

"No, you and *Sidra*," Emily clarified. "I know that what

happened was pretty bad, but I thought that she apologized.
At least that's what Alex *told* me."

"She *did*," Malajia confirmed. "Look, can we just go? I
don't want to miss the opening. I hear that Quincy is
supposed to be juggling basketballs."

Chasity stared in disbelief, before standing from her seat.
"Oh I *gotta* go see that shit," she laughed. "One of those balls
are gonna smack him right in that big ass head of his."

"And Mr. Bradley is supposed to be playing the damn
flute," Malajia added, amused.

"Wait *what*?" Chasity laughed.


"Sahara, you already know that Ma isn't gonna let you
spend the week down here... Yes, I know you're on spring
break... My bed is not big enough for *both* of us to sleep in
anyway... You don't want to sleep on this floor, trust me...
Girl, you have another two weeks and you'll be down here
for the tour, and I'll *think* about letting you spend the
*weekend*... Semaj's goal in life is to annoy you. He's your
little brother get over it... I gotta go, love you, bye."

Alex shook her head in amusement as she hung up her
cell phone. It was always a pleasure talking to her family
back home, especially her sister. Having spent most of her
afternoon and early evening curled up on the couch with her
grammar textbooks, the half hour conversation with her sister
was a welcomed break.

Sidra walked through the door. "Hey Alex," she sighed.

Alex looked up "Hey sweetie," she returned. "How was
your study group?"

"Boring," Sidra huffed, flopping down on the couch next
to Alex. "I would've much rather studied by myself."

"I hear you," Alex chuckled. "I made some salmon and
rice, you want some? I didn't put it away yet."

Sidra shook her head. "No thanks, not really hungry,"
she declined, removing her jacket.

Alex scratched her head as she studied Sidra. Her

demeanor hadn't been the same since she left for spring break. "How's your brother doing?"

"He's good," Sidra assured. "The baby is good too."

"He's still sticking to his guns about not being with India?"

"God, I *hope* so," Sidra replied. "So far, so good."

"Good," Alex breathed. "Still can't believe the girl lied about getting an abortion... She's *all* the way crazy." Although Alex was relieved to hear that Sidra's niece or nephew was safe, she still couldn't believe that India would lie about such a thing. She only prayed that that was the end of the drama with Sidra's family.

"Yeah," Sidra agreed.

"Is something else bothering you?" Alex wondered. "I mean, crazy aside, things seem good on the family front... You've been kind of down lately."

"Just have a lot on my mind," Sidra answered. "I got in a fight with James a few days ago."

Alex looked shocked. "Oh really? About what?"

Sidra shrugged. "Apparently I'm acting like a bitch and he doesn't like it," she vaguely replied.

Alex frowned. "He called you a bitch?" she charged, angry.

Sidra quickly shook her head. "No, he'd never do that, I was just summarizing," she answered, somber. "He told me to call him when I cool off and well...that was like four days ago and I'm *still* not cool."

Alex rubbed Sidra's shoulder. "All couples argue from time to time. It'll be okay," she soothed.

Sidra shrugged. "I guess," she muttered. "Honestly, that's not all that's been bothering me," she admitted, playing with some of her hair. "I'm feeling a lot of tension around me."

Alex looked confused. "What do you mean?"

"Well Mark is pissed at me over what I said to Malajia and I'm not sure, but I think that *Malajia* might still be pissed at me too... Maybe even the others."

"Did any of them *say* anything?" Alex asked.

"No, not necessarily," Sidra replied. "They *talk* to me, but things seem weird." She sighed. "The girls even went out and didn't invite me."

"You mean to that talent show?" Alex asked, recalling Malajia coming into her room earlier that day, asking her to come. "You weren't here, Sid. *I* didn't even go."

"But they *asked* you right?" Sidra threw back. Alex sighed. "Me not being in the house never stopped them from inviting me places with them. That's what *cell phones* are for."

Alex tried to choose her words carefully. She'd noticed the tension herself, but decided against making the girls sit and talk it out. After all, Alex was trying her best to change her intrusive, meddling ways. "Um…I don't really know what to say. I've been pretty preoccupied lately, so I haven't noticed much."

"I know, I just… I don't *like* this," Sidra sulked. "It's like everything I say, gets a negative reaction…and I'm not saying anything differently than I was before… I want things to be back to normal."

"A lot was said Sidra, and sometimes it takes a little longer for the raw feeling to go away," Alex pointed out. Sidra just sighed. "I know you apologized but…maybe you should just talk to Malajia again."

"Maybe," Sidra pondered. She gathered her belongings and stood from the couch. "I'm gonna go work on this paper now. Thanks for letting me bug you."

"You're not bugging me sweetie. I'm here for you anytime," Alex returned.

Sidra offered a slight smile and headed up the steps.

Malajia broke a piece of brownie and placed it into her mouth. "Damn this is a good ass brownie," she said to herself as she tapped the keys of her laptop. Hearing a knock at the door, she glanced over at it. "It's open."

"Hi," Sidra greeted, walking in.

Malajia looked up. "Hey."

"Um...I was gonna go pick up a cinnamon bun, wanted to know if you wanted one," Sidra offered.

Malajia shook her head. "No, I'm good." She went right back to looking at her laptop.

Sidra stood there. Unsure of what to say next. After her earlier conversation with Alex, she spent the next few hours in her room, trying to work on her paper. Hearing Malajia's voice prompted her to go to the other girl's room. Sidra had hoped that the encounter wouldn't be awkward, that what she perceived would be all in her head. But alas, that was not the case. Malajia seemed stiff when talking to her.

"So um...how was the talent show?" Sidra asked at an attempt to start another conversation.

Malajia took a deep breath. "As bad as you can imagine," she commented, unenthused. "Quincy got busted in the face with one of the basketballs he was trying to juggle. And Mr. Bradley's flute fell apart while he was blowing in it," she informed, rubbing her arm. "Chasity's screamin' ass laugh almost got us kicked out...or was that *mine*?" she tried to remember. "No, it was hers." She waved her hand. "Anyway, some of those fools had a nerve to have props."

Sidra chuckled. "Well, it's a good thing they didn't have hoola hoops up there. You might've been tempted to go up there and embarrass yourself like you did during the contest that we had back in our high school."

Malajia stared at her screen as Sidra laughed at the memory. "Right," she muttered. Normally being poked fun by her friends wouldn't bother her; it was what they did. But when it came to Sidra, Malajia was having a hard time taking her little jabs as just jokes.

"Now, if they had a *pole* up there, you would be a *pro*," Sidra teased.

Malajia slowly turned and looked at Sidra, who was clearly amused. "Really, Sidra?" she calmly put out. Both her voice and her face were void of any amusement. Sidra, catching Malajia's look, stopped laughing. *Shit, she's pissed.* Sidra put her hand on her chest. "Mel, I—I'm sorry, I was just—"

"You were just joking, yeah I know," Malajia sneered, holding her intense gaze.

Sidra's face fell. She had no intention of insulting Malajia; she was just trying to fall back into old verbal jousting habits. The tension could be cut with a knife. "Um, I'm just gonna go," she murmured. "Sorry to bother you."

"Uh huh," Malajia muttered as Sidra made a hasty departure out of her room, shutting the door behind her. She rested her elbows on her desk and put her head in her hands. "Chill Malajia, chill," she whispered to herself.

# Chapter 28

"Yo, these tacos are good as shit," Mark declared, taking a bite of one.

Malajia stared at him with disgust. "You hype as shit eating that dry ass taco," she hissed.

Chasity chuckled as Alex busted out laughing. "Tearing that thing up, all outside and shit," Chasity commented.

"I know, right?" Malajia agreed, glancing at Chasity before turning back to an annoyed looking Mark. "Who the hell eats tacos from the caf, outside?"

"They not from the caf, you asshole," Mark snapped. "And how you talking shit and you *just* asked me for a bite?"

"I don't remember that shit," Malajia denied with a wave of her hand. The sunny weather was bringing everyone out to the quad that Tuesday afternoon. Mark, Malajia, Chasity, and Alex were sitting on a bench, watching passersby.

"You on time out, yo. I'm sick of your shit," Mark grumbled, earning a laugh from Malajia.

"You two will be sixty years old *still* putting each other in time out," Alex chortled, opening a bottle of juice.

"He better hope I'm still *with* his black ass at sixty," Malajia ground out.

Mark took another bite of taco. "Shut up. Who *else* you gonna be with?"

Malajia sucked her teeth at him. "Chaz," she said, turning towards Chasity. "You and Jason wanna double date with me and Mark tomorrow night?"

"I just said you on time out," Mark cut in, before Chasity

had the chance to respond.

Malajia snapped her head at him. "Boy shut the hell up!" she barked, smacking his hand. The force from the slap sent the rest of Mark's taco falling out of his hand on to the ground. Remorseful, Malajia put her hand over her mouth. "Oops."

Mark stared at her, eyes narrowed. "You owe me another fuckin' taco," he slowly put out, voice calm.

Malajia tried not to laugh. "Okay."

"I want a *homemade* taco, and you gotta make it butt naked."

Malajia snickered, while Chasity made a face in disgust.

Alex looked over, eyes wide. "In *whose* kitchen is she making a damn taco, naked?!" she exclaimed.

"Yeah, you can count us out of that double date," Chasity affirmed. "Nobody feels like y'all nonsense."

"You just mad that Jason ain't asking *you* for no naked tacos," Mark jeered. Malajia busted out laughing, giving his arm a playful slap.

"No, I promise that's not why I'm mad," Chasity threw back, tone even, sarcastic.

"Nobody answered my question about where Malajia is making these damn naked tacos," Alex cut in, agitated. "*Nobody* wants to see that."

Hearing her phone ring, Chasity rolled her eyes. She pulled it from her pocket; letting out a groan, she went to put it back.

"Who is that?" Alex asked. "Your phone rang like four times since we've been out here."

"Yes, I know that, I've heard it," Chasity spat. "And like the *last* four times, I'm ignoring it."

When her phone rang again, Alex grabbed Chasity's hand; the hand that held her phone. "Sperm donor?" she asked, looking at Chasity's screen.

Mark snickered while Malajia put her hand over her face, shaking her head in the process. "Yo, you wild, Chaz," Mark commented, amused.

Alex rolled her eyes at Mark, then focused her attention back on Chasity, who was steady ignoring another phone call. "Sweetie—"

"No," Chasity interrupted, having an idea what Alex was about to say.

Alex squeezed Chasity's hand. "Chasity, answer it," she urged, calm. Chasity looked at her. "Come on, it could be important, this is now call number six," Alex insisted.

Malajia gave Chasity a slight nudge. "Busted boots has a point," she put in, earning a snicker from Chasity.

Angry, Alex reached over and tried to grab Malajia's shirt, but was blocked by Chasity's arm.

"What? I was *agreeing* with you," Malajia hurled at Alex.

Alex put her hands up as she turned away from Malajia. "Nope, not worth my energy," she grunted. She took Chasity's phone from her hand and hit the answer button when it rang again. "Don't curse, your dad is on the line," she quickly put out as Chasity was about to react.

Annoyed, Chasity snatched the phone from Alex. She rolled her eyes as she placed it to her ear. "Yes," she bit out. "Why? ...What? ...I'm hanging out, *why?*..." she frowned. "You're *where?* ...You don't think you should've *asked* me first?—Uh huh...uh huh... Fine, give me like ten minutes."

"What's up?" Alex charged, seeing Chasity's confused look as she hung up her phone.

"My dad just said he's around the corner from campus and wants to come see me," Chasity informed, irritated.

"Really? Like *now?*" Malajia replied, shocked.

"Apparently *so*," Chasity confirmed.

Malajia's mouth dropped open. "Well shit, I guess he *wasn't* lying when he said that he would see you soon," she commented. "When did he first call you, two days ago?"

Chasity rolled her eyes. "Please," she ground out, standing from her seat. "I might as well get this over with."

"You going back to the house?" Alex asked.

"Yeah," Chasity answered, pushing her hair behind her

ear.

"I'll go with you, I gotta grab my jacket," Alex announced, standing up. "It's freezing in that damn English building."

Chasity stared at her. "Yeah, I didn't need to know all that," she mocked.

Alex sucked her teeth, then playfully poked Chasity on the arm. "Smart ass," she said. "Bye guys," Alex waved to Mark and Malajia as she and Chasity walked off.

"Damn, I wish I didn't have to go to this stupid class. I'd go and get another look at Chasity's sexy ass father," Malajia muttered, playing with a few strands of hair.

Mark glanced at her. "Really? You just gonna say that shit while I'm sitting right here?"

"Yup," she answered without a qualm. Her laughter at Mark's annoyance faded when she saw Sidra walking up the brick path. Her eyes locked with Sidra as the girl walked past. Sidra smiled slightly and offered a slight wave. Malajia returned the wave with a head nod and small wave of her own. She let out a heavy sigh when Sidra kept walking.

Malajia felt a little bad. She knew that normally, she would yell Sidra's name to annoy her. And Sidra would sit down with them, make a comment about Malajia being loud, before settling into comfortable conversation. She wondered if they would ever go back to normal.

"Don't feel bad." Mark's voice cut into Malajia's thoughts.

"For *what*?" Malajia asked, tone sullen.

"For not being all extra friendly with Sidra," he clarified. "She deserves to feel that distance."

Malajia let out a sigh. She understood Mark's gripe with Sidra. She appreciated the way that he was protective over her feelings. But although she wasn't too fond of Sidra, Malajia didn't want everyone else taking on her feelings. "Mark, I know you're still—"

"You damn *right* I am," Mark cut in. "The shit she said was foul babe. And the fact that she expects you to just go back to how things were even though she apologized, is some bullshit."

"You don't think her apology was sincere?" Malajia questioned.

"No, I'm not saying that," Mark clarified, balling up the paper in his hand. "I'm sure she meant it, but—and I love Sidra to death, you *know* that—but she's never been held accountable for shit that she says... She says what the hell she wants and expects all to be fine and well when *she* wants them to."

Malajia just sat there and listened as Mark spoke to her. What he was saying, mirrored her own thoughts.

"It shouldn't have taken her a freakin' *week* to apologize to you," Mark spat. "I don't care *what* she was going through. *You* had nothing to do with that, and she took that shit out on you...that's not right."

"Yeah," Malajia sighed, resting her arm on his shoulder. She leaned her head on it. "You're right babe."

"And I'm *still* not understanding why she ain't out the damn group," Mark fussed.

Malajia lifted her head up and looked at him. "What are you talking about?"

"Why she still in the group and shit?" he repeated. "When *I* put a fuckin' pair of glasses on a damn dinner table, y'all had me standing outside y'all house staring through the damn window all lonely, goin' to Easter egg hunts without me and shit."

"You still feel some kind of way about that?" Malajia observed, fighting to keep her laughter contained.

"Hell *yeah* I feel some kind of way," Mark threw back. "Y'all don't kick me out the group."

Malajia shook her head. "I don't think a kick out would resolve this anyway," she chortled.

"Oh, but it did for *me*?" Mark challenged.

"Are you gonna set David up on blind dates with glasses again?" Malajia threw back.

"Nah," Mark chuckled.

Malajia ran her hand over his head. "Thanks though, babe," she said, giving him a kiss on the lips. "Anytime," Mark smiled, touching her chin. "Want me to loosen the caps on her iced coffees?" Malajia laughed. "No, crazy."

Chasity walked through the house door with Alex following close behind. "Remind me to never walk with you again," Chasity griped as Alex shut the door behind her. "What did I do?" Alex asked, amusement in her voice. "You had like a half hour conversation with everybody you saw on the way back here," Chasity hissed, heading for the kitchen.

"You are worse at exaggerating than Malajia's behind," Alex chuckled. "Let me go get this damn jacket and get to this class. Another paper due." She let out a huff. "I swear, graduation can't come fast enough."

"*Still* giving me your life story when I didn't ask for it," Chasity sneered, nonchalant as she grabbed a bottle of water from the refrigerator.

Alex flagged Chasity with her hand, trotting up the steps. A knock at the door stopped her in her tracks. Alex turned around on the steps. "Is that him? Is that your dad?" She was excited as she made her way back down the steps.

Chasity sat her water on the counter. "Girl, calm your ass down," she ground out, going to the door. Opening it, her face was void of any pleasantries. Her father was standing there.

"That was quick," she mentioned, unenthused.

Derrick Parker offered a small smile. "I told you that I was minutes away," he reminded.

Chasity stared at him, resisting the urge to roll her eyes, or slam the door in his face. Sure, she'd texted him the directions to her campus house while walking back with Alex, but she almost wished she hadn't; seeing him was not high on her list of things to do.

"Can I come in?" he asked after a moment.

Chasity let out a sigh. "Yeah," she muttered, moving aside to let him in.

"Thank you," he said, grateful. Once he stepped inside, he moved in for a hug. "Good to see you," he said.

Chasity casually backed up, preventing the embrace from taking place. "Right," she uttered, shutting the door.

The disappointment was clear on Derrick's face, but he decided not to harp on it. He looked up at the smiling Alex, who was standing on the steps. "Hi," he waved.

Chasity shot a glare Alex's way. *Will she take her smiling ass on somewhere?!* "Dad, this is Alex. Alex, this is Derrick," she quickly put out.

"Hi Mr. Parker," Alex beamed. She'd never met Chasity's father face to face before, but she did remember the ski resort hotel that he'd put them up in over winter break their freshman year. "It's nice to meet you, and thanks again for the whole ski resort thing—"

"Alex, don't you have an ugly ass jacket to go get?" Chasity hissed, staring daggers at Alex.

Alex met her gaze and pointed at her. "Right. I'll go get that."

Chasity followed her progress as Alex walked back upstairs. She shook her head. *I know her ass is standing by the steps listening*, she thought.

"Nice place," Derrick commented, looking around the living space. "Living quarters have gotten a lot better over the years."

"This isn't the army, nobody says living quarters," Chasity sneered.

Derrick chuckled a bit. "Noted."

Chasity stared at him for a moment; she wasn't interested in small talk. "Dad...what are you doing here?" she asked, directly.

Derrick rubbed his chin, then pointed to the couch. "Can I sit?"

Chasity gave a slight nod. Derrick sat down on the couch

and patted the cushion next to him. Chasity sat on the accent chair across from the couch.

Derrick chuckled. "You're not going to make this easy, are you?"

Chasity ran her hand through her hair. "*What* are you doing here?" she repeated, patience wearing thin.

"I wanted to talk to you."

She frowned in confusion. "You could do that over the phone, *if* you actually *called*," she bit out.

Derrick glanced down at his hands, then let out a deep sigh. "Chasity listen—"

"You played me," she cut in, angry. "You begged me to talk to you after Brenda died and when I finally did, you blew me off, just like you *always* did."

"I am sorry for not contacting you these past few months," he replied. "I mean it, I know that I was wrong and if it means anything—"

"It doesn't," Chasity spat.

"I got nervous, okay," Derrick blurted out, flustered. "I—all I knew was that I wanted to talk to you but I had no idea what to actually *say* to you." He rubbed his face when she held her angry gaze on him. "I didn't say it was a *good* excuse, but it's the only one that I *have*."

Chasity shook her head at him.

"I had hoped that my Christmas gift to you would've made up a little bit," he added.

Chasity felt like she was about to snap. She sat up in her seat. "Are you f—seriously?" she hissed. Derrick couldn't say anything, "I didn't *want* a goddamn bracelet," she barked. "I wanted you to call me after you promised you *would*. What is *wrong* with you?"

Derrick found it hard to hold eye contact with Chasity. As much as she tried to hide it, she was clearly hurt. "A *lot* apparently," Derrick admitted, somber. "Can't say that I was surprised that you returned it to me… I didn't mean it as an insult, I promise."

"I think we've already established that your promises

don't mean shit," she spat, sitting back in her seat.

Derrick took a deep breath. "I know that I deserve everything that you've thrown at me," he admitted. "I know that I have not been the father that you deserved; I've always been distant—" he sighed. "Sure, I can chalk it up to my relationship with Brenda or my lack of relationship with my *own* father, but those are just more, meaningless excuses for me not being who I was *supposed* to be for you... It's nobody's fault but my own, I know."

Chasity didn't say anything; she just sat there trying not to get up and leave.

Derrick adjusted his position in his seat. He knew that Chasity wasn't trying to hear what he was saying; he understood why. But he had to make her listen. "Chasity, I know that I've said this before, and I know you don't believe me, but I really *do* want to have a relationship with you," he pleaded. "A *real* father-daughter relationship... One that you *deserve*. Just give me a chance, please."

Chasity let out a quick sigh. "I'm no longer interested," she hissed, defiant.

Derrick's face fell.

"We haven't had one *this* long; what's the point?" Chasity added, digging the knife in deeper. "You're about *six months* too late for that chance. I don't care anymore."

"I think you *do*," her father contradicted, eyeing her intensely. "If you *didn't*, then...you wouldn't be this upset."

"I can be angry and *still* not care," Chasity threw back.

"You can, but...that's not you," he insisted.

Chasity frowned. "Please don't sit here and act like you know *anything* about me," she ground out.

"I know *some* things," Derrick countered.

"Oh what? That my favorite color used to be *pink* and I liked dressing in frilly dresses and shit when I was five years old?" she sneered. "Yeah, a *lot* of shit has changed since then," she added when Derrick chuckled a bit.

Derrick shook his head; Chasity's smart mouth never ceased to surprise him. "Noted... So how about I start *getting* to know you," he proposed.

"I don't trust you enough to allow that," Chasity replied.

"So let me start *earning* it," he insisted, determined.

Chasity rolled her eyes. "Starting with face to face conversations... I'll be here in Virginia for a while for work. I'd *love* to come visit you more often. Maybe we can go on dates."

"*Dates*?" Chasity sneered.

"Father-daughter dates," he clarified. "I'm talking days where I pick you up and we spend the whole day together...like we *used* to do when you were little."

Chasity frowned. Before Derrick had started letting Brenda's erratic behavior drive a wedge between the two of them, they did used to spend days together, just the two of them. She remembered how much fun she had with him. Then the pleasant memory faded when she remembered how quickly things changed when he started treating her like she didn't exist.

"I know you're hesitant," he began, sensing how she felt. "And I don't blame you. But I'm sitting here telling you that I want to make this work... I don't want to miss out on another important moment in your life... I don't want to miss out on your life *period*."

Chasity rubbed her face and took a deep breath. She was silent as she thought.

*I know he messed up, but if he's coming to you and trying to make amends, just talk to him at least...like you did for me. You may not see it now, but you will need him one day.*

The words from Brenda's letter to Chasity played back in her head. As hesitant as she was about believing him, she felt like she at least should try. "Fine Dad...fine," she answered finally.

Derrick broke into a smile. "Yeah?" he asked.

Chasity shrugged slightly. "It's on *you* so...what do you wanna do?" she threw back.

Derrick beamed at the possibilities. He clasped his hands

together. "Okay, so I was thinking tomorrow after your last class, if you're not busy, I'll pick you up and we'll go to an amusement park, maybe the movies, do a little skating and have dinner afterwards," he proposed.

Chasity stared at him in wide-eyed, stunned silence for several seconds. "Just wanna pack every summer activity into one day, huh?" she commented,

Her father let out a laugh. "Too much?"

"*Way* too much at once," she confirmed. "We can start with dinner, but I can't do it tomorrow."

"Sorry, I'm sure you're busy most of the week. Friday then?" he proposed, hopeful.

Chasity nodded. "That'll be fine."

Ecstatic, Derrick nodded. "Okay perfect. I'll find a nice place and make a reservation."

"Okay," she agreed, standing from her seat.

Derrick too stood. "I'll call you later tonight with the info…I promise," he smiled.

Chasity offered a slight smile. "Okay," she repeated.

Derrick held his hand out. After hesitating for a moment, Chasity placed her hand in his. He held on to it. "See you Friday," he said.

She nodded as he walked out the door. As soon as it shut, Chasity slowly turned around and glanced up the steps. Just as she suspected, Alex was standing at the top, a smile on her face.

"I really hate you," Chasity sneered.

Unfazed, Alex bolted down the steps with delight. "I'm so happy for you, Chaz," she gushed.

Chasity looked confused. "Stop it," she dismissed.

"No, I *won't* stop," Alex pressed, excited. "I'm serious, this seems like it'll be the start of an actual relationship with your father, which I know deep down, you need...and *want*." Alex gave Chasity's arm a rub when she didn't respond, electing to glance off to the side instead. "Come on Mama, it's okay to let your guard down sometimes," Alex said, sincere. "You did it with *us*, and look how that turned out."

Chasity squinted her eyes at Alex. "Not your best argument, right now."

Alex giggled. "Now, *you* stop it," she countered.

"You might want to get your ass to class before you get locked out," Chasity suggested.

Alex gasped. "Damn it!" she panicked, running for the door. She paused and turned around. "Your favorite color used to be *pink?*"

Chasity frowned as she pointed to the door.

Alex laughed and ran to class.

David removed his sweat jacket as he got comfortable on Nicole's bed. "Can you pass me the popcorn?" he asked, holding his hand out.

Nicole grabbed the bag of popcorn from her lap and handed it to him.

"Thanks," he mumbled, grabbing a handful. He'd come over to Nicole's room forty-five minutes ago to watch a movie with her. Although the images flashed across the screen, David wasn't paying attention; his mind was plagued with other things.

Nicole's long sigh broke the silence. "This movie is so dry," she muttered of the lackluster movie.

David busted out laughing as he ate his popcorn. "I wasn't gonna say anything."

Nicole stood up and stretched, then grabbed the remote. "I'm sorry, I should've known that these movies would be crappy," she muttered. "Pilfered them from my Grandpa's stash."

"No, it's okay," David assured, smiling. "*My* collection isn't much better than this."

Nicole sighed again as she turned the TV off.

David adjusted the glasses on his face. "You wanna go to an *actual* movie?"

Nicole shook her head. "No, not really," she answered, pushing her hair behind her ear. "There's nothing out that I really wanna see."

David shrugged as he looked at his watch. "Yeah, me neither," he agreed. Nicole stared at him. It looked like she had a question, but was afraid to ask. "What's on your mind?"

Nicole hesitated for a moment. "David—I want you to know that I'm an affectionate person," she began finally. David looked confused; that came out of nowhere. "Okay," he replied. "Is there a reason why you said that?"

"Is that something that you have a problem with?" she asked.

David was taken aback. "No, why *would* I?"

"I guess I'm wondering because every time I go to give you a kiss, or even *touch* you, you pull away," she pointed out.

*Goddamn it David.* He put his face in his hands as he let out a long sigh. "Shiiiit," he mumbled. Not at her, but at himself.

"If you're not, or don't like it, just tell me," Nicole pressed.

David looked up at her, apologetic; he was kicking himself on the inside. She'd noticed his standoffish behavior, just as he had feared. Reaching his hand out for hers, he smiled. "I have no problem with it," he assured.

She walked over and put her hand in his. "You sure?"

David nodded. "I didn't mean to make you feel otherwise," he said. "Okay?"

Nicole smiled. "Okay," she said, moving in for a hug. She parted from their embrace and sat next to him. She looked at him, then after a moment, she touched his face.

Nicole was attracted to David; she liked him, she cared for him, and in that moment, being that close to him, she couldn't help herself.

Before David knew what was happening, Nicole leaned

in and planted a kiss on his lips. It shocked him, but after a moment, he welcomed it.

*It's fine, don't make any sudden movements and you won't embarrass yourself.* Their first real kiss, a kiss that started out sweet, but quickly turned to something more passionate. Feeling himself stir to life, David pulled his head back from Nicole.

"What's the matter?" she breathed, wide-eyed.

*I'm freakin hot and bothered, that's the damn matter,* he thought, catching his breath. "Um, nothing," he lied. "Everything is fine."

She frowned. "Then why did you *stop?*" she bit out.

David's eyes widened at her tone. "Sorry I was um—I think I'm sitting on my wallet," he stammered. "I was just trying to adjust my position."

Nicole raised an eyebrow. "Well, are you comfortable *now?*"

David's eyes shifted. "Uh huh."

Nicole leaned in again. "*Good,* now where *were* we?"

Before her lips could connect with his, David moved his head once again and this time Nicole didn't take the rejection lightly. "Damn it David!" she barked, delivering a slap to his chest.

"Ow!" he wailed as Nicole stood from the bed. "What did you do *that* for?"

"See *this* is what I was talking about," she snapped, pointing at him. "I give you a little kiss and you start acting all stupid."

"A *little?*" he quipped. The way Nicole was kissing him, he felt like she could grab for his jeans any moment.

"We're a couple, why can't I make out with you?" Nicole was agitated; David was being hard to read and she didn't like it.

"I never said you *couldn't,*" David argued.

"But that's what you're *acting* like," she threw back. She tossed her arms in the air in frustration. "What's the problem David?"

David pinched the bridge of his nose. "Umm…" He didn't know what to say and his lack of response was unnerving to Nicole.

"Are you seeing someone else?"

David looked confused. "Huh? *God* no, of course not," he assured, standing from the bed.

Nicole backed away when he tried to approach her. She looked at him, sadness in her eyes. "Then…is it *me*?" she asked. "Are you not attracted to me?"

David's heart sank. *I'm such a fuckin' idiot.* He took a step towards her. "Nicole—"

"I mean, I know that I'm not skinny like most of the girls you hang with—" She looked down at her ripped jeans and baggy school t-shirt. "I know that I'm not a fashion queen or—"

"Nicole, stop," David urged. Nicole folded her arms and turned away in a huff. "There is *nothing* wrong with you. I find you absolutely beautiful."

"You don't have to lie to me," she spat.

"I'm *not* lying," David promised. "I think you're perfect."

"Then what *is* it?" Nicole pressed, looking back at him, eyes pleading.

David struggled on the inside. He couldn't figure out what would be worse: Nicole being mad at him, or laughing at him.

Fed up with not getting an answer, Nicole pointed to the door. "I think you should go."

"No, wait, let me just—" David rubbed his head and let out a sigh. "Nicole, the problem isn't you…it's *me*," he put out.

"And that would be *what*, David?" she asked, annoyed.

David shook his head as he tried to gather his thoughts. "The thing is…I'm a—um..." He let out a quick sigh. "I'm a virgin." He braced himself for a reaction, *any* reaction. But what he got was silence.

Nicole stared blankly for several seconds. "Come

again?" she finally sputtered.

David looked down at the floor for a moment. "Yeah," he confirmed. "I'm a virgin."

Nicole was shocked. In her twenty years of life, she had yet to deal with a man her age who hadn't already had sex. "Oh...*wow*."

David rolled his eyes. *Great, she thinks I'm pathetic.* "Look it just never happened for me," he explained. "I mean—" he tossed his hands up in frustration as Nicole just stood there listening. "No girl was interested in me when I was younger and as I got older, I stopped *caring*. I just concentrated on my studies. It never really bothered me until *now*."

"Why does it bother you?" she wondered.

David was frazzled. He'd never had to explain to anybody about his virginity in the past and in a matter of weeks, he'd had to explain himself to two people. "I mean— because—"

"David," Nicole cut in, sensing that he was uncomfortable. "You should've told me sooner. If I would've *known* that you were saving yourself—"

"I'm not saying that I'm saving myself for marriage or anything like that," he interrupted. "It's not like I don't *want* to...I don't know *how* to and I'm afraid of embarrassing myself."

Nicole smiled.

"It's not funny," David grunted.

"No sweetie, I'm not laughing at you," she assured. "You can't embarrass yourself around me. I may not be a virgin, but I'm no sex expert."

David folded his arms but didn't say anything.

Nicole tilted her head. "Listen, the last thing that I want to do is make you uncomfortable or to feel like I'm putting pressure on you."

"No, stop, you've done nothing wrong," David assured, sincere. "*I* handled this whole thing stupidly. This is *my* fault." He put his hand on his chest. "I'm sorry for making you feel insecure; that was the last thing that I wanted."

Nicole nodded, then smiled once again. "I think it's respectable," she said after a moment.

David chuckled. "Yeah right."

She put her hands up. "No, I *mean* it," she promised. "There's something sexy about knowing that my man hasn't had any other woman touch him."

David pointed at her and resisted the urge to laugh. "Stop it."

Nicole giggled. When David held his arms out for her, she crossed the room to embrace him.

# Chapter 29

Sidra sat in the library, tapping her pencil on the table. Feeling so much tension in the house, she decided that her homework had a better chance of getting finished if she went to the library. After sitting at a corner table for a half hour, not doing anything but stare at math problems, she soon realized that her excursion was for nothing.

"This is pointless," she huffed, gathering her books and standing from the table.

Walking out of the library and heading down the steps, she glanced ahead of her and smiled as she saw Josh walking up the steps.

"Hey you," she beamed.

Josh returned her smile with one of his own. "Hey. You leaving?" he replied, stopping in front of her.

Sidra nodded. "Not getting anything done in there…too quiet."

"Well, I'll welcome the quiet," Josh said, adjusting his book bag on his shoulder. "My house is pretty loud right now. Mark got the damn radio up on a hundred, trying to do the robot."

Sidra laughed "The *robot?*"

"The robot," Josh confirmed, laughter in his voice. "The oldest damn dance in the world and needless to say, he looks quite stupid." He shook his head. "Jason is pissed 'cause he's trying to watch TV and Mark keeps asking him if he's doing it right."

"Wow. Yeah I'd be pissed too," Sidra commented,

laughter subsiding.

"Well, I'll see you la—" Josh's words were cut short when he saw a friend of his from across the stairs. "Hey Taylor."

"Hey Josh," the girl smiled. "You finish that data management homework yet?"

"No, going inside to work on it now," Josh answered, gesturing to the library entrance.

Sidra found herself staring at the voluptuous, scantily clad girl. *It's not that warm out here for her shorts to be that damn short*, she thought. *Butt all the way out...heifer.* Sidra really didn't approve of some of the girls that Josh was talking to nowadays.

"When you're finished, why don't you come over and *not* watch a movie with me," Taylor crooned, twirling her long extensions around her finger.

Josh chuckled as he rubbed his chin with his hand. "I'll think about it," he returned. Sidra rolled her eyes.

"Fair enough," Taylor said with a slight nod. "See you later, sexy."

"Later," Josh said, following Taylor's progress as she sauntered down the steps. He looked up to find Sidra staring at him. "What?"

"She's a little underdressed, isn't she?" Sidra sneered.

"That's left up to a matter of opinion," Josh replied, adjusting his book bag yet again.

Sidra rolled her eyes. "It's more than *opinion*," she ground out, pushing her hair over her shoulder. "The whole *world* could see her behind," she scoffed, gesturing her hand in the girl's direction. "I'm just saying her outfit, the whole invitation for what we *know* isn't a movie night, calling you out of your name, it makes her seem a little desperate, don't you think?"

Josh stared at Sidra, all traces of smile gone from his face. "You're being a little judgmental, don't you think?"

Sidra was taken aback by the stern tone of his voice. "Um, I'm *not* being judgmental."

"You *seriously* don't think so?" Josh countered. His tone was calm, but the seriousness was prevalent. "You don't even *know* that girl and you're standing here making assumptions about her, based on a two-minute conversation that didn't even *involve* you."

Sidra stared at him, shocked and speechless.

"Taylor happens to be a kind, funny, and smart woman. Her grades even rival *David's* and just because she doesn't dress or act how *you* think she should, you insult her character," Josh ranted.

Sidra folded her arms in a huff. "Wow, I see how quickly you defend someone who calls you 'sexy'," she hissed.

"What's *that* supposed to mean?"

"Come on Josh admit it, your taste in women nowadays is a bit questionable," she spat, tone smug. "They all call you 'baby', 'sexy'...what, they don't remember your name?" She punctuated her dig with a slight chuckle. "Anytime *I* make a comment, you get all defensive over them."

Josh didn't find it funny. "Just because *you* don't think I'm sexy, doesn't mean that others *don't*," he hissed. "And *again*, you're worrying too damn much about who I'm seeing."

Sidra's smile faded. "That's *not* what I—"

"Don't worry about whose calling me *what* and worry about fixing your problems with the boyfriend that you *chose* to be with," Josh spat, moving around her to continue up the steps.

She spun around. "Josh, I'm sorry, I didn't mean it," she pleaded at his back. She couldn't believe that she had just made him think that he wasn't attractive to her.

Josh stopped and turned around. "Yes, you *did*," he snapped. "Just like you *always* mean to say the shitty things that you've *been* saying. Then you think that saying 'sorry' with those pouty lips and beautiful eyes of yours will immediately fix it."

Sidra held her wide-eyed gaze as she stood there

speechless.

"You feel some kind of way because Mel isn't exactly back to normal with you yet? Well I don't *blame* her," Josh fussed, saying what he wished he would have said the many times that Sidra had complained to him about Malajia's behavior. "You judged her so damn bad and she didn't deserve that."

Sidra felt her heart sink into her stomach and looked away, down at the concrete step under her feet.

"Everybody has been pacifying your shit for *years*, and brushing it off as 'Princess Sidra being Sidra'," Josh ranted. "You don't expect anybody to check you, but have *no* problem checking other people, when the *one* person you *should* be checking is your damn self."

It was clear to Sidra that Josh had been holding in his feelings about her behavior for a while now. If there was one person's opinion of her that mattered more than anybody else's, it was Josh's. And to hear him chastise her like that, hurt. Not because Josh was doing it, but because her behavior *caused* him to do it.

Josh took Sidra's silence for indifference and rolled his eyes. "I gotta go," he huffed, walking off, leaving her standing there.

Feeling a tear fall from her eye, Sidra looked around as she wiped it with her hand. She hoped that no one had witnessed the verbal lashing that had just taken place; she was already embarrassed enough. Clutching her books to her chest, she walked the rest of the way down the steps.

Chasity pulled in front of an upscale restaurant in downtown Paradise Valley. Electing not to use valet, she pulled into a parking spot across the street. Chasity had mentally prepared herself for this dinner since Derrick had proposed it days ago. But now that she was in front of the place, her stomach was in knots.

"I'm here," Chasity said into her car speaker system.

"Is he there?" Trisha asked through the phone.

"I *just* got here," Chasity chuckled. "Stop acting like it's my first day of school."

"Fine," Trisha chortled. "I still don't know why you decided to drive. Hell, if you didn't want him to pick you up, he makes enough money to send you a car...or a limo. Ooh you should've told him to get you a limo."

Chasity shook her head as she grabbed her clutch from the passenger seat. "I am perfectly capable of driving myself," she sneered.

"I know this, but still," Trisha threw back. "Did you talk to him at all today?"

"No," Chasity answered.

"Oh?" Trisha questioned. "Well, you two have been talking every day for the past few days so I'm sure there's a reason. He's probably already in there waiting on you."

"Probably," Chasity dismissed.

Trisha was right; Derrick made good on his promise to call Chasity the evening that he visited her. If that didn't shock her, the fact that he called the next day before she went to her first class did. Then the day after, with their last conversation lasting practically an hour. The fact that he really did seem to be making an effort, made Chasity let down her guard about dinner.

"I want you to try to enjoy yourself tonight okay?" Trisha said. "And order the most expensive shit you can get, he got it."

Chasity laughed a little. "Noted."

She disconnected her phone from the car blue tooth and placed her phone to her ear as she turned the car off. The evening breeze felt good as she stepped out of her car. "Okay, I'm about to go in. I'll call you when I get home."

"Love you baby. Call me later."

"I will." Ending the call, Chasity crossed the street and walked inside the restaurant. After speaking briefly to the hostess, she was seated. *Not a bad place*, she mused to herself. Checking the silver watch on her wrist, she looked up as her server approached.

"Hi, I'm Camille, can I start you off with something to drink?" the polite woman asked.

Chasity smiled. "No, not yet, I'm waiting for someone," she said. "I'm actually a little early," she added, glancing at her watch once more.

"Okay no problem. I'll check back in a few minutes."

"That's fine, thanks," Chasity said as the woman walked away. She took a deep breath and reached for the compact mirror in her purse. Seeing her phone light up, she glanced at the message. Confused, she called the sender.

"Hello?" Alex answered.

"Alex, what the hell are you trying to send me?" Chasity barked in the phone.

"I was trying to send you an emoji," Alex giggled.

Chasity sucked her teeth. "Girl, you know your phone is old as Jesus. All I see are x's."

There was a pause on the line. "Did you just say Jesus?" Alex wondered, confused.

Chasity snickered.

"Anyway, I was sending you a thumbs up. But since you called, I want to wish you luck tonight," Alex said.

"Thanks."

"Don't forget to come tell me how it went when you get in," Alex insisted, excited. "I'll be up...working on more damn papers."

"I will," Chasity chuckled.

"Oh and Malajia had to run to the library, but she asked me to tell you to bring her back a steak." Alex laughed when her message was met with silence.

Chasity narrowed her eyes, even though Alex couldn't see her. "She wants a fuckin—you know what, tell her greedy ass I said no, and fuck off."

"Will do," Alex promised, amusement in her voice. "Later sweetie."

Chasity shook her head as she ended the phone call. Then laughed to herself. "That girl really asked for a whole goddamn steak," she mused of Malajia. Fifteen minutes later, Chasity was nursing yet another glass of lemon water. She ran her hand through her hair as she let out a long sigh. "Dad come on," she muttered. "Got me sitting here looking dumb. What are you doing?" Ending her solo conversation, she picked up her phone. She sent a text then sat the phone back down.

Camille approached again. "Hey, just checking on you," she smiled.

"*Still* waiting," Chasity muttered.

"Oh…Well, traffic is pretty hectic around this time down here, maybe they got stuck," Camille offered, sweet.

Chasity stared up at the bubbly woman. It was clear that she was trying to reassure her and for that, Chasity didn't want to give her attitude. She forced a smile. "Yeah, I'm sure that's what it is."

"I'll be back."

Chasity nodded as she glanced back at her phone. Her father had yet to respond and she didn't want to admit it, but she was beginning to worry. Another fifteen minutes later, her worry gave way to frustration. She'd even called him and he didn't answer.

The server approached for the fifth time. "Miss?—"

Chasity looked up, fighting to keep her annoyance from showing on her face. "Look, I'll make sure you get an extra tip for all your running but he's *still* not here yet," she said, traces of frustration in her voice.

The server held up her hand. "I know… You're Chasity right?" she said, tone soft.

Chasity shot her a quizzical look.

"Um…The guy—Mr. Parker called…he's not going to be able to make it," she carefully delivered. Both tone and face were sympathetic.

Chasity's face fell. "What?" was all that she could get out. As if on cue, she heard a notification on her phone. Glancing down, a message popped up from Derrick.

*"I'm so sorry Chasity, I won't be able to make it.*

*Something important came up. I'll make it up to you, I promise."*

"You fuckin' bastard," Chasity quietly uttered to herself as she stared at the message.

Camille stood there, not knowing what to say; she felt bad for the young woman sitting in front of her. "Um...he actually said for us to tell you to get whatever you want and he'll take care of the bill."

Chasity grabbed her purse and retrieved a twenty-dollar bill from it. "No, I'm fine, thanks," she ground out, handing the money to Camille. "Sorry for all your trouble."

"Oh wow, thank you." Grateful, she watched as Chasity stood up from the table. "Are you sure that you don't want anything? There are a lot of good dish choices here."

"No, I lost my appetite," Chasity bit out, walking away.

Walking out of the restaurant, Chasity felt her blood run cold. It took everything in her not to call Derrick and leave her extensive catalogue of profane-laced phrases on his voicemail. But she knew it wouldn't matter. In the end, her father wasn't there; a curse out wasn't going to change that.

Angry and disappointed, Chasity folded her arms across her chest as she slowly made her way back to her car.

After driving around for half an hour, in an attempt to calm herself down, Chasity entered the house, took a deep breath and headed upstairs. Seeing Alex's light on under her closed door, she walked over and knocked.

"Come in," Alex called from the other side.

Chasity opened the door slightly and stuck her head in. "Hey," she said, tone sullen.

Alex smiled as she closed her textbook. "Hey Chaz, you're back early," she observed.

"Yeah," Chasity replied, tone not changing.

Alex sat in anticipation of the evening's events. She couldn't wait to hear how her dinner went. "So? How was it? How was dinner?"

Chasity stood there in silence for a few seconds. "I wouldn't know, he never showed." The disappointment was clear in her voice.

Alex's face immediately fell. "Wait, what?"

"He stood me up," Chasity clarified.

"Oh shit," Alex muttered. She couldn't believe it. She held a sympathetic look on her face. "I'm sorry sweetie." Chasity's face showed her disappointment as she glanced at the floor.

"You might not have shown it, but I know how much it meant to you," Alex added.

"Yeah," Chasity mumbled, then took a deep breath. "It's whatever. It's fine," she quickly dismissed. "I just came to tell you, because you asked me to let you know how it went."

"Are you okay?" Alex asked, tone not masking her concern.

Chasity nodded. "Yep, I'm fine. Goodnight Alex," she quickly put out. Feeling her emotions bubbling up, Chasity turned and proceeded to walk away.

"Chasity," Alex called. Chasity stopped but didn't turn around. "Do you wanna come in and keep me company?"

"No, not really," Chasity replied, back still facing Alex.

"Please?" Alex insisted. She could sense that Chasity's feelings were hurt and she didn't want her friend to lock herself in her room, where Alex knew that Chasity would sulk alone. "I could use the break."

Hesitating for a moment, Chasity let out a sigh then turned around and closed the door behind her. Alex moved her books and papers from the bed and placed them on the floor, giving Chasity room to sit next to her. Chasity sat down with her back against the wall, staring out in front of her, saying nothing.

Alex looked at her. She wanted to say something, she just wasn't sure of what to say. She could only imagine what Chasity was feeling. Reaching for a plate on the other side of her, she picked it up and held it out. "I made some smore's," she announced. "You want one?"

Chasity shook her head.

Alex sat the plate down. "So um…what happened exactly? What did he say?" she began.

"Something important came up, is what his message said," Chasity spat. "He told the damn *restaurant* before he even told *me*."

"Oh," Alex said, trying to choose her words carefully. "No explanation?"

Chasity slowly shook her head. "Nope. Knowing him, it was probably work…or he just didn't want to come," she sneered. "Talking about he'll make it up to me."

Alex tilted her head as she held her gaze on Chasity. "Well, *maybe* you two can set up another—"

"There's not going to *be* another time," Chasity snapped, upset. "This bastard played me *twice*, lied to me *twice*. I'm not giving him another fuckin' chance to make me look stupid." She let out a sigh. "I should've known something was up. He called me every day for the past few days, and the *day* that we were supposed to meet up, I don't hear from him at *all*." She looked down at her hands. "I think he already knew when he woke up this morning that he wasn't going to come."

Alex felt terrible. She couldn't help but even feel a bit responsible for Chasity's let down. She was the one who had answered Chasity's phone when he'd called, she was the one who had talked Chasity into letting her guard down. "I—I don't know what to say sweetie," Alex sputtered.

"There's nothing you *can* say," Chasity spat. "He's a liar, he's unreliable and he's fuckin' stupid… *I'm* stupid for even thinking that tonight would be any different than it's *always* been."

"You're *not* stupid," Alex declared, tone stern.

"Yes, I *am*," Chasity insisted, holding her gaze on her hands, twisting a silver ring around her finger.

Alex watched in silence as Chasity placed two fingers on the bridge of her nose and closed her eyes. After a moment of deep breathing from Chasity, Alex saw tears start to fall.

As much as Chasity tried to hide it, she could no longer keep her emotions and feelings in; her father had hurt her. Unlike the many times before, she didn't expect it. She sniffled as Alex put a comforting hand on her shoulder. "I'm so sorry, Chaz," Alex consoled. She felt like crying herself, but knew that she had to keep it together.

Chasity sniffled again as she put her hands at her sides. Her face was streaked with tears. "I know it was only a stupid dinner," she managed to say through her sobs. "But I was looking forward to it you know," she admitted, rubbing her eyes. "I guess I just thought that maybe…that maybe for *once*, he would put me first."

Alex just listened intently as Chasity poured out her feelings. "I guess I shouldn't be surprised," Chasity continued. "Why would he do something that he's never done before?"

"Chasity you don't have to explain the reason why you're upset," Alex placated. "You had every right to feel hopeful that your father would keep his word. Just like you have every right to feel let down that he *didn't*." Chasity was quiet as more tears fell. "I can't imagine how you feel… I wish there was something I could do or say to make you feel better." Alex felt like kicking herself. To think that at one point in time, she was envious of Chasity's life because of what she had. Alex didn't stop to think then, what Chasity *didn't* have.

"I never wanted to admit it, but I look at what you guys have with your family," Chasity cried. "Your *dads* and…I realize that I missed out on so much by not having *mine*, and it's not fair… It's not fair."

As much as Alex tried to avoid it, she could no longer keep her own tears in. "No, it's *not* fair," she agreed, tone caring. She wiped her eyes with her hand. "You didn't deserve that *then* and you don't deserve it *now*. There is nothing that you did, for Brenda, your father or *anybody* for that matter to treat you like you didn't matter." Alex rubbed Chasity's shoulder. "I hate that this is happening to you."

"Me too," Chasity agreed. "You would think that I would be over it by now."

"How can you be over it, when you're still going *through* it?" Alex questioned, sincere.

Chasity shrugged. "My father really doesn't give a shit about me...and I'll just have to live with that."

"You know what, fuck him," Alex fumed. She didn't know Derrick Parker as a person, but in that moment, she despised him, like she despised anyone who hurt her friends. "He's an idiot because he is missing out on you. With *everything* that you've been through, you've *still* managed to evolve into the beautiful woman that you are and it's his damn loss so screw him."

Chasity couldn't help but chuckle through her tears at Alex's sudden outburst.

"Seriously...it's *his* loss," Alex reiterated, calming herself. "I know it doesn't fill the void that you have, but at least you have your mom. You know you're her world."

"Yeah, I know," Chasity agreed, taking a deep breath.

"And you have *us*," Alex smiled. "We're not blood, but we *are* family...as dysfunctional as it is."

"Dysfunctional is right," Chasity chortled.

Alex laughed. "*Completely* dysfunctional," she joked. "But in all seriousness, just know that you have people who love you."

"I know," Chasity nodded.

Alex smiled. "I'm gonna hug you now," she put out. Chasity just looked at her. "So don't swing on me." She then gave Chasity a long hug, something that Chasity needed in that moment. "You feel a little better?" Alex asked once they parted.

Chasity nodded, wiping her eyes.

"You want a smore now?"

"I want a *tissue* now," Chasity threw back, eyeing the wetness on her hands.

Alex reached over on her nightstand and grabbed her box of tissues for Chasity. "Tissue, then smore," she pressed, smiling.

"Why do you keep trying to feed me those damn smores?" Chasity wondered, taking tissues from the box.

"'Cause its comfort food," Alex explained. "And if you don't take one, I'll eat them all and lord knows my butt don't need to get any bigger." When Chasity made a face and glanced away, Alex playfully backhanded her on the arm. "Hush up," she said, as Chasity laughed a little.

Malajia approached the front step of her house. Letting out a deep sigh, she opened the door. Sidra, who was in the kitchen stirring food on the stove, looked over at her. "Hi," she said, tone soft.

Malajia looked at her as she closed the door. "Hey."

There was a somber tone in Malajia's voice and on her face. Sidra wondered, given the current state of their relationship, if she should even attempt a conversation. But it didn't matter. Resentment or not, Malajia was still her friend and Sidra wanted to know if she was okay. "You alright?" she asked finally.

Malajia folded her arms. "Not really," she admitted.

"A lot on your mind?" Sidra asked, turning the stove off.

"You could say that," Malajia replied, tone even.

Sidra nodded as she tried to figure out what else to say to Malajia. She was avoiding asking the question that she knew she should be asking; she was afraid of the answer that she would receive.

"Have you spoken to Chaz today?" Sidra asked. "I heard about what happened with her father the other day…that sucks."

"Yeah, it does," Malajia agreed.

"I know she's been at Jason's, but I figured that you would talk to her… How is she doing?"

Malajia sighed as she ran a hand along the back of her neck. "You know Chaz, she pretends like she's fine when we know she's really not," she said. "Her dad is a fuckin' joke."

Sidra glanced at the food in the pot. "Well, you know it's hard for her to admit when she's hurt," she muttered, then glanced at Malajia. "It's hard for *any*body to admit that they're hurt…or even that they're *still* hurt."

Malajia fixed her gaze on Sidra. She had a feeling that Sidra was addressing *her* with her last comment. Mark had told her about what Josh had said to Sidra just the day before. "You talking about Chasity or me?" Malajia asked, point-blank.

Sidra faced Malajia as she slowly walked out of the kitchen. "Does it apply to you?" she hesitantly put out.

Malajia glanced away.

Sidra looked down at her hands. She was afraid that she might have lost her friend forever because of her carelessness and insensitivity. For the first time in a long time, Sidra was feeling the consequences of her words. "Malajia…I know you want to say something to me… Please just say it," she pleaded.

Malajia looked at Sidra once again; her gaze was stern, a little cold even. The conversation that she had with Mark stuck in her head. It was time for her to come clean. "Okay," Malajia began. "I know when you came to my house over break, I said that I was fine. Truth is, I'm *not* fine Sidra. Not even a little bit."

Sidra's heart sank. She had a feeling, but hearing it, hit her. "I figured," she said.

"I know that you're sorry for what you said, but the fact that you even *said* it to me…" Malajia paused as she tried to gather her thoughts.

"I didn't mean to hurt you," Sidra said, voice cracking.

"Yes, you *did*," Malajia contradicted. "You may regret it *now*, but you meant to at the time."

Sidra fought back her tears as she stood there and took what Malajia was saying. She knew that she needed to hear it, and for them to truly heal, Malajia needed to say it.

"I've ignored a lot of shit that you've said before," Malajia vented. "The countless comments about me being a whore, the comments about me staying with Tyrone for attention, when you found out that he was abusing me—"

To have what she had said, thrown back at her, was a reality check for Sidra.

"You saying shit like that to me—I'm starting to think that deep down, you don't care about me like you *say* you do," Malajia spat.

"That's not true," Sidra denied, emotional. "Of *course* I care about you Malajia, I love you. You're my sister."

Malajia shook her head. "I really want to believe that, Sidra," she said. "God knows I hate fighting with you. You're my oldest friend, one of my favorite people." Malajia took a deep breath as tears began to prick the back of her eyes. "I *wish* I could let this go like the other times but…you just keep stabbing me with your words, and my wounds don't heal that fast anymore."

Sidra let out a long sigh. "I understand…I get it now," she said, apologetic.

"I'm not saying that I *won't* put it behind me but…I just need a little more time before I can look at you without being angry again," Malajia concluded.

Sidra nodded in acceptance as Malajia headed up the steps. "Take all the time you need," she sadly called after her. "Just know that I'm still your friend and I'll be here whenever you decide not to hate me anymore."

Malajia paused for a moment. "I don't hate you Sidra…I *can't*," Malajia assured, before continuing up the steps.

Upon hearing the door close, Sidra let out several deep breaths and fought to keep her building tears from falling.

# Chapter 30

Alex tossed several bags of chips into her shopping cart, before reaching for a jar of dip.

Malajia stared at her. "You hype as shit you got paid today," she teased, earning a soft backhand to the arm.

"Hush," Alex chortled. "While I *am* excited for my paycheck, that's not why I'm shopping. I just want to make sure we stock up on snacks."

"Alex, Sahara will be here for a *day*," Malajia pointed out. "And you out here buying up the whole aisle of chips."

"Well, my sister loves chips," Alex explained, shrugging. "And so does *your* greedy butt, so stop complaining before I ban you from having any." With Sahara arriving on the Paradise Valley campus tomorrow for the campus tour, Alex was beyond excited. Not only would her sister be on campus for a day, but Alex was leading the tour for her group.

Malajia sucked her teeth. "We *both* know you can't keep me from the snacks," she jeered, putting some salsa into the cart. "You remember how I found those cookies you hid."

Ignoring Malajia's comment, Alex did a mental count of the items in her cart as she pushed it down the aisle. Malajia's smart comments aside, Alex was happy that Malajia had tagged along to the grocery store with her. Alex wanted to talk to Malajia about something, and this seemed like the perfect opportunity.

"So, I want to ask you something," Alex began as Malajia examined a box of crackers on a shelf.

"What's up?" Malajia wondered, eyes not leaving the box in her hand.

"Well, since we'll be doing the tour as a group tomorrow—"

"Which you know, I'm still irked about," Malajia cut in. "It's gonna be like eighty degrees outside tomorrow, ain't nobody tryna spend the day touring a bunch of high school kids around."

Alex rolled her eyes. "Complaining won't change the fact that you're doing it," she pointed out. Malajia made a face in retaliation. "But seriously, I want to know with things being a little strained—"

Malajia, having an idea as to what Alex was getting at, looked at Alex as she spoke.

"Between you and Sidra…will it be weird for you two to be in the same tour group?" Alex asked. "I mean, I wanted us to do this together, but if it's gonna be—"

"Alex, Sidra and I are grown. We coexist in the same *house* so yes, I'm sure we can coexist on a tour group for a few hours," Malajia cut in, placing the box of crackers in the cart.

Alex let out a sigh. "You sure?"

"Yes," Malajia assured. "Look, like I told y'all before, I don't *hate* Sidra. We're still friends, I just—" She let out a quick sigh.

"You just need time, I know," Alex finished.

After Malajia and Sidra's conversation about the state of their friendship a little over a week ago, Malajia sat down with the other girls to tell them what was going on. Although Sidra and Malajia weren't arguing, in fact they were cordial, Alex knew that both women were hurting. She wished that she could fix things.

Malajia pushed some of her hair over her shoulders. "Yeah…I'm getting there."

"Look Mel, as much as I want everything between you two to be normal again…and I can't believe I'm saying this but…take the time you need, you know," Alex said, shocking

Malajia. "I know she hurt you, so you're entitled to feel how you want for as *long* as you want."

Malajia stared at Alex. "What? You mean you're not gonna force a sit down between us? Talk our ears off about how important it is for us to resolve our issues *right* away?" she teased.

"Hey, I told you before, I'm trying to change," Alex chuckled. "After what happened between Em and I last semester—trust me, I won't be overstepping my boundaries anytime soon."

"The baby had to cuss you a new ass for you to realize that," Malajia joked, putting more items in the cart.

"Funny," Alex hissed, then glanced down in the cart. "Hold on, where did all of this stuff come from?"

"I put it in the cart," Malajia shrugged, looking at her phone.

Alex looked confused. "*Why?*"

Malajia looked at her, eyes wide. "I thought I was helping you shop for your sister."

Alex began placing items back on a shelf. "Girl you— nobody eats salted caramel peanuts but *you* and they're high as hell, I'm not paying for that."

Malajia watched as Alex placed her items on one shelf. "They don't even *go* there," she jeered.

"Shut up and keep moving before somebody notices that," Alex demanded, pushing the cart out of the aisle. "Between you and Chaz, I can never shop in peace."


Jason retrieved two beverages from the donut shop cashier and handed one to Chasity. "Extra whipped cream for you," he said.

"Thanks," Chasity returned, grabbing straws from the nearby holder. After the test filled day that they'd had, frozen hot chocolates were a perfect treat for them both.

Walking out of the shop, Chasity took a sip as Jason pointed to a nearby bench. "You wanna sit over there?" he asked.

Chasity glanced at the bench in question. "Not with that big ass, stalking bird sitting over there," she sneered.

Jason chuckled. "As soon as we go over there, the bird will fly away," he assured.

"Oh I'm *sure* it'll fly away, right after it shits on us," she grunted. Jason couldn't help but laugh.

He pointed to a bench across the path. "The one over there is bird free."

Crossing the student littered path, the couple were just about to take a seat, when Mark walked up and flopped down on the bench in a huff.

"Dawg, we were just about to sit here," Chasity charged, pushing her hair behind her ear with her free hand.

"So, *sit down*," Mark threw back.

"We wanted to sit *alone*," Jason chimed in.

"Tough luck, you don't own the bench bruh," Mark huffed, setting his book bag on the ground.

"Just go to the one over *there*," Chasity demanded, pointing.

"There's a big ass bird over there, barkin' all loud and shit," Mark ground out. Jason shook his head in amusement, as Chasity looked confused. "Eatin' that old ass gum off the ground."

"Birds don't *bark*, dickhead," Chasity spat.

"*Exactly*, that's why I'm not fuckin' with him," Mark threw back.

Chasity put her hand up in surrender. "It's too damn hot to go back and forth with you," she directed at Mark, sitting down next to him, with Jason taking a seat on the other side of her.

Mark eyed the frozen beverage and started salivating. "Yo Chaz, let me get a sip of that."

"If you think you're putting your crusty ass lips on my straw, you got another damn thing coming," Chasity scoffed, tone even.

Mark quickly licked his lips. "Come on they not crusty.

Let me get some," he pressed, reaching for her cup.

Jason reached behind Chasity and delivered a smack to Mark's arm. The loud, dramatic yelp that Mark made, nearly had Chasity spitting out her drink as she tried not to laugh.

"Damn Jase, that was uncalled for," Mark spat out, examining his arm. Jason just gave him a long, fiery stare. Mark sucked his teeth. "I don't want that frozen ass chocolate milk anyway," he grunted, grabbing his book bag from the ground and standing up. He stopped just before leaving. "How much was it?"

"Three dollars," Jason answered.

"Bet," Mark rejoiced, hurrying off.

Chasity shook her head. "That was a total waste of five minutes," she jeered.

Jason chuckled, taking a sip of his drink. After a brief pause, he glanced at Chasity, who was concentrating on her drink. "So…have you heard from *him?*" he wondered.

Chasity shrugged. "I wouldn't know 'cause I blocked him," she said of Derrick.

Jason shook his head as he let out a deep sigh. "Chaz, you *have* to let me cuss him out one good time," he fumed. He was furious with Chasity's father. When he learned of how the man had stood Chasity up, Jason wished that the flaky hotel chain manager, turned owner, was standing in his face so he could give him a piece of his mind…or deliver a punch.

Chasity patted Jason on his leg. "I appreciate that, but he's not even worth it," she resolved.

"He let you down."

"Always *has*," Chasity clarified. While she was upset for a few days following the incident, Chasity pulled her emotions back and decided to cut her losses. "I just won't put myself in another position like that."

"He *still* deserves to be cussed out," Jason maintained.

"Oh he *was*, by my mom," Chasity revealed.

Jason chuckled. "She laid into him, huh?"

"Hell yeah," Chasity confirmed, amusement in her

voice. "When he couldn't get ahold of *me*, he called *her* and she called him *everything* under the sun. She put together cuss combinations that I would've *never* thought of."

Jason laughed.

"She told him if he ever comes near me again that she would burn his house, car, *and* hotels to the ground."

Jason grimaced, then shrugged. "Well I can't say he wouldn't deserve it," he commented. He then looked at Chasity as she stared out at the scenery in front of her. "I still wish there was something that I could do to make things better for you," he said. "I mean, I know you said you're over it—"

"I'm not," Chasity admitted, tone even. "But I'm not gonna cry about, I'm not gonna scream about it, I'm just gonna...move on. I don't have time for the bullshit anymore."

Jason grabbed her hand and held it. "I hear you," he said. "We have plenty of good things coming our way."

"Hope so," she replied, twining her fingers with his.

Their comfortable silence was interrupted when Mark started running towards them, cup of frozen hot chocolate in hand, and a fearful look on his face.

Jason looked perplexed. "Yo, what are you running—"

"I kicked the barking bird by accident, he's fuckin' chasing me!" Mark yelled, approaching the bench.

Seeing the running bird suddenly take flight, Jason and Chasity jumped up and started running.

"Don't leave me!" Mark shouted after them.

Sidra jotted down notes in her notebook. Frowning at what she had just written, she immediately erased it. She sighed as she tapped her pencil to her chin, then reached for her empty mug. Peering inside of it, she sucked her teeth. "I need more coffee."

Just as she went to stand up, Emily stumbled in, carrying a box. "Oh no!" Emily shrieked as the box tumbled out of her hands.

Sidra bolted up and darted over to help. "You okay?" she asked.

Emily giggled as she picked the box back up with Sidra's help. "Yeah, sorry for the noise."

"No, you're fine," Sidra assured, helping place the box on Emily's bed. "I was about to get up, *anyway.*"

Emily grabbed a pair of scissors from her desk and sat on her bed. Sidra watched as she sliced open the box. "Mommy, really?" Emily muttered, pulling several clothing items from the box.

"Your mom sent you clothes?" Sidra asked, eyeing the contents.

Emily let out a sigh as she rubbed her forehead. "Uhhh, yeah…I don't think she got the memo that I don't dress like this anymore," she grimaced, eyeing a long flower maxi dress. "Well, it's the thought…I *guess.*"

Sidra folded her lips inward, trying to refrain from saying anything smart. "Yeah, it's the thought that counts," she agreed.

Emily glanced up. "You can say that they're ugly," she chortled.

Sidra put her hand up. "Nope," she refused.

Emily tossed the dress back into the box. "Well, they *are.*"

Sidra grabbed her cup and headed for the door. "I'm gonna get a coffee refill, you want anything while I'm downstairs?"

"No, thank you." Emily looked at Sidra; she saw the sadness on Sidra's face and heard it in her voice when she spoke. She, Alex, and Chasity had promised to stay out of the situation between Malajia and Sidra. But as Sidra's roommate, Emily couldn't stand to see her look so broken every day. "Sidra," Emily called, prompting her to turn around.

"Huh?"

"You okay?" Emily wondered.

Sidra smiled and nodded. "Just need coffee."

"Well, when you're finished your coffee and homework, you wanna come to dinner with me and the others?" Emily asked.

Sidra smiled slightly. This had been the fourth night in a row that Emily had invited her to dinner, and each time Sidra had declined. Not because she didn't *want* to go, Sidra just felt that she *shouldn't*.

"Sweetie, you know I appreciate the fact that you want me—"

"Come on Sidra, I don't like how you've been alienating yourself," Emily blurted out, tone caring. Sidra looked down at the floor. "You know that's *Chasity's* thing, not yours," she joked.

Sidra couldn't help but chuckle. "I know and I used to get on her about doing that," she recalled. She took a deep breath. "I know that I'm being standoffish Em, and I don't mean to be. I miss hanging out with you guys but...I just don't want to say or do anything to dig myself in a deeper hole."

"With Malajia?" Emily asked, rubbing her arm.

"Yeah," Sidra muttered. "And *Josh* and *Mark* and—I've been doing a lot of reflecting and I've come to realize that I haven't been—Um...I just don't want to upset anybody else."

Emily stood from the bed and folded her arms. "Sidra, we a*ll* have said and done things that may not have been the best," she began. "And we *all* have learned that shutting yourself off from everyone and sulking alone is not how we need to deal with issues... I mean, it's not like you were *shunned*."

Sidra sighed. "I know and I appreciate everybody just letting me and Malajia deal with this on our own," she said, grateful.

Emily took a step towards Sidra. "You're hiding Sidra, and it's not right," she said. "We miss you."

"You *shouldn't*," Sidra pouted. "I'm a snobby,

judgmental bitch."

Emily tapped Sidra on her arm. "Stop, that's my friend you're talking about," she teased. "You're not a bad person. You made a mistake, it happens. You learn and you grow." She raised her hand. "Take it from a former reclusive alcoholic."

Sidra pointed at her. "You're admitting that you *were*?"

"Well, I was on the *verge*," Emily amended. She tilted her head and smiled. "Will you please come to dinner?"

Sidra hesitated for a moment, then let a smile come through. "Yeah, I'll come."

# Chapter 31

"Does anybody know when graduation pictures will be taken?" David asked, squirting ketchup on his steak. Mark glared at him, a disgusted look on his face. "You nasty as shit, putting ketchup on your steak," he grunted. "Where's the steak sauce?"

David narrowed his eyes at Mark as snickers resonated around the cafeteria booth. "Stop minding my business," he sneered.

"I'm guessing they'll have us take them during senior week," Alex answered, grabbing a pickle from her plate and taking a bite. "Makes sense, I guess."

"Yeah, final grades will be in before then, and they probably want to make sure that they only take pictures of people who are *actually graduating*," Josh added.

"They learned their lesson *last* year, wasting all that damn film," Malajia laughed.

"I know right?" Chasity chimed in. "People were cheesin' hard as shit in those pictures. Like that was gonna change the fact that they failed."

Alex playfully tapped the laughing Chasity on the arm. "That's not funny," she said, then soon broke into laughter.

"Y'all are going to hell," Mark grumbled, rubbing his arm, which was covered from elbow to wrist in a bandage. "These fuckin' scrapes hurt like shit."

Josh looked at him. "Mark, what the hell *happened* to your arm, anyway?" He'd been held up in the library most of the day; he hadn't seen Mark until they arrived at dinner.

Chasity erupted with laughter as Jason snickered hard, drinking his soda.

Mark shot Chasity a death stare. "Shut...up...Chasity," he bit out.

"Mark, you know that shit was funny," Jason laughed, wiping his mouth with a napkin. "*You* would've laughed if the shoe was on the other foot."

Mark pointed at them and opened his mouth to fire off a retort, when he realized that Jason had a point. "Shut up," was all that he could say.

"Are you gonna tell us what happened?" Alex pressed.

Malajia shook her head as she rolled her eyes. She'd heard the story when she met Mark at the campus infirmary. She was both embarrassed and annoyed. "Some big ass bird knocked his tall ass down," she spat out.

Chasity's laughter grew louder as tears spilled down her cheeks. Mark rolled his eyes.

"Wait, *what*?" David laughed. "How did a little bird knock you down?"

"*First* of all, that fuckin' vulture wasn't *little*," Mark argued. "And I don't care what *nobody* says, it was barkin'."

"Oh God, will you *stop* with that fuckin' *lie*?" Malajia snapped, slamming her hand on the table.

Mark flagged her with his hand, ignoring her outburst. "Look, the bird didn't knock me down... It knocked my hot chocolate out of my hand while I was running."

"And that scared the shit out of him, so he tripped over his own foot and took a big ass spill," Jason filled in, amused.

"Yo, he rolled like *eight times*," Chasity cut in, laughter filling her voice.

"Fuck you, I rolled *twice*," Mark fussed. He pounded his fist on the table. "Whatever. *Those two*," he said, pointing at Jason and Chasity, "just stood there, laughing and shit."

"Come on, I *did* come over to help you up, but you got an attitude and smacked my hand away." Jason recalled.

"I didn't need your pity," Mark groused.

Jason shook his head. "Well, you shouldn't have *kicked* the damn thing," he muttered. "Serves you right."

During the conversation, Emily walked over with Sidra beside her. "Hey guys," she beamed, causing them all to look up and greet her. Emily then gestured her hand out in front of Sidra. "Look who I brought with me."

"We know, we can *see* her," Chasity mocked.

Emily had a silly look on her face, and even Sidra couldn't help but snicker. "Well...okay," Emily said, as room was made for both her and Sidra.

"Hey guys," Sidra meekly put out as she adjusted herself in her seat. She smiled slightly when she received greetings in return. Sitting there with the group, although they spoke, Sidra felt awkward.

"Long time, no see," David smiled at her.

"Yeah, I've been busy with um...homework and stuff," Sidra replied. "My professors seem like they want to pile every little assignment they can think of, on us right now."

"I know that feeling," Alex agreed. She then glanced over at Sidra, who was looking down at her hands. "You're not gonna grab anything to eat?" she charged.

Sidra shook her head, as she looked at Alex. "No, I'm not hungry right now...filled up on coffee."

"Oh," Alex said. She had a feeling that Sidra was a bit uncomfortable, given the circumstances. She felt bad for her. "So um, about this campus tour—"

"Alex, I *told* you already that I'm not doing it," Chasity abruptly cut in. Alex rolled her eyes. "I don't *like* people, *especially* teenagers."

"Girl, you're fresh out the teen years yourself. Hush on up," Alex ground out.

"Chaz, you might as well get over it, 'cause Alex will just breathe on us until we agree," Malajia joked.

Alex made a face at Malajia. "Look, Sahara is excited. She *loves* hanging with us when we're together," Alex explained, reaching for her glass of water. Chasity rolled her eyes. "And you *have* to come Chaz because besides *me*, *you're* her favorite."

Malajia's mouth fell open as Chasity's frown was replaced by a smile. "Really?" Chasity gushed, playing with a few strands of her hair.

Alex chuckled at the sudden change in Chasity's attitude. "You are *so* damn conceited," she said.

Chasity shrugged.

Malajia waved her hand in Alex's direction. "You tell Sahara we got a problem," she hurled at Alex. Alex looked confused. "I thought we was cool. We were making up dances and shit the last time she was here, and she just gonna choose the fuckin' *scorpion* over *me* as her next fave?" she fussed, pointing to Chasity.

Emily looked confused. "Did you just call Chaz a scorpion?"

Malajia folded her arms. "I did," she grunted. "With her growing up in the desert ass… poisonous ass heffa," she fussed.

Alex shook her head in amusement at Malajia's dramatics.

"Shut your corny ass up," Chasity spat. "And those dances you made up was wack any-damn-way. You probably lost points for that *alone*."

"My dances were better than *yours*," Malajia argued, glaring at Chasity.

"Bitch, you a damn lie," Chasity threw back.

"Wait a minute Malajia, we can't *all* be her favorite. She overlooked *us too*," Emily interrupted, gesturing to herself and Sidra. "It's no big deal."

"Emily, *y'all* don't count. Nobody expects you to be *anybody's* favorite," Malajia jeered, shaking her hand in Emily's direction.

"Oh come on!" Emily exclaimed, humor in her voice.

Sidra simply shook her head, while examining her nails.

"You know it's true," Malajia harped. "But me, I should be *everybody's* favorite. I'm hilarious."

Mark rubbed Malajia's arm. "It's okay baby, you're *my* favorite," he smiled.

Malajia shot him a side-glance. "Don't nobody wanna be your favorite. You got your ass beat by a bird and shit," she sneered, to which Mark immediately removed his hand from her arm.

"Fuck you! You're on time out," he barked, pointing at her. Malajia broke into laughter as Mark stood up. "Come on guys, let's go get this basketball game started," he directed to the guys.

"Awww, I'm just playing, my chocolate daddy," Malajia teased, reaching for his hand.

"Naw, don't touch me," Mark fussed, moving his hand out of her reach as the other guys moved from the booth. Malajia continued her laughter as the guys headed on their way.

"You better stop messing with him," Alex advised, pointing to Malajia.

"Or *what*? You heard him say before, I'm stuck with his ass," Malajia dismissed. "Plus, he ate my last brownie this morning. He deserved it."

Sidra pushed her hair over her shoulder as she glanced at the exit. "What happened to Mark's arm?" she wondered; she'd noticed the bandage when she'd first sat down, but elected not to mention it at the time.

"He busted his ass running from some pigeon," Malajia nonchalantly replied. "He's alright."

Alex glanced back and forth between Malajia and Sidra. Malajia was right; they seemed cordial. She only hoped that that would continue during her sister's visit.


"Why are we even going over there?" Chasity asked as she and Malajia ambled through the campus away from the other girls after dinner.

"'Cause I wanna watch my man play basketball,"

Malajia explained, pushing her hair behind her ears. "Don't you wanna go watch *your* man play?"

"I'd rather go and watch *TV*," Chasity jeered. "I already had to sit through football; I didn't sign on for basketball." Malajia laughed as she nudged Chasity. "So rude," she joked. "I'm not gonna front, I'm only going so I can yell at Mark from the bleachers."

Chasity shot Malajia a confused look. "For *what*?"

"'Cause I'm sick of his ass putting me on time out," Malajia griped. "I'm gonna fuck his focus *up*. I will show my *entire ass*."

Chasity stared at Malajia for several seconds before shaking her head. "Yeah, *that's* gonna stop him from putting your simple ass on time out," she drawled sarcastically.

"Mind your business," Malajia spat. After a few moments of silence, Malajia took a deep breath. "So...Sidra looked uncomfortable at dinner, didn't she?" she mentioned.

"Yeah, I know," Chasity agreed, folding her arms.

"She probably didn't want to come in the *first* place," Malajia said.

"Probably not," Chasity replied. She glanced at her. "You feel bad?"

Malajia thought for a moment. "Not about *my* feelings, but..." she let out a sigh. "Mark's still upset, because *I'm* upset and Josh lit into her pretty bad so...I know she's feeling it."

"Well, she brought that on herself," Chasity concluded. "I'm not gonna lie though, her walking around looking like her dog died every-damn-day, is depressing."

"I know right? Like you don't have *enough* shit to be depressed about," Malajia said.

Chasity narrowed her eyes at her. "Thanks," she spat out, sarcastic.

Malajia giggled. "I'm messing with you," she declared, waving her hand. She then took a long breath. "I just...I care about everybody you know. And even though things are how they are now...I still worry about her."

"Sidra will be fine," Chasity placated.

Malajia shrugged. "Yeah," she sighed. Then hearing a notification on her phone, glanced at it. *'Just so you know, you're still on time out.'* Malajia sucked her teeth at Mark's message. "I thought his ass was supposed to be playing ball," she griped. She looked up as Chasity began walking in another direction. "Where are you going?"

"I'm not subjecting myself to you and Mark's nonsense all damn night," Chasity threw over her shoulder. "You annoy him on your own."

Malajia stomped her foot on the ground as she stopped walking. "Bitch don't be selfish! I didn't want to walk over by myself," she yelled after her.

Chasity kept walking, ignoring her. Malajia sucked her teeth. Realizing that she didn't even feel like going anymore, Malajia took off to catch up to her.

David clutched his books to his chest as he trotted down the steps of the Science building.

"David, you got the answers to that Physics test?" Mark asked, approaching him.

David frowned as he halted his stride. "You don't even *have* Physics," he pointed out.

Mark shrugged. "So? That don't mean I don't wanna know if you got the answers to the test."

David stared blankly, then shook his head. "Are you ever *not* gonna be weird?" he wondered, moving around Mark to keep walking. "I gotta go."

"What's your problem?" Mark asked, following.

"Nothing, why?" David huffed.

"'Cause you girlin' for no reason," Mark countered, walking alongside him.

"Do you have any idea how offensive it is to say that I'm girlin'?" David sneered. "That's like saying that only *women* have attitudes or bad days."

Mark rolled his eyes and let out a groan. "Fine, David. You have an *attitude*, that's why I asked you what your problem was," he mocked. David narrowed his eyes. "You sure you don't need a hot water bottle for your cramps you little bitch?"

David backhanded Mark on the arm, earning a laugh from him. "Shut the hell up," David barked. He then took a deep breath. "I'm fine though, just tired. That Physics test was a little rough, had me up until four this morning, studying."

Mark patted David on the back. "Well, if we would've studied *together*, you wouldn't have been up so late," he said. David stared at him. "*You* don't *have* Physics!" he erupted. Mark busted out laughing again. David shook his head.

"I'm hungry; you wanna get the other guys and go get some hoagies?" Mark asked, adjusting his book bag.

"Sounds good, I'm starving myself," David said, running a hand across his stomach. Looking out ahead of him, David successfully hid a frown as he saw Quincy approaching. *Just great*, he thought.

"What's up fellas?" Quincy smiled. "Mark, how many tests have you failed today bruh?" he goaded.

Mark let out a loud, phony laugh to accompany Quincy's boisterous laugh. "That's why your momma is bald, shut up," Mark threw back, laughter halted.

Quincy sucked his teeth at Mark, then turned his attention to David, who stood there unenthused. "How's it goin' man?" he asked.

David looked at him. "Fine," he sneered.

Quincy nodded, then gave David a pat on his shoulder. David looked at his arm, then back at Quincy. "I admire you man."

David looked confused, as did Mark. "You admire me for *what*?" David questioned.

"You know, for holding it together," Quincy vaguely replied.

The confusion never left David's face. *What the hell is this fool talking about?*

Mark sucked his teeth. "Man Q, shut your non-articulating-a-response ass the hell up and get ready to take this L on the courts later," he barked.

"Yeah a'ight," Quincy returned, unfazed. "Remember, your ass lost *last* game."

"Ain't nobody ask you that. Just step your bald ass on," Mark threw back. Quincy laughed as he walked away. Mark then turned to David, who looked like he was seething quietly. "You cool?"

*What the fuck was he talking about?* David continued to wonder. *Weird ass dude.* It wasn't until David felt a nudge that he snapped out of his thoughts. "What?"

"You cool?" Mark repeated.

David feigned indifference. "Oh, yeah I'm cool," he lied. "Let's just um…go get these hoagies."

# Chapter 32

Alex beamed with excitement, running down the steps; a knock had sounded on the door. "She's here, she's here," she squealed mid-run.

"Oh my God, the house is shaking!" a voice yelled from upstairs.

Alex hopped down the last step and glared up the staircase. "Go to hell Malajia!" she barked.

"Alex, I swear to God Chasity said that, *not* me," Malajia argued from her room.

Alex's mouth fell open as she heard Chasity's laugh. "*Really* Chasity?!" Hearing nothing but laugher from upstairs, she sucked her teeth. "Ignorant ass," she muttered, opening the door. "Sissy boo!" she squealed at the sight of Sahara standing there.

As Alex wrapped her arms around her sister, another voice yelled from upstairs. "Shut your corny ass up! What the hell is a 'sissy boo'?"

Alex let out a loud sigh as Sahara busted out laughing. "I'm gonna choke them, I swear," Alex grunted.

"Hi girls!" Sahara yelled up the steps as she set her overnight bag down by the couch. Within moments, Malajia, Chasity, and Emily made their way down the stairs.

They were met with Alex's angry gaze. "Now *who* said—"

"Emily," Malajia cut in, pointing to a shocked Emily.

"I don't even *curse*," Emily denied, pointing to herself.

Alex shook her head. "Malajia, I know it was *you* that

time," she hissed.

Malajia waved her hand at Alex. "You don't know shit," she dismissed as she gave Sahara a hug. "I'm hugging you even though you said Chasity was your favorite," she jeered.

Sahara laughed as she looked at Alex in shock. "You told them?"

"I *had* to. *That* one wouldn't have come if I didn't," Alex laughed back, pointing to Chasity.

Sahara's mouth fell open. "Is that true?" she asked Chasity, feigning hurt.

Chasity stared at her for a moment. "Nooooeeeessss, yes," she slowly put out, inciting a laugh from the girls. "Yeah, I can't lie," Chasity chuckled.

"Yo, you stupid as shit Chasity," Malajia bellowed with laughter, holding her hand to her chest. "You got her hopes all up and shit."

Alex shook her head, "Rude ass," she commented, then looked at her sister, who was still laughing. "Where is the rest of your group?"

"Oh, they're in the cafeteria. I decided to walk over here first," Sahara answered.

"Okay let's get going then," Alex glanced at her watch. "Anybody seen Sidra?"

Emily shook her head as she rubbed her shoulder. "She was gone when I woke up this morning," she informed.

Alex put her hands on her hips. "I wonder where she is. She knows that we have to start this thing soon," she said, glancing at her watch yet again.

"Whelp, Sidra isn't here. So much for doing this as a group, I'm going back to sleep," Chasity quickly put out as she headed for the stairs.

Alex grabbed the back of her shirt. "Keep your skinny ass down here," she demanded through clenched teeth.

Chasity smacked Alex's hand. "Bitch if you rip my shirt you're gonna pay me for it and you *know* you can't afford it," she spat out.

Alex released her and folded her arms in a huff. "Stop

being difficult and let's *go* please," she ground out.

Malajia looked at Sahara as she pointed to Chasity, who was adjusting her shirt. "Aye Sahara, Chasity just called your sister a broke bitch," she goaded. "She still your favorite?"

Sahara looked like she was trying to hold in her laugh. She nodded. "Yeah."

Malajia sucked her teeth and tossed her hands in the air. "Come *on* damn it! I'm fun as shit, at *least* replace me with Alex," she said, exasperated.

"How are you trying to take *my* place?" Alex put out. "I'm her first—"

"Bitch you only a first by default 'cause you her sister and shit," Malajia loudly interrupted. "If y'all weren't related, you, that old ass phone, them hot ass jeans, and those boots would be at the bottom of the list," she harped. Alex held a frown as Malajia continued. "You'd be after Emily and shit."

"Why do *I* have to be low on the list?" Emily asked, amusement in her voice.

"Yeah, you don't wanna ask that," Chasity joked as Malajia shot Emily a knowing look.

"You *know* you corny," Malajia jeered.

"Oh come on!" Emily exclaimed as Sahara snickered hard.

Alex rolled her eyes at her friends. "Sahara, you have to ignore them," she ground out. "Come on, we have to go check in. I'll call Sidra on the way."


Sidra swirled the last bit of caramel latte around in her cup. "This was too damn sweet," she griped to herself. "I'm gonna get a sugar rush." After a tense phone call with James the night before, Sidra found it hard to sleep. She got up early with the intention of going to the fitness center to go get a workout in, hoping that it would tire her out enough to be able to sleep a bit before the high school tour.

But in route to her destination, Sidra decided to ditch the

workout idea all together and stopped at the donut shop for a caffeine pick me up. Instead of going back to the house to meet the others, Sidra sat by the pond, staring at the ducks while drinking her latte. Secretly hoping that nobody would call her to ask where she was.

Her hope was shattered when she heard her phone ring moments later. Sidra glanced at the caller ID, then sighed as she put the phone to her ear. "Hey Alex... Um, I'm around... I know... Listen I—" She let out a sigh. "Okay let me change and I'll meet you guys over there... I know, I won't be long." Ending the call, she took a deep breath and stood up from the bench. Hosting a tour was the last thing that Sidra wanted to do. With everything on her mind, she would have much rather spent the day alone.

*You promised Alex*, she thought, walking around to the front. In passing by the guys' house to get to hers, she ignored the sound of the guys' door opening. Sidra only stopped when she heard her name being called.

She spun around to find Josh walking out of the house.

"Huh?" she stammered, eyes wide.

"Alex is looking for you," he informed, walking up to her. "She stopped by not too long ago."

"I know, I just spoke to her," Sidra replied, pushing her hair behind her ears. She felt like she was fighting to make eye contact with him. She felt like if she looked at him for more than a moment, she would start to cry. Their friendship had become so strained and Sidra hated it. She missed him. "Thanks for telling me though," she quickly put out.

Josh nodded. He watched her turn to walk away. Just as he was about to go his own way, Josh stopped. "Sidra," he called, she turned around.

"Yes?" she answered.

He ran a hand over the back of his neck. "Look, I know things between us aren't—"

"It's my fault," Sidra cut in, tone somber.

"That's not what I was going—"

"Josh, you don't have to explain anything," Sidra cut in

once again.

"You going to let me finish?" he asked, tone and face stern.

Sidra shut her mouth and just nodded.

"Now I know that things are a little strained right now," Josh began. "But I see how sad you've been and it doesn't sit well with me."

Sidra just stared at him as he spoke.

"I know you think that everybody is pulling away from you but that's not true…and I may be annoyed with you, but I don't want you to think that I'm not here if you need to talk to me," he said. "I'm *still* your friend and I just want you to be okay."

Sidra felt tears forming behind her eyes. All the sadness that she had been feeling was coming to the surface. When things were wrong, Josh was the first person that she would run to; he always made her feel better. But now that she was giving him space, Sidra found herself keeping her feelings buried behind her usual façade.

"*Are* you okay?" Josh pressed when she didn't answer. "Do you want to talk?"

Sidra forced her tears back down and cleared her throat. "I'm okay Josh, you don't have to worry about me," she said, moving hair from her face. "But thank you for being concerned…for thinking about me."

"I always *will*," he said, then gave her a soft tap on her shoulder. "I'll see you later."

Sidra nodded as Josh walked away. "I miss you," she said to herself as she watched him round the corner.


Alex held a hand up. "Okay everybody!" she bellowed over the chatter. She also grabbed the attention of Malajia, Chasity, and Emily, who were standing to her side. The fifteen high school students that were facing them in front of the steps of the cafeteria, finally hushed.

"You hype as shit with a folder," Malajia ground out,

folding her arms.

Alex shot her a side-glance, but decided against engaging in an argument. Instead, she focused her attention back on the teens. "So, we're just waiting for one more person and we'll get this tour on the road," she said, glancing at her watch.

"Is Sidra still coming?" Emily asked, looking at Alex.

"She *said* she was," Alex answered, unsure. With Sidra being so down lately, Alex wondered if she would even be up to the tour; if she should have pressed her in the first place.

"So, I know we already introduced ourselves a little earlier, but do any of you have any questions while we wait?" Alex asked the teens.

One of the boys smiled. "I got a question for Chasity," he said.

"And that *is*?" Chasity returned.

"You got a man?"

Chasity narrowed her eyes at the boy in front of her as her friends and the teens snickered. She had caught the kid staring at her while she spoke to the group earlier, and the entire time after. He had licked his lips on more than one occasion. She bit back the urge to say something smart. "Yes," she replied curtly.

The young man, who looked a lot younger than seventeen years old, folded his arms and stared at her, lust in his eyes. "I'm sayin' you can't have friends?" he pressed. His female classmates sucked their teeth and let out groans.

Chasity held her frowning gaze on him.

"Frank, just quit," Sahara scoffed.

"I mean, come on. I know I got something that *he* don't got," he boasted, holding his arms up.

"Yeah, your mama's tit still in your mouth, little boy," Chasity hissed, earning loud laughter from Malajia and the teen girls, including Sahara, who was pointing at him.

"Oh wow," Emily commented, trying to hold her laughter.

"Ahhhhh!" Malajia bellowed. "He got breast milk on his

lip and shit," she teased, as Frank looked around embarrassed. "*And* his pants tight as shit."

"Balls probably suffocating like shit," Chasity sneered, pushing her hair over her shoulder. Malajia roared with laughter.

"They need CPR and shit," Malajia added.

"One of 'em probably jumped back up to get away from those fuckin' tights," Chasity added, Malajia laughed louder.

"That's enough you two," Alex chided, a stern look on her face.

"You better look at *him* like that," Chasity spat out. "You ain't touring *me*, don't get embarrassed."

Alex waved her hand at Chasity dismissively as the laughter subsided. Then a smile appeared on her face as she saw Sidra walk up. "You made it," Alex beamed.

Sidra forced a smile in return as she greeted everybody. "Yeah," she said, adjusting the bracelet on her wrist.

Smiling, Alex faced the group once again. "Well, if everybody is done insulting the babies—"

"Wait, *who* insulted somebody?" Sidra asked, curious.

Chasity raised her hand, unfazed. "And I'll do it again," she muttered.

Sidra shook her head in amusement. She almost regretted not getting there earlier; she could have used a good laugh.


Alex was enthusiastic as she led the tour for her sister's group. Although her friends would have preferred not to participate, they were actually involved. Even Sidra, though she kept quiet unless a question was asked of her. The eager high schoolers seemed to be enjoying themselves, much to Alex's delight.

"So how are the parties here?" one girl asked.

"They're fun when you're a freshman, then they start getting wack," Malajia joked. "It be hot as shit in that gym."

Alex looked confused. "Stop acting like you weren't

partying *after* freshman year," she reminded. "Stop lying to these babies."

"I said the *gym* parties be wack," Malajia threw back. "The clusters is where it's at, *especially* the first weekend after break. Upperclassmen *stay* with drinks."

"Not that you should be *drinking*," Alex quickly cut in, looking at the group. "In fact, you may not even *want* to." Chasity and Malajia rolled their eyes. "Oh you *will*," Chasity contradicted. "Maybe not *all* the time, but trust me, you'll have a drink...or five."

"Yup," Malajia agreed. "Just make sure the RA's or those flashlight guards around campus don't catch you, and you'll be good."

Alex shook her head. "Don't encourage that mess," she chided.

"No point in lying to them," Chasity pointed out.

"I agree Alex," Emily said. "I mean, why hide the reality from them?" She looked at the group. "I just want to say to you guys, don't *ever* use alcohol as a way to deal with stress...from experience, it's not pretty."

"Y'all better listen to her, she was drinking like a fish sophomore year," Malajia cut in, gesturing to Emily. "I mean, like a big ass whale, and those hangovers she had, made her look terrible...just *terrible*." Malajia caught Emily staring at her. "What? Am I *lying*?"

"No, but come on, all *that*?" Emily ground out.

Malajia was taken aback. "I think I liked you better when you didn't talk back," she joked. Emily stuck her tongue out at her in retaliation.

"Thanks for sharing that Em," Alex smiled, proud. "Not *all* of you will drink, but if you *do*, do it in moderation, eat before drinking, and be *careful*. Don't leave your drinks unattended, and stay around people you trust to look out for you." Alex looked at Sahara, who was listening intently. "Except for you, *you* don't drink at all."

"Yeah okay," Sahara replied, flinging her long wavy hair over her shoulder.

Alex shook her head. "Don't make me tell Ma," she warned.

"Sahara, tell her to stop being a snitch bitch," Malajia ground out, earning a backhand from Alex.

"How's the food here?" someone else asked.

"Please," Malajia scoffed. "Y'all went to the caf for breakfast, I'm sure you got a taste of that dry ass food." Sidra giggled. "It's not bad," she contradicted.

"Yeah okay," Malajia returned, pushing some of her hair over her shoulder. "They be recycling the wing dings and shit."

Chasity snickered hard.

"They put the leftovers in the campus diner and Alex be eatin' them by the *bucket* full," Malajia continued.

Alex stared daggers at Malajia.

"One time, one of 'em had a bite mark on it," Malajia continued, earning a pluck to her arm from Alex. Malajia busted out laughing.

"You always *lying*," Alex huffed. "Guys, you gotta know by now that Malajia is Miss Exaggeration," Alex directed at the group. "You can't take *anything* that she says seriously."

"I'm not exaggerating about those wing dings," Malajia mumbled.

"You know what *I'm* worried about?" a girl began after a few seconds of silence.

"What's that?" Alex wondered.

"Having to live with someone you don't know," she answered. "How was it for *you* girls, meeting your roommate freshman year?"

The girls shot glances at each other, before breaking into laughter as they recalled their first encounters with one another.

"I hated *both* my damn roommates freshman year," Malajia commented. Alex and Emily looked at her with shock.

"Oh come on Malajia, hate is a strong word," Alex

chuckled.

"I *know*, and I *meant* it," Malajia agreed. "Y'all irked my *entire* existence."

Sidra pointed to Chasity. "*She* was completely and utterly *evil*," Sidra recalled, humor in her voice. "I mean the meanest, harshest, most foul-mouthed person that I ever met."

Chasity shrugged. "She's not lying," she confirmed. "I wanted my own room and when I walked in and saw *this* prissy ass chick in there, I wanted to drag her ass out by her ponytail," she said, pointing to Sidra.

Sidra giggled.

The group of teens were amused as the girls shared their first experiences.

"Yo, it was like living in a room with your annoying ass mom and a wimpy mute," Malajia jeered, gesturing to Alex and Emily. "*And* I had the top bunk. That was some bullshit. Emily wouldn't even give me her bed."

Emily busted out laughing.

"You act like rooming with *you* was a damn joy," Alex hurled at Malajia, who shot Alex a challenging look.

"Excuse you, I am an *amazing* roommate. I'm fun as shit," Malajia argued, pointing to herself. "Isn't that right Chaz?"

"Nope," Chasity immediately threw back.

Malajia sucked her teeth and flagged Chasity with her hand. "She lying like shit. *We* became best friends when we started rooming together sophomore year."

"Whatever," Chasity ground out.

"Malajia, between your loud voice, your constant teasing, pointless lying and...must I reiterate, that *loud voice*—I was ready to choke you on *more* than one occasion," Alex maintained. "So cut that out."

Malajia made a face at Alex. "Like I said, I'm a fun roommate, so fuck you."

Alex shook her head again, then adjusted the folder in her hand. "But first impressions aside, we eventually learned to see past the exterior. We learned to accept our differences and we became friends," she said. "Over these past four years, we've *all* been through so much and we just get closer and closer as a group... If you find a group of people like that while you're in college, consider yourselves lucky...I know *I* am." Alex smiled at her friends, who stared at her.

"See, she always on some ole' mushy shit," Malajia blurted out, inciting laughter from everyone but Alex, who just gritted her teeth.

"You know what—"

"I'm just messing with you boo boo," Malajia laughed, cutting Alex's angry words off. "You know I love your wide ass."

"She's right though," Emily cosigned. "*Alex*, I mean... You may sometimes feel like you're better off alone when you come to college, but...you're not. You need a strong set of friends. It makes the years so much better."

Sidra smiled at their words, but deep down she wondered if her bond would ever go back to being as strong as it was with some of the group. *Keep it together, Princess,* she thought.

Seeing another tour group in passing, the girls stopped when they noticed the guides.

"Jason, *you're* touring?" Chasity asked, seeing him and a few of his football teammates.

"Yeah, the athletic department called me," Jason answered. "Sports players," he added, gesturing to a few teens in his group. "Has she cussed any of you out yet?" he joked to her group.

"Just *him*," Sahara laughed, pointing to Frank, who glanced away.

Jason shook his head in amusement, then noticed that all of the girls in Chasity's group were staring at him, smiling. Some were twirling their hair around their fingers, others had their hands on their chests. He chuckled.

"Oh Lord," Alex muttered, knowing how Chasity could react to other females making googly eyes at her boyfriend.

Chasity glanced at the girls and frowned. "Aye yo, put all those damn teeth back in your mouths, he's spoken for," she hissed.

Jason laughed. "Chaz, babe—"

"Shut up," Chasity spat at him. Jason, amused, put his hands up in surrender.

Malajia frowned when she noticed another one of the guides. "Carl, how you touring potential students when you failing like shit," Malajia shot at the football linebacker.

Carl sucked his teeth. "Why you always gotta start?"

Malajia focused her attention on the guy running up to Jason's group.

"My bad, thanks for waiting for me," Mark panted.

Malajia frowned. "How *you* touring with the athletes and shit?" she hurled at him.

Mark shot her a frown. "Whatchu' mean?" he threw back. "*I'm* athletic."

"Boy you ain't on no damn team," Malajia spat out. "You all deceiving people and shit."

Mark stared at her, eyes flashing. "They ain't even need to *know* all that," he barked. "Don't be showing off in front of the group."

Malajia flagged him. "Whatever, that's why none of the girls are smiling at your black ass," she bit out.

Mark pointed to a young lady from Malajia's group. "*She* is," he countered.

Malajia immediately spun around. "What?" she barked at the girl, who just giggled and moved away.

Alex put her hand over her face and shook her head. She sighed at her group. "Ignore them. They're a couple and they do this all the time," she said of Malajia and Mark.

"We gotta finish up, movies later?" Jason cut in.

"Yeah, see you guys," Alex waved to them.

"He always talking shit," Malajia muttered as the guys' group walked off.

"*You* just started with *him*!" Alex exclaimed.

"Nobody asked you," Malajia bit out, folding her arms.

"We have a few more sites to see. Does anybody have any more questions before we continue?" Alex asked, ignoring Malajia's response.

A girl raised her hand. "Um, Sidra you said earlier that you were a Criminal Justice major?"

Sidra nodded.

"How is it? Do you plan on becoming a lawyer? If so, what kind? And what law schools are you looking at after you graduate?" the girl asked.

Sidra took a second to process all of the questions. "Well, the Criminal Justice program here is really good... It's tough but that's not a bad thing," she answered, pushing her hair out of her face. "I'm not sure what side of law that I want to be in *just yet*, still deciding... and I'm looking at a few law schools here in Virginia, Pennsylvania and um...California."

"*California*?!" Alex exclaimed, as the other girls looked at Sidra.

"Wow, that's so far away," Emily added, tone sad.

Sidra looked back at them with wide eyes. She'd forgotten that the only person she had mentioned the possibility of going to California with was James. "I'm just looking right now," she replied.

"She ain't going to no damn California," Malajia mumbled, waving her hand at Sidra. Sure she was upset with her, but Malajia didn't know how she would deal with Sidra being all the way on the other side of the United States. She was used to only living two hours from her. "She better keep her ass on the East Coast."

Sidra shook her head. "Yeah, so that's basically it," she said to the girl who asked the question.

"Thank you," the girl smiled, grateful.

"Sure," Sidra returned.

"*I* have a question," another girl asked.

"Sure Larria, what's your question sweetie?" Alex acknowledged.

"Chasity, is that all your hair?"

Chasity looked confused as snickers rang through the group.

"Ooh, no you didn't," Sahara chuckled, shaking her head.

Chasity held her same confused look. "What kind of—"

"Yeah, it's all hers," Malajia eagerly cut in, before vigorously running her hands through Chasity's long hair, parting some in the process. "See? No tracks."

"Bitch, get off me!" Chasity barked, knocking Malajia's hand out of her hair, then slapped it.

"Ouch!" Malajia yelped, rubbing her hand. "Childish."

Sidra couldn't help but laugh along with the group.

"Yeah, if I find friends like you girls when I come here, my college experience is gonna be freakin' *hilarious*," Sahara mused.

"You're right about that, little sis" Alex chortled, putting her arm around Sahara. "A hundred percent."

# Chapter 33

Alex tossed a pillow to Sahara, who was lying on the floor. After touring and hanging out most of the day, the girls were finally able to relax in Alex's room for some much-needed sister time.

"Thanks for letting me stay the night here," Sahara said, grateful.

Alex waved her hand at her. "Don't mention it," she smiled, opening a bag of chips. "Ma already told me that no matter *what* I said, she was gonna send you with an overnight bag."

Sahara giggled. "I'm sure she *did*," she said, opening some sour cream and onion dip. "Semaj is spending the night at a friend's, and Dad is working overnight too? Yeah, Ma is gonna enjoy that quiet."

"I don't blame her," Alex laughed. She reached down and dipped a chip into some dip. "So what did you think of the tour? You still thinking about coming here?"

"You already know this school is my first choice," Sahara mused. "I didn't need a tour to sway me... But I *will* say that I had fun with you guys today... I wish y'all could be here when I come in the fall."

"I know," Alex sighed. "But you'll be fine."

"Will *you* be fine?" Sahara asked.

That question caught Alex off guard. "What do you mean?"

Sahara shrugged. "I mean, you'll be graduating in like a month or so, which means that that's it, you'll no longer be coming back to school with your friends. You'll no longer see them every single day... How are you gonna deal with that?"

Alex pondered Sahara's question. She felt a somber cloud fall over her. She was excited to graduate and embark on a new chapter in her life, but Alex didn't have a minute to stop and think that the days of being around the group, that had become a second family to her, would be over. "Wow," was all that Alex could get out. "I um—" her thoughts were interrupted by the door slowly opening.

Alex and Sahara watched as Malajia slowly crawled into the room and over to the pile of snacks that were sitting in front of Sahara. Alex held a scowl and Sahara put her hand over her mouth to keep from busting out laughing as they watched Malajia slowly grab a bag of chips, and the dip, then slowly crawl backwards out the door.

"Shhhhh," Malajia whispered, closing the door.

"Malajia!" Alex erupted as Sahara busted out laughing. "What the hell is wrong with you?"

"Oh, you saw me?" Malajia said, sitting halfway in the room.

"Girl," Alex pinched the bridge of her nose. "What is your greedy behind doing stealing our snacks? You have your own downstairs."

Malajia pointed in the hallway. "*Chasity* wanted—"

"Why you always gotta drag me down with you?" Chasity barked from the hallway.

Alex narrowed her eyes. "Chasity, where is your sneaky behind?"

Chasity poked her head in the room. She was standing right next to the door, waiting on Malajia.

Malajia pointed up at Chasity. "She told me to come in here and get the sour cream and onion chips 'cause she don't like plain," Malajia told.

Chasity nudged Malajia with her knee, inciting a laugh from her. "You snitchin' ass bitch," she huffed. "And you grabbed the wrong fuckin' bag anyway."

Malajia glanced down at the plain bag of chips in her

hand. "Oh shit," she laughed.

Alex shook her head then turned to Sahara, who was finding the whole thing amusing. "To answer your question, I'll be fine with it. I could use the break from these fools," she spat.

David plopped his book bag down on the floor as he sat at the library table across from Nicole. "Sorry I'm late," he said. "I was helping one of my classmates with an assignment."

"That's okay," Nicole replied, jotting down notes in her notebook. She glanced up at David. "Okay, don't be mad."

David shot her a confused look and stopped unpacking. "Be mad about what?"

Nicole fiddled with the pencil in her hand. "Um...so okay—"

"What is it?" David pressed when she hesitated.

"I may have let it slip to someone that you were a virgin," she admitted.

David's mouth fell open. "What?!" Nicole flinched at the bass in his voice. David glanced around as his loud voice carried. He'd almost forgotten that he was in the library. "Nicole, you *what*?"

"I'm sorry," she said, remorseful.

David put his hands on his head and let out a frustrated huff. News and gossip had a way of spreading through campus quicker than wildfire. "My damn *friends* don't even know. I told you that in confidence."

Nicole looked down at the table, silent.

"Nicky, why did you do that?" David ranted.

Nicole put her hands up. "David, I'm sorry, I just... My friend and I were talking about relationships and I started telling them how great you are and we got on the topic of sex and...." She let out a quick sigh. "It just slipped out. I didn't mean to tell your business—*our* business."

David put his head in his hands. He was mortified. *Shit!*

*Now I'm gonna have to tell the others.* "Great, this is great," he muttered, sarcastic.

Nicole reached over and touched his arm, holding on. "I'm *really* sorry David," she pouted. "But in all honesty, you don't have to be ashamed of it."

"Easy for *you* to say," David grunted, lifting his head. Shaking his head, he sat back in his seat, staring at her. "Who did you tell?"

Nicole's eyes shifted. "Um…"

David frowned. "*Who* did you *tell?*" he repeated slowly.

Nicole shook her head and let out a sigh. "It was Quincy," she quietly admitted.

David held a blank look on his face as he tried to keep from flying off the handle any more than he already had. Although on the inside, he was burying himself in a hole. Thinking back to what Quincy had said to him days prior, David pinched the bridge of his nose and let out a long sigh. "That explains the comment that he made," he ground out.

"*What* comment?" Nicole wondered.

"It doesn't even matter," David hissed, gathering his belongings. He couldn't figure out if he was more upset at the fact that Nicole had told his business in the first place, or that she had told it to her ex. "I gotta go."

Nicole let out a sigh as David stood from the table. "I'll make it up to you I promise sweetie," she said, tone pleading.

"Yeah," David spat out, walking away.


Sidra rolled her eyes as she held her phone in front of her face.

"You *do* realize that I can see you right?" James ground out.

Sidra stared at the phone. She'd almost forgotten that James had called her via video phone. "Sorry," she muttered. "I forgot that you don't like to see any emotion but happy."

James let out a sigh. "That's *not* what I meant, and you know that," he threw back. "I can't believe you're still dwelling on our little spat. That was three days ago."

Sidra narrowed her eyes. "Oh yeah," she mocked. "I forgot that you expect me to get over shit right away *too*. My fault."

"Now you're being condescending," James hissed. "That's not attractive."

Sidra sucked her teeth. James was right; she was still annoyed with him. So much so that she almost refused to answer his phone call that day. But, not wanting to seem immature, she reluctantly answered. Sidra was now regretting that decision.

"Now look, I'm sorry that you took what I said the wrong way honey, and I know I was short with you, but...I had a lot on my plate that day," James said, tone calm.

"You should have just told me to call you back," Sidra argued.

"And if I would have done that then this whole thing would be about the fact that I wasn't there when you needed me to be," James returned. "I don't know what you want from me anymore."

"I *want* you to act like you care about what I'm going through," Sidra harped. "And not make me feel like I'm being childish by feeling how I feel."

James rubbed his face with his hand as he let out a deep sigh. He too was regretting this phone call. "Look Sidra, I get that you're dealing with the fact that your friends are pulling away from you, and I feel bad for you," he began. "But I don't have time to listen to you go on about it every time we talk. I don't want to hear you upset every time we talk. I listen to people's sob stories all damn day and when I talk to my girlfriend, I want it to be positive."

"So basically, you're telling me to keep my problems to myself," Sidra cut in, angry. "Got it."

"Sidra, you whining about your issues like a teenager isn't going to change what's going on," James spat out. "Stop being down on yourself. Suck it up."

Sidra's eyes widened; her mouth dropping open in

shock. *No the fuck he did not just say that to me.* "Suck it up? As in just shut up about it?" she fumed.

"That's not what I meant."

Sidra stared at the phone. "I think it *is* what you meant," she contradicted. "I'm not whining to you, I am *venting* to you. I spend all day keeping my feelings to myself and making everybody think that I'm okay. I just want to be able to talk about what I *truly* feel, to the person I thought I should...but you don't want that. You just want the perky, smiling, happy, stuffy-ass Sidra. Not the emotional, smart-mouthed, stressed, *real* one. So that's fine, I'll give you what you want."

"Sidra—"

Sidra plastered on a phony smile. "Everything is fine. Have a good day at work honey," she put out in her best nice voice, before hanging up, cutting off James's protest.

Smile immediately faded, she threw her phone on the floor. Feeling herself getting ready to cry, she put her hands over her face. Sucking her tears back in, Sidra stood up from her bed and headed out the door.

Sidra's journey took her to the guys' house. Hesitating, she eventually knocked on the door. She entered when she heard a voice on the other side tell her to come in.

"Hi Mark," she said, closing the door behind her.

"Hey," Mark said, shoving his wallet into his pocket.

"Um...is Josh here?" she asked.

"Nah," Mark said, shaking his head. "He's at work."

"Oh," Sidra said, tone low. *It's just as well, he doesn't want to hear my problems*, she thought. "Thanks."

Mark stared at her as she slowly headed back for the door. Like the others, he hated seeing Sidra look so lonely and sad. He was still on Malajia's side regarding her feelings about Sidra, but Sidra was still like a sister to him. "Sidra," he called.

She turned around. "Yeah?"

Mark rubbed the back of his neck as he let out a sigh. "You want some juice or something?" he asked.

Sidra let a small smile come through. Normally an offering of a beverage wouldn't be a big deal. But coming from Mark, especially with their recent tension, she found it sweet. "Juice?"

"Yeah, you lookin' kind of thirsty," Mark replied.

"No, I'm fine," she declined, smile still on her face. "Thanks though."

"Sure," he said as Sidra walked out the door.

As soon as the door closed, David trotted down the stairs and walked into the kitchen. Mark watched as David rummaged through cabinets, then the fridge, all without saying a word.

"Uhhhh, you just not gonna speak bruh?" Mark groused.

David looked up at him. "Sorry," he said. "Do we have any beers?"

"Hell no, don't nobody drink that nasty shit," Mark scoffed.

David sucked his teeth as he ran his hand over his head. "We have any liquor?"

Mark shook his head. "Nah, I finished that off last night," he said. "You actually asking for *drinks*? What's up with you man?"

David let out a deep sigh. "I'm just um…I'm pissed off and I need to calm myself down."

Mark patted David on his shoulder as he nodded. "Say no more, I got you," he assured, then pulled out his phone.

David stood there, confused, as Mark made a call.

"Boo boo!" he bellowed into the line. "I'm *always* loud sugar. Yo, y'all got a bottle over there?... Who all over there?... Tell Jase and Chaz not to leave yet, I'm coming over with David… Just have the bottle ready."

David looked at Mark as he hung up the phone. "You guys don't have to drink with me," he said.

"Man, you already know we don't pass up an

opportunity to drink," Mark quipped. "Come on."

David closed his eyes as he took a sip of his vodka.
"God, why didn't I mix this?" he grimaced at the taste.
"'Cause you a grown ass man dawg, you don't need no
juice," Mark teased, giving David a pat on his back.
David patted his chest as the strong liquid poured down
his throat. It had been fifteen minutes since he and Mark
walked over to the girls' house. And he'd spent every second
of it sipping on vodka. He took another sip. "Ugh!"
"David, stop nursing the thing. Drink up bruh," Mark
urged. He gave David another pat on his back, causing David
to spill some of his drink. "Oops," Mark chuckled.
"Yo, will you stop slapping him so he can stop spilling
his damn liquor all over the floor?" Chasity hissed, handing
Jason a bag of chips before sitting on the couch next to him.
"This carpet old as shit anyway," Mark dismissed.
Chasity smirked. "Yeah, you ain't lyin'," she agreed,
reaching into the chip bag.
Malajia shook her head as David took another quick sip
of his drink. "David, I don't know why you let Mark talk you
into that," she ground out. "He telling you to drink it straight
and his ass got a whole cup of cranberry juice mixed with
his."
David jerked his head around and frowned at Mark, who
was trying to hide his cup. "You lied to me!" David wailed.
Mark laughed.
"I watched him pour the juice in his cup, too," Jason
laughed. "Swore he was sneaky."
David's mouth fell open. "We were supposed to drink
this straight *together*," he recalled, pointing to his glass.
"Man my bad, that shit is *nasty* straight," Mark reasoned,
laughter in his voice.
David shook his head. "Well, to hell with it, I'm almost
done now," he resolved, taking another sip.
Malajia fanned herself. "This drink got me hot and

hungry," she said. "What time is Alex getting off work? I'mma need for her to lug one of those nasty pizzas home."

"She gotta close with Josh tonight," Chasity informed, taking a sip of juice.

"There better be liquor in that cup Chasity," Malajia sneered, pointing.

"I told you before, I'm not drinking anymore of that five-dollar vodka that you keep buying," Chasity returned. "That shit had my head about to explode last time."

"Nobody told you to lose that drinking game," Malajia threw back. "Got all drunk and your horny ass was grabbing Jason's manhood in front of everyone."

Chasity nearly choked on her drink. "I did *not!*" she exclaimed. She glanced around the room and everyone was nodding their heads.

"Yeah sis, you *did*," Mark laughed.

Chasity looked at Jason; she had no recollection of the event in question. "Really?" she mouthed.

Jason nodded enthusiastically, smiling at her. "In a goddamn vice grip."

Chasity narrowed her eyes at him. "What *else* did I do?" she hissed.

Jason chuckled. "I'll remind you later," he crooned. Chasity sucked her teeth and snatched the bag of chips from him.

"Yeah, you were tore down that night," Malajia added. "Shit *me too*. Alex said that I tried to squeeze her boobs for whatever reason... I probably thought they were pillows or some shit."

"Wow," Jason chortled, eating chips.

Mark stared at Malajia. "You wanna squeeze a boob while I watch?" he teased.

Malajia shot him a side-glance. "No, but I'll squeeze a *dick* while you watch, jackass," she shot back. Mark frowned as he flipped her the finger. "Yeah, that's what I thought," she spat out, taking a sip of her drink.

David chuckled as he finished his drink. Leave it to his

friends to lighten his mood. Holding the empty glass in his hand, his mind began to wander. Remembering his earlier conversation with Nicole, David cleared his throat.

"Hey, can I ask you couples a question?" David began, grabbing the attention of the room.

"What's up man?" Mark prompted.

David adjusted himself in his seat. "Okay so..." he was interrupted when the door opened.

"Hey guys," Emily smiled.

"You smilin' hard as shit Em," Mark teased. "Where you comin' from?"

"The library," Emily replied.

Mark sucked his teeth. "That ain't no reason to smile," he jeered, taking a sip of his drink.

"Nah, she on her way to go see Will and shit," Malajia announced.

Emily giggled. "Not until later tonight," she said, sitting on the arm of one of the chairs. "I'm meeting him at his second job...he bartends at a restaurant in the mall."

"She hype as shit, explaining what Will doin' and shit," Mark teased.

Emily shook her head in amusement.

"Anyway David, what were you about to say?" Mark wondered.

David ran a hand over his head, deciding if he even wanted to bring up what was on his mind. The alcohol running through his system was giving him a bit of courage to speak. "Okay so, you guys are in a relationship...how would you feel if your significant other was still friends with their ex?" His question was met with silence and frowns.

"This about Nicole?" Chasity asked. David glanced down at the floor. "Her silly ass *still* think that shit is cute?"

"Chaz," Jason warned. Chasity flagged him with her hand.

"Oh, that would be no problem," Mark answered, to which Malajia shot him a knowing look.

"Oh *really*?" she challenged.

"Yeah, 'cause that shit wouldn't happen, I'd kill that muthafucka," Mark grunted. "I betta not *ever* see his ass."

"That makes two of us babe," Malajia sighed.

David put his hand up. "I'm sorry, I didn't mean to bring up bad memories."

"No, it's cool," Mark said. "I mean in different circumstances...I don't know."

David looked to Jason. "Jase? Would *you* be okay with Chasity being friends with her ex?"

"Chasity doesn't *have* an ex," Jason stated, Chasity shrugged; it was the truth. "But if she *did*... As long as there is nothing funny going—"

"Stop lying," Chasity cut in, earning a snicker from Jason. "You know damn well, you would not be okay with me hanging out and talking to someone I used to fuck."

"Well shit," Mark chuckled. "Well when you put it like *that*."

"I would punch Mark in his fuckin' face and cut up all his drawls if he *ever* got friendly with one of his raggedy, bum ass ex's."

"Really? Cut up my drawls? No other clothes, *just* the drawls?" Mark sniped; Emily snickered.

"Damn right," Malajia maintained. "Your balls gonna be chaffed like shit in those hard ass jeans."

Mark shook his head.

David sighed. "So, I'm *not* overreacting when I get upset about it?" he looked to them for confirmation.

"Not at all," Malajia confirmed. "I don't get why she's still doing it. Like, how you in a relationship and gonna be all extra friendly with someone you used to bang? ...Sorry David."

David shrugged. "It's the truth." He looked at Chasity. He had yet to get her opinion, and he needed it from all who were present. "Chaz, how would *you* feel—" He closed his mouth when he saw Jason shaking his head 'no.' Chasity shot him a lethal side-glance.

"David, *please* don't get your face ripped off, bringing

up Jason's ex," Malajia advised.

"Uh sorry. Almost forgot about that," David apologized. He looked to Emily. "Em? Would you be okay with Will talking to his ex?"

Emily examined the pale pink polish on her nails. "Well...Will's ex is *dead*, so..."

Everyone regarded Emily with shock.

"*Damn* Em!" Malajia wailed.

Emily looked up from her hand, oblivious. "What?" she asked, eyes wide. "Oh God, no I didn't mean it like that!" she exclaimed, waving her hand.

"That was some mean shit, Em," Mark jeered. "You been hanging with Chasity too damn much."

"Don't blame that shit on me," Chasity threw back.

Emily was mortified. "No seriously, I didn't mean it like that—I'm not mean, I was just—I'm just gonna go upstairs now."

"You make sure you keep your evil energy confined to *your* room," Malajia joked as Emily headed up the steps.

"Cut it oooouuuut," Emily whined before closing her door.

David leaned forward and sighed. "I mean, she insists that they're just friends... I do trust her, I just hate that she tells him *everything*. She even told him that I was a damn virgin." As soon as the words flew out of his mouth, David wished that he could've taken them back. *Fuck! This damn liquor! I'm never drinking again.*

David hesitantly glanced up and saw all eyes on him, shocked. "You heard me huh?" he sputtered, letting out a nervous laugh.

"Hold up," Mark said, putting his hand up. "You said you're a *what*?"

David let out a long sigh. "I'm a virgin," he sulked. "There, it's out."

Jason sat there, mouth open. "Sooooo, you never did...anything?" he slowly put out. David shook his head. "I mean like...*nothing*?"

"He *said* no," Chasity spat at Jason.

Jason was confused by her attitude. "What did I do?"

"Just 'cause *your* fast ass lost yours at like fifteen, doesn't mean *he* had to," Chasity hissed.

"*Sixteen*, smart ass," Jason shot back.

Malajia reached for her drink. "Yo, I had *no* idea David," she said, taking a sip. "That's a first. The guy being a virgin and the girl not."

"Come on guys, it's not uncommon for a grown man to be a virgin," David pointed out.

"Yes, it is," Jason joked, earning a backhand from Chasity. "I'm joking," he insisted, laughing. "David, it's nothing to be ashamed of, bro."

David shrugged, then looked over at Mark. The guy was staring at him, a sympathetic look on his face. "What's with *you*?" David asked.

Without warning, Mark walked over and threw his arms around David. "My brother, I didn't know you weren't gettin' none," he blurted out.

David rolled his eyes as Jason snickered. Malajia shook her head.

"You shoulda *told* me bro," Mark added, releasing David from his embrace. "I coulda hooked you up with one of *my* girls," Mark ducked when a pillow came flying at him.

"*What* fuckin' girls?" Malajia barked.

"Aye, chill your ass out. This is between me and my virgin brother," Mark hurled at her, pointing. He turned to David who had his eyes narrowed at him. "Now look, I would've gave you Marilyn's number."

"Dick suckin', *snaggle tooth* Marilyn?" Chasity blurted out, earning a laugh from Malajia and Jason. "You wanted to subject him to having her named carved on his man parts?"

"You are so damn ignorant!" Malajia roared with laughter.

David nudged Mark away from him. "Mark, it's no big deal."

"The fuck it *ain't*, boy you better *go* over there and get some damn service from your girl," Mark teased. "I heard she a freak too."

David elbowed Mark in his ribs. "Watch your damn mouth!"

"I'm playing, I'm playing," Mark laughed, rubbing his ribs with a hand. "No disrespect, I'm just messing with you man. Don't rush into something you're not ready for...even if it *does* make you look like a punk." He laughed louder when another pillow came flying at him.

# Chapter 34

Sidra cradled her cell phone to her ear as she walked into the restaurant within the mall. "Mama, I've said before that I'm fine," she answered, bite in her voice.

"Judging by that tone, that is a lie," Mrs. Howard returned.

Sidra rolled her eyes as she glanced up at the ceiling. Still flustered from her conversation with James earlier, on top of everything else that she was dealing with, Sidra decided to take a solo excursion to the mall. Not in the mood to do any actual shopping, she decided to get a bite to eat.

Sidra's sour mood didn't improve when her mother called her to check in on her. "What do you want me to say?" she huffed, glancing around for the hostess.

"Look Sidra, I don't like that you've been so depressed lately," Mrs. Howard said, tone stern. "This isn't my Princess."

"Why does everybody seem to be under the impression that 'Princess' Sidra is supposed to put on a happy face all the damn time?" she barked into the line. She immediately regretted the outburst when she was met with silence. "Mama, I'm sorry."

A sigh came through the line. "It's okay Sidra, I know you've been going through a lot," she placated. "I wish I could mend things for you."

"I know, but we both know you *can't*," Sidra sighed. Not seeing the hostess appear, she headed for the bar. "Anyway, I'm about to grab something to eat, I'll call you later."

"Okay baby, I love you."

"Love you too."

Sidra let out another sigh as she sat down. "Hi, can I have a menu please?" she asked, voice tired as she dug around in her purse.

The bartender turned around and smiled. "Hi Sidra."

Sidra glanced up from the contents of her bag. "Will? Hi," she returned. "You work here? I thought you were still at the movie theater."

Will handed her a menu. "I'm still there," he confirmed. "This is my second job. Gotta finish furnishing the apartment."

Sidra managed a small chuckle. "I hear you."

"You here by yourself?"

"Unfortunately," Sidra sighed, glancing at the menu.

"Well, I won't say that. There's nothing wrong with taking yourself out to dinner."

"I agree," Will smiled, resting his hands on the counter top. "So, what can I get for you?"

Sidra studied the menu. "Um…I'll take the coconut shrimp please," she said, handing the menu back to Will.

"I'll get that in," Will replied. "Anything to drink?"

Sidra thought for a moment. "Ginger ale," she said. When Will went to fulfill her order, she called him, prompting him to turn around. "Can you make that a strawberry daiquiri please?"

"Virgin or non?"

"Non," Sidra replied. After the time that she had been having, the way that she had been feeling, she felt that she could use a drink. When Will began to prepare her beverage after placing her order, Sidra looked at her phone and watched James' number flash across her screen. "Screw him," she huffed to herself. She had no interest in talking to him. She smiled when the drink was placed in front of her. "Thanks," she said, and took a sip.

"Hey Em, were you still coming to meet me here at

work?" Will asked into the phone. "Oh you're at the mall? ...Okay, um..." He glanced back at the bar. "I just wanted to let you know before you walk in here that your friend is here at the bar... Sidra... Yeah, she's been here for a few hours and um...she's pretty drunk... Okay, see you in a few."

Will hung up and approached the counter. "Sidra," he called.

A visibly intoxicated Sidra glanced up at him as she played with a cube of ice in her glass. "Hey," she beamed. "Hey, can you get me another drink?"

"Um, I don't think that's a good idea," Will said. "You seem to have had enough."

Sidra frowned. "I'm a paying customer *William*, and I *want* another damn drink," she barked, slamming her glass on the counter. Luckily for her, the glass didn't break.

Will stared at her, nervous. He didn't know what to do and certainly didn't want to upset her. "Uh—" relief set in when he saw Emily walk through the door. "Thank God," he breathed, moving around the counter, leaving Sidra sitting there.

"I'm so glad you're here," he said to Emily, intercepting her before she could reach the bar.

Emily looked over at Sidra. "How many drinks did she have?" she asked.

"I swear, I only gave her two," Will stammered, putting his hand up. "I was called to another section and another bartender took over," he said as Emily looked at him. "When I got back, I saw that she'd switched from the frozen drinks to vodka and cranberry... She had like *four* of them."

Emily winced. "She's gonna feel that in the morning," she muttered. She knew all too well the effects of over drinking. Plus Sidra wasn't that much of a drinker, so Emily could imagine the hangover in her future. She looked at Will. "Thanks for calling me, I'll check on her."

"Okay," he sighed.

Emily giggled at the sick look on his face. "Why do you look nervous?"

"Y'all women scare me sometimes," Will returned, before walking away to tend to his work.

Emily shook her head, then walked over to the bar. She tapped Sidra on the shoulder, prompting her to turn around. "Hey sweetie," she said.

Sidra looked at her. "Em—Emily," she slurred, throwing her arms around her. Emily steadied herself as Sidra's drunk weight nearly made her stumble. "What are you doing here? You shouldn't be at a bar."

Emily took a seat next to her. "I'm not tempted to drink," she said, adjusting herself in her seat. "So um...how are you feeling?" she slowly put out as Sidra's eyes started wandering. Emily counted the empty glasses in front of her. "Decided to have a few drinks huh?"

Sidra nodded. "I just needed to relax a bit," she slurred. "But I'm good now... In fact, I think one *more* wouldn't hurt." She raised her hand to get the bartender's attention.

"No, I think you've had enough," Emily cut in, pulling Sidra's hand down. "Can you just get her some water please?" she asked the bartender when he walked over.

Sidra snatched her hand from Emily's grip. "I don't want any fuckin' *water* Emily," Sidra snapped.

Emily put her hands up in surrender as Sidra held her fiery gaze on her. "Okay, okay Sid," she relented. She turned to the bartender. "Um can you get her some *vodka* please?" Emily asked. When Sidra smiled, and turned away, Emily signaled for the bartender to come close. "Give her water and tell her it's vodka please," she whispered. "Make up something about it tasting like water." The bartender nodded and did as she asked.

Emily watched as Sidra grabbed the glass and took a sip. "Ooh, it's nice and cold," she slurred.

"Uh huh," Emily agreed. "Um Sidra...did you drive?"

Sidra nodded as she concentrated on her drink.

"Can you give me your car keys please?"

"No," Sidra spat. "I'm not gonna drive home Emily, I'm not stupid."

"I didn't say that you *were*," Emily returned, tone calm. "I'm just trying to look out for you." She then eyed Sidra's purse on the counter and slowly moved it to her lap. Emily spotted the plate of uneaten food on the bar. "Maybe you should eat something."

"Not hungry," Sidra returned.

Emily just sat there, staring at her. She knew that Sidra sitting at a bar alone wasn't like her. Let alone getting drunk, without anyone to look out for her, knowing that she drove. For Sidra to put herself in a potentially dangerous situation like that only meant that she was allowing her troubles to overtake her.

"Are you okay Sidra?" Emily asked as she removed a small straw that had gotten stuck in Sidra's curled hair.

Sidra set her empty glass down and looked at Emily. "Sure Em, I'm just fine," she said. "Don't I look fine? Am I still pretty?"

Emily signaled for the bartender to give Sidra another glass of water. "You look beautiful as always, Sidra," she replied. "But judging by what you're doing right now…you're not fine."

"I *am* fine," Sidra hissed. "I'm just fine, like *always*. I'm *fine* with the fact that I damaged my friendships."

"Sidra, you didn't—"

"I *did*!" Sidra yelled, causing Emily to flinch. Sidra glanced around as Emily touched her arm. "I'm sorry."

"It's okay, just try to calm down," Emily said, tone caring. Emily held a sympathetic gaze on Sidra as she watched tears fill her eyes.

"I'm fine though," Sidra lied through her tears. "Just need a few more glasses of this vodka."

"Sidra, maybe we should go. Will can take you home—" Emily suggested, making a move to help Sidra from her seat.

Sidra smacked her hand away. "Get off me Emily," she snapped. "I don't need you to tell me what to do."

"I'm not *trying* to," Emily assured her, glancing around. She wanted to get Sidra out of the bar, but worried that she would cause a scene. She knew that if she got Will to help that Sidra might throw a complete tantrum. This wasn't a Sidra that Emily was used to seeing. "I just want to make sure you're okay."

"I *said* I'm fine," Sidra fussed.

"Sidra, please calm down," Emily pleaded. "Um, do you want to talk to somebody? You want me to call your mom?"

"I'm a grown ass woman Emily," Sidra hissed, wiping her eyes. "I don't need you to call my damn mother."

Emily retrieved Sidra's phone from her purse. "Okay, okay," she said, searching through Sidra's call log for someone to calm her down. "James, you want to talk to James?" Emily's eyes widened with shock as Sidra tried to snatch the phone from Emily's hand. "I will throw that phone in the fuckin' trash if you try to call him," she snarled.

Emily just sat there, holding the phone out of Sidra's reach as Sidra rambled on.

"That stuffy ass bastard wouldn't want to talk to me anyway 'cause I'm not *happy*," Sidra mocked. "He only wants *happy* Sidra, *perky* Sidra, the Sidra who won't cuss his old ass the fuck *out*... Stupid bastard—"

Emily didn't know what to say. "Um—"

"All he wanna do is talk about his stupid job and stupid art...who the fuck likes *art*? Nobody wants to go to a boring ass art gallery." Sidra turned to Emily. "Do I *look* like I would enjoy some damn art gallery?"

Emily shook her head. "No, no you don't," she placated.

"It's *boring*," Sidra ranted. "And why does he only wear suits? Where are the fuckin' jeans, some sweats—*something*... Who wears a *tie* every day?... Dressing like Mr. rusty ass office man every fuckin' day... Stupid ass prude."

Emily contained her urge to giggle. Sidra was annoyed with James for behaving and dressing like *she* did.

"Stupid, old fuck—I don't want to talk to him. I don't even *like* him anymore."

"You what?" Emily questioned. "You don't like James anymore?"

"Not as my *boyfriend*," Sidra slurred. "I can't be myself around him. He doesn't care about the *real* me. He doesn't have time for me, *work* comes first."

Emily stared at Sidra as tears started pouring down her face. "I—I can't believe I said that just now... I *do* like him, I *care* about him...but I— I don't care about him *enough* and I don't think I ever will." Sidra put her hands over her face. "What is *wrong* with me? He's a good guy...I just—I think I just don't *want* him... I just don't want to be how I *am* anymore."

Emily's eyes were wide. Sidra was rambling, slurring, but her truth was coming out. "What *do* you want?"

Sidra played in her hair with one hand and twirled a glass with the other. "I want—I want my friendship with Malajia to go back to normal—I miss her... I want James to leave me alone and I want—I want Josh."

"You want Josh?" Emily didn't know if she'd heard her correctly.

"I—I want Josh," Sidra stammered, staring out in front of her. "I miss Josh. I want to talk to Josh... I want *Josh*."

Emily wasn't certain, but she almost felt like Sidra, in her drunken state, had just confessed that she wanted to be with Josh. Or maybe, she just wanted his friendship back to normal. In any case, Emily knew who to call.


Emily stood off to a corner, making sure to keep a close eye on Sidra; she was still at the bar, with her head in her hands. When she saw Josh walk in, Emily breathed a sigh of relief. "Sorry, I know that you were at work," she said.

Josh removed his Pizza Shack apron. "It's fine, I was getting off anyway," he said. He glanced over at the bar when Emily pointed. His heart sank; Sidra looked sad and lonely sitting there. He looked back at Emily. "You have her car keys?"

Emily handed Josh Sidra's entire purse. "They're in there," she said. "I felt that you were the only one she would talk to right now. She kept yelling at me... She doesn't know you're here."

"No problem, I got it from here," he assured.

"You sure?" Emily asked, pushing her hair behind her ears.

Josh headed for her. "I'm sure," he said.

He set Sidra's purse on a stool next to him and touched Sidra's arm. Sidra slowly lifted her head and looked at him through half-lidded eyes. Then her eyes lit up. "Josh," she said.

Josh smiled and sat down next to her. "Em told me that you had a few too many," he said. "She thought that you could use a designated driver."

Sidra was too busy staring at Josh's face to hear what he was saying. She slowly reached out and touched the corner of his eye. "You look tired," she slurred.

"I just got off work," Josh said. "I'm fine though."

Sidra moved her hand to his cheek. "You came here to see me after working all day?" she asked.

"Of course," Josh returned.

Sidra felt a wave of emotion overtake her. "You—you always look out for me. You're always here when I need you."

"You're my best friend," Josh said. "I told you, I'll *always* be here."

Sidra moved her hand to Josh's shoulder as she continued to stare into his brown eyes. "You're so handsome," she slurred, blinking slowly.

Josh chuckled. "Thanks," he said as she gripped his shirt fabric in her hand.

"No really, like you're *really* cute... attractive ...adorable...handsome." Sidra touched his arm. "You've been working out...your arms are really strong."

Josh patted Sidra's hand, amused. "I appreciate it honey," he placated. "Come on, let's get you out of here."

Sidra grabbed his hand as he made a move to get up. "I'm sorry Josh," she said.

Josh frowned in confusion. "For what?"

"For ruining your relationship with December," she said out of nowhere.

Josh stared at her and sighed. He wasn't expecting to hear that. "That wasn't your fault, Sidra."

"In a way it *was*... She was stupid to break up with you, Josh," Sidra slurred. "She was lucky to have you...*any* woman is lucky to have you...and I'm sorry that I talk shit about your new girlfriends... They're really pretty."

Josh shook his head; he'd never seen Sidra drunk ramble before. "They aren't my girlfriends," he said. "But I appreciate it, and don't worry about it Sid—"

She gripped his hand. "I'm so—sorry that I've been a bitch, I'm sorry that I hurt your feelings... I don't want to be a bad friend to you. I can't take it when you're mad at me. I'm sorry...."

Josh moved some of Sidra's hair from her face as he smiled. "Yeah, you're not gonna remember *any* of this in the morning," he teased. "I already forgave you and I'm not mad at you... You drive me crazy sometimes, but I'll always care about you."

"Really? Even when I'm depressed and whiny...and crazy and...rude...and—and..."

"*Yes*, and you're not as bad as you're making yourself out to be, so cut it out okay," Josh said, tone comforting.

Sidra let a few tears spill as Josh stood up from his seat. "I'm sorry," she muttered.

"I know, it's okay," he placated, moving her seat back from the bar.

The room was spinning as Sidra felt his arm wrap around her waist. *He is such a good man...why didn't I see that? Why did I pick James? ...Why am I even with James? Why am I not with Josh? He means everything to me, why am I not with him...I want to be with Josh ...I...shit!*

Sidra's eyes widened as the words in her mind pounded in her head. In her drunken state, she realized that the feelings she had for her best friend ran deeper than she thought. "The fuck?" she muttered as Josh gently grabbed her from her seat.

"Can you walk?" Josh asked, completely unaware of what was going on in Sidra's mind. Sidra stared at him as if she didn't recognize him as he tried to steady her in his arms. "Sidra, can you walk or do you need for me to carry you?" Sidra opened her mouth to speak. The truth serum was in full affect. *I don't want to be James's girlfriend anymore. I want to be your girlfriend.* Sidra had every intention of telling him, but as she went to speak nothing came out but vomit.

Josh flinched as Sidra threw up all over his shirt. "Nice," he sighed, sarcastic.

# Chapter 35

Sidra laid in her bed, arm thrown over her face, groaning. "God, my insides hurt."

Emily, who was making her own bed, looked over at her. "I'm not surprised," she commented. "You had a lot to drink."

Sidra struggled to sit up, before Emily walked over to help her the rest of the way. Sidra lowered her head as she felt a wave of nausea hit.

"You gonna throw up?" Emily asked.

"I think so," Sidra moaned.

Emily grabbed the nearest wastebasket and handed it to Sidra. Sidra grabbed it and held it in front of her face.

"I think it went back down," Sidra said.

Emily made a face of disgust. "I sure don't miss *those* days." Sidra held the basket in place as Emily went back to making her bed. "Do you remember anything from last night?"

"Um, not really," Sidra replied. "How did I get here?"

"Josh brought you back here," Emily informed.

Sidra felt her heart jump at the mere mention of Josh's name. She remembered part of the previous evening's events, even in her drunken state. She remembered the revelation about both James *and* Josh. She thought that she had imagined it, but as Sidra laid in bed that morning, the thoughts came back. *I want my best friend, and I have a boyfriend. What the fuck am I gonna do?!*

"Oh," was all that Sidra could get out as she put the trashcan down.

"Yeah," Emily replied, placing a pillow on her bed. "He slept on the floor while you were passed out in your bed. Until I got back from Will's, that is."

Sidra ran her hand through her disheveled hair as she let out a sigh. *He is so sweet.* "Thanks for filling me in, Em," she said, grateful.

Emily smiled and nodded. "Sure, I hope that you feel better." Emily started to walk out of the room. "Oh, I gave Josh your phone. You seemed pretty mad at James last night, so I didn't want you to make a drunk phone call to him."

"Thank you, that would've been…not good," Sidra said, cringing at the mere thought of calling him the night before. She could only imagine how that conversation would have gone.

Emily stared at Sidra as she stood in the doorway. "Um, I know you said you don't remember much, but you *did* mention that you missed Malajia, among other things…" she said. "*Maybe* you should go talk to her again. I'm sure she misses you too—"

Sidra shook her head. "No, I'm giving her the space that she needs," she said. She rubbed the back of her neck. "Um, Em…anything else that I may have said last night, can you please not mention it to anybody?"

"I wouldn't do that," Emily smiled. "Your rants are safe with me."

Sidra managed a grateful smile as Emily walked out of the room. When the door closed, Sidra's smile faded.


"Ooh, let's stop and grab some chicken sandwiches from the diner after I'm done in the post office," Malajia beamed, practically skipping along beside Chasity. "I left my money back in the room, but you know I'll pay you back."

Chasity snapped her head towards Malajia. She took one look at the goofy smile on Malajia's face and her eyes became slits. "*That's* the real reason you wanted me to walk you," she bit out. "Your freeloading ass wanted me to buy you lunch."

Chasity was already irritated that Malajia bugged her to walk to the post office with her. The idea that Malajia only wanted to use her for a lunch purchase had Chasity ready to slap the smile off Malajia's face.

Malajia put her hand up and gasped. "Chasity, I am shocked and appalled by your accusation," she mocked, feigning hurt.

Chasity stopped walking and spun around with the intention of walking away. Giggling, Malajia grabbed her arm, stopping her. "I'm kidding. *I'll* treat *you*," she placated. "My dad finally loosened the reins on his damn wallet and put more money into my account."

"In that case I'm ordering *every* damn thing," Chasity sneered, walking along side Malajia once again.

"Don't go overboard," Malajia warned, earning a narrowed eyed glare from Chasity.

"Malajia—"

"I know, I know," Malajia pacified as Chasity continued her tirade. Both girls stepped inside of the post office. Approaching the counter, Chasity glanced over and rolled her eyes as she saw Jackie approaching.

Chasity sucked her teeth. "This is the last time I walk anywhere with you," she sneered to a confused Malajia, who was trying to retrieve something from her purse. "I swear, every time we're out, you attract roaches."

Malajia, having caught sight of Jackie, busted out laughing so loud that nearby students craned their necks to see what was so funny.

Jackie, having heard the remark, squinted as she stopped in front of them. "*Ladies*," she hissed, tone not hiding her disdain.

"*Roach*," Chasity bit back, inciting a loud squeal from Malajia.

Malajia was laughing so hard that tears formed in her

eyes. "Roach…hilarious."

Jackie sucked her teeth as she clutched a box of roses. "Yeah, that's real cute," she spat out. She honed her gaze on Malajia, who retrieved her ID from her purse. "Picking up another package, I see," Jackie spat.

"Still in my *business*, I see," Malajia threw back. Ignoring Jackie's gaze, she handed the mail handler her ID. He smiled and pointed to a small box on the other end of the counter.

Malajia reached over and grabbed it. "How long was this sitting out here?"

The worker's eyes shifted. "Umm, not sure. That package was sitting up here with a few other boxes when I came in."

Chasity stared at him. "So y'all just set peoples' packages on the counter now?" she sniped. "Is that what the fuck goes on around here?"

"I know right, somebody could've snatched my shit," Malajia fussed. "Y'all disrespectful up in this piece."

Jackie moved aside as she discretely removed a tag from the box of flowers that she was carrying. "Too bad you didn't get roses like *I* did," she boasted, shoving the tag in her pocket.

Chasity tilted her head. "Nobody wants those dead ass flowers you stole from that crazy man at the gas station," she bit out.

Malajia chuckled as she examined the address label on her package. "He probably wiped his ass with them and shit," she mocked.

Jackie sucked her teeth. "Whatever," she muttered as she stormed off.

Malajia frowned as she examined the box. "The hell is up with my parents not putting a return address on these damn packages?" she complained. "Damn, they act like I don't know it's *them* sending them."

"Did you ever *ask* them why they do that?" Chasity wondered, heading over to her own mailbox and checking her mail.

Malajia looked guilty. "Uh…nah, 'cause I haven't thanked them for them," she hesitantly put out.

Chasity opened her mailbox. "Oh yeah, *that's* not rude as shit." she threw back, sarcastic.

Malajia waved her hand dismissively. "Please, *they* know I'm appreciative," she defended. "Hell, if they cared that much, they would've cussed me out about it… They don't even *mention* it."

Chasity looked up from her mail, confused. "So, they've sent you packages damn near every month since we got back here, and never did they *once* ask you if you've gotten them?"

Malajia shook her head.

Chasity stood there, frowning. That didn't make sense to her. If Chasity didn't let Trisha know that she received a package from her own mother, Trisha called *her* to make sure that she in fact *did*. She shook her head. A lot of what Malajia and her family did, made no sense to her. "Whatever," she dismissed, flipping through the mail.

"You get anything good?" Malajia asked, peering over Chasity's shoulder.

"Hell no," Chasity chuckled as the two women walked out of the post office.

Upon rounding the corner, where the parking lot was located, Malajia bobbed the box up and down in her hand. "I wonder what it is *this* time," she mused. "I hope it's those cookies I like." The smile on her face immediately faded as a car drove past. Startled, Malajia dropped the box on the ground. Malajia froze, flashing back to an incident in a car with a similar color, make and model.

Chasity, who was glancing at her watch at the time that the car passed, looked at Malajia, face full of concern as Malajia started mumbling something to herself. "Malajia," she called.

Malajia closed her eyes. "Stop it Malajia. Stop it. Stop it," she mumbled to herself. In that moment, she couldn't hear anything but her own voice trying to calm herself down. Chasity clapped her hands in front of Malajia's face, snapping her out of her trance. "Malajia," she barked. Malajia looked at her. "What the fuck just happened?" Malajia ran her trembling hands over her face and took a few deep breaths. *Malajia, stop it. Every time you see a car like that you can't freak out!* "I'm fine," she said finally, breathing steady. "Don't worry about it. I'm fine. I just—I'm fine."

Chasity stared at Malajia as she retrieved her box from the ground. She opened her mouth to speak, but Malajia cut her off.

"Chaz I'm cool, I promise," she insisted. "Come on, let's go get this food before it gets crowded." Malajia forced a smile. "You better come on before I renege on my plans to treat."

Chasity held a skeptical gaze. "Okay," she relented.

Malajia knocked on Mark's door and waited for a response.

"It's open," he called.

Malajia walked in. "You didn't even say 'who is it'?" she mentioned, closing the door behind her.

"I knew it was you," Mark assured, not looking up from his notebook.

Malajia frowned in confusion. "How?"

"You got a girly tap," Mark teased. "And no *other* chick comes by to see me."

"Yeah well…they just better *not*," Malajia muttered, setting the box that she was holding down on his nightstand. "What are you doing?"

Mark put his pencil down and leaned back in his seat stretching. "Trying not to throw this fuckin' accounting book out the damn window," he grunted.

Malajia giggled. "You want me to come back?"

Mark signaled for her to come over to him. "No, I need

the break," he said. Malajia walked over to him as he pushed his seat back from his desk. Malajia straddled his lap and put her arms around his neck.

"You stressed?" she asked.

Mark rubbed his face. "It's fine," he said. "I just...*hate* Accounting," he vented. "It's boring, and freakin' tedious... I don't even want to *do* this shit."

Malajia looked at him. This was becoming a regular conversation. "What do you *really* wanna do?" Malajia asked as she rubbed her hand over the short waves on his freshly cut hair.

Mark thought for a moment. He had never stopped to think about that. "To make some good money when I graduate," he replied. "So...I guess I better stop bitchin' huh?"

"Well, bright side, you'll be able to do *our* taxes once we start working," Malajia pointed out.

"Fuck taxes," Mark grumbled, earning a laugh from Malajia.

"You're so simple," she teased. She gestured her head to the box on his nightstand. "I got another package today. Some spring ass candies," she chuckled. "I swear it's like a ton of pink and blue wrappers in that box."

Mark reached over for the box. "You shoulda' said that when you first walked in," he joked. "You know I like free shit."

Malajia shook her head at him. They were so much alike, it was hilarious to her. The amusement faded from her face as she let out a sigh. "So um...I had a little freak-out episode today," she announced.

Mark stopped peeling the foil off a piece of chocolate candy and looked up at her. "What do you mean?"

She ran her finger across the collar of his t-shirt. "When I was out with Chaz today, I thought I saw..." she took a deep breath. "I thought I saw Tyrone's car."

A mask of anger appeared on Mark's face. "What?"

"I'm sure it wasn't him," she placated. "There are a

million tan cars. And his didn't have tinted windows... I think the memories just freaked me out a bit, but I'm fine now." Although the moment had passed and she felt fine now, she didn't want to keep it from Mark.

"Malajia, I swear to God, if I ever see him—"

Malajia put her hand on his shoulder. "Baby, I'm sure it wasn't him," she cut in.

Mark, along with Jason, had already given Tyrone a serious beating over what he had done to both Malajia and Chasity over a year ago. But she knew that if Mark ever got a chance to face Tyrone again, that he wouldn't let up.

"I haven't seen *or* heard from him at all... I wouldn't be surprised if he's not even living here in Virginia anymore," Malajia insisted.

"I still think that six months wasn't enough fuckin' time in jail," Mark fussed. "That weak ass verdict."

Malajia shook her head. She understood Mark's annoyance; she felt the same way when she learned of the sentence herself over a year ago. "Yeah well, he pled guilty to assault and the six months plus probation and anger management classes seemed to be what they thought to be punishment enough," she said. "The restraining order that I have is still in place...all the more reason why I *know* that wasn't his car. He wouldn't show up on campus, knowing that he can go back to jail."

Mark let out a sigh; he was worked up. Just the mention of Tyrone's name sent him into a fit of rage. But his anger wouldn't help ease Malajia's mind, which was what he really wanted to do. He relaxed his frown. "If you say it wasn't him, then I'll go with that," he said.

Malajia nodded. "I didn't mean to get you all worked up."

Mark touched her face. "It's okay," he assured. "I *want* you to come tell me stuff like that."

Malajia nodded again, before wrapping her arms around him and hugging him. Parting from their warm embrace, Malajia reached for the box of candy, but Mark moved it out of her way.

"Nah dawg, you burnt," he teased, much to her shock.

"And you go *right* back to being a jackass," Malajia ground out, folding her arms.

Mark laughed. "Yeah, yeah, love you too," he threw back, giving her a piece of candy.


Sidra took a sip of ginger ale from her glass before pouring more from the bottle. After sleeping most of the day away, along with the worst part of her hangover, Sidra was finally feeling well enough to get herself together and come downstairs.

"Come in," she called, when she heard a knock on the door. Upon seeing the guest enter, she felt butterflies in her stomach.

"Hey, I see you finally made it out of bed," Josh smiled, walking over to her.

Sidra just held a slight smile on her face as she watched him retrieve her phone from his pocket. She found it hard to speak, afraid of what she might say. It didn't help that Josh seemed to have gotten more handsome overnight to her.

"I came to give you back your phone," he said, holding it out to her. "I would've brought it over sooner, but I didn't want to wake you."

Sidra took the phone from him. "Thank you," she said.

"And... Of course I came to check on you," Josh admitted.

"I'm okay," she replied, scratching her head. "I will probably never drink again in my *life*, but I'm okay."

Josh chuckled. "Well, if you can stick to that, more power to you."

Sidra glanced at her fluffy slippers. "I appreciate everything that you did for me last night."

"You don't have to thank me."

"No, I *do*... Especially for not cussing me out for throwing up on you."

Josh winced. "You remember that, huh?"

"Yeah, that's the *last* thing that I remember actually, before everything went dark."

"You were awake, just…limp after that. Then you started mumbling stuff," Josh replied.

Sidra's eyes widened. *Shit! Did I say any of that shit I was thinking?!* "Umm, what—what was I mumbling?" Josh thought for a moment. "Nothing that I could understand."

Sidra breathed a sigh of relief. "Thank God," she muttered. She let out a sigh as she set her phone on the counter. "Again, I'm sorry."

"You can stop apologizing, Sidra," Josh placated. "Shit happens. That shirt had pizza sauce on it anyway," he said, hoping to ease her guilt and embarrassment. He tapped her shoulder. "Don't worry about it."

Sidra nodded. "Okay."

"Anyway, I gotta get going," he said, heading for the door.

"Um Josh," Sidra called, halting his progress.

"What's up?"

Without saying anything, Sidra walked over and hugged him. She closed her eyes as she relished the feeling of him hugging her back. When he went to part from their embrace, Sidra held on, prompting Josh to put his arms back around her.

"You okay?" he wondered.

Sidra, feeling slightly embarrassed, let go of him. "Yeah…I'm good."

Josh nodded. "In that case… I'll see you later."

Sidra gave a slight wave as he walked out of the door. Going back to the kitchen, she looked at her phone and saw a missed call from James. She let out a sigh. "Shiiiit," she grunted to herself. Dialing him back, she put the phone to her ear. "Hi James," she said when he answered.

"Hi…how are you feeling today?" James asked.

"I'm okay," she answered. "You?"

A sigh came through the line. "I'm okay too," he replied. "Listen Sidra, I'll be in your neck of the woods in a few days… I would like to come see you."

Sidra was silent for a moment. "Oh, okay," she answered.

"Is something wrong?" he asked, picking up on her hesitation.

"No…I just didn't think that you would want to see me, especially because of how things have been between us."

"That's *exactly* why I want to see you," he vaguely replied. "Look um…when I finalize the details, I'll give you a call, okay."

"Okay, sounds good," Sidra nodded.

"See you soon."

Sidra stared at the phone after James ended the call. Something in his voice sounded different. He didn't sound upset, or happy, he sounded…indifferent. She wasn't surprised; the feeling was mutual. She sighed as she grabbed her cup of soda from the counter and took another sip.

"Fine," Alex huffed, then looked at Malajia. "You don't think we should—"

"Nooo, they burnt I said," Malajia snapped, interrupting Alex's suggestion.

Alex sucked her teeth.

Sidra nervously fiddled with a napkin as she sat across from James at a restaurant. She awoke that morning to a phone call from James telling her that he was going to be in town sooner than he thought. He had requested a quick lunch.

"You sure you don't want a drink or something?" James asked her as the waiter set his glass of rum and soda in front of him.

Sidra shook her head. "No, I think I had enough alcohol to last me a while," she replied. She studied him. "You seem tired."

James sighed as he took a sip of his drink. "I *am*, in more ways than one," he vaguely replied, setting the glass back down. "So do *you*."

"Same here," Sidra returned, rubbing her arm. "But I'll be okay."

"I know you will," James said, staring at her.

Sidra just nodded. It was silent for a few minutes while the couple waited on their meals. "So you're here on business, right? New client?" Sidra asked, attempting to make conversation.

"Discussing a new opportunity," James replied.

"Really? What's that?"

James took a deep breath as he rubbed his face with his hand. "I um…I'm mulling over the possibility of starting my own firm," he said.

Sidra's eyes lit up. It was something that James had spoken about before. Starting his own law firm was one of his life goals. "That's great James," she gushed, her smile then faded. "But why do you look so sick about it?"

Her boyfriend hesitated. "Because, *should* I decide to do

it…I'll be starting it in California."

Sidra's eyes widened. "Ca-California?" she stammered. Any ill feelings that she had for him vanished; dread took its place. She was barely seeing him as it was, and he lived in Washington DC. If he moved to California, she would *never* see him. Despite her recently discovered feelings for Josh, James was still her boyfriend and she still cared for him. Sidra knew that if he left, that she would miss him. "That's so far."

"I know," James agreed. "But you know that I'm originally *from* there. My family still lives there, my alma mater is there, and…it's just a great opportunity for me."

Sidra sat back in her seat and folded her arms. "Wow," she sighed. "I'm happy for you. Really James, I am," she assured.

"Yeah?" he wondered, eyes hopeful.

Sidra nodded. "Yes," she promised. "I just can't help but wonder about the future of our relationship."

James glanced down at the table as Sidra spoke.

"I mean, where we're living *now*… If you go…what happens to *us*?"

James lifted his gaze and held it on her, sadness in his eyes. "Sidra—"

"I mean, I'll be graduating soon, and depending on where I go to law school…I suppose I could visit you, so *you* wouldn't have to do all the visiting, you know?"

"Sidra—" he repeated.

"You already know that one of my school options is in California, so that might work out perfect," she rambled. She was so into planning their visitations that she wasn't hearing James call her name. It wasn't until he snapped his fingers, that she stopped her rambling.

"Sidra," he said once again, voice stern.

Sidra looked at him. "Yes?"

James took a deep breath before taking another sip of his drink. He ran his hands down his face as he tried to gather his words.

Sidra, noticing the hesitation, frowned in concern. "James, what's wrong?"

James pulled himself together long enough to focus on her. "Sidra, I think—I think it would be best for *both* of us, if…if we go our separate ways."

Sidra stared at him, confused. "I'm sorry, what?"

"I think that we should end this relationship."

Sidra felt as if the wind was being knocked out of her. When she had agreed to meet him for lunch, she had figured that James wanted to discuss the state of their relationship due to the many disagreements that they were having. She had no idea that James would end it. "You—you're breaking up with me?"

Seeing tears form in Sidra's eyes, nearly broke him. "I'm sorry, sweetheart," James said as she began fanning her face in an effort to keep the tears from spilling down her cheeks. "But we *both* know that things haven't been right between us lately… I just feel that, we both need space. I feel that you're at a place in your life where you're growing and changing and I—" He took another deep breath. "I know that I work too much—I just need to focus on my career… You deserve someone who has time for you… I don't want to hold you back from finding that."

Sidra didn't know what to do. She wanted to cry, but felt that she shouldn't. She was angry, sad, confused, hurt. "This is my fault," she sputtered.

James's eyes widened. "Sidra. I'm not blaming you—"

"No, it *is*," she insisted, upset. "I knew who you were when I—when I agreed to a relationship. You tried your best to make time for me, to make me feel spec—" her voice cracked. "You didn't do anything wrong. It's *me*, *I* changed, I—*I* messed us up, I—I'm sorry."

James watched with sadness as Sidra grabbed her purse. "Sidra, don't leave, I don't want you to feel like this is your fault. I really *do* feel that this is best for both of us," he pleaded. "And who knows, in time, maybe we'll cross paths again."

Sidra couldn't focus on the comforting words that James was saying. All she could focus on was the fact that her heart was breaking into a million pieces. "I have to go," she sniffled, standing up.

James sat back in his seat, letting out a heavy sigh. "Please, don't leave like this," he pleaded. "Please, I still care about you—"

"I have to go," Sidra repeated, slinging her pocketbook over her shoulder. She had to get out of there before she completely lost it. "Goodbye James."

James watched in agony as Sidra made a hasty departure. Tears began to cloud his eyes, "Goodbye Sidra," he mumbled to himself. Wiping his eyes with his hand, he took another sip of his drink.

Sidra nearly ran through the restaurant parking lot to her car. Sliding into the front seat, she snatched on her seatbelt. As she stuck her key into the ignition, she felt the weight of her emotions crush her. She put her hands over her face and broke down in a hysterical cry.


Sidra sat in her car for what seemed like forever, just staring out the front window. She'd cried so much that her insides hurt. Watching James leave the restaurant nearly twenty minutes ago was gut wrenching. When he pulled off, the reality set in that she would never see him again. Tears filling her eyes again, Sidra dialed a phone number.

"Hi sweetie," Mrs. Howard answered, voice cheerful.

"Hi Mama," Sidra sniffled.

Taking notice of Sidra's pained voice, the cheer left Mrs. Howard's voice, replaced by concern. "What's wrong Sidra?" Sidra didn't answer, she just cried. "Princess, what happened?"

Sidra rubbed her eyes with one hand as she held the phone with another. "James broke up with me," she managed to say through her tears.

A gasp came through the line. "Oh sweetie, I'm so

sorry," Mrs. Howard sympathized. "But, what *happened*? Why did he do that?"

"'Cause I ruin everything," Sidra sniffled.

"That's not true my love." She felt helpless as she listened to Sidra's cries through the phone. "God, I hate that you're going through this, I wish there was something that I could do… You know what, why don't I come down there tomorrow?" she proposed. "I'll come for the night. Grab a nice hotel room and have you come spend the night with me. How does that sound?"

"Sounds nice," Sidra said, wiping her eyes yet again.

"Okay good, then it's settled," Mrs. Howard confirmed.

"Okay… Mama, I gotta go," she said, tone low.

"Baby are you sure you don't want to stay on the phone?" Mrs. Howard pressed. "I don't mind if you cry."

Sidra wiped a few more tears from her eyes. "No, I just want to get home."

"Are you driving?"

"Yes," Sidra sniffled.

"Sidra, you be careful, you hear? If you're too emotional to drive, then you sit there until you feel like you're ready."

*I've been sitting here long enough,* she thought. "I'm okay," she insisted. "See you tomorrow?"

"Yes, definitely."

Sidra ended the call and set the phone in the passenger's seat. She gripped the steering wheel as she felt another sob coming on. At this rate, Sidra didn't know how much more she would be able to take. She felt like she could cry forever, but she knew that she had to pull it together to be able to make it back home. Taking several deep breaths, Sidra smoothed her hair from her face and started her car.

Alex fanned herself as she stood on the front step of the girls' house. Malajia who was sitting on the step, glanced up at her. "Why you fanning your hot ass all over top of me and shit?" she griped.

Alex nudged Malajia in her back with her knee. "Hush," she hissed.

"Ow!" Malajia barked back, reaching behind her and giving her back a rub.

"Your smart-ass comments and this humid air can't steal my joy today," Alex said. "Guess what I found out today."

"That Eric really *does* have a girlfriend?" Malajia sneered, then jumped up from the step as she felt Alex move behind her.

Alex shook her head. "As insensitive as that *was*, I'm not gonna knee you again *or* let it get to me," she said, then smiled.

"Well what's got *you* all happy today?" Malajia wondered, still rubbing her back.

"It's official," Alex beamed. "Come the fall, Sahara will be a freshman here at Paradise Valley University."

Malajia smiled. "Awww, good for her," she gushed. "I know she's hype."

"Girl yes, she was screaming all in my ear." Alex chuckled, recalling the earlier conversation with her sister. "I just wish that I could be here next semester to help her get settled, you know? ...Help guide her."

"Well, go ahead and fail a few classes. Then you're *guaranteed* to be here next semester," Malajia joked, to which Alex laughed.

"I can mentor her from a far," Alex said, with a wave of her hand. Seeing a car pull up in front of their house, Alex squinted to see who it was.

"Oooh, Chaz is gonna be pissed someone parked in her spot," Malajia said.

"There are no assigned spots," Alex frowned.

"Tell *her* that," Malajia chuckled of Chasity. Both girls stared as the woman got out of the car.

Malajia's eyes nearly popped out when she saw who the visitor was. "Ms. Vanessa," she sputtered.

"Uh, I gotta get to class," Alex quickly put out as she hopped off the step. She had no idea what Sidra's mother was doing there, but if it had to do with the tension between Sidra and Malajia, she wanted no part of it.

"Alex your classes are done for the day," Malajia sneered as Alex hurried off.

"Nah uh, I got a bonus class," Alex threw over her shoulder.

Malajia held her narrowed eyed gaze on Alex's hasty departing figure. *Lying ass.*

"Hi Malajia," Mrs. Howard smiled, approaching. She gave Malajia a warm hug. "How are you doing?"

"I'm fine," Malajia answered, still stunned. "Umm, what are you doing here?"

Mrs. Howard chuckled. "I'm not here to yell at you, if that's what you think," she joked. "I came to visit Sidra... I'm here to pick her up. She's spending the night with me at my hotel room."

"Oh," Malajia replied, pushing her hair over her shoulder.

"She didn't tell you?" Mrs. Howard questioned.

Malajia shook her head. "No, she didn't mention it."

Mrs. Howard glanced at her nails. She was aware that Malajia and her daughter were at odds. It bothered her. "I guess that would make sense, since you two aren't really speaking," she said.

Malajia took a deep breath. "Look Ms. Vanessa—"

Mrs. Howard put her hand up, silencing Malajia's words. "Malajia, I'm not upset with you... If my tone came off that way, then I'm sorry."

"It didn't," Malajia assured. "Listen, I know that you're on Sidra's side, and you have every right to be, she's your child... I just—I just don't want to lose *my* relationship with you or for my mother to lose *her* relationship with you, because of this."

Mrs. Howard adjusted the purse strap on her shoulder. "Yes, it's true that I side with Sidra on *many* things...but when she's wrong, she's wrong," she said. "*Our* relationship is just fine Malajia."

Malajia let out a sigh. "I appreciate that…and I know *my* mom was upset—"

"Evelyn and I have already talked," Mrs. Howard cut in. "She loves Sidra still… It's like when your child does something that annoys you…you may be upset with them, but you still love them…and that's how your mother feels. So, don't worry about that."

Malajia nodded.

Mrs. Howard smiled slightly before heading for the front door. She paused and looked back at Malajia. "I know that your mother and I agreed to stay out of this, but…I just have to say this to you."

Malajia stood there in anticipation of what Mrs. Howard was about to say.

"You have *every* right to feel how you're feeling…to react how you're reacting," Mrs. Howard began, tone caring. "Sidra—she was out of line for how she behaved and what she said. She knows that. And…she really *is* sorry."

Malajia folded her arms and glanced at the ground. "I know she is," she admitted.

Mrs. Howard managed a smile. "As long as you know that…I hope you two can get back to normal soon."

"Me too," Malajia admitted, somber. "She's upstairs. You want me to go get her for you?"

Mrs. Howard smiled. "No, I'll get her," she said, then walked into the house.

Malajia let out a long sigh, before making a beeline for the guys' house.


Sidra was relaxing on the plush mattress as her mother handed her a plate of French toast, fruit, and turkey bacon. "Thanks, but I had like three croissants earlier," Sidra said. "Not trying to be miserable *and* fat."

Mrs. Howard chuckled. "Girl, your metabolism is like lightning right now…enjoy it while it lasts," she said.

Sidra managed a giggle as she grabbed a piece of bacon.

That morning, she awoke after spending the night with her mother at the hotel, feeling even more tired than she was the night before. Which was weird to her, because she'd fallen asleep early after watching a movie and having another cry.

Mrs. Howard sat next to Sidra on the bed. "How are you feeling this morning?" she asked.

Sidra thought as she took a bite of her food. "A little better, I guess," she sighed.

"Well, you seemed to have cried a lot of your frustrations out yesterday...sometimes that's needed."

"Yeah," Sidra agreed, placing her plate on the nightstand. "I guess reality hit me hard... James is really gone, like—it's really over."

"I'm trying to wrap my head around what happened sweetie," Mrs. Howard said.

Sidra looked down at her hands. "To be completely honest Mama, it's kind of complicated."

Mrs. Howard put her hand on Sidra's shoulder to comfort her.

"Bottom line...he did what was best for him and I can't blame him for that," Sidra sulked. "And...he deserves someone who doesn't have feelings for someone else."

Mrs. Howard frowned, wondering if she had heard her daughter correctly. "What do you mean, for someone else?"

Sidra looked at her mother. "Yeah," she alluded.

Mrs. Howard was confused. Sidra had never mentioned another man that she was interested in other than James. "Well don't just sit there quiet, who are you talking about?"

Sidra wasn't sure if she was going to tell her mother or not, but since the words came out, it was time to come clean. "Um...Josh."

Mrs. Howard's eyes looked like they could have popped out of her head. "I'm sorry...you said Josh? As in *Joshua Hampton?*"

Sidra nodded.

Mrs. Howard put her hand on her forehead as she tried to wrap her head around what she'd just heard. "Sidra—what—

*when* did this happen?"

Sidra sighed. "I just recently figured it out...but I think that subconsciously...it might have been for some time now," she revealed. "My interactions with him for *months* now, have made me feel a lot different than normal... I *see* him differently now... I'm *really* freaked out by this."

"Why are you freaked out?"

"Because!" Sidra exclaimed; she let out a huff. "This is *Josh*. He went from being just my best friend to being..." she was frazzled as she tried to express her feelings. "Mama, like...I physically *want* him—" She looked embarrassed. "Sorry."

"Hey, you're grown," Mrs. Howard said, putting her hand up.

"I just...this whole thing is a *mess*," Sidra vented. "I'm *so* confused. I feel like I mentally cheated on James and may have unintentionally sabotaged my relationship with him— and *now* I don't know how to even *act* around Josh anymore or what I'm even supposed to do with these feelings."

"You have to talk to him," Mrs. Howard urged.

"Who James?" Sidra frowned. "No, I can't tell him that, it would kill him."

"No sweetie, you need to talk to *Josh*."

Sidra shook her head. "I can't...not after I rejected him when he told me how he felt about me," she sulked.

"Sweetie, you didn't *know* then," Mrs. Howard placated. "You didn't intentionally hurt Josh... You can't punish yourself for that."

Sidra sighed as she folded her arms. "Yeah well, whether it was intentional or *not*, I rejected him and now...he's moving on."

"That doesn't mean that he still doesn't love you Sidra... Deep feelings like that don't just disappear," Mrs. Howard said. "Now yes, he may be moving on, but that's because he still thinks that there is no chance for you two...which is *why* you need to talk to him to see where his head's at."

Sidra sighed once again as she pondered her mother's

words. "I just—I can't."

Mrs. Howard put her hand on Sidra's cheek. "Just *think* about it," she pressed.

*Me thinking about it isn't going to change the fact that I'm still not doing it.* Despite the words in Sidra's head, she just nodded.

# Chapter 37

Malajia moved around Emily and placed her bowl in the kitchen sink. "Damn Em, can I get to the sink?" Malajia jeered.

"I'm not even blocking the whole sink," Emily laughed.

"I know. I just wanted to mess with you since you ate the last of those donuts."

Emily thought for a moment. "*You* did."

Malajia sucked her teeth. "Nobody asked you for the truth," she hissed, to which Emily laughed again.

"I gotta get to class," Emily said, heading for the door. "Are we still going to the movies later?"

Malajia nodded. "You hype as shit you don't have to miss out on the fun anymore," she teased.

Emily let out a groan as she walked out the door. "I can never live that down."

"Nope!" Malajia yelled after her as the door closed. She giggled to herself. Hearing her phone ring, she grabbed it from the pocket of her shorts and put it to her ear. "Which one of your kids do you need to vent about?" Malajia answered, voice filled with amusement.

"Girl, *all* of 'em," Mrs. Simmons threw back. "Hello hon."

Malajia laughed a little "Hi Mom, what's up?"

"Well, your father is working on the budget for the month, so he wanted to know how much money he needs to put in your account to carry you until next month."

Malajia looked surprised. "Say *what*? Dad is actually

*asking* me how much money I want?" she asked, playing with a few strands of her hair.

"I know, right?" Mrs. Simmons agreed. "So come on, how much do you need?"

Malajia thought for a moment. "A thousand," she blurted out.

"Girl!—"

Malajia laughed. "Sike Mom, sike," she quickly put in, cutting her mother's rant short. "If you guys can spare two hundred, I'd appreciate it. I still have a little left over from last month anyway."

"What? You actually *saved* money?"

"Not on *purpose*," Malajia jeered. "Haven't been doing too much of nothing but studying... Now *next* month might be a different story. Senior week is coming up and I'm gonna need money to partake in all of the foolishness."

"Girl, as long as you're *graduating* on time, I'll make sure your dad hooks you up next month."

"Yeesss Mommy," Malajia rejoiced. "While you're at it, can you get Dad to send me another package? I'm almost out of those snacks."

"*What* package?" Mrs. Simmons asked.

Malajia frowned. "The packages that you guys been sending me like every month since I've been back to school...the ones with the snacks and cards, and sometimes little stuffed animals." Malajia scratched her head when her mother didn't respond. "Mom, seriously."

"Malajia, I *am* serious," Mrs. Simmons insisted. "Your father and I haven't sent any packages to you. What address did they come from?"

Malajia's face held a confused stare, even though her mother couldn't see her. "Um...they didn't have a return address on them." A weird feeling came over her. "You think that one of the girls could have sent them?"

"Geri and Maria are here now, I'll ask them."

"No, can you just put Geri on the phone please?" Malajia asked. She ran her hand through her hair as she waited for her mother to do as she asked. *What the hell?* She thought.

"Hey, it's my favorite sister," Geri beamed into the line after another moment.

"Hey!" Maria wailed from the background.

Geri laughed. "Well, it's *true*," she teased. "What's up girl?"

"Geri, question, did you send me any packages at all this semester?" Malajia asked, voice lacking any humor.

"Um, no sis, I *haven't*," Geri answered. She then asked Maria the same question. "Maria said, she didn't either. And you know Tanya is busy dealing with that newborn of hers, so she don't have time to send anything but smoke signals, asking for help."

Malajia would normally laugh and joke along with Geri at their oldest sisters' expense, but her mind was too preoccupied. "Valentine's Day, did you send me a card?"

"Why would I send you a card for Valentine's Day?" Geri wondered, bewildered.

Malajia gave a hard shrug. "I don't know, it just seemed like something you would do," she argued.

There was a pause on the line. "No, it *doesn't*," Geri denied. "Malajia, I haven't sent you *anything*," she confirmed, her voice now void of any humor. "What's going on sis? Is some weirdo sending you shit?"

Malajia opened her mouth to speak, but was cut off when her mother got back on the phone. "Malajia, I don't like this shit, who would do that? All of your friends are there with you."

Malajia ran a hand across her forehead. She was already freaking out; she didn't want her family to do the same. "You know what, don't worry about it," she placated. "Now that I think about it, it could have been Mark. He's been doing cute stuff like that lately... It's fine. I'll cuss him out for you though."

"Malajia—"

"Mom it's fine, really, sorry I got you upset," Malajia quickly cut in. "Listen, I gotta get to class, I'll call you later tonight okay."

"You better, especially after you ask Mark if it was him who sent them."

"I will. Bye." Malajia set her phone on the counter after she ended the call. A worried look was frozen on her face.

"Alex, I'm not stopping anywhere else after I leave this damn movie theater," Chasity barked into the line. "I don't *care* if I'm right around the corner from you... Nobody told you to forget that you had off today... Was probably hype as shit walking into work." Chasity laughed at the thought. "What? ...Fine Alex, you owe me some damn lunch and I don't want no pizza... In like twenty. Bye." Chasity punctuated her response by hanging up on Alex.

Having agreed to pick up movie tickets for the group after class for an anticipated new release, Chasity was standing in line waiting.

Hearing somebody call her name, she turned around and immediately let out a groan. "Goddamn it," Chasity huffed.

"So, what, you don't want me to go *anywhere*?" Jackie hissed.

Chasity rolled her eyes. "You can go wherever the fuck you *want*, just don't fuckin' talk to me when you see me," she bit back.

Jackie sucked her teeth. "And *now* I'm not allowed to be mature," she drawled sarcastically.

"And you're *still* talking to me," Chasity barked. "What do you expect Jackie?" she questioned when Jackie folded her arms in a huff. "I'm *never* gonna like you."

"How long are you gonna hold this grudge?" Jackie spat.

Chasity smirked. "You *obviously* have no idea."

"Whatever Chasity. People can change you know, I'm sure *you* have."

"*You* haven't changed *shit*. You're still the same jealous ass, trouble-making bitch that I met freshman year," Chasity sneered. "Get away from me. You're contaminating my fuckin' space."

Jackie rolled her eyes. "Look, I didn't come in here to argue with you," she sniped. "I just came in here to pick up movie tickets for me and my man, but since it's apparent that I don't belong *anywhere* but in a damn hole according to you and your friends, I might as well leave."

"If you don't get your cryin' ass away from me," Chasity snapped. "I don't give a fuck about what you do. Just. Don't. Talk. To. Me."

Jackie shook her head, then eyed a message on her phone. "My man is outside anyway."

"Uh huh. Tell that crack head from the corner store I said what's up," Chasity mocked.

"Whatever." Jackie turned and stormed out, without another word.

Chasity shook her head. "Raggedy bitch," she mumbled to herself. Glancing out the glass window, she caught eye of a tan car pulling up in front of Jackie as she waited on the curb. Seeing a familiar person get out of the car, her eyes widened. *Is that fuckin' Tyrone?*

Chasity watched in horror as he opened the passenger door for Jackie to get in. Chasity held her stare as Jackie walked up to the door. *No... that's not him, you trippin'*, she told herself. She turned away, then quickly turned back around. This time she was able to get a clearer look at his face, even though he was looking at Jackie. *That is him!* She watched as Tyrone got into the car and sped off. "Shit," she hissed to herself.

Malajia hurried down the steps to find Mark in the kitchen. "What is your greedy ass doing in our fridge?" she fussed.

"Shut up," Mark threw back. "Were you *not* just in *our* fridge last night, eating up all our leftovers?"

Malajia looked confused. "I brought my *own* damn food over to your place last night," she recalled.

Mark glanced up from the contents of the refrigerator, a dumb look on his face. "Yeah well...y'all ain't got shit in here anyway," Mark grunted, closing the refrigerator. "Now I gotta go to class hungry. My stomach gonna be all loud and shit."

Malajia giggled as Mark approached her. "You coming over later?" she asked.

"You cookin'?" Mark joked.

"What do you want, greedy ass?" Malajia barked.

Mark laughed. "Just playing. Yeah I'll be over after I get some studying in." He gave Malajia a quick kiss. "Love you, even though you ain't got no food."

"Love you too, even though you get on my fuckin' nerves," she threw back.

Mark chuckled, then walked out the door. Malajia headed into the kitchen and proceeded to search the cabinets.

"Damn, we slippin' up in here, not one snack," she said to herself, closing the cabinet. Hearing a knock at the door, she glanced over. "It's open."

Jason rushed in. "Hey Mel," he panted, heading for the steps.

"What are you so out of breath for?" Malajia wondered.

"Was halfway to class when I realized that I left my damn wallet in Chaz's room last night," Jason informed.

"Uh huh. Stop using your *other* head every time you come over to see Chaz, and maybe your *actual* head would be clear enough to remember your shit," Malajia teased.

Jason stared at her, a blank expression on his face. "You held on to that one for a long time, didn't you?" he mocked of Malajia's comeback.

Malajia laughed. "Kind of."

Jason shook his head as he headed up the steps to Chasity's empty room.

Malajia grabbed her book bag from the floor and glanced at her watch. *On time for Business Management for once. No door shut in my face today*, she thought, heading for the door.

She opened the front door but didn't look outside; a

notification from her phone had her attention. Opening the text, her eyes widened in shock. Malajia looked up and her eyes landed on a familiar figure standing on the other side of the gate, several feet away, staring back at her.

Malajia backed away from the door and slammed it shut. "Jason!" she screamed, dropping her book bag and phone to the floor.

The sound of his name screamed in alarm sent Jason running down the steps, where he found a hysterical Malajia sitting on the floor against a wall. He rushed over and kneeled beside her. "Malajia, what's wrong?" he panicked. Her hands were shaking and she began to hyperventilate. "Talk to me, what's wrong?"

"T-Tyrone is outside," she managed to get out.

Anger immediately masked Jason's face. He bolted up.

Malajia grabbed Jason's arm as he went for the door. "No Jason, don't leave me, please!" Malajia cried, holding Jason's arm in a firm grip.

Jason crouched back down near Malajia and tried his best to console her. "Okay, I'm not going anywhere," he promised. He grabbed his phone from his pocket and quickly dialed a number. "Mark, where are you?" he said once the line picked up. "You need to get back here; Malajia said she saw Tyrone outside of the house... Yeah... I got her, just hurry up." Jason hung up the phone and glanced towards the window, not seeing anything. He was both in protective and destroy mode. If he could get his hands on Tyrone again, Jason wasn't sure if he would be able to let up like he was forced to do last time. But knowing that his friends always came first, Jason just held Malajia as she began to cry.


Mark paced the room.

"Mark, you gotta relax," Alex said, tone calm as she set a glass of water in front of Malajia.

Malajia was sitting at the dining room table, looking and feeling physically spent. After witnessing her abusive ex-boyfriend outside of her complex, Malajia spent the time clinging to Jason until Mark arrived. It didn't take long for the rest of the group to be informed and their presence to be requested at the house.

"Naw, fuck that," Mark fumed, continuing his pace. "What the fuck was he doing here, yo?"

"That's so creepy," Emily said with a shiver.

"That's an *understatement*," Chasity agreed. She remembered the feeling that came over her when she listened to Jason's urgent message after she got out of class. A mix of anger and fear.

"Jason, you didn't see him?" Alex asked.

Jason shook his head as he stood behind Chasity, his hands on her shoulders. "I heard Mel scream and I ran down here... I didn't get a chance to look out the door."

"Did anybody see him walking around campus today?" Josh asked. He rubbed the back of his neck when the group answered, "No."

"He could have dipped out the back way off campus," David pointed out. "You know we're right near the backroads."

Malajia rubbed her eyes with her hands. "I *know* that I saw him, I'm not crazy," she said.

"Sweetie, *nobody* is suggesting that," Sidra placated, shooting her a sympathetic look.

Malajia took a deep breath. "I just... I got a text message and I freaked out, then I opened the door and—"

"*What* message?" Mark questioned.

Malajia grabbed her phone and clicked on said message. Mark took the phone and looked at it. It was from an unknown number. The message consisted of an old picture of Malajia sleeping with the text '*miss you like this*'.

"The fuck is *this*?" Mark asked, angry.

"I think that might've been taken when I was asleep over his place when we were still together," Malajia informed. "I kept getting weird blurry pictures, but now that I see the whole thing...they were part of *this* picture."

"Is that his number?" Alex frowned.

"I don't *know* Alex!" Malajia erupted, upset. "He could've changed his number, or is using someone else's phone. He's good for doing shit like that."

Alex put her hands up. "Malajia, I'm sorry, I didn't mean to—"

Malajia slammed her hand on the table repeatedly. Chasity, who was sitting at the table across from her, jumped. "I can't *believe* this shit! What does he *want*? Why is he *here*?"

Chasity ran her hands through her hair as she contemplated making things worse. "Umm I hate to add to this crazy shit but…there's something that I need to tell you Malajia," she began.

Malajia looked at Chasity as she fiddled with her hands. "What is it?"

"Umm, I think that there is a possibility that Tyrone could have been here on campus before," Chasity said.

The group looked confused. "What makes you say that?" Jason asked.

"Because Jackie is here…and I think that she might be with him now."

Malajia looked perplexed.

"Wait Chaz, Jackie is dating *Tyrone*?" Alex questioned.

"I think *so*," Chasity said.

"How do you know that?" Mark asked.

"While I was at the movie theater yesterday Jackie came in and we had words. She said her man was outside, so she left and the next thing I saw was her getting into his car," Chasity informed.

Malajia felt like she was holding her breath. "How do you know it was his car?"

"Because he got *out* of it and opened the door for her," Chasity answered.

"Did he see you?" Jason asked, angry.

"No," Chasity said. "At least I don't think so."

"Oh my God," Sidra gasped. "*That* explains why Jackie

is always picking with you, Malajia."

Malajia put her hand up. Jackie was the furthest thing from her mind; there was something *else* that she needed to know. "Wait, what color was his car?" she sputtered to Chasity.

"Tan," Chasity answered.

Malajia's breathing became labored. "Tinted windows?" Chasity nodded. Malajia put her hand over her chest. "He—he's been here. I *knew* I saw that car on more than one occasion on this campus, he's *been* here, I knew it—"

Worked up, scared, and angry, Malajia felt another panic attack coming on as memories of her violent relationship flooded back to her. And Tyrone had been watching her for who knew how long.

Mark rushed over to her and put his hands on her face. "Baby, look at me, calm down please," he pleaded. Malajia started hyperventilating and it sent Mark into panic mode. He felt helpless. "*Please* calm down," he urged.

Alex rushed over to Malajia and tried to aid in calming her down. Emily, frozen in fear, put her hands over her mouth in shock.

Jason, seeing that Mark could break at any moment, headed over to him. "Bro, come on, step outside," he said.

Mark, not wanting to upset Malajia more than she already was, decided to comply. He backed away from her and made his way to the door, with Jason following behind him. On his way out, Mark punched the wall behind the door, creating a hole.

"Oh my God!" Alex shrieked. Alex didn't care about the hole; she was concerned with Mark's anger and his hand.

"He's cool, I got him," Jason assured as they walked out the house.

Chasity watched as Malajia put her hands over her face and started shaking. Malajia's state was scaring her. The rest of the group were trying to keep their composure.

"Josh, David, can you step outside too, please?" Sidra requested.

David and Josh did as they were asked.

"I'm about to call an ambulance," Alex panicked, reaching for her phone.

Chasity leaned forward. "Malajia," she called, voice stern. When Malajia didn't remove her hands from her face, Chasity slapped the table, causing Malajia to flinch, "Malajia!" she barked.

"Chasity, don't yell at her," Alex hurled.

"Be *quiet* Alex," Sidra demanded, earning a stunned look from Alex. "Go get a cool towel or something for her."

"Malajia, focus," Chasity urged as Malajia removed her hands from her tear streaked face. "Look at me," Chasity ordered. Malajia slowly made eye contact. "Calm down, you're gonna give yourself a heart attack."

Malajia stared at Chasity as her breathing steadied. Malajia then reached her hand out and Chasity grabbed hold of it.

Emily slowly walked over to Malajia and put her hand on her shoulder. "Are you okay?" she asked, worried tears in her eyes,

Malajia managed a nod as her breathing returned to normal. "I'm sorry."

"Don't you dare apologize, you hear me?" Alex stressed, walking over and grabbing Malajia's other hand. "You have *every* right to be upset."

Malajia let out a deep sigh.

"Why can't he fuckin' fall into a hole somewhere?" Sidra fumed. "Does he *not* know that you have a restraining order against him?" she asked, recalling what Malajia had told the group over a year ago.

"He knows," Malajia assured. Before Malajia could say another word, the door opened and in walked the guys.

"She's okay for now," Alex informed as Mark walked over to Malajia.

Mark sat down next to her and just looked at her as he rubbed his hand, which was starting to swell. Malajia let go of Chasity and Alex's hands and threw her arms around

Mark. He just whispered some consoling words as he held her.

"We were talking outside and we think it's best to call the police," Josh said.

"I agree, but per the terms of Malajia's restraining order, it says he can't come within fifty feet of her," Sidra said. "That gate outside has to be more than fifty feet away, so *technically*, other than rattling her nerves, he didn't break any laws."

"What about the car?" David asked. "She said she saw it around campus."

"Unless you took a picture of the license plate each time you saw it, he can say it's not his," Sidra informed. "The windows are tinted so his face wasn't seen." She rubbed her shoulder. "I don't mean to sound like I'm discrediting anything, I just—"

"You're just stating the facts, we know," Josh finished, calm.

"Okay future lawyer, so what *do* we do?" Chasity asked Sidra. "Since it's apparent that he can just walk around staring at people and shit."

"He's not supposed to have any contact with you at all. So if we can prove that he sent those messages, then the police can do something," Sidra informed. "You've been getting strange calls too, right Malajia?"

Malajia nodded as she parted from Mark's embrace. "Yeah, but from different numbers," her voice was drained. "After I block one, another one is used."

"What about the packages that you've been getting?" Alex asked, recalling what Malajia had mentioned the other day after her conversation with her mother and sister.

Malajia shook her head and sighed. "I threw away all of the boxes," she said. "And after my parents said that they didn't send them to me, I threw out the stuff that was in there…the shit that I didn't *eat* anyway." She put her face in her hands. "…I don't know. There was no return address on those packages so that probably can't be traced to him *either*."

"It's okay Malajia," Sidra assured. "We'll figure this out… He's not gonna get to hurt you again."

"Especially not if *I* have anything to do with it," Mark fumed. "I will tear this fuckin' campus apart."

"I'm with you on that," Jason cosigned.

Chasity pinched the bridge of her nose with her fingertips and sighed. Jason wrapped his arms around her. "I'm not gonna let him touch you again," he whispered to her.

"I'm fine," Chasity replied.

"Chaz, I think *you* should get a restraining order on him too," Alex suggested.

"I don't think he's interested in getting to me," Chasity said.

"He put his hands on you *too*," Alex fumed.

Chasity glanced at Jason, whose anger was coming through once again. "Yes, I *know* that, thanks for the reminder."

"I'm *concerned*," Alex argued. "He beat you up because you went to help Malajia, what if you're in that situation again. *Then* what?"

Chasity rolled her eyes.

"Look, here's what's going to happen," Jason cut in, tone stern. "Until this muthafucka' is caught, *none* of you ladies are going anywhere by yourself." The girls were silent as he spoke. "I'd *prefer* that you don't go without one of us guys."

"I agree," Josh chimed in. "Alex, no matter what my schedule is, when you have to go to work, call me and I'll walk you."

"If Josh is in class or something, *I'll* do it," David chimed in.

Alex nodded. "Thank you."

Jason glanced around the room. "Everybody agree?"

"Yeah," they collectively said.

Jason glanced down at Chasity, "I *mean* it, Chasity," he

urged. Knowing how stubborn and defiant she could be. "I don't want you going anywhere without me. *Especially* at night."

"I heard you, Jase," Chasity assured. She had no intention of putting up an argument; the last thing that she wanted was for herself or any of her friends to be hurt. She was putting on a brave front, but Chasity was scared.

"We all about to be having a bunch of damn sleepovers," Mark cut in.

"I'm all for it," Alex chuckled. "I'll make sure to bring plenty of pizza home." She looked around when the room went silent, "Really? Y'all are *still* hating on my damn pizza?"

"Alex, stop acting shocked, it's unbecoming," Sidra sneered, examining her nails.

Alex made a face at her in retaliation.

# Chapter 38

"Did you eat breakfast today?" Mark asked as he walked alongside Malajia in route to her class.

Malajia pushed her hair over her shoulder. "Yeah, a little," she said. She glanced at him. "You?"

"Don't worry about me," he said. Mark, like Malajia, was still on edge. So much so that his appetite was almost nonexistent. His focus was on making sure that Malajia was taking care of herself.

"Yeah, well I *am* worrying about you," she threw back. "I don't need you passing out on me. When we finish with classes today, I'm gonna make you dinner, and you *better* eat it."

"As long as you don't make that dry ass meatloaf that you normally make, I'll eat it," he joked.

Malajia stared at him. "Boy, I've never made meatloaf," she hissed. He broke into laughter. "Always lyin'."

Mark put his arm around Malajia as they continued to walk. Malajia glanced ahead of her and her eyes locked on Jackie, sitting on a nearby bench.

Mark glanced over at Malajia as she halted her steps. "What's wrong babe?" he wondered, stopping his walk.

Malajia gestured to Jackie as she stared at her.

"What *about* her?" Mark asked, confused.

Malajia hesitated for a moment "Mark...I have to go talk to her," she said.

Mark frowned. "Nah, fuck that," he hissed, trying to nudge Malajia along. She put her hand on his arm to stop him. "No Mel, you don't need to get into no bullshit ass argument with Jackie."

"I'm not trying to argue with her," Malajia insisted.

"Malajia, I'm serious, you don't need to get involved in that," Mark barked.

Malajia looked at him. Under any other circumstances, Malajia wouldn't give Jackie's life a second thought. But in this case, Malajia felt that a conversation was warranted. "Mark," she said, tone calm. "I get it but…knowing what I know about Tyrone and knowing what I've *been* through with him, I can't in good conscious not try to warn her about him… I'm a woman first and I would want someone to tell *me*."

Mark rubbed his face with his hand.

"I promise, I won't be long," she said, touching his arm.

Mark sighed. "Do what you need to do… I'll be over here waiting for you," he said.

Malajia nodded, then walked in Jackie's direction, while Mark watched her like a hawk. Malajia slowly approached the bench where Jackie was sitting.

"Jackie," she called.

Jackie's head jerked around and she immediately bolted from her seat. "Malajia, what—"

"I didn't come over here to argue with you," Malajia calmly interrupted.

"Oh, *that's* new," Jackie sneered.

Malajia rolled her eyes. "Jackie you know that *you're* the one who starts—" She put her hand up. "Whatever Jackie, like I said, I'm not trying to argue, I just want to talk to you."

"About what?" Jackie hissed, folding her arms.

"About your boyfriend," Malajia said. Jackie's eyes widened. "As in *Tyrone*… I know you're with him."

"And *how* do you know that?"

"Does it really *matter* Jackie?" Malajia questioned. Jackie rolled her eyes. "I'm starting to believe that you knew that he and I used to date."

Jackie sucked her teeth.

"It's true huh?" Malajia pressed. "You knew and that's why you've been up my ass this whole time."

"Yes, I know about you two, *and* what?" Jackie challenged, furious.

Malajia shook her head. Jackie's immaturity was not what she wanted to focus on. "Look Jackie, I'm not sure *how much* you know about our past relationship but—"

"Don't come over here trying to tarnish my man's name because you still want him."

Anger masked Malajia's face. "*First* of all, there is *nothing* on the face of this goddamn earth that would make we want Tyrone's ass again, okay," she bit out. "Second, don't tell *me* about tarnishing his damn name, because you have *no* idea what I went through with him." Malajia glanced at Jackie's arm. "But judging by that bruise on your wrist, maybe you *do*."

Jackie glanced down at her wrist and caught sight of the bruise in question. "Whatever bitch, I fell."

"Yeah, I *fell* a few times when I was with him *too*," Malajia threw back.

Jackie rolled her eyes. "Look, I don't know what you're implying, but my relationship with Tyrone is fine okay. He's not concerning himself with what you're doing so stop getting in *our* business."

"I don't give a fuck *about* him, and frankly I don't give two shits about *you either*," Malajia flashed back. "But because I have a conscious, I'm trying to *warn* your stupid ass. When he doesn't get his way, he makes you feel like shit, he puts you down, he puts pressure on you and when he *really* feels like he has a hold on you, he gets violent... This is not me tarnishing his image, these are *facts* and I have the medical bills to prove it."

"Spare me the bullshit Malajia," Jackie spat out. "Tyrone treats me just *fine* okay. I know what to do to keep my man happy, unlike *you*,"

"Oh you mean by fuckin' him on the first date?" Malajia

hissed. Malajia had no intention of engaging Jackie in a verbal battle, but Jackie's bad attitude was heightening the feelings of disdain that Malajia already had for her.

"Cute," Jackie sneered. "Just concern yourself less with *my* man. He wasted his time with you and now he's happy with *me*. So get out of my face and leave us alone with your lying ass."

Malajia flipped her hair over her shoulder as she stared Jackie down. "Fine, suit yourself," she ground out before turning to walk away. She paused and turned back around. "Oh yeah, I think you should know that *your man* was standing outside *my* house the other day."

Jackie's eyes widened. "So what he was on campus? *I* still go here."

"See that would make sense in any other situation, but *this* one," Malajia goaded. "*You* don't live on campus anymore, and you have *no* classes near the housing complex that *I* live in so you really wanna justify that?"

Jackie stood there, face masked with anger.

"Yeah," Malajia confirmed. "He was outside of my house, and I'm pretty sure he's been texting and calling my phone from different numbers. Which is fuckin' hilarious since you seem to think that *I'm* the one who wants *him*," she sneered. "He's not even supposed to be in *contact* with me at all, so that crazy bastard is willing to risk his fuckin' freedom just to *mess* with me. So baby girl, you might want to take that anger that you have with *me* and save it for *him*." Malajia folded her arms. "On second thought, being angry takes too much energy. So save it 'cause you'll need it to defend yourself when he slaps the shit out of you. Good luck."

Jackie stood and watched in seething silence as Malajia headed off in Mark's direction.

Sidra removed a freshly washed item from her laundry basket and folded it. Placing the item on the bed, she surveyed the color-coordinated piles and chuckled. "God, I am so anal," she said to herself, grabbing another item.

Sidra had thrown herself into her schoolwork as well as cleaning and laundry duty. It was far from fun, but it kept her mind off her feelings, which was what she needed. Hearing a knock on the door, Sidra looked up from her laundry pile.

"It's open," she called softly. Seeing Malajia stick her head in, Sidra gave her a small smile.

"Hey, David dropped some donuts off. You better come get one before Alex eats them all," Malajia said.

Sidra giggled. "You mean before *you* eat them all?"

"Yes, before *I* eat them," Malajia amended. "I'm working on this long ass paper for class and it's making me hungry."

Sidra shook her head in amusement. "Thank you for letting me know, but I don't want any."

Malajia nodded. "Okay."

Sidra folded another shirt. "How are you holding up?" she asked.

Malajia shrugged. "I'm going crazy on the inside," she admitted, "I don't like feeling afraid, you know?"

"I know, and I'm praying that he just goes away," Sidra said, tone caring.

"Yeah, me too," Malajia muttered. She shook her head as she held onto the doorknob. "I told my parents... My dad tried to come down here."

"And I don't blame him," Sidra replied. "*My* dad would post up in a hotel too."

Malajia quickly shook her head. "No, he said he was gonna sleep *here* on the *couch*."

Sidra couldn't help but snicker.

"I mean, I love my dad and I *get* it but nah, I wasn't having that," Malajia said. "He be snoring all loud, bones be crackin', sweating all over the couch cushions and shit."

"Will you stop it," Sidra laughed. She admired how Malajia could still make a joke when Sidra knew that she was terrified.

Malajia couldn't help but chuckle. "I told him that I'm safe with Mark and you guys here with me... I told him that I'll check in every day," she said. "That seemed to satisfy him for now."

"Well good," Sidra said. "I'm here for you. Whatever you need okay?"

Malajia managed a smile as she nodded. "Thank you."

"Malajia," Sidra called as Malajia went to walk out the door.

Malajia opened it again. "Yeah?"

"You um...you don't have to knock before coming in here," Sidra said.

Malajia was taken aback. "Seriously?" she said. "And here I am, trying to be respectful." She scratched her head. "Isn't that what you *wanted* all these years?"

Sidra sighed. "No...I mean—I—" She fiddled with the shirt in her hand. "I *thought* that's what I wanted, but I *don't* anymore so you can go back to barging in here like you're crazy."

Malajia smiled. "Okay then, don't say anything when your things go missing," she quickly put out.

"No, Malajia that's not what—"

"Too late," Malajia cut in, grabbing a calculator off of a dresser and darting back out the room. "Damn it, this is Emily's," she huffed, tossing the item back on the dresser, then walking back out and shutting the door behind her.

After a moment, Sidra let a giggle come through.


Malajia removed the flash drive from her laptop then breathed a long sigh. "Finally finished this bullshit," she said to herself. Glancing at her notebook, she frowned. "Shit!" she yelped, bolting out of her seat and darting out the door. She walked next door and knocked. Upon being given the okay to enter, Malajia walked in.

"Chaz, I need you to do me a huge favor," Malajia said.

Chasity looked up from the homework sprawled out on

her desk. "What?"

"Can you *please* walk me to the Science building? I need to go to the computer lab."

Chasity frowned. "*Now*?!"

"Yes," Malajia insisted. "Look, I just finished working on my paper for class and I forgot that it's due tomorrow. Like *first* thing in the damn *morning* tomorrow…and I need to print it out."

Chasity sucked her teeth; she was clearly annoyed. "Why do you *always* wait until the last minute to do shit?"

"'Cause I'm a procrastinator and it's something that I *clearly* need to work on," Malajia threw back. "Look, I would do it tomorrow, but it closes at eleven and doesn't open back up until eight in the morning which is exactly when that class *starts*. That paper makes up a lot of my final grade and I can't afford to not turn it in…*please* Chaz?"

Chasity ran her hand through her hair. "Malajia, I don't think we should be going all the way across campus to that damn building at ten something at night…not with Tyrone's ass still around."

"I know, but Josh went to get Alex from work, David is with Emily at the library, and Jason and Mark went to the store…" she let out a quick sigh. "It's not like we're walking by ourselves. They said walk in *pairs*…you're my 'pair'."

Chasity rolled her eyes. "Malajia, just use *my* printer."

"For twenty pages?"

Chasity winced. "Yeah, I don't even have that much ink," she admitted. "Shit."

"I haven't gotten any messages or seen him for the past week… Campus security is always lurking in the damn buildings at night, so I think we should be okay… It'll be fast."

Chasity had a bad feeling, but decided to ignore it. "Fine," she sighed.

Malajia clasped her hands together. "I owe you one."

"Yeah, yeah you *do*," Chasity agreed, grabbing her phone from the desk.

Both girls walked downstairs and headed for the door. "Where are you two going?" Sidra asked, clicking the TV volume down.

"We're going to the computer lab in the Science building," Malajia answered. "I have to print my paper."

"You're not supposed to be going out alone," Sidra said, tone sharp.

"We're *not* alone," Malajia pointed out. "We won't be long."

"I'll walk with you too," Sidra offered.

"In what, your nightgown?" Malajia jeered. Sidra looked down at her nightgown and slippers. "Chaz and I will be fine."

Sidra sat there, worry written on her face. "You have your phone?"

"Yeah," Chasity answered.

"Okay…be careful, please," Sidra urged.

"We will," Malajia promised, and walked out the door with Chasity behind her.

# Chapter 39

"Why does this campus seem extra creepy tonight?" Chasity said, looking behind her.

"Because you're thinking too much," Malajia pointed out, then nudged her. "Will you stop looking behind you like you're crazy?"

"No," Chasity hissed.

"You're making me nervous," Malajia bit out.

*You should be*, Chasity thought. "Fine, I won't say anything else, but I'm still gonna look… You can't take *everything* away from me."

Malajia chuckled. "Very well."

Upon entering the Science building, the girls headed to the computer room. Malajia quickly turned on one of the computers and slipped her flash drive in. "I hope they don't have the raggedy printer hooked up," she said.

"You mean the one that takes like five minutes to print one page?" Chasity asked, turning on the computer in front of her.

"Exactly," Malajia said, typing some keys on the computer. When she hit print, she glanced over and waited for the printer to come to life. As soon as she heard the sounds of a page printing, Malajia let out a groan. "Damn it! This school cheap as shit!"

Chasity laughed. "You're gonna be here for like an hour."

"No *we're* gonna be here for like an hour," Malajia

corrected. Chasity sucked her teeth. "So just get comfortable."

"Say something else and I'll leave your 'waiting 'till the last minute' ass right here," Chasity warned.

Malajia opened her mouth to protest, but Chasity shot her a warning glance, prompting Malajia to close her mouth.

Fifteen minutes later, Malajia was losing her patience. "This fuckin' thing jammed like *three times* already and only printed like five pages," she complained.

"Yes, I know. I've been sitting here listening to you bitch about it," Chasity said, tone even.

Malajia made a face as she glanced at Chasity. "Why don't you come over here and *fix* it, computer expert," she sneered.

"That is not a *computer,* you moron," Chasity threw back.

"Chasity, can you stop arguing with me and just take a look at it please?" Malajia huffed. "I want to get out of here as badly as *you* do."

Chasity tossed her hands up. "Whatever Malajia," she huffed, standing up. "Don't ask me to walk you another damn place."

"I appreciate you," Malajia gushed as Chasity walked over to the printer. "And to show you how much, I'm gonna go to the vending machine and get you some candy."

"Bitch don't front, you're gonna get *you* some candy," Chasity sneered, opening the top of the printer.

Malajia laughed. "Well, now I'm gonna get *you* some *too*," she amended. "I might even get that guard that's been passing by here every five minutes some too."

"Just hurry the hell up," Chasity hissed as Malajia walked out of the computer lab.

Chasity let out a loud sigh as she started tinkering with the printer. "I swear to God, tuition is too fuckin' high for these broke ass printers," she huffed to the empty room. After a few more seconds, Chasity had cleared the jam and closed the printer. She rubbed the back of her neck as the rest of Malajia's paper started printing again. Shaking her head, Chasity went back over to her computer and frowned when she noticed Malajia's phone sitting next to the computer that she was working on.

"Always forgetting shit," she ground out, grabbing the phone. She walked to the door and opened it. Her eyes widened as she came face to face with a tall figure that had appeared from behind the door. Before Chasity could scream or react, she was grabbed and slammed into the wall behind her. The force from the impact was enough to make her black out and fall to the floor.

Malajia stared at the vending machine, which was located down the hall and around the corner from the computer lab. She'd been standing there for far too long, trying to decide on what to purchase. "What kind of candy would that picky heffa want?" she asked herself, before digging into her pocket to retrieve some money. "She gon' eat whatever I get her." She purchased one pack of candy, then placed more money in the machine. "Ooh, they finally restocked those chocolate covered peanuts," she beamed to herself.

"It's nice to know that you still like those," a male voice said.

Recognizing the voice, Malajia immediately spun around and backed up against the machine. Her eyes widened and fear froze on her face as she saw Tyrone standing in front of her, smiling.

"Hi Malajia," he said.

Malajia was too scared to speak. She just stood there staring at him, gripping the sides of the machine for support.

Ignoring the fear on Malajia's face or her labored breathing, Tyrone just smiled. "You're even more beautiful than I remember," he said. "I mean, I've seen you around campus but could never get close enough to you."

*Scream Malajia!* She thought. *The guard will hear you, Chasity will hear you, just scream!* No matter what her head said, her mouth wouldn't listen; she was paralyzed with fear.

"I missed you so much," Tyrone continued.

Malajia swallowed hard as she tried to keep herself from having another panic attack. "Get away from me," she managed to say finally.

"Nah, I think I like being close to you again," he insisted, rubbing his chin with his hand. He stared at her. "You been enjoying those packages that I've been sending you?"

Malajia's mouth fell open; she should have known from the beginning.

"Don't worry, I didn't do anything to the stuff inside," he assured, assuming her thoughts. "I just wanted to send you all of your favorites… I wish I could have seen your face light up when you opened them…and when you got your roses. I left them on the front step for you."

"You came to my fuckin' *house?*" Malajia stammered, angry.

"No, I paid a delivery man," Tyrone said, "I know that the ones that I *originally* mailed were taken so I wanted to replace them."

"God, why are you stalking me?" Malajia asked, trying to keep herself from shaking. "What do you *want?*"

Tyrone held an icy gaze on her. "I want to give us another chance."

Malajia's terror turned to fury as her ex stood in front of her. Not only had he abused her and hurt her friend, but he had just admitted to stalking her, and he had the nerve to stand in her face and propose getting back together. "You must be fuckin' crazy if you think that I would *ever* get back—"

"Why *not?!*" Tyrone erupted, causing her to flinch. "Is it because you're with *Mark* now?" He nodded his head.

"Yeah, I know about that…and to think, you always told me that I had nothing to worry about when it came to him."

He took a step forward. Malajia pressed her body against the machine and put her hand out. "Don't—"

"I'm not going to hurt you," Tyrone assured. "I still love you and I *really* want us to get back together. I'm willing to overlook you messing around with Mark, if you're willing to overlook me messing with Jackie."

Malajia went to move, but he blocked her path. "Just leave me the hell alone!" she cried out.

"She never meant anything, just an easy lay," Tyrone insisted. "I was gonna dump her ass right away. But when I found out that she knew *you*, well… I knew that I could use her to get on campus… I don't want her, I want *you*. I've always wanted *you*."

Malajia stood there as Tyrone kept talking; she was looking for a way to escape.

When she didn't say anything, Tyrone began to lose his patience. "You just gonna let me pour my heart out and not say anything back?" He took another step and got in Malajia's face.

She put her arm out to keep him from coming any closer. "Get away from me!"

Tyrone grabbed her hand and pushed it down. "I *said* I'm not gonna hurt you!" he barked. "Should I though?" he taunted, a crazy look in his eyes. "*Should* I hurt you, especially after you got rid of my baby?"

Malajia's eyes widened. *How the fuck did he find out?!* Nobody besides her mother and her close friends knew about her abortion. "I don't know what you're talking—"

"You're lying!" he yelled.

Malajia jumped again at the bass in Tyrone's voice. Her eyes were filling with tears. *Where is the damn security guard?*

"Yeah, I know about that *too*," Tyrone revealed. "So no need in trying to deny it."

Tears spilled down Malajia's face. "I'm—"

"Don't beat yourself up for it," Tyrone said, tone now calm. "You did what you had to do." He nodded his head again, rubbing his hands together. "We can always make *another* one."

"I'd rather die than let you touch me again," she hissed, anger full in her voice.

"I doubt that," Tyrone taunted, calmness gone. "You can't tell me that you don't still have feelings for me Malajia."

"The only feeling I have for you is hatred you fuckin' psycho," Malajia hissed.

Tyrone put his hand up, and Malajia flinched. "You're trying me. You're really trying my fuckin' patience Malajia," he spat out. "You're *going* to give me another chance."

"I'm not giving you *shit*."

"See I love you and that feeling isn't going away," Tyrone insisted, "You *owe* it to us to give me another chance... I did six months in *jail* and finished my damn program... I went through *hell* because I fell in love with *you*... You *owe* me and you *owe* me another baby."

Malajia looked around. "Tyrone I swear to God, if you don't get away from me, I'm gonna fuckin' scream, and you'll go back to jail."

"Scream for *who*?" he taunted. "You think someone is gonna hear you? The guard ain't here and your pretty little friend...what's her name, Chasity?"

Malajia's eyes widened.

"I *doubt* she'll hear you right about now."

Malajia made a move to run, but was still blocked by Tyrone. "What the fuck did you do to her you sick bastard?!" Malajia screamed in anger, stomping her foot on the floor.

"You're concerning yourself with the wrong shit, Malajia!" he yelled back.


Chasity slowly opened her eyes and blinked several times. Glancing down, she realized that she was on the floor.

She tried to push herself up, but the pain from her head and back made her lay still for a moment. Chasity had no idea how long she was out as she tried to piece together what had happened. She stared at the chairs in front of her as the memories flooded back.

*Tyrone, that was Tyrone*, she thought, remembering her assailant's face.

She slowly turned her head. The door was cracked open. *Shit. Malajia!*

Making another effort to stand, Chasity used a nearby chair for support. Scared and hurt, she wanted to cry, but knew that she couldn't. She had to know if Malajia was okay. She grabbed her phone, which had fallen on the floor, and sent Jason a text message.

*'Come to the Science building, Tyrone is here, Malajia is in trouble, I'm hurt, hurry up.'*

Slowly stuffing the phone into her pocket, Chasity, as quietly as she could, made her way out of the lab. Holding onto the wall for support, she slowly inched her way down the hall.

She paused for a moment when she felt her head pound then slowly sat on the floor. "Shit. Get up, get up," she whispered to herself. She prayed that Jason got there soon.

Hearing voices, Chasity crawled the rest of the way to the end of the hall. Peering around the corner, she saw Malajia standing against the vending machine, Tyrone within inches of her face. "Shit," Chasity whispered to herself.

Slowly, she pushed herself back up from the floor. As much as she wanted to run to Malajia's aid, she was too hurt. She wanted to yell out and distract him, but she was too weak for her voice to carry. Looking for something to cause a distraction, Chasity noticed a trash can by the wall. She inched over to it and with the little strength that she had, kicked the metal can over.

The noise made Tyrone turn around, giving Malajia the opportunity to knee him in the groin and take off running. Although in pain, Tyrone managed to grab Malajia's leg. She took a hard fall to the floor, screaming at the top of her lungs as Tyrone dragged her towards him.

"I'm not fuckin' done talking to you, bitch!" he yelled.

"Get off me!" Malajia screamed, kicking him in the face. Tyrone grabbed his face with one hand and his aching groin with another. Seizing the opportunity, Malajia jumped up from the floor and took off running. Tyrone, realizing that there was no way that he could catch her in his condition, bolted in the other direction.

Malajia rounded the corner. When she felt someone grab her arm, she screamed and spun around to find Chasity leaning against the wall. "We gotta get out of here," she panicked.

"I don't think I can run," Chasity managed to say.

Malajia grabbed Chasity to steady her. "Are you okay? What did he do to you?"

"He slammed me into a wall," Chasity answered, pained. "It happened so fast—are *you* okay?"

Malajia shook her head. Before Malajia could say anything else, she heard Mark and Jason yelling their names. Malajia looked around. "We're by Dr. Rosen's classroom!" she yelled.

Within seconds, Jason and Mark came sprinting around the corner. Jason rushed to Chasity and Mark rushed to Malajia.

"Did he put his hands on you? Are you hurt?" Mark charged.

"Please, get me out of here," Malajia cried, clinging to Mark.

"Are you okay?" Jason put his hands on Chasity's face and examined her.

Chasity shook her head as tears spilled from her eyes.

"He slammed her into a fuckin' wall," Malajia fumed, holding on to Mark.

Jason saw red. "I'm gonna fuckin' kill him."

Chasity grabbed Jason's arm as he was about to take off in search of Tyrone. "Jason no!" she managed to yell. She knew that if Jason went after Tyrone, that he might in fact kill him. His life would be ruined, and Tyrone wasn't worth that. "Just take me to the hospital," she begged, tears spilling down her face. Jason looked like he was ready to explode; she tugged on his arm. "Jason, please."

Jason rubbed his face with his hands. He was furious but Chasity needed him right now. He quickly scooped her up in his arms.

"I'll drop y'all off at the hospital on the way to the police station," Mark said.


Sidra paced the floor of the living room as the rest of the group sat in stunned silence. "I can't believe this," Sidra huffed.

"What the hell did he *do*? Follow them?" Alex fumed.

Having arrived back from work nearly two hours ago, Alex never expected for herself or anyone else in the group to get a phone call telling them about what had happened at the computer lab. She was beyond furious.

"We should've left sooner," Josh said, angry. "If I hadn't been stalling trying to get my schedule for next week, I would've been back to walk them."

"I should have gone with them," Sidra said, still pacing.

"Then what would have happened to *you*?" Josh frowned. Sidra let out a sigh. "Having you there wouldn't have stopped that crazy bastard from doing what he wanted to do."

"Nobody can blame themselves," David placated. "None of us had any idea that this was going to happen."

Emily cradled a pillow to her chest. "How long has it been since they called?" she asked.

"*Too* long," Sidra answered, frustrated.

Alex stood up. "We need to go be with them," she said. "Half of us will go to the hospital with Chasity, and the others to the police station to be there for Malajia," she ordered.

"I have my car keys right here," Sidra announced, reaching into her purse that was sitting on the table.

As everyone went to leave, the door opened.

"Malajia," Emily breathed as Sidra darted over and gave her a hug.

"Are you okay?" Sidra asked as she continued to embrace Malajia.

"Physically, yes," Malajia said. When they broke from their embrace, Malajia grabbed her arm. "My arm is just sore...I fell on it."

Emily jumped up from the couch. "I'll get you some ice for it."

"Where's Jason and Chasity?" Josh wondered.

"They're still at the hospital," Mark answered, tone eerily calm. "They did a few scans on her... They'll probably keep her overnight for observation, but they said that as far as they could see, she'll be fine."

"I'm going to the hospital," Alex insisted.

"I was gonna go back myself, but she said that there is no need for anybody to come," Malajia muttered, still shaking. "You know how she is."

"I don't give a damn *what* she says. I'm going to see her for myself," Alex fussed.

Sidra guided Malajia over to a chair and sat down next to her.

"He followed us," Malajia said as Alex and Emily huddled around her. She rubbed her face with her hand as she recalled the chilling details. "...he lurked around the backroads and watched the house until we left." She put her head in her hands. "I can't believe this happened. I should've never left the house. And I dragged Chasity into my shit yet again."

"Malajia stop that," Alex scolded.

"Yeah," Emily agreed. "Tyrone is out of his freakin' mind."

"The police better put his ass *under* the jail this time," Sidra fumed. "Not *only* did he violate his restraining order

like a hundred times over, they can add stalking and fuckin'
assault again to his rap sheet."

"I went to the station," Malajia revealed, running her
hand over her hair. "They said they're going to pick him up
tonight... They're going to his apartment."

"*Good*," Josh said. "A slap on the wrist isn't gonna work
*this* time."

Mark stood silent as the conversation took place. Each
word that Malajia spoke about the incident made his anger
rage faster and faster. "Baby," Mark called, causing Malajia
to look up at him. "I'm gonna run out for a minute, I'll be
back okay."

Malajia frowned in skepticism. "Where are you going?"
When Mark just stared at her, she slowly stood up from her
seat. "Mark?"

"Yes," he answered.

"Where are you *going*?" Malajia repeated, both worried
and angry.

"I have to make a run."

"Can you drop me off at the hospital?" Alex asked.

Malajia held her stern gaze on Mark as realization set in.
"No...he *can't*," she answered.

Alex looked confused. "Why *not*?"

"Because he's not *going* to the hospital," Malajia
concluded.

"He's *not* getting away with this," Mark fumed, going to
the door.

"Mark, don't!" Malajia yelled.

"Bro, let the police handle this," Josh urged, approaching
Mark.

Mark pointed at him. "Don't test me Josh!" Mark hurled,
halting Josh's steps. "The police should have *never* let his ass
the fuck out in the *first* place."

"This time they *won't* let him out," David added.

"Well then I need to get to him before *they* do," Mark
raged, grabbing back for the doorknob.

"Don't get yourself locked up Mark," Alex cut in,

worried. "Don't let him ruin your life."

"Mark I'm *begging* you, don't go over there," Malajia panicked, tears in her eyes.

Mark pointed to Josh and David. "Watch her," he demanded before walking out the door.

"Mark!" Malajia hollered after him. As the door slammed shut she put her hands over her head. "Shit!"

"We can't let him go beat up Tyrone," Alex said. "Not with the cops already going to arrest him, if they're not there *already*."

"There's no stopping him," Sidra said.

Malajia grabbed on Sidra's arm. "Sidra, can I use your car?"

"No, you're not going over there, are you crazy?!" Sidra exclaimed.

"I can't let Mark do this, he could go to jail. I can't—I need to go," Malajia argued.

"*I'll* drive you," Josh offered, heading for the door. "David, stay here and watch the other girls."

"You got it," David agreed.

"No Josh, you're not—"

"Give me the damn keys Sidra," Josh demanded, holding his hand out.

Sidra stared at him, eyes wide before taking a deep breath. "Fine," she huffed. "But I'm going with you both."

"No—"

"*My* car, *my* rules," Sidra cut in, stern, shutting Josh's protest down.

"Sidra," Malajia insisted, "you don't—"

"I'm not letting you walk out that door without me, *again*," Sidra said, interrupting Malajia. She grabbed Malajia's hand. "Let's go."

"Maybe we should *all* go," Alex proposed.

"No, go to the hospital," Malajia said. "Chasity and Jason *both* need you guys there."

Alex nodded in agreement as she watched the three walk out the door. "I'll get Chaz's car keys," she said, heading for the steps. "Jase is probably punching walls right now."

Josh honked the horn. "What the fuck—Move damn it!" he barked at the slow-moving car in front of him.

"Josh go around him," Sidra ordered.

"I *can't*, it's one lane," Josh threw back, agitated.

Sidra shook her head, then looked at Malajia, who was sitting in the back seat next to her. "We're gonna get to him in time," she placated.

"This traffic is moving like fuckin' snails right now," Malajia seethed. "God why did he have to leave?"

"Because Mark loves you and his job is to protect you," Sidra said. "So don't be mad at him."

"I'm *not*, I just don't want him to go to jail," Malajia said.

"Neither do *we*," Josh chimed in from the front. "We'll get to him if this car FUCKIN' MOVES!" The bass in his voice caused both girls to flinch. "Sorry."

"*Don't* be," Sidra said.

"*Finally*," Josh huffed when the car turned a corner, allowing him to speed up. Rounding the next corner, Josh's eyes widened as he saw two police cars and an ambulance, lights flashing, parked in front of Tyrone's apartment complex.

"Is Mark's car here?" Sidra asked as Malajia glanced around for it.

"Yeah," Josh said, pointing to the familiar car parked on the sidewalk. "Shit!" he panicked, putting the car in park. The three of them jumped out of the car and darted for the scene; they were stopped by two police officers.

"Hold up, you can't pass through here," one officer said.

"Our friend could be in there," Josh barked, pointing to the open apartment door.

"I don't care, you're not getting through," the officer barked back.

Malajia looked around in a panic for any signs of Mark.

Her eyes focused on a familiar figure sitting inside of one of the police cars. Her eyes widened. "Mark!" she yelled, trying to push past the officers.

"Shit," Josh reacted, glancing. "Where the fuck is the *other* guy? The one you're *supposed* to have in handcuffs?"

"Why is he in the backseat of the car? Why is my boyfriend in your damn car?!" Malajia raged.

"Are you arresting him?!" Sidra wailed.

The other officer glanced back at the car in question. "Calm down," he urged.

"Don't tell me to calm down," Malajia argued.

The officer put his hand up at her. "Seriously, calm down," he said.

Malajia put her hands over her face as she tried to keep from busting out crying. The officer looked at his partner. "It's cool," he said. His partner nodded to him and he put his arms down. "You two, stay put," he said to Josh and Sidra.

"We're not leaving," Sidra ground out.

"Don't have to, just don't move." He then guided Malajia in the direction of the car that held Mark. As they walked over, he glanced at her. "I spoke to you at the police station earlier."

Malajia squinted slightly as she looked at him; she did in fact recognize him.

"Tyrone Edmonds is being arrested as we speak," he said, gesturing to the commotion going on within the apartment.

"Why is my boyfriend in handcuffs?" Malajia asked him. "Is he being arrested?"

"No... We put him in here to calm him down," the officer answered. "We were inside when your boyfriend pushed his way into the apartment. He went straight for Tyrone and we grabbed him before he could lay a hand on him."

Malajia stared in the car. Mark was staring out ahead of him, furious.

"If we hadn't been here..." the officer shook his head.

"We're just glad that we *were*. Your boyfriend was so mad, this could have very well been a murder scene."

Malajia closed her eyes and silently thanked God that that wasn't the case. She put her hand on the window. "Are the cuffs necessary?"

"Yes, until we get the assailant in the other car and out of here... Don't worry, we didn't hurt your boyfriend." Malajia nodded as the officer reached inside the car and rolled down the window slightly. "You can talk to him," he said as he stood close to the car.

She leaned close to the window. "Hey," she said softly.

Mark glanced at her. "Hey."

"Do the cuffs hurt?"

"Not really," Mark answered, tone even. "What are you doing here, Malajia?"

"Trying to stop you from doing something stupid," she replied. "Luckily, the cops already *did*."

"He deserved to get the shit beat out of him again," Mark fumed. "For you, Chaz, Jase *and myself*."

"*Then* what?" Malajia asked. "You'd be in jail...your life would be over."

"I'd get off," he scoffed.

"Mark, stop it," Malajia fumed. Tears started filling her eyes and Mark let out a heavy sigh.

"Mel, don't cry."

"I saw the ambulance—then saw you in this car and—I *know* you're mad, *I'm* mad too... But I can't lose you, okay," she cried.

"Okay...you won't," Mark assured her. He leaned his head back against the hard seat. Although he wished that he could have gotten to Tyrone before the cops arrived, Mark knew that if he had, he wouldn't have let up.

Malajia glanced over at Sidra and Josh as they looked on from feet away. She gave them the okay sign before glancing at the apartment door. "They're bringing him out," she announced to Mark.

"Don't look at him," Mark ordered.

Malajia complied and held her gaze on Mark. She flinched when she heard Tyrone yell her name, followed by the officers ordering at him to remain quiet.

"Focus on me," Mark said to her.

"Okay," she said, reaching her hand in the car and touching Mark's shoulder. "Is he gone?" she asked Mark.

Mark craned his neck to see. The police car that held Tyrone pulled off. "Yeah," he said.

"What's the ambulance for?" Malajia asked.

Mark hesitated for a moment. "Jackie was in there," he revealed.

Malajia frowned and quickly spun around to see an officer walk Jackie out of the complex and to the ambulance. She was holding her jaw and it looked like she had blood on her arm. Malajia stared as Jackie's eyes locked with hers. Malajia slowly shook her head as Jackie glanced at the ground, before being loaded into the ambulance.

# Chapter 40

"I swear to God, after these finals are done, I'm gonna flood the bathroom and slide down the steps butt ass naked," Mark announced, shifting his books from one arm to the other.

Jason frowned in disgust at him. "In *whose* house, do you think you're doing that nasty bullshit?" he griped.

Mark busted out laughing.

"You know the floors have *carpet*, right?" Josh pointed out. "So you're gonna slide your dumb ass down wet carpet?"

"Okay, *clearly* I didn't think my idea through enough," Mark chuckled. "I should've waited to announce it."

"No, you shouldn't have announced that shit at *all*," Jason barked, still annoyed by Mark's silly idea.

Josh shook his head in amusement. "This is going to be an interesting two weeks," he mused. "Our last time cramming for finals…don't know whether to be happy or sad."

"Man, I'm mad as shit," Mark cut in. "These professors are gonna *kill* us with these tests."

"Can't be any worse than they already *have* been," Jason reasoned, adjusting his book bag.

"True," Josh shrugged. When he saw a young lady walking by, he smiled. "Hey," he said to her as she passed.

"Hey," the girl smiled back, continuing on her way.

"You *stay* with a new chick nowadays," Mark teased. "Where was this Josh for the *first* three years of school? You bang that one *too*?"

"Why you all up in the man's business?" Jason laughed before Josh could answer.

"Look, *I'm* only banging *one* chick right now, so I'm living vicariously through Josh," Mark joked.

"I don't know if I should be more amazed that you could say something so simple, or that you actually know what 'vicariously' means," Josh commented after a few seconds.

Mark made a face at him.

Josh shook his head. "Anyway, like I've said before, I'm not banging every damn girl you see me with."

"Nah, you a hoe, just admit it," Mark joked, earning a laugh from Jason and an eye roll from Josh.

"Anyway…how are the girls doing?" Josh asked, changing the subject. "I mean, when they're *not* putting on a brave face in font of everyone… It's been a couple weeks."

"Now that he's locked the fuck back up and *will* be for a long time…they're fine," Mark said of Tyrone. "Still wish that I could've stomped the shit outta him first, smashed his face through the fuckin' window or *something*."

"Bro, I was in the hospital *snappin*'," Jason recalled, upset. "Chasity was hysterical when they tried to take her away to give her a CAT scan. I couldn't go with her, and knowing what that bastard did and that he was still out there… I almost punched a damn doctor when he told me to calm down."

"Yeah, I hear you," Mark agreed. "Sitting in that police car, I just kept thinking about how to get out those damn handcuffs."

"I'm surprised your parents didn't cuss you out when they came down here for winding up handcuffed." Josh said.

"Shit, Mom ain't cuss me out, but she did *smack* me like eight times," Mark grunted, rubbing the back of his head.

Josh laughed. "She didn't smack you *eight* times, you always lying."

"Okay, like *twice*," Mark corrected. "*Your* mom was on some gangsta shit Jase," he joked.

Jason couldn't help but shake his head in amusement as he recalled the interaction with his parents, who had driven to campus after the incident. "Yeah, knowing how mad I was and the fact that Chasity was hurt...she was going *off*," he said. "Between her and Ms. Trisha—pray for me and Chaz when we get married y'all. Those women are crazy."

Josh chuckled, then sighed. "I'm just glad he's off the street...it's finally over."

"Yeah," Mark muttered. "Now I done got mad all over again. I need a burger, let's go to the caf."

"I gotta go to class," Jason said.

"Fuck that class." Mark laughed. "Sike naw, let me get my ass to class too before I fail and shit."

"Then you'd *really* get smacked eight times," Josh teased.

"More like *ten* and all my shit thrown on the curb," Mark chuckled, walking off.


Chasity sat on the couch and slid down to the floor in dramatic fashion, inciting a laugh from both Sidra and Malajia.

"The hell is wrong with you?" Malajia laughed.

"I'm *sick* of this college shit," Chasity complained, stomping her foot on the floor repeatedly. She was already feeling the pressure of her upcoming exams.

"You only have computer classes," Sidra pointed out, leaning over the couch. "They can't be *that* bad."

"They *are*, you former ponytail wearing heffa," Chasity griped, inciting another laugh from Sidra. "I swear to God, they're coming up with all new shit. Half the stuff that's gonna be on the finals, wasn't even *taught* this semester."

"Girl, I hear you," Malajia sympathized. "My business classes are trippin'." She held her hand up. "Team repeats?" she joked.

"Fuck no," Chasity sneered, slowly sitting up. Malajia put her hand down. "This school ain't getting any more of my damn tuition money. I'm out this bitch." She looked down at her clothes, which now had lint on them. "This carpet is fuckin' nasty."

"Blame Alex for that," Malajia said as Chasity stood up from the floor. "She's been dodging her floor duties for the past two weeks."

Sidra frowned in confusion. "No, *you* had floor duties—"

"Sidra, shut up," Malajia cut in; Sidra giggled. "The vacuum broke and I wasn't sweeping *shit*."

Sidra shook her head. She was glad that the banter with Malajia was getting back to normal. She didn't think she'd miss being told to 'shut up', so much.

Chasity rubbed her lower back as she sat back on the couch.

"Your back still bothering you?" Malajia asked, looking at her.

"Only when I do stupid shit, like what I just did," Chasity jeered. The reminder of Tyrone's assault lingered in the manner of soreness for the past couple weeks. "I'm fine though. Wasn't the first time I was slammed into a wall."

"That's not funny," Sidra chided, frowning.

"I'm not laughing," Chasity returned, placing a pillow behind her back.

Sidra shook her head as she and Malajia sat down on the couch. "How long will Tyrone be in jail?" Sidra asked.

"A *long* time," Malajia answered. "He could *die* in there for all I care."

"Agreed," Sidra said. "Have you seen Jackie?"

"Nope," Malajia answered. "Not since she was put in the ambulance the night Tyrone was arrested... I tried to tell her."

"You did, and that's on her that she didn't listen," Sidra said.

Malajia sighed. "Yeah well... I didn't listen *either* when I was involved with him so..." Malajia admitted. She looked at Chasity. "Ms. Trisha call you today? It's almost time for her daily 'check in and threaten you' phone call."

"Shut up," Chasity hissed. "And no...I think she's finally letting up."

"What is she threatening you for?" Sidra asked, curious.

Chasity rolled her eyes. "She keeps telling me that if I keep any more secrets from her, like what happened with Tyrone that winter, that she's gonna barricade me in the house...like I can't break a damn door down," she ground out.

Malajia chuckled. "Yeah, she was *hot* with you when she found out," she recalled. "I'm surprised you even told her what happened *this* time."

Chasity ran a hand through her hair. "I had no *choice*," she said. "I was acting so damn belligerent in the hospital, they called. I *had* to tell her."

"She got here in record time," Malajia recalled. "She must've been going at *least* ninety on the highway."

"God, she was on *twenty*," Chasity added, adjusting her position in her seat. "She was yelling and cussing up a storm. Then she cried for like ten minutes, then got *mad* again and started plotting some criminal shit," she said. "Like some 'I'm breaking into the jail and setting fire to his cell' shit."

Malajia chuckled. "Ms. Trisha ain't no joke."

"She's fuckin' crazy," Chasity added. "Like, she wasn't lying when she said she was on some other shit when she was a teenager."

"Girl, *my* mom told me that when they got that phone call from me that night, that my dad got in the car with one shoe on, holy sweatpants, and no shirt with his jiggly ass stomach," Malajia recalled, amusement in her voice. "He had a bat and a damn weed whacker in the back seat."

"What the hell was he gonna do with the weed whacker?" Sidra laughed.

"Whack Tyrone's balls off," Malajia said.

"Wait, what did your *mom* say to him?" Sidra asked.

"Evelyn's ass was right in the car *with* him, with a bonnet, some flip flops, and her old ass robe on," Malajia said. "They was gonna go tear that block up...which they *would* have done if the van didn't stall."

Chasity laughed. "Was probably mad as shit, sitting in that driveway."

"Girl, my dad was cussin' so loud, he woke the neighbors," Malajia laughed. "Then started kicking the damn van."

Sidra chuckled. "At least they made the effort and even came down the next night," she said. "It's good to know that no matter how old we get, our parents are still there for us, you know."

"Yeah," Malajia smiled. "Never thought how much I'd appreciate them and everyone *else's* damn parents after everything came out... It was nice that they all came down for the day to make sure we were all okay."

"Well, we don't call each other family for nothing," Sidra shrugged.

"Even David's dad, who hardly ever gets mad...like *ever*, was steaming," Malajia said.

Chasity shook her head. "I couldn't focus on anything he was saying. I just kept staring at his glasses...them things are thick as shit, yo," she joked.

Sidra playfully threw a throw pillow at Chasity. "You stop that," she laughed. "He can't afford to shave the lenses down."

"Shit, *I'll* pay for it," Chasity laughed. "Eyes were big as shit."

Malajia cracked up laughing, "I'm telling David you in here talking about his dad."

"Shit, *he* knows it's true," Chasity threw back.

Emily tapped her pen against her notebook as she reached for her cup of soda. Taking a sip, she coughed as some of the cola went down the wrong pipe.

"You okay, over there?" Alex called from behind the counter.

Emily patted her chest as she reached for a napkin. "Yeah, I'm fine," she assured, cough subsiding. Feeling restless and needing a change of scenery from the four walls of her bedroom, Emily had decided to meet Alex at work and wait for her to get off.

Alex grabbed a cup of water and headed over to Emily's table. "You sure?" she pressed, taking a seat across from her in the booth.

Emily nodded. "Yeah, stupid soda went down the wrong pipe."

Alex winced. "Ugh, I hate when that happens," she sympathized. She folded her arms on the table as she studied Emily. She looked troubled. "You okay?"

Emily flipped a page in her notebook. She was finding it hard to concentrate on her homework assignment. "Um...just a little antsy."

Alex nodded. "Finals?" she assumed. "Yeah, I'm on edge myself."

Emily wrote something in her notebook. "No, I'm actually not stressed over finals this time around," she said. "Which is surprising."

Alex frowned in concern. "Well then, what *is* it?"

Emily looked up, sighing. "The principle from Paradise Valley Elementary School wants to have a meeting with me," she revealed.

"Really?"

"Yeah...she left a message yesterday," Emily added. "I have *yet* to return the phone call."

"How come?" Alex wondered.

"Because I'm nervous," Emily admitted. "My assignment ended over a month ago. I just figured that she would just give my grade to my professor and be done with it... What could she *possibly* want to talk about?"

Alex tilted her head. "Well sweetie, you'll never know if

you don't return the phone call," she pointed out. "What do you have to be nervous about?"

"Maybe they realized that my teaching methods suck and all the kids failed their tests and they want to yell at me about it," Emily sulked.

Alex couldn't help but chuckle at Emily's dramatic response. "Come on Em, you know that's not true." Emily rolled her eyes. "You said yourself, you enjoyed working there and everybody told you that you did an amazing job… Stop doubting yourself and return the phone call."

Emily sighed as she ran her hand over her hair. "I'll get up the nerve eventually," she promised. Glancing up at the restaurant entrance, a bright smile appeared on her face.

Alex turned around to see what had made Emily so happy. "Ahhh, makes sense," she teased, seeing Will walk in, holding Anthony's hand. "Hey Will."

"Hey Alex," Will greeted, making his way over to the booth.

"Hi Anthony," Alex cooed at the smiling little boy. "Do you remember my name, cutie?"

Anthony glanced up at his dad before looking back at Alex. "Alice," he blurted out, much to Alex's confusion.

Emily put her hand over her face and busted out laughing; Will shook his head in amusement.

Alex slowly turned and faced Emily, folding her arms. "Really? *Alice?*" she spat.

Emily put her hand up as she tried to control her laughter. "I swear to God, I didn't teach him that," she promised. "Chasity told him that was your name the last time he was over at the house."

Alex shook her head. "I'm gonna *kill* her," she muttered, standing up. "You guys want anything?" she asked Will, who had sat down in Alex's place.

"Nothing for me thanks, but can I get a kid's order of breadsticks for my little man?" he replied.

"Sure thing," Alex smiled at Anthony. "My name is *Alex*, cutie pie," she cooed.

"Alice," Anthony repeated, innocent. Alex shook her head as Emily snickered again.

"Yeah, I'mma kill that devil," Alex promised, walking off.

Will chuckled. "Starting trouble already huh?" he said to Anthony, who began playing with a piece of balled up notebook paper.

"Aww, he's innocent," Emily smiled, ripping another piece of paper from her book and balling it up.

Will stared at her with adoration as he watched her hand the paper ball to the amused Anthony. "How are you doing?" he asked her.

Emily smiled at Anthony as he played with the paper. "I'm okay," she returned. "Things are finally getting back to normal after all of the craziness."

"You know, I wish you would have told me about that then," Will said. "I could have helped... I feel bad for what your friends went through."

Emily looked at him. She recalled the shock that had been frozen on Will's face once she finally told him what had her practically MIA for over a week. She had regretted not filling him in sooner. "I know, and I'm sorry... I just didn't think that you needed to be involved. You have your son to look out for."

"And I always *will* but that doesn't mean that I can't look out for *you too*," he pointed out.

Emily blushed as she glanced down at the table. "Noted," she said.

Will reached over and patted her hand. "Glad everything is okay now," he said. He glanced at Anthony playing. "So um...since you're a teacher and all, would you mind teaching Anthony a few things?" he asked, changing the subject.

Emily looked up at him.

"I mean, I know he's only *two* but—"

"It's not too early for him to learn things," Emily assured. "*Sure*, I can."

Will smiled, grateful. "Thanks," he said. "With me

working so much, I don't get to go over things with him as much as I should, and—"

"Will, you don't have to explain, I'll be happy to do it," Emily interrupted as she moved her cup of soda out of Anthony's reach. "I can even put together some lesson plans that you can have for when I leave after graduation. That way you can keep up with it."

The smile left Will's face. The last thing that he wanted to think about was Emily leaving Virginia. He knew that graduation was inevitable for her, but Will was keeping it out of his mind for as long as possible. He didn't want to think about not seeing Emily again.

"Yeah," he muttered.

"Something wrong?" Emily asked, noticing his sudden change in demeanor.

"No, nothing's wrong," he deflected. "Hey, I know I keep mentioning this, but I still wanna cook you dinner."

She smiled at him.

"I mean…not *now* 'cause I don't have good pots yet," Will amended; Emily laughed. "But I'mma get them before you graduate, and *then* cook you dinner."

"Okay, sounds good," she chortled.

"Great," Will beamed. He looked over and saw Anthony rip another piece of paper from Emily's book. He tossed his hands up. "Dude!"

# Chapter 41

David pushed his glasses up on his nose as he walked towards the library. He glanced at his watch and let out a sigh. His class had run over due to finals review. Now, he was late to meet his friends at the library.

"Hope they were able to get a private room," he muttered to himself. Glancing up, he locked eyes with Nicole, who was walking in his direction. *Great*, he thought.

Nicole stopped in front of him. "Hey," she said. "In a hurry?"

"*Kind* of. Study group," he answered.

Nicole adjusted her book bag. "Yeah finals week," she chuckled. David glanced at his watch again. "Um…I haven't seen much of you."

"You've seen me," David contradicted.

"I know but not *much*," Nicole reiterated. "I've been worried about you… Especially over the past couple weeks. It's like you were always tied up."

David ran his hand over the top of his head. "Yeah, sorry… I was dealing with a serious matter… I didn't have time to really spend with you."

Nicole frowned. "You didn't have *time* for me, but yet I saw you around campus practically joined at the hip with your *friends*," she bit out. "I mean walking to class with them, to eat, the library… You were barely in your room, you barely answered your *phone*… So you had time for them but not for *me*?"

"Nicole, the serious matter had to do *with* my friends and

I needed to be there for them," David argued. "It's over now but at the time it was serious."

"Well what *was* it? Was anybody in danger?" Nicole's eyes widened. "Oh shoot, did it have anything to do with what happened in the Science building a few weeks ago? I heard about the incident but...no names were given."

"You don't need to concern yourself with it," he ground out. "Everything is fine now. I have to go."

Nicole spun around to meet David's departing back. "David...if something was going on, why didn't you tell me? You don't think that I had a right to know?"

David stopped walking and faced her again. "It wasn't my place to tell you... I'm not the type of person to tell people's business."

Nicole stared at him as a realization set in. "You're still mad at me for telling *your* business," she concluded. David looked away. "*That's* why you've been distant, even *now*."

"What do you want me to say Nicole?" David knew that Nicole was right. Add in the fact that she had been hanging around Quincy more and more, and it all had David on edge. He had tried to forget about it, but he couldn't. He'd managed to put it in the back of his mind while dealing with the Tyrone drama. But now that that was over, David's ill feelings for his girlfriend had resurfaced.

Nicole tossed her hands up and let out a sigh. "I *said* that I was sorry," she pouted. "He didn't even *tell* anybody—"

"That's not good enough, Nicole," David spat out. "It's bad enough that you keep talking to your ex, *whatever* he was to you—"

Nicole was taken aback. Never had she seen David so upset before. "So this is about me talking to Quincy?"

"This is about you telling *Quincy* my damn personal business," David barked.

"David, I get that you're angry okay. But I seem to think that if I told this to one of my girlfriends and not *him*, that you wouldn't be so mad."

"I would *still* be mad," David hissed. "But yes, the fact

that this guy knows my business is taking my anger with you to another level."

"Don't be insecure," Nicole spat.

"*Excuse* me?"

"So *what* I used to sleep with Quincy? We're not sleeping together *now*. He was my friend *before* you and he'll be my friend *after* you. So I'll *continue* to talk to him about whatever I *want*," she hurled. "You don't like it, then don't date me. You don't like the fact that people know you're a virgin then how about you *screw* me, so you'll no longer *be* one."

David narrowed his eyes at Nicole, then shook his head. "Yeah, *that's* mature," he spat out.

Nicole let out a sigh as David walked away. "David, I'm sorry."

"Forget it," he threw over his shoulder as he continued on.

Nicole let out a huff and stormed off in the other direction.


David had not calmed down when he walked into the private study room within the library. He sighed loudly as he flopped down in one of the empty chairs.

"What's wrong David?" Alex asked, looking up from her textbook.

"Yeah, you flopped down hard as shit in that chair…you *know* you hurt yourself," Malajia chuckled, writing something on her paper.

David rubbed his leg. "No, I'm fine," he sulked.

Malajia got close to his face, studying him. David looked at her, perplexed.

"Why are you all up in his damn face?" Chasity wondered, both confused and amused. "Breathing all on his damn neck and shit."

Malajia shot her a glance. "You want me to breathe on *yours*?"

"I told you about being gross," Chasity ground out, pointing her pencil in Malajia's direction. Malajia giggled, adjusting herself in her seat.

"You don't *look* fine, brother," Malajia concluded, folding her arms on the tabletop. "You might as well spill it." David let out a sigh.

"You a straight A nerd, so we know that you ain't fail no test," Malajia said, tapping her chin with her finger. "Did Quincy say something to you again?"

"No," David muttered.

"Wait David, you had words with Quincy before?" Alex charged.

"Alex, shut up, we tryna get the scoop," Malajia quickly cut in, waving her hand in Alex's direction. "So, was it Nicole?"

"I don't wanna talk about it right now," David bit out, grabbing a textbook from his book bag. "I need to go over these notes."

Malajia snapped her fingers, ignoring David's request. "Ooh, are you mad 'cause Quincy had his arm around her the other day?"

"What?" David replied, shocked. "He had his arm around her?"

Malajia winced. "I guess you didn't know about that, huh?"

David slammed his book on the table. "And she got a freakin' nerve to question why I have a damn issue," he mumbled, then stood up and left.

Alex shot Malajia a venomous glance as David shut the door behind him. "Mel, really?"

"What? It ain't *new*, she's *always* hanging around him," Malajia defended. "*Clearly* he had an argument with her, by the look on his face… She prolli rubbing grease on Q's bald head after he shower and shit."

Alex smacked her hand against her face. "Malajia—I just can't, with you." She shook her head. "Look, couples argue all the time," she said. "It's probably not that serious."

2

"No, I think David still feels some kind of way about what Nicole did," Chasity put out, adjusting herself in her seat.

"Well, besides her refusal to stop hanging with Quincy, what else did she *do*?" Alex pressed.

"She told Quincy that David is a virgin," Malajia informed, to which Alex's mouth fell open.

"Wait, David is a *virgin?*" Alex questioned, unsure if she heard correctly.

"You late as shit, Alex," Chasity snapped. "Just stop talking from now on."

Alex tossed a balled-up piece of paper at her.

"Nicole is trippin' with that Q shit," Malajia griped. "In all seriousness, it's really bothering David and she act like she don't care."

"I guess her issue is, Quincy was her friend before David came along," Alex cut in. "So Nicole doesn't feel like she should change her behavior, even though she's in a new relationship."

"I thought I told you to stop talking," Chasity spat out, inciting a snicker from Malajia.

"Chasity, I swear to God, I'm about to smack you," Alex warned, pointing.

"You're not but how-muthafuckin-*ever*," Chasity dismissed getting back to the subject. "She needs to respect her damn relationship and stop telling her man's business to someone he's not comfortable with…simple bitch."

"Chasity, I'm not disagreeing with you," Alex assured, putting her hand up. "But until she *really* stops to think about how what she's doing is affecting her boyfriend, she's not going to see anything wrong."

Malajia stared at Alex. "You know what, I take back everything I said about you being nosey all these years—we need the *old* Alex back," she griped, shaking her hand in Alex's direction.

Alex tossed her hands in the air. "God, I swear I can't win."

"Nope, you need to go to Nicole and pull a 'Will'," Malajia harped.

Chasity chuckled. "Really, 'a Will'? That's a thing?"

"Yup. Anytime somebody goes and gives someone's significant other, a nosey ass talking to, it's a 'Will'," Malajia explained. "So, are we doing a 'Will'?"

"No, I don't think that a 'Will' would work in this situation," Chasity said. "We'll have to try something else."

Alex tossed her hands in the air. "I don't want you two to make this a *thing*," she huffed.

"I feel you," Malajia added, ignoring Alex. "What Alex did was *way* beyond overstepping, and deserved more than a slap and some water being thrown in her face."

"I'm sitting right *here!*" Alex wailed, annoyed.

"Alex, shut your loud ass up," Chasity hissed. "We're in the library. Don't get me kicked out, I'm trying to study."

"Whatever Chasity. Stop acting like you haven't been kicked out of the library for being loud before," Alex huffed.

Chasity looked confused as Malajia raised her hand. "No, that was *me*," she admitted. "But that was *only* because Mark tried to steal the cookies I was hiding."

Alex stared at Malajia for several seconds before shaking her head. "Anyway," she began. "You guys are talking crap about *me* overstepping. Lest you forget, *I'm* not the one talking about talking to David's girlfriend, *you two* are."

"Lest *you* forget—you can get the fuck up and walk away if you want no part," Chasity huffed.

"I know right? Fuckin' up the plans and shit," Malajia threw in, waving her hand at Alex.

Alex rolled her eyes as she tossed her hands up in the air. As much as she was trying to keep her nose out of other people's business, David was like a brother to her. Him being upset didn't sit right with her. Her interest was peaked. "What do you have planned?"

Chasity thought for a moment. "I don't know yet."

Malajia sucked her teeth. "Bitch, you got me all hype for

some evilness and you ain't *got* shit?" she snapped.

"No wait, I got it, and Malajia, shut up," Chasity spat out.

Malajia snickered.

"So what? You wanna ambush her? Threaten her? Talk to her, what?" Alex wondered.

Chasity shook her head. "None of the above," she vaguely replied. "Just...make her understand how David feels...but be *extra* with it."

Malajia was intrigued. She slowly rubbed her hands together. "Sounds sneaky and bitchy," she smiled. "I'm in, *whatever* it is."

Alex rubbed her forehead with her hand. "You two are gonna give me heartburn," she sighed. Chasity and Malajia both shot her confused glances.

"The fuck does that have to do—"

"Chasity, just shut up, I know it didn't make any sense," Alex spat. She was about to say something else, when the door to the room opened. "Em, Chasity and Malajia wanna teach David's girlfriend a lesson, you wanna join in?"

Emily, who paused midway through entering, stared blankly. She knew that she was late getting to their study group, she expected to miss some conversation, but she didn't know exactly *how* much. "Um...what is she doing *now*?"

"She's hanging around her ex too much and she told his basketball-sized head ass that David was a virgin," Malajia answered. "And she don't get why David is mad."

Emily's mouth fell open. "Wait, *huh*?"

"Emily, you asking too many damn questions. Never mind, you out the plans," Malajia snapped.

Emily looked baffled as she slowly backed out of the room and closed the door.

This time Malajia looked confused. "Did she just really leave back out?" she asked.

Alex chuckled. "She wants no part of your nonsense, and I don't blame her."

Malajia tossed her hands in the air. "Damn, we're only teaching a *lesson*. We not going full on 'Alex'," she ground out.

"Come on!" Alex erupted, jumping up from her seat. "Damn, was I *that* bad?"

"You already *know* you were, sitcho' ass down," Chasity demanded, pointing to the chair that Alex jumped up from.

Alex rolled her eyes and flopped back down. "Whatever," she mumbled.

"She got yelled at and shit," Malajia teased of Alex, who just sat there playing in her hair.

Nicole stood outside of the English building as she glanced at her watch. *Where are you David?* She wondered. She had been waiting on David for the past ten minutes to get out of his class, hoping to catch him before he went to his next class. She hadn't spoken to him since their little spat the day before, and she just wanted to get past it.

Glancing up as the door opened, she saw Malajia and Chasity walk out. As the girls headed down the steps, Nicole managed a smile. "Hi girls."

Malajia forced a smile back; Chasity's face was void of any smile. "Hey Nicole," Malajia said, clutching her books to her chest.

"Did you two see David come out of his class by any chance?" Nicole asked.

Chasity and Malajia glanced at each other. "Yeah, we saw him," Chasity answered.

"Yeah, he should be out soon," Malajia added. "We were just having a conversation about relationships and shit."

Nicole shifted her weight from one foot to the other. "Oh?" she replied.

"Yeah, he just wanted some advice on some personal stuff," Chasity goaded, pushing some of her hair behind her ear.

"You mean you haven't talked to him?" Malajia asked,

eyes wide.

"No, I haven't," Nicole sputtered. "I think he's—" she sighed. "Um, *personal* stuff?" she zoned in.

Chasity nodded. "Yeah, he just wanted some advice on sex, *that* kind of stuff."

Malajia slowly shifted her gaze to Chasity as she spoke. While they had discussed their plan that morning, they didn't have any exact details on what they were going to say to Nicole once they saw her. Malajia was intrigued as to where Chasity was taking the conversation.

Nicole frowned, confused. "Advice on *sex*?" she questioned. "I mean, um… Why would he ask *you two* about sex?"

"He just wanted to know if you might like some of the things that he's done in the past, that's all," Chasity said, nonchalant.

Nicole looked confused. "What do you mean, things that he's done in the past?" she asked. "I thought he was a virgin."

"Oh, he *is*," Malajia assured.

"He never had actual sex," Chasity confirmed; she paused. "I let him go down on me once though—"

Malajia began coughing as she nearly choked on her own saliva. That completely took her by surprise. "You bitch," she coughed to Chasity as Nicole's eyes widened in shock.

"He *what*?!" Nicole fumed. "He went—he *what*? Oh my God, don't you have a boyfriend?!"

"Yeah," Chasity confirmed, calm. "Oh that happened *way* before we got here to school…in like eleventh grade."

Malajia stared at Chasity, mouth open. Chasity glanced at her, making gestures with her eyes. While Nicole put her hands over her face in shock, Malajia nudged Chasity. "Bitch what the hell?" Malajia whispered, angry.

"Shut up and fuckin' contribute," Chasity whispered back through clenched teeth.

Malajia pointed her finger at Chasity in a warning

manner, before looking back at Nicole. "Um yeah—Oh my God Chasity, he went down on *you too?*"

Nicole removed her hand from her face. "*Too?*"

"Yeah, me and David messed around a bit too, before we came here," Malajia sputtered. "I mean, it was innocent… We just played with each other… Like, I jerked him off a little bit and I let him play in my butt with a straw—"

Chasity snickered loudly as she turned away, trying to avoid busting out laughing.

The look of shock never left Nicole's face.

"But that's waaaay behind us now," Malajia assured with a wave of her hand. "Right Chasity?" she looked over and saw that Chasity was laughing silently, with her back turned. "Chasity," Malajia called, nudging her.

"Huh?" Chasity replied, turning around. It was clear that she was laughing so hard that her eyes were tearing up.

"That's all behind us now, right?" Malajia pressed, staring at Chasity.

"Right, right," Chasity agreed, wiping her eyes with her hands. "*Way* behind us. We're just friends now."

"Wait, how can he still—"

"Hang out with us after we let him explore our nether regions?" Malajia finished. Chasity closed her eyes as she fought to contain her laughter. "Chasity, don't you do it, I swear," Malajia warned, as she too tried not to laugh. She knew that as soon as Chasity started her high-pitched laugh, that she too would break and laugh.

Nicole just stood there, horrified.

"I mean, what's the problem Nicole?" Chasity goaded. "We were friends *way* before he started dating *you*, so it shouldn't be an issue, right?"

Nicole opened her mouth to answer, but could only focus her attention on David as he walked down the steps. He approached the three girls, skepticism on his face.

"Hey…what's going on?" he wondered. Malajia and Chasity never held a conversation with Nicole, not alone anyway. He was curious as to what they could be talking about.

Nicole was too angry to speak; she just stood there glaring daggers at him.

"Um nothing, we gotta go," Chasity quickly put out. "See you later tonight," she added, before giving a confused David a long kiss on his cheek.

"Yeah, see you," Malajia added, giving David a kiss on his other cheek, before giving it a pinch. "You're so cute with your glasses," she cooed. David was already confused, but that was taken to another level when Malajia grabbed his behind and gave it a squeeze.

"Hey!" David exclaimed, moving away from Malajia.

"Nice and firm," Malajia grinned. "Got any straws?" she crooned as she and Chasity walked away.

David followed their progress with his eyes, then turned back to Nicole. "They're acting weird," he said, shaking his head in the process. "Anyway, hi Nicole."

"Why didn't you tell me that you had sexual experiences with Chasity and Malajia?!" Nicole snapped, unable to restrain her anger any longer.

David frowned. "I *what*?!" he wailed.

# Chapter 42

Sidra crossed her legs as she sat on a bench, skimming her homework before class. She was so engrossed in the words on her paper, that she didn't see Josh sit next to her. It wasn't until Sidra lifted her head up that she saw his figure out of her peripheral. Startled, she turned and let out a scream.

Josh dug his finger into his ear as he laughed. "I forgot how loud your scream is," he teased.

She playfully backhanded him. "You scared me."

"Sorry," he said. "You looked like you were focused. I didn't want to disturb you."

"That's okay," she said, setting her notebook on her lap. "How are you doing?"

Josh ran a hand over his head. "I'm good," he answered, "Just tired…had tons of homework and of course studying." He sat back in the seat. "How's your stress level so far?"

Sidra shrugged. "It's fine," she answered. "At this point I think my GPA and overall grades are in pretty good standing, so even if I bomb on my finals, I should still be okay." She chuckled. "Not that I *plan* on bombing."

"Yeah, I don't see that happening either," Josh agreed, amusement in his voice.

Sidra stared at him as they both sat in comfortable silence for a few moments. With things being so crazy lately, she hadn't gotten much one on one time with Josh; she couldn't figure out if that was a good or bad thing.

"So," Josh began, breaking through the silence. "How nervous are you that we'll be leaving soon?"

Sidra thought for a moment. "Pretty nervous," she admitted. "We'll no longer be under the protective umbrella that is this campus, so we'll have to really...*adult*."

Josh chuckled. "I hear you, though some of us have been 'adulting' longer than others."

"True," Sidra sighed. "Do you plan on going to grad school?"

Josh nodded. "*Hell* yeah," he answered. "I watched my family struggle over the years and I know that the more education that I have, the better the job...and I can not only help myself, but them as well."

Sidra stared at him with adoration. "I really admire that about you Josh," she said. "You have a big heart and always look out for everybody in your life... You're such a good person."

Josh blushed. "Thanks...I *try* anyway."

"You don't *try*, you *do*," she insisted. "Do you plan on going to grad school *here*?"

Josh immediately shook his head. "Nah, I think I'm done with Virginia," he said. "I'm looking at this one in Delaware... They allow for some of the classes to be taken online, so I can have a flexible work schedule if need be."

"You plan on still working at the diner while you're in school?"

"No, I hope that my bachelors will get me something *away* from the food industry," he chortled. "I'll just look for a desk job while still working in my dad's shop."

Sidra shifted in her seat. "Josh, I don't see you as a corporate person," she said.

Josh looked taken aback. "Why not?"

She put her hand up. "No sweetie, that's not a bad thing," she assured. "I just see you in a different position." Josh just stared at her. "I mean, you've always liked working with cars, you've been fascinated with them since you were little. Hell, when we were in middle school you used to sit on my front step. Every car that drove past, you could name the make and model."

Josh smiled. "You remember that huh?"

"Of course," Sidra smiled back. "I just think that you should stick to what you love, that's all I'm saying... With your master's in business, you can manage your own car shop. Or just take over your dad's shop for that matter. You can get a business loan, hire mechanics, and really expand it," she advised. "The shop does great work, but imagine how far it can go with a true business mind behind it."

Josh pondered Sidra's words and nodded. "Wow Sid," he gushed. "I'll have to consider that...thanks."

"Sure," she replied.

"Have you narrowed down a law school yet?" he asked her.

"Other than the three I was already looking at, no."

Josh hesitated for a moment. "You still considering the one in California?"

Sidra sighed. "I don't know," she admitted. "I um...I have a lot to think about."

"Well, what does James think about the possibility of you moving to California?" Josh asked, curious.

Sidra smirked. "James doesn't think much of what I plan on doing right about now," she vaguely replied. She had yet to let her friends know about her break up with James. "Which is okay."

Josh looked sympathetic. "Sounds like you guys are fighting again," he assumed. "I hope whatever is going on, that you two can get past it... I just want to see you happy, you know?"

"I know," Sidra said, looking at him. "And James and I aren't fighting." Her response was in fact true. She had accepted that she and James were through, and was no longer mad at him. She wished him well.

"Well, good," Josh said, giving Sidra a pat on the arm.

Sidra stared at him once again as Josh watched the scenery in front of them in silence. *Maybe Mama was right, maybe I should just tell him,* she thought. But how would she begin that conversation? Should she start by coming clean about her break up? Or just ask him if he still had feelings for her? Or should she just come out and tell him *her* feelings? *Just wing it!* As she opened her mouth to speak, Josh started speaking.

"This is off topic, but can I ask you a silly question?" he began.

"Sure."

"Okay so…" he shifted in his seat. "As a woman, would you prefer going out to dinner or being cooked dinner?"

Sidra was taken aback by the question. "Wow, that really *was* off topic," she teased.

"Well, I'm curious," he replied. "Since I'm broke as all hell…for *now* anyway, I can't afford to take anybody to a really nice restaurant. So I just wonder if instead of me trying to play myself and find somewhere cheap, if it would be a better gesture just to cook dinner myself…or *try* to cook at least… What do you think?"

Sidra feigned a smile. She knew that his question was general, but she wished that it was in reference to her. "Honestly Josh, no matter what you do, whether you cook, go on a picnic or to an inexpensive restaurant… As a woman, and knowing the type of man you are, I'd love whatever you decide and would appreciate it," she answered honestly.

"Really?" he asked. "Even someone like *you*?"

Sidra sighed. *Ouch.* "Josh, I *know* I come off as a snob—"

"That's not what I meant," he cut in.

"I know, but it's true," Sidra insisted. "But… Yeah, I *would*." She took a deep breath. "You have someone you're planning on cooking for?" she asked, even though she feared the answer.

Josh shrugged. "I don't know, maybe," he replied. "Still deciding."

Sidra looked down at her hands. *Yeah, I figured.*

Josh glanced at his watch. "Damn, I'm about to be late," he panicked, jumping up from the bench. "Thanks for the talk, and advice."

Sidra managed a smile. "Anytime," she said, watching him hurry off. A feeling of dread came over her. She'd figured her feelings out too late; Josh had moved on from her. "This sucks," Sidra whispered to herself, then went back to going over her homework.

"Yo, will you rack the damn balls?" Mark griped, rubbing chalk on his pool stick. "You stalling like shit."

Jason stared him down as he set his pool stick on the table. "Who are you talking to?" he challenged. "What's stopping *you* from racking the damn balls?"

"I don't know," Mark answered truthfully, shrugging.

Alex chuckled as she leaned over the table. "*I'll* do it," she offered. Taking a little study break, Alex, Jason and Mark decided to pass the time with a game of pool in the SDC game room.

"I'm starving, Alex, why you ain't bring us no food? You fuckin' up," Mark complained as Alex set up the balls.

"I didn't *work* today, greedy," she threw back.

Mark sucked his teeth. "Where's David? He said he was meeting us here."

Jason shrugged, then glanced over at the entrance. "There he is," he announced.

"About time," Mark charged as David walked into the room. The look on David's face made it clear that he was in no mood for nonsense.

David let out a huff and pointed to Jason and Mark. "You two," he spat, much to their confusion.

"What?" Jason questioned.

"Damn you just got here, what we do?" Mark added.

David put his hands up. "Your women are freakin' crazy," he ground out.

"So what *else* is new?" Jason chuckled.

"No seriously," David ranted.

His tone wasn't missed. "What's the problem?" Mark asked.

David grabbed a pool cue from a nearby stand. "Yesterday, they told Nicole this made up story about how I had a sexual experience with them before coming here freshman year."

"Wait *what*?" Jason barked, angry.

"What the fuck would they do *that* for?" Mark asked, equally upset.

"I have *no* freakin' idea," David fussed. "I didn't say anything yesterday because I seriously thought that this was gonna blow over, but Nicole is *pissed* 'cause she thinks I lied to her."

Alex stood there with her hand over her mouth. "Oooooh," she muttered.

Jason looked at her, frowning. "You *knew* about this?" he charged.

Alex put her hand up. "I had no idea that they were gonna do *that*," she assured, backing away. "Um…for the sake of not incriminating my girls, I'm gonna just stay out of this…over there with the arcade games." She continued to slowly back away from the pool table. "David, just know that I had *nothing* to do with this," she said. "I did not pull another 'Will.'"

"What the fuck is a 'Will'?" Jason ground out.

"Y'all making up new words and shit? And ain't tellin' nobody?" Mark added.

Alex laughed nervously. "Nope, gotta go." The guys watched Alex make a hasty departure, hitting her leg on a nearby table in the process. "Damn it!" she wailed, grabbing her leg.

Mark shook his head. "Ole' clumsy ass," he muttered of Alex. He then looked at David. "Look man, on behalf of our simple ass women, we apologize. They're gonna fix this shit, *believe* that."

"Yeah, they've lost their damn minds," Jason cosigned.

David shook his head. "Now Nicole is feeling insecure about me being around them," he complained. "Talking about she can't compete with them, especially since they had something from me that she hasn't." David let out a frustrated sigh. "I already have enough on my damn mind due to finals... Now I have to worry about her possibly never speaking to me again."

"She might be mad *now*, but Mark is right, this *will* get fixed," Jason assured.

David just sighed as he chalked his pool stick.


Chasity and Malajia sat on the couch in their house, quiet as Jason and Mark stood in front of them, visibly irritated. Both men had their arms folded, stern stares held on their faces.

"We heard about your little escapade from yesterday," Mark grunted. He and Jason had left the pool hall earlier than they'd wanted to; this conversation with their girlfriends wasn't something that could wait.

Chasity glanced up. "What escapade are you talking about?" she asked, innocently.

Malajia put her hand up. "I don't know what escapade *means* so...whew," she said, moving her hand over her head. "That went right over *my* head." Both Malajia and Chasity knew that what they did would get back to the guys, but they weren't going to be quick to own up to it.

Jason glanced at Mark. "I don't think that was the right word to use," he said.

"*They know* what I mean," Mark huffed.

"True," Jason agreed, turning back to the girls. "But let me rephrase. We heard about that bullshit story that you told Nicole yesterday," he spat out.

Chasity stared at him. "You seem upset my love," she placated. "You want me to blow you?"

Malajia snickered as Jason narrowed his eyes; he wasn't amused.

"Yeah Mark, you wanna play in my butt with a straw?"
Malajia offered. Chasity too snickered.

"This is *funny* to you both?" Jason hissed.

"No," Chasity and Malajia responded in unison.

"But…we *still* don't know what you're talking about,"
Malajia lied. "*What* story?"

"Yeah, I was studying all day yesterday sooooo…"
Chasity added, shrugging.

"You really gonna stick with that, 'I don't know shit'
story?" Jason grunted.

"Till the wheels fall off," Chasity threw back.

"Yup," Malajia answered.

Jason and Mark were trying their best to remain calm.
"So, y'all gonna sit here and act like you ain't tell Nicole that
y'all messed around with David before?" Mark questioned,
angry.

"We have no recollection of what you are referring to,
you sexy thing," Malajia said to Mark as Chasity shook her
head.

Mark put his hand up. "Malajia, I got kicked out of
accounting class today because I told the professor to shove
his book of debits in his rotten mouth," he barked. "I swear to
God, I am in *no* mood to play with you right now."

Malajia looked confused. "Why would you even *say*
that—"

"In *no* mood!" Mark snapped, clapping his hands.

"Y'all gonna have the whole fuckin' school, thinking
that David was with our women," Jason fumed.

Chasity rolled her eyes. "There is *no* way that these
people on this campus, are gonna believe that bullshit."

"*Nicole* did," Jason pointed out.

"Yeah well, she's simple," Chasity spat.

Malajia raised her hand. "I second that," she said. "And
she ain't gonna say shit *anyway*. She won't further embarrass
herself."

"Oh, what happened to you wouldn't be mad if I had

dealt with someone *before* you?" Chasity threw to Jason when he rolled his eyes. "Your attitude makes you seem like a bit of a liar right now."

Jason fixed Chasity with an angry gaze. His silence spoke volumes. Clearly, he was in no mood for Chasity's deflection, or her smart mouth.

Her eyes shifted. "Malajia told me to say that," Chasity blamed.

Malajia's head snapped towards her. "Huh?!" she exclaimed.

When Jason sucked his teeth, Chasity let out a frustrated sigh. "Do these people *not* remember who the fuck I am? Why would *anybody* believe that I would let David even *talk* to me before I came here," she pointed out. "Hell, I didn't let *you* touch me until a year later."

"Don't get cute Chasity," Jason spat out. "Y'all were wrong for doing that bullshit."

"*Way* wrong," Mark cosigned. "Getting all in that man's business like that. Y'all know that shit was foul. David been trying to convince Nicole that y'all were lying ever since yesterday... Gettin' him in trouble and shit."

"*She* started it," Malajia argued.

Mark stared at her. "Really? *That's* your defense?"

Malajia frowned. "*Yes*, that's my defense, and a damn *good* one. She was playing your boy and *we did* something about it."

"What, are y'all *Alex* now? Sticking your noses where they don't belong?" Jason fussed. "You know better than that, Chasity. You know how *you* feel when people get in *our* business. What's wrong with you?"

Chasity stared at him, lust in her eyes. She couldn't help it, but Jason's anger was turning her on. "You *sure* you don't want me to blow you?" she offered.

"Cut it the fuck out," Jason ranted, pointing at her. "That look isn't gonna let you off the hook this time."

"Mark, I already know I'm on time out, can we just drop this?" Malajia huffed.

"No," Mark spat. "Now whose idea was this?"

Chasity and Malajia glanced at each other, then looked back at the guys. "Alex's," they muttered in unison.

"Nice try," Jason countered.

"She already said she had nothing to do with this, 'cause she was there when David told us what y'all said," Mark added.

Jason fixed his stern gaze upon the women. "*Whose* idea was it?" he drew his question out slowly.

As Malajia sat there quiet, Chasity slowly pointed to Malajia. Malajia, caching the gesture, gave Chasity's hand a hard slap. "What?!" Malajia bellowed.

"Ouch!" Chasity wailed as she grabbed her hand.

"No, no, *no*," Malajia hurled at Chasity, repeatedly flinging her hand in Chasity's direction. "*I* didn't come up with the idea, this was all *her*," she pointed to Chasity. "I didn't even *know* that she was gonna say that David gave her tongue action, she caught *my* ass off guard."

"And you just *had* to follow along with it, huh?" Mark spat at Malajia.

"Hey, *I* was being a good friend and being supportive of Chasity's decision to make Nicole look dumb as shit," Malajia argued, putting her hand over her chest.

"Bitch please, I didn't say *shit* about no straws in your ass," Chasity threw at Malajia. "That was all *you*. You nasty fuck."

"Oh like you've never had anything stuck up your ass before!" Malajia argued.

"What?!" Chasity wailed, annoyed.

"Hey shut up!" Mark boomed, silencing the girls' arguing. "Malajia, don't put this all on Chasity. *You* were the one who grabbed David's ass... Yeah, he told me about that too," he added when Malajia's eyes widened. "What the fuck was *that* all about?"

"Hey, now, damn it... It was a necessary gesture in order to pull our plan off," Malajia sputtered. Seeing that the guys were unconvinced, Malajia folded her arms and sat back in her seat. "I'm not getting none for a while, *am* I?" she asked, looking at Mark.

"Nope," Mark spat. "You better get that porno DVD and get to working that finger."

"Fine, I get myself off faster *anyway*," Malajia mumbled.

"Excuse me?!" Mark barked.

"Nothing," Malajia lied.

"Jason, I'm sorry alright," Chasity said. "But shit, what's done is *done*. What do you want from me?"

"So you're saying I have *no* right to be annoyed with you right now?" Jason asked, angry.

"I didn't *say* that," Chasity pouted. She put her arms out and started whining. "Look, baby you know I'm not right sometimes. But I love you, and *you* love *me* so come hug me. I wanna have your babies."

Malajia put her hand over her face and busted out laughing. "I swear to God, I hate you sometimes," she laughed of Chasity.

Jason rolled his eyes. "I can't deal with you right now," he grunted. "You drive me fuckin' crazy."

Chasity dropped her arms and looked shocked as Jason turned around and headed for the door. "Jason you're *really that* mad at me? You're walking out on me?" she threw at his back. "I'm offering you the chance to impregnate me and you're walking *out*?"

"Shut uuuupppp!" Malajia roared with laughter as she backhanded Chasity on the arm.

"Good night Chasity," Jason spat, slamming the door behind him.

"It's not even *night* time you fuckin' dick," Chasity spat back.

The door swung open. "Say *what*?" Jason barked, sticking his head in, startling her.

"I didn't—"

Mark looked back at Jason. "She said, 'it's not even'—"

"Mark, shut your snitch ass up!" Chasity yelled at Mark

as Jason stared daggers at Chasity. She caught his stare. "I didn't say anything," she lied. Jason just shook his head and headed back out the door, slamming it again.

Mark shook his head. "Y'all better hope David can fix this mess with his girl," he warned. "And y'all *better* apologize to him."

"Fine," Malajia huffed. "I'm sorry."

"I said to *him*," Mark fussed. He then headed for the door. "Malajia, don't call me later either, I mean it. You're on time out."

"I *heard* you," Malajia pouted.

"You get on my damn nerves," Mark grunted, walking out and closing the door.

Malajia looked at Chasity. "We just got our asses handed to us by our damn men," she said after a few seconds of silence. "Ain't this some bullshit?"

Chasity just shook her head.

Malajia, then held her hand out for a high five. "It was so worth it, wasn't it?"

"Yup," Chasity agreed, victoriously hitting Malajia's hand.

"You were really gonna let Jason get you pregnant again?" Malajia chuckled.

"*Fuck* no," Chasity barked.

Malajia laughed.

# Chapter 43

Sitting on the steps outside of the English building, Alex sighed as she looked over the red marks on her essay. "How did I get a C on this paper?" she griped. "Makes no damn sense."

"Talking to yourself, huh? Finals must really be taking its toll," a male voice teased.

Alex glanced up. "Funny Eric," she said.

Eric removed the book bag from his shoulder and sat down on the step next to her. "No really, talking to yourself is a sure sign that you're losing it," he joked.

"No, I think *answering* yourself is," she countered, giving Eric a nudge. Bad paper aside, Alex's mood had quickly flipped at the sight of him. For them to be able to have a conversation without sniping was a relief to her.

"True," Eric chuckled. "So how's it going?"

"Okay," she answered, then showed him her paper. "Not happy about this C."

"You still *passed*," Eric pointed out.

"Yeah I know, but this is *English*, my *major*. I should be pulling A's in *everything*," she sulked.

"Well what was the reason for the C?"

Alex rolled her eyes. "Professor talking about 'too much of your opinion, not enough facts'," she complained, reciting the words written in red ink. "Um, *excuse me* for exercising my right to express how I feel about the topic at hand."

Eric ran his hand along his chin as he hesitated for a moment. "I feel you but um…when they assigned the topic…did they *ask* you for your opinion on it?"

Alex's mouth dropped open. "Ugh…point taken," she huffed.

Eric laughed.

Alex stared at him as he glanced at his watch.

"So…how's everything with *you*?"

Eric looked back at her. "Things are good…ready to graduate in the winter."

Alex looked stunned. "You're not graduating with *us*?"

Eric shook his head. "No, some of my credits from my school in Maryland didn't transfer here, so I'm about two classes behind," he answered. "It's okay though, I already knew that, coming here," he said when Alex held a sympathetic gaze.

"Well, you know what, as long as you graduate, that's all that matters," Alex consoled, placing her hand on his leg.

"Appreciate that, and I know," he smiled.

She removed her hand from his leg. Alex was dying to confirm what Stacey had told her so long ago, but didn't know how to bring it up. She pushed her hair out of her face. "So umm, how does your *girlfriend* feel about you graduating in the winter?"

Eric shot her a knowing look. "You are not subtle at *all*," he chortled; she broke into laughter. "*So* obvious."

"I know, I've been told how transparent I am when it comes to trying to find out information," Alex agreed.

"I'm sure you already know that that girl is my cousin," he said. "She's now friends with your friend Stacey, so I know she told you."

"Yeah, yeah she did," Alex confirmed.

"Cuzzo runs her mouth quite often," Eric chuckled.

"Eric, will you go out to eat with me?" Alex blurted out.

The proposal took Eric by surprise and it showed on his face. "I'm sorry?"

"Will you go out with me?" she repeated. "I mean, I can't afford much but some tacos or something, but…*will* you?"

Eric ran his hand over his head as he contemplated.
"Alex I don't—"

"Just as friends—um *former* friends, or however you feel about me these days," she cut in. "I just want us to talk… I don't want to leave here without—" Alex ran her hands over her hair; she was frazzled. "Eric, I don't know how things with us will end up…I just—I just want a chance to sit down and talk to you… Is that okay?"

Eric pondered Alex's words. He found the gesture to be sincere. He'd spent months trying to get Alex to go out with him with rejection after rejection, and now she was the one to ask him. He looked at her and offered a slight smile. "Sure," Eric said. "Just let me know when."

Alex's smile was big and bright. "Next Friday?"

"Sounds good," he agreed. He stood up and Alex glanced up at him. "Just give me a call when you have a specific time…my number is still the same."

Alex nodded. As Eric walked into the English building, she glanced back at her paper. Suddenly that C meant nothing to her; she could handle it.


"Yoooo, how you feel knowing your homeboy bagged your girl a long time ago?" Quincy goaded Mark as he dribbled the ball around him.

Mark folded his arms as he watched Quincy make a basket. "You hype as shit doing all that and I'm not even playing anymore," he sneered. "*And* you hype as shit tryna tease me about some shit that ain't even *true*."

Quincy grabbed the ball from the floor and walked back over to Mark. "What do you mean it ain't true?"

"What I *said*, dickhead," Mark threw back. "The girls lied about it."

Quincy rubbed the top of his head. "Damn, I just *knew* I had some shit on you," he joked.

"Yeah, yeah. Give me my damn ball so I can go study," Mark said.

Quincy tossed it to Mark. "Nicole is pretty pissed about it," he chuckled. "Your boy is in trouble."

"Don't worry about what trouble *my boy* is in," Mark hissed, shaking his hand in Quincy's direction.

Quincy looked confused. "What's *your* problem?"

Mark opened his mouth to speak, but he realized that this was David's battle to fight, not his. "Nothing yo," he sneered. "I gotta get out of here."

Quincy wiped the sweat from his brow with his t-shirt. "A'ight, go head and change your tampon and I'll see you on the court tomorrow," he jeered at Mark's departing back.

"Your mother, bitch," Mark threw back, walking out the door.


Mark headed into his house and dropped his books on the dining room table. "What you cooking?" he asked as Jason opened the oven.

"French fries and before you ask me, no, you're not getting any," Jason said, closing the oven, interrupting Mark's excitement.

Mark put his arms down. "Fine, don't nobody want those dry ass fries anyway," he griped, flopping down in the chair. He grabbed a book and opened it. "You need to call Chaz and get some 'cause I don't like your damn attitude."

"Already got some," Jason chuckled.

Mark's mouth fell open. "Bro, how you gonna give in? We was supposed to be holding out until David and Nicole work things out."

"I *never* said that shit," Jason threw back, grabbing salt and pepper from the cabinet. "I said I was *annoyed* with her, I didn't promise to withhold anything."

"So, I guess the look *did* wind up working, you wuss," Mark grunted.

Jason nodded emphatically, unfazed by Mark's goading.

Mark slammed his hand on the tabletop. "Damn it! So I been handling my business *solo* for two days for *nothing*?"

he barked.

Jason stared at the spot Mark had just slapped. "Wipe the fuckin' table off," he demanded.

Mark busted out laughing as he opened a notebook. "Shit, I gotta commit now," he said, ignoring Jason's request. "If I give in now, Mel will think I'mma punk, and I can't be havin' that shit. She be disrespectful."

Jason shook his head. "Suit yourself."

David barged through the door and Mark tossed his arm up. "David, you make up with Nicole yet?" Mark charged, eager.

David looked perplexed. "Um no, not yet."

"Whatchu' waitin' on?!" Mark bellowed. "Hurry the fuck up or I'mma start using *your* socks next."

"Come *on*!" Jason barked at Mark, disgusted.

"I *will*, right in David's sock," Mark joked, flipping pages in his book.

"Nasty bastard," Jason grunted, grabbing a plate from the cabinet.

The look of confusion never left David's face as he slowly sat down at the table. "Anyway, I *did* talk to her, told her that the story was a lie... Then Nicole told me that she told Quincy," he spat.

"Uhh yeah, he was tryna come at my neck about it while we were playing ball," Mark said. "I told him it was a lie."

David removed his glasses and rubbed his eyes. "That girl don't freakin' get it," David snarled. "I'm *tired* of her running to him for every little damn thing."

Jason removed the fries from the oven and sat them on the counter. "David, you want my advice?" he asked.

"Sure," David sighed.

"You really need to sort this out before you leave," Jason suggested. "'Cause both of them will still be here and I know that makes you uncomfortable. So you two need to either come to an understanding about this, or..."

"Yeah, I know," David sighed, picking up on Jason's thoughts.

"You really wanna break up with her?" Mark asked.

"No, of *course* not," David said, holding his hands on his head. "But what am I gonna do? I can't make her stop talking to him... She made that clear." He sighed again. "Maybe I'm just being insecure."

"May*be*," Jason agreed, to which David's mouth fell open.

Mark chuckled. "Damn Jase, tell him how you *really* feel."

Jason walked to the table and sat down. "Don't take it the wrong way," he said, looking at David. "Now granted, she needs to respect the fact that you don't want her talking to him about your business. You have every right to request that."

David just sat there, listening intently as Jason spoke.

"But man, unless they're messing around, and unless he is trying to disrespect your relationship...do you think it's really okay to ask her to stop being friends with him?" Jason wondered. "How would you feel if Nicole asked you to stop being friends with the girls?"

David thought for a moment then sighed. "I'd never allow that," he admitted.

"Exactly," Jason said.

"Yeah David, I mean Q is a bald-headed jackass—"

David couldn't help but snicker at Mark's words.

"But from what I get from him...even though they had a brief past...he ain't checkin' for Nicole like that," Mark said. "They been friends for years, *before* they even came here."

"Either you trust her or...let her be," Jason added.

David rubbed his eyes once again. "I hear you."

"Umm, whatever decision you make bro...can you get some first?" Mark teased. Jason busted out laughing as David shot Mark a glare.

"Really?" David sneered.

"I'm saying, a hand job or *something*," Mark stressed. "I'm just lookin' out for you, you too damn *old*."

"I hate you sometimes," David hissed, flipping Mark off.

Mark just laughed.

"I can't believe you girls really did that," Sidra said, cutting up an apple. "How mad is he?"

"I don't know," Chasity grunted, opening her bottle of juice. "He didn't sound too mad over the phone."

"Shit, *Mark's* probably more mad than David and shit," Malajia griped. "Holding out on me and shit...*me*." She pointed to herself. "His dumb ass resisting all this fineness."

Sidra shook her head and chuckled. "Well maybe *next* time you'll think twice before you pull an 'Alex'," she teased.

Malajia made a face. "Nobody asked you."

Sidra shook her head. "Look, bright side; David is probably the easiest to win over out of the four of them, so you should have no problem getting him to forgive you," she said.

Chasity stared for a moment. "Is it rude that I really don't give a fuck if he does or *not*?" she jeered.

"Yes, yes it is," Sidra said.

"Just checking," Chasity muttered.

Malajia snatched open the fridge. "David need to bring his ass on so we can get this over with." As if right on cue, a knock sounded at the door. Malajia darted over and opened it, smiling as David walked in. "Thanks for coming."

"Sure," David said.

Sidra took a seat at the dining room table and began eating her apple.

Chasity gestured for David to sit on the couch as she glanced at Sidra. "Just gonna sit right there huh?"

"Yup," Sidra confirmed, chewing.

David sat on the couch; Chasity and Malajia sat on the chairs across from him.

"So look, we called you over here, because we were told to apologize—" Chasity's words were interrupted by Malajia nudging her. "We *wanted* to apologize," she amended.

"Yeah, we didn't mean to cause problems between you and Nicole," Malajia added. "We were just trying to help."

"Trying to help *what* exactly?" David asked.

Malajia took a deep breath. "We didn't like the fact that Nicole was disregarding your feelings by doing what she was doing," she explained. "We just felt that maybe if she knew how you felt...then maybe she would stop?" she looked to Chasity for help; she felt her explanation didn't make sense.

"Yeah, I don't know what you were trying to say," Chasity jeered, shaking her head. Malajia sucked her teeth.

David leaned forward. "I know what you meant Malajia," he assured. "I appreciate that you girls were trying to look out for me...but that was a bit much."

"We know that we went overboard, and we're sorry," Chasity said. "In my defense, I didn't think that she would actually *believe* that shit... Hell, why would *anybody*?"

David looked offended when Chasity started laughing.

Chasity stopped. "Yeah I didn't mean it like—dude you forgiving us or *not*?"

Malajia smacked her face with her palm. "A little more remorse, a little less bitch, okay?" she chided.

"Fine," Chasity huffed. She looked at David and smiled her biggest phoniest smile. "David, will you find it in your near-sighted heart to forgive myself and my friend for our role in creating a rift between you and your girlfriend?"

Malajia joined in by plastering a huge smile on her face. "And will you forgive me for squeezing your butt cheeks?"

Sidra nearly choked on the apple that she was eating. They had left that part out of the story when they told it to her.

David shook his head as he tried hard to keep from laughing. "You two drive me nuts, you know that?" he said. Chasity and Malajia both stared at him, eyes hopeful. "Yes, I forgive you," he said, standing up. "Just *please* don't do anything like this again."

"Yeah, you don't have to worry, I'm hanging up my 'Alex' mop," Chasity assured, standing from the couch.

Malajia busted out laughing. "You said 'mop'."

Sidra tried not to laugh. "Really Chasity?"

"What? So now everybody wanna act like she hasn't been called a 'mop' before?" Chasity griped.

David chuckled as he held his arms out. "Give me hugs," he said. Both girls obliged. "I'll put in a good word for you both, with the fellas," he promised, walking to the door.

"Fuck them," Chasity muttered.

"No fuck *yours,* at least *yours* is still giving you some," Malajia cut in, shaking her hand in Chasity's direction. She turned to David. "Go ahead David, put in *all* the words you need to."

"You got it," David laughed, walking out.

Malajia snapped her head toward Chasity. "You almost fucked up the apology with your ignorant ass mouth," she hurled, pointing.

"Hey, hey! I have a fuckin' final at eight in the damn morning tomorrow, I don't have *time* for this shit," Chasity threw back.

"Girl, tell me about it," Sidra chimed in. "I'm team eight o'clock class too."

"I can't believe I'm this stressed out," Chasity complained, running her hand through her hair. "I'm about to pull my fuckin' hair out."

Malajia stared at her. "If you do, can I have it?" she asked.

Sidra busted out laughing at the irritated look on Chasity's face.

Emily fidgeted with the rings on her fingers as she focused on the silver apple trophy sitting on the desk in front of her. As the door opened, Emily took a long, deep breath. After getting through one of her finals that morning, the last thing that Emily wanted to be doing was sitting in the principal's office at Paradise Valley Elementary.

"Hi Emily," the female voice beamed, entering the room.

Emily rose from her seat and shook her hand. "Hi Mrs. Washington," she said.

The principal smiled and waved a hand at her. "I've told you before, you can call me Breanne," she offered, sitting behind her desk. "We're informal around here."

"Yes, I remember now," Emily replied.

Breanne shuffled some papers around on her desk. "So how is everything going?"

Emily rubbed the back of her neck. "Pretty good," she answered. "I have finals this week, so been busy."

"Ah yes, then graduation," she beamed.

Emily nodded. "Yeah, in two weeks actually."

"Exciting," she said. Emily just smiled. "I appreciate you taking the time out of your busy schedule to meet with me."

"I'm sorry that it took so long for me to return your phone call," Emily said.

"That's okay, I know how hectic college course work is," Breanne replied. "I'm sure you're wondering why I wanted to see you."

Emily shifted in her seat. "Kind of," she admitted. Emily might have seemed coy and calm, but on the inside she was freaking out. *Oh God! Is she gonna take back my A? Did a child fail a test because of my lesson plan? What does she want?*

"When you were here during your student teaching assignment, you did a wonderful job," Breanne gushed. "The children loved you, *Olivia* loved you—you made the children excited to learn, which is what we love. And *you* seemed to really love working here."

Emily's smile could have lit the entire school. "Thank you," she replied, grateful. "I admit that I was nervous the entire time but—I really *did* love working here. I always wanted to be a teacher, but until I did *this*, I didn't believe that I could do it... Now, I know I *can*."

Breanne nodded. "*I* know you can as well," she smiled. "What are your plans after graduation?"

Emily thought for a moment. "Not sure really," she admitted. "I mean, of course I'll get my certification and look for a teaching job. But just not sure where, you know?" Breanne nodded again as she refrained from speaking right away. Something that made Emily nervous.

"Emily...how would you feel about staying here in Paradise Valley after you graduate?" she asked.

Emily looked confused. "Umm, I haven't thought about that," she answered. "I mean, I like it here, but unless I had a job offer, I don't see why I *would*."

"Well...consider this your job offer."

Emily's eyes widened. "Excuse me?" She wasn't sure if she heard correctly.

Breanne chuckled. "I would like to offer you a job teaching here at Paradise Valley Elementary after you graduate," she clarified. Emily was speechless. "Olivia is moving out of the state with her husband at the end of this semester, and we couldn't think of a better person to take over her class."

"Wait," Emily put her hand up as she caught her breath. "You want to offer *me* a job?"

"Yes," the principal confirmed. "We will pay for your certification, and should you pass, which I know you will...the position will start in September." She folded her arms on her desk. "Would that be something that you would be interested in?"

Emily felt that she could jump out of her seat and hug the middle-aged woman in front of her. But a wave of nervousness hit her. If she stayed in Virginia, she would have no family here. Her friends were leaving upon graduation, how would Emily handle truly being on her own?

"Umm, as much as I appreciate the offer and as much as I would love to work here I—" Emily took a deep breath. "I just need to consider some things... Can I think about it?"

"Absolutely," Breanne smiled. "Take all the time you need. Just know that should you decide to join us, you would be a welcome addition to our family."

"Thank you so much," Emily smiled, grabbing her book bag from the floor. She stood up and Breanne rose from her desk and extended her hand.

"If you have any questions or concerns, please don't hesitate to contact me," she offered.

Emily shook her hand. "I'll be in touch," she promised.

Upon leaving the office, Emily closed the door behind her and leaned her back against it. She needed a moment to take everything in.

"Oh my God," she whispered to herself as both excitement and worry took over her.


Sidra cradled her phone to her ear as she flipped through pages in her textbook. "No Mama, I haven't told him," she said into the line. "I don't know I—" she let out a sigh and rolled her eyes. It seemed like Sidra couldn't speak to her mother lately without the woman bringing up her feelings for Josh. She almost regretted telling her. "Mama—yes I know—" She let out a quick sigh, grabbed her textbook, and stood up from the table. "Listen, I have to get to my final... Yes, I'll call you later."

Ending her call, she jumped when Mark barged through the door. "What the hell?!" she screeched.

"My bad, is Malajia in her room?" Mark panted, shutting the door.

"Yeah, what's wrong?" Sidra asked, frowning.

"I'm fuckin' horny and stressed out," Mark answered, heading for the steps.

Sidra's face took on a disgusted look. "Eww, you could've kept that to yourself," she grimaced, grabbing her travel cup of coffee from the table.

"*You asked* me," Mark pointed out as Sidra headed for the door.

"Don't remind me," she returned, walking out.

Mark darted up the steps. "Boo boo!" he yelled.

"What?!" Malajia yelled from her room.

"Get naked!"

Malajia snatched open the door to find him standing in front of it. "What?" she repeated.

Mark took off his shirt. "Come on, I got like twenty minutes before I go take this damn final."

Malajia slowly folded her arms. "Oh what? David made up with Nicole?" she hissed.

Mark frowned. "What? Fuck them, I don't care no more," he dismissed, waving his hand. He grabbed her arm and tried to pull her close. "I'm done holding out."

Malajia moved her arm from his loose grip. "That's nice, but now *I* feel like holding out."

Mark once again frowned. "For *what*?"

"'Cause I *feel* like it," she ground out, folding her arms. "You don't hold out on me for three days and think there won't be any damn consequences."

Mark's mouth fell open. "You really gonna be petty?"

"Yup," Malajia maintained. "Now go away, I gotta go study."

"Well…when you gonna be ready?" he pouted.

"I don't fuckin' know," she barked, then pointed downstairs. "Go."

Mark opened his mouth to protest, but was distracted by Chasity's door opening. She pulled her phone from her ear, and took one look at Mark's shirtless body and turned her lip up.

"Ugh," Chasity scoffed, heading for the steps.

Mark smirked. "Hey Chaz, can I borrow one of your socks?"

Chasity stared at him as she headed for the steps. She then put her phone back to her ear. "Jason, Mark just asked to jerk off in my socks," she quickly told, then ran down the stairs with Mark quickly leaning over the banister.

"Fuck you, you snitch!" he yelled after her.

"Jason, Mark just called me a bitch." Chasity lied, shutting the front door behind her.

"No I didn't! Why you lyin?!" Mark yelled, kicking the banister. He put his shirt on, then looked at Malajia, who was still standing in her doorway. "Baby—" The look on her face told him that he better not dare say another word. He sighed as he headed down the steps. "You know, how is it that *I'm* in trouble now when *you* messed up first? This is some bullshit," he spat.

Malajia shook her head. "Are you done?" she mocked.

"Yeah, I guess," he grunted.

Malajia leaned over her banister as she watched him walk to the front door. She broke into silent laughter when she heard him bump into something.

"Damn it! I hit my knuckle!" he barked.

Malajia pushed her hair behind her ear as her laughter subsided. "Mark," she called.

"Huh?"

"Bring your dramatic, clumsy ass up these steps before I change my mind," she teased. She barely got the words out before Mark darted up the steps, a smile plastered to his face. She shook her head. "You get on my damn nerves," she said, walking into the room, with Mark close behind.

# Chapter 44

David grabbed his head and let out a deep sigh after handing in his Physics final. *Thank God this is over. One more to go*, he thought, standing up from his seat. He glanced around the empty classroom; he was the last student remaining. *Hmm, that's a first*, he thought, amused.

He moseyed out of the classroom and down the hallway, towards the exit. He chuckled to himself as he watched many of his stressed and tired fellow seniors make their way through campus.

Seeing Chasity and Jason approach along his path, he waved slightly. "Hey guys."

"Don't talk to me!" Chasity barked; David was taken aback.

Jason put a hand up, touching Chasity's shoulder with the other. "Don't worry about it, it's stress," he chortled of Chasity. "She's on her way to her last final."

"Oh," David nodded.

"The fuck you nodding for?" Chasity hissed, causing Jason to snicker as David just shook his head.

"Hey chill out, it's almost over," Jason ordered, guiding her in the direction of the Science building. "We'll catch you later, man," he threw over his shoulder at David as they continued on.

David kept walking. Hearing Mark's loud voice behind him, he spun around.

"Move David, mooooovvve!" Mark yelled, sending

David darting out of the way.

"What's wrong?!" David hurled at his departing back, perplexed.

"I forgot my calculator, I'm gonna fail like shit without it!" Mark yelled behind him, mid-run.

David straightened his shirt out. Just as he was about to walk again, Malajia ran up and grabbed his arm.

"You see Mark's black ass run past here?" she asked.

"Uh yeah, he said he was going to get his calculator," David answered, scratching his head.

"Fuck! He's going to get *my* damn calculator," Malajia griped, adjusting the strap on her sandal. "*His* broke the other day."

David laughed. "You mean *yours* didn't break?" he teased.

Malajia stood upright and made a face. "Shut up," she hissed. "He play too much, I need it for my *own* shit."

David watched as Malajia took off running. "My friends have officially lost it," he mused, walking yet again.

He made his way to his room and dropped his book bag to the floor. Playing back the message on his answering machine, David smiled as he picked the phone up and dialed a number.

"Hey Dad, just got your message," he said, when the line picked up.

"I figured you would be in class when I called," Mr. Summers said into the line.

David flopped down on his bed. "Yeah," he confirmed. "Just one more final this week and I'm finished."

"I am so proud of you and am beyond excited," Mr. Summers beamed. "My son and only child, a college graduate."

David chuckled. "Yeah...can't believe how fast four years went." He removed his glasses. "But I still have years to go before I'm finished school...with me going for my master's degree, then my doctorate in biology." David rubbed his eyes. "It's a lot, but if I want to be a disease specialist, then it's what I need to do."

"I have no doubt that you will finish," Mr. Summers said. "You've been talking about being in the medical field since you were young."

"Yeah...when Mom got sick...that's when I decided on what field I wanted to be in." David sighed as memories of his late mother filled his head. "Hopefully I can cure some of these fatal illnesses, help save some lives, you know?"

"I'm sure you will... She would be so proud of you."

"I miss her," David returned, somber. "Even more now that I'm hitting these milestones... It sucks."

There was silence on the line as Mr. Summers tried not to lose his composure. "Your mother is looking down on you...and because you have her as an angel, you're sure to be great at everything you do."

David managed a small smile. "Yeah...hopefully she can send down some advice on women and relationships, because that's one thing that I'm *not* great at," he joked.

Mr. Summers laughed. "Hey, I'm old as dirt and I'm *still* not great at it," he joked in return.

David too laughed.

"Your mother would just tell you to always be honest about how you feel. Be kind, trust your instincts, make sure the woman you choose isn't just pretty, but has a good mind as well. She'd also tell you to be respectful, and don't just talk, but listen," Mr. Summers continued.

"I remember, she used to say the last thing to *you* a lot," David recalled, amused.

"Yeah, apparently I talk a lot."

David chuckled. It had been a while since he'd spoken to his father; he was glad for the conversation. He felt better than he had in days.

"Anyway, I'm sure you have better things to do than sit on the phone with an old man," Mr. Summers said. "I'll talk to you later."

"Talk to you later," David smiled, then hung up the phone.

Nicole was flipping through pages of her textbook with one hand as she grabbed popcorn from a small bowl with another. A knock on the door snapped her out of her studies. She jumped up and opened it. Her eyes widened when she saw Alex standing there, holding both Chasity and Malajia's arms in a grip.

"Um, hi," Nicole stammered.

Chasity and Malajia's faces held unenthused looks, while Alex smiled bright. "Hey Nicole, do you have a minute?" Alex asked.

Nicole was confused. The girls were the last people she expected to see at her door, especially Chasity and Malajia. "Uh yeah, you want to come in?"

"No," Chasity griped, earning a squeeze to her arm from Alex. "You wanna stop that before I punch you in your fuckin' face?" she hurled at Alex.

"Alex, your grabby ass just pinched me," Malajia griped.

"Shut it up, you two," Alex demanded through clenched teeth, shooting both of them glances. She then turned her attention back to Nicole, who held her hand on the door. "Yes, we'd like to come in," Alex said, walking into the room and hauling both girls with her.

Nicole moved aside to let them in, then shut the door behind them. She walked over and stood in front of them, folding her arms.

"These two little mischievous, lying, storytellers, came to say something to you," Alex began, letting go of their arms.

Malajia sucked her teeth as Chasity rolled her eyes. "Isn't lying and storytelling the same thing?" Malajia mocked. "How you gonna call us names and be redundant with it?"

"Do you even know what redundant *means*?" Alex threw back.

"I know what *fuck you* means," Malajia barked back.

Alex sucked her teeth.

Nicole pushed some of her twists behind her ear. "Is this about David?" she wondered.

"Yes, yes it is," Alex confirmed. She glanced at the girls. "Ladies? I'm sure Nicole is very busy as are *we*. Let's make this quick."

"Fine," Malajia sighed. "Look Nicole, I know David already told you this but—"

"We lied about David. He never touched us that way, and we apologize," Chasity quickly spat out.

Malajia snapped her head towards her. "Damn bitch, how you cut my apology off?" she barked.

"You were taking too fuckin' long," Chasity snapped back.

"The hell is *your* problem?" Malajia threw back.

"I have cramps," Chasity bit back.

"So, pop a goddamn pill," Malajia bit out.

Alex put her hands up. "Hey, hey, stop it!" she cut in. "Nobody wants to be subjected to your pointless arguing."

Malajia waved her hand at Alex dismissively. "Look Nicole, we *are* sorry. We went too far, we know that."

Nicole, while she appreciated the apology, was still upset about the whole thing. "Why would you lie about that? What was the point?"

Alex folded her arms and looked back and forth between Chasity and Malajia. She found this amusing.

Chasity stared at Nicole for several pain-filled, seething seconds. "You're irritating me," she spat.

Nicole gasped.

"I swear to God," Alex muttered, before giving Chasity a nudge towards the door. "Girl, go get a hot water bottle and lay your behind down," she ordered.

Not hesitating for a second, Chasity walked out of the room without saying another word.

Malajia looked at Alex. "I have cramps too, can I go?"

Alex held a narrowed-eyed gaze on Malajia for several seconds. "Girl, go on," she huffed.

Malajia threw her head back. "Yeeessss," she rejoiced, then paused and grabbed her stomach in dramatic fashion. "Uh—I mean, ouch."

"Go," Alex fumed, pointing to the door. Alex shook her head as Malajia walked out, closing the door behind her.

"Wow…they seem like a lot to deal with," Nicole mentioned.

"Yeah well, I'm used to it," Alex commented, folding her arms. "Look, I can vouch for them, they're sorry. And David had no idea about any of this, so don't be mad at him."

"I don't get why they would lie though," Nicole harped. "That makes no sense."

Alex took a deep breath. She knew that her friends were wrong in what they did, but she understood their reasoning. "Look…in their *own* way, they thought that they were looking out for David."

"What do you mean?"

Alex ran her hands over her hair. She looked at Nicole, who was looking to her for answers. She wasn't sure how much she wanted to divulge. Alex was trying her best to keep her nose out of her friends' business. "Um…"

"In all honesty Alex," Nicole softly cut in. "I don't want you guys to think that I'm doing something to intentionally hurt or upset him."

Alex let out a sigh. "Umm Nicole, you…" she paused. *Don't you go and say something to make things worse.* "I'll just say this… When you two talk, just try to see things from his perspective," she vaguely replied. "Just think about how *you* felt over these past few days, when you thought that what was said was true…if that makes *any* sense."

Nicole nodded after a moment. "I guess it does."

"Good," Alex smiled. "Well, I need to get to the library. See you around."

Nicole watched as Alex headed for the door. "See you."

Alex left and shut the door behind her, leaving Nicole alone to ponder her words.

Mark took a long sip of his soda as he leaned back in his seat at the girls' dining room table. "So," he began, scanning the room, eyeing each one of his friends. "Everybody who's done or *will* be done with their finals before Friday, raise their hands."

Immediately, all hands besides Alex's shot up in the air. Alex put her hand on her face and shook her head as laughter rang out around her.

"God, I have two finals on Friday," Alex griped.

"Ahhh, you mad as shit," Mark teased.

"How the hell am I the *only* one who has finals on Friday?" Alex complained.

"'Cause your professors are assholes," Chasity chuckled, taking a sip of water.

"Tell me about it," Alex agreed, leaning back in the accent chair where she sat. "This is some bull."

"Damn, you salty as shit you gotta be in class on Friday," Malajia laughed.

"Gotta remember her studies and shit," Mark added.

"Gotta carry her book bag and shit," Jason teased.

"Gonna be staring out the window at everybody else having fun and shit," Chasity added.

Alex clenched her jaw as her friends' teasing continued.

"Gotta eat breakfast so her stomach won't be growling all loud in the quiet and shit," Malajia put in.

Emily just laughed at the taut look on Alex's face.

"You're just gonna keep going with it, huh?" Alex ground out.

"Yep, gotta sit in those small ass plastic seats and shit," Malajia mocked.

"Gotta sit in that hot building and shit," Josh laughed, earning praise for joining in.

"Yes Josh!" Mark laughed, giving Josh a high five.

"Gotta flip pages and shit," Jason laughed.

"Gotta read words and shit," Chasity added.

Sidra laughed hysterically as she tried to form words. "Wait, wait, I got one," she began, then thought for a moment. "Gotta, umm…"

"Damn it Sidra, you fucked it up!" Malajia snapped when Sidra hesitated. "We could've kept it going."

"I'm sorry," Sidra said through her laughter. She looked at Alex, who was clenching her jaw. "Alex, I'm sorry, but that's pretty sad."

Alex rolled her eyes. "Whatever," she sneered.

David sat up in his seat. "So—"

"David it's too late, you had your chance to join and you ain't say shit!" Mark barked, pointing at him.

"Huh?" David replied. "I wasn't even gonna *say* anything about Alex's final."

"Oh," Mark laughed. "My bad, what were you gonna say?"

"Your loud ass made me forget," David hissed.

A knock at the door broke through the group's chatter. "I'll get it," Emily announced, standing from her seat. She darted for the door and opened it. "Hi Nicole," she said when she laid eyes on the guest.

Everyone turned around and looked at her. Nicole waved nervously.

"You want to come in?" Emily offered, moving away from the door.

"No thank you. I wanted to know if David would come take a walk with me," Nicole answered.

"David," Mark announced, loud. "Nicole said she wanted to know if you would take a walk with her."

David stared at him, annoyed. "I *heard* her," he hissed. "I'm right *here*."

"Well then get the fuck out and go walk with her then," Mark demanded, earning snickers from around the room. Malajia broke into full laughter when she saw the salty look on David's face.

Not wanting to engage in the back and forth with Mark, David just shook his head and walked out the door with Nicole.

"Mark, you always gotta be the one," Alex ground out, scratching her scalp.

"Shut up before I plaster my balls right on your class window while you taking that Friday final," Mark threw back, earning disgusted looks from most of the girls.

"Boy please, what are those two shriveled ass raisins gonna do?" Chasity sneered.

Jason spat out his soda as he busted out laughing.

"Shut *up* Chasity!" Mark barked at her.

David shoved his hands into his pockets as he and Nicole took a stroll outside of the gate of the complex. "What brings you by?" David asked her as he felt the breeze from the night air blow past him.

Nicole looked at him. "I think it's time we talk," she answered. "I mean *really* talk...not argue."

"Sounds good," David agreed.

Nicole walked over to a bench and sat down; David joined her. "Look," she began, adjusting a twist. "I know that what the girls said wasn't true...they apologized to me earlier."

"You know *now*?" he ground out. "I've been telling you that for *days*."

Nicole looked down at her hands. "I know you have," she said. "Look...I just—"

David let out a deep sigh as he remembered the conversations that he'd had with his friends and his father. *Stop acting like an ass*, he said to himself. "Nicole listen, I don't want to fight with you anymore," he cut in.

"You don't?" she asked, hope in her voice. David shook his head and she let out a sigh of relief. "I don't want to fight with you either... I'm sorry that I didn't believe you."

David shrugged. "I mean...I act like I don't trust *you*, so why should you trust *me*?"

Nicole touched his shoulder. "David, that's not true."

"It is," David insisted. "Look, as much as I hate the fact that you talk to Quincy—"

"I'm sorry for telling him your business," she cut in. "I know how wrong that was."

David nodded. "Thank you, but in all honesty...I talk to my friends about a lot of stuff too, so I get it...I think—no, I *know* that my real issue is that I feel a bit threatened by your relationship with him."

"You don't *have* to be," Nicole said. "We don't like each other in that way... What happened between us is behind us. He's just my friend, that's all."

"I get that now," David assured. "And I'm trying not to let my insecurities affect me, but...they are."

"David, I will refrain from telling him certain things," she promised. "I won't give hugs anymore...I'll even limit my time with him and any other guy friend that I have... whatever makes you comfortable."

David removed his glasses and rubbed his face. "I don't want you to—" He let out a huff. "This isn't your issue... It's *mine*," he said, pointing to himself. "I'll be leaving you here and—I don't want you to think that you have to not be yourself because your boyfriend is too damn insecure to trust you."

Nicole stared at him. "David I—"

"You deserve someone better than me."

She frowned. "Are you trying to break up with me?" she questioned.

"I don't *want* to, but—"

"Then you're not *going* to," Nicole cut in. She grabbed his hand and held it. "Summers, you overthink things."

"Sometimes," he admitted.

"*All* the time," she chuckled. "Now look, I know you're leaving and I know that you probably think that I'll be better off with someone who is nearby...but I *won't* be... I like *you* and I really want to give our relationship a chance. And I'm not going to stop the things that I do because I feel that you're insecure; I'm doing it because I respect you and this relationship."

David managed a smile. "So, you're still willing to work with this stammering nerd?"

Nicole giggled. "If you're still willing to work with this country girl, who used to participate in ménage a trois."

David frowned. "Wait what—"

Nicole laughed. "I'm joking," she assured. She pinched his cheek. "You should've seen your face."

David shook his head in amusement. "Funny." He put his arm around her and drew her close. Nicole leaned her head on his shoulder. He glanced up at the sky. Seeing a large, twinkling star, David smiled. *Yeah, you'd like her Mom,* he thought.

# Chapter 45

"How did you do?" Malajia asked Sidra when she walked out of class.

Sidra shook her head and let out a sigh. "About as well as I possibly *could*," she answered, drained. "All I can do now is pray."

Malajia chuckled. "Back to being dramatic, huh?"

"I think I'm entitled right now," Sidra threw back, humor in her voice. "How do *you* think you did on your finals today?"

Malajia glanced at the ceiling. "Let's just say that as much sleep that I've lost studying for these damn finals…if I don't pass, I'm flooding every single classroom at this school."

Sidra giggled. "Come on, let's get out of here." As both women went to walk towards the exit, they heard someone call Malajia's name.

Turning around, they saw Jackie approaching.

"What Jackie?" Malajia asked, unenthused.

"I didn't come over here to start any shit," Jackie assured, putting her hand up as both Malajia and Sidra held piercing gazes on her.

"What do you *want*?" Sidra charged.

"I just want to know if Malajia would sit down with me for a few minutes," Jackie said, tone sincere. "I just want to talk to you."

Malajia stared at Jackie. She was skeptical; nothing good ever came from talking to Jackie. But in light of recent events, Malajia couldn't help but wonder what Jackie wanted to say to her.

"What? Girl bye, no," Sidra scoffed as she turned to walk away. "Come on Mel."

Malajia grabbed Sidra's arm, stopping her. Her gaze never left Jackie. "No wait... It's okay."

Sidra frowned. "Seriously?"

Malajia looked at Sidra and nodded. "Yeah...I'll catch up with you a little later."

Sidra let out a sigh. "Okay," she agreed and continued on her way.

"Sidra," Jackie called.

Sidra stopped and turned around, an annoyed look on her face.

"Look...about the whole jumping situation..." Jackie looked nervous. "I'm really sorry."

Sidra stared at her; she wasn't interested in Jackie's apology. As far as she was concerned, the girl went to too many lengths to be a troublemaker. If she never saw Jackie again after graduation, she would be happy. Sidra sucked her teeth. "Please," she muttered, then walked away.

Malajia shrugged at the defeated look on Jackie's face. "Well, what did you expect?" she said in defense of Sidra.

"*That*, I guess," Jackie sighed. "Umm, can we go to the cafeteria?"

"Fine," Malajia agreed, walking towards the exit.

Malajia sat across from Jackie in a booth at the dining hall. Malajia's appetite was nonexistent; her turkey sandwich and sour cream and onion chips went untouched.

Jackie picked at her cheese fries. "Last finals huh?" she quipped, taking a sip of her soda. "Must be nice... I practically have to start over since I flunked out sophomore year."

"Jackie," Malajia cut in, unenthused. "You asked me here because you said you wanted to talk... What do you have to say to me?"

Jackie took one last sip of her soda and pushed the cup aside. She clasped her hands together as she took a deep breath. "I um…I've been doing a lot of thinking over the past couple weeks… Since everything with Tyrone went down and I just feel the need to come clean."

Malajia's stern facial expression didn't change. "About?"

Jackie ran her hand over her braids. "I…I knew Tyrone was sending you those packages… the Valentine's Day card…the flowers…"

Malajia folded her arms. "Figured," she hissed.

Jackie took another deep breath. "I umm…I'm *also* the reason why um…Tyrone found out about your abortion."

Malajia's eyes widened in shock. "How the fuck did *you* know about my damn abortion?" she barked.

Jackie put her hands up in an effort to keep Malajia from flying off the handle. "Just hear me out—"

"What kind of shit are you trying to pull?"

"You remember when I mentioned that my friend Trina got an abortion?" Jackie asked.

"*No*," Malajia sneered.

"Okay well, she did…in March of last year," Jackie said. "I went with her and um… I was tired of sitting while she was getting it done, so I started wandering around looking for the bathroom… I happened to pass by the recovery room and…I saw *you* in there."

Malajia pinched the bridge of her nose. *Fuck!*

"You were sitting in one of the chairs and your eyes were closed," Jackie recalled. "You had a blanket wrapped around—"

"Yeah, I remember," Malajia hissed, looking back at her, angry.

"Well, at that time…I thought that it would be a good idea to take your picture," Jackie shamefully admitted. "I hated you all and I just figured that if I ever ran into you again, that I could use it against you."

Malajia shook her head as she eyed Jackie in disgust. "Nice...you seized the opportunity during a traumatic time to try to humiliate me," she sneered. "And you wonder why we see your so' called 'change' as bullshit."

"Maybe it *was* then...I'm not proud of that, but I did it and I kept the picture," Jackie confessed. "Anyway I met Tyrone at a party that fall... He had gotten released from jail not too long before that—"

"Did he tell you *why* he was in jail?" Malajia cut in.

"He told me that he got caught trying to rob somebody," Jackie said.

Malajia rolled her eyes. "Yeah, 'cause that sounds a *lot* better than woman beater," she sneered.

Jackie sighed. "I guess that was his thinking," she said. "We hooked up that same night and he tried to leave me alone, talking about he just wanted to smash and that was that...but I didn't listen. I got in my feelings and kept calling him and popping up to where he was. And eventually, he gave in and we started *talking*, talking."

Malajia just sat there listening as Jackie continued with her story.

"He was always distant and I thought he was seeing other women... So one night after he went out, I started going through his shit...came across one of his phones in the top of his closet and started going through it and...I found pictures of *you*... I asked him—in my exact words, 'why do you have pictures of that whorish bitch in your phone?'"

Malajia narrowed her eyes as she shook her head.

"He cussed my ass out and told me that you were his ex-girlfriend and that you were the love of his life—"

"Tyrone didn't love me, I refuse to believe that," Malajia spat.

"I can see why you feel that way," Jackie admitted. "I started going off on him and telling him about *my* experiences with you and he kept *defending* you... Then I asked him how can he think so highly of someone who got an abortion." She glanced down at the table. "He called me a liar and threatened me… I showed him the picture that I saved, which was date stamped and…he completely lost it… That was the first time that he hit me…right in my face."

Malajia ran her hands over her face as she tried to take it all in. Jackie's revelation struck a memory. "Last fall huh?"

Jackie nodded. "Which is around the time that I started receiving weird messages…including a picture of a damn ultrasound."

Jackie fiddled with her hands as the guilt set in. "I…just wanted him to myself. I wanted us to have a chance to be happy and he wasn't giving us that chance because he became obsessed with *you*… And instead of blaming him, I blamed *you*…which was fucked up since you didn't even *know* who was sending you shit."

"No, I didn't," Malajia confirmed. "You called me a liar when I tried to tell you about him…what made you start believing me *now*?"

Jackie hesitated for a moment. "When he came back to the house that night—the night that everything went down…he told me to get out and when I didn't leave, he attacked me," she revealed. "He hit me so hard I thought he broke my jaw…." She rubbed the side of her face where she had been hit; it was still sore. "After we fought, he told me what he did… He was so damn *cold* about it…like he didn't give a fuck that he stalked you and attacked someone to get to you… After I talked to the police about what he did to me, they told me the *real* reason why he did six months in jail."

"Well…at least you know the truth."

"I do," Jackie promised. She fixed a sympathetic gaze on Malajia. "No matter *how* I felt—you didn't deserve what he did to you…and Chasity didn't either."

Malajia's expression softened as she heard the sincerity in Jackie's voice. "Despite what you've done…*you* didn't *either*."

Jackie managed a small smile and nodded slightly. "Malajia we'll probably never see each other again, so I just want to say that I'm truly sorry for my part in this… If I hadn't brought you up again, maybe none of this would have happened... I knew he used me to have a reason to come on campus... If I could take it back I would...if I could take back a *lot* of shit, I *would*."

"Your apology is noted," Malajia said.

"And...I want you to know that you will *always* have my respect," Jackie said. "You went through all that and you still managed to come out of it and move on to someone who makes you happy now... I hope that I can find the same."

Malajia tapped her hand on the table. "My advice? ...Talk to someone about it...it helps you move on," she advised. "And just be a better person. Grow up...you do *that* and you'll be okay."

Jackie smiled once again. "Thank you for talking to me."

Malajia nodded. "Take care of yourself Jackie," she said, then stood up. "And finish school, if you can."

"I will," Jackie promised.

Malajia gave another nod and then walked out of the cafeteria. Although she knew that she would never consider Jackie a friend, Malajia did in fact wish her the best. She was glad that she could finally put their feud and Tyrone behind her.


Alex sat at the desk and let out a sigh as her last final was placed in front of her. *God, my stomach hurts*, she thought, picking up her pencil. She couldn't be sure if it was actually the final that made her nervous, or the fact that she was meeting Eric for their agreed upon dinner later that evening. *Focus*.

"You have one hour," the professor stated, bringing Alex out of her own thoughts. "If you finish early, you are free to leave."

Alex nodded and took a deep breath. As the professor took a seat behind his desk, Alex glanced out the window. She frowned when she saw Mark, Jason, Chasity, and Malajia outside teasing her. *Of course, my Friday final would be on the damn first floor where everybody can see me.* She glanced at the professor, who was focused on the papers in front of him. Alex watched with agitation as they pointed and laughed at her. When Mark accidentally bumped the glass, making a loud noise, the professor looked over and jumped up.

"Hey!" he barked, walking over to the window.

Alex, as well as her other classmates, laughed as they watched Malajia, Jason, and Chasity run away, then watched Mark try to jump over a flower bed. When he tripped and fell in the dirt, Alex thought that she was going to fall out her seat laughing.

"Get out of here!" the professor yelled. Mark stumbled to his feet and ran away, dusting his pants off in the process.

Alex shook her head as she began to write. She had to admit, her friends as silly as they were, loosened her up a bit.


"How you fall?" Malajia scolded, turning around and glaring at Mark, who was dusting more dirt off his jeans.

"So, *nobody* was gonna tell me about those flowers sitting there?" Mark hissed, standing upright.

Malajia looked like she could've slapped him. "You *saw* them!" she erupted. "You even said, 'yo, these some dope ass flowers' when you stepped *over* them to get to the freakin' window."

"How was I supposed to know that they'd still be there when I jumped back over?" Mark questioned.

Chasity and Malajia stared at him with pure disbelief. They couldn't believe how stupid he was at times.

"Yo, what the fuck are you *on*?!" Chasity exclaimed as Malajia tossed her hands in the air in frustration.

Jason laughed. "Ladies, don't give yourselves a headache over this idiot," he teased.

"Shut up Jason," Mark threw back. "Fuck y'all, I'm gonna go change."

"Nobody cares," Jason hissed back.

Mark sucked his teeth, then bent down to tie his sneaker. Eyeing some dirt lining the path, Mark grabbed a handful, then stood up. He slowly walked past and said, "Now *you* gotta change too, bitch," throwing the dirt at Jason. Mark managed to hit Jason's white t-shirt with it, before taking off running. Jason, furious, chased after him.

Chasity shook her head and folded her arms, watching the guys run at top speed down the path. "Bet money Mark busts his ass again."

Malajia let out a loud sigh. "What did I get myself into with his simple ass?" she huffed.

"Years of migraines," Chasity joked.

Malajia sighed again. "It's not even funny, 'cause it's true," she complained, earning a giggle from Chasity. She looked over at Chasity as they started walking. "So umm, I sat down with Jackie the other day," she informed.

"I hope you checked for fleas when you got home," Chasity returned, nonchalant.

Malajia laughed. "I did, and I was all clear," she returned. "No but she admitted to a *lot* of shit. The girl is a hot ass mess, but I can honestly say that I'm over all that damn drama."

"So you're saying that talking to her was good for you?" Chasity asked.

"It answered some questions that I had," Malajia alluded. "I just plan on leaving any drama from this school, *here* at this school."

"Makes sense," Chasity agreed, pushing her hair behind her ear.

"Do you think *you* would ever sit down and talk to Jackie?" Malajia wondered.

"Fuck no," Chasity answered. Malajia chuckled. "I don't care why she did the shit that she did, nor am I interested in any apology that she would try to form with her dry ass lips."

Malajia snickered.

"I'm foreal, like…I'm happy you got what you needed out of that, but when it comes to me, I just don't care,"

Chasity shrugged.

"Fair enough," Malajia said as they continued their pace.

Alex took a sip of her soda as she sat across from Eric. She smiled as he took a bite of his quesadilla. She glanced down at her plate of tacos.

"Nothing says 'date' quite like tacos and quesadillas," she joked, grabbing one.

Eric swallowed his bite. "Hey, lest you forget, I *like* Mexican food," he returned.

Alex let out a sigh. She wished that she could afford a dinner at a place a lot fancier than Tacos' 'n Things near the mall. After all that she put Eric through, she felt that he deserved something better.

"No, but still, I've been getting less hours because of me studying for finals and—"

Eric put his hand on the table. "Alex, this is nice, stop," he smiled. "Hell, I might've brought you here *myself* for a date," he mentioned. "I'm on financial aid and *not* working."

Alex giggled. She felt a bit better. "Well, I'm glad that you like the food."

Eric nodded as he took another bite. "So, how much hell did you get when you told your friends that you were going out with me today?"

"I didn't tell them," Alex chuckled. "Not so much in the mood for 'fuck buddy' jokes, or being called 'mixed signals'."

Eric busted out laughing at the name. "Oh shit, who called you 'mixed signals'?"

Alex narrowed her eyes at him. "The Devil," she sneered.

Eric laughed once more. "Damn...that's pretty funny."

Alex shook her head in amusement. "Fine, I deserve it," she agreed.

"Nah, I'm not gonna say that...*entirely*," he returned. "But, I *do* have to wonder, what made you finally want to go out with me after all this time?"

"I felt like I owed it to you," she shrugged.

"Oh really?"

"Yeah," she maintained. "Like I said the day I asked you, I just didn't want to leave here without hanging out with you one more time."

Eric stared at her for a moment as she gave a nervous smile. There was no humor on his face. "Alex…if you don't be honest with me, I'm getting up and walking out of here."

Alex's eyes widened. "Are you serious?" she hissed.

"A hundred percent," he confirmed.

"Eric, I already *told* you—" she grabbed his arm when he began to stand from his seat. "Okay, okay," she relented, causing him to sit back down. "Don't leave."

Eric folded his arms on the tabletop and fixed a gaze. "Well?"

Alex took a deep breath. *Here comes the awkward conversation.* "Look, in all honesty…I miss you…And I wanted to see where your head is at."

"As far as?"

"As far as…*we* are concerned." Alex gestured her finger back and forth between the two of them. "I don't want to leave here not knowing what can happen with us."

"How do you know that I don't have a girlfriend, Alex?" Eric asked, point-blank.

"You said that that girl was your cousin," she pointed out.

"I know, but there are *other* girls on this campus," Eric threw back.

Alex folded her arms, a defeated look on her face. "Well…*do* you have one?" she asked, not really wanting to know the answer.

Eric rubbed his face, then sighed. "No, I don't," he confirmed.

Alex was both confused and annoyed. "Then why even go through all of that to make me think that you did, just now?" she spat.

"Games aren't so fun when it's at your expense, huh?" He flashed back.

Alex shook her head. "Nice," she ground out, sarcastic. "So you turning down my coffee invitation when we first got back, was *that* a game *too*?"

"No," Eric answered. "At the time I wasn't sure that I could handle being around you so...I didn't."

Alex nodded. "Fair enough," she said. Alex was smiling on the inside, *he's free!* "So, yeah..." she leaned forward. "I know that I hurt you and I'm deeply sorry for that... And I know that you're a good man and I'd like to see what it would be like to date you...*date*, date, not just...you know."

Eric smirked. "Oh you mean, you don't want to just use me for my body huh?" he joked.

Alex couldn't help but chuckle. "Exactly. Not that that wasn't a good time," she quickly amended, putting her hand up. "A *great* time."

Eric blushed slightly. "Yeah...it was," he agreed.

Alex smiled. "So?" she pressed. "What do you say?"

Eric pondered her proposal. This was something that he had wanted since he'd met Alex. He fixated on the hopeful look on her face and let out a deep sigh. "I say...no," he answered, carefully.

Alex's face fell. She felt her heart drop into the pit of her stomach. "I'm sorry?" she sputtered.

Eric felt terrible; he wished that he could block out the look on her face. "I'm sorry Alex."

Alex felt tears begin to fill her eyes. She'd put herself out there and had gotten rejected. She fanned her face in an effort to dry the forming tears.

"Don't cry," he pleaded, voice caring. "It's not that I don't *want* to Alex, it's really not."

"Then what *is* it?" she asked, voice cracking. "Is it because you think I'm still bitter over my ex?" she wiped a tear that had spilled down her cheek.

"No, that's not why," he assured.

"Are you still mad at me?"

Eric shook his head. "No."

"Then—then what *is* it Eric?" Alex questioned, tears spilling.

Eric leaned forward as he gathered his words. "Alex…be honest, do you *really* want another long-distance relationship?"

"Huh?" she ground out, grabbing some napkins from the table.

"Seriously," he pressed. "You're leaving and who knows *where* you'll end up living," he pointed out. "As smart as you are, in your field, you can end up in New York somewhere… I have another semester to go here in Virginia, and after that, who knows where *I'll* be—"

"We can make it work," Alex broke in.

"I repeat, do you *really* want to start another long-distance relationship?" he pressed, desperate to get her to see his point. "Do you really want to start a new relationship right now…*period*?"

Alex wiped her eyes as he spoke. "You *do* think I'm still bitter," she concluded.

"No, I *don't*."

"Yes, you *do*," she insisted, hurt. "Eric, I promise, I've put that behind me. I no longer judge other men based on the actions of one… I'm not angry anymore."

"Alex…you spent your teen years in a relationship that went nowhere… Then you spent your college years being angry over it," he said. "Now that you have whatever closure you need…don't you think you need to experience being single, *without* the anger?"

Alex pondered Eric's words.

"Who knows, maybe you'll find that I'm not your type *after* all," he pointed out.

"No, you *are* my type," she assured. "And I just don't want to lose you."

"Hey, I'm more than happy to be just your friend… *now*," Eric smiled. "And who knows, if we're meant to be…we'll *be* one day. But it would be selfish of me to allow you to commit yourself without you actually *finding* yourself."

Alex hated to admit it, but Eric had a point. She was amazed by his selflessness when it came to her; she only wished that she could have seen it sooner. Who knows what they could've been. "Okay," she sniffled.

Eric reached out and touched her arm. "This isn't easy for me, you know," he said. "I miss you too and I'm probably gonna kick myself in the back of the head later for this. But at this moment…it seems like the right decision… Go put that degree to good use with the career that you always wanted. Hell, go on a few dates to test the waters…just don't tell me about them."

Alex giggled through her tears. "I promise, I won't," she said. "But I don't want to hear about *your* dates either."

"I'll be sure to keep my imaginary girlfriends to myself," Eric laughed.

"Funny," she chuckled.

Eric stood up and walked over to her, then wrapped his arms around her. She welcomed the embrace and held on to him. "You'll be okay," he consoled.

"I hope so," she muttered into his shoulder. "Thank you."

"Anytime."

# Chapter 46

Mark had his hands over his face, pleading to the computer screen. "Please, please, please please," he repeated.

"You still praying for that email, huh?" Josh teased, patting Mark on his shoulder.

"Don't touch me Joshua!" Mark barked.

Josh shook his head.

Alex tapped the keys of her computer. She, Mark, and most of the group were huddled in the computer lab. They were checking for emails from the university, letting them know their final grades and confirmation of graduation.

"I'm glad that they finally integrated a new system for this instead of sending the info to our mailboxes," Alex chuckled. "Can you imagine the crowd—"

"Alex, shut the fuck up, will you!" Mark erupted.

Alex glared at him. "Don't get mad at *me* because you're scared that your slacking behind won't graduate with the *rest* of us."

Malajia rolled her eyes at Alex, then rubbed Mark's back. "Ignore her baby, she just mad 'cause her hair shrunk in the shower this morning," she sneered.

Chasity, who was drinking some of her bottled water next to Alex, spat it out as she busted out laughing.

"Damn it Chasity!" Alex bellowed, wiping the water droplets from her face and her computer.

Chasity was too busy laughing to bother saying sorry.

"Damn, watch it shrink some more now," Malajia teased

of Alex's hair.

"Shut up," Alex spat back.

"Uh huh, stop teasing my baby," Malajia threw back, accompanied by a middle finger in Alex's direction.

Mark watched the email pop up on his screen. But he just stared at it.

"Come on bro, open it," David urged, excited.

"Open *yours*," Mark demanded.

"Don't *need* to," David replied, adjusting his glasses. "Had a meeting with the dean this morning. Not only am I graduating, but I was told that I am graduating Suma Cum Laude of the Science department. And because I have the highest GPA of the graduating class, I will be giving the valedictorian speech," he beamed.

"Oh my God, that's awesome David," Sidra beamed, hugging him tightly as the rest of his friends congratulated him.

"I know your Dad is so excited right now," Josh smiled.

David nodded. "Yeah, he is," he confirmed. "I already know he's gonna cry." He adjusted his glasses. "The only thing that worries me is giving the speech—"

"David, just throw in some big words and nobody will care *what* you say," Mark cut in, on edge. He glanced at David. "Sorry."

"Open the email Mark," David urged, pointing to the screen. "I'm sure you didn't fail."

"Please, Mr. Slacker?" Alex laughed. "I wouldn't be surprised."

"How did *you* do?" Sidra hissed at Alex.

"Oh, I *passed* of course," Alex boasted, reading her email. "Although I wish I would have gotten an honor within my department."

"Oh, you mean like Magna Cum Laude?" Chasity asked, placing the top on her water.

"Or Cum Laude?" Josh added.

Alex looked at them both. "Yeah," she confirmed. "I

thought my overall GPA was going to be good enough, but *clearly* I was wrong." she sulked. "I guess they're harder to come by than I *thought*."

"Oh," Chasity commented. "Well I guess I'm a badass 'cause I got Magna Cum Laude for Computer Science."

Alex's mouth fell open in shock.

"Same here for Math," Jason beamed, giving Chasity a high five.

Josh raised his hand. "Cum Laude for Business Administrating," he chimed in.

Alex looked at Chasity. "*Magna Cum Laude*? Really?"

Chasity nodded. "You mad I was blessed with beauty *and* brains," she mocked.

"Chasity, how did you, Miss I-can't-pass-math-without-a-tutor get honors?" Alex wondered, shocked. Chasity frowned.

"She had a *damn* good tutor," Jason hissed at Alex, folding his arms. "And she's smart as shit, so stop hatin', it's annoying."

"I'm not—"

"Yes, you *are*," Jason cut in, stern. "How about saying 'congratulations'?"

"Geez Alex, what's gotten into you?" Sidra wondered of Alex's snarky attitude. "*I* was *just shy* of getting Cum Laude and you don't see *me* being spiteful."

"Oh shit, that's right, you missed by one point, right?" Malajia asked, looking at Sidra.

Sidra nodded. "Yup, got a 3.3," she said.

Alex let out a loud huff. "My GPA pissed me off," she complained, folding her arms.

"She salty she got in trouble," Malajia goaded. Alex clenched her jaw. "She got a whole dozen of rotten eggs sitting on her salty ass face."

Alex sucked her teeth as her friends laughed around her.

"She mad, she ain't no *Laude*," Malajia teased.

"Shut up Malajia," Alex grunted.

Jason glanced at Mark, who was still staring at his screen. "Mark, if you don't open that email, I'm gonna do it *for* you," Jason urged.

"Okay, okay," Mark relented, putting his hands up.

"Baby, if you weren't gonna graduate, I'm sure you would've been called to the department head's office already," Malajia consoled.

Mark sighed. "I know, just…give me a minute," he said. He hoped and prayed that his class clown behavior didn't catch up to him. "Here goes nothing."

He slowly clicked the mouse to open the email while his friends huddled around him in anticipation. Losing her patience, Malajia snatched the mouse from him. "Mel—"

"Shut up, you taking too long," Malajia interrupted, waving her hand at him. She clicked open the email and all eyes stared at the screen.

Mark silently read the words before jumping up from his seat, knocking his chair over in the process. "I muthafuckin' passed!" he bellowed. "I'm out this bitch!" He was met with hugs, handshakes and congratulations.

"See, you had nothing to worry about," Josh said, giving Mark a pat on his shoulder.

Mark let out a sigh of relief. "Man, that was brutal…but I did it *and* got a 3.5 GPA."

"You got a 3.5?!" Alex exclaimed. Her words mirrored the shocked looks on everyone's faces.

"What?" Mark asked, confused.

"*You*? Mr. 'fuck that class', got a *3.5*?" Malajia asked. She was pleasantly surprised. His GPA was higher than hers.

"Oh yeah, I fooled y'all. I'm actually smarter than I pretend to be," Mark said, snapping his fingers. "Muthafuckin' Cum Laude for Accounting baby."

"But…you never went to *class*," Alex was still in disbelief as Mark received praise and high fives from the other honor recipients in the room

"I *did* actually," Mark laughed at the dumb look on

Alex's face. "You mad you thought I was dumb and shit."

Malajia did a dance. "My man is smart, my man is smart," she sang. "You gonna make me some money, huh baby?"

"Naw, you doubted me too, you ain't gettin' shit," he joked, then laughed when Malajia's mouth fell open. "I'm messin' with you."

Alex opened her email again. "*What* did you say your GPA is, Mark?" she asked.

"3.5," he answered. "Why?"

When Alex didn't answer, Mark got close to the screen. "She got a 2.9! I beat her!" Mark laughed, then got close to Alex's face. "You mad, I beat you! You salty as shit cuz! Ole' C average having ass! You thought you was getting a B and shit!"

"You spit on me!" Alex wailed, shoving Mark away from her.

"Naw that was your tears," Mark laughed.

"Whatever," Alex sneered. "I'm gonna go have a talk with my damn professors, this doesn't seem right."

"Ah who cares," Malajia dismissed, waving her hand. "Girl we're done, loosen up."

"Well what was *your* GPA?" Alex asked her.

"A two point I-don't-*give*-a-fuck, I'm *done*," Malajia rejoiced. "I don't care if it was a *one* something, as long as I can walk across that damn stage."

"Yeah, senior week starts tomorrow," David pointed out. "Our last week here… I say we make the most of it. The stress of college is officially over."

"Yeah, you're right," Alex smiled after a moment. "Between the party, senior picnic, and games—it's gonna be fun."

Mark stood by his computer screen. "Yo Alex, pull out that flip phone and take a picture of me and my B average," he taunted, posing.

Alex narrowed her eyes at him as he busted out

laughing.


Emily cut a piece of steak with her fork before placing it into her mouth. Will watched as she chewed then swallowed the food. "Well?" Will asked, anxious.

"That has to be the best steak and potatoes that I've tasted," she smiled.

Will chuckled. "You don't have to lie," he joked. "Anthony just threw his mashed potatoes at my face, so I know it couldn't be *that* good."

Emily giggled. Instead of hanging out with her friends that evening, Emily elected to accept Will's offer of a homecooked dinner at his apartment. "No, it's good, I promise," she assured.

"Thanks," he replied, cutting a piece of his steak. "So...are you excited? You graduate Sunday."

"Yeah, I know," she replied, reaching for her juice.

Will took notice of the tone of Emily's voice. "You don't *sound* excited."

"I *am*, I think it's just surreal right now," Emily admitted. "I mean in a week I'm officially entering yet another chapter in my life...full fledge *adulthood*." She tapped her fork on the plate. "I'm excited, but at the same time I'm...."

"Scared?" Will finished.

Emily looked at him. "Yeah."

Will held a sympathetic gaze on her. "Emily, I know what it's like to fear being on your own but, I'm doing it," Will placated. "And *you* can too."

Emily poked at her food some more and sighed. She appreciated Will's words, but she just couldn't shake her fears.

"Have you made a decision about your job offer yet?" Will asked, cutting through the silence.

Emily shook her head. "No, not yet."

"What did your family and friends say when you told

them about the offer?"

Emily sat back in her seat. "My dad is *very* supportive, says that he'll set me up in an apartment here until I can manage on my own," she answered "And my mom? Well...she's excited for me...and she offered to move here to Virginia."

Will laughed. "Is she serious?"

Emily chuckled. "I can honestly say that I don't know," she said, amused. "But, she knows that's not happening."

"Well, at least she didn't threaten to make you turn down the job," Will joked, taking a bite of his food.

"I know right? I guess she really *is* trying to change," Emily mused, folding her arms. "My friends...I haven't told them yet."

Will looked confused. "Why *not*?"

Emily shrugged.

"Afraid that they might try to talk you out of it?"

Emily shook her head. "No. They would encourage me to take it... I just don't need all the voices right now," she replied. "This is something that I need to decide on my own."

"Makes sense," Will agreed, nodding. "But I just want to say that..." He took a deep breath as Emily stared at him, anticipating his words. He wanted to express how happy he would be if she stayed in Virginia, but in listening to what she'd just said about wanting to come to the decision on her own without any persuasion, Will decided to keep his thoughts to himself. "Whatever you decide...I'll support you."

Emily smiled. "Thank you Will."

Will nodded and returned her smile with one of his own. He glanced over at the highchair and chuckled. "Little man is knocked out."

Emily looked over at the sleeping toddler. "Aww, he has mashed potatoes all over him," she giggled.

Will shook his head. "The day wouldn't be complete without him covering himself in his dinner."

Emily giggled as she grabbed a napkin and began to

gently wipe the food from Anthony's face. One thing was for sure, if she decided not to accept the offer, she was sure going to miss spending time with Will and Anthony.

Mark busted out laughing as he stepped out of the post office. "Yo, some of them people mad as shit about their graduation pictures."

"That's a shame too, because they're being strict with the re-shoots," Sidra said, pushing her hair over her shoulder.

The group, after leaving lunch, took a journey to the campus post office to retrieve their graduation photos that they had taken the week prior. Photos in hand, they were now ambling through campus.

"Naw, they should allow do overs 'cause that photographer was doing stupid shit on purpose, tryna make people laugh and shit," Malajia griped, holding her photos in her hand.

"Caught you slippin' huh?" Jason laughed.

Malajia rolled her eyes, "Right in mid-fuckin' laugh," she ground out, showing one of her pictures.

Mark snickered. "Yo, your mouth is big as shit," he teased of Malajia's open mouth picture.

Malajia glared at him.

"You can see every last one of your molars," David chuckled.

"Shut up David," Malajia hissed. "That's why all your pictures have a damn glasses glare."

David flipped through his pictures and put one in her face. "*This* one doesn't."

Malajia waved her hand at him dismissively. "Fuck you."

"Malajia, I don't know what you're so mad for," Alex cut in, fanning herself with her pictures. "You have *plenty* of beautiful pictures to choose from as your main photo."

"That is not the *point*," Malajia snarled, pinching her fingers together.

"Then what *is* the point?" Alex wondered.

"I needed *all* of my pictures to be perfect," Malajia harped.

"Don't get mad at us because you look like a fool in one of your pictures," Chasity said. "I told you before about laughing at stupid shit."

"So, *I'm* the *only* one who laughed?" Malajia asked, pointing to herself. Her mouth fell open when everybody nodded. "That's 'cause y'all corny."

"He wasn't *funny!*" Chasity exclaimed, over Malajia's complaining.

"He was *hilarious*," Malajia argued.

"Nah babe, his jokes were wack sauce," Mark added, amused. "And you know *my* stupid ass laughs at anything."

"Really," Jason agreed. "He actually sat there and said, 'your mama is so dumb, she jumped out the window and went up'."

Malajia let out a loud laugh. "Hilarious!"

"No, it was stupid and insulting to our mothers," Alex sneered.

Malajia sucked her teeth at Alex, then glanced over at Chasity, who was laughing to herself. "See?!"

"I *just* really thought about it," Chasity admitted, laughter subsiding.

Malajia sighed as she shoved her pictures into her purse. "That's fine, 'cause I'll print that ugly picture right out and give it to my sister Tanya, since she never sent me no money while I was here," she muttered.

"So…which one of these activities are we going to do today?" Emily asked, tilting her head as she stared at one of her pictures. "Is one of my eyes lower than the other?"

Alex glanced at her picture. "No, you look pretty," she chortled. Emily shrugged. "But whatever you guys decide, you'll have to count Josh and I out."

Sidra looked at her, frowning in confusion. "Why?"

"We have to work," Josh ground out.

"I thought you both said that *last* week was your final

week," Sidra recalled.

"We *did*," Alex confirmed. "But they put us on *anyway*."

"For three damn hours," Josh griped. "Today better be *it*."

Alex patted his shoulder. "I hear you."

"Well, while y'all will be slinging pizzas we'll be at…" Mark thought. "What *is* going on today?"

"I think tonight is bingo night," David answered. His response was met with complaints.

"*Bingo?*" Mark barked. "Man, ain't nobody tryna play no corny ass bingo."

"Who comes *up* with this bullshit?" Chasity sneered. "Last night it was 'bonfire and smores' night, like *why?*"

"I thought that was a cute idea," Emily giggled.

"I wasn't eating marshmallows from a bag that people dug their nasty ass hands in," Chasity griped. Emily laughed.

"They fuckin' up with the senior week. I hope that the picnic on Friday makes up for it," Malajia cut in. "They better have some *good* food and not caf food."

Sidra busted out laughing. "Can you imagine if they *did* have cafeteria food there?"

"Everybody would leave like shit," Malajia concluded, amusement in her voice.

"We might as *well* just go to bingo tonight…what *else* is there to do?" David shrugged, circling back to the topic at hand.

"You hype as shit you wanna play that senior citizen game," Mark mocked. "What's their prize? *Pencils* and shit?"

David shook his head. "Two hundred dollars," he announced.

"Yeah? I'm on that," Mark said, changing his tune. "Bingo it is… We should bring liquor and do some shots."

"No, stop trying to get drunk all the time," Alex chided.

Malajia shook her hand in Alex's direction. "Don't kill our joy 'cause you gotta play with pizza cheese while we're having fun."

"She gonna play, how many shreds come in a pack, and shit," Mark laughed.

Alex let out a huff as she stomped away from the group.

"How many tickets are you getting for graduation again?" Mrs. Howard asked into the line.

Sidra placed a stack of folded clothes into a suitcase. "Six, I think," she answered.

"That's *it*?" Mrs. Howard sneered. "As much as tuition is and that's all they give?"

Sidra giggled. "Mama, we have a large graduating class—"

"They're having it at the football field, I'm *sure* they can fit some extra chairs out there," Mrs. Howard cut in, annoyed. "Makes no sense."

"Sorry, but I can't do anything about that," Sidra placated. "Five will cover you, Daddy and the boys. Just give the last one to Grandma."

"Which *one*?" Mrs. Howard pointed out.

Sidra smacked her forehead with her hand. "Crap," she huffed. "I'll see what I can do about extra tickets," she promised.

"Keep me posted," Mrs. Howard said. "How much do you have packed? Your father will be there sometime tomorrow to get some of your things."

Sidra looked around her cluttered room. "Not *enough* yet," she chuckled. "But I'll have it together before he gets here."

"I know you will," Mrs. Howard said. There was a pause on the line. "So...have you told Josh yet?"

Sidra frowned. "How did we go from tickets, to packing, to *Josh*?"

"Sidra—"

"No, I *haven't*," Sidra cut in, sitting on her bed.

"You *need* to."

Sidra rolled her eyes. "I have to finish packing and the

phone keeps slipping so I have to hang up, now. I'll talk to you later."

"Okay Princess."

"Bye." Sidra hung up the phone and tossed it on her bed, running a hand through her hair. She knew her mother was right. But she also knew that talking to Josh about her feelings for him at that point was not an option…at least not at that moment. Needing to focus on something else, she walked into the hallway.

"Hey, are your families hounding you for additional tickets?" Sidra asked, walking into Chasity's room where she and Malajia were.

"No, there's only two people I care to see. Everybody else can get out my face," Chasity ground out.

"Damn, only inviting Ms. Trisha and Grandmom, huh?" Malajia chuckled.

"That's what I *want*, but of course what *I* want doesn't matter," Chasity sneered, removing items from the top of her closet. "The rest of my tickets are being given out against my will."

"To *who*?" Malajia wondered.

Chasity shrugged.

Sidra leaned against the door. "My mom is having a fit. There are a lot of my family members who want to come," she griped. "But I can't do anything about it."

"Shit, you know how big *my* family is," Malajia said. "Six sisters, Mom, Dad, brother-in-law… Mom told them little ones to lap it up in one seat."

Sidra giggled. "Dana will *not* be pleased," she mused of Malajia's fourteen-year-old sister.

"Yeah well, Miss Diva will get over it," Malajia dismissed. "She better hope that Melissa stopped peeing on herself. She gonna be salty as shit with a soggy lap."

Chasity shook her head in amusement. "Get out my room," she chortled.

Malajia laughed. "Sidra, just go see if they have any extra tickets," she advised. "I'm sure *Carl* ain't graduating."

Sidra shook her head. "Yeah, I'll do that," she agreed. "Are you both taking some of your stuff home before graduation day too?" she asked, looking around at Chasity's suitcases.

"Mom is coming down to get some of my stuff before Friday," Chasity replied, unzipping a bag. "I have *way* too much shit."

"Yeah, my dad is coming tomorrow," Sidra said.

"Shiiit, I'm putting all my shit in one of the cars that will be coming down here Sunday," Malajia said, adjusting an earring in her ear. "*And* I'mma wait until the last minute to pack...just like old times."

"Your dad is going to curse you out," Sidra warned, folding her arms.

"*Just* like old times," Malajia joked.

Sidra shook her head as she glanced at her watch. "Are we still going to bingo?"

"Yeah, let's go get these damn guys," Malajia said.

# Chapter 47

Alex sighed as she and Josh approached the block of The Pizza Shack. "Our last rodeo here, my friend," Alex mused, giving Josh a soft tap on his shoulder.

Josh smiled. "Yeah, I know," he said, then glanced at her. "Are you going to miss it?"

"The people, yes. The type of job, no," Alex replied. "I mean, don't get me wrong, I enjoyed working here and it helped me out financially, I just—"

"Don't want to work as a waitress anymore," Josh filled in, amusement in his voice. "Trust me, I get it. I hope to only be making food in my own house, *not* in somebody's restaurant."

"Exactly," Alex chuckled. "I wish us *both* luck with finding a job doing something that we really want to do."

Josh nodded as they approached the door. "If I had a drink, I'd toast to that." He opened the door for Alex to walk in before following after her.

They both surveyed the space with their eyes. "It's dead in here," Josh complained, seeing the two patrons sitting. "They really could've taken us off the schedule."

Alex moved around to the counter. "Well, it *is* finals week for the rest of the campus…maybe people will get tired of studying and come get some food," she placated. "I just wonder where the *other* waitresses are. He normally puts two or three on at a time."

Josh went around the counter and grabbed an apron. Any words that he was about to say were halted when Leroy came out.

"Hey you two, can I see you in my office for a moment?" he requested.

Josh and Alex glanced at each other in confusion. "*Both* of us?" Alex asked.

"Yeah, both. Now please?" Leroy urged, heading for his manager office.

Josh stared at the back of Leroy's head as he walked away. "What the hell is *his* problem?" he sneered of Leroy's tone.

"I know, it's not like we're late," Alex added, scratching her head. "At least I don't *think* we are."

Josh and Alex made their way to the office. Alex opened the door. As she and Josh walked through, they heard a loud "surprise!" come from Leroy and several of their coworkers.

"Are you serious?" Josh smiled, eyeing the balloons and streamers around the room, along with a cake, ice cream, sodas and sandwiches laid out on a small table.

"Absolutely," Leroy smiled.

Alex headed over and gave her coworkers and boss a hug. "Aww, you guys shouldn't have," she gushed. "But it's nice that you *did*, thank you."

"You're welcome," Leroy replied. "We couldn't let you leave here without throwing you a little something." He handed both Alex and Josh an envelope. "You two have been a part of this crazy place for three and a half years, and although we wish you much luck and success…you will be missed."

Alex placed her hand on her chest; she was getting emotional. This was just another reminder that this part of her life was coming to an end. "I'll miss you guys too."

Leroy nodded. "Those are your last checks, along with a little something extra from me," he announced, gesturing to the envelopes.

Josh opened his envelope and retrieved the contents. It was his last Pizza Shack paycheck, along with a personal check in the amount of a hundred dollars. Josh smiled as he shook Leroy's hand. "Thanks man, we appreciate this," he said.

"Don't mention it," Leroy said.

Alex glanced out the door. "I think there are people waiting for service out there," she observed.

"I got it," a fellow waitress smiled, darting out of the door.

"Alex, you're not actually on the schedule, that was just a ruse to get you here," Leroy chuckled. "So have some food...not pizza—"

"Thank God," Alex joked, laughing.

"Trust me, I get it," Leroy agreed. "So enjoy yourselves, you deserve it." He shook both of their hands once more. "I mean it, best of luck to you both."

Alex and Josh said their thanks you's and smiled as Leroy headed out of the office for something. As their coworkers began to head for the food, Alex looked at Josh and playfully nudged him.

"I'll miss working with *you too*," she said.

"Likewise," Josh replied, giving her a soft nudge back. Alex stuffed her envelope into her pocket as Josh made a beeline for the food.


"Yo, when they gonna call my damn number?" Mark complained, holding up his marker as he stared down at his bingo paper.

"There is no guarantee that they're going to call your number," David said, shaking his head.

Mark sucked his teeth as another number was called. "Come on man!" he barked, slapping his hand on the table.

David shook his head again as he marked the number on his sheet. He looked around the room. "The others ditched us," he observed.

"Yeah, I knew they was lying when they said they'd be back," Mark grunted. "This shit is wack, bee."

Hearing a door open, David glanced up. "Hey Malajia,

came back to join us?" he smiled.

"Hell no, this shit is boring," Malajia said, leaning over Mark. "Y'all put those markers down and come over to the next room with me," she demanded.

"What's going on over there?" David wondered, interest peaked.

"I'm tryna win this two hundred bucks," Mark hissed, cutting Malajia's would-be reply off.

Malajia grabbed the marker from Mark's hand. "Boy, you got like one number marked out of both of those sheets," she jeered. "You ain't winning jack shit, now come on."

Mark let out a loud sigh as he allowed himself to be led from his seat by Malajia, grabbing his arm. "Fine," he grunted.

David stood up from his seat. As he got ready to depart with Mark and Malajia, a final number was called. David looked at his sheets of paper and tossed his arms up. "Ooh! Bingo! Bingo, I won!" he bellowed, quickly marking the number on his paper.

"Let me get that real quick," Mark demanded, reaching for the paper.

"Back up off me bro," David ordered, holding the paper out of reach.

Mark sucked his teeth as he watched David trot to the front of the room. "Man, fuck this game," he ground out.

Malajia giggled. "My sentiments exactly," she agreed, pulling Mark out of the door.

Upon entering another room within the SDC, Mark shook his head as he saw his other friends in there, listening to music blaring from Jason's phone. "Y'all are some liars," Mark hurled.

"You already knew we wasn't going back in that dry ass room," Chasity said, flagging him with her hand.

"I know, Mr. Bradley was talking all slow and shit," Malajia laughed.

"Who won the money?" Jason asked, changing the song on his phone.

"David's dweeb ass," Mark groused. "I sat in that hot ass room for an hour for *nothing*."

"Well, at least *one* of us won," Emily smiled, sitting on one of six chairs that were arranged in a circle.

Before Mark could say anything, David barged through the door, smiling as he held up his winnings. "Say 'hi' to the winner."

"Shut up," Mark bit out, earning a snicker from David.

"See, I was going to treat everyone to some donuts later, but you just sniped yourself out of any," David threw back, pocketing his money.

"Bet money I get a donut," Mark mumbled, folding his arms.

Malajia handed Mark a water bottle that she grabbed from a nearby table. "Here, sip on this you sore loser," she teased.

"What's this?" Mark asked, taking the bottle.

"Vodka and cranberry, sip it and get some damn cheer," Malajia demanded, gesturing for him to take a sip. Mark did as he was told as Malajia held her hands up. "So, while you two were playing bingo, the rest of us decided on something *fun* to do," she announced.

"Come on now, bingo was fun—"

"Bingo was *not* fun, *David*," Chasity snapped, shooting him a glare. David shot her a stunned look.

Sidra busted out laughing. "You seem pretty pissed," she teased, looking at Chasity.

"'Cause he's not gonna keep lying about that bullshit," Chasity griped.

"Anyway," Malajia cut in. "We're gonna play musical chairs."

Mark paused mid-sip. "Musical chairs?" he frowned.

"Yup."

"For shots?" Mark asked.

"You know, I *suggested* that, but everybody told me no," Malajia replied, pointing at Mark. "But we *did* say that whoever loses has to run through the sprinklers by the president's house."

"Naked?" Mark asked.

"Eww, no!" Sidra shrieked. "You freak."

"Sidra, you *know* you wanna see one of us dudes naked...*especially* since James ain't been around," Mark teased.

His words took Sidra by surprise. It had been a while since anybody had mentioned James, and she had *yet* to share the news of her break up.

"You know what Sidra, now that Mark's nasty ass mentioned it...where *has* James been?" Malajia wondered, looking at Sidra, whose eyes had gotten wide.

"Umm...he's just been busy with work, that's all," Sidra answered, fiddling with her fingers.

"Hopefully you'll get to see more of him when you graduate," Emily placated. "I know it must suck not being able to spend that much time with him."

Sidra scratched her head. "Uh huh," she muttered. "Here's hoping."

Chasity glanced at her; Sidra looked frazzled. "You alright?" she asked.

"Uh huh," Sidra assured, voice on high. "So umm, running through the sprinklers right?" she was desperate to change the subject.

"Yup," Malajia confirmed.

Mark downed the rest of his drink. "You know what...I'm with it," he mused. "Y'all know 'competition' is my middle name."

"It's *Moses*," Malajia sniped, folding her arms.

Mark quickly pointed at her. "Damn it Malajia!"

"Wait, your middle name is *Moses*?" Jason laughed. "Old ass middle name."

"Well, my grandfather was allowed to pick my middle name and his ass was all into the bible so...*Moses* I got stuck with," Mark explained. "What's *yours*, Bartholomew?" he hissed at Jason, who looked at him confused. Malajia busted out laughing.

"No, it's *Kyle*," Jason ground out.

Mark stood there with a silly look on his face.

"The fuck is a Bartholomew?" Chasity questioned as Malajia continued to double over with laughter.

"Whatever," Mark grunted. "Let's get this game started."

Malajia put her hand over her chest as her laughter subsided. "He said Bartholomew and was salty about it," she mused, fanning herself. "Anyway, who's gonna control the music?"

Before anyone could answer, the door opened and in walked Alex and Josh.

"We thought you guys had to work," Emily said.

"Yeah, *we* thought so too," Josh chuckled, shutting the door behind him. "They ended up throwing us a little party."

"Aww, that was nice of them," Emily beamed.

"Any leftover food?" Mark asked.

"Yeah, plenty," Alex answered, sitting on one of the chairs.

Mark tossed his arms in the air. "Then *where* are the leftovers?" he charged. "How y'all have a party and shit with leftovers and you ain't even bring none to share? That's some selfish shit."

"How do you know that we *didn't* bring any?" Alex ground out.

"Where *is* it then, huh?" Mark threw back, folding his arms.

Josh stared at him, annoyed. "At the *house* you greedy bastard," Josh snarled, earning snickers. Mark stood there, salty. "We went home first, then I texted Sidra, asking if y'all were still at bingo and she told us you were *here*."

Mark rubbed the back of his head. For once, he had no comeback. "Alright, musical chairs!" he belted out, clapping his hands in the process.

"Really?" Josh questioned, confused.

"Yep, loser has to run through the sprinklers naked," Mark lied, gesturing for Alex to get up from the chair.

"Wait, what?!" Alex exclaimed.

"Loser runs through the sprinklers by President Bennett's campus house, but not naked. Don't listen to him," Sidra corrected, adjusting a bracelet on her wrist.

Alex shook her head. "Very well."

David held his hand out for Jason's phone. "I'll control the music," he offered. "I'm not playing." His revelation was met with complaints.

"You corny bro," Mark grunted.

"Hey, I already won something today, I'm not going to test my luck," David replied unfazed. Jason handed him his phone and David stood off to the side. "So how are we doing this? First person to be eliminated? Last person?"

"Naw, let's make it interesting. Fourth person to be eliminated gotta run through the sprinklers, and the *last* person eliminated gotta knock on the front door," Mark proposed.

"Bet," Josh agreed, rubbing his hands together.

Placing a few more chairs in the circle, the group, minus David, took their places. "I'm not running through no damn sprinklers, so get ready to go down," Mark boasted.

"Trash talking already, huh?" Josh quipped.

David started the music and watched in amusement as his friends carefully circled the chairs.

"Malajia, stop touching the chairs," Alex barked.

"*You're* touching them *too*," Malajia threw back.

"I am *not*," Alex argued.

Malajia didn't get a chance to respond because the music stopped, sending the group scrambling for a seat. Sidra darted for the last seat, leaving Emily standing confused.

"Emily, you ain't even *try*," Malajia laughed.

"I could have *sworn* there was an extra seat," Emily laughed, placing her hand on her head.

"Naw, your excuses are not wanted, hit the bench, you out," Mark ordered, pointing to the spot near David. Emily sighed as she headed over to the spot.

Jason removed one of the chairs from the circle and

David clicked the music back on, sending everyone back around.

"Shit!" Josh yelped, tripping over Mark's foot and stumbling as his friends grabbed the available chairs once the music stopped.

"You okay?" Sidra panicked, seeing Josh nearly fall into the wall.

"Damn Mark, you tripped me!" Josh barked at Mark.

"Why was you all up on my neck *anyway* bruh?" Mark taunted from his seat. "You mad, you out."

Josh flipped him off. "I'm fine Sidra," he said to her, standing over by David and Emily. "He plays too much."

"Naw, you *lose* too much," Mark teased, removing another chair.

"Bet money Sidra get out next," Malajia predicted, as the music started again.

"Underestimate me if you *want* to," Sidra threw back, walking around a chair.

"Malajia, shut up so we can hear the music," Alex hurled, minding her step.

"Take your ass back to—" The music stopping cut Malajia's rant to Alex short.

As the group dove for seats, Malajia tried to push a seat away from Sidra. The chair ended up sliding across the floor, sending Malajia sliding to the floor with it. "Ooooooh!" she belted out as her body stretched out on the hardwood. The room erupted with laughter and Sidra snatched the chair away from Malajia and sat in it.

"That's what the hell you get!" Alex yelled at Malajia, who was sprawled out on the floor.

Mark was nearly in tears. "Yoooo, baby!" he roared. "How you slide like that?"

"That's what your cheating behind *gets*," Sidra hissed.

Chasity was crying with laughter. "You see her face?"

"You hear that *sound* she made?" Jason laughed.

Malajia rolled over and sat up. "Fuck y'all!" she yelled at them.

"Malajia, if it were any of *us*, you'd be laughing too," Josh pointed out, laughter in his voice.

"So nobody is gonna help me up?" Malajia barked, dusting her arms off. When the laughter continued, she jumped up in a huff. "You know what, that's fine. At least *my* ass was the third to lose, so next one of y'all laughing asses get ready to run through those sprinklers."

"Yo Mel, can you slide like that in the bedroom later?" Mark teased, still laughing.

"Fuck you Mark," Malajia fussed, joining the loser side.

The music started again, sending the remaining group cautiously circling the remaining chairs. "Yo, I'm scared as shit right now," Mark mentioned, passing a chair.

"Who you tellin'?" Alex chuckled. Running through sprinklers was not on her to-do list. She didn't plan on tackling her hair until the day before graduation; getting it wet beforehand would derail that notion entirely.

"Mark, stop grabbing the fuckin' chairs," Jason barked, smacking Mark's hand off the top of a chair.

"You minding my business too much, bee," Mark threw back.

Sidra let out a groan. "David, you can stop it at any time now," she huffed, noticing the longer than usual play time.

Without notice, David quickly stopped the music. Everyone grabbed a chair, but Alex and Chasity both darted for the same one. As both girls went to sit down, Alex, using her bigger hips to her advantage, knocked Chasity out of the seat, sending her falling to the floor.

"Goddamn it you fat fuck!" Chasity snapped, grabbing her wrist.

"Call me what you *want*, but *I'm* not running through the sprinklers," Alex boasted, clapping her hands.

"Damn bitch, I thought you had more fight than that," Malajia mocked, folding her arms.

Chasity glanced back at Malajia as she rubbed her wrist. "She fuckin' tripped me in the process," she fumed.

"I am sorry about that, but your foot was under mine,"

Alex laughed.

Jason walked over to Chasity and helped her up from the floor. "You okay?" he asked, amusement in his voice.

"No, my damn wrist hurts," Chasity complained.

Jason grabbed her wrist and examined it. "Aww, I'm sorry. But you still gotta run through those sprinklers," he teased.

Chasity snatched her arm from his grasp and headed for the others.

"Ahhh, you thought Jason was gonna get you out of the sprinklers," Mark mocked, pointing.

"Shut up, at least *he* helped her up," Malajia hissed at him.

Mark tossed his arms in the air. "Malajia, I'll pull the splinter from your ass later on, what's the problem?" he threw back.

Malajia flipped him off.

Sidra, Mark, Jason, and Alex stared each other down as the music began playing. They hadn't gotten around the chairs one good time before the music stopped. Alex tried to take a seat, but Jason beat her to it, sliding himself and his seat back. Alex lost her footing and slid into the cluster of removed chairs, screaming in the process.

"Why you always gotta knock shit over?!" Mark barked at her, standing from his seat.

"That's exactly what the fuck you get," Chasity snarled at her.

Alex quickly jumped from the floor and pointed at Jason. "Did you really have to move the seat like that?!" she wailed. "You already *had* it."

"That was payback for my baby," Jason threw back, taunting as he pointed to Chasity. "I got you babe."

Chasity flashed a smile at him as she twirled some hair around her finger. Alex meanwhile, just rubbed her leg as she let out a loud huff.

"This is the *last* damn game I play with y'all behinds," Alex grumbled, moving aside.

"Jase helped Chaz up from the floor *and* got Alex back for her," Malajia hurled at Mark. "What good are *you*?"

"That shit Jase did don't matter, Chaz *still* gotta run through the sprinklers!" Mark belted out.

"What does that have to do with helping your girlfriend off the damn floor?!" Malajia yelled back.

"You distracting me from the music," Mark barked, as the music began again.

"Stay in there Sidra," Emily encouraged, clapping. Sidra gave a quick thumbs up as she rounded a chair.

"Yeah, win it for the sisters," Alex added.

"Shut *up*," Chasity spat out, earning an eyeroll from Alex.

Malajia snickered. "She mad, nobody wants her encouragements," she teased.

Seeing David glance down at Jason's phone, Mark smiled slyly. "Jason, David just dropped your phone," he quickly belted out.

Jason's head snapped towards David, who looked confused as he stopped the music. Jason was too late. Sidra and Mark dove for the final seats, leaving Jason standing there annoyed. He glared at Mark, who just made taunting faces at him.

"I should kick your lying ass out that chair," Jason threatened.

"That still won't change the fact that you out the game, football boy," Mark threw back, then flinched and slid back when Jason made a move towards him.

"Jase, chill out," Chasity called after him.

Realizing that going back and forth with Mark was pointless, Jason flagged him with his hand and walked over to join the rest of the eliminated group.

Mark stood up and got close to Sidra's face. "Last round Princess, you ready to ring that doorbell?" he taunted.

"Do you *have* to be this close to my damn face?" Sidra hissed.

"Yep," Mark threw back, unfazed by her attitude with

him. He pointed to David while holding his intense gaze on Sidra. "David, drop that beat," he ordered.

David shook his head as he started the music for the last time.

Sidra and Mark made their way around the remaining seat. "I hope you got a loud knock," Mark taunted.

"Why are you still *talking?*" Sidra ground out.

"'Cause he just wants to make noise, don't lose your focus Sidra," Alex put in from the sidelines.

"You better not push her or trip her Mark," Josh warned.

Sidra tried to fight the smile building inside of her at the sound of Josh's protective words. It wasn't rare, but it meant more to her now.

Mark ignored him as he held his focus. When the music stopped, determined not to lose, Mark screamed at the top of his lungs as he lunged for the chair.

"Oh come on!" Alex yelled of Mark's unnecessary loudness.

The scream startled Sidra; she hesitated. Mark quickly sat down and began clapping loudly.

"Yeeeessss! I told y'all I wasn't losing!" he boasted.

His friends watched him clap loudly as he did a dance in his seat.

Malajia was embarrassed. She pinched the bridge of her nose as a defeated Sidra walked over.

"Your man his freakin' issues," Sidra huffed.

Malajia lifted her head and stared at Mark, who was sliding the chair across the floor as he continued to celebrate his victory. "I know, I know," she agreed.


"That sprinkler looks like it's gonna soak you to your soul," Mark laughed, giving Chasity a soft nudge as the group stood on the lawn outside of the president's campus house. The property was off in a corner of the grounds; students rarely had a reason to be back there.

"Must we relive me punching you freshman year?"

Chasity hissed, glaring at Mark; his smile quickly faded. "I *told* you about touching me."

"How are you *still* mean?" Mark threw back.

"Chaz, ignore him," Jason cut in, placing his hand on Chasity's shoulder. "Look, you're a fast runner so you shouldn't get too wet."

"This sprinkler is old as shit," Chasity griped.

"Probably got old ass mosquito water in it and shit," Malajia teased.

Chasity stomped her foot on the ground and let out a whine. "Come on, Sidra trade me," she proposed, looking at Sidra, who stood next to her with an equally annoyed look on her face. "You run through the sprinklers and *I'll* knock on the door."

"Nope," Sidra refused. "I don't feel like dealing with my hair until Saturday night."

Chasity rolled her eyes and faced the spraying water.

"Girl, just do it so we can get out of here," Alex egged on, laughter in her voice. "And try not to scream, you don't wanna wake up President Bennett."

"Please, President Bennett don't live in this raggedy ass campus house," Malajia sneered, flipping her hair over her shoulder. "It's just there for looks."

"Then what's the point of me knocking on the door?" Sidra wondered, confused.

"'Cause you lost and that was the rules," Mark grunted. "Stop tryna get out of shit... You too Chasity. Get to running."

Chasity sucked her teeth. "Fine," she sighed, moving closer to the grass. "It looks cold though... I'm anemic."

"You've been taking your iron pills, I'm sure you'll be fine," Jason assured, amused.

"Yo, if you fall, I'm gonna die laughing," Malajia said.

"Don't tempt me," Chasity snarled; Malajia sucked her teeth. She looked back at the group. "Sooo when you say run *through*, you mean...."

"Just *do* it!" they yelled at her.

"*Okay*, shit." Chasity let out a loud huff, then took off running through the grass. "This water doesn't have to be this fuckin' cold!" she shrieked as the water hit her.

"You're gonna wake up the president!" Alex laughed.

"Fuck her!" Chasity yelled, running back through the water to get to the sidewalk. As she nearly made it, Mark ran and jumped on the grass and blocked her way, trapping her in the sprinkler's spray. "Move!"

"Bask in the wetness," Mark laughed, as he heard complaints from the others. He kept blocking Chasity's way, until she punched him in the stomach. He let out a yelp and doubled over.

"That's *exactly* what you get," Jason hurled at Mark, who knelt down in the grass and coughed. "You play too damn much."

Malajia shook her head. "Sidra, trade me boyfriends," she grunted.

"No, I'm okay," Sidra threw back.

Chasity folded her arms to her chest and stood back with the group. Jason laughed as he put his arms around her.

"Never noticed how wavy your hair gets when it's wet," Alex teased.

Chasity narrowed her eyes at her. "Yeah? At least my length still shows when it's wet," she threw back.

Alex grabbed a few strands of her naturally wavy hair and held it. "Funny, but *mine* is dry now, so…"

"You okay bro?" Josh asked Mark, who was slowly standing to his feet.

Mark held his stomach as he slowly walked over. "Naw, I *told* y'all she punches like a fuckin' boxer." He tapped Sidra and pointed to the door. "Go knock so I can go to the bathroom. She done stirred up my goddamn dinner."

"Just EWW!" Malajia snapped, stomping her foot on the ground.

Sidra let out a sigh as she headed off in the door's direction. She glanced back at the group, who were egging her on. "This is so stupid," she complained, reaching the front step. She slowly walked up and hesitated for a moment, then slowly raised her hand to knock.

"Sidra Ophelia Howard is about to knock on your door!" Mark yelled at the top of his lungs.

Sidra flinched, then her eyes widened when she saw a light flick on from the window.

"Shit!" Sidra shrieked, then quickly tapped on the door before taking off running with the rest of the group.

Once the house was out of their view, they stopped running. "Who the hell is in there?" Sidra wondered, glancing back.

"Good job with getting your knock in still," David chortled, giving Sidra a pat on her arm. "What do you guys want to—" David's words were halted when he heard a small thunderclap. He frowned. "Is that—"

"Yup...rain," Josh confirmed when raindrops started falling. It took only a second for the trickle to become a downpour. Students who were enjoying the night air began to scream and scatter.

"Aww shit," Jason chuckled as the rain poured. "No point in even running."

"Are you kidding me?!" Alex shrieked, holding her hands out.

Chasity busted out laughing. "Ha! Now *everybody's* wet," she boasted. She pointed to Alex. "Go ahead and make wet hair jokes *now*, 'shrinkage'."

Malajia busted out laughing along with the rest of the group, as she tried to shield her face from the rain.

"Malajia, you have a butt load of weave tracks that's getting wet," Alex sneered.

"Fuck these tracks, I'm getting my hair redone on Saturday," Malajia teased. "You mad you can't tease me, 'mop n fro'."

Alex sucked her teeth as she and the group continued walking through campus. But after a minute or two, she just smiled. "This may very well be the last time that we all get caught in the rain together," she mused.

"I didn't know that was a thing," Mark griped. Alex sucked her teeth. "My bad, I gotta go to the bathroom."

Alex shrugged. "Just noting moments like this, that's all."

# Chapter 48

Ms. Smith arranged the folders on her desk, then adjusted her blazer. Senior exit sessions were something that she looked forward to more so than freshman sessions. She anticipated how much the students had changed, especially her most memorable students.

She looked up and smiled as the first student of the day entered her office. "Miss Howard, it's so nice to see you again," she beamed.

Sidra smiled as she took a seat in front of Ms. Smith's desk. "It's been a while, huh?" Sidra mused.

"Four years," Ms. Smith chuckled. "Shocked to see you without the business suit."

Sidra glanced down at her jean capris and turquoise short-sleeved top. "Yeah," she agreed. "I've found that wearing that every day comes off a bit stuffy."

"Did you think that you were stuffy before?"

"A little," Sidra answered.

Ms. Smith fixed the collar of her blazer. "Well, if it means anything, you always looked very polished."

Sidra managed a smile.

"So Miss Howard, how have the last four years been for you?" Ms. Smith wondered.

"They've been good," Sidra answered.

Ms. Smith took notice of the difference in Sidra. She didn't have that smile plastered to her face. The one that Sidra used when she let Ms. Smith know during their first visit that everything was perfect in her world.

"That's good to know."


"Miss Harris, I must say that I can see a difference in you from the other times that I've met with you," Ms. Smith smiled.

Emily looked Ms. Smith in her eyes as she pushed some of her hair behind her ear. "Really?" she grinned.

"Yes," Ms. Smith confirmed. "You seem more confident. You're not constantly looking at the floor or your hands..."

"I'm happy that it's noticeable to you," Emily said.

"Is it noticeable to *you*?"

Emily nodded. "It is, I guess," she replied. "I'm not going to lie, even though I've found some confidence, the old insecurities in me sometimes resurface."

"No matter how old you get, there will always be times where you feel a bit insecure about something," Ms. Smith said. "That doesn't mean that you're reverting, just continue to find your strength in those moments."

"I'll try to keep that in mind," Emily promised.


"Don't worry Ms. Smith, I'm not gonna ask about parties or boys," Malajia joked, crossing her legs in her seat.

Ms. Smith chuckled. "Ah, you remember."

"Yeah," Malajia replied. "I remember sounding like a desperate idiot." She let out a little laugh. "Anyway, I think I'm partied out and I'm only worried about *one* man now so..."

"I take it that these last four years have caused you to take life more seriously," Ms. Smith observed. It was clear that the woman before her wasn't the same scantily clad teenager, who had the attention span of a toddler. "I knew that it would eventually happen. As much as you tried to deny it."

Malajia's smile faded as she thought about everything that she had been through. "Yeah well…when you've been through enough serious things…you tend to change your outlook on life," she said, reflective. "What I thought was important back then…just isn't anymore."

"And what things are those?"

Malajia shrugged. "Like, looking for attention in the wrong places for one. I was so focused on people seeing me, that I didn't pay attention to who was actually *looking* and…I ended up in situations that I wish I *hadn't*."

A mask of concern fell upon Ms. Smith's face. "Do you want to talk about that?"

Malajia shook her head. "I don't want to give that part of my experience here anymore of my attention," she said. "Just know that I've learned from it."


"Miss Parker, you're not frowning today," Ms. Smith observed, adjusting herself in her seat.

"Do you *want* me to?" Chasity threw back.

"No," Ms. Smith chuckled. "So how have things been for you over these past years?"

Chasity slowly shook her head. "Not easy," she admitted.

"Yeah, unfortunately some students have a hard time adjusting to college, while some breeze through."

"That's not what I mean," Chasity clarified. "College itself wasn't that hard…it was dealing with life *outside* of it."

Ms. Smith listened intently. "I could tell when I first met you that you had a rough life," she said, tone caring. "Your anger…I knew it had to come from somewhere."

"Yeah well, I've gone through more than I *should* have in these twenty-two years of my life," Chasity replied, moving some of her hair from her face. "I'm just trying to keep my anger from surfacing as much as it has in the past."

"Miss Parker, you putting your anger aside to allow yourself to enjoy life, despite the things that you've been through, shows a lot of growth."

"Yeah, I said I'm *trying* to," Chasity returned. "A lot of it is still there."

"It may *never* go away," Ms. Smith pointed out. "But the key is in how you manage it and to not let your past stop you from enjoying your future."


"Miss Chisolm, how have things been going for you?" Ms. Smith smiled when Alex sat down.

"Great," Alex smiled. "I'm sooo excited to be graduating. I can't believe that four years are up already."

"Been a good experience for you, I take it?"

Alex crossed her leg and folded her hands over her elevated knee. "For the most part," she said. "Not going to lie, these past years came with some mess."

"I can imagine."

"Yeah, things got pretty rough for me at times," Alex recalled. "I lost some relationships, gained some trust issues..."

"I'm sorry to hear that," Ms. Smith sympathized.

Alex nodded. "Thanks." She took a deep breath. "To be honest, I let it consume me for a while and yes it did cause some friction in my friendships but now...I feel like I'm no longer bitter; I feel like I'm over it."

"That is great to hear, for bitterness can cause us to have a negative outlook on situations and people who may not deserve it," Ms. Smith pointed out.

Alex knew that all too well. "Tell me about it... It costed me a potential new relationship," she sulked.

"Well Miss Chisolm, the bright side is that now you can experience your life *without* the negativity," Ms. Smith smiled.

"I agree and I'm looking forward to it."


"Miss Howard, you look a bit troubled," Ms. Smith

observed.

"*Do* I?" Sidra wondered. The things on her mind, from Josh, to where to go to law school, to leaving her college world behind, had Sidra feeling a bit scattered.

"Yes…are things okay?"

Sidra thought for a moment. In the past, she would have put on a smile, tossed her ponytail over her shoulder and given a polite "everything is fine." But at this point in her life, she had grown tired of that façade. She no longer cared. "I don't think so," Sidra admitted. Ms. Smith just stared at her, listening. "To be honest…I think I'm losing my mind."

"Why is that?"

"Because when I first got here, I had this plan of how things would be. I knew exactly what I wanted and I was so certain about things and now…" Sidra let out a sigh. "I'm walking around confused and—I don't have it together anymore."

"You're twenty-two years old, not having it together at this age is normal," Ms. Smith chuckled. "This time in your life is for testing the waters, figuring things out… It's okay if your plan derails a bit."

"You sure? Because I feel like I'm twisting in the wind," Sidra said, adjusting the bracelet on her wrist. "There are things that I feel, that I can't say… I don't know where I want to continue my education… I'm confused a lot—I don't know." Sidra shook her head.

Ms. Smith leaned forward in her seat as she studied the woman in front of her. She smiled. "*That's* the Sidra that I wanted to meet freshman year," she mused.

Sidra looked confused.

"The person that you were hiding behind that prim appearance," Ms. Smith clarified. "The *real* you… I like her, she's relatable."

Sidra managed a chuckle. "She's a hot mess."

"No, she's *human*," Ms. Smith corrected. "And she'll be just fine."

Sidra smiled slightly. "I hope you're right."


"What are your plans after graduation?" Ms. Smith asked Emily.

Emily smiled. "Well, I was offered a job here in Virginia," she answered. "At the school where I did student teaching."

Ms. Smith's smile was bright. "That's wonderful," she beamed. "Are you going to take it?"

Emily sighed. "I *want* to."

"What's stopping you?"

"The usual," Emily answered, adjusting herself in her seat. "Fear, uncertainty, being on my own…"

"Fear of *what*?" Ms. Smith pressed.

"If I stay here, I'll be totally on my own…and as much as I have changed, I admit that I was able to do that because of my support system here at this school—my friends were here to help me through it," Emily explained. "What if I get out there on my own and realize that I still need them— *someone* as my crutch to help me maintain this new Emily? What if I fall on my face? What if I fail?"

"Emily, you're letting that old you surface again," Ms. Smith said, caring. "The you that talked yourself out of everything. The you that wanted to run home because you were scared of new experiences… The you that almost flunked out because you didn't use your voice…"

"I know, I *hated* that person," Emily sulked.

"Then don't *be* her. You know what you want, you just have to take a chance and go for it."

Emily stared at her. "What if I fall?"

"Then…you get back up," Ms. Smith said.

Emily slowly nodded as she pondered everything that was just said to her. "Okay."


"Miss Simmons, the fact that you have gone through

whatever it was that you have and came out of it okay and with a positive outlook is admirable," Ms. Smith commended.

"Thanks…I mean I'm not saying that there aren't times that I don't regret some things but—"

"Hindsight is twenty-twenty; remember that," Ms. Smith cut in. "We always see things clearer after they happen."

"Tell me about it," Malajia muttered. "But as much as I wish I hadn't gone through those things…I know it helped me change. I see myself and the people close to me differently."

Ms. Smith smiled.

"I mean…I never thought in a million years that the man that I *despised* would become the love of my life. I never thought that a bunch of girls who irked my entire face, and who were *not* one of my eighty sisters would become…my *sisters*." Malajia smiled to herself. "It's just crazy how life happens, you know. And how much one can grow."

"I know exactly what you mean," Ms. Smith agreed. "You should be proud of yourself for your growth and perseverance."

"I am," Malajia assured.


"What is one thing that you've learned over this time?" Ms. Smith asked.

Chasity stared at her. "You mean from classes or just about life in general?" she questioned.

"Let's try *both*, if you don't mind."

Chasity examined her nails. "Well…as far as classes go, I learned that I don't hate math as much as I thought I did," she said. Then she shook her head. "No I'm lying, I do. I hate it and I suck at it but at least I can get through it now."

Ms. Smith chuckled. "It's wonderful that you improved."

"Yeah well, I have my boyfriend to thank for that," Chasity joked.

"So you learned that even though you thought that you couldn't do something, you realized in the end you could."

Chasity tilted her head. "I guess."

"And the other thing?"

Chasity thought for a moment. "I learned that…I'm not alone," she said, catching herself off guard. "I used to think that I didn't matter to anybody…that I *had* nobody…that nobody *cared*."

Ms. Smith held a sympathetic gaze. "That's a tough way to feel."

"It's tough to *live* through," Chasity confirmed. "It was…lonely. But now I know that there are people in my life who I *do* matter to, and who matter to *me*… I know that despite how some people *still* act towards me…I am in fact, loved. And aside from my degree…that was something that I needed."

Ms. Smith felt like shedding a tear. Seeing how far the woman before her had come, she wanted to give her a hug, but knew that that would not be professional. "Miss Parker…that's an amazing thing to learn and I truly hope that you can continue with that positivity… I hope that the worst is behind you."

Chasity smirked. "As much as I hope that too, I know that won't be the case," she said. "Life is life and stuff happens, but at least now I know that no matter what else is thrown at me…I won't have to face it on my own…so no matter what, I'll be okay."

Ms. Smith smiled. "That, you will."

"You know, I remember you telling me, during our freshman session that not everybody needed another mother," Alex recalled. "And that not everybody handles things the same way."

Ms. Smith smiled and nodded as Alex continued.

"And I not only heard that from *you*, but from many people in my life, and I just thought they'd get over it. That I was doing what I felt was best for my friends and that I was right in how I felt things should be handled," Alex revealed.

Ms. Smith nodded. "That didn't go over well with the people in your life, did it?"

Alex chuckled. "No, not at all," she admitted. "I have been cussed out *many* times over it... But it wasn't until I started going through my *own* stuff that I started to realize that, maybe everybody had a point. I mean...no matter what people told me or suggested...I knew that I had to deal with my situation, and my feelings, in my own way and in my own time."

"That's a tough pill to swallow, realizing that you may have been wrong," Ms. Smith said. "But you seem to handle it well."

"Oh it took time, trust me...and many more arguments, and water thrown in my face but...I get it," Alex reminisced. "Everyone's business, is not *my* business. And the only person's issues that I need to focus on fixing are my *own*."

Ms. Smith leaned forward in her seat. "I tell students all the time, take from college, not just the things that you've learned from class, but take the real-life lessons as well. And I'm happy to see that you're doing it."

Alex smiled. "Yeah, I can honestly say that these were some of the hardest, but the best years of my life," she mused. "I wouldn't trade them for anything... I'd do it all over again."

"The good thing is that you don't have to," Ms. Smith chuckled. "But, it's good to know that you would. It means that you got the best out of this experience."

Alex nodded and smiled. "Yeah, I did."

# Chapter 49

David held up his maroon-colored graduation gown. "Wow, finally I get to hold this in my hands," he mused. "And my Suma Cum Laude sash."

"You hype as shit," Mark joked. "You'll have that damn thing on for two hours at the most then it'll be thrown in the basement somewhere."

The day before graduation and the senior class was picking up their cap and gowns before having to go to graduation practice. David and Mark were getting ready to head out to meet the others.

David laughed. "Maybe *yours* will be, but I'm cherishing this."

"Shiiit, I'm getting this big ass gown framed," Mark admitted. "This shit going right on my wall. Unlike *you*, I ain't gettin' no more."

"Well my friend, there is nothing wrong with just a bachelor's degree," David assured. "I know you'll do well with it."

"Thanks man," Mark smiled. He glanced at his watch. "Yo, we gotta go."

David hung his gown and sash on his closet door. "Yeah, time for graduation practice."

Mark began walking out the door and David started following. Then David looked over on his bed. "Hey, where'd my cap go?"

Mark turned around. "Say what?"

"My graduation cap," David clarified, pointing to the

space where he'd left it before going to turn in his post office key.

"I didn't see your cap bro. Maybe you misplaced it," Mark shrugged.

David scratched his head. "I *know* I left it on the bed." He looked at Mark, worried. "I left my door unlocked; you think someone could have taken it?"

Mark shot David a confused look. "Why would some random person come in your room just to take a damn cap?" he ground out. David opened his mouth to respond, but Mark put his hand up, stopping him. "Chill David, it'll turn up."

David let out a sigh. "You're right," he huffed. "I'll check behind the bed or something when I get back."

Mark gave David a pat on his back as they left.

Emily wiped a tear from her eye as she sat on the bench in front of the football stadium entrance.

Alex sat next to her, concerned. "Sweetie, what's wrong?" she charged.

Emily wiped another tear. "I just handed my mailbox key in," she sniffled, then laughed at the look on Alex's face. "I know, I know, I'm pathetic."

Alex giggled. "No, you're not," she placated. "Trust me, I've been getting emotional too. I shed a few tears when I picked up my cap and gown earlier."

Emily just nodded as she wiped another tear.

"Y'all crying at the wrong shit," Malajia sneered. "The *real* reason to cry is because y'all won't have the pleasure of living with *me* anymore."

Emily snickered as Alex twisted her lips to the side. "No, that would be a reason to *celebrate*," Alex threw back.

"Boooooo!" Malajia howled as she gave the thumbs down sign. Alex flagged her. Malajia looked at her watch. "Where the hell is Mark and David? The damn practice is about to start."

"I don't know about *you* guys, but I'm nervous," Sidra

said, adjusting the headband on her head.

"Why?" Josh asked, looking at her.

"Because, somebody is bound to fall while walking up to get their degree...and I swear to God, if it's me, I'll be humiliated." Sidra said.

"Shit if *I* fall, I'm laying my ass right there," Chasity joked, opening a pack of crackers. "Hand me my shit and leave me be."

Malajia laughed. "I'll come and fall out with you," she promised. "Right on the grass."

Emily giggled, then the smile left her face. "Guys...*I'm* nervous for tomorrow too," she admitted.

"Yeah, I don't blame you. *You* might be the one to bust your ass...you can't walk in heels," Malajia teased.

Emily shook her head. "That's not what I meant, but thanks for jinxing me," she ground out.

"Why do *I* keep getting sarcastic Emily?" Malajia complained, folding her arms.

Chasity handed Malajia a cracker. "Here, put this in your mouth and shut up," she ordered. Amused, Malajia took the cracker and bit it.

"No but, I talked to my mom today and she told me that Jazmine is coming to graduation," Emily revealed.

"*Why?*" Chasity scoffed, frowning.

"Does she still got that caterpillar on her face?" Malajia asked, referencing Jazmine's bushy eyebrows.

"Malajia—"

"No, it's a legitimate question," Malajia quickly cut in, interrupting Alex. "She gonna end up scaring people and shit."

Emily stared at Malajia, wide eyed. "Um...I don't know. I haven't seen her."

"You know you have to ignore her," Alex pointed out, pointing to Malajia. Malajia just sucked her teeth in return.

"Anyway," Emily said, going back to her original train of thought. "That girl *still* hates me. *Especially* since Mommy put her out after she called herself berating me to her." She sighed. "I'm afraid that she's gonna say or do something to ruin the day for me."

"Emily, if she tries it, punch that bitch," Sidra hissed, taking Emily by surprise. "Seriously, don't let her ruin anything for you... She could stay her miserable ass home for all that."

Chasity stared at Sidra. "Shit...you actually took the words out of my mouth," she said. "I'm so proud."

Sidra chuckled.

Alex put her hand on Emily's arm. "Em, try not to worry about it. Your parents and your brothers will be here to check her if need be," she placated.

Emily let out a sigh. "I guess you're right," she said, tone unconvincing.

Malajia was about to say something else, when she looked over and saw Mark and David walk up. "'Bout time."

"*Good morning*," Mark sneered to her.

Malajia put her hand up. "Oh right, good morning... 'bout time," she spat out.

Mark shook his head in amusement. He looked at Jason. "How does it feel to be back at your old stomping grounds?" he asked of the football field. "It's been a while, huh?"

Jason looked confused. "I was just here *yesterday*."

Mark busted out laughing.

"Jase, I heard a few of your teammates are entering the draft," Josh announced.

"I know," Jason replied. "I'm happy for them and I wish them luck."

Mark put his hand up. "Look bro, I *know* you already said that you didn't want to go pro but...just know that you only have one year after you graduate to enter the draft—" Jason rolled his eyes. "All I'm saying is, think about the money man."

"It's not always about money," Chasity cut in, knowing Jason's feelings about playing professional football. "He's said time and time again that it was only paying for school. He doesn't want to play."

"But…the *money*," Mark harped. Jason couldn't help but laugh at the desperate look on Mark's face.

"Mark, even if he *did* play, *you* ain't gettin' none of that money," Malajia cut in. "It's going right to Chasity."

Chasity snickered as Jason shook his head in amusement.

"Jase, just keep me in mind as your manager. I can handle the groupies for you," Mark joked.

"Boy, I'll step on your shin if you think you going *anywhere* near groupies," Malajia hissed. "Stop having dumbass dreams and let's go get this practice over with."

Mark lowered his head. "Fine," he muttered.

Malajia closed the cabinet door and sighed. "Everything is gone besides these bags of that dry ass generic popcorn that Alex bought," she said, turning around. She leaned her back against the sink as she looked at Chasity, who was standing in the kitchen with her.

"I kept telling her that nobody eats that shit, but like always she doesn't listen," Chasity said, examining her nails.

Malajia let out a long sigh, but didn't respond.

Chasity glanced up at her; she frowned slightly at the down look on Malajia's face. "What's wrong with you?"

Malajia hesitated. "This is our last night here," she said after a moment. "I mean…our *last*, last night… Tomorrow, we *graduate*. It's unreal."

Chasity stared at her. "You're not about to *cry*, are you?" she jeered.

Malajia chuckled. "No…at least not *yet*."

Chasity folded her arms. "I wish that I could say that the four years here flew by, but I *can't*," she said.

"I know right?" Malajia agreed. "Waaay too much shit happened for time to fly…like how much more could we *possibly* go through?" She sighed again. "Chasity…I'm really going to miss you."

"Are you breaking up with me?" Chasity joked, inciting

a chuckle from Malajia.

"No, you asshole," Malajia threw back, amusement in her voice. "But I'm gonna miss...being *around* you every day, talking to you—"

Chasity just stared at Malajia as she spoke.

"When I met you, you were this evil ass bitch, who I couldn't *stand*," Malajia recalled. "I hated *everything* about you besides your clothes and your hair—"

Chasity shook her head in amusement.

"And you became my best friend...my sister," Malajia paused for a moment to prevent herself from getting choked up. "You saw me through so much and—I just...I don't know what I'm gonna do if I can't bug you anymore."

"There's always the phone."

"It's not the same," Malajia sulked.

"Yeah, I know," Chasity agreed, she sighed. "Look honestly...and you'll *never* hear me say this again," she began. "But...I'm gonna miss you too."

Malajia smiled bright. "Yeah?"

"Yeah," Chasity assured. "I don't know how the hell it happened, but you went from this stupid ass, simple twit who annoyed me *every* second of *every* minute of *every* day, and you *still* do actually—"

"Seriously?" Malajia sneered.

"*However*," Chasity amended. "You became *my* best friend. You were there for me when I thought I didn't need anyone... You checked me when I needed it, 'cause I *did* need it at times."

"*All* the time," Malajia joked.

"I didn't say that," Chasity threw back. "Look, you don't have to worry. I know I'm stuck with you and I'm okay with that."

"You damn *right*, you are," Malajia agreed. "And for the record, I am your *only* best friend okay," she stressed. "Ain't no 'Alex' mess with that 'you all are my best friends', no bitch, you get *one* best friend and it's *me*... It's bad enough I gotta share you with the other three, but that title is *mine*."

Chasity tried not to laugh. "Okay," she agreed.

"And while I'm on it, don't you even go making any more friends after we leave here," Malajia threw out, shaking her hand in Chasity's direction. "Your friend quota is filled, no new friends."

Chasity looked at Malajia as if she was crazy. "You done?"

"I am, but I mean it…let me call you and hear another bitch in the background that ain't somebody I know. I'mma drive down from wherever the hell I live and I'll beat your ass like I did at the cabin."

Chasity frowned. "Still lying about that shit? You did *not* beat my ass," she snarled.

"Maybe not, but I gave you work," Malajia joked.

"Want me to choke you again?"

"Want them ribs kicked again?" Malajia threw back.

Chasity flipped her the finger. "Cheap ass shot that was," she jeered.

Malajia laughed, "I apologize." Chasity flagged her with her hand. "You know what, let's have a shot."

Chasity watched as Malajia reached under the sink. "A shot of *what*?"

"This liquor I bought," Malajia answered, pulling a small bottle of alcohol from the cabinet.

"Come on Malajia, I'm not trying to be all hungover for graduation," Chasity complained as Malajia grabbed two small plastic shot glasses from a drawer.

"It'll be just one shot, you can't get drunk off of a shot," Malajia pressed.

"It's all *dark*," Chasity griped of the contents.

"It's *one* shot," Malajia threw back. "Come on, don't be corny. Have one shot with your bestie, in our house, on our last night here, before everybody come back and starts breathing all in the bottle and shit."

Chasity stared with disgust at the smiling Malajia. "Fine," she hissed, teeth clenched. She took the cup from Malajia and held it out for her to pour. "Don't fill it all the way up."

"Shut up," Malajia returned, filling her cup. She set the bottle down and raised her shot to Chasity's. "Here's to our friendship," she smiled.

"Yeah, yeah," Chasity sneered, tapping her cup to Malajia's.

"On three," Malajia said.

Malajia quickly counted to three and both girls threw their shot back. Malajia spat the majority of hers out as some of the strong liquor spilled down her throat. Chasity's got caught in her throat and she had no choice but to swallow it.

"God, what the fuck *was* that!" Chasity yelled, patting her chest repeatedly. She angrily threw her cup in the sink.

Malajia put her hands on her head. "Yoooo, I did *not* expect that," she said, coughing. "My chest is on *fire.*"

Chasity rubbed her watering eyes. "I swear to God, I'm about to cry," she griped, rubbing her chest. "It's burning my fuckin' soul."

Malajia held her hand over her chest as she started laughing.

"Malajia what *proof* is that?" Chasity barked.

Malajia couldn't stop laughing as she grabbed the bottle. "Oh shit, it's a hundred and fifty-one!"

"One fifty-one?!" Chasity exclaimed, coughing. "You trying to kill me you stupid bitch?"

"I didn't *know,*" Malajia laughed. "I just saw it was on sale."

"*And* it's cheap?" Chasity ranted. Malajia was hysterically laughing as Chasity grabbed her stomach. "I think it's burning my ovaries... I swear to God, it just ate through my insides... Yep, my uterus is gone."

Malajia wiped tears from laughter from her face. "I love you bitch," she said through her laughter.

"Love you too...just not right now," Chasity threw back,

patting her chest again.


David looked around at his friends as they sat at the girls' dining room table. Instead of going to the last party that was going on that evening, the group decided to spend their last night together in the house, playing cards.

David smiled. "Well guys...our last night."

"I know...it's surreal," Alex said, a hint of sadness in her voice.

"You sure we shouldn't go to that party?" Mark proposed, throwing out a card.

Alex shook her head. "No, I think we're right where we need to be."

"Whatever *that* means," Malajia teased. Alex sucked her teeth and Malajia laughed. "I'm just messing with you. It's my last night with you; you gotta let me get my digs in."

Alex tossed her hands up. "Very well, have at it."

Malajia became excited as she shifted in her seat. "Yeeesssss, free reign on 'Alex' jokes," she beamed.

Alex folded her arms in anticipation as laughter erupted around her. "What is your dig of choice Malajia Lakeshia Simmons?" she goaded. "My clothes, shoes...hair...phone—"

"Hair, ooh *gotta* be the hair," Malajia cut in, enthused. She pointed at Alex's wild, wavy locks and cleared her throat. "Alex your hair is...it's cool as shit, and I actually like it."

Alex looked totally shocked. "You *what?*" she asked in disbelief.

Malajia nodded. "Yeah, I mean it *does* look like a mop," she joked, laughter in her voice. "*But*...I respect the fact that you embrace your natural hair and don't let anybody... including *me*, sway you from sticking with it and you always should."

Alex was stunned. After years of enduring jokes from Malajia about her locks, she was touched. "Awww, Mel," she gushed. "Does this mean that deep down you wish *you* had my hair?"

"No, I want *her* hair," Malajia said, gesturing to Chasity who shook her head.

"Can't win them all," Alex chortled, putting her hands up. "But thank you and I'm going to actually miss your silly teasing…can't lie, you're pretty funny."

Malajia tossed her hands up. "See, I *told* you I'm hilarious."

"She ain't say all that," Mark jeered, tossing out a card.

Malajia shot him a glare.

Mark looked back at her and smiled at the anger on her face. "You know I love you."

Malajia tried to stay angry, but couldn't. She blushed and looked away. "You make me sick," she joked.

Josh tossed a card out. "I swear, I *still* don't know how you two even *happened* as a couple," he teased of Mark and Malajia.

"Neither do *we*," Mark and Malajia both said in unison. They pointed at each other.

"Jinx!" Malajia quickly said.

Mark slammed his hand on the table. "Damn it."

Josh laughed. "No seriously," he said. "I mean, seeing how we all met and interacted with each other when we first got here—Chaz when I first met you, you almost hit me with your *car*, and cussed me out about it—" Josh recalled, gesturing to Chasity.

"Oh come on, that was like eighty years ago," Chasity threw back, eyeing her cards.

"I know, and I'm *still* traumatized," Josh laughed. "No, but my point is that despite how we first met, I look at you like a sister now, so it's just funny how life works."

Chasity smiled at him. "Well…I'm sorry for almost hitting you with my car, even though you ran out in front of it," she chortled. "No but I get it… I came here an only child and I'm leaving with a bunch of siblings that I never wanted."

"You *know* you love us," Alex goaded.

Chasity shrugged. "Sometimes." She looked at Jason. "*And*, I'm leaving here with a man."

"A damn good, *patient* man," Jason stressed, grabbing her hand and giving it a kiss.

"Yes, I'd have to agree," Chasity said. "*Extremely* patient."

"You're worth it," Jason returned. "I love you."

"Love you too," Chasity replied.

"You two make us sick," Mark jeered, speaking for Malajia, who spat her drink out as she laughed. "Why can't y'all argue like *us*?"

"You *just* sat there and told Mel that you loved her in front of everybody," Jason pointed out.

"Yeah, but I made her *mad* first," Mark threw back, a sad attempt to make a point.

Jason looked confused, then shook his head and grabbed his drink. "I don't even know why I respond sometimes."

Mark laughed.

"You know what's funny?" Alex cut in, laughter in her voice. "Everyone who came here single, is leaving with a significant other, and the one who came here in a *relationship,* is leaving here *single*."

Sidra's eyes shifted as she threw out a card, but she kept silent.

"Damn, sorry Alex," David consoled.

Alex waved her hand. "Oh it's fine," she assured. "Everything worked out how it was *supposed* to. I'm over it."

"Still no luck with Eric, huh?" Sidra asked, sympathetic.

Alex shrugged as she looked down at the table. "Well...we went to dinner last Friday," she revealed. The girls' faces were shocked.

"How you keep that from us?" Malajia charged. "Damn, you holdin' out the scoop."

"Are you guys gonna date now?" Emily asked, enthused.

Alex sighed. "Well...no," she answered. "But we talked and...we're friends again."

"Why does it feel like you're leaving stuff out?" Chasity asked.

"Because I *am*," Alex confessed. She ran her hand over her hair. "Truth is, I asked him to date me and he told me no."

"Oooohhh!" Mark belted out, then put his hand over his mouth when he saw the look on Alex's face. "My bad."

"Wait, are you *serious*?" Sidra frowned. "I thought that's what he *wanted* all this time."

"It wasn't like that Sid," Alex assured. "It's just not the right time and I won't go into every single detail right now, but... We talked about it, he made a lot of sense and... Like I said, we're friends again so, I'm good."

"Well, as long as you're okay, that's all that matters," Emily said.

"I *am*," Alex smiled.

"Yo, you know what *else* is funny?" Mark said.

"What's that?" Alex wondered.

"I ain't seen Sidra in a ponytail in a *minute*," Mark teased.

Sidra put her hand over her face and laughed. "Yeah well, it was time to give the edges a break," she joked, smoothing her hair with her hand.

"Sidra, I can definitely see a change in you," Alex said. "*Aside* from the hair... You seem a lot less porcelain for lack of a better word."

"Porcelain?" Malajia sneered. "Alex, you was just on my good side, don't make me go back to the hair jokes."

"It's too late, you already complimented me and you can't take it back," Alex teased, then stuck her tongue out at Malajia.

"No, I know what she meant Mel," Sidra cut in, tone calm. "I um...I'm learning that it's okay to not have it together. I know that I'm not perfect so why should I continue to *pretend* to be?"

"I don't think you pretended to be perfect," Emily said.

"I *did*," Sidra contradicted. "And in doing so, I became

self-centered and judgmental." She took a deep breath. "I don't like that person...that person *hurts* people." She looked at Malajia. "And I'm sorry."

Malajia just looked down at the table.

"Look, we've *all* said and done things that has hurt people," Alex cut in.

"*I* haven't," Mark lied, at an attempt to break the seriousness.

"I beg to differ," David contradicted. "Need I remind you about said 'blind date' incident?"

"Naw, I'm good," Mark laughed.

Emily looked around the table, after a few moments of silence and took a deep breath. "Guys, can I tell you something without you teasing?"

"Naw," Chasity said.

"Nope, not at all," Malajia added.

Emily shook her head as the girls broke into laughter.

"We're joking, go ahead," Malajia gestured.

Emily put her hands on the table. "I just want to say that... I want to say thank you to all of you for helping to make me the person that I am now," she began as the room fell silent. "You guys dragged me out of my shell, cussed me out when I needed it, supported me and helped me—" she felt tears fill her eyes. "Guys, when my brothers weren't talking to me, you filled that void... Girls...even though I annoyed you, you still stuck by me and forced me to get my mess together... Even though you had your own stuff going on, you still were there for *me*. You made the *scariest* time in my life, one of the *best* times of my life, and I'm gonna miss each and every one of you." Emily wiped the tears from her face as her friends sat around her, silent.

Mark rubbed his eyes. "Damn onions," he muttered, inciting chuckles from the room.

"Emily...I can speak for everybody when I say that it has been a pleasure to watch you blossom into the woman that you are. I know you feel that we only had an impact on you, but you impacted *us* as well," Alex said. "We're going to miss you too, and anytime you need us for *anything*…just call us. But I know that you're strong enough now to handle everything that life throws at you, on your own."

Emily smiled through her tears. "Thank you," she said.

"Anybody else wanna get sentimental?" Mark joked.

"No but you guys already know…y'all are my peoples for life."

"Couldn't have said it better myself," Josh smiled.

Malajia cleared her throat. "*I* actually have something else to say," she began, grabbing everyone's attention. "Sidra," she called.

Sidra looked up at her. "Yeah?"

Malajia paused for a moment. "I forgive you."

Sidra stared at her, emotion showing on her face. "You do?"

Malajia nodded. Sidra, overcome with emotion, stood up from her seat and made her way over to Malajia, who too stood from her seat.

"I love you," Malajia said as she embraced the emotional Sidra.

"I love you too," Sidra sniffled.

"Damn onions!" Mark repeated, rubbing his eyes.

"Awww, you guys, I thought I was done crying," Emily gushed, putting her hand over her face.

"Now *this* is what I call, leaving on a good note," Alex beamed, clasping her hands together.

Chasity stared at Alex with disgust. "Your corny ass always gotta ruin shit," she jeered.

Alex laughed. "I'll miss you too cranky," she threw back.

Mark clapped his hands, then looked down at the table. "Who's winning this game?" he wondered, eyeing the cards scattered along the table.

"I don't think anybody knows," Jason chortled.

"So everybody just been throwing cards out for no reason?" Mark asked, picking up several cards. "Who's three is this? That ain't even a good card to play."

David raised his hand. "That would be mine," he laughed.

Mark sucked his teeth. "Fuck this game, let's play some spades."

"No!"

Mark flinched at the united voices of his friends' protest.

# Chapter 50

Jason laughed as his mother clung to him, gripping him in a hug. "Mom, I didn't even *graduate* yet."

"I'm just so proud of you," Mrs. Adams gushed, tears spilling down her face.

Jason patted his mother's back and shook his head in amusement at his father and brother. He'd expected to see his family at the stadium, but Jason was surprised when they knocked on his door as he was about to head out to graduation.

"She started crying ever since she got in the car earlier," Kyle Adams teased.

Jason stared at him. It was still hard to believe that his little brother was seventeen years old. It seemed like only yesterday, he was just thirteen. "I'd still like to know when your voice got so deep," Jason teased.

Kyle laughed. "I have no idea brother."

Mr. Adams gently took hold of his wife's arm. "Nance, come on, you're going to wrinkle the man's gown," he said. "Plus we have to go find some seats."

"I heard they're filling up pretty fast, so you better get going," Jason urged as his mother finally released her grip.

"I'm not trying to hear that," Mrs. Adams returned, straightening out Jason's collar. "You won way too many games for this school, so they just better have some seats saved for the family of their star."

Mr. Adams lowered his head and shook it. "Good God, don't start."

"She's gonna cuss people out, watch," Kyle chuckled.

"Mom, I am *begging* you, control it okay," Jason urged. "I'm *not* the only graduate."

Mrs. Adams waved her hand dismissively as she smiled. "Baby, you have nothing to worry about. I would *never* ruin your day," she assured.

Jason stared at her, unconvinced. "Mom—"

"I promise," she cut in, putting her right hand up. She gave him another hug as her husband and other son walked out of the house. "I'm proud of you."

"I know," Jason smiled, hugging her back. "See you soon."

"See you soon," Mrs. Adams beamed.

"Nancy!" Mr. Adams boomed from outside.

Jason laughed as he watched his mother roll her eyes and walk out the door.

"Ahh, Mom you got screamed," Kyle teased, earning a smack to the back of the head by both of his parents.

Jason busted out laughing at the salty look on his brother's face. "Uh huh, that's what you get." Shutting the door, he looked at his watch. "Guys!" he shouted up the steps. "Come on, we gotta go!"

"A'ight!" Mark yelled back.


David stood in his room and let out a loud sigh as he placed his hands on his head in a panic. Josh and Mark walked through his open door.

David faced them. "I still can't find my cap," he fumed. "I looked everywhere. There is nothing left in this room but a damn suitcase... The office won't give me another one. I'm screwed."

"Everything will be fine David," Josh placated.

"Josh, I'm giving a damn valedictorian speech in front of the *whole* student body, faculty, and families and I'm the *only* fool without a graduation cap," David ranted. "I don't know where the hell it *went*."

Mark stood there, one of his arms behind his back. He glanced at Josh. "Okay umm, I *might* know what happened to your cap," he began.

David frowned. "What do you mean? Where is it?"

"I took it," Mark admitted.

The discovery made David see red. "Are you freakin' kidding me?!" he erupted. "Dude, I've been stressing over that and you had it *all this time?*"

"Yes," Mark answered, nonchalant.

David looked like he was ready to explode. "Why?!" He tossed his arms up. "You just *had* to get one more stupid prank in on me before we left. Is that what it was?"

"David man, it's not like that," Mark assured.

"Can I just have the damn thing please, so we can get going?" David fussed, folding his arms.

"Go ahead, give it to him," Josh said, gesturing to David.

David in turn frowned at Josh. "*You* knew he had it *too?*"

Josh didn't answer as Mark pulled David's hat from behind his back. He held it, tilting it so that David could see the top of it.

All of David's anger left as he set his eyes on the top of the cap, covered in pictures of his mother. David slowly took the cap and stared at it. He was speechless. "Wow umm...how—"

"I called your Dad and asked him to email me some pictures of her," Mark said, pointing to the cap. "I just printed them out and put them on there."

David looked at Mark, overcome with emotion.

"I figured since she can't *physically* be here, that you can still have her with you if that makes sense," Mark explained.

Josh smiled, proud of his friend's kindness. He gave Mark a pat on the back. "This was all him, too," Josh said to David. "His idea."

David took a step forward and still unable to speak, he held his hand out for Mark to shake. Smiling, Mark shook his hand before pulling him into a hug.

"Thank you," David sputtered, as they parted. "This is—*thank* you."

"You're welcome," Mark returned.

David wiped a tear from his eye. "Damn it," he chuckled.

"It's cool bro, it's just the onions," Mark joked.

David laughed. "Right, we'll go with that." He carefully placed the cap on his head and took a deep breath. Smiling at his brothers. "I'd say we're ready."

"Agreed," Josh replied. "Let's go close this chapter."

"Girls, y'all look perfect, get out the mirror and come on!" Alex hollered up the steps as she adjusted the tassel on her graduation cap. "We gotta go!"

She smiled as the girls headed down the stairs.

"I had to fix my eyeliner," Sidra said, heading down.

"Yo, my dad is trippin'," Malajia complained, adjusting her gown.

"Why?" Emily chuckled.

"'Cause he mad that he gotta park far from the stadium," Malajia griped. "So now he cussing people out and shit. I *told* his old, decrepit knee having ass to get here early so he can get the good parking spots. He don't listen."

"At least you know where you get it from," Chasity joked, fixing a curl with her finger.

"Yeah, I wonder what you get from *your* dad," Malajia threw back.

"The ability to run," Chasity jeered.

Malajia stared blankly for a moment. She regretted her comeback. "Shoulda left that one alone huh?"

"Probably," Chasity threw back, nonchalant.

Emily fiddled with her necklace. "Girls, are you *sure* I look okay?" she panicked. "I feel like my curls are falling already."

"Oh, they are," Chasity confirmed.

Emily let out a whine.

"But they look fine," Sidra cut in, amused. "Your hair has a wavy look to it."

Alex stood there, watching her friends converse. Seeing them all in their caps and gowns. Realizing that they were no longer the sheltered, prudish, angry, and spacy teenagers that she first met, but mature, loving, strong women, who had managed to change her life. Never imagining being friends with them in the first place, now she couldn't imagine her life without them.

"Look at us," Alex gushed, halting their talking. They looked at her. "We did it…we really did it."

The girls just smiled back in agreement.

Alex felt a tear form. "I am so proud of each and every one of you," she said, emotional. "And I love you all…just please remember that, no matter *where* we all end up."

"We love you too," Sidra said, as the other girls said the same.

Alex held her arms out. "I know how much you all hate these, but this occasion calls for a group hug," she proposed. She was pleasantly surprised when the girls moved in for one big embrace.

"Congratulations girls," Emily said.

"Emily, you breathed *right* on my neck," Chasity scoffed, breaking the embrace.

Emily laughed. "I had nowhere else to breathe," she explained.

"Alex, I think you spit on me a little bit," Malajia joked.

"I didn't even say anything!" Alex exclaimed, humor in her voice.

Sidra shook her head. "These robes are hot," she complained, fanning herself.

"Yeah, let's get out of here," Alex agreed, heading for the door. She opened it and looked back inside as the girls walked out. "Bye house," she pouted.

"Alex, you still got a bag in your room, you'll be back here after graduation," Malajia pointed out, earning a playful backhand to her arm from Alex.

"Oh wait, we need a picture," Sidra said, facing them, holding up her phone.

"We gotta grab somebody to take it for us." Malajia glanced around outside. "Carl!" she yelled.

Carl, graduation gown in hand, stopped walking and looked at her. "Hey, it's graduation day. I'm not for no mess from you," he said, pointing at her.

"Boy shut up, you hype you graduating," Malajia teased as he walked over to them. "Sike naw, congratulations, now take this picture of me and my girls," she demanded, gesturing for Sidra to hand him the phone.

Carl shook his head as he held the phone up. "I feel sorry for Mark," he jeered.

"I feel sorry for your *cap* 'cause it can't fit on your big ass head," Malajia threw back.

Carl smirked and stood back, gesturing for the girls to move close together. "Y'all ready?" When they confirmed, he snapped the picture. "That's nice," he smiled.

"Thank you, Carl," Sidra smiled.

"Ooh, let me see," Malajia cut in, snatching the phone. Her eyes widened when she made a discovery. "I'm not in the picture!" she erupted.

Chasity busted out laughing along with the other girls.

"He zoomed me out!" Malajia fussed.

"Uh huh, you don't get smart with me and think I'm gonna do what you want," Carl ground out.

Malajia sucked her teeth, then looked over at Chasity, who was still laughing. She narrowed her eyes. "Bitch, you got a disrespectful ass laugh," she hissed.

"*Don't* she," Alex agreed, laughing.

Chasity was unfazed by Malajia's attitude; she found the situation hilarious.

"Carl, Malajia is sorry, can you *please* take a real picture of us?" Emily asked, handing Carl back the phone.

"Only for *you*, my future cousin-in-law," he teased.

Emily looked away in embarrassment. She'd almost forgotten that Carl was Will's cousin. Carl signaled for the girls to move in close again.

"I'm not getting on the end this time, I'm not playing with him," Malajia said, switching her position.

"Smile beautifuls," Carl prompted, before taking a perfect picture of them.


David sat in his seat on the graduation stage, nervous. As he listened to commencement take place, his mind was clouded with the speech that he was about to give. Speaking in front of a classroom of twenty made him nervous. He could only imagine how standing in front of nearly a thousand people would make him feel.

He took a deep breath when he heard his name being called. *Here goes nothing*, he thought, slowly standing as a loud, welcoming applause rang through the stadium. David chuckled to himself as he heard a familiar voice yell his name. *Mark will forever be loud*, he mused.

He took another deep breath, and gave the top of his cap a touch before walking to the podium. He placed his hands on both sides of the wood stand and glanced down. He'd memorized his speech, but was secretly wishing that he had the papers in front of him in case he forgot anything. *Chill out...you got this.*

He looked up, staring at the crowd of eager excited faces in front of him. "Good morning President Bennett, faculty, graduates, friends and family," he began.

"Yeaaaaahhhh!" Mark shouted, earning laughter from the crowd.

David couldn't help but laugh.

Mr. Bradley, who was sitting on the stage, pointed at Mark. "Mr. Johnson...I'm *so* glad you're graduating," he joked, earning more laughter.

"Likewise," Mark said, pointing at him.

David shook his head in amusement as the laughter subsided. "When I was told that I would be giving the valedictorian speech, I was honored and excited...and nervous," he said. "My mind started going crazy trying to think about what to say to you all... How can a shy, nerd, encourage an entire graduating class? ...Well, I finally got my thoughts together and...here goes nothing." He smiled as he adjusted the honors sash on his shoulder. "Ever since I was a child, I had a plan... Yes at seven years old, I had a grown-up plan, yes I was *that* weird." He smiled when he achieved some laughter from the crowd. "I knew that as long as I kept with that plan, that everything in my life would go exactly how it should."

"But as the years went on and life happened, I realized that things don't exactly *go* as planned... I never expected to lose my mother at fifteen years old, but going through that made me realize what it was that I really wanted to do with my life... I also never expected, when coming here four years ago, that my time here wouldn't be just about books... The friends that I came here with and the ones that I met here wouldn't let that happen for me," he smiled to himself. "I never expected to be part of a group of people who are *polar opposites* of one another, and despite our differences, they accepted me for who I was...even though they never shied away from the glasses jokes. Thanks guys," he joked. "But...those people became my family, and it taught me that forming strong friendships is another part of the college experience...which some may not realize, but it's *just* as important as studying hard."

"So yeah...for me, life did not go as planned, and I'm pretty sure that it's the same for many of you... Some of us may have jobs already secured, some of us may not. Some of us will go on to further our education, some of us will stop at our bachelor's degree. Some of us may end up with careers in our chosen field, some of us may end up in a career that they never thought they would be in... But no matter *what*, I just want all of you, myself included, to strive to do whatever makes us happy. Follow your own dreams no matter where they take you, and I know it gets hard sometimes, but always try to stay positive... Think about it, we came in here freshman year with *way* more people than this… Not everybody made it here today, but *we did*, and that's an accomplishment in *itself.* So, whenever you feel discouraged, or start to doubt yourself, just remember that you made it this far, and if you can do *this*, you can do *anything.*"

He smiled again. "Another thing, for those of you who decide not to take your education further, don't think that your learning and lessons are over…" he laughed when he heard some groans. "Oh no, learning *never* stops. Because when it comes to life…class is *always* in session… This ride called life will be a bumpy one, but it'll be well worth the trip… So my fellow gradates, go out there and live… Congratulations, and thank you."

David smiled bright as applause and cheers rang throughout the stadium. He took a breath and looked around as applause continued. Spotting the faces of his loved ones, both friends and family, he nodded. *Piece of cake.*

# Chapter 51

"Move, it's *hot!*" Malajia barked, shaking her six sisters off, who had her engulfed in a group hug. Graduation was now over; the class had gone from students to alumni. Malajia, like the rest of her friends, had separated along the grounds outside of the stadium, surrounded by family, who couldn't seem to stop gushing.

"Take that hot behind robe off," Geri laughed.

"*They* won't *let* me," Malajia griped, pointed to her parents who were snapping countless pictures of her. She posed for a few, then tugged at her gown. "Please, it's like ninety degrees."

"It's not even that bad out," Tanya, the eldest Simmons daughter teased, giving Malajia's arm a soft poke.

"Ain't nobody heard from you in four years, don't make no comments," Malajia jeered, then laughed when her sister glowered at her.

"Malajia," the youngest daughter Melissa said, tugging on Malajia's gown.

"Yes munchkin?" Malajia answered, touching the top of the little girl's ponytail covered heard.

"You look pretty," Melissa gushed, wrapping her arms around Malajia's waist.

Dana rolled her eyes. "God, she says that to *everybody*."

Malajia picked up her baby sister, "Don't get mad 'cause she's lying when she says it to *you*," she bit back. Then let out a huff. "Dang you heavy mama." Malajia looked at her mother. "Mom, she's heavy as crap what are you feeding her? Butter and cheese?"

Mrs. Simmons sucked her teeth. "The girl is six and her weight is normal," she hissed, gesturing for Malajia to put Melissa down.

Mr. Simmons gathered his family around. "Malajia you gave us hell these past four years," he joked, laughter in his voice. "But you did it. You accomplished what you set out to, and we are *all* very proud of you."

Malajia's smile was bright. "Thank you Daddy," she gushed, giving him a hug. She then looked at him. "Can I get fifty dollars for old times sake?"

Mrs. Simmons laughed as Mr. Simmons let out a groan as he reached for his wallet. "Fine," he grunted, slapping a fifty bill in her hand.

"Yesssss!" Malajia rejoiced, throwing her head back.

Mark sidled up to her and grabbed hold of the bill. "Ooh, dinner on you?" he joked.

Malajia snatched her hand away. "Nah brotha."

Mark chuckled, then extended his hand for Malajia's parents to shake.

Mrs. Simmons flagged him with her hand as she moved in for a hug. "You'll always get a hug from me," she smiled.

"Thanks," Mark smiled back. Then looked at Mr. Simmons, hopeful, holding his arms out.

"I don't think so," Mr. Simmons bit out, earning a chuckle from Mark and an eye roll from Malajia.

"It was worth a try," Mark teased, extending his hand.

Mr. Simmons reluctantly shook it. "Congratulations Mark... I'm *surprised*."

"Dad, don't be ignorant," Malajia chided, annoyed as her mother gave a swift backhand to his arm.

"It's cool Malajia," Mark dismissed. "Thank you, sir," he returned, respectful.

"Mark, where are your parents? I wanted to say hi," Mrs. Simmons asked, craning her neck.

"Oh, Dad is talking to Josh's parents, and Mom is probably in the gift shop buying up all the sweatshirts," Mark answered.

"I might as well go find her, I want to get a few things from there *myself*," Mrs. Simmons said, walking off.

"Ooh, Mom, can you buy me—"

"No!" Mrs. Simmons interrupted, cutting off Dana's question.

Malajia shook her head then looked at Mark, who had his cap and gown in his hand. "Why did you take yours off?" she asked.

"It's too damn *hot*," Mark barked.


Chasity cradled the assortment of flowers in her arm. "That went faster than I thought it would," she said to her mother and grandmother, who stood in front of her.

Grandmother Duvall clasped her hands together with glee. "To see you walk across that stage, and that smile—I'm *so* happy and proud," she gushed.

"God, she's about to cry again," Chasity teased.

Grandmother Duvall playfully flagged her with her hand. "Such a smart behind," she said.

Chasity giggled as she gave her grandmother a kiss on her cheek. "Thank you though."

"Girl, when they called your name, I screamed so loud," Trisha beamed, touching the honors sash on Chasity's gown.

"Yes, I know," Chasity chuckled. "I *heard* you. You're embarrassing you know that?"

"I don't give a good goddamn, I'm a proud mother," Trisha returned, unfazed. "Your Uncle John would've yelled too, but he lost his damn voice screaming at that baseball game he was at the other day."

Chasity shook her head, then turned around when she felt a tap on her shoulder. She successfully fought the urge to roll her eyes at her cousin Melina. It was known that they didn't care for each other, so why she was there was weird to Chasity.

"How much did they pay you to come here?" Chasity

asked.

Melina smirked. "Grandmom promised not to kick me out for another two months," she returned, folding her arms.

"Make it *one* month," Grandmother Duvall jeered, pointing a warning finger at Melina.

Melina chuckled at her grandmother, then looked back at her younger cousin. "No seriously, all spite and snarky comments aside...I'm proud of you cousin."

Chasity stared at her, skeptical. "Thanks."

"You went and turned all that negative into something positive and I'm not gonna lie, it's pretty inspiring," Melina continued.

Chasity stood there; she wasn't sure what to make of this nicer Melina. "Thank you," she said. Though she still had her reservations, Chasity was willing to be cordial. She stepped back and put her hands up in a fighting stance as Melina moved in for a hug.

Melina laughed. "Girl, what are you *doing*?"

"I thought you were tryna fight me!" Chasity exclaimed. "You were about to catch these hands."

Melina laughed again. "No, I'm good," she said, then gave Chasity a hug.

"Chasity, you might not want to hear this or even *care*, but...Brenda would be so proud of you," Grandmother Duvall said, touching Chasity's arm. "I *know* she would."

Chasity looked at her. "I know," she said after a moment. "Thanks." For once, she actually believed it.

Trisha smiled at her daughter, then looked at her watch. "Melina, go find your father and stepmother," she ordered. "They're probably in that gift shop tearing up that credit card."

"Nah, Uncle John is in there looking for girls to pick up," Chasity joked as Melina scurried off. "Y'all know he's cheating on her."

Grandmother Duvall shot Trisha a stern look as she laughed. "Patrisha."

"Mom, it's true, *everybody* knows," Trisha laughed. She

glanced over and smiled when she saw Jason and his mother heading over. "My future son-in-law," she beamed, giving Jason a hug.

Chasity shook her head as her mother and Jason greeted each other.

"How does it feel to be the mother of a graduate?" Trisha asked Mrs. Adams as the two women embraced.

"Amazing," Mrs. Adams beamed, parting. "Got one more to go with Kyle…*wherever* his behind wandered off to."

"Some girl caught his eye," Jason joked.

"Of course," Mrs. Adams jeered. She looked at Chasity. "You look beautiful sweetheart," she smiled, giving her a hug.

"Thanks," Chasity returned.

"Jason, way to go with that Athletic Achievement award," Trisha commended. "Well deserved."

"Yeah, and so is that five hundred dollars they gave him," Chasity added.

Jason smiled. "Thanks. I already knew about the award, but the money was a surprise…a *pleasant* surprise."

Mrs. Adams adjusted the bracelet on her wrist. "I wish they would have given more than six tickets," she said. "Your other uncles were pissed that they couldn't come."

"I told them to sneak in a lawn chair," Jason said.

"I wish you would've said something, I gave the extra one that I had to Sidra," Chasity said, looking at Jason.

"They'll be alright," Jason dismissed with a wave of his hand.

"Wish you would've given it to *me*," a male voice calmly interrupted.

The group turned around and all laid eyes on Derrick, standing there with flowers in hand. He managed a nervous smile as the angered expressions of Trisha, Chasity, and even Jason burrowed through him.

"You've *got* to be kidding me," Trisha ranted. Chasity just stood there staring at him, angry. "How the hell did you get into her graduation without a ticket?"

Derrick let out a sigh. "I umm—I didn't, I was outside the gate," he revealed.

"Why are you even—" Trisha paused, then glanced at Mrs. Adams, who was standing there stunned. "Oh Nancy, I haven't introduced you to Chasity's absent father," she ground out. "Derrick, this is Nancy, Jason's mother."

Derrick extended his hand. "Nice to meet you."

"Likewise," Mrs. Adams replied, although she was uncomfortable with the tension. "Uh, let me go find the rest of my family."

"Yeah, I'll go with you," Jason said, holding a stern gaze on Derrick.

"Nice to see you again, Jason," Derrick said, looking him in the eye.

"Yeah," Jason spat. He was no longer interested in playing nice with Chasity's father. The man had let Chasity down one too many times for Jason's liking.

Trisha stopped Jason as he went to walk off with his mother. "Jason, take Chasity with you," she ordered. Jason stopped and grabbed Chasity's hand. Trisha looked at her and gave her a nudge. "Go on, don't let this mess ruin your day. I'll handle it," Trisha assured.

Chasity didn't say anything, she just allowed herself to be pulled away by Jason.

Derrick took a step in her direction. "Chasity—"

Chasity turned around, anger in her eyes. "Don't," she spat, before continuing her departure.

Watching her walk away, Derrick let out a deep sigh.


Sidra removed her gown and slung it over her arm. "I can't believe I'm finished," she smiled to Josh, who stood in front of her.

"I know," he agreed. "This degree feels good in my hand. Mom already told Dad that she's hanging it up in her house."

Sidra giggled. "Yeah, I heard that," she said, moving hair from her face. "Your Dad didn't seem too fazed by it."

"That's because he told her that *he* gets my master's degree," Josh replied, laughter in his voice.

Sidra's response was interrupted by Josh's sister, running up and wrapping her arms around him.

"JJ, I swear I cried the entire time," Sarah Hampton said, holding on to her baby brother.

Josh chuckled as he held on to her. "Between you and Mom, y'all could have filled a damn lake with your tears."

"Yeah well, they're happy tears, so that's okay," Sarah replied, parting from their embrace. Her tears weren't just about Josh graduating, but at the fact that they were back on good terms; she finally had her brother back. Sarah looked over at Sidra. "So proud of you too," she smiled, giving Sidra a hug.

"Thanks Sarah," Sidra smiled back.

Sarah sighed happily as she pushed some of her hair twists out of her face. She looked back and forth between Josh and Sidra. "Y'all look good standing there together," she said.

"Sarah, go find Mom," Josh ordered, shooting her a stern look.

"I'm just saying," Sarah teased, walking off.

Josh shook his head in her direction and looked at Sidra. "Sorry about that," he said. "She's been in my ear lately about us being good together. I told her it wasn't gonna happen."

Sidra looked away; she secretly mirrored Sarah's thoughts.

"Why isn't James here?" Josh asked, cutting into Sidra's thoughts.

"Huh?" she replied, looking back at him.

"It's your graduation and he's not here...that's not cool,"

Josh said, stern.

Sidra pushed her hair behind her ear as she glanced down at the ground. "He umm…he just couldn't make it," she said, unconvincing.

Josh looked confused. *How could your man not be here on the most important day of your life? Who does that? What is wrong with him?* "Okay," was all that he said. He didn't want to argue with Sidra about her absent boyfriend. Not on a day that was meant to be happy. "Well, I'm sure my people are ready to get out of here," he began. "I guess I'll see you back in Delaware."

"Yeah, see you," Sidra smiled.

Josh held his arms out. "Congratulations Princess."

Sidra moved in for an embrace. "Same to you." She went to give Josh a kiss on his cheek as they parted from their embrace, but he moved his face too soon and Sidra's lips accidentally touched his. Although accidental, neither one parted right away. A few seconds later they quickly jumped back.

Sidra touched her lips with her hand. She was mortified. "I'm so sorry."

"My fault, I moved my face," Josh panicked. "I would never purposely do that, especially since you have a boyfriend."

All sorts of emotions ran through Sidra. "It's not your fault," she assured, frazzled. "It was an accident."

Josh nervously ran his hand over the back of his neck. "Yeah," he said. "Umm, I gotta go."

"Okay." Sidra looked down at her shoes. "See you."

"See you."

Sidra looked up in time to see Josh walk away. She touched her lips with her fingers once again. Even though she hadn't meant to kiss him, she didn't regret it. In fact, she wished that it had been longer, and passionate. *What the fuck are you doing?!* she yelled at herself. Sidra put her hands on top of her head and let out a loud groan.

The voices of her family startled her.

"Your brothers bought every rose they could find," Mrs. Howard chuckled, watching her three sons eagerly place the flowers into their sister's hand.

"Thanks boys," Sidra said.

"You cool, sis?" Marcus asked, noticing the unenthused tone of Sidra's voice.

Sidra shook her deep thoughts off. "Yeah, I'm fine, just hot that's all," she said, fanning herself. It was true in more ways than one.

"Yeah, it *is* blazing out here," Mr. Howard commented, taking the flowers and Sidra's cap and gown from her. "So, what do you want to do, college graduate?" he smiled. "Anything you want."

Sidra shrugged. "Dinner is fine," she said.

"Oh no, this day is too great to celebrate with *just dinner*," Mrs. Howard dismissed with a wave of her hand. "I already called the rest of the family; I'm throwing you a party at the house tonight."

Sidra wasn't much in the mood to entertain a bunch of people. "Mama—"

"Baby, let these people come and shower you with praise and gifts," Mrs. Howard pressed.

Sidra giggled. "Yes ma'am," she relented.

Mr. Howard glanced at his watch. "Good God, that means another grocery store run," he huffed. "Alright, let's round it up."

Mrs. Howard grabbed Sidra's arm to halt her departure as the guys walked off in search of the car.

Sidra shot her mother a questionable glance. "What's wrong?"

Mrs. Howard looked at her. "Saw that kiss," she said.

Sidra's eyes widened. "Huh?"

"Yeah," Mrs. Howard confirmed. "You okay?"

Sidra shook her head. "No. No, I'm not," she admitted. "I'm in love with him and...I can't bring myself to tell him."

Mrs. Howard held a sympathetic gaze as tears started forming in Sidra's eyes. She quickly touched her face. "No, no, don't cry. It'll be okay," she placated. She hadn't meant to upset her daughter. Sidra wiped her eyes. "Everything will work itself out."

Sidra sighed. "Okay."

Mrs. Howard took hold of Sidra's hand. "You ready to go?" Sidra nodded, then headed off with her mother beside her.

Emily fussed with her hair. "I sweated out every *part* of my curls," she complained, then put her hand up when her mother snapped several pictures. "Mommy, I look all hot."

"No you don't, you look perfect, my angel," Ms. Harris beamed, snapping more pictures.

"How much space do you *have* on that thing?" Mr. Harris joked to his ex-wife.

"*Too* much," Emily chortled. She put her hand over her mother's camera, which was now right in her face. "Mommy," she giggled. "Stop."

Ms. Harris lowered the camera. "Okay, I'm sorry," she relented. "I just want to capture every moment."

"I know," Emily smiled as her mother touched her face.

"I'm so proud," Ms. Harris gushed, giving Emily a hug.

"You know what *I'm* proud of?" Dru commented. "Besides you graduating, of course," he amended when Emily looked at him.

"What's that?" Emily asked.

"The fact that Mom and Dad have managed to be around each other all day and have not argued *once*," Dru teased, resulting in claps from himself, Emily, and Brad as they faced their parents.

"Will you stop it?" Mr. Harris laughed.

"Yes, your father and I are in a better place now," Ms. Harris added. "Besides, even if we *weren't* we would *never* ruin Emily's day."

"Shoot, back in the day—"

"Dru, leave her alone," Emily chuckled, giving her

brother a playful backhand to his arm. She looked around. "You guys see Jaz?"

"She left right out and went to the car," Mr. Harris said. "She had no *choice*, I told her to. Her attitude was getting on my nerves."

Emily shook her head. "Daddy, I'm not even surprised," she spat. "I don't even know why she *came*."

"Because you're her sister and she had no *choice but* to come and support you," Ms. Harris ground out. "Maybe she can *learn* something from you and get herself together."

"She *needs* to, 'cause I'm sick of her sleeping on my couch," Dru commented.

Emily rolled her eyes at the thought of her sister's attitude, but was determined not to let that ruin her day.

"Oh, have you decided on your job proposal?" Mr. Harris asked, enthused.

"Yes," Emily said.

"Well?" Mr. Harris pressed, when Emily neglected to say anything else.

She looped her arm through her father's arm. "I'll tell you later."

"Fine," Mr. Harris said. "You going up to Jersey for—"

"Wait does this mean you're moving back to Jersey?" Ms. Harris cut in, hopeful.

"No Mom," Emily chortled. "I'll just be there for two weeks."

"I'll take that," Ms. Harris smiled. "Your room is ready for you... *If* you decide to stay at the house," she quickly amended. "I know you might want to stay at your brothers."

Emily just smiled. "My old room at the house is just fine," she said, relishing the happy look on her mother's face. Hearing someone call her name, Emily's smile got even brighter. "Will," she breathed.

Will walked over and gave her a hug. "I wish I could've gone in there, but I'm not a student," he said, regretful. "I couldn't even *sneak* in."

"It's okay," Emily assured. "Where's Anthony?"

"With my parents," Will replied. "All these people would have made him too excited."

Emily giggled. "Yeah, I'm sure." She looked at her family who were staring at her, smiling. It just dawned on her that this was the first time that they were meeting Will. "Will, this is my family… Family, this is my friend Will."

Will smiled and shook hands as her family introduced themselves. "Glad to meet you all," he said.

Dru cleared his throat. "Likewise," he said.

Emily frowned; her brother's voice got noticeably deeper. *Please don't embarrass me*, she thought.

"So uh, what is your intention with my sister?" Dru asked.

Mr. Harris gave Dru a hard slap on his back as Will went to open his mouth. "Go check on your sister in the car," he ordered.

"Thank you, Daddy," Emily said, grateful.

"Oh, the interrogation *will* happen," Dru assured, reaching to rub the spot where he was hit. "Just wait."

Emily rolled her eyes as Dru walked off. "Don't pay him any mind," she muttered to Will, who in turn laughed.

"It's cool," he assured.

Ms. Harris stared at Will and folded her arms. "Will," she said, tone stern.

Emily shot her mother a skeptical look as Will looked nervous.

"Yes ma'am?" he replied.

Emily just held her gaze. She didn't know what to expect, what her mother would say. She just hoped that whatever her mom did say, wouldn't run Will off. Her mother had that affect.

Ms. Harris just stared at him, before breaking into a smile. "It's nice to meet you, young man."

Emily breathed a sigh of relief.

Will smiled back. "Nice to meet you too."

Emily was beaming as Will put his arm around her and

continued to converse with her family.


Sahara took the cap from Alex's hand and placed it on her own head. "Perfect fit," she grinned, doing a twirl.

Alex laughed. "Yeah, don't get comfortable with it," she teased. "A lot of money, sweat, stress, and tears earned me that cap."

Sahara moved the tassel out of her face. "That's okay. I'll have my *own* in four years."

"That, you will," Mrs. Chisolm agreed, smiling.

"I can't *wait* to get here in August," Sahara said, fiddling with the tassel. "I already started packing."

"You haven't even graduated *high school* yet," Alex chuckled. "You still have another two weeks."

"Don't remind me," Sahara grimaced.

"Don't worry, you can still keep packing," Semaj commented. "*I'm* counting down."

Sahara shot her little brother a glare. "Shut up," she hissed.

"Okay, you two don't start your nonsense," Mr. Chisolm sternly cut in. He lightly smacked Semaj's back. "Come on boy, let's go get this car."

Alex followed their progress until they disappeared through the crowd.

"So?" Mrs. Chisolm began, smoothing down her maxi dress. "How do you feel?"

Alex let out a deep sigh as she nodded. "Accomplished," she replied, pushing some of her hair out of her face. "Relieved and a little sad." She looked around for her friends, but couldn't see them. She knew that they had probably been whisked off by their loved ones, but Alex wished that she could have seen them one last time before leaving campus for good.

"It's a shame that you guys couldn't all sit together during graduation," Sahara said.

Alex looked back at her sister. "I know but they sat us by

department, so…we had different majors."

"Makes sense," Mrs. Chisolm said. "You know the rest of the family is already at our house, waiting for us to get back."

"Oh Ma, you guys didn't have to throw me anything," Alex said.

"Like *hell* we didn't," Mrs. Chisolm threw back. "Baby, you accomplished something that *none* of us have. You graduated *college*, and you thought that I wasn't going to throw you something? Please."

Alex chuckled.

"She made everybody cook and decorate," Sahara whispered to Alex, who in turn laughed.

"You damn right," Mrs. Chisolm said, startling Sahara, who hadn't meant for her to hear. "If your aunts weren't here at graduation, they'd have their behinds right up in that house too." She pointed to Sahara. "And so would *you.*"

Sahara shrugged. "Well, in *this* case, I wouldn't mind," she smiled, then shook her head. "But I'm glad that I'm *not* there. It's too hot in that house to be in that kitchen."

Alex shook her head, then let out a scream of delight when Stacey rushed up to her. "Girl, I was hoping to see you before I left," she squealed, giving her a big hug.

"You already knew I wasn't gonna miss it," Stacey said, flinging her hair over her shoulder. "I snuck my butt right on in there. I'm happy for you sis."

"Thank you Stace," Alex smiled back. "Just one more year left for you and *you'll* be wearing this hot thing too," she added, pointing to her gown.

"And trust me when I say, I can't wait for that day," Stacey returned, then greeted Alex's mother and sister with a hug.

"It's good to see you Stacey," Mrs. Chisolm said. "Your mother is counting down the days until you get home."

"God, I know," Stacey scoffed. "She's been blowing my phone up… Three years and she *still* gets sad when I leave." She let out a happy sigh. "Well, I'll let you guys go."

"Thanks for coming," Alex said, grateful. "You're still one of my best friends. I hope you know that."

Stacey smiled. "I know," she said, before walking away.

"Sweetie, we should probably get to the car and pull out before everybody else does," Mrs. Chisolm suggested.

Alex nodded, then proceeded to walk. As she passed through the crowds, she caught glimpses of the buildings. She smiled as she reminisced about meals that she had shared in the cafeteria, the classes that had both stressed her and challenged her in the buildings. She let out a giggle as she recalled the funny things that she and her friends had gotten into. The prank war, the curfew that had them running for cover many nights, the food fight; then there were things that were not funny that stirred up in her memories as she walked. The fight with Jackie, the arrest, the many arguments, the serious situations that involved her friends... Everything that she had endured, both good and bad, had shaped her into the person that she was now.

She stopped and stared at Wilson Hall, the first place that she had lived when she arrived on campus her freshman year. She smiled at the fond memories, then continued walking, giving a nod to Torrence Hall, where she spent most of the times when she wasn't in her own dorm.

Walking through the parking lot, she found it harder to keep composed, but somehow she maintained it. As her family piled into the car, she held her hand on her door and looked back one last time at the place that she had called home over the past four years. She let out a long, happy sigh as she gave a nod. "Thanks for the memories," she said to herself, before stepping into the car and shutting the door.

# Chapter 52

Alex stared at her cell phone sitting on the table in front of her before taking the ink pen in her hand and crossing an item off in her notebook. *Another one bites the dust.* Tossing the pen on the table, she let out a frustrated sigh as she placed her head in her hands. She glanced up when her mother walked into the kitchen.

"Alex honey, everything okay?" Mrs. Chisolm asked, removing the empty coffee mug from in front of Alex.

"No, I just got turned down for another job," Alex explained.

Mrs. Chisolm sat the mug in the sink before heading back to the table and taking a seat, facing Alex. "I'm sorry to hear that sweetheart, but you're stressing yourself out about this. That isn't good for you."

"It's been a *month*," Alex griped.

Mrs. Chisolm chuckled. "So?"

"Ma, this degree is supposed to get me a good job, like *now*," Alex fussed, folding her arms. "I expected to maybe chill for a week, *two* weeks at the most, then be able to find a job." She let out a huff. "It's now a month later and I've applied to every company that I can think of online and *nothing*... The jobs that I really want aren't replying and the ones that I applied for just to make a little bit of money are rejecting me." She pointed to her phone. "Just got a call from that bank teller position that I interviewed for two weeks ago... no go," she sighed. "I'm tempted to call the diner to get my waitress job back."

Mrs. Chisolm reached over and patted Alex's hand. "Alexandra, there is no law that says that you will find a job right after you graduate," she said. "These things take time. And you wouldn't want to jump into something that you're not going to like."

"I get that but *right now*, I need to make some money," Alex said. "I feel like a bum, sitting up in my parents' house."

"You *shouldn't*," Mrs. Chisolm replied, sincere. "You know you can live here as long as you need to."

Alex sighed as she closed her notebook. "Thanks Ma."

"How are your friends making out? Have you spoken to them?"

"Yeah, I have," Alex said, adjusting herself in her seat. "Some of them are working and some aren't."

"See, you're not alone," Mrs. Chisolm placated. "You'll find something in your own time."

"Yeah, I guess you're right," Alex muttered. *I'll probably be jobless forever*, she thought, despite what her mouth said. "Thanks Ma, I'm gonna go hang out with Stacey for a little bit."

"Okay, try to cheer up my love."

"I'll try," Alex said, standing up from the table.


Malajia rolled her eyes as she spoke on the phone. "Dad, I already told you, I'm not tryna work at no insurance company," she griped, picking up her glass of mojito. "Dad—I swear if you bring me another application I'm gonna spit on it... No, I didn't just say that... Look, I gotta go, see you in a bit."

"Dad ready for your ass to get out of his house, huh?" Chasity joked, grabbing her glass of water.

Malajia shook her head as she placed her phone back in her purse. She and Chasity were having lunch in a restaurant near the Baltimore harbor. Chasity, feeling stir crazy in her house, decided to take a trip down from West Chester to Malajia's neck of the woods.

"Girl, that man has been irking my face about me working at his company," Malajia complained. "Talking about 'those benefits though'," she mocked.

Chasity let out a chuckle. "Sounds like he's just trying to look out," she said. "He probably figures that after a month of not finding anything, that maybe you need some help."

Malajia grabbed a crab leg from a bowl. "I hear that, but I told him that I'll find my *own* job," she said, giving the leg a crack. "The right one will come along eventually."

Chasity frowned as she watched Malajia work on her crab leg before taking the meat out of it. "That looks like a lot of work," she observed.

Malajia dipped her crabmeat into some seasoned butter, "It *can* be if you don't know what you're doing," she chortled.

Chasity shook her head as she took another sip of water. "I don't like to work for my food," she said.

Malajia pointed a finger at Chasity's plate. "You don't know what you missin'," she said. "You got that dry ass pasta and shit."

Chasity laughed a little. "I don't even *want* it."

Malajia picked up another crab leg and pushed it in Chasity's direction. "Here, stop being a crab snob and try one of these."

"The fuck is a crab snob?" Chasity sneered.

"*You*," Malajia threw back. "Now try it. I'll even crack it for you *this* time."

Chasity turned her lip up as she moved Malajia's hand away. "Nah, I'm good," she declined. "I don't feel well anyway."

Malajia placed her crab bits into her mouth. "Why? What's the matter?" she asked between chews.

"I don't know, I think I might have eaten something bad the other day," Chasity assumed, running a hand over her mid-section.

Malajia scrunched her face up. "Eww," she grimaced.

"I know, right?" Chasity agreed.

"Hope you feel better booski," Malajia said, cracking another crab leg.

"Thanks," Chasity muttered. "So, how many jobs *have* you applied for?"

Malajia glanced at the ceiling as she thought. "Four or five maybe...*six*... I don't know," she answered. "I think the reason why I'm having a hard time is because I'm applying out of state... I'm not tryna stay here in no Baltimore."

"Where are you trying to live?"

"West Chester." Malajia then busted out laughing at the look on Chasity's face. "I'm joking...but not that far. Probably Philadelphia. They have a lot of good marketing jobs out there."

Chasity looked confused. "I thought you wanted to work in fashion design," she recalled.

"Fuck them clothes," Malajia scoffed, with a wave of her hand. "I stopped being interested in that, sophomore year... I actually *enjoyed* my marketing classes, so I figured I'd give that a try. My degree is in business so, I should be okay."

Chasity was impressed. "Look at you trying to be all successful and shit," she teased.

"I know, right?" Malajia threw back, amusement in her voice. She took a sip of her drink. "What happened with that interview that you went on last week?"

Chasity rolled her eyes. "It was some *bullshit*, is what it was," she complained. "What they tried to offer me was insulting."

"Damn, they *still* wanted to hire you after all that attitude?" Malajia mocked.

Chasity sucked her teeth. "I did not *have* an attitude, I was totally professional...bitch."

Malajia laughed. "Well, hopefully we *both* will get something soon...unless you still want to freelance for a while," she said after a moment.

Chasity shrugged. "I mean yeah, I'll do it for a while...I

designed a few websites a few weeks ago. A few of Mom's clients. But freelancing can get sporadic and I feel like I should get something more steady," she said.

"Girl all that money you have—"

"All that money my *mother* has," Chasity corrected. "I'm not gonna be living off of her. Just *no*, I'm too old for that."

Malajia waved her hand. "Bitch you better than *me*. My black ass would be right up in that house, spending up all those credit cards."

Chasity shook her head. "She already doesn't want me to move out," she said. "I told her she's crazy as hell."

Malajia giggled. "Well, at least you know where you get it from."

Chasity nodded in agreement.

Sidra sat at her family's kitchen table holding two letters in her hands, staring at them. Hearing the front door open, she placed both letters on the table and craned her neck to try to get a view of the person entering. She offered a slight smile when she saw Marcus.

"Hey college grad," Marcus mused, heading straight for the fridge.

Sidra chuckled. "Marcus, it's been a month, you can stop saying that now."

"Nah, you earned that title," he replied, grabbing a bottle of orange juice from the fridge and shutting the door. Bottle in hand, he walked over and sat down in a chair across from his sister.

Sidra stared at him as he began drinking the juice from the container. "Really? No glass?"

Marcus shook his head as he took another sip. "Oh the rest of this is mine anyway, no need for a glass," he dismissed. Sidra shook her head, then went back to looking over her letters. "What are you up to?"

She sighed. "Reading these letters from the law schools

that I applied to," she answered.

Marcus sat up in his seat. "Yeah?" he asked, excited. "Did you get into them?"

"Two of the three," Sidra answered, eyes not leaving the papers. "The one in Pennsylvania and the one in California."

"Which one is better?"

"They *both* have great programs," she replied. "But...the one in California is higher ranked."

Marcus stared at her. "California?" he sulked. "Damn sis, the other side of the country?"

Sidra sighed. She almost wished that she hadn't applied to the prestigious law school in the first place, then her decision would have been easier. "I know...I probably won't even *go*. The one in Pennsylvania is close enough where I can commute." She ran her hands over her hair and leaned her elbows on the table. "I don't know. I have until August to decide either way...classes start in September."

Marcus nodded as he took another sip of juice. "Well...I hope you stay close, but whatever you decide to do I'll support you," he said, sincere.

Sidra gave a smile. "Thanks." She folded the papers and set them aside on the table. "How's the baby?" she asked, changing the subject.

Marcus smiled a big smile. "Growing," he beamed.

"You excited?"

"*Very*," Marcus answered, confident. "Can't wait."

Sidra folded her arms on the table. "You still plan on going for custody once the baby is born?" she asked.

"Oh most definitely," Marcus confirmed. "I'll try joint at first and see how that goes."

Sidra nodded. "Still think you should go for full though," she advised.

"We'll see how it goes," Marcus replied.

"Well, if I can help you in any way, let me know... I won't be an actual lawyer by the time the baby is born, but maybe I can do some research for you or something."

"I appreciate that, but I'll be fine," Marcus promised.

"Okay," Sidra said, standing from her seat. "Anyway, I'm gonna go get this mess on top of my head done. Are you gonna stick around for a while?"

"Probably, yeah."

"Okay, see you," Sidra replied, walking out of the kitchen.


Emily poured herself a glass of lemonade and walked into the sunroom of her mother's house. "It's nice out today," she mused, sitting down beside her mother, who was taking a sip of her water.

"Yeah," Ms. Harris said, setting her glass back down. She looked at Emily. "You ready to leave yet?"

Emily chuckled at the out of nowhere question. "No Mommy, I'm enjoying my time here with you."

Ms. Harris giggled. "I just want to make sure," she said. "Don't want to run you off again."

"I promise you have been perfectly fine," Emily assured. Her initial decision of only visiting New Jersey for two weeks, turned into a month as Emily had found herself comfortable staying under the same roof as her mother. Something that Emily was happy about; she had missed being around her mother. "And the room feels so much bigger with Jaz not being here."

Ms. Harris nodded as she reached for her bowl of fruit salad. "Have you two talked?"

Emily slowly shook her head. "Nope."

"Do you *want* to talk to her?"

"Not really," Emily answered honestly. "Honestly Mommy, I'm in a really good place in my life right now, and the last thing that I want or *need* is Jazmine's negativity."

"Well, I can't say that I'm not disappointed," Ms. Harris said. "I would love for you and your sister to have a good relationship—"

"With all due respect, I don't want to talk about her," Emily requested.

Ms. Harris gave a small smile. "Sure," she complied. "Let's focus on the positive." She stared at her daughter. "Like your job."

Emily took a deep breath. She had revealed her decision to accept the job offer in Virginia about a week after graduation. "Yeah," she said. "I hope I made the right decision."

"As much as I had hoped that you would have decided to move back here to Jersey…I'm glad that you took the job. I think that it will be a good opportunity for you."

Emily smiled as she looked at her mother. "Thanks," she said. "I can't lie, I'm scared, but…I'm excited."

"I know you're scared honey," Ms. Harris placated. "But I *also* know that you'll be okay." Ms. Harris hoped that her words brought Emily some comfort, but deep down she was nervous too.

"Thanks," Emily smiled. "I gotta go with Daddy next week to check out an apartment."

"Oh?" Ms. Harris replied. "You already found a complex?"

Emily smiled and nodded.


Jason sat at a table in a restaurant, on a quiet street in West Chester. His palms were sweaty; he was nervous. Wiping his hands on a napkin, he took a sip of his ice water. He barely got a chance to look at his watch, when he felt a light tap on his shoulder.

He looked up and smiled. "Hi."

"Hi, sorry I'm late," Trisha smiled back, taking the seat across from him. "Traffic was crazy coming from Philly."

"That's fine," Jason said. He pointed to the menu in front of Trisha. "Umm, the waiter dropped the menus off."

Trisha picked it up and glanced at it. "I'm probably going to get my usual," she said. "I come here all the time."

Jason nodded. "Makes sense." He couldn't help but feel nervous as Chasity's mother sat before him. He knew why he'd wanted to meet with her, he just wasn't sure how the visit would go. "I already know what I want to eat; I looked at the menu already. So we can order whenever you're ready."

Trisha signaled for a waiter. After placing their orders, Trisha folded her arms on the table. "It's good to see you Jase, how have things been post-graduation?" she asked him. Being pulled on several business trips over the past weeks, Trisha hadn't gotten a chance to see her potential son-in-law lately. "Chaz said you found a job?"

"Yeah, nothing major, just entry level tech support for an insurance company," he nodded, reaching for his glass of water. "I also got accepted to the grad school that I wanted to get into...I'll be starting in the fall."

"Yeah? Congratulations," Trisha beamed. "Where is the school located?"

"Philadelphia. Close enough for me to commute while working," he replied.

Trisha smiled. "Well, although I'm not your mother, I am proud of you as if I was," she gushed.

"Thanks," Jason replied, glancing down at the table.

Once the food arrived, Trisha took a few bites of her meal, then took a sip of her wine. "So, career talk aside...you asked me here to lunch and you asked me not to tell Chasity," Trisha began, fixing him with a gaze. "What's going on, sweetie?"

Jason set his fork down. "I know, and thanks for coming, by the way."

She smiled. "Of course."

"I *did* ask you here for a reason," Jason promised. He reached into his pocket and pulled out a little black box, setting it on the table.

Trisha looked confused.

"I need your opinion," he clarified, putting his hand up. "Can you look at it and tell me what you think?"

Trisha grabbed the box. "Oh, I thought you were giving this to *me*," she joked.

Jason couldn't help but laugh. "Nah, that would be weird *and* inappropriate," he returned as he watched her open the small box.

"It's a ring," she observed.

"Yeah," Jason said. "What do you think about it?" Jason watched with nervousness and anticipation as Trisha pulled the ring out of the box and examined it.

Trisha stared at the delicate polished white gold ring, with the solitaire marquee cut diamond in the middle. "It's beautiful," she complimented. "Simple, with a good-sized diamond, which is *always* a plus."

"It's my grandmother's...*was* my grandmother's," he replied. "She gave it to me."

Trisha placed the ring back in the box. "Really?"

Jason nodded. "So...you like it?" he pressed.

"Yes," she confirmed. "You want me to get it appraised for you?"

Jason shook his head as he tugged at the cloth napkin on the table. "Do umm...do you think that *Chasity* would like it?"

"I'm sure she *would*," Trisha said.

"I mean...do you think that she would actually *wear* it? ...Every day?" Jason pressed.

Trisha chuckled. "Chaz changes up her jewelry a lot, but I'm sure if you asked her to wear it then..." she paused as she stared at Jason; realization set it. "Wait...this isn't a 'just because' gift for her, *is* it?"

Jason smiled and shook his head. "No...it's a 'forever' gift."

Trisha's mouth fell open in shock. Feeling overwhelmed, she started fanning her face with her hands. "Oh my God, an engagement ring. My baby is getting married."

Jason chuckled a bit at her reaction. "I haven't even *asked* her yet," he said. "And she would still have to say *yes*."

"Oh boy please, she'll say yes," Trisha assured with a wave of her hand. She placed her hand over her chest and let out a happy sigh. "You want to marry her?"

"Yes," Jason answered, serious. "Do I have your blessing?"

"Abso-fuckin'-lutely!" she blurted out, loud.

Jason put his hand over his face and shook his head in both embarrassment and amusement.

"Please, I've been planning your wedding since she introduced me to you," Trisha said. "She didn't know it then, but *I* did."

"Well, thank you," Jason said as he picked the box back up. "You really think that she'll like the ring? I mean...I know it's not big or flashy... It's kind of old—"

"Jason, I *promise* you, she'll love it... Not only because it's a beautiful ring and has meaning but...because *you're* giving it to her, *that alone* will make her love it."

Jason smiled. He was brimming with excitement. With Trisha's full approval, he was one step closer to asking Chasity that big question.

Trisha picked her wine glass up as Jason placed the box back into his pocket. "So how do your parents feel about you wanting to get married right now?"

"They're supportive," Jason said. "They know that my decisions are mine and I don't rush into things that I haven't thought through. Whether it's now or *five years* from now... I'm still going to propose, so...why wait?"

Trisha nodded with approval. "I agree with you," she said, giving his hand a pat. "So...how are you going to do it? Can I be in on it? Ooh, can I plan your wedding?"

Jason stared at her wide-eyed. "Umm...I don't know yet, I don't see why not, and...you gotta talk to Chaz about that."

Trisha laughed at Jason's answers to all three of her rambling questions. "Fair enough."


"You need to make sure you get yourself a set of jumper cables," Josh urged, wiping his hands on a towel.

"Why do I need cables when I can just come to my

favorite mechanic shop and get everything taken care of?" a smiling woman crooned, twirling a few strands of hair around her finger.

Josh smirked. It was clear that this woman, who looked to be twice his age, was flirting with him. "Because in order to *get* here to your favorite car shop, your car needs to be *running*," he countered.

The woman giggled.

"Your engine is perfectly fine, it's just a precaution," Josh added.

"I will go and purchase some cables as soon as I get out of here," she promised, adjusting her purse strap.

Josh smiled. "Good." He pointed to an open door leading to another room. "My sister will assist you with your bill."

The woman smiled and headed on her way. "Tell your father I said hi," she threw over her shoulder.

"Yeah, I'll do that," he muttered as she disappeared through the door. Josh walked over to another car, popped the hood and leaned forward to get a closer look.

"Hey you."

Startled by the sound of Sidra's voice, Josh bolted up, hitting his head on the top of the hood.

"Be careful," Sidra panicked, walking into the open garage.

Josh stepped back from the car and chuckled. "I'm fine," he assured, giving his head a rub. "What's up? Can't remember the last time that I actually saw you in this garage."

"Yeah, I know," Sidra returned, leaning against a wall. "You know grease and engines aren't really my thing." She pushed some of her hair over her shoulder. "But I knew you'd be here, and I wanted to see you."

Sidra spent the majority of her time nowadays being plagued by thoughts of her grad school choices and her feelings for Josh. She thought that by limiting her time with him—which was easy because Josh worked so much—that her feelings and her need to see him would somehow subside. But as the weeks passed, Sidra realized that wasn't the case. Not being able to stand it anymore, she decided to pay him a little pop up visit.

"I'm flattered," Josh replied. "How have things been?"

Sidra shrugged. "Fine, I guess."

"You don't sound too sure."

*That's because I'm not.* "No, things are okay… Just have some decisions to make about some stuff and it has me a little on edge," she amended. She pointed to the car that Josh was standing near. "I see *you're* keeping busy."

Josh chuckled. "Yeah umm, didn't realize how much Dad worked all day until I offered to fill in for him for the past week." He rubbed the back of his neck. "But it's good that he's taking some time off."

Sidra found herself staring at him. She never would have imagined how much a man with a grease stained shirt and hands would turn her on, but alas Josh had her feeling things that she never imagined she would. "Umm, yeah," she said, snapping out of her trance. "I'm sure he's enjoying the relaxation."

"No, he's calling me every five minutes," Josh grunted. "I've started ignoring the calls. His shop is in good hands."

*That, it is,* she thought. She hesitated for a moment. "Umm...what are you doing tomorrow? After work that is."

Josh shrugged. "Nothing that I know of," he answered. "Probably just relax or something."

"Do you want to go out to dinner?"

Josh nodded. "Sure, why not?" he said. "But I thought that Mark had Mel come visit him this week. And is David back from vacation with his dad?"

Sidra fiddled with her hands. "Yes, Mark did and no, David isn't back from Vegas yet," she replied. "I was really just asking for the *two of us* to go to dinner."

Josh looked surprised. Sure, they'd been out to eat together on many occasions, but *he* usually asked *her*. It was a nice gesture for her to ask him. "Uh sure, yeah," he smiled.

Sidra smiled back, but her insides were churning.

Although she knew that to Josh, it would be nothing more than a dinner between two friends, to her it felt like she was asking him out on a date. "Okay great... I know this place downtown—"

"Do I have to wear a suit?" he joked. "I know the kind of places that you like."

Sidra giggled. "No, a regular shirt is fine." She headed towards the exit. "Eight okay?"

"Yeah, I'll be finished here like six tomorrow, so that's perfect."

Sidra nodded. "Okay."

Josh watched as she nearly bumped into a crate on her way out of the garage. "You alright?" he asked, slightly amused.

"Yep, I saw that," she lied, walking out.

Josh shook his head in amusement as he went back to his task with the car.

Sidra stepped into her car and shut the door. Taking a deep breath, she placed her hands on the steering wheel, smiling to herself. As she was about to start the car, she heard a sound come from her cell phone, indicating that she had a message. She grabbed her phone from her purse.

"I really need to turn this loud tone down," she muttered, unlocking the phone. Her eyes widened as she saw the name of the message sender. "James?" she grunted to herself. She read the message on the screen.

*'Sidra, I hope you're doing well. I know this is probably inappropriate, but I'd like to see you. Please let me know if that is okay and when you have some time.'*

Sidra closed her eyes and slammed her head against the back of her seat. "Come on, not this, not *now*," she complained aloud. She tossed her phone in her bag, not bothering to respond. James had broken up with her, and she was finally okay with it, and now he wanted to see her. Sidra didn't know what his reason was, but all she knew was that she didn't want him on her mind.

# Chapter 53

Plastic bag in hand, Malajia sauntered into an office building and up to a front desk. Removing her sunglasses, she smiled at the young woman. "Hi, can you call Mark Johnson's desk please?" she asked.

The young woman looked at her computer. "Do you know his extension?"

"I know what *department* he's in," Malajia returned. "Accounting department." She stood and waited as the receptionist located Mark's information and called his desk. Malajia fingered the curls on her head as the receptionist let Mark know that he had a visitor.

"He'll be right down, Ms.—?"

"Simmons," Malajia replied. "Thank you." Malajia moved to one of the empty chairs and sat down. It took less than five minutes for Mark to emerge from the elevator. She smiled and stood up.

"There's my working man," she gushed as Mark shook his head in amusement.

"I thought I told you that I'd see you later," he chuckled, giving her a hug.

"I was bored as shit, waiting at your house," Malajia returned. "So I figured I'd bring you some lunch." With Mark's parents out of town on vacation, Malajia took Mark up on his offer to come take advantage of the empty house and spend a few days with him. She originally planned on waiting in the house while Mark worked, but going stir crazy without him, she elected to do a surprise visit at his job.

Mark stared at the bag that she eagerly held up. "Good lookin' I didn't really wanna spend money on lunch, you always come through."

"Yeah, I know," Malajia boasted. She stared at him as he opened the bag and peered inside.

He threw his head back. "Yesssss," he rejoiced. "You brought the left-over lasagna."

Malajia giggled as she ran her hand along his arm. "Look at you lookin' all sexy in your work clothes," she cooed, eyeing Mark's attire of black dress pants, black button-down shirt and red tie. She already thought that he looked good in just regular clothes, but he cleaned up even better.

"Cut that out, this is a place of business," he said, feigning seriousness.

"Fuck this business," Malajia returned, earning a laugh from him. She then glanced around to the receptionist. "Sorry," she apologized of her vulgarity.

The receptionist just offered an amused smile.

"I'm on lunch now, so let's go sit in the park across the street," he proposed. Malajia nodded as they headed for the building exit.

Sitting on a park bench, directly across from Mark's building, Malajia enjoyed the warm breeze. "How's your day so far?" she asked Mark, who was eating his food.

He shrugged. "It's fine," he answered. "Still transitioning from the training process, to actually doing the work…it's frustrating."

"*What* is?" Malajia wondered.

"Fuckin' *accounting*," Mark replied. At the urging of his father, Mark applied for several accounting jobs upon returning home from college. He was shocked that in less than two weeks, he had interviewed for and was offered a job, working in a major accounting firm downtown. Although Mark was grateful for the job and the money that he was offered, he still couldn't bring himself to actually *like* the work. "It's boring."

"Well babe, use your degree to get something *else*," Malajia urged, tone comforting.

Mark sighed as he dug into his container of leftovers. "Nah, I don't think I'll be lucky enough to get another job so soon," he sulked. "Plus, I don't know what else I want to *do*... I chose accounting because I know that it makes good money and...the money here *is* good."

"I get that Mark, but good money don't mean *shit* if you're not happy," Malajia pointed out, touching his arm.

"The way I look at it, it's only eight hours a day," he reasoned. "After that, I don't have to think about it... Plus, this money will get me my own place, which I can't freakin' *wait* for."

Malajia laughed. "Still mad your mom painted your room, huh?"

"Hell yeah! You don't paint my shit olive green," he barked. "Talking about they turning it into a 'sitting room'," Mark griped. "The fuck is a sitting room?"

Malajia again laughed. "You find any places yet?"

"Nah, still looking."

Malajia adjusted herself in her seat and leaned back as she stared at the scenery in front of her. "Well, your misery with this job aside... I'm happy that you have one," she said. "At least you're not still looking, like *me*."

Mark looked at her. "You'll find something," he assured.

"I hope *so*. This shit is getting annoying," Malajia complained. "I'm tired of all those damn kids in my parents' house. I want out... Dana running her mouth about not a damn thing important, Taina touching all my shit, and Melissa fat ass staring in my face every time I eat something."

Mark laughed. "Isn't Melissa six?"

"That don't mean she ain't pudgy," Malajia jeered. "No but...I gotta find something..." she sighed. "I feel useless."

Mark put his arm around her and pulled her close to him. "Shut that up," he chuckled. "There is nothing useless about you, just keep applying... If I see something open up here,

I'll give them your resume."

"Thanks, but I can't work here with you," Malajia replied.

Mark looked offended. "Why the hell *not?*"

"'Cause we'll get in trouble for sneaking off for quickies all the time," Malajia joked.

Mark pointed at her. "Good point."

"*That* and you would irk my entire face if I had to work with you every day," she quickly slid in.

Mark sucked his teeth and moved away from her. A gesture that Malajia found hilarious.


Alex laid sprawled out on the carpeted floor in her bedroom as she cradled the cordless phone to her ear. "It's so damn hot," she complained into the receiver.

"Tell me about it," Emily giggled. "Try *packing* in this heat."

Alex sat up and began fanning herself with her hand. "When do you head back to Virginia?"

"Next week," Emily beamed, tossing a throw pillow on her bed before flopping on it. "My dad secured the place for me a few weeks ago. They just have to put the carpet in and I'll be all set."

Alex smiled, although Emily couldn't see her through the phone. She remembered the joy that she felt when Emily told her of her job offer, weeks ago. "Em...I'm so proud of you," she gushed.

"Thank you, Alex," Emily smiled back.

"I mean it," Alex insisted. "I mean not *only* do you have a job, but you get to go back to Virginia...I would love to live back there...I miss it."

"Yeah," Emily agreed. "But maybe you'll be able to live somewhere *else* and build *new* memories."

Alex shrugged. "Yeah well, I need to get a *job* first before I start talking about living somewhere."

"Still no other interviews?"

"Girl—yeah, I had a few interviews for a bunch of crappy positions that I didn't even *apply* for," Alex grunted. "Seriously, this one company pulled my resume off of a job site and called me for an interview. I went, it was for customer service, which I was just going to take to hold me over." She adjusted her position on the floor as she continued with her story. "Emily, they got me in the office and started showing me a picture of *butt plugs*."

"Of *what*?!" Emily broke out laughing.

"You heard me," Alex returned. "You should've seen the look on my face. They expected me to work customer service for a freaking sex toy manufacturing company…like, *eww*."

Emily couldn't stop laughing.

"I'm glad you find this funny," Alex grumbled.

"Well…every type of company needs customer service," Emily replied at an attempt to make Alex feel less embarrassed.

"Yeah well, they can get someone else to service those butt plugs," Alex grimaced, earning more laughter from Emily. Alex shook her head, then hearing her cell phone ring, grabbed it from the floor. With her cell phone acting up lately, Alex had elected to call Emily on the house phone, leaving her cell lying next to her. "Em, hold on a second." Alex set the house phone down and put her cell to her ear. "Hello?"

"Good afternoon, may I speak with Alexandra Chisolm please?" a polite female voice requested on the other end.

"Yes, this is she," Alex answered, leery.

"I'm Marlene Webster and I'm calling from Wharton Press. I received your resume and I wanted to know if you would be interested in interviewing for the assistant editor position that we have available."

Alex's mouth fell open. She had been dying to get an interview with an actual publishing company. She then recalled something. *I thought that I applied for the editor position, not assistant editor*, she thought. "Oh yes, absolutely," she beamed. Despite their obvious mix-up, Alex didn't want to pass up the opportunity for an interview. She quickly grabbed a notepad and pen from her nightstand and jotted down the information that Marlene provided. She was brimming with excitement. "Thank you so much, I'll see you on Monday."

"Great, see you then," Marlene replied.

Alex ended the call and let out a squeal of delight. In the middle of her solo celebration session, she remembered that Emily was on the other phone. She grabbed the house phone and put it to her ear. "Em, I got an interview!"

"I heard," Emily returned. "Congratulations. Knock 'em dead."

"Thanks sis," Alex replied, scratching her scalp with her free hand. "I just wonder why they're interviewing me for an assistant position when I didn't apply for it."

"I'm sure you'll find out when you go to the interview," Emily placated. "Just don't go in there trying to argue with them about it. I'm sure they have their reasons."

Alex was taken aback by Emily's words. "Excuse me Miss Harris?" her tone was laced with amusement.

"Alex, you know how you get," Emily returned.

Alex giggled, "Fine, your words are noted baby sis."

Emily too giggled. "Well, I have to run some errands, I'll talk to you later."

"Okay, oh are you going to the cookout at Chasity's house next week?" Alex quickly cut in. "It's on a Saturday. When are you leaving Jersey?"

"I'm leaving Sunday to go start packing the rest of my stuff from my dad's and yep, I'll be there," Emily promised.

"Good, see you then."


Sidra ran a brush through her long, straight locks as she glanced at her reflection in the mirror. "Should have curled this," she muttered to herself as she placed her brush on her dresser.

A small knock on her room door made her turn around. "Mama, is my hair too flat?" she asked as her mother entered the room.

"No sweetie," Mrs. Howard replied, walking over to her.

"I swear, sometimes I want to cut it," Sidra fussed, running her hand through her hair.

"*Please* don't," Mrs. Howard replied, inciting a giggle from Sidra. "All those years growing this, girl you better keep it."

Sidra shook her head as she grabbed a perfume bottle from her dresser, giving her neck and wrist a spritz.

"Have you decided on which law school you're going to yet?"

Sidra resisted the urge to roll her eyes. *If one more person in this family asks me that.* "Not yet… Still weighing my options."

"Sidra, I'm not going to stand here and lie to you, I don't want you to go to California. The other school is *just* as good," Mrs. Howard blurted out. Sidra looked at her. "I know that you're grown and it's your decision—"

"I'm still weighing my options," Sidra reiterated.

Mrs. Howard took that as a request to be quiet about the topic. She put her hands up in surrender. "Okay," she relented. Her eyes roamed down Sidra's length. "You heading out?"

"Yeah, going to dinner," Sidra replied.

"Oh? You meeting up with one of the girls?" Mrs. Howard smiled. It had been a while since Sidra had hung out with her friends.

Sidra hesitated for a moment. "Um no…I'm going to dinner with Josh."

Mrs. Howard's eyes widened. "Oh?" she repeated. "Is this a regular dinner or a…"

"It's not a date," Sidra assured, even though she felt like it was one. "Just a dinner between friends."

"Between friends who are in *love* with each other but the other doesn't know it," Mrs. Howard bluntly declared.

Sidra let out a sigh. "That sounds…harsh."

"It's the *truth*. I hope you're going to talk to him about how you feel."

This time Sidra did roll her eyes. Between Josh, and the texts from James, Sidra didn't want to add an argument with her mother to her already plaguing thoughts. Sidra grabbed her purse from her bed. "I gotta go," she said as she walked out of her room.

Sidra leaned back in her car seat as she adjusted the volume on her car radio. "I promise I had no idea how long the wait would be," she said to Josh, who was seated in the passenger's seat next to her.

"I don't expect anything less on a Friday night," Josh shrugged, adjusting the collar on his shirt.

Sidra had pulled up to her suggested restaurant nearly ten minutes ago, to find Josh standing outside. She was annoyed when he told her that it would be a half hour to a forty-five minute wait for a table. "I knew I should have made an actual reservation," Sidra griped. "Don't know what I was thinking."

"Sidra, it's fine," Josh assured. "It's not like we haven't had to wait to eat before."

Sidra shrugged. "You want to go somewhere else?"

"Nah, we're already here," he returned. "Might as well wait."

Sidra nodded as she focused on changing the music station. She had to admit, although this was not the ideal start to her dinner with Josh, she was pleased for the quiet time, sitting in her car.

"So… Since we won't be eating for some time, we might as well catch up," Josh suggested.

"True," she replied, looking at him. She didn't know where to begin. "Have you hung out with the guys lately?"

"I played ball with Mark last week, but other than that, I haven't seen them. I spoke to Jase the other day and David has been busy traveling with his dad."

"I think it's so cool that Mr. Summers saved up to be able to take David on a few trips after he graduated," Sidra smiled. "It's his only child, I don't blame him."

"Yeah," Josh agreed. "David got accepted into that grad school in Ohio…full ride."

"Yeah, he told me last week," Sidra revealed. "He's so excited. It's a great school for science."

There was a pause as the two friends listened to the R&B music coming through the speaker. Sidra looked at him. "Are you still starting grad school in the fall?"

"Yep, right here in Delaware," Josh beamed. "I can still help out at the shop when I'm needed and work my other job, while taking my classes."

Sidra looked confused. "You went back to working at the diner?"

"*Hell* no," Josh blurted out. "I got hired as an insurance underwriter. Been there for about two weeks…right downtown."

Sidra smiled. "That's great Josh," she said. *Wow, we really haven't talked.* "How do you like it?"

Josh shook his head. "Let's just say…you were right, I'm not a 'desk job' person."

Sidra nodded. "I knew you *wouldn't* be."

"But it will tide me over for now, at least until I figure out how to expand this car business," Josh said. "In the meantime, I'll be using that money to find a place."

"Not staying with your dad, huh?"

"Not at twenty-two I'm not," Josh chuckled. "No, I need my own place."

"I don't blame you," Sidra said, pushing some of her hair behind her ear. "It would be weird making dinner for someone in your dad's house." She immediately closed her eyes after the words spilled from her lips. *Shit!* She hadn't meant to bring the subject to Josh's potential girlfriend, nor had she meant to sound so snarky while saying it.

"Well, you're right," Josh agreed, either not picking up

on it, or ignoring Sidra's tone. "Nothing says 'loser' like bringing someone back to your parents' house." He ran his hand over the back of his neck. "Not that I *would*."

"You're not a loser Josh," Sidra said, staring at him as he focused his gaze out of the window.

Josh just smiled. "Look, I've been meaning to say this to you, I don't even think you still remember but... I'm sorry again about that kiss at graduation."

Sidra glanced away. She did in fact remember it; it was on her mind constantly. "I already told you that that wasn't your fault," she said.

"Yeah but...still," Josh said. "Did you tell James?"

Sidra slowly shook her head. "There was no need to."

"Okay then."

Sidra took a deep breath as silence once again filled the car. "Josh, can I ask you something?"

"Of course," Josh replied, still gazing out of the window.

She struggled with the next words forming in her throat. "Um...if I had told you that I loved you back when you told me how you felt... Do you think we would still be together now?"

Josh's head snapped toward her. He frowned. "What kind of question is that?"

"One that I'm curious about."

"It's an *irrelevant* one because you *didn't* say it back, and we're *not* together," Josh hissed.

"Josh, I'm not trying to fight with you, I honestly want to know...do you think that a relationship with us would— *would've* worked?"

Josh was still confused as to why Sidra went there. She already knew how he felt and how she didn't, so why was she asking at all? "Honestly Sidra, I don't know," he spat out.

She looked taken aback. "Oh?"

"Yeah, I don't know if we could've made the transition," he said. "Yes, we're best friends but we're also too different."

"I disagree," Sidra threw back. "We want a lot of the

same things."

"You want a fancy lawyer, and you got one, so again, why are you asking me that question?" Josh ground out, fixing her with a stern gaze.

Sidra stared at him. It was clear that she had upset him, although that was not her intention. She couldn't tell if his response was out of anger, or if he really felt that being with her would never work, despite how he felt. She couldn't bring herself to find out the truth; she was embarrassed enough.

"You're right, I shouldn't have asked you that. I'm sorry," she said.

"You have no idea what it's like to be in a position to have feelings for someone and they don't return them…it's torture," Josh ranted. "I have worked to move on from my feelings for you and I don't need you bringing it up as some pointless 'what if' question."

Sidra sat there and took everything that Josh was saying. She knew she deserved it. "I know that I hurt your feelings Josh, and I'm sorry."

"I'm not blaming you for that… It was my own fault for falling for someone who I knew I had no chance of being with."

"What if you—" Sidra put her hand over her face as the words got stuck in her throat. *What if you had a chance? Ask him?!* "I'm sorry," she repeated as tears pricked her eyes.

Josh let out a sigh, not noticing the glassiness in her eyes. "I sometimes wish that I never told you," he said. Sidra stared at her hands. "The last thing that I ever wanted to do was hurt our friendship and ever since I told you…it hasn't been the same."

"You're right, it hasn't," she agreed, somber. At that moment, Sidra realized that it was better to keep her feelings to herself. Their relationship was strained enough. If they actually gave it a shot and failed, she would lose Josh forever. She couldn't handle that, but she also knew that she couldn't stick around while he ended up with someone else.

"We have about ten more minutes," Josh said, breaking through the silence. "Might as well take the conversation back to the original topic."

"If that's what you want," Sidra muttered, discretely wiping the tear from her eye.

"Decided on which law school you're going to yet?"

Sidra sat there staring at the steering wheel in front of her. She'd been asked that question over and over for the past few weeks, and it didn't get any less irritating to her. She wasn't sure, at least until now. "Yes," she answered after a few seconds of silence. "I know which one I'm going to."

Josh stared at her in anticipation. "Well, is it a secret?" he asked, an attempt at a joke.

There was no humor in Sidra's eyes as she gazed at him. "I'm going to California."

A somber look fell over Josh's face. "Oh…well, I'm sure it's a great school."

"It is."

Josh nodded as he looked away. He never thought that she would actually move to the other side of the country. While he was happy for her opportunity, he couldn't help but think about the possibility of not seeing Sidra again. "I'm excited for you…I know you'll do well."

"Thank you."

Josh ran a hand over his cut hair. "We should go see about our table," he said, opening the car door.

"Yeah," Sidra mumbled as he stepped out of the car.

# Chapter 54

"Mom, I'm trying to work," Chasity hissed, looking up from her laptop.

Trisha sipped on her latte as she sat across from Chasity at a local coffee shop. "Why did you even *come* here with me if you were just going to *shush* me the entire time?"

Chasity shot her a confused look. "'Cause you said 'Chasity, I promise I'll let you get your work done, just come check out this place with me'." Chasity was approaching a deadline on a design for one of her clients, and had only agreed to hang out with her mother on the condition that she let her work on her laptop.

Trisha laughed. "Well look...you can't blame me for enjoying your company."

"Yeah well...you need a damn man," Chasity mumbled, looking back at her screen.

"What?" Trisha frowned.

"Huh?" Chasity deflected, typing on her laptop.

Trisha shook her head as she took another sip of her drink. "Smart ass," she hissed. "How many design jobs have you done this week?"

"This is my third," Chasity answered. "Luckily, these clients don't want much right now. Just a basic design and set up."

Trisha nodded in approval. "I still don't know why you won't sign on as a full-time designer for *my* company."

"Because I don't want to *work* for you," Chasity ground out, looking at her.

"What's wrong with working for me?" Trisha asked, offended. "You did my websites for years...that, and I'm a *great* boss."

"Yes, I know you are. But I didn't spend four years in college to get a degree just to work for my mother, who I *know* will pay me more that she's supposed to, and buy me an apartment, and call it 'needed office space'," Chasity argued.

Trisha couldn't help but chuckle; Chasity had a point. "I just want to make sure you're taken care of."

"Mom, I'm not a teenager anymore," Chasity threw back. "You don't have to make up for lost times or past mistakes with me. I'm here and we're good."

Trisha let out a sigh.

"You've done enough for me, I just want to make things happen on my own, you know...like get a damn apartment."

Trisha let out another sigh. "I understand...although I think you're exaggerating just a bit...but I get it. You're capable of making your own way," she said. "Just...hold off on looking for an apartment until you talk to Jason."

"Talk to Jason about *what*?" Chasity asked, confused.

Trisha's eyes widened. She hadn't meant to say that; she just didn't want Chasity to choose a place before Jason popped the question. She figured that they could look together. But because Chasity had no idea that Jason was planning this, she needed to keep it under wraps. "Um...I just figured that he would want to go with you when you look...that's all."

Chasity shook her head and went back to her work. "Jason has enough on his plate right now. I'm sure he'll have no problem with whatever I decide to get."

Trisha took another sip of latte.

"*You* can come with me when I look, if you want," Chasity offered. Trisha's eyes lit up. "I mean since, you know buildings and codes and shit."

"Regardless of that sorry ass reasoning, I would *love* to go with you," Trisha returned. "I'll even pull up some properties for you."

"Very well," Chasity sighed, running a hand over her stomach.

Trisha took notice of the nauseated look on Chasity's face. "You okay?"

"That nasty coffee you made earlier, got my damn stomach acting up again," she complained.

"*You* made that," Trisha returned.

"Right," Chasity recalled.

Trisha shook her head. "You've been having stomach troubles for a few weeks now; you think you should go see a doctor?"

"No…it's probably something I ate, combined with the fact that my damn period will be starting soon," Chasity assured. "I'm fine."

"Well…okay," Trisha said, trying her hardest not to make a fuss. "Are you working this weekend?"

"No, I'll be at your cookout Mom," Chasity replied, unenthused.

"Cranky much?"

"It's hot and it's gonna be like fifty-leven people in the house," Chasity griped.

Tisha laughed. "Fifty-leven? Is that a new number?"

"It is," Chasity sniped.

Trisha shook her head in amusement.


"Ms. Trisha, I don't think that proposing to Chasity in front of a bunch of people is a good idea," Jason said into his cell phone as he approached the front steps of his family's home. "Because, you know how embarrassed she gets… I just want it to be the two of us…" He rolled his eyes as Trisha kept talking into the phone. "No disrespect, but no… Tell you what, I'll let you know the day that I'm going to do it, how's that?" Jason chuckled at Trisha's response, "Noted. I have to go…bye."

Jason shook his head as he opened the front door and

tossed his briefcase on a nearby stand. "Hey Dad," he greeted, removing his tie.

Mr. Adams jumped up from the couch, a large envelope in hand. "There's my first born."

Jason eyed him skeptically. "Uh...okay," he chortled, heading for the kitchen.

Mr. Adams followed him. "How was work?"

"It was okay." Jason pulled open the refrigerator and peered inside. "Are there any leftover ribs from last night?" he asked.

"Uh no, Kyle polished the rest of them off for lunch," Mr. Adams replied.

Jason shut the refrigerator with a sigh. "Of *course* he did," he muttered. He spun around to find his father standing before him. "Dad, you're acting weird," he observed. "What are you holding?" he asked, pointing to the envelope in his father's grasp.

"Curious Jase, is everything all set with your grad school yet?" Mr. Adams asked, ignoring Jason's question.

"No, not yet. I'm still sorting through some financial stuff...why?" Jason tilted his head. "Dad, what's in the envelope?" he pressed when his father hesitated.

Not saying a word, Mr. Adams handed Jason the envelope.

Jason stared at the heading. "It's from the professional football league," he observed. Opening the envelope, Jason quickly skimmed a letter. He frowned. "They want me to enter in the draft," he read, confused. "Who did this? I'm not playing pro, I've *said* this."

"Jason, this didn't come from the university, this came from the professional league...the *professional league* son," Mr. Adams beamed.

There was no happiness on Jason's face. "Yes, I read that," he sneered.

"All I'm saying is just *think* about it," Mr. Adams urged.

"I've *thought* about it, and my answer is *still* no," Jason hissed, moving around his father. "I'm working and I'm about to go to grad school, is that not good enough?"

"Jason, I never said that what you're doing isn't good enough. You know I'm proud of you," Mr. Adams returned, facing Jason's departing back. "Just listen for a moment."

Jason halted his progress and turned around.

"Grad school...is expensive, and I know you plan on taking out loans to pay for it... You plan on moving soon and I know that your job isn't paying you as much as you want—"

"I'll get the money that I want when I finish grad school, Dad," Jason interrupted.

"*One* year on a team, and you won't *have* to take out any loans. You'll be able to pay for school, get a house, and can afford to hold out for the job that you *really* want... Not to mention that you plan on asking Chasity to marry you...you can set the *both* of you up," his father pressed.

"How many one-year contracts do you know about in the league Dad?" Jason argued. "Try *five* years," he answered when his father couldn't answer. "So, they will own me for *five* years of my life...you really want that for me?"

"Contracts can always be negotiated," Mr. Adams assured.

Jason shook his head. He knew that his father always hoped that Jason would go pro, but he thought that the man would have respected Jason's vision for how his life should go. At least he *hoped* that his father did—this conversation proved otherwise. "Dad, while I appreciate the fact that you don't want me to struggle... I'll be fine. I'll get to where I want to be in time. My plan, *as it stands,* will *get* me to where I want to be."

"Life doesn't always go according to plan son, so...just keep an open mind," Mr. Adams said.

"Yeah," Jason muttered, walking out of the kitchen.


Alex smoothed her blazer down as she took a seat in front of a large desk. She'd never been as nervous as she was at that moment. Finally having an interview for a job that she actually wanted, she didn't want to make any type of mistakes that could spoil it.

"Thank you for agreeing to the interview," Marlene beamed.

Alex smiled. The light-brown skinned woman before her looked to be in her mid-fifties. "Thank *you*," she returned.

Marlene picked up a piece of paper and glanced at it. "Let me give you a little bit of background on our company," she began.

Alex nodded.

"Wharton Publishing Company currently does the editing, publishing and distribution for City Speak Magazine—"

"I know that magazine!" Alex cut in, enthused. She winced at herself for interrupting.

Marlene chuckled. "I'm glad to know that."

Alex giggled. She had researched the company several days before coming to the interview.

"We handled only that magazine for about five years and just a year ago, we started producing books... No major names just yet, mostly small-time authors are under our publishing house, but a few of them have won awards for their books and our name is starting to circulate throughout the publishing world... Our clientele is growing, and so is our need for more editors."

Alex smiled as she shifted in her seat. "And that's where I would come in?"

Marlene nodded as she stared at Alex's resume. "You graduated from Paradise Valley University with a bachelor's degree in English?"

"Yes ma'am, I enjoyed every one of those classes and knew since I was a teenager that I wanted a career in the English field, specifically in editing," Alex said. "I figured my need for fixing things would come in handy."

Marlene chuckled at Alex's attempt at a joke. After grilling Alex for the next half hour with interview questions,

Marlene leaned back in her seat and smiled. "I must say, I like the way that you carry yourself Alexandra. You're smart, enthusiastic and confident... I have a few other interviews to conduct this week, but I must say that you are seriously a front runner for the assistant editor position."

"Thank you so much," Alex replied. She was pleased with how the interview was going and she thought that Marlene, although serious, would make a great boss. But there was still one nagging issue that was still plaguing her.

"Do you have any questions for me?"

Alex took a deep breath. *Alex, don't ruin it*, she thought, but decided to ignore her own voice. "Yes, I have one... I applied for an editor position and you called me for the *assistant* editor position...why is that?"

Marlene leaned forward. "Honestly, you have no experience," she stated bluntly. "Unless you would count editing your college papers, which I *don't.*"

Alex glanced down at her hands. "I see."

"Now, the assistant editor position will allow you to get your foot in the door. You'll be able to learn the job, learn the industry, and *then* you can move on to regular editor."

Alex nodded. "That makes sense, I guess," she said. She hoped that her solemn mood wasn't noticed.

"Should you be offered the position, and do well...you'll be in your desired position within a year or so."

Alex sat there, nodding. She couldn't help but feel a little disappointed. "Well...thank you for explaining that to me and I hope to hear from you."

Marlene stood up. "No matter who I decide to go with, you should hear from me by the end of the week." She extended her hand as Alex rose from her seat.

"I look forward to hearing from you," Alex said as she shook Marlene's hand.


Malajia stormed into her house and snatched her blazer off. "This shit is *hot!*" she barked, throwing it on the couch.

Geri walked out of the kitchen, sandwich in hand. "What are you in here complaining about *now?*" she teased.

Malajia made a face at Geri as she placed her hands on her hips. "What are you doing here?" she hissed. "Stop eating up our damn lunch meat."

Geri flagged Malajia with her hand as she sat down on the couch. She reached over and picked up the red jacket, examining it. "You got all these sweat stains," she laughed.

"It's fuckin' ninety degrees outside!" Malajia wailed.

"Nobody told you to wear that hot ass business suit," Geri threw back.

Malajia chuckled as she flopped down on the love seat. "I had an interview today," she informed.

Geri's interest peaked as she took a bite of her sandwich. "Yeah? Where at?"

Malajia ran her hands through her hair, scratching her scalp. "Some staffing company downtown," she said.

"How do you think it went?"

Malajia shrugged. "I think it went okay… I don't know, I think I was talking too much. That man was staring at me like I was crazy."

"He probably noticed your pit stains," Geri pointed out.

Malajia thought for a moment, before putting her hand over her face and burying her head on the seat cushions. "Damn it! You're probably right," she whined.

Geri laughed, but she reached over and gave Malajia's leg a pat. "I'm just messing with you," she placated. "I'm sure you did fine."

Malajia lifted her head up. "*I hope* so, I'm tired of this not-having-a-job bullshit," she complained. "I'm tryna move…and you know, just be an adult."

"From one adult to another," Geri said. "A job will come…you'll be dreading the office life soon enough."

"Yeah," Malajia sighed.

"And, if you *really* wanna get out of here before you're financially ready, you can always stay with *me.*"

Malajia turned her lip up. "Girl, ain't nobody tryna sleep

on that one ass couch you got in that medium ass living room," she jeered.

Geri narrowed her eyes. "Forget you then!"

Malajia broke into laughter. "Sike, I appreciate it, but I'm cool."

Geri shook her head. "You know you have a way of making people regret being nice to you. Ignorant ass heffa," she ground out.

Malajia laughed again. "I know right?" she agreed. The humor left her face. "I kinda want to live with Mark though."

Geri nearly choked on her sandwich. "*Already*?" she asked, in between coughs.

Malajia stared at Geri, expressionless as her sister patted her chest to relieve the coughing. "Really, all those dramatics?" she bit out.

"I was really *choking*!" Geri exclaimed, setting the rest of her sandwich down. "Anyway…like I said, already?"

"We've been together a little over a year," Malajia argued. "And we were in each other's rooms all the damn time while we were in school… I don't think it'll be that much different."

"Really? That's your only reason?" Geri asked, tone laced with sarcasm.

Malajia let out a sigh. "No…I miss him when I'm not with him and when I stayed with him while his parents were gone, I kind of got a glimpse of what it would be like to actually live with him and…I was happy… I love that crazy, silly ass fool."

Geri smiled. She was happy that her sister was able to find happiness. Especially after Malajia's tumultuous relationship with Tyrone. "I know you do," she said. "But I have to ask…do you think *he's* ready for that? Full time cohabitation?" Geri asked. "Have you brought it up to him?"

"His ass *better* be," Malajia hissed. "And no, I *haven't*. I'm waiting to get a damn job so I can contribute… Or maybe I'm lying and I'm really waiting for him to bring it up to *me*."

Geri held a sympathetic gaze on her sister. She watched as Malajia stood from the couch.

"Anyway, I gotta get out of this hot ass polyester, I'm gonna miss my train."

"Where are you going?" Geri asked, watching Malajia head for the steps.

"Chasity's house," Malajia answered. "There's a cookout on Saturday."

Geri looked confused. "It's *Wednesday*."

"*And*?!" Malajia threw back. "Damn, can I miss my friend enough to go visit her for a few days before everybody else gets there sucking up her air and shit?"

Geri chuckled. "Did she invite you?" she wondered.

"Nope," Malajia revealed, heading up the steps.

# Chapter 55

Mark, plate piled high with cookout food in his hands, made his way to one of the round umbrella-covered picnic tables that were set up in the massive backyard of Trisha and Chasity's West Chester home. By the time Mark had arrived, the cookout was already in full swing. The grounds were filled with family and friends. The abundance of food and drinks had Mark ready to move in.

"Yo, I'm about to go jump in that pool," Mark said, picking up one of his ribs.

"Go ahead and be the only soggy one running around here," Jason said, taking a sip of his beer.

Mark shrugged and pointed to Jason's drink. "Yo, why you drinking that wack ass beer? Where's the cognac?"

Jason chuckled, mid-sip. "This was the first thing that I grabbed."

"Still no excuse," Mark hissed, taking a bite of a rib.

Jason stared at him. "You talking shit to *me* and you got a whole wine cooler sitting right next to you."

Mark quickly knocked the bottle of red cooler that was sitting next to him off the table, spilling the contents on the patio. "That ain't mine," he lied.

"Boy! You better pick that shit up!" the guys heard Chasity scream from the house.

Mark flinched, then scrambled to retrieve the now empty bottle from the ground, inciting laughter from Jason. "My bad Chaz! I'mma pour some water on this beautiful granite to wash it off," he promised, nervous.

Jason kept laughing. "You flinched hard as shit you little bitch," he teased.

"Yo, her voice got deep as shit," Mark returned, pouring water on the spot.

"Hey," Jason beamed, seeing Josh and David walk over to their table, each guy giving a handshake.

"Y'all hype as shit, y'all rode here together," Mark teased as Josh and David sat down.

"Shut up," Josh chuckled.

"Man, it feels like forever since I've seen you guys," David smiled, folding his arms on the tabletop.

"I'm sure it has, mister travel man," Mark said.

David looked confused. "Was that supposed to be an insult or a joke?" he laughed.

"Neither, it was too corny for both," Mark admitted, humor in his voice.

Jason scooped some potato salad on his fork, then craned his neck to get a look at the grill. "I think Chasity's uncle is taking the steaks off the grill." He barely got his words out before Mark jumped up.

"Bet, I'm on those," Mark said, wiping his hands on a napkin.

Josh frowned in confusion. "You already got a whole plate of food sitting right in front of you," he observed, pointing to the full dish.

"Don't worry about what I got on my plate, engine grease boy," Mark jeered, walking away, with Josh breaking into laughter.

"Let me get my plate before he eats up everything," Josh announced, humor still in his voice, as he got up from the table to follow Mark to the grill.

"Yeah, I better get my share too," David chortled, following suit.


Malajia stirred some sugar into a large glass pitcher of lemonade, before pouring some lemon-flavored vodka into it.

She poured some in a cup and took a sip. "Oh my God yeeeeessss!" she bellowed, tossing her head back. She pushed the cup in front of Chasity, who was cutting up some pineapples and placing them into a clear bowl. "You gotta taste this."

Chasity moved the cup away from her. "No."

Malajia frowned. "Come on, it's good," she pressed. "It's not even strong."

"I don't want any," Chasity replied, tone calm. "I'm still messed up from that drink you made *last* night."

"Hell, me too," Malajia agreed, laughter in her voice. "No bullshit, I think I'm still drunk." Malajia then shook her head as she watched Chasity take a bite out of a piece of pineapple. "That damn piece is all small, just put the whole thing in your mouth," she grunted, taking another sip of her drink.

Chasity stared at her for a moment. "Nope, not even gonna touch that," she said, resisting the urge to make a vulgar joke. She looked up when her cousin walked into the kitchen.

"Chasity, where is the other container of pasta salad? The one outside is almost gone and Aunt Trisha wants me to put the new one out," Melina asked.

Chasity pointed to the refrigerator. "In the fridge," she answered.

Malajia watched as Melina retrieved the large container of salad from the refrigerator, and headed back through the glass doors to the backyard. Malajia then turned to Chasity. "I think she was sweating over the hot dogs—"

Chasity busted out laughing as Malajia continued.

"Naw, she was glistening all hard, standing over the grill earlier and shit," Malajia complained as Chasity was laughing hysterically.

"You are so fuckin' *stupid*," Chasity laughed.

"You can't tell me that she wasn't sweatin' all in the greens she was making," Malajia continued.

"She didn't even *make* any greens," Chasity pointed out.

"We don't even *have* any greens."

"Yeah well, she was sweatin' on *something*. And I think it was the hot dogs. I'm not eatin' those," Malajia threw back. "Wide ass, ham stick."

Chasity laughed again. "The fuck is wrong with you?"

"I don't like her 'cause she used to treat you like shit," Malajia grunted. "I don't care *how* nice she is to you now, to *me* she'll always be a sweaty, ham stick."

Chasity shook her head. "I can't even argue with that," she admitted. "Grandmom, are any of the other salads empty out there?" she asked when her grandmother walked into the kitchen.

"*All* of them," Grandmother Duvall chuckled. "I came in here to get some more."

"You already know that Mom is gonna be mad if she sees you helping," Chasity chastised. "She told you to relax. You got dizzy the other day remember? *I'll* bring them out."

Grandmother Duvall waved her hand at Chasity dismissively. "Hush girl, my pressure was just up a little bit. I'm fine now," she argued, heading for the refrigerator. "*You* should relax; you're looking a little pale."

"She's just light-skinned, Granny," Malajia teased, earning a giggle from Chasity's grandmother.

Chasity rolled her eyes. "I'm hungover," she grunted. "But foreal, I'll bring them out in a minute, go sit down," she ordered.

Grandmother Duvall put her hands up in surrender. "Okay." As she headed back to the door, Malajia poured some of her special lemonade into a cup.

"Psst Granny, you want some lemonade?" she said.

"Oh sure sweetie," Grandmother Duvall smiled, taking the cup.

"Grandmom, there's liquor in that," Chasity barked, backhanding Malajia on the arm.

"And?" Grandmother Duvall dismissed, taking her cup and walking out of the house.

"Yeeesss, Granny!" Malajia bellowed, holding her arms

up, only to be jolted out of her celebration when Chasity backhanded her again. "Ouch!"

"If she gets drunk and starts singing gospel songs, I'm locking you in a room with her," Chasity sneered.

"Shit, I'll probably be singing *with* her," Malajia laughed, rubbing her arm.

"Hey sisters!" Alex squealed, entering the kitchen through the living room. She was beaming as she gave Malajia and Chasity big hugs.

"About time you got here, bantu knots," Malajia said, looking at Alex's knotted hair. Alex narrowed her eyes at her. "They look cute though."

"I did these because I was gonna try a twist out, but…it's just too hot so I left them in there," Alex explained.

Chasity stared at Alex's head. "I never noticed how small your head is," she teased.

"Funny," Alex chuckled. She looked behind her. "Emily should be right behind me, we rode here on the bus together."

Not a moment after she said that, Emily walked in, carrying a bag. She let out a squeal of delight as she embraced Chasity and Malajia. "I missed you," Emily gushed. "Chaz, I don't remember your house being this big."

"It hasn't changed in size since you were here last time, Em," Chasity teased.

Malajia's eyes zoned in on the bag in Emily's hand. "Whatchu got there?" she asked, pointing.

"Oh, I wanted to bring something," Emily smiled, handing the bag to Chasity. Chasity reached her hand in and retrieved the frozen item. She looked perplexed.

"You brought a half-gallon of sorbet to a cookout?" Chasity drew her question out slowly. Emily nodded enthusiastically. "Um…for *what*?"

"Right? And didn't even bring a *gallon*," Malajia added. Alex just shook her head at Malajia. "Cheap ass cookout gift and shit."

Emily shrugged. "Well Chaz, since it's your house, I brought it for you and your mom to share." Chasity and

Malajia stared at her.

"What about *me*? I've been here since Wednesday, you ain't bring *me* nothing," Malajia complained.

Emily once again shrugged. "Well...*you* don't *live* here," she said, causing Alex to bust out laughing at the salty look on Malajia's face.

"You know what, you have made a great point Emily," Chasity agreed, pointing at Emily. She looked at the container. "It's rainbow too. I'm gonna eat this whole damn thing."

Malajia reached her hand out to try to touch the container. "You gonna share?"

"Fuck no," Chasity threw back, moving the carton out of Malajia's grasp.

Emily giggled as she leaned over the counter. "Is *everybody* here?" she asked.

"Everybody but Sidra," Malajia answered, taking another sip of her drink. "I talked to her a little earlier; I think she's on her way."

"Anybody notice that she seems a bit down?" Alex wondered. "I mean, even though everything between you and her are finally resolved Mel, it seems that some other stuff is bothering her. At least that's what *I* notice when I talk to her."

"Sidra is probably just in one of her moods," Malajia dismissed. "I know she's still trying to decide what law school to go to so maybe that's been stressing her a bit." She looked at Alex. "Don't go bringing that up either. Nobody wants to hear you breathe out fussy bus stuff today."

Alex's mouth fell open in shock. "I'm not going to do that."

"She lying like shit," Chasity commented. Malajia and Emily nodded in agreement.

Alex just flagged them with her hand dismissively as she headed for the patio. "Where's the food? Shut up Malajia," she said, walking out.

"I ain't even say anything, fat ass," Malajia hurled at

Alex's departing back. Emily snickered loudly as Chasity shook her head.

"Hey girls," Sidra said, walking in from the living room.

"Sidra!" Emily shrieked, giving her a hug.

Upon hearing Sidra's name, Alex turned around and darted back for the door, only to be met by Malajia pulling it closed. "Malajia stop being childish, you're a college graduate for Christ sakes!" Alex barked, pulling on the door.

"Nope, you told me to shut up. You stay your ass out there and look through the glass," Malajia taunted, making faces at Alex.

Alex sucked her teeth and pulled the other glass door handle, opening it. Malajia held a stupid look on her face as Alex walked in and gave Sidra a hug.

"Damn it Chasity. Fuck your rich ass house with double glass doors and shit," Malajia griped, pushing the door back open.


"Jase, I just heard you say pineapple upside down cake," Mark said, looking up from devouring his food.

Jason frowned, holding his gaze on Mark for several seconds. "I said, I'm about to go get another *plate*," he bit out.

Josh and David busted out laughing as Mark sat there looking silly. "Soooo, there's no cake, is what you're saying?" Mark slowly asked.

Jason vigorously rubbed his face with his hands in agitation.

David scooped up some pasta salad onto his fork. "I'm going to go visit Nicole in a few weeks," he announced before putting the food into his mouth. "She wants me to meet her grandparents."

"If this conversation ain't about no damn cake, I ain't tryna hear it," Mark blurted out, then laughed when David shot him a glare. "I'm joking. Y'all *do* remember I'm simple right?"

"How could we *forget*?" Josh chuckled.

"Yeah, she invited me down to North Carolina for a weekend," David continued.

"That's cool bro, I'm glad that you two worked everything out," Jason commended.

David nodded in agreeance. "Things have been good. We're talking all the time, making plans and stuff," he said. "I just figure that if things are meant to work out, they *will*. If not, they *won't*. But for now…things are good."

Mark put his hand up. "So does this mean that you will *finally* get some ass?" he asked.

Jason snickered and Josh just shook his head as he tried not to laugh. "Yeah, you *really* had to remind us that you're simple," Josh commented, sarcastic.

David was silent as he put some ketchup on his hamburger. "I already *did*," he revealed.

For a long moment, no one spoke, shocked into silence.

"Bullshit!" Mark barked, pointing.

David put his right hand up. "Swear to God," he said.

"*When?*" Jason asked, curious.

"I went back down to school to visit her a week after we graduated," David revealed. "Remember, everybody else still had like two weeks left of—"

"We know the damn college schedule," Mark interrupted, earning a chuckle from David. "Why you holdin' out on the details? We're your brothers man. Josh, did *you* know?"

Josh put his hands on his chest. "I had no idea," he assured. "I'm just as shocked as everyone else."

"Come on guys, you mean to tell me that you ran and told somebody after *your* first experience?" David questioned.

"Hell yeah!" Mark bellowed as Josh and Jason nodded in agreement.

David flagged them with his hand as he went back to eating his food. "Well…I'm telling y'all *now*, so get over it."

"I'm telling the girls," Mark quickly put out. "Baby! I got some beans to spill!" he yelled in Malajia's direction. David reached across the small table and grabbed Mark's arm in a panic. "Chill man!"

"Naw, fuck that, ain't no secrets in this group," Mark threw back. Malajia walked over with Sidra in tow.

"Why *you* always gotta be the loud one?" Malajia said to Mark as she ran her hand along the top of his head. "What do you want?"

"Yo, I—" Mark glanced at David and laughed at the panicked look on his face. He decided to keep it to himself, for now. "Can you go fix me a plate of potato salad?"

Malajia stared at him. "You called me over here just for some salad?" she barked. "You got me chopped." She gestured to Jason. "Jase, Chaz needs your help with something in the kitchen."

"Okay," Jason said, getting up from the table.

Mark shook his head in amusement as Malajia walked off. "So damn disrespectful," he joked, getting up to follow her. "Can you at least get me some ice?"

"How many cubes, lazy?!" Malajia threw over her shoulder.

"Damn this burger is good," David mentioned, taking another bite. He grabbed his plate and stood up. "I'm about to grab another one before they're gone."

"I don't think the food is in any danger of running out any time soon," Sidra chortled as David hurried for the grill.

"Yeah, it looks like they bought up the whole supermarket," Josh commented as Sidra sat down in an empty seat.

Sidra tapped the soda can in her hand with her fingernails. It was a little awkward, just the two of them. She hadn't really spoken to or seen much of Josh since their tense conversation in her car the night of their dinner. That was over two weeks ago. "You still helping your dad out at the shop?" she asked in an attempt to start a conversation.

Josh leaned back in his seat. "Here and there. Dad came

back to work a few days ago, so now I'm mostly just working the one job for now," he answered. He held his gaze on her. "You still going to California?"

Sidra stared back, before nodding, providing a silent answer to Josh's question.

Josh reached for his drink. "You tell the others yet?"

"Not yet," Sidra replied. "Wanted to finalize some stuff first...now that I have. I *will*."

Josh nodded. "Well... Congratulations again," he said.

Sidra forced a smile. "Thanks." She opened her mouth to say something else, but a loud noise startled her. She and Josh stood up and looked over at a nearby table to see Mark bent down.

"My bad," Mark apologized to a group of people, picking up the fallen plate and drink from a table that he bumped into.

"This is the last time your ass is allowed over here," Chasity hissed.

"It was an accident!" Mark yelled

"Why were you dancing so hype *anyway*?! You didn't even have to *do* all that!" Chasity yelled back.

Mark pointed to Malajia. "*She* made me do it, backing up on me all hard and shit," he defended.

Malajia stood there laughing at the scene. "My bad," she said to him.


"All of that food...every last thing was hittin'," Mark complimented, rubbing his stomach, before Malajia took a seat on his lap.

"You *would* know, 'cause you damn near ate it all," Josh laughed, adjusting the watch on his wrist. Mark just shrugged.

Night had fallen and with everybody else either in the house or gone for the evening, the gang remained outside, seated around one of the tables. The nearby torchlights, accompanied by the moonlight and lit citronella candle, provided a peaceful, calming, environment after the hustle and bustle of the day.

"Who made that potato salad?" Mark asked. "It tasted better than Sidra's mom's."

Sidra looked at him, pointing. "I'm telling," she joked, earning snickers from the group.

"No but seriously, did your grandmom make that?" Mark pressed, looking at Chasity.

Chasity shook her head. "*I* did," she answered.

Mark twisted his lip up. "Parker, your light skin ass is lying like shit," he hurled.

Chasity chuckled. "I *did* make it," she insisted.

"Not believing it. You ain't make shit but that dry ass corn," Mark jeered, waving his hand at her.

Malajia slowly turned and looked at him, face masked with anger. "*I* made the damn corn," she revealed.

Mark had a silly look on his face for a moment before giving Malajia's back a rub. "And it was the *best* unseasoned corn that I ever had, my love," he amended; Malajia softly elbowed him in his ribs.

"Whatever," Malajia sneered. "No but Chaz *did* make the salad, I watched her," she assured, adjusting her position on Mark's lap. "I kept eating it when she turned her back."

Chasity stared at Malajia. "Your greedy ass is going home *tonight*," she spat.

"Yeah a'ight," Malajia dismissed. "I ain't got no job yet, I got nothing *but* time to be here."

"Jase, trade me women for a day so I can get some more potato salad," Mark joked, earning a hit to his leg from Malajia, a disgusted look from Chasity, and a confused stare from Jason.

"Oh, you tryna trade me now?" Malajia snarled as Mark rubbed his leg. "For some potatoes and mayonnaise?"

"I'm just playing," Mark laughed.

"I swear to God, the thought of me being Mark's woman is making me want to throw up," Chasity complained.

"You and me *both* baby," Jason added, rubbing her arm.

Chasity grabbed her stomach. "No seriously," she said, before getting up from the table and heading for the house.

"You see what you did, you idiot," Jason barked, getting up to follow her.

Alex shook her head in amusement. "Mark, you're going to mess around and end up by yourself," she jokingly predicted.

"You mean like *you* are?" Mark immediately threw back.

"Ooh!" Emily blurted out, then immediately covered her mouth.

"Oh shit," Josh snickered.

Alex's face was masked with anger as her friends desperately tried not to bust out laughing at Mark's comeback. "*Still* a butthole," she grumbled, folding her arms.

After a few moments, Jason and Chasity returned to the table.

"You okay sissy boo?" Alex asked as Chasity sat down in her chair.

Malajia waved her hand in Alex's direction. "Nah, don't be calling her no damn sissy boo. Only *best friends* can give one another nicknames," she hurled at Alex, who sat there looking perplexed. Malajia then looked at Chasity. "You okay, my vanilla pudding cup?"

"Malajia, shut up," Chasity barked, causing Malajia to bust out laughing. She ran her hand through her hair. "I'm fine. I just ate too much."

"*When*?" Jason asked, looking at her. "I barely saw you eat today."

Chasity stared back at him. "Didn't know you were here *watching* me all day," she sarcastically spat. Jason just shook his head.

Emily folded her arms, as she got comfortable in her seat. "I'm glad that we were able to get together again," she began. "Even if it was only for a few hours."

"Yeah...once everybody starts grad school, or jobs wherever they may be, who knows if we'll get this chance again," David added.

"Yeah, you're going to Ohio David," Alex smiled. "You excited?"

David gave an enthused nod. *"Very.* I can't wait to get my courses started."

"You hype as shit you about to start school again," Mark teased.

David laughed a little. "Hey, I look at it as being one step closer to getting my career started," he shrugged. "So, yeah, I'm hype."

"As hype as you were about losing your virginity?" Mark blurted out.

David's mouth fell open in shock as the girls all stared at him. *"Seriously* Mark?!" he snapped.

"You and Nicole finally did it?" Malajia squealed.

"Say it louder, I don't think the people down the street heard you," David grunted.

Malajia threw her head back. "You and Nicole finally did it?!" she yelled at the top of her lungs. David couldn't help but laugh a little as laughter erupted around him. *"Now* they did," Malajia boasted.

"Yep, walked right into that one," David admitted, running his hand over his head.

"That's a big step for you, I'm happy that you two are at that place," Alex smiled, patting David's arm.

"So, who initiated it?" Malajia asked, eager.

David looked uncomfortable as he fidgeted in his seat.

*"Damn* the initiation, David did you smack her ass?" Mark goaded. "Ooh ooh, wait, I *gotta* know, did you take your glasses off?"

"Yo, I just wanna know how quick you busted one," Chasity joked.

Jason tossed his hands up. "Chasity come on!" he barked, annoyed as she started laughing. "Really?"

"I was wondering the same thing!" Malajia exclaimed, pointing at Chasity.

"You two are so nasty," Sidra scoffed.

David put his hands over his face and pulled down. "See, *this* is why I didn't say anything at first," he ground out.

Emily giggled. "Okay guys, leave him alone," she said.

"Nah, let's keep going. So David, did you know where to put it, or did she have to show you?" Mark mocked.

David tossed his hands up in frustration and sat back in his seat.

"Emily is right; leave him alone," Alex cut in. "He's suffered enough."

"Thank you," David replied, grateful. "Let's talk about something else please."

Sidra was silent for a moment then took a deep breath. "I um…I'm moving to California." The table fell silent. She stared at her hands. "I'm leaving next month."

"Sidra…you really decided to go to the school out there?" Alex asked, surprised.

"Yeah," Sidra answered, tone sullen. "It's a good school. One of the top… I would be stupid *not* to go."

"Then why don't you seem happy about it?" Malajia asked, tone serious.

Sidra was taken aback by the question. "I *am* happy," she insisted.

Malajia shook her head and turned away. "Okay."

"Damn sis, the other side of the country huh?" Mark asked. Sidra nodded. "An expensive ass plane ride."

Sidra forced a smile. "I'll be back up this end to visit whenever I get a break," she assured. Her friends sat there, quiet. She knew that they didn't believe her. She didn't even believe that herself.

"Hey, don't be worried Sid," David assured her. "With Em moving back to Virginia and me moving to Ohio—"

"Man, don't nobody care about no damn only a-six-hour-drive-away ass Ohio," Mark spat out.

David gritted his teeth as Mark laughed.

"I'm just messing with you, I have to get it all out. I don't know the next time I'mma see you after you leave," Mark explained.

"Yeah well, fuck you," David mumbled.

# Chapter 56

Alex took a bite of her burger then wiped her mouth with a napkin. She grabbed her cup of vanilla milkshake and took a long sip.

Stacey stared at Alex, giggling, as she reached for a French fry. "Hungry, I see," she teased.

Alex set her cup down. "Girl, I haven't eaten all day," she said. Alex was so busy wracking her brain about the job that she interviewed for two weeks ago, that she had forgotten to eat. She was ecstatic when Stacey called, asking her to meet up for lunch downtown. "I'm going crazy about this job situation."

"Still haven't heard from the publishing company, huh?" Stacey asked, holding a sympathetic glance.

Alex shook her head, sighing in the process. "No, and she said that no matter what, that she'd call me by the end of that week," she grabbed a fry and leaned back in her seat. "I was probably so pathetic that she forgot about me." She punctuated her sullen reply by stuffing the fry into her mouth.

"Come on Alex, you know that's not true," Stacey placated. "Something probably came up."

"Yeah, a better candidate," Alex sulked. Stacey shook her head. "No really… What if I blew it because I questioned the position that she interviewed me for?"

"You have a right to ask whatever you want," Stacey said, grabbing half of her sandwich. "You applied for one thing, and they interviewed you for something else. You were right to question."

"I guess you're right," Alex said as Stacey took a bite of her sandwich. "It may be for the best. It's not what I wanted anyway."

"So, if they were to call you right now and offer you the job, you'd turn them down because it's not what you want to do?" Stacey asked.

"I never wanted to be anybody's assistant."

"Who says you have to *stay* that?" Stacey questioned. "You told me what she said to you. You don't have any *experience* Miss-know-it-all." Alex feigned hurt as Stacey giggled. "You'll learn and work your way up."

Alex ran her hand over her hair. "Yeah, yeah. You and your red hair have a point."

"Ooh you like it?" Stacey smiled, wrapping a few strands of her curled locks around her fingers.

"It's cute," Alex replied. She took a few more bites of her food.

"Paul went into the army," Stacey began, earning a shocked look from Alex.

"Say *what*?"

Stacey nodded. "Yeah, you know his aunt lives on my block and she runs her mouth, so that's how I heard... Figured I'd tell you before it gets around the neighborhood."

Alex shrugged, "Well, whatever works for him... He has a kid to take care of, so I guess he needed to do *something*," she said. "Not my business or my problem, but I wish him well."

Stacey looked pleasantly surprised. "Look at you, being all mature and stuff."

"Girl, I have so much going for me—or I *will* as soon as I get this job stuff together," Alex said. "I don't have time to be bitter towards anybody anymore. I mean it, I wish him well."

"And Victoria?"

Alex paused in mid-sip of her milkshake. "I hope she doesn't die," she sneered, earning a laugh from Stacey. The sound of Alex's phone ringing made her nearly drop her cup. She quickly grabbed it from her purse and answered.

"Hello...yes, this is she...Yes, it's good to hear from you again...okay... No, I understand. I'm sorry to hear that... Okay... Okay... Umm, yes, sure... Yes... Okay great... Thank you."

Stacey sat in anticipation as Alex ended the phone call. "Well?"

"That was Marlene, she just offered me the job," Alex squealed with delight.

Stacey gave the excited Alex a high five. "I *knew* you'd get it. Congratulations sis."

Alex was smiling from ear to ear. Sure, it wasn't her ideal position, but it was a start and she was looking forward to getting paid for learning.


Sidra flipped through channels on her television as she enjoyed the quiet of her house. With her parents out, she spent the majority of her alone time in the living room, surrounded by snacks, catching up on shows.

Hearing a knock at the door, she glanced at it. Annoyed by the interruption, she let out a huff as she stood up and headed for the door. Not bothering to look out of the peephole, she opened the door and her eyes nearly popped out of her head at the sight of the person standing on the other side.

"Hi Sidra," James said.

Embarrassed by her messy hair, tights and T-shirt, she slammed the door in his face. "Shit, shit! What is he doing here?" she whispered to herself. She glanced in the nearby mirror and started fussing with her hair. Then after a moment, she dropped her hands. *Wait a minute, I don't give a damn how I look right about now.*

She opened the door again and stood with her hand on it. "Hi James," she said.

James held a bouquet of white roses in his hand. "I'm

sorry to barge in on you like this, but my texts went unanswered, so I did the *mature* thing and popped up."

James chuckled, but Sidra's face was void of amusement. "You want to come in?" she asked after a moment.

"Yes, please," James said.

Sidra moved aside and let him in, shutting the door behind him. She walked over to the couch and moved her abundance of unhealthy snacks to the coffee table. She then pointed to an empty cushion. "You can sit," she offered.

James didn't hesitate to take a seat next to her. "You look pretty," he complimented.

"Liar," she sneered.

"No, I mean it," James insisted. He handed her the flowers. "These are for you," he said as she took them from him. "Congratulations on graduating."

"Thank you," Sidra replied, giving the flowers a sniff. "They're pretty."

James smiled as he adjusted himself in his seat. "You're welcome... I wish I could have seen you walk across that stage."

Sidra sat the flowers down on the coffee table. "Yeah, people don't tend to invite their ex's," she sniped. Then took a deep breath. "I'm sorry, that was rude."

James glanced down at his hands, before looking back at her. "No, it was warranted," he agreed.

"James, I have to ask...why are you here? Why are you contacting me?" she wondered.

"I just wanted to see you," he admitted. "I really feel like we left off on a bad note."

Sidra let out a huff. "James—"

"No, seriously," he cut in, gently touching her hand, which was resting at her side. "I admit, I could have handled things better."

"I don't think that there is *any* good way to handle a break up," Sidra argued. James sighed. "I mean face it...you weren't happy, so you did what you had to do."

James ran his hand over his head. "Yeah," he sulked.

Sidra looked away. "Neither was I," she admitted, shamefully. "So despite how much it hurt...you did the right thing."

James was silent for a moment. "Sidra..." he let out another sigh. "Everything was so perfect...at least *I* thought it was... I mean, we had the distance thing but we were making it work," he said. "What went wrong?"

Sidra fought the tears forming in her eyes. James was looking to her for answers, and she didn't know what to say. She didn't want to hurt him more than she already had. "I just...I realized that I...I was going through a lot and, I was frustrated and confused... I took everything out on you and..." She ran her hand through her hair. "*I* was what went wrong...and I'm sorry."

James held his gaze. "I'm sorry too," he said. "I saw us being this great power couple."

Sidra chuckled a bit. "Yeah, with our expensive business suits and briefcases."

"Don't forget our matching travel coffee mugs."

Sidra smiled briefly. "Yeah...well, hopefully you'll find that non-neurotic woman who understands your busy life and shares your love of caffeine."

"And I hope that *you* find someone who has all the time in the world for you," James said, tone filled with sincerity.

Sidra smiled at him.

"So," he began, feeling a bit lighter. "I'll be moving to California in a few weeks. It's official; I'm starting my own firm."

"That's great James, I'm happy for you," Sidra gushed. "I'll be moving to the west coast *myself* in a few weeks."

James's eyes lit up. "You got in?"

Sidra nodded. "Yeah."

James was clearly pleased. "You're going to a great school," he approved. "Who knows, maybe one day when I'm not up to my eyeballs in cases and you're not neck deep in the books...maybe we can grab a friendly cup of coffee."

Sidra thought for a moment. "Yeah, maybe we can," she agreed.

James rubbed his hands across his pant legs. "Well, I've taken up enough of your time," he said. "I should get going."

Sidra stood up and walked James to the door. She stood there as he opened the door and walked out. He paused and turned around to face her. They stared at each other for a moment. He reached out and touched her face. "Take care of yourself Princess."

"You too," Sidra returned. She watched as he walked to his car, and waited for him to drive away before she shut the door.


Chasity laid on her bed, staring at the ceiling. She'd been laying there for the past five minutes. Her mind was racing a million miles a minute. She'd thought that lying down after leaving her private bathroom would help calm her.

It didn't.

She closed her eyes briefly as a soft tap sounded on the door. She didn't answer.

"Chasity?" Trisha softly called.

"Yes?"

"Sweetie, you remember that we have an appointment to go see that apartment at three, right?" Trisha said from the other side of the door.

Chasity looked at the clock on her nightstand. It was two fifteen. It would take them at least a half hour to get to the apartment complex on the outskirts of Philadelphia. She was in no way ready. "Mom, can you push the appointment back?"

"Umm sure, I guess I can," Trisha said. "What time?"

"Just not three," Chasity answered.

"Okay I'll call them," Trisha assured. "Are you okay? You sound terrible," she asked after a moment.

"I'm fine, just tired," Chasity answered.

"Okay, I'll let you know what the new time is."

"Great." Chasity's last word was said low enough only for her to hear. The alarm on her phone went off for the second time. Three minutes after she laid down, it sounded and she ignored it. But the loud beeping was annoying her; she knew she had to get up. Slowly rising from her bed, she walked into the bathroom. Taking a deep breath, she picked up the pregnancy test that was sitting on her sink. She stared at it, face void of expression. She then threw the stick in the trashcan, along with the box.

She walked back out of the bathroom and over to her bed. She grabbed her phone when it rang. "Hey Jase," she answered, after checking the caller ID. "Tomorrow night? Nothing…meet you where? …Okay, what time? …Yeah, I'll be there. Okay…okay. Love you too. Bye."

As soon as she hung up the phone, she heard another knock. "*Yes* Mom."

"Is four okay?"

"Four is fine, Mom," Chasity replied, tone dry. She sat down on her bed and dialed another phone number.

Emily opened a fresh pack of sheets and tossed the empty plastic in the trash. She placed the sheet to her nose and inhaled.

"Don't tell me you do that every time you buy something new," Will laughed.

Emily made a face at him. "No. I just like the smell of fresh sheets…that sounds weird."

"It *looks* weird," he teased.

Emily waved her hand at him. "You came over here to make fun of me?" she chortled.

Will smiled and headed over to help Emily make her queen-sized bed. He was excited that Emily had accepted the job offer in Virginia, and that she had moved into her new place two weeks ago. He was even more excited that her place was in *his* building. "No, I came to check on you."

"I'm fine," Emily insisted. "That's not the first time that I've seen a bug."

"Not judging from the way that you screamed when you saw it."

Emily playfully tossed a pillow at him. "Stop, that spider was huge...like a tarantula," she whined.

"It was *not* a tarantula," Will laughed.

Emily folded her arms and shook her head at him. "*Whatever* species it was...thank you for coming over yesterday to kill it."

"No problem," Will said, placing a pillow on Emily's bed. "So, when do you start your certification classes?"

"Next week," she answered.

"Excited?"

"Very," Emily replied.

"That's good, I'm excited *for* you," Will smiled. "Hey, how about you let me take you out?"

Emily smoothed out her comforter. "You don't have to do that."

"But I *want* to," he insisted. "Think of it as a 'congratulations' dinner."

Emily stared at his hopeful face. She pushed her hair behind her ears. "With the cost of this rent, I think we both should be eating *in*," she joked.

Will shook his head in amusement. "Okay Miss Kill-joy, we'll celebrate indoors. My schedule is pretty crazy for the next few days, but on my day off, me and you."

Emily shrugged. "Okay, sounds like a plan." Hearing her house phone ring, Emily looked down at the cordless phone resting on her nightstand.

"Tell Ms. Kelly I said hi," Will teased, heading out of the room.

"Shut up, you don't even know it's her," Emily giggled, picking up the phone. "Hello? ...Hey Mommy."

Will's loud laugh could be heard from the hallway.

Emily shook her head as she sat down on her bed. Emily's mother had made it a point to call her nearly every day since she'd moved back to Virginia.

"Emily, I know you said that I don't need to check in on you every day, but I can't help it," Ms. Harris said, amusement in her voice.

"It's okay Mommy. I can handle your daily phone calls," Emily replied. "As long as you're not doing random pop-ups, we're good."

A laugh came through the phone. "That has been noted."

Emily too laughed as she stared at the cream carpet on the floor. "Thanks for sending me the bed stuff. The pink looks pretty in here."

"You're welcome." There was a pause. "Emily...I am so proud of you."

Emily smiled. "That was out of nowhere," she said. "...You are, really?"

"Absolutely...your determination to live your life on *your* terms, no matter how many times I tried to stifle that...you are inspiring sweetheart."

"I never thought of myself as inspiring," Emily blushed.

"You *should*...okay I've bothered you enough. Have a good day sweetheart and...Jazmine said that she wants to talk to you."

"Wait *what*?" Emily spat, hearing that last part being said quickly. "No, I don't need her nonsense. What does she even *want*?"

"I don't know sweetie, but she's your sister so just answer if she calls. I have to get to this store; I'll talk to you tomorrow."

Emily opened her mouth to speak, but was cut off when she heard dead air. She hung up the phone and tossed it on the bed. "I'm not answering that heffa's phone call," she mumbled to herself as she folded her arms.


Jason sat on a bench in a park across the street from a restaurant. He was anxiously awaiting the arrival of Chasity. He had called her the day before to invite her to dinner and had planned on picking her up, but with her having a few things to handle, she told him that she would meet him there. He sent her a text and not even five minutes later, Chasity was approaching him.

He stood up to meet her.

"Why are we over here?" Chasity asked him after they parted from a quick embrace.

"It's better than sitting in the restaurant foyer, waiting on our table to be ready, isn't it?" he asked.

She let out a sigh. "Yeah, I guess."

Jason took notice of Chasity's tone. "You alright?"

"Uh huh," she quickly put out.

He pointed to the bench. "We have a few more minutes," he said, as she took a seat, with him following. He rubbed his hand over his head.

"You look tired," she observed, looking at him.

"Nah, I'm cool. Got stuck on a long call today," Jason explained. "I wanted to jump through that phone and strangle that dumbass with the computer cord that he *did not* have plugged in."

Chasity stared at him, no amusement on her face. "Sorry babe," she said.

"It's fine, comes with the job," he dismissed. "How was your day? Did you get any new clients?"

She shook her head as she stared at him. "No…but I got a positive pregnancy test."

Jason's eyes widened. He didn't know if he'd heard her correctly. "I'm sorry?"

"I'm pregnant," Chasity confirmed.

Jason was in shock and it showed on his face. They had made sure to be more careful after Chasity fell pregnant their junior year. "Umm…" he pinched the bridge of his nose as he tried to keep himself composed. "You just found out today?"

"I took a home test *yesterday* but went to the doctor for a blood test *today*…both positive, so yeah," Chasity shrugged.

"*That's* why you've been sick."

She sighed. "I had a feeling a while ago but my period started...or I *thought* it started...turns out it wasn't." She looked at him. "Are you mad?"

Jason looked at her. His eyes were bright and he let a smile come through. "No, of *course* I'm not mad," he assured. He put his arm around her. "Why would you ask me that?"

Chasity shrugged. "Was just wondering."

"I'm...actually *excited*," he admitted.

She tilted her head. "Yeah?"

"*You're not?*" he wondered, picking up on her expression and tone of voice.

"It's not *that*...I guess I am, it's just not an ideal time," she replied honestly.

"It never *is*," Jason replied. "We're both adults who love each other and we have an opportunity to bring a baby into this world together...what's not to be excited about?"

Chasity smiled slightly, although on the inside she was nervous. Sure, the money that she was making from her freelance jobs would take care of her for the time being, but a baby was a different story. Jason would be taking on graduate school full time while still trying to manage the job that he had now, a job which clearly stressed him out. She tried to keep her worries from showing on her face, especially when Jason seemed so happy.

"You're right," she said finally.

Jason pulled her in for a kiss before embracing her. As he held on to her the words of his father rang through his head. "Life doesn't always go according to plan." *I gotta figure this out*, he thought. He stood up and grabbed her hand. "Come on, our table should be ready. Time to feed *both* of my babies."

Chasity shook her head as she stood up. "You're so corny," she teased.

Jason laughed. "Yeah well, get used to it."

# Chapter 57

Malajia leaned over the counter as she held her phone in front of her face.

"You look mad as shit," Mark observed, through videophone.

"Hell *yeah* I'm mad," she grunted. "Them buffalo wings was nasty as shit." She grabbed a piece of celery from the empty wing container and took a bite. "I would've been better off just eating these dry ass celery stalks."

Mark shook his head. "You sure tore *all* six of them up, while I was talking to you," he chortled. "With no dressing."

"Yeah well, I was hungry and the dressing wouldn't have helped." Talking to Mark on his lunch breaks came to be something that Malajia looked forward to. Today of all days, her conversation with him was needed.

Malajia's mood wasn't missed on Mark. "What's wrong muffin?"

Malajia smiled slightly at the nickname before the sullen look came back. "I didn't get that job," she sulked.

"For real?"

"Yeah…they filled it last week," she answered, twirling her bitten celery stalk around in the small container of dressing. "The only reason I found out was because my desperate ass called them to follow up."

"Awww, I'm sorry boo," Mark sympathized. "Something else will come along."

"It's been almost *three months* Mark," Malajia harped.

"I know babe."

"It's not fair," she whined. "Everybody else is doing *something*. If they're not working, they're going to grad school… I'm just sitting here like a cute bump on a useless ass log."

Mark chuckled. "Malajia, try not to stress yourself."

"Easier said than *done* Mr. Sixty-thousand dollar salary," she sneered. "You gonna pay for me to get a place?"

"Shiiiittt, I'll help you *look* for one," Mark jeered.

Malajia sucked her teeth. "Whatever," she muttered. "How's your apartment hunting going? You find anything yet?"

"Uhhh, working on that," he said. "Look, I don't like seeing your pretty face on the floor. We need to do something fun, why don't we go to an amusement park on Saturday?"

She looked confused. "What the hell is *that* gonna do?" she sneered. "It's all hot."

"*Hopefully* it'll make you have some fun," he threw back. "Now stop being an asshole and just say yes."

Malajia turned her lip up. "You think talking to me like that is gonna make me go with you, you jackass?" she hissed.

Mark laughed, "I'll buy you a funnel cake."

"You'll buy me *two* funnel cakes and a churro," she demanded. "And one of those expensive ass park cups with unlimited refills…and ice cream dots."

Mark again laughed. "Whatever my greedy baby wants," he promised.

"Well then, you have yourself a date," she smiled.

"Good. Now get off my phone, I gotta get back to this dry ass job," Mark said.

"Bye," Malajia giggled, before ending the call. Setting the phone on the counter, she continued to dip her celery as she let a smile come through. She had something to look forward to. Taking a bite of the dressing covered stalk, Malajia grimaced. "Eww! The fuck is this blue cheese? I asked for *ranch!*" she yelled to an empty room.

Jason sat at his family's dining room table, looking over several papers. He had his elbow on the table, with his head resting on his hand. The sandwich and chips on his plate went untouched. Rubbing his eyes with his hand, he let out a sigh.

"You *still* haven't eaten that sandwich?" Mrs. Adams observed, putting her hand on his shoulder.

Jason glanced up at her then put his hand over one of the papers. "I guess my eyes were bigger than my stomach," he said.

Mrs. Adams moved around him and sat down in the seat next to him. She moved the plate away from him. "It looks good, so if you're not going to eat it, I'll take it off your hands."

"Be my guest," Jason said, gesturing for her to eat it.

She smiled and took a bite of the turkey club sandwich. "Are those your graduate school papers?" she asked between chews. "I thought you were all set with everything."

"I am," he confirmed. "I just um…am having some second thoughts about things."

Mrs. Adams frowned slightly. "About *what*?" she wondered. "I thought that you wanted to go to that school."

"I do," he assured.

"Then what are the second thoughts about?"

Jason rubbed his face. "I just don't think it's the right time for me to enroll full time right now."

"Why *not*?"

"It just *isn't*," Jason replied, bite in his voice. "Some things came up and I just don't think it's a good time for me to go right back to school."

Mrs. Adams looked concerned. All Jason talked about since graduating undergrad was getting his master's degree. He seemed so excited about starting in the fall. She didn't understand why he was changing his mind now.

"Jason...delaying your education is something that you swore you would *never* do," she pointed out, voice calm. "What could have come up to make you change that?"

Jason just sat there, silent.

She looked at the forms her son was trying to hide. "Jason, what are those papers?" she asked him.

"Don't worry about it."

"No, I think I *will*, because whatever they *are*, they have you sitting here looking troubled and talking crazy," she argued. When he didn't respond, she tapped the hand that was covering the papers. "Jason."

Knowing that his mother would not let up, Jason let out a loud sigh and reluctantly moved his hand.

She grabbed the papers and read the first few lines. His mother frowned. "Why are you looking over these draft papers?" she questioned. "I thought you threw these out."

"Dad put them in his desk," Jason answered. "I went looking for something else and found them...so I started reading them."

"Why are you even *reading* them? You don't want to play professional," she pressed, putting the papers back on the table. "You don't need to waste your time with that and I don't even know *why* your father held on to them."

Jason took a deep breath. "I guess he figured I'd need them one day," he muttered.

A bewildered look was frozen on her face. "Why would you need them?"

"Mom...Chasity is pregnant," Jason blurted out.

Mrs. Adams's eyes nearly bulged out of her head. "What?"

He nodded. "Yeah...found out a few weeks ago," he confirmed.

"Why didn't you tell me *then*?" Mrs. Adams asked, keeping her composure.

"We just wanted to wait to make sure everything was okay—anyway yeah, she is," he confirmed. "And...we need money, like *now*." He ran his hand over his head. "She's working freelance, but she's going to try to get a fulltime job, which I *know* she doesn't want. *My* job pays a lousy salary and my hours will need to be cut a little to accommodate some of these classes that I have to take... We're looking for an apartment, but I want to get us a house and—"

"Jason...I'm sure you two can make things work... I thought Chasity had money."

"Her *mother* has money and Chasity doesn't want help from her... I don't blame her. We're adults, we need to figure things out on our own," Jason said.

"So, what do you plan on doing then? I hope you're not thinking about going into this damn draft."

"I have no *choice*," Jason vented, looking at his mother. "It's only five years, *if* that and...I'll see if I can negotiate a signing bonus or something to start us off... I need to set my family up and *then* I can go back to school."

"What if you get hurt?"

"I'll deal with it," Jason threw back.

"Damn it Jason—" Mrs. Adams pinched the bridge of her nose. She knew as much as she wanted to argue him down about this rash decision, that she could not talk her stubborn son out of doing anything that his mind was set to. But she had an idea of who could. "Did you talk to Chasity about this?"

"I don't *need* to," Jason spat out. "I'm doing what's best for us."

"You can't make a decision like that without talking to her," Mrs. Adams insisted. "Granted, you two might not be married yet, but you will be one day and you need to get in the habit of consulting one another on decisions like *this*."

"It'll just upset her."

"If she finds out you made this decision without her input, how upset do you think she'll *really* be?" Mrs. Adams asked. Her tone was calm, but on the inside she was shaking. She was scared for her son. She commended him on wanting to provide for his family, but she didn't want him to throw away everything that he worked so hard for while doing it.

Jason took in everything that his mother had said to him. *I'm not changing my mind.* "I'll talk to her first," he agreed.

Mrs. Adams breathed a sigh of relief. "Good," she said, patting his hand. *God, please change his mind*, she thought.

"I swear as many baby clothes as your grandmother keeps buying, that child won't need anything until they turn two," Trisha mused into her phone as she folded some white onesies. "Some of these are pink," she observed, looking in a bag that her mother had dropped off earlier.

Chasity shook her head as she sat at a small table in a restaurant, sipping on iced tea. "I told her to stop buying that pink mess," she griped. "I *hate* the color first of all, and it's going to be a while before we know what I'm having."

"It's *clear* that your grandmother hopes that you have a girl," Trisha concluded, amusement in her voice.

Chasity had no idea how her mother and grandmother would react to the news of her being pregnant. She had just finished school, and she and Jason weren't even married. But she was pleasantly surprised when not only her mother and grandmother didn't get upset, they were genuinely happy and excited.

"Yeah, I don't think I'll be good with a girl…she'd probably have my attitude," Chasity said, dreading the possibility.

"Yeah well, at least you'd know how to deal with it," Trisha joked. She paused for a moment. "How long have you been sitting there?"

"Just ten minutes," Chasity answered.

"I should've come with you."

"I already told you that I don't need a mediator, I can handle this on my own," Chasity said. She looked at her watch.

"Okay, well don't sit there for too much longer," Trisha urged.

"Trust me, I got a good five minutes left in me, *if* that,"

Chasity replied. "I'll see you later." Hanging up her phone, she placed it in her purse then took another sip of her tea. "Shit tastes like metal," she complained.

Feeling a tap on her shoulder, she turned around. "Hey," she said, unenthused.

Derrick walked around to the seat across from her and sat down. "Thanks for meeting with me," he smiled. "Nice to see you."

"Nice of you to show *up* this time," Chasity ground out.

Derrick's smile faded. "I deserved that." He tapped his hands on the tabletop. His calls to Chasity since popping up at her graduation had gone unanswered. So he was both surprised and delighted when she'd called him a few days ago. Wanting to see her face to face, he proposed that he take a day trip from New York and meet her for lunch to talk. "Did you order yet?" he asked after some silence.

Chasity nodded. "Here comes the waiter if you want to go ahead and get your order in," she said, pointing in the young man's direction.

Derrick smiled and placed his order when the waiter stopped at the table. "I have to admit that I was surprised when you called me," he began. "I didn't think I'd hear from you again."

"Trust me, that was the plan," Chasity replied, folding her arms.

"Well, whatever the reason, I'm glad that you changed your mind," Derrick said. "I just want to start off by saying that I'm so—"

"Save it," Chasity calmly cut in. "I don't want any more apologies from you."

"Not even if they are *sincere*?" her father asked.

"It doesn't matter," she replied, shrugging slightly. "I've accepted the fact that you and I aren't meant to have a real relationship...and its fine."

"Can I at least explain why I didn't show up that day?" he pleaded.

Chasity stared at him before slowly shaking her head.

"No," she answered.

Derrick let out a sigh as he pinched the bridge of his nose. He had hoped that this lunch would allow him to start on the path of making amends with his daughter. It was clear that by her words and her demeanor that she no longer cared. "Chasity, I know that I made mistakes...a *lot* of them," he began, somber. "And, if it means *anything*, I wish that I could go back and change everything that happened."

"That's not possible, so it's no point in even saying it," she said.

Derrick sighed again.

"Look, I know that you were affected by Mom and Aunt Brenda's lie too... I hope that Mom can acknowledge that and hopefully apologize for lying," Chasity said.

"Their lie is no excuse for me not being what I needed to be for you. I knew a hundred percent that you were mine since you were three years old..." Derrick explained. "So, *none* of what happened should have affected my relationship with you...I know that."

Chasity nodded. "Okay." She took a deep breath. "Look, despite what I'm saying, I'm not here to bash you," she assured. "That's not why I wanted to talk to you."

He sat there, dreading his next question. Not even sure if his heart could take the answer. "Chasity...are you about to tell me that you're completely cutting me out of your life?" he asked. "Judging by your demeanor, your lack of anger at me...it seems like you're completely done with me."

Chasity tilted her head as she stared at him. "I wish that I *could* be done with you Derrick," she answered honestly. He glanced down at the table. "But I can't... I can't make decisions based on my own feelings anymore...no matter how much I *want* to."

He looked up from the table and locked eyes with her. He was grateful to hear that she would not be completely erasing him from her life, but was curious as to why she wasn't, if it was what she really wanted to do. "Not that I'm not happy to hear that but... What's stopping you, if you don't mind me asking?" he asked. "Because it's not like I wouldn't deserve it."

Chasity took another deep breath. "The fact that I'm pregnant, is what's stopping me," she revealed.

Derrick sat there in stunned silence. "You mean like, for real? Like right *now*?"

Chasity watched him sit back in his seat and place both hands on his head. He was clearly in shock. "You okay?" she nonchalantly asked.

"Uh...I could use a drink," he replied. No matter the state of their relationship, he would always consider Chasity to be his little girl; the thought of her having a baby had him thrown for a loop. His arms fell to his side. "Wow."

"So that being the *case*, I decided that it would be a good idea to keep communication open with you," she said.

Derrick leaned forward. The idea of him being a grandfather was quickly filling him with joy. "Honey, *whatever* you want or need, I promise you, I'll provide it," he said.

"*Again*, with the promises," she ground out.

"Chasity, I *mean* it," Derrick stressed.

Chasity eyed him intensely. "There is only one thing that I want from you," she said after a moment.

"Name it," Derrick smiled.

She paused as she tried to form her words. She meant it; she wasn't there to snipe at him. But she wanted to make sure that he understood her. "What you couldn't be for *me* as a *father*...just be for my child as a *grandfather*," she replied.

Derrick felt overcome with emotion. Her words both cut him like a knife and made him feel grateful at the same time. To face his failure as a father, but to be given the opportunity to make up for it in the form of a do-over with his grandchild... Derrick was overjoyed to be given the chance, even though he knew that he didn't deserve it.

"If I keep you out of their life, that would be selfish of me," she continued as Derrick wiped his eyes with a cloth napkin. "And...I can't repeat a selfish cycle."

Derrick reached out and gently grabbed hold of Chasity's hand. He was pleasantly surprised when she didn't pull away from him. "Chasity, I want you to know that I appreciate you allowing me to be a part of your child's life...and *I promise* that I'll be everything that he or she needs me to be."

Chasity held her gaze. "I truly hope that you *do*," she said, eyes pleading. "Just know that you only get *one* chance," she stressed. "The first time you disappoint my baby—"

"Chasity, on my *life*, you have *nothing* to worry about," Derrick promised, getting choked up. "I hear you loud and clear and I'll be the grandfather that they deserve."

Chasity gave a slight nod. "Okay," she agreed. "Okay," she repeated as she sat back in her seat.

Derrick smiled at Chasity as he watched her grab her phone. "Thank you," he said, grateful. "I mean it, thank you and I appreciate you."

Chasity read a text message. "Uh huh, don't thank me just yet. Mom wants you to call her so she can threaten you."

Derrick put his hand over his face and let out a laugh. He then reached for his cell phone. "Calling right now, tell her to bring it on," he challenged, dialing. "I'm not going anywhere."

# Chapter 58

Malajia danced in her seat as she pulled apart her funnel cake. "I don't know if it's just because I'm hungry, but this is the best damn funnel cake that I've ever eaten," she mused.

"How you hungry and you just ate a big ass churro and that damn ice cream?" Mark chuckled. "What, you pregnant or something?"

"*Fuck* no!" she barked. "Period just went off, we straight dawg."

Mark shrugged. "Well, hurry up and eat it so we can go get on some more rides."

Malajia put a piece of the fried dough into her mouth. She pushed the plate in front of him. "You want some?"

"Since when do you share food?" he mocked.

"Since you thought about me enough to try to cheer me up," she said. She then smiled. "Thanks, by the way. I needed it."

Mark broke a piece. "You don't have to thank me, you know I got you," he replied, before putting the food into his mouth.

Malajia blushed. "Okay, stop being all sweet. I gotta get into battle mode if I'm gonna beat you in those games," she said, waving her hands.

Mark took a sip of his drink. "You got me chopped if you think you beating me in *any* games," he threw back. "That big ass bear is *mine*."

"What the hell are *you* gonna do with it anyway?" Malajia wondered, amused.

"I'mma use that shit as a pillow."

Malajia laughed. "So stupid."

After finishing their food, the couple made their way to the games. "That bear is *mine*," Malajia boasted, holding her water filled gun at her target.

"You keep telling yourself that like it's actually gonna happen," Mark jeered, adjusting his gun.

Intensity on their faces, as soon as the game operator gave the signal, Malajia and Mark fired their water guns. "This shit is jammed!" Malajia yelped, when her water gun stalled.

"Ahhh, your gun defective like shit," Mark taunted.

Malajia sucked her teeth as she smacked the gun several times with her hand. The gun started working just as Mark's horse reached the top of the hill. "This is some bullshit!" Malajia fumed, slamming her water gun down on the counter, as Mark jumped out his seat with his arms in the air. "Y'all owe me another chance!" Malajia demanded.

"Who won? *I* did, that's who?" Mark boasted. He then got right in Malajia's face and taunted her as she folded her arms and held a scowl on her face. "Who ain't got no bear? *You* that's who. You lost!"

"You don't have to rub it in my face, you asshole," Malajia hissed.

Mark, unfazed by Malajia's anger, laughed loudly until he was stopped by the game operator.

"Sir, you didn't actually win," the teenager cut in.

Mark and Malajia both looked at him. Mark frowned. "*Sir?*" he scoffed. "I ain't that much older than *you*."

"Mark, he's probably like sixteen and you're twenty-three. Sit your old ass down somewhere," Malajia demanded.

Mark waved his hand at her dismissively. "Fuck that, how did I *not* win?" he asked him. "My horse *clearly* beat hers. Stop tryna cheat me out of my damn bear."

"You hype about that damn bear," Malajia muttered.

"Shut up, you," Mark threw at her, before turning his attention back to the worker.

"You were also playing against the people over there." He pointed to two players seated on the other side of the counter. "The lady over there won."

Mark craned his neck to see, then sucked his teeth. "We ain't see them, so they don't count," he fussed.

Malajia busted out laughing as she stood from her seat. "You salty," she teased, getting close to Mark's face. "*You* don't get a bear either. You mad as shit."

Mark held an angry gaze. "You just spit on me."

"And?" Malajia laughed. "You act like you ain't have my fluids on you before."

"Stop acting nasty in front of the teenager," Mark bit out, earning another laugh from Malajia.


"We done rode damn near every ride and played every game," Mark commented, rubbing the back of his neck. "I'm tired like shit." Night was beginning to fall and after spending all day at the amusement park, both Mark and Malajia were worn out.

Malajia gave the large stuffed bear in her arms a tight squeeze. "Me too," she agreed. "Thanks for my bear." She was pleasantly surprised that after finally winning an oversized stuffed animal while playing another game, that Mark passed the prize directly to her.

"Yeah, you're welcome," Mark replied. "It's not like you would've let me keep it *anyway*."

"You damn right," Malajia giggled. She smiled when Mark grabbed her free hand and held it as they continued to walk through the park.

"You ready to get out of here?" Mark asked, glancing at her.

Malajia was in mid-nod when something caught her eye. "Not just yet," she alluded.

Mark frowned. "Babe, what else can we *possibly* do?"

Malajia smiled and pointed to a ride. "That," she beamed.

Mark looked as well. His eyes widened. "The sling shot ride?" he panicked. "Nah bruh, you on your own with that one."

Malajia sucked her teeth. "Oh come on, you're not scared are you?" she teased.

"Hell *yeah*, I'm scared," he admitted, unashamed. "I'm not foolin' with that."

Malajia stomped her foot on the ground. "You rode every freakin' roller coaster in this place," she argued. "We've been tossed, twisted, dropped and spun around all damn day and you're scared of a little sling shot?"

"*Little?*" Mark barked. "Malajia, that thing will shoot us to the fuckin' moon. I ain't goin'. You on your own."

"You'll really let me ride alone?" Malajia ground out.

"Nah, you got your bear. Put his purple ass in the seat next to you."

Malajia narrowed her eyes at him. His stubbornness and refusal to do what she wanted was pissing her off. "Mark...let's get on the damn ride," she demanded.

"I said no!"


"I swear to God, if we die, you'll be on permanent time out," Mark ground out, clutching the handles of the ride.

"Well, *duh*," Malajia laughed, tightening her strap.

After a verbal standoff lasting another ten minutes, Mark finally relented. A decision that he was regretting.

"Yo, you promised to blow me in the car if I do this," Mark reminded, closing his eyes. "I'm cashing in on the way home."

"You got played boy, I ain't doing that bullshit," Malajia refused.

Mark snapped his head towards her. "Fuck you!"

Malajia laughed as the ride operator checked their straps.

"Yo my man, let me off," Mark pleaded as the worker chuckled.

"No, leave him on," Malajia cut in. "We're already on

here."

Mark closed his eyes as he felt the ride pull back and set. "Oh God, please. I don't wanna die," he complained.

"Stop bitchin'," Malajia barked. "You're embarrassing me."

"Malajia I'm not playing, tell them to let me off," Mark panicked. "I gotta go to the bathroom."

Malajia rolled her eyes. "No you *don't*."

Mark took a deep breath as he heard the operator speak over the speaker. He shut his eyes tight. "Mel, if I fall out, tell my mom that I didn't scream like a bitch."

Malajia giggled. She'd never seen Mark so nervous before and it was both amusing and cute to her. "We're not going to die," she promised. "Stop whining, I'm here with you." She reached for his hand. He grabbed hold of it and squeezed it. Malajia sat there, eyes closed, just waiting.

"Marry me Malajia," Mark blurted out.

Malajia's eyes snapped open and her head jerked in his direction. "What?!" she yelled right before the ride took off sending them screaming into the sky.


Mark quickened his step to try to catch up to Malajia, who was walking ahead of him at a hurried pace. "Mel, will you stop?"

"No, fuck you," Malajia snapped.

"Why are you mad?" he wondered.

Malajia stopped walking and stormed up to him, pointing. "I can't believe you did that shit."

"Did *what*?" he asked, confused. "You're mad because I said 'marry me Malajia'?"

"Yes! On a damn ride," she harped.

Mark shrugged. "What's wrong with *that*?"

Malajia could have slapped him. He was so clueless. "You take some of the most important words that a girl wants to hear and you blurt them out on a damn amusement park ride because you were scared of dying... Does that sound fuckin' *romantic* to you?"

"That's *not* why I said that," he assured.

Malajia folded her arms and eyed him skeptically. "So, you *weren't* scared for your life?"

"Oh no I *was*," Mark admitted.

Malajia shook her head. "Don't say stuff like that if you're not serious, Mark," she said, tone serious.

He raised an eyebrow. "You don't think I'm being serious?"

"I know you play around a lot," she ground out. "That's what you *do*."

"Have I ever played around when it came to my feelings for you?" Mark asked. Malajia shot him a knowing look. "Okay, *maybe* in the beginning of our relationship but not *now*."

"Whatever Mark," Malajia spat back. "Bottom line, don't take something like that and say it like it don't mean shit…that's not cool."

Mark stared at her. He reached out and grabbed her hand and she jerked it away. "You're right, I shouldn't have asked you like that…I'm sorry," he admitted. She looked away from him. Mark got down on his knee. "I should've asked you like *this*."

"Asked me like *what*?" Malajia sneered, facing him again. Her eyes widened when she saw him on one knee. She unfolded her arms. "Wait…what are you doing?"

Mark smiled as he grabbed her hand and held it. "Malajia Lakeshia Simmons—"

"Oh my God," Malajia breathed. "Wait, are you *serious*?" she felt tears prick her eyes. "You better not be playing with me."

"Hush your face," Mark chuckled.

Malajia fanned her eyes with her free hand. She couldn't believe what was happening.

"Malajia Lakeshia Simmons," he repeated. "Will you marry me?"

Tears spilled from Malajia's eyes. "Okay, so like, are

you really serious?" she sniffled.

Mark nodded. "Yes."

"Even with me not having a job right now?"

Mark chuckled. "Yes, even without you having a job."

"Even though—"

"Nothing can ever be a simple 'yes' with you, can it?" Mark joked.

Malajia let a laugh come through her tear-streaked face. She recalled the many questions that she had asked Mark when he first asked her on a date. "Yes," she answered. "Yes, I'll marry you."

Mark's smile was bright as he reached into his pocket.

"You already bought a ring?!" Malajia squealed, giving his arm a playful slap.

"Of course," Mark chortled, opening the small grey box. Though he'd only purchased the ring a week ago, he'd knew that he wanted to propose since they'd graduated. He wasn't sure how he actually wanted to do it, but he realized that it didn't need to be perfect; it just needed to be sincere.

Malajia eyed the silver ring with the small three princess cut diamond studs. "Awww," she smiled.

"Don't 'awww' it! You're making me think it's too small," Mark said, almost embarrassed.

"No babe, I love it," she gushed, holding her left hand out. She watched as Mark slid the ring onto her ring finger. Mark stood up and Malajia jumped into his arms, holding on tight. The lack of job or apartment no longer mattered to her. All the things that she endured were behind her. Malajia was engaged to the love of her life, and that made her the happiest that she had ever been.

"I love you," Malajia sobbed into his shoulder.

"I love you too, you big baby," Mark replied, holding onto her.


Jason smiled when Trisha opened the door. "Hey Jase," she greeted, adjusting her purse strap. "She's in the den."

"Okay thank you," he returned, stepping inside the house.

"I'm on my way out, but can you do me a favor and make sure that stubborn woman in there finishes her food?" Trisha requested. "She doesn't need to be pulling that 'I'm not hungry' mess."

Jason chuckled a bit. "Yeah, I'll make sure." He was happy that Trisha was excited about her future grandchild, but according to Chasity, her mother had been fussing over her too much. All of the extra attention was getting on Chasity's nerves. Jason, on the other hand, found it amusing.

"See you later," Trisha said, walking out. She then turned back in. "And hopefully when I get back, she'll have that pretty ring on her finger," she whispered.

Jason shook his head. "I'll do it when the time is right, I told you that already."

Trisha put her hands up in surrender. "Okay, I'll back off," she promised.

Jason headed for the den as Trisha walked out of the house, shutting the door behind her. He understood why Trisha was concerned. He'd gone to her expressing his interest in proposing to Chasity, but almost two months had gone by and he still hadn't done it. He wanted to plan something perfect, but by the time he'd figured it out, she'd told him that she was pregnant. He felt that if he asked her soon after, that she might think he was doing it just because she was pregnant, and he didn't want her to feel that way.

Jason rubbed the back of his neck as he entered the den. He was stressed and needed to talk to Chasity and he wasn't sure how the conversation would go. "Hey," Jason said, prompting her to look up from her laptop that was sitting on her lap.

"Hey," she replied as he walked over.

Jason sat down on the ottoman in front of the chaise lounge chair that Chasity was in. She put the laptop on the floor next to her and he reached out and put his hand on her stomach. "Hey to you too," he directed to her stomach, smiling.

Chasity giggled.

Jason glanced at her plate of half-eaten sandwich. "You're not going to finish that?"

Chasity rolled her eyes. "Don't listen to Trisha's ass, I ate like three times already, I don't want that damn sandwich," she hissed. "I almost threw it at her."

Jason laughed a little. "She's just being a doting soon-to-be grandmother," he placated.

"She's being a pain in my black ass," Chasity returned, annoyed.

Jason adjusted his position on his seat. "So...how did the conversation with your dad go the other day?"

"It was okay," Chasity answered. "We have an understanding."

"So, I don't need to drop him?" Jason asked.

"Not at this time, but I promise to let you know if you need to," Chasity returned jokingly. She knew that Jason wasn't too fond of her father, and her boyfriend had every right to feel that way. But he, like herself, knew that it wouldn't be fair to keep him from their child. So he, like herself, was willing to give Derrick a chance to prove himself.

"Well...that's good," Jason said. "We don't need any negative shit in our lives right now." Chasity nodded in agreement. "Were you working?" he asked, pointing to her laptop.

Chasity glanced at it, then back at him. "No, I was shopping actually," she said. "Buying work clothes."

Jason looked bewildered. "You need work clothes to work from home?" he chuckled.

"No, I need them to work in an *office*," she clarified. "I got a job. I start in two weeks."

Jason frowned. "Doing *what*?"

"Junior designer for a tech company," Chasity explained.

"I thought you didn't want to work for anybody."

"I *don't*, but it'll be fine for now," she replied. "The

apartment that we looked at, the one that we actually *like*. For that price, they want both of us to show steady income. And right now, I don't have that."

"What about the other ones that we looked at?"

"*Clearly*, I didn't *like* those," she threw back.

Jason rubbed his eyes. This was what he didn't want. "You know what, you don't have to worry about that. I'll take care of the apartment by myself."

"And just *how* do you think you're going to do that?" Chasity asked. "*Your* income *alone* won't cover it. Not to mention, you have to consider your school expenses…stop being dramatic and unreasonable," she said. "I'm fine to work. It's not a big deal."

"It *is*—" Jason took a deep breath. "I'm going into the draft," he blurted out. "So, tell them you don't need that job. Stick with your freelance, and eventually I can help you start your own company, if you want."

Chasity stared at him for a few seconds. "I'm sorry, I thought I heard you say that you're going into the draft. As in the *professional football* draft." Her voice was calm, almost humorous, and her face was void of anger.

"Yeah, I did," he confirmed. Chasity just held her gaze on him. Jason was shocked. "I mean, it's only a few years that I'll have to commit to them. The money from the contract can get us a house, we can put some in savings, get everything we need for the baby… It can set us up. *I* can set us up."

Chasity held her stare.

Jason studied her face. "Are you listening?"

"Uh huh," she confirmed.

"What are you thinking?"

"I'm thinking about how you plan on playing football while sitting your ass in a classroom," she hissed.

Jason pinched the bridge of his nose. *And there it is.*

"You're not doing that bullshit, are you fuckin' crazy?" she snapped.

Jason put his hands together. "Chasity it's the best thing

for us right now."

"So, the best thing for us is *you* doing something you swore you would never do?" she fumed. "What you *clearly* don't *want* to do?"

"You're about to start working at a damn company that isn't your own," he threw back. "Something that *you* don't want to do."

"Jason cut that shit out, you know it's not even the same," Chasity argued. "I can quit if I don't like it. You *can't* quit when you're tied to a fuckin' five-year contract." She was livid with him. "And who says you're guaranteed to get money up front? Who says that the contract isn't *just* five years? What if you get hurt? Do you even know where you'll end up?"

"I know the team *here* wants me," Jason said.

"It doesn't matter what they *want*? It matters who *gets* you!" she yelled out. "You could end up in California, or Alaska, or fuckin' Utah. You ever been to Utah? Do you *want* to go to some dry ass Utah?"

"No, no I don't want to go to Utah," he replied, calm.

"I didn't think so," she sneered. "Take your ass to school like you want to and kill that draft bullshit."

"Chasity, it's not that simple anymore. It's not just *you* and *I* anymore, we're about to have a *child*."

"You don't think I know that?" Chasity barked, folding her arms. "This little thing in here is sucking up all my food and energy so, yeah I'm aware."

"Yeah well, I have to sacrifice in order to do what's best for *both* of you…" Jason ground out. "We need money and this is how I can get it for us. It's not that big of a deal Chaz."

"If it's not that big of a deal, why did you wait a week to tell me that you decided to do this?" she threw out, taking him by surprise.

"What?"

"Your mother called me," Chasity revealed, annoyed.

Jason rolled his eyes. "Why am I not even fuckin' surprised?" he grunted. "She had no right to do that."

"I'm not even mad at her for telling me. If my son was trying to make a dumb ass decision, I'd probably tell his girlfriend too."

"If you knew, then why didn't you say anything to me?" he asked, confused.

"I figured maybe you'd find some damn sense, but *clearly* I was mistaken."

Jason rolled his eyes. "The insults aren't necessary," he bit out.

"Neither is what you're trying to *do*," she argued. "I'm not letting you do this."

"Look, not to be an asshole right now. But you can't stop me," he said. Chasity looked at him like he was crazy. "I'm telling you because it's the right thing to do, but I don't need your permission."

Chasity smirked. "That's real cute," she said.

He sucked his teeth. "Whatever Chasity," he said, tone calm. "I didn't come over here to argue with you... I just think that this is the best thing right now and I *still* plan on going to school, I'll just be pushing it back a few years... My parents sacrificed for me, so, I can sacrifice for *mine*... It's fine."

Chasity took a deep breath as she tried to calm herself down. She understood where Jason was coming from and she appreciated it, but she couldn't let him go through with what he was trying to do. "Jason, I get it," she began. "I know you want to take care of everybody and you think that money will do that but...you know I grew up having money and it didn't do shit for my happiness. All I wanted was a stable family... to have parents who were happy and *present*...I would've traded everything that I was able to buy for that... Money doesn't mean shit if you're not happy."

Jason let out a sigh. "Our child wouldn't grow up like you did."

"I know that," she assured. "But if we start off with the mentality that having money trumps being at peace and happy...what message do you think that will send?"

Jason was silent for a moment. "I get what you're saying."

Chasity grabbed his hand and held it. "We'll be okay Jase," she promised. "We'll make it work."

Jason sighed. "Financial aid won't cover everything for my school…so with the extra bills…I just—"

"Stop," she cut in. "You're gonna give yourself a heart attack worrying so much."

Jason took a deep breath. "You're right…okay," he agreed. "I'll um, I'll see if I can take some of the courses online, that way I can pick up more hours at work if I need to."

"You can do whatever you feel you need to do as long as it has nothing to do with damn football."

"Okay," he smiled. "In all honesty, thank you for talking me out of it."

Chasity gave a nod. "Yeah no problem, 'cause your ass would've been by yourself in Utah," she jeered. Jason laughed. "There was no way I was ever moving there."

"Yeah, I hear you." Jason felt like a weight had lifted from his shoulders. He would have done what he had to do, but was happy that he didn't have to be pressured to. The fact that she believed in his dreams enough to pass up on an easy life for herself, was admirable to him. If he had the ring with him, Jason would've asked Chasity to marry him right then and there.

# Chapter 59

Emily twirled the last bit of spaghetti from her plate and put it into her mouth. She then giggled as the sauce dripped on her shirt. "I think I got more sauce on my clothes, than in my mouth," she said.

"Yeah, you're lucky you're pretty, because you eat sloppy as hell," Will joked, earning a balled-up napkin tossed at him. Emily, knowing that Will had worked a double and probably wouldn't have the time or energy to cook for himself, invited him over to her scarcely furnished apartment for a spaghetti dinner. They were lost in conversation for over an hour.

Emily blushed as she pushed some of her hair behind her ear. "Thank you for the compliment though."

"You don't have to thank me for saying that," he smiled back. He then watched as Emily removed her short-sleeved cardigan, revealing a white, spaghetti strap tank top underneath. The fabric was form fitting, something that he rarely saw her in. He focused on her shape, then shook his head with vigor in an effort to snap his thoughts back to more pure ones.

"How was work today? Tiring I bet," Emily asked.

Will ran his hand over the top of his head. "Yeah, it was," he confirmed. "I'm glad that my parents kept Anthony overnight for me, otherwise I would have had to get up even earlier than I normally would have to drop him off."

"Will, I told you before that I would have watched him for you," Emily said.

"I couldn't ask you to do that."

"What do you mean? We have so much fun together," Emily giggled of Anthony. "I let him throw things at me and he laughs at my jokes, it's a win win."

Will laughed.

"And besides, I live right below you, so you wouldn't have to travel an extra half hour just to get to your parents."

"*Speaking* of which, Mom will be calling me soon to come get him," Will said, glancing at his watch.

Emily pointed to Will's plate as she took a sip of her orange juice. "You might want to hurry up and finish your food then."

Will nodded as he took a bite of his food. "So uh, did your sister ever call you?"

Emily rolled her eyes as she adjusted her position on her carpeted living room floor. She told Will what her mother had said about Jazmine wanting to call her; she was hoping that he had forgotten. She ran her hands down the front of her jeans. "Yeah, she did…twice."

Will looked at her. "Did you answer?"

Emily shook her head. "There are only two reasons why my sister would call me after all this time," she began. "Either she wants to cause me trouble, or she wants something *from* me…and I don't have time or the headspace for *either*."

"Well…maybe she wants to apologize," he pointed out, careful.

"Jazmine has animosity for me because of how Mommy treated *me* over *her*," Emily explained. "It wasn't my fault, but she *blames* me for it, and I don't see how after twenty-one years of that much ill-feelings, how she would all of a sudden, out of the blue want to apologize… I don't buy it."

"I guess I can understand that," Will said, rubbing his chin. "Hopefully one day she will."

"I wouldn't hold my breath," Emily muttered. "Subject change please."

Will put his hands up in surrender. "Okay," he agreed. "I

enrolled in Paradise Valley University."

Emily's eyes lit up at his announcement. "Are you serious?" she asked. Will nodded. "That's awesome," she squealed, giving him a hug. A gesture that he welcomed. She broke apart much too soon for his liking. "I'm so happy for you."

"Thanks... It's only part-time—"

"It doesn't matter; you're going back to school like you wanted. It wouldn't matter if it was *one* class," she said. "I'm proud of you."

Will held a smile on his face. The woman sitting in front of him had truly become a companion, even if it was platonic. Something that he sometimes wished he hadn't agreed to. He was starting to want more, and he wasn't sure if Emily was ready for that. "Thank you. If it means anything Ms. Harris, I'm proud of you too."

Emily tilted her head and smiled back. "Why thank you." She put her hands up. "Yay, we're doing great at being adults."

Will chuckled. He found her corniness adorable.

"And listen, no matter what you say, I want you to let me help you out with Anthony," she insisted. "You'll be working full time and taking classes, which if my memory serves me correctly, are far from easy....so you'll need all of the extra help and... I'm your friend so I want to help."

"Emily," Will began, adjusting his position on the floor. "I want you to know that I appreciate you."

"Thank you," Emily beamed.

"I really mean it," he reiterated. "With everything that I go through... When I feel like it's too much, just knowing that I have you in my life, makes things feel lighter. It's not just about the things that you do, it's just...you."

Emily was so busy focusing on the kind things that Will was saying about her that she wasn't paying attention to the intensity in his eyes while he was looking at her. "Well, I care about you."

"I care about you too," he said to her.

This time Emily noticed. The way that he was looking at her was different. It didn't scare her, but it was new and it made her nervous. She pointed to his plate. "You done with that?" she quickly asked, before grabbing both of their plates. Not waiting for a response from him, she stood from the floor.

*Emily don't go making a fool of yourself,* she thought, putting the plates into the sink and turning on the water. Grabbing the small bottle of dish liquid and glancing into the sink, she saw that Will had just dropped both of their cups in there. She looked up at him, "I would've gotten those—"

Emily was caught off guard when Will gently grabbed her, turned her around and planted a kiss on her. *Oh my God, what?!* she panicked. Her initial shock caused her to pull away, but that lasted only for a moment. When she realized what was happening, she was mad at herself for stopping him. When Emily didn't move or push him away again, Will took that as an okay to move in for another kiss. Closing her eyes, Emily dropped the bottle of dish soap in the sink and wrapped her arms around his neck. Will put his arms around her small waist and pulled her to him as the kiss intensified.

Emily had never experienced a kiss so intense, not even when she lost her virginity. What Will's lips were making her feel was new. By the way her body was reacting, it was also welcomed.

The sound of Will's phone ringing in his back pocket snapped them both out of their passionate make out session. Both stood there, breathing heavily.

*What was that? What does this mean? What the hell? I hope I didn't have sauce on my face.* Although her nervous thoughts returned, her lips said nothing as she just stared at his shirt. She felt vulnerable.

Will silently cursed as he retrieved his phone. He didn't answer, but he did look at the caller ID. He let out a heavy sigh. "It's Mom, I guess it's time for me to pick Anthony up," the regret and disappointment was clear in his voice.

"O—okay," she stammered, folding her arms to her

chest. "Yeah, you should go."

Will put the phone back into his pocket. "I could pretend that I didn't hear it," he said, staring at her.

In that moment, Emily wanted more than anything for Will to ignore that phone call. But she knew that if he stayed, she might cross a line that she wasn't sure she was ready for, that *they* were ready for. "No, you should go," she said.

Will nodded. "Okay," he agreed. He touched her hair and leaned in for one more kiss, but Emily moved her head back, stopping him.

"You should go," she insisted.

"You're right," he relented. He walked away from her and headed for the door. "Call you tomorrow?" Will asked, looking back at her.

Emily just nodded and watched as he walked out, gently closing the door behind him. In shock, she slowly sat down on her kitchen floor, her mind running wild with what had just taken place.

She touched her lips with her hand and smiled.


Mrs. Howard darted for the door when she heard the doorbell ring. Her face lit up when she saw Malajia standing there, doing a silly dance. "You're so silly, get in here girl," she chuckled.

Malajia laughed and gave Mrs. Howard a hug before walking into the house. "Oooh, I smell food, what did you cook?" Malajia asked as Mrs. Howard shut the door behind her.

"Pot roast."

"I'm on that, you might as well fix me a plate," Malajia said.

"I'll put a plate out for you," Mrs. Howard said, amusement in her voice. "How long are you staying?"

Malajia eagerly rubbed her hands together. "As long as it takes for that food to get done," she joked. After talking to Sidra the other day, Malajia decided to take a day and visit her friend. She wanted to make sure that she got a visit in before Sidra left for California, which would be in just a few days. Malajia looked at the steps.

"She's upstairs," Mrs. Howard said, picking up on Malajia's thoughts. "She's been packing all day."

Malajia took notice of the saddened look in Sidra's mother's eyes. "Can't believe she's really going huh?" she asked.

Mrs. Howard shook her head. "No...I can't," she answered. "Virginia was one thing—"

"I know it's far," Malajia placated. "But this is what she wants."

"I don't think it is," Mrs. Howard contradicted.

Malajia frowned. "What do you mean?" she questioned.

"Nothing, I shouldn't have said that. You should go on up. I have to check on dinner," Mrs. Howard stammered, before retreating for the kitchen.

Malajia held a skeptical look on her face as she followed Mrs. Howard's progress until she disappeared. Malajia then headed up the steps.

Sidra was sitting on her bed, folding clothes when she heard a tap on her door. "Come in." Her eyes widened when the door opened. "Malajia," she gasped. "What are you doing here?"

"I came to see you," Malajia smiled, shutting the door. "I know you're leaving soon and—*damn* you have a lot of shit," she observed, looking around.

Sidra chuckled slightly. "Tell me about it," she agreed, looking at the many piles of clothes that had yet to make it into any suitcase. "My parents are going to have to ship half of this stuff to me." She moved some clothes to the side so Malajia had a place to sit. "There is no way that I'm going to be able to take all of this mess on the plane."

Malajia just nodded. She looked on the bed and picked up a bracelet. "Oh look, the bracelet that I borrowed from you sophomore year," she recalled.

"No, you *stole* it," Sidra contradicted.

Malajia shrugged. "Eh, tomato, tomato," she dismissed.

Sidra looked confused. "That's not even the same thing," she pointed out, earning a laugh from Malajia. "Something is wrong with you."

"Yeah, I know," Malajia agreed, twirling the blue sapphire bracelet in her hand.

Sidra stared at it. "You want it?"

Malajia looked up at her. "No, I couldn't take it," she said. "You pitched such a bitch over it when I *borrowed* it from you," she teased.

Sidra giggled. "It's okay, I want you to have it," she insisted.

Malajia smiled, pleasantly surprised and flattered. "Thanks Sid," she said, placing the bracelet on her wrist.

Sidra gave a nod. "Sure…and congratulations again," she said, tapping Malajia's left hand. "I can't believe you're getting married."

Malajia's smile was bright as she looked at her engagement ring. She couldn't wait to share her good news with everyone. Sidra was the third person that she had told. "I never thought that you and Mark would *ever* end up where you are now," Sidra added, "but I am *truly* happy for you."

"Thank you hunny bunny," Malajia gushed. "I'm happy too."

"When is the wedding?"

"Girl, I don't know," Malajia said with a wave of her hand. "I want to wait until I'm working and we get a place… I ain't tryna get married jobless and still living at home."

Sidra laughed. "Gonna say 'I do' then go back to my parents' house and shit," Malajia continued, earning more laughter from Sidra. "It's gonna be awkward banging in that full-size bed I got in my room… Dana's sneaky ass will probably be in the closet listening and shit."

Sidra tapped Malajia's leg. "Will you stop it."

"Gotta be quiet and shit."

"Stop it nasty," Sidra chided. "How do your parents feel about you getting married?"

"My mom and sisters are hype as shit," Malajia answered.

"I knew they *would* be," Sidra replied, pushing her hair behind her ears. "And your dad?"

Malajia flagged the air with her hand. "Dad is being an ass as usual," she griped. "Talking about dating Mark is one thing, but marrying him is another... He still thinks that Mark is the same as he was when we were younger... He doesn't take him serious and it's pissing me off."

"Don't let that get to you," Sidra advised. "As long as you two are happy with how you are, that's all that matters... Your happiness matters to your dad too...he'll get his act together."

"Yeah well, he *better*," Malajia muttered. She twirled her new bracelet around her wrist. "Can you believe our little devil is gonna be a mom?" she gushed.

Sidra chuckled. "I know right," she said. "When I talk to Chaz she seems so...I don't know how to put it."

"Like she's excited but she's afraid that she's gonna break him or her?" Malajia finished.

Sidra pointed to her. "Exactly," she said. "But she'll be a great mom. She'll make sure that her child will have everything that she didn't have, growing up."

"Yeah...I'm happy for her," Malajia smiled. "You know that Godmother title is mine, right?"

"Yes, I know that," Sidra chortled. "Well deserved... You'll make a great Godmother and when it's your time, you'll make a great mom too."

"Yeah I'm not trying to find that 'mom' thing out right now," Malajia quipped. "I need to be able to give a child back if they get on my nerves."

"Okay, if you say so...but you know twins run in Mark's family right?" Sidra revealed. "His father's side."

"Sidra I will punch you in the left boob if you mention twins to me again," Malajia sneered, earning a laugh from Sidra.

"Well whatever happens, just let me know when

everything is way ahead of time and I'll fly back," Sidra promised. "Wedding, baby showers, *anything*."

Malajia nodded as she stared at Sidra. She couldn't believe that Sidra would no longer be within driving distance from her. "You're really leaving," she said.

Sidra let out a sigh. "Yeah, I am."

"You know…your mom said that she didn't think that you were happy."

Sidra frowned. "She what?"

"I mean I don't think she *meant* to…but that's what she implied," Malajia corrected

Sidra shook her head. "Unbelievable," she hissed, standing up.

"I mean…is she right?" Malajia asked. "Are you happy? Do you really want to go?"

"Why does everybody keep asking me that?" Sidra barked.

"Because maybe everybody can see that there is something wrong with you," Malajia threw back, standing up. "Sidra even when *I* talk to you about it…you never seem excited."

"I *am* excited!" Sidra snapped.

"Excited people don't tend to yell in anger and stomp their foot on the floor," Malajia pointed out, remaining calm. Malajia folded her arms as Sidra too folded her arms in a huff. "Why are you really going?"

"Because it's a good law school there and lest you forget, I want to be a lawyer," Sidra hissed.

"Is it because that was *James's* old school?" she asked, remembering what Sidra had told her about James's alma mater a while back. "Did he talk you into going?"

"If the reason for you coming over is to give me shit about my decision to leave, then you can go," Sidra bit out, walking over to her door.

"You're mad 'cause I'm right," Malajia pressed.

"You're *not* right."

"So your decision had *nothing* to do with him?" Malajia

goaded.

"James had no effect on that decision. Nothing that I *do* concerns him anymore," Sidra blurted out.

Malajia looked confused. "You're his girlfriend," she said.

Sidra let her arms drop. "No...I'm not," she revealed. "James broke up with me."

Malajia's mouth fell open. "What the fuck?!" she belted out. "Wait—What? Why? *When?*"

Sidra sighed. "It was before we graduated," she answered. "We just...weren't working anymore."

"Does anybody know?"

"Other than my mother...no."

Malajia ran her hands through her hair. "Sidra—*why* didn't you *tell* me?"

"We weren't speaking then," Sidra pointed out.

"I don't *give* a fuck," Malajia barked. "If you would have told me, I would've been there to help you through that...or at least *tried* to anyway."

"Malajia it doesn't even matter now," Sidra said. "I'm not even angry at him...we're okay. We're gonna try to be friends...*eventually*."

"I'm sorry Sidra," Malajia sympathized. "Break ups suck."

"Yeah but...it's *okay*."

"Well, I don't get it... What happened?" Malajia pressed. "He seemed so into you."

"He *was*," Sidra agreed. "He was a great boyfriend... I just stopped being into *him*." She let out another sigh. "My feelings changed."

"I thought he was the type of man that you wanted."

"So did *I*," Sidra agreed. "Turns out...I was wrong."

Malajia was confused, yet intrigued. She never imagined that Sidra would want a type of man who wasn't the wealthy, well-dressed, successful type. "Well sweetie...what type *do* you want?"

Sidra didn't even know how she'd come to spill what

she already had to Malajia. Maybe she was tired from the packing, maybe she was too stressed to keep her thoughts straight, or maybe she was sick of dealing with everything alone. Regardless, Sidra had gone this far, so she figured she might as well finish it. "Umm…Josh."

Malajia was taken aback. "You want a man like Josh?" she asked. "Didn't think he was your type."

"Not *like* Josh," Sidra clarified. "*Josh.*"

Malajia stood there. It had taken a moment for what Sidra had just said to register, but when it did, she let out a loud gasp. "You've *got* to be fuckin' kidding me!"

Sidra shook her head. "I'm not."

Malajia put her hands on her head. "You—hold on!" she couldn't believe it. "When he told you junior year how he felt—"

"I didn't *know* then," Sidra cut in, feeling the guilt come back. "I really didn't…I just… Things started changing, I started seeing him differently. Feeling differently *about* him…"

"Sidra this is crazy, you *have* to know that."

"I *do*," Sidra admitted. "But I can't help it…I can't turn this off. I've *tried*."

"Just like *he* did," Malajia concluded. Sidra looked at the floor. "Whoa…after all these years—"

"After all these years, I now realize that I'm in love with him."

Malajia put her hand over her heart. "How does he feel about that?" she wondered. "He *has* to be happy. This is what he's been dreaming about… How does he even feel about you leaving, knowing that things can *finally* work out for you two?"

Sidra held her gaze on the floor. Not saying a word.

"Sidra," Malajia called.

Sidra headed back over to her bed. "I should finish packing," she muttered, passing Malajia. "You should get downstairs, Mama should be finished dinner."

Malajia grabbed Sidra's arm, prompting her to spin

around. "Sidra, how does Josh feel about you leaving?"

Sidra rolled her eyes. "Let go of me please."

"No, I think I'll hold on," Malajia insisted. "My nails are long and pointy, so jerk away from me if you *want* and I promise I'll scratch you."

Sidra was agitated. "I don't have TIME FOR THIS!" she yelled.

"I don't care how loud you get," Malajia maintained.

Sidra sucked her teeth. "Look Malajia, it's complicated."

"How so?"

"Can you let go of my damn arm?" Sidra barked.

"No," Malajia refused. "What's complicated? You two are *finally* on the same page. I'm surprised that he isn't over here trying to stuff his tall ass into your suitcase."

Sidra shook her head. "Josh is…he supports me," she said. "He wishes me well."

Malajia studied Sidra's face. There were tears filling her eyes, even though she tried to avoid Malajia's gaze. "He doesn't know, *does* he?"

Breaking down, Sidra shook her head. "No," she admitted as the tears fell. "I couldn't tell him."

Malajia let go of Sidra's arm and tried to put her arms around her to comfort her, but Sidra backed up.

"I'm okay," Sidra sniffled. "I just…I can't. He moved on."

"Only because he thinks you don't *want* him," Malajia pointed out.

"He told me that we were better off being just friends anyway…that a relationship between us probably wouldn't have worked."

"When the hell did he say *this?!*" Malajia exclaimed. "Joshua is lying out his ass and you *know* that."

"It doesn't even *matter*," Sidra barked, wiping her eyes. "I hurt his feelings, ruined his relationship—he had to watch me be with James when he felt that I should have been with *him*… I put him through all of that and now because I finally figure *my* shit out, I'm supposed to expect him to drop his life and just run to me?" she argued. "That's not fair to him."

"No, what's not *fair* is not being honest with him about how you *feel*," Malajia contradicted. "You're not giving him a chance to finally get what he wants and that's *you*. That's selfish Sidra. And you're gonna fuck around and watch him *really* end up with someone else."

"I won't see *shit* because I won't *be* here," Sidra sneered.

Malajia slowly shook her head. "You're running from him…all the way to freakin' *California*," she concluded, coming to a realization.

"Call it what you *want*, but I'm leaving in three days," Sidra spat out, wiping more tears from her face. "So are you going to still stand here and argue with me, or are you going to help me pack?"

Malajia let out a long sigh. She wished that she could talk some sense into Sidra. She felt that the girl was making a huge mistake. "Sidra—"

"Malajia, can you just help me pack please?" Sidra cut in, voice trembling. The tears started again and she sniffled. "I just need you to help me, *please*?"

Malajia held a sympathetic gaze. She threw caution to the wind and threw her arms around Sidra; this time Sidra allowed the hug and even returned it. Malajia realized that she wasn't going to change Sidra's mind and that made her sad. "I'm gonna miss you."

"I'll miss you too," Sidra cried, holding on to her.

# Chapter 60

Alex cradled the desk phone to her ear as she typed on a laptop. "Are you serious? It's eight thirty?" she asked, eyes not leaving the screen.

"Yeah," Chasity answered, holding the phone to her ear as she tossed some items into a box. "You still at work?"

"Yeah," Alex chuckled. "I *clearly* lost track of time." With everyone in the publishing office gone since six o'clock, Alex had taken advantage of the quiet to work on her assignments. Between that and chatting on the phone with Chasity, she'd lost track of time.

"Girl, you better take your ass home," Chasity advised, folding some towels.

"I will, in a few," Alex assured. "Just want to give this article one final look over."

"So, I'm guessing that despite all of your whining, you actually *like* the job?" Chasity jeered.

Alex smiled as she sat back in her seat. "I do, actually," she admitted. "I mean, at first I didn't think that I could get pass the whole 'assistant' thing, but I'm really learning a lot... They even started giving me articles to edit on my own... Well, of course they'll triple check me, but hey, it's a start."

"Yeah, it's a start," Chasity agreed.

"I just heard today that they plan on opening an office in New York," Alex beamed, reaching for her half empty cup of coffee. "My boss said that she might take me with her when she goes to check it out."

"It's crowded and busy up there, but you're a people person so you'll do fine," Chasity said.

"Thanks sis, I'm really excited for where my life could go," Alex mused.

"You're gonna get up there and start wearing business suits and straightening your hair and shit," Chasity teased.

Alex laughed. "*Suits*, maybe. My *hair? Never*," Alex promised. "I wear this 'mop' proudly and will never change that."

Chasity giggled. "Yeah well, I hope not. It looks good on you," she said. She looked around her messy room and let out a groan.

"Still packing, huh?" Alex assumed. "When do you move into your new place?"

"Well, some of the stuff is going tomorrow morning, but we should be all moved in by the weekend," Chasity answered. With Chasity starting her job and providing the second income that the apartment complex needed to see, the lease was signed and both Jason and Chasity were anxious to move in. Chasity glanced at her watch. "As a matter of fact, Jason should be on his way over here to help me get the rest of this stuff together."

"I'm surprised that Ms. Trisha isn't there, helping you," Alex said.

"Yeah, me too. Especially since her ass started crying when I signed the damn lease," Chasity replied. "But she said that she had to help my grandmom with something so here I am…doing this by myself, for the time being."

"Well, at least the baby is there with you," Alex chuckled.

Chasity was silent for a moment. "If one of y'all make *one* more corny ass comment about me being pregnant, I swear to God, I'm not telling any of you when its born," she hissed.

Alex laughed. "Hey, we're family so we're entitled to make as many jokes, and comments as we *want*," she said. "I'm gonna be right at the hospital when you're giving birth so just get ready."

"Yeah well, fuck you," Chasity sneered. Hearing a knock at the door, she headed out of the room. "Jason's here, I gotta go," she announced, walking down the steps.

"Okay, I'll call you tomorrow."

"Okay, bye," Chasity said before opening the door to let Jason in. Her eyes zoned in on a large paper bag in his hand. "What's that?" she asked, pointing to it.

"Umm, food," he quickly answered.

"Are there brownies in there?"

Jason slowly shook his head. "Do you *want* brownies?" he drew his question out slowly.

"Yeah, but I'll make some later," Chasity said, going for the staircase. "Now come on, I still have a lot to do."

Jason, bag still in hand, took a few steps towards the couch. "Umm Chaz, I kinda want to eat first," he said.

She turned around and looked at him, frowning. "Jason, you're already late and I wanted to get this done so I can go to sleep. I'm tired," she bit out.

"I get that and I'm going to help you," Jason assured, tone calm. "I've been running around and packing all day myself. I didn't get to eat so I just want to do that before I go tackle your stuff... Can you give me like twenty minutes?"

Chasity sucked her teeth. "Whatever yo," she hurled, heading for the staircase.

"You want me to bring you up something?" he asked at her departing figure.

"Yes, your ass up here to help me," she spat back.

Jason shook his head in amusement. When he heard her room door slam, he set his bag down and looked around the living room.


What started out as twenty minutes, turned into a half hour. Annoyed and tired, Chasity sat in the middle of her bedroom floor, folding clothes and wrapping breakable items. "I shoulda did this shit earlier this week. Waiting around on his ass," she griped to herself. "He didn't eat all day, well I haven't *slept* all day, so spare me."

Her solo rant fest was interrupted by the sound of Jason calling her. Chasity rolled her eyes as she moved over to her closed door and pulled it open a crack.

"Chasity," he called again.

She held her hand on the door. "What Jason?"

"Can you come here for a minute, please?" he asked from downstairs.

Chasity rolled her eyes. "For *what*?" she huffed.

"I just need you to come here for a minute."

"Jason, you're supposed to be up *here*," she snapped.

"I know that and I'm coming, but I need you for a minute," he persisted.

"I don't fuckin' feel like it," she griped.

"It will only take a minute," Jason promised. "I have something to show you." She didn't say anything. "I promise I'll help afterwards."

Annoyed, Chasity jumped up from the floor and snatched the door the rest of the way open. "He's on my goddamn nerves," she muttered to herself.

As she headed down the staircase, she noticed flickering light. Stepping down the last stairs, Chasity forgot about her agitation as her eyes set on the living room. The fireplace was lit, helping to illuminate the space. Several candles were placed around the room, from the top of the fireplace to the coffee table, and end tables. The space in front of the fireplace had fresh rose petals in the shape of a large heart. Jason was standing in the middle of it.

Chasity was surprised, confused, and intrigued as she stood there looking at him. "What's all this?" she asked.

Jason held his arms behind his back, smiling. "You know, I had a million ideas of how to do this," he began. "Racked my brain over it... I didn't want to embarrass you, but I also wanted to make it special for you."

Chasity's eyes roamed the romantic space once more as she listened to him talk. Just the effort that he went to, to do this for her, made her melt. But she was curious as to what the occasion was. "Make *what* special?"

Jason removed one hand from his back and held it out for her. Chasity walked over and took it, letting Jason pull her into the rose shaped heart with him. Holding on to her hand, he took a deep breath. "This space right here, where we're standing, holds meaning for me," he said.

"Yeah?" she asked.

"Yeah," he confirmed. "It was the place where I first told you that I loved you...among *other* things."

Chasity smiled as she glanced down at the floor. "I remember," she said.

"Even though I *said* it to you that night...I actually fell in love with you the first time I saw you through the gate of the football field...and when I first *spoke* to you well...I was scared for my life." He let out a chuckle "...and later, my man parts," he joked.

Chasity let out a laugh. "I'm sorry about that."

"Nah, I deserved it," Jason admitted, recalling the incident outside of his dorm freshman year. "But I learned a lesson that night...you were clearly not like anyone that I've ever come across and that was what I wanted...what I *needed*."

Chasity didn't know if it was the sincere and loving things that Jason was saying to her, or her hormones that were making her emotional, but she felt that she could bust out crying at any moment.

"Chasity, I can honestly say that I love you more and more every day, and I want that to continue for the rest of our lives."

Before Chasity could say anything, Jason got down on one knee in front of her. *Oh my God!* She thought as her eyes widened. With her hand still secure in one of his hands, he pulled the other one from behind his back, holding out a small black box. Emotions overtaking her, tears began spilling from Chasity's eyes as she put her free hand over her mouth, unable to speak.

"Chasity...the love of my life...will you marry me?" Jason asked.

*Girl, stop crying like a baby and answer him!* Chasity yelled at herself as she tried to compose herself long enough to speak. Kneeling before her was a man who loved her even at her worst. He was everything she wanted and needed, and the fact that he wanted to spend the rest of his life with her was overwhelming, in a good way.

"I'll stay down here as long as you need me to," he teased.

Chasity removed her hand from her mouth and with a tear streaked face, nodded.

"Yeah?" Jason smiled.

"Yes," she replied, smiling back.

Jason removed the ring from the box and placed it on Chasity's finger. Jason rose from the floor, put both of his hands on her face and kissed her before pulling her into a loving embrace. He breathed a sigh of relief; he had been nervous since he spoke to Chasity earlier that day. He was grateful to Trisha for not forcing her ideas on him and allowing him to do it *his* way, and for staying out of the house while he planned his proposal.

Chasity broke from the embrace and looked at her ring. "It's so pretty," she gushed.

Jason smiled. "My grandmom would be happy to hear you say that," he said. "It was hers."

Chasity smiled as she leaned her head on his chest.

"Oh, I really *did* bring you brownies," Jason announced, pointing to a small container on a nearby end table.

Chasity quickly glanced over at them. "My fuckin' hero," she rejoiced, earning a laugh from her fiancé.


Sidra played with the strap on her purse as she sat in the front seat of her mother's car. Having just arrived at the airport, Sidra was gathering all of her nerve to get out of the car.

"What time does your flight leave again?" Mrs. Howard asked.

Sidra stared at the time on the clock on the dash; it read seven o'clock. "Nine," she answered. "I'm early."

"Well, it's always good to check in early so that you don't have to rush."

"Yeah, I know," Sidra muttered. Having had an emotional night saying goodbye to her family, the car ride with her mother that morning was spent in silence. Sidra felt that there was nothing left to say.

"I'll ship some more of your stuff to you next week okay?" Mrs. Howard said, looking over at her daughter.

"Okay...thank you."

"And once you get settled, your father and I will come out to visit you," her mother continued. "It's been years since I've been out to the west coast, but I'm sure it's still beautiful."

"Yeah, and hot," Sidra chuckled. "Might have to go back to my ponytails to keep my hair out of my face." She grabbed a few strands of her straightened hair.

Mrs. Howard nodded. Then after another moment, reached over and wrapped her arms around Sidra, who hugged her in return. Parting from the embrace, Mrs. Howard wiped the tears that spilled out of her eyes.

"I'm sorry, I said that I wouldn't do that anymore," she sniffled.

Sidra smiled a little. "It's okay Mama," she assured. "I'm gonna miss you too... Just think of it like I'm going back to Paradise Valley...that wasn't so bad right?"

"Virginia is not California honey," Mrs. Howard pointed out. "I can't jump in the car and get to you within a matter of hours if you need me."

Sidra reached out and wiped a missed tear from her mother's face. "I'll be fine, and so will *you*," she assured.

"If you decide to live out there permanently, I don't know if I *will* be." Mrs. Howard pushed some of her hair behind her ear. "Okay, I'm going to stop being dramatic. I expect for my babies to grow up and leave." She patted Sidra's hand. "I guess I secretly wished that my only Princess would stay close to me."

Sidra smiled at her. "I'll *always* be close to you," she promised. "And I'm sure you'll get sick of me, because I'm going to call you every single day."

"You *better*." Giving one more hug, Mrs. Howard hit a button, popping open the trunk. "Okay, you should get going."

Sidra stepped out of the car and walked around to the trunk to grab her suitcase and carry-on bag. She made a stop by the open window and looked inside. "I'll call you when I land."

Mrs. Howard nodded. "Have a safe trip Princess."

Sidra smiled and gave a wave before walking into the building. She looked back just in time to see her mother's car pull off. Letting out a long sigh, she made her way to the check in line.

As she proceeded to check in for her flight and check her suitcase, she began to feel butterflies in her stomach. Knowing that it was nothing more than nervousness, Sidra tried to focus on positive thoughts. *You know what, this will be good for me. I can focus entirely on my career… At least I have one friend out there… It's pretty there… Everybody else is moving on with their lives, why shouldn't I? Yeah…this will be good for me.*

Grabbing her ticket from the baggage handler, Sidra picked up her carry-on bag. As she was getting her necessary identification items back in order, she heard a voice call her name. Frowning in confusion, she spun around to see Josh standing there.

"Oh shit!" she shrieked, completely taken by surprise. She dropped her bag in the process.

Josh reached down and grabbed it for her. "Sorry."

"Um it's okay. Josh what are you doing here?" Sidra asked, ignoring how fast her heart was beating. She purposely did not tell any of her friends what time she was leaving because she didn't want to face anymore sad or questioning faces. It was hard enough to say goodbye to Josh over the phone; she didn't know how she would be able to handle it if he was in front of her.

"I don't know exactly," he answered after a moment.

Sidra raised an eyebrow. "You don't know why you're *here*?" she questioned.

Josh rubbed his face. "Yeah that sounded stupid," he admitted. "I'm here because I wanted to see you off."

"How did you know I'd be here at this time?"

"Your mom told me," he answered. Josh called Sidra's house the night before because Sidra's cell phone had died. When her mother picked up, Mrs. Howard made a point to let Josh know what time Sidra's plane would be leaving in the morning.

Sidra rolled her eyes. "Nice," she muttered in anger. "What *else* did she tell you?"

"Nothing really," he said.

Sidra pushed some of her hair behind her ear. Despite her behavior, Sidra was happy to see Josh, even if it was for only a few moments. "You want to sit down with me for a few?"

"I do," he said. "But don't you have to get up to TSA?"

"I have a few minutes for you Josh," she assured, pointing to a bench off to the side.

Josh smiled as he and Sidra made their way over to the bench and sat down. "How long is your flight?" he asked.

"Almost six hours," she answered. "Luckily my e-reader is fully charged."

"At least the weather is supposed to be nice today…here *and* there," he informed.

Sidra looked at him. "You're keeping up on the weather in California now?" she chortled.

"Of course," he replied. "No matter where you go, I'll always wonder if you'll be okay…so if checking the weather gives me peace of mind, then so be it."

Sidra stared at him adoringly. "I appreciate that."

Josh gave a nod. "Sidra, why isn't James here seeing you off?" he asked out of the blue. Sidra pinched the bridge of her nose. "This is the second time he hasn't been around for you," Josh pointed out. "That's not cool."

Sidra realized that she couldn't make excuses for James anymore. Her lying about the situation was making James out to be the bad guy, and that wasn't what she wanted. Together or not, James was a good man and she didn't want to tarnish him. "Josh, James isn't here because we are no longer together."

Josh frowned in confusion. "*Excuse* me?"

"It's true," Sidra sighed.

The confusion didn't leave Josh's face. "What *happened*?"

"It doesn't even matter at this point," Sidra returned. "He isn't here because he isn't obligated to be, not because he's neglecting me so…there it is."

"You're not going to tell me what happened?" he pressed.

"What *difference* does it make?" Sidra asked, exasperated.

*What do you mean?! It makes all the difference!* Josh thought, then sighed. *No, no it doesn't because with James or not, she still doesn't feel the same as I do for her.* "I guess you're right," he agreed. "I know how bad breakups can be… Are you okay at least?"

"I *will* be," she answered.

"Then that's all that matters," he said. "Hey, well maybe it's a blessing in disguise because you won't have to do the long-distance thing anymore."

"Yeah," she sulked. She looked at her watch. *God, why is time moving so fast.*

Josh too looked at his watch. *I need more time.* "Look, I just want to say that…despite how I may have acted—I'm really happy that you're taking this opportunity… Do I wish you could have the same opportunity *closer*? Yes, but nevertheless… I'm happy for you and proud *of* you."

Sidra was finding it harder and harder to keep it together. The more he spoke, the longer he sat there next to her, the harder it was getting for her to maintain control of her feelings. She realized just how much her heart was breaking, knowing that what she wanted, she couldn't have. That there was a chance that she wouldn't see him again for a long time.

"I'm going to miss you Joshua," she blurted out.

Seeing her eyes glisten as she held her gaze on him and hearing the sadness in her voice made Josh want to shed tears himself. "I'll miss you too," he said. "And listen, no matter what happens or where we both end up…you will always be my best friend." He grabbed her hand. "Anybody I'm with will just have to get over it."

Sidra managed a small chuckle.

"I mean it," he promised. "I'll always be here for you. I'm just a phone call away."

Sidra wiped a fallen tear with her fingers. "The same goes for you," she said. "Even with our three-hour difference…I don't care if it's two in the morning…just call me… I'll always pick up for you."

Josh stared at her. *And I'll always love you*, he thought. In that moment, Josh couldn't help it, a tear was forming. In an effort not to embarrass himself, he quickly rubbed his eyes and stood up. "You should probably get upstairs," he urged.

Sidra slowly stood up. "Yeah, you're right," she agreed.

Josh grabbed her bag and they slowly walked to the elevator. Unbeknownst to the other, they were both trying to keep from breaking down. "You need me to go up with you?" he asked as she pushed the elevator button.

She faced him and shook her head. "No. You wouldn't be able to get pass TSA anyway, so there's no point," she said, taking her bag from him. "But thank you…as always."

Josh nodded as the door opened. As people filtered out, the two embraced. Josh held on to her longer than he should have. He was trying to convert everything about Sidra to his memory. He didn't know the next time that he would get to see her. If he thought that it was appropriate, he would have kissed her.

"I gotta go," Sidra said, pulling from the embrace. Josh took a step forward as Sidra stepped inside. She held her finger on a button, keeping the door open.

He waved slightly to her. "Have a safe flight."

Sidra nodded, letting tears fall freely. "Have a safe drive back."

"Call me when you land," he said.

"I will." More tears fell from Sidra's eyes as she held her finger on the button. She didn't want the doors to close, but she knew that she had to let the button go—she had to let *him* go.

Josh dreaded the idea of those doors closing in his face. They would shut, and Sidra would walk out of his life and it was destroying him. Succumbing to his emotions, Josh let a few built up tears fall from his eyes. "Goodbye Sidra."

Sidra sniffled as her own tears poured. Not taking her eyes off him, she finally let the button go. "I love you Josh," she said just as the doors closed.

# *College life 501;*
## *Post-Grad Management*

The Final Book

The College Life Series

**Coming soon!**

Made in the USA
Las Vegas, NV
13 August 2021

28098199R00413